A CRAZY IMPULSE

*H*e looks at me, and I feel a ripple of something flutter through me. Am I really going to do this?

"So, Lulu? What do you say? You want to go to Paris for just one day?"

It's totally crazy. I don't even know him. And I could get caught. And how much of Paris can you see in just one day? And this could go disastrously wrong in so many ways. All of that is true. I know it is. But it doesn't change the fact that I want to go.

So this time, instead of saying no, I try something different.

I say yes.

GAYLE FORMAN

Includes

JUST ONE **DAY** - JUST ONE **YEAR** - JUST ONE **NIGHT**

YA

speak

BOOKS BY GAYLE FORMAN

Sisters in Sanity

If I Stay

Where She Went

Just One Day

Just One Year

Just One Night
(novella)

I Was Here

Leave Me

GAYLE FORMAN

JUST ONE **DAY**

SPEAK
An imprint of Penguin Random House LLC
375 Hudson Street
New York, New York 10014

USA * Canada * UK * Ireland * Australia
New Zealand * India * South Africa * China

penguin.com
A Penguin Random House Company

First published in the United States of America by Dutton Books,
a member of Penguin Group (USA) Inc., 2013
Published by Speak, an imprint of Penguin Group (USA) Inc., 2013,
This omnibus edition published by Speak,
an imprint of Penguin Random House LLC, 2017

Art on page 79 courtesy of Shutterstock.com

THE LIBRARY OF CONGRESS HAS CATALOGED THE DUTTON BOOKS EDITION AS FOLLOWS:
Just one day / Gayle Forman.
p. cm.
Summary: "Sparks fly when American good girl Allyson encounters laid-back Dutch actor
Willem, so she follows him on a whirlwind trip to Paris, upending her life in just one day and
prompting a year of self-discovery and the search for true love."—Provided by publisher.
ISBN 978-0-525-42591-5 (hc)
[1. Voyages and travels—Fiction. 2. Self-actualization (Psychology)—Fiction.
3. Love—Fiction. 4. Actors and actresses—Fiction. 5. Europe—Fiction.] I. Title.
PZ7.F757876Jus 2013
[Fic]—dc23
2012030798

Speak ISBN 9780142422953
This omnibus edition ISBN 9780451478795

Designed by Danielle Delaney
Printed in the United States of America

5 7 9 10 8 6 4

*For Tamar: sister,
travel companion, friend—
who, incidentally, went and
married her Dutchman*

All the world's a stage,
And all the men and women merely players:
They have their exits and their entrances;
And one man in his time plays many parts....

From William Shakespeare's *As You Like It*

PART ONE

One Day

One

AUGUST
Stratford-upon-Avon, England

---

*W*hat if Shakespeare had it wrong?

To be, or not to be: that is the question. That's from Hamlet's—maybe Shakespeare's—most famous soliloquy. I had to memorize the whole speech for sophomore English, and I can still remember every word. I didn't give it much thought back then. I just wanted to get all the words right and collect my A. But what if Shakespeare—and Hamlet—were asking the wrong question? What if the real question is not whether *to* be, but *how* to be?

The thing is, I don't know if I would have asked myself that question—*how* to be—if it wasn't for *Hamlet*. Maybe I would have gone along being the Allyson Healey I had been. Doing just what I was supposed to do, which, in this case, was going to see *Hamlet*.

— — —

"God, it's so hot. I thought it wasn't supposed to get this hot in England." My friend Melanie loops her blond hair into a bun and fans her sweaty neck. "What time are they opening the doors, anyhow?"

I look over at Ms. Foley, who Melanie and pretty much the rest of our group have christened Our Fearless Leader behind her back. But she is talking to Todd, one of the history grad students co-leading the trip, probably telling him off for something or other. In the Teen Tours! Cultural Extravaganza brochure that my parents presented to me upon my high-school graduation two months ago, the Todd-like graduate students were called "historical consultants" and were meant to bolster the "educational value" of the Teen Tours! But so far, Todd has been more valuable in bolstering the hangovers, taking everyone out drinking almost every night. I'm sure tonight everyone else will go extra wild. It is, after all, our last stop, Stratford-upon-Avon, a city full of Culture! Which seems to translate into a disproportionate number of pubs named after Shakespeare and frequented by people in blaring white sneakers.

Ms. Foley is wearing her own snow-white sneakers—along with a pair of neatly pressed blue jeans and a Teen Tours! polo shirt—as she reprimands Todd. Sometimes, at night, when everyone else is out on the town, she will tell me she ought to call the head office on him. But she never seems to follow through. I think partly because when she scolds, he flirts. Even with Ms. Foley. Especially with Ms. Foley.

"I think it starts at seven," I say to Melanie. I look at my watch, another graduation present, thick gold, the back engraved *Going Places*. It weighs heavy against my sweaty wrist. "It's six thirty now."

"Geez, the Brits do love to line up. Or queue. Or whatever. They should take a lesson from the Italians, who just mob. Or maybe the Italians should take a lesson from the Brits." Melanie tugs on her miniskirt—her bandage skirt, she calls it—and adjusts her cami-top. "God, Rome. It feels like a year ago."

Rome? Was it six days ago? Or sixteen? All of Europe has become a blur of airports, buses, old buildings, and prix-fixe menus serving chicken in various kinds of sauce. When my parents gave me this trip as a big high-school graduation present, I was a little reluctant to go. But Mom had reassured me that she'd done her research. Teen Tours! was very well regarded, noted for its high-quality educational component, as well as the care that was taken of its students. I would be well looked after. "You'll never be alone," my parents had promised me. And, of course, Melanie was coming too.

And they were right. I know everyone else gives Ms. Foley crap for the eagle eye she keeps on us, but I appreciate how she is always doing a head count, even appreciate how she disapproves of the nightly jaunts to local bars, though most of us are of legal drinking age in Europe—not that anyone over here seems to care about such things anyway.

I don't go to the bars. I usually just go back to the hotel rooms Melanie and I share and watch TV. You can almost always find American movies, the same kinds of movies which, back at home, Melanie and I often watched together on weekends, in one of our rooms, with lots of popcorn.

"I'm roasting out here," Melanie moans. "It's like the middle of the afternoon still."

I look up. The sun is hot, and the clouds race across the sky. I like how fast they go, nothing in their way. You can tell from the sky that England's an island. "At least it's not pouring like it was when we got here."

"Do you have a pony holder?" Melanie asks. "No, of course you don't. I bet you're loving your hair now."

My hand drifts to the back of my neck, which still feels strange, oddly exposed. The Teen Tour! had begun in London, and on the second afternoon, we'd had a few free hours for shopping, which I guess qualifies as culture. During that time, Melanie had convinced me to get my hair bobbed. It was all part of her precollege reinvention scheme, which she'd explained to me on the flight over: "No one at college will know that we were AP automatons. I mean, we're too pretty to just be brainiacs, and at college, everyone will be smart. So we can be cool *and* smart. Those two things will no longer be mutually exclusive."

For Melanie, this reinvention apparently meant the new heavy-on-skimp wardrobe she'd blown half her spending money on at Topshop, and the truncating of her name from Melanie to Mel—something I can't quite remember to do, no matter how many times she kicks me under the table. For me, I guess it meant the haircut she talked me into.

I'd freaked out when I'd seen myself. I've had long black hair and no bangs for as long as I can remember, and the girl staring back at me in the salon mirror didn't look anything like me. At that point, we'd only been gone two days, but my stomach went hollow with homesickness. I wanted to be back in my bedroom at home, with my familiar peach walls, my collection of vintage alarm clocks. I'd wondered how I was ever going to handle college if I couldn't handle this.

But I've gotten used to the hair, and the homesickness has

mostly gone away, and even if it hasn't, the tour is ending. Tomorrow, almost everyone else is taking the coach straight to the airport to fly home. Melanie and I are catching a train down to London to stay with her cousin for three days. Melanie is talking about going back to the salon where I got my bob to get a pink streak in her hair, and we're going to see *Let It Be* in the West End. On Sunday, we fly home, and soon after that, we start college—me near Boston, Melanie in New York.

"Set Shakespeare free!"

I look up. A group of about a dozen people are coming up and down the line, handing out multicolored neon flyers. I can tell straightaway that they're not American—no bright white tennis shoes or cargo shorts in sight. They are all impossibly tall, and thin, and different looking, somehow. It's like even their bone structure is foreign.

"Oh, I'll take one of those." Melanie reaches out for a flyer and uses it to fan her neck.

"What's it say?" I ask her, looking at the group. Here in touristy Stratford-upon-Avon, they stand out like fire-orange poppies in a field of green.

Melanie looks at the flyer and wrinkles her nose. "Guerrilla Will?"

A girl with the kind of magenta streaks Melanie has been coveting comes up to us. "It's Shakespeare for the masses."

I peer at the card. It reads *Guerrilla Will. Shakespeare Without Borders. Shakespeare Unleashed. Shakespeare For Free. Shakespeare For All.*

"Shakespeare for free?" Melanie reads.

"Yeah," the magenta-haired girl says in accented English.

"Not for capitalist gain. How Shakespeare would've wanted it."

"You don't think he'd want to actually sell tickets and make money from his plays?" I'm not trying to be a smartass, but I remember that movie *Shakespeare in Love* and how he was always owing money to somebody or other.

The girl rolls her eyes, and I start to feel foolish. I look down. A shadow falls over me, momentarily blocking out the glare of the sun. And then I hear laughter. I look up. I can't see the person in front of me because he's backlit by the still-bright evening sun. But I can hear him.

"I think she's right," he says. "Being a starving artist is not so romantic, maybe, when you're actually starving."

I blink a few times. My eyes adjust, and I see that the guy is tall, maybe a full foot taller than I am, and thin. His hair is a hundred shades of blond, and his eyes so brown as to almost be black. I have to tilt my head up to look at him, and he's tilting his head down to look at me.

"But Shakespeare is dead; he's not collecting royalties from the grave. And we, we are alive." He opens his arms, as if to embrace the universe. "What are you seeing?"

"*Hamlet,*" I say.

"Ah, *Hamlet.*" His accent is so slight as to be almost imperceptible. "I think a night like this, you don't waste on tragedy." He looks at me, like it's a question. Then he smiles. "Or indoors. We are doing *Twelfth Night.* Outside." He hands me a flyer.

"We'll *think* about it," Melanie says in her coy voice.

The guy raises one shoulder and cocks his head toward it so his ear is almost touching his very angular shoulder blade. "What you will," he says, though he's looking at me. Then he saunters off to join the rest of his troupe.

Melanie watches them go. "Wow, why are they not on the Teen Tours! Cultural Extravaganza? That's some culture I could get into!"

I watch them leave, feeling a strange tug. "I've seen *Hamlet* before, you know."

Melanie looks at me, her eyebrows, which she has overly plucked into a thin line, raised. "Me too. It was on TV, but still . . ."

"We could go . . . to this. I mean, it would be different. A cultural experience, which is why our parents sent us on this tour."

Melanie laughs. "Look at you, getting all bad! But what about Our Fearless Leader? It looks like she's gearing up for one of her head counts."

"Well, the heat was really bothering you . . ." I begin.

Melanie looks at me for a second, then something clicks. She licks her lips, grins, and then crosses her eyes. "Oh, yeah. I totally have heatstroke." She turns to Paula, who's from Maine and is studiously reading a Fodor's guide. "Paula, I'm feeling so dizzy."

"It's way hot," Paula says, nodding sympathetically. "You should hydrate."

"I think I might faint or something. I'm seeing black spots."

"Don't pile it on," I whisper.

"It's good to build a case," Melanie whispers, enjoying this now. "Oh, I think I'm going to pass out."

"Ms. Foley," I call.

Ms. Foley looks up from ticking names off her roll-call sheet. She comes over, her face so full of concern, I feel bad for lying. "I think Melanie, I mean Mel, is getting heatstroke."

"Are you poorly? It shouldn't be much longer now. And it's lovely and cool inside the theater." Ms. Foley speaks in a strange hybrid of Britishisms with a Midwestern accent that everyone makes fun of because they think it's pretentious. But I think it's just that she's from Michigan and spends a lot of time in Europe.

"I feel like I'm going to puke." Melanie pushes on. "I would hate to do that inside the Swan Theatre."

Ms. Foley's face wrinkles in displeasure, though I can't tell if it is from the idea of Melanie barfing inside the Swan or using the word *puke* in such close proximity to the Royal Shakespeare Company. "Oh, dear. I'd better escort you back to the hotel."

"I can take her," I say.

"Really? Oh, no. I couldn't. You should see *Hamlet*."

"No, it's fine. I'll take her."

"No! It's my responsibility to take her. I simply couldn't burden you like that." I can see the argument she's having with herself play out over her pinched features.

"It's fine, Ms. Foley. I've seen *Hamlet* before, and the hotel is just over the square from here."

"Really? Oh, that would be lovely. Would you believe in all the years I've been doing this, I have never seen the Bard's *Hamlet* done by the RSC?"

Melanie gives a little moan for dramatic effect. I gently elbow her. I smile at Ms. Foley. "Well, then, you definitely shouldn't miss it."

She nods solemnly, as though we are discussing important business here, order of succession to the throne or something. Then she reaches for my hand. "It has been such a pleasure traveling with you, Allyson. I shall miss you. If only more young people today were like you. You are such a . . ." She pauses for a moment, searching for the right word. "Such a good girl."

"Thank you," I say automatically. But her compliment leaves me empty. I don't know if it's because that's the nicest thing she could think to say about me, or if it's because I'm not being such a good girl right now.

"Good girl, my ass." Melanie laughs once we are clear of the queue and she can give up her swooning act.

"Be quiet. I don't like pretending."

"Well, you're awfully good at it. You could have a promising acting career of your own, if you ask me."

"I don't ask you. Now, where is this place?" I look at the flyer. "Canal Basin? What is that?"

Melanie pulls out her phone, which, unlike my cell phone, works in Europe. She opens the map app. "It appears to be a basin by the canal."

A few minutes later, we arrive at a waterfront. It feels like a carnival, full of people hanging about. There are barges moored to the side of the water, different boats selling everything from ice cream to paintings. What there isn't is any kind of theater. Or stage. Or chairs. Or actors. I look at the flyer again.

"Maybe it's on the bridge?" Melanie asks.

We walk back over to the medieval arched bridge, but it's just more of the same: tourists like us, milling around in the hot night.

"They did say it was tonight?" Melanie asks.

I think of that one guy, his eyes so impossibly dark, specifically saying that *tonight* was too nice for tragedy. But when I look around, there's no play here, obviously. It was probably some kind of joke—fool the stupid tourist.

"Let's get an ice cream so the night's not a total write-off," I say.

We are queuing up for ice cream when we hear it, a hum of acoustic guitars and the echoey beat of bongo drums. My ears perk up, my sonar rises. I stand on a nearby bench to look around. It's not like a stage has magically appeared, but what has just materialized is a crowd, a pretty big one, under a stand of trees.

"I think it's starting," I say, grabbing Melanie's hand.

"But the ice cream," she complains.

"After," I say, yanking her toward the crowd.

"If music be the food of love, play on."

The guy playing Duke Orsino looks nothing like any Shakespearian actor I've ever seen, except maybe in the movie version of *Romeo + Juliet* with Leonardo DiCaprio. He is tall, black, dreadlocked, and dressed like a glam rock-star in tight vinyl pants, pointy-toed shoes, and a sort of mesh tank top that shows off his ripped chest.

"Oh, we *so* made the right choice," Melanie whispers in my ear.

As Orsino gives his opening soliloquy to the sounds of the guitars and bongo drums, I feel a shiver go up my spine.

We watch the entire first act, chasing the actors around the waterfront. When they move, we move, which makes it feel like *we* are a part of the play. And maybe that's what makes it so different. Because I've seen Shakespeare before. School productions and a few plays at the Philadelphia Shakespeare Theatre. But it's always felt like listening to something in a foreign language I didn't know that well. I had to force myself to pay attention, and half the time, I wound up rereading the program over and over again, as if it would impart some deeper understanding.

This time, it clicks. It's like my ear attunes to the weird language and I'm sucked fully into the story, the same way I am when I watch a movie, so that I *feel* it. When Orsino pines for the cool Olivia, I feel that pang in my gut from all the times I've crushed on guys I was invisible to. And when Viola mourns her brother, I feel her loneliness. And when she falls for Orsino, who thinks she's a man, it's actually funny and also moving.

He doesn't show up until act two. He's playing Sebastian, Viola's twin brother, thought dead. Which makes a certain sense, because by the time he does arrive, I am beginning to think he never really existed, that I've merely conjured him.

As he races through the green, chased after by the ever-loyal Antonio, we chase after him. After a while, I work up my nerve. "Let's get closer," I say to Melanie. She grabs my hand, and we go to the front of the crowd right at the part where Olivia's clown comes for Sebastian and they argue before Sebastian sends him away. Right before he does, he seems to catch my eye for half a second.

As the hot day softens into twilight and I'm sucked deeper into the illusory world of Illyria, I feel like I've entered some weird otherworldly space, where anything can happen, where identities can be swapped like shoes. Where those thought dead are alive again. Where everyone gets their happily-everafters. I recognize it's kind of corny, but the air is soft and warm, and the trees are lush and full, and the crickets are singing, and it seems like, for once, maybe it can happen.

All too soon, the play is ending. Sebastian and Viola are reunited. Viola comes clean to Orsino that she's actually a girl, and of course he now wants to marry her. And Olivia realizes that Sebastian isn't the person she thought she married—but she doesn't care; she loves him anyway. The musicians are playing again as the clown gives the final soliloquy. And then the actors are out and bowing, each one doing something a little silly with his or her bow. One flips. One plays air guitar. When Sebastian bows, he scans the audience and stops dead on me. He smiles this funny little half smile, takes one of the prop coins out of his pocket, and flips it to me. It's pretty dark, and the coin is small, but I catch it, and people clap for me too, it now seems.

With the coin in my hand, I clap. I clap until my hands sting. I clap as if doing so can prolong the evening, can transform *Twelfth Night* into *Twenty-Fourth Night*. I clap so that I can hold on to this feeling. I clap because I know what will happen when I stop. It's the same thing that happens when I turn off a really good movie—one that I've lost myself to—which is that I'll be thrown back to my own reality and something hollow will settle in my chest. Sometimes, I'll watch a movie all over again just to recapture that feeling of being inside something real. Which, I know, doesn't make any sense.

But there's no restarting tonight. The crowd is dispersing; the actors drifting off. The only people left from the show are a couple of musicians passing around the donation hat. I reach into my wallet for a ten-pound note.

Melanie and I stand together in silence. "Whoa," she says.
"Yeah. Whoa," I say back.

"That was pretty cool. And I hate Shakespeare."

I nod.

"And was it me, or was that hot guy from the line earlier, the one who played Sebastian, was he totally checking us out?"

Us? But he threw *me* the coin. Or had I just been the one to catch it? Why wouldn't it have been Melanie with her blond hair and her camisole top that he'd been checking out? Mel 2.0, as she calls herself, so much more appealing than Allyson 1.0.

"I couldn't tell," I say.

"*And* he threw the coin at us! Nice catch, by the way. Maybe we should go find them. Go hang out with them or something."

"They're gone."

"Yeah, but those guys are still here." She gestures to the money collectors. "We could ask where they hang out."

I shake my head. "I doubt they want to hang out with stupid American teenagers."

"We're not stupid, and most of them didn't seem that much older than teenagers themselves."

"No. And besides, Ms. Foley might check in on us. We should get back to the room."

Melanie rolls her eyes. "Why do you always do this?"

"Do what?"

"Say no to everything. It's like you're averse to adventure."

"I don't always say no."

"Nine times out of ten. We're about to start college. Let's live a little."

"I live just plenty," I snap. "And besides, it never bothered you before."

Melanie and I have been best friends since her family moved two houses down from ours the summer before second grade. Since then, we've done everything together: we lost our teeth at the same time, we got our periods at the same time, even our boyfriends came in tandem. I started going out with Evan a few weeks after she started going out with Alex (who was Evan's best friend), though she and Alex broke up in January and Evan and I made it until April.

We've spent so much time together, we almost have a secret language of inside jokes and looks. We've fought plenty, of course. We're both only children, so sometimes we're like sisters. We once even broke a lamp in a tussle. But it's never been like this. I'm not even sure what *this* is, only that since we got on the tour, being with Melanie makes me feel like I'm losing a race I didn't even know I'd entered.

"I came out here tonight," I say, my voice brittle and defensive. "I lied to Ms. Foley so we could come."

"Right? And we've had so much fun! So why don't we keep it going?"

I shake my head.

She shuffles through her bag and pulls out her phone, scrolls through her texts. "*Hamlet* just let out too. Craig says that Todd's taken the gang to a pub called the Dirty Duck. I like the sound of that. Come out with us. It'll be a blast."

The thing is, I did go out with Melanie and everyone from the tour once, about a week into the trip. By this time, they'd already gone out a couple times. And even though Melanie had known these guys only a week—the same amount of time

I'd known them—she had all these inside jokes with them, jokes *I* didn't understand. I'd sat there around the crowded table, nursing a drink, feeling like the unlucky kid who had to start a new school midway into the year.

I look at my watch, which has slid all the way down my wrist. I slide it back up, so it covers the ugly red birthmark right on my pulse. "It's almost eleven, and we have to be up early tomorrow for our train. So if you don't mind, I'm going to take my adventure-averse self back to the room." With the huffiness in my voice, I sound just like my mom.

"Fine. I'll walk you back and then go to the pub."

"And what if Ms. Foley checks in on us?"

Melanie laughs. "Tell her I had heatstroke. And it's not hot anymore." She starts to walk up the slope back toward the bridge. "What? Are you waiting for something?"

I look back down toward the water, the barges, now emptying out from the evening rush. Trash collectors are out in force. The day is ending; it's not coming back.

"No, I'm not."

Two

---

*O*ur train to London is at eight fifteen—Melanie's idea, so we will have maximum shopping time. But when the alarm clock starts beeping at six, Melanie pulls the pillow over her head.

"Let's get a later train," she moans.

"No. It's already all arranged. You can sleep on the train. Anyway, you promised to be downstairs at six thirty to say good-bye to everyone." And I promised to say good-bye to Ms. Foley.

I drag Melanie out of bed and shove her under the hotel's weak excuse for a shower. I brew her some instant coffee and quickly talk to my mom, who stayed up until one in the morning Pennsylvania time to call. At six thirty, we trudge downstairs. Ms. Foley, in her jeans and Teen Tours! polo shirt as usual, shakes Melanie's hand. Then she embraces me in a bony hug, slips me her business card, and says I shouldn't hesitate to call if I need anything while in London. Her next tour starts on Sunday, and she'll be there too until it begins. Then she tells me she's arranged a seven-thirty taxi to take me and Melanie to the train station, asks once again if we're being met in London (yes, we are), tells me yet again that I'm a good girl, and warns me against pickpockets on the Tube.

I let Melanie go back to bed for another half hour, which means she skips her usual primp time, and at seven thirty I load us into the waiting taxi. When our train arrives, I drag our bags onto it and find a pair of empty seats. Melanie slumps into the one next to the window. "Wake me when we get to London."

I stare at her for a second, but she's already snuggled up against the window, shutting her eyes. I sigh and stow her shoulder bag under her feet and put my cardigan down on the seat next to hers to discourage any thieves or lecherous old men. Then I make my way to the café car. I missed the hotel's breakfast, and now my stomach is growling and my temples are starting to throb with the beginnings of a hunger headache.

Even though Europe is the land of trains, we haven't taken any on the tour, only airplanes for the long distances and buses to get us everywhere in between. As I walk through the cars, the automatic doors open with a satisfying *whoosh*, and the train rocks gently under my feet. Outside, the green countryside whizzes by.

In the café car, I examine the sad offerings and wind up ordering a cheese sandwich and tea and the salt and vinegar crisps I've become addicted to. I get a can of Coke for

Melanie. I put the meal in one of those cardboard carriers and am about to go back to my seat when one of the tables right next to the window opens up. I hesitate for a second. I should get back to Melanie. Then again, she's asleep; she doesn't care, so I sit at the table and stare out the window. The countryside seems so fundamentally English, all green and tidy and divvied up with hedges, the fluffy sheep like clouds mirroring the ever-present ones in the sky.

"That's a very confused breakfast."

That voice. After listening to it for four acts last night, I recognize it immediately.

I look up, and he's right there, grinning a sort of lazy half smile that makes him seem like he just this second woke up.

"How is it confused?" I ask. I should be surprised, but somehow, I'm not. I do have to bite my lip to keep from grinning.

But he doesn't answer. He goes to the counter and orders a coffee. Then he gestures with his head toward my table. I nod.

"In so many ways," he says, sitting down opposite me. "It is like a jet-lagged expatriate."

I look down at my sandwich, my tea, my chips. "This is a jet-lagged expatriate? How do you get *that* from *this*?"

He blows on his coffee. "Easy. For one, it's not even nine in the morning. So tea makes sense. But sandwich and crisps. Those are lunch foods. I won't even mention the Coke." He taps the can. "See, the timing is all mixed up. Your breakfast has jet lag."

I have to laugh at that. "The doughnuts looked disgusting." I gesture toward the counter.

"Definitely. That's why I bring my own breakfast." He

reaches into his bag and starts unwrapping something from a wrinkled piece of waxed paper.

"Wait, that looks suspiciously like a sandwich too," I say.

"It's not, really. It's bread and *hagelslag*."

"Hachuh what?"

"*Hach-el-slach*." He opens the sandwich for me to see. Inside is butter and some kind of chocolate sprinkles.

"You're calling *my* breakfast confused? You're eating dessert for breakfast."

"In Holland, this is breakfast. Very typical. That or *uitsmijter*, which is basically fried egg with ham."

"That won't be on the test, will it? Because I can't even begin to try to say that."

"*Out. Smy. Ter.* We can practice that later. But that brings me to my second point. Your breakfast is like an expatriate. And, go ahead, eat. I can talk while you eat."

"Thank you. I'm glad you can multitask," I say. Then I laugh. And it's all just the weirdest thing, because this is just happening, so naturally. I think I am actually flirting, over breakfast. About breakfast. "What do you even mean, an expatriate?"

"Someone who lives outside of their native country. You know, you have a sandwich. Very American. And the tea, very English. But then you have the crisps, or chips, or whatever you want to call them, and they can go either way, but you're having salt and vinegar, which is very English, but you're eating them for breakfast, and that seems American. And Coke for breakfast. Coke and chips, is that what you eat for breakfast in America?"

"How do you even know I'm from America?" I challenge.

"Aside from the fact that you were in a tour group of Americans and you speak with an American accent?" He takes a bite of his hagu-whatever sandwich and drinks more of his coffee.

I bite my lip to keep from grinning again. "Right. Aside from that."

"Those were the only clues, really. You actually don't look so American."

"Really?" I pop open my crisps, and a sharp tang of artificial vinegar wafts through the air. I offer him one. He declines it and takes another bite of his sandwich. "What looks American?"

He shrugs. "Blond," he says. "Big . . ." He mimes boobs. "Soft features." He waves his hands in front of his face. "Pretty. Like your friend."

"And I don't look that way?" I don't know why I bother to ask this. I know what I look like. Dark hair. Dark eyes. Sharp features. No curves, not much in the boob department. A little of the fizz goes out of my step. Was all this just buttering me up so he could hit on Melanie?

"No." He peers at me with those eyes of his. They'd looked so dark yesterday, but now that I'm up close, I can see that they have all kinds of colors in them—gray, brown, even gold dancing in the darkness. "You know who you look like? Louise Brooks."

I stare at him blankly.

"You don't know her? The silent film star?"

I shake my head. I never did get into silent films.

"She was a huge star in the nineteen twenties. American. Amazing actress."

"And not blond." I mean for it to come out as a joke, but it doesn't.

He takes another bite of his sandwich. A tiny chocolate sprinkle sticks to the corner of his mouth. "We have lots of blondes in Holland. I see blond when I look in a mirror. Louise Brooks was dark. She had these incredible sad eyes and very defined features and the same hair like you." He touches his own hair, as tousled as it was last night. "You look so much like her. I should just call you Louise."

Louise. I like that.

"No, not Louise. Lulu. That was her nickname."

Lulu. I like that even better.

He reaches out his hand. "Hi, Lulu, I'm Willem."

His hand is warm, and his grasp is firm. "Nice to meet you, Willem. Though I could call you Sebastian if we're taking on new identities."

When he laughs, little crinkles flower along his eyes. "No. I prefer Willem. Sebastian's kind of, what's the word . . . passive, when you think about it. He gets married to Olivia, who really wants to be with his sister. That happens a lot with Shakespeare. The women go after what they want; the men wind up suckered into things."

"I don't know. I was glad when everyone got their happy ending last night."

"Oh, it's a nice fairy tale, but that's what it is. A fairy tale. But I figure Shakespeare owes his comedy characters those happy endings because he is so cruel in his tragedies. I mean, *Hamlet.* Or *Romeo and Juliet.* It's almost sadistic." He shakes his head. "Sebastian's okay, he's just not really in charge of his own destiny so much. Shakespeare gives that privilege to Viola."

"So you're in charge of your own destiny?" I ask. And again, I hear myself and can hardly believe it. When I was little, I used to go to the local ice-skating rink. In my mind, I always felt like I could twirl and jump, but when I got out onto the ice, I could barely keep my blades straight. When I got older, that's how it was with people: In my mind, I am bold and forthright, but what comes out always seems to be so meek and polite. Even with Evan, my boyfriend for junior and most of senior year, I never quite managed to be that skating, twirling, leaping person I suspected I could be. But today, apparently, I can skate.

"Oh, not at all. I go where the wind blows me." He pauses to consider that. "Maybe there's a good reason I play Sebastian."

"So where is the wind blowing you?" I ask, hoping he's staying in London.

"From London, I catch another train back to Holland. Last night was the end of the season for me."

I deflate. "Oh."

"You haven't eaten your sandwich. Be warned, they put butter on the cheese sandwiches here. The fake kind, I think."

"I know." I pull off the sad wilted tomatoes and smear off some of the excess butter/margarine with my napkin.

"It would be better with mayonnaise," Willem tells me.

"Only if there was turkey on it."

"No, cheese and mayonnaise is very good."

"That sounds foul."

"Only if you've never had the proper sort of mayonnaise. I've heard the kind they have in America is not the proper sort."

I laugh so hard that tea comes spurting out my nose.

"What?" Willem asks. "What?"

"The *proper* sort of mayonnaise," I say in between gasps of laughter. "It makes me think that there's, like, a bad-girl mayonnaise who's slutty and steals, and a good-girl mayonnaise, who is proper and crosses her legs, and my problem is that I've never been introduced to the right one."

"That is exactly correct," he says. And then he starts laughing too.

We are both cracking up when Melanie trudges into the café car, carrying her stuff, plus my sweater. "I couldn't find you," she says sullenly.

"You said to wake you in London." I look out the window then. The pretty English countryside has given way to the ugly gray outskirts of the city.

Melanie looks over at Willem, and her eyes widen. "You're not shipwrecked after all," she says to him.

"No," he says, but he's looking at me. "Don't be mad at Lulu. It's my fault. I kept her here."

"*Lulu?*"

"Yes, short for Louise. It's my new alter ego, *Mel*." I look at her, my eyes imploring her not to give me away. I'm liking being Lulu. I'm not ready to give her up just yet.

Melanie rubs her eyes, like maybe she's still sleeping. Then she shrugs and slumps into the seat next to Willem. "Fine. Be whoever you want. I'd like to be someone with a new head."

"She's new to this hangover thing," I tell Willem.

"Shut up," Melanie snaps.

"What, you want me to say that it's old hat for you?"

"Aren't you Miss Sassy-pants this morning."

"Here." Willem reaches into his backpack for a small white container and shakes out a few white balls into Melanie's hand. "Put these under your tongue to dissolve. You'll feel better soon."

"What is this?" she asks suspiciously.

"It's herbal."

"Are you sure it's not some date-rape drug?"

"Right. Because he wants you to pass out in the middle of the train," I say.

Willem shows the label to Melanie. "My mother is a naturopathic doctor. She uses these for headaches. I don't think to rape me."

"Hey, my father is a doctor too," I say. Though the opposite of naturopathic. He's a pulmonologist, Western medicine all the way.

Melanie eyes the pills for a second before finally popping them under her tongue. By the time the train chugs into the station ten minutes later, her headache is better.

By some unspoken agreement, the three of us disembark together: Melanie and I with our overstuffed roller bags, Willem with his compact backpack. We push out onto the platform into the already-hot summer sun and then into the relative cool of Marylebone Station.

"Veronica texted that she's running late," Melanie says. "She says to meet her by the WHSmith. Whatever that is."

"It's a bookstore," Willem says, pointing across the interior of the station.

The inside of the station is pretty and redbricked, but I'm disappointed that it's not one of those grand stations with the clattering destination boards I was hoping for. Instead, there's just a TV departure monitor. I go over to look at it. The destinations are nowhere that exotic: places like High Wycombe and Banbury, which might be very nice for all I know. It's silly, really. I've just finished up a tour of big European cities—Rome, Florence, Prague, Vienna, Budapest, Berlin, Edinburgh, and now I'm in London again—and for most of it, I was counting the days until we went home. I don't know why now all of a sudden I should be struck with wanderlust.

"What's wrong?" Melanie asks me.

"Oh, I was just hoping for one of those big departure boards, like they had at some of the airports."

"Amsterdam's Centraal Station has one of those," Willem says. "I always like to stand in front of it and just imagine I can pick any place and go."

"Right? Exactly!"

"What's the matter?" Melanie asks, looking at the TV monitors. "Don't like the idea of Bicester North?"

"It's not quite as exciting as Paris," I say.

"Oh, come on. You're not still moping about that?" Melanie turns to Willem. "We were supposed to go to Paris after Rome, but the air traffic controllers went on strike and all the flights got canceled, and it was too far to go on the bus. She's still bummed out about it."

"They're always on strike for something in France," Willem says, nodding his head.

"They subbed Budapest in for Paris," I say. "And I liked Budapest, but I can't believe I'm this close to Paris and not going."

Willem looks at me intently. He twists the tie on his backpack around his finger. "So go," he says.

"Go where?"

"To Paris."

"I can't. It got canceled."

"So go now."

"The tour's over. And anyhow, they're probably still striking."

"You can go by train. It takes two hours from London to Paris." He looks at the big clock on the wall. "You could be in Paris by lunchtime. Much better sandwiches over there, by the way."

"But, but, I don't speak French. I don't have a guidebook. I don't even have any French money. They use euros there, right?" I'm giving all these reasons as if *these* are why I can't go, when in truth, Willem might as well be suggesting I hop a rocket to the moon. I know Europe is small and some people do things like this. But I don't.

He's still looking at me, his head tilted slightly to the side.

"It wouldn't work," I conclude. "I don't know Paris at all."

Willem glances at the clock on the wall. And then, after a beat, he turns to me. "*I* know Paris."

My heart starts doing the most ridiculous flippy things, but my ever-rational mind continues to click off all the reasons this won't work. "I don't know if I have enough money. How much are the tickets?" I reach into my bag to count my remaining cash. I have some pounds to get me through the weekend, a credit card for emergencies, and a hundred-dollar bill that Mom gave me for absolute emergencies if the credit card wouldn't work. But this is hardly an emergency. And using the card would alert my parents.

Willem reaches into his pocket, pulls out a fistful of foreign currencies. "Don't worry about that. It was a good summer."

I stare at the bills in his hand. Would he really do that? Take me to Paris? *Why* would he do that?

"We have tickets for *Let It Be* tomorrow night," Melanie says, assuming the Voice of Reason. "And we're leaving on Sunday. And your mom would freak out. Seriously, she'd kill you."

I look at Willem, but he just shrugs, like he cannot deny the truth to this.

And I'm about to back down, say thanks for the offer, but then it's like Lulu grabs the wheel, because I turn to Melanie and say, "She can't kill me if she doesn't find out."

Melanie scoffs. "Your mom? She'd find out."

"Not if you covered for me."

Melanie doesn't say anything.

"Please. I've covered for you plenty on this trip."

Melanie sighs dramatically. "That was at a pub. Not in an entirely different country."

"You *just* criticized me for never doing things like this."

I have her there. She switches tacks. "How am I supposed to cover when she calls my phone looking for you? Which she'll do. You know she will."

Mom had been furious that my cell phone didn't work over here. We'd been told it would, and when it didn't, she called the company up in a tizzy, but apparently there was nothing to be done, something about it being the wrong band. It didn't really matter in the end. She had a copy of our itinerary and knew when to get me in the hotel rooms, and when she couldn't manage that, she called Melanie's cell.

"Maybe you could leave your phone off, so it goes to voice mail?" I suggest. I look at Willem, who still has the fistful of cash spilling out of his hand. "Are you *sure* about this? I thought you were going back to Holland."

"I thought so too. The winds are maybe blowing me in a different direction."

I turn to Melanie. It's on her now. She narrows her green eyes at Willem. "If you rape or murder my friend, I will kill you."

Willem tsk-tsks. "You Americans are so violent. I'm Dutch. The worst I will do is run her over with a bicycle."

"While stoned!" Melanie adds.

"Okay, maybe there's that," Willem admits. Then he looks at me, and I feel a ripple of something flutter through me. Am I really going to do this?

"So, Lulu? What do you say? You want to go to Paris? For just one day?"

It's totally crazy. I don't even know him. And I could get caught. And how much of Paris can you see in just one day? And this could all go disastrously wrong in so many ways. All of that is true. I know it is. But it doesn't change the fact that I want to go.

So this time, instead of saying no, I try something different.

I say yes.

Three

The Eurostar is a snub-nosed, mud-splattered, yellow train, and by the time we board it, I am sweaty and breathless. Since saying good-bye to Melanie and hastily exchanging plans and info and meeting places for tomorrow, Willem and I have been running. Out of Marylebone. Down the crowded London streets and into the Tube, where I got into some sort of duel with the gates, which refused to open for me three times, then finally did, before snapping shut on my suitcase, sending my Teen Tours! baggage tag flying underneath the automatic ticket machine. "I guess I'm really going rogue now," I joked to Willem.

At the cavernous St. Pancras station, Willem pointed out the destination boards doing that shuffling thing before hustling us to the Eurostar ticket lines, where he worked his charm on the ticket agent and managed to exchange his ticket home for a ticket to Paris and then used far too many of his pound notes to buy me mine. Then we rushed through the check-in process, showing our passports. For a second, I was worried that Willem would see my passport, which doesn't belong to Lulu so much as to Allyson—not just Allyson, but fifteen-year-old Allyson in the midst of some acne issues. But he didn't, and we went downstairs to the futuristic departure lounge just in time to go back upstairs to our train.

It's only once we sit down in our assigned seats on the train that I catch my breath and realize what I've done. I am going to Paris. With a stranger. With *this* stranger.

I pretend to fuss with my suitcase while I steal looks at him. His face reminds me of one of those outfits that only girls with a certain style can pull off: mismatched pieces that don't work on their own but somehow all come together. The angles are deep, almost sharp, but his lips are pillowy and red, and there are enough apples in his cheeks to make pie. He looks both old and young; both grizzled and delicate. He's not good-looking in the way that Brent Harper, who was voted Best Looking in the senior awards, is which is to say predictably so. But I can't stop looking at him.

Apparently I'm not the only one. A couple of girls with backpacks stroll down the aisle, their eyes dark and drowsy and seeming to say, *We eat sex for breakfast.* One of them smiles at Willem as she passes and says something in French. He replies, also in French, and helps her lift her bag into the overhead bin. The girls sit across the aisle, a row behind ours, and the shorter one says something, and they all laugh. I want to ask what was said, but all at once, I feel incredibly young and out of place, stuck at the children's table for Thanksgiving.

If only I'd studied French in high school. I'd wanted to, at the start of ninth grade, but my parents had urged me to take Mandarin. "It's going to be the Chinese century; you'll be so much better able to compete if you speak the language," Mom had said. *Compete for what?* I'd wondered. But I've studied Mandarin for the last four years and am due to continue next month when I start college.

I'm waiting for Willem to sit down, but instead he looks at me and then at the French girls, who, having deposited their things, are sashaying down the aisle.

"Trains make me hungry. And you never ate your sandwich," he says. "I'll go to the café for more provisions. What would you like, Lulu?"

Lulu would probably want something exotic. Chocolate-covered strawberries. Oysters. Allyson is more of a peanut-butter-sandwich girl. I don't know what I'm hungry for.

"Whatever is fine."

I watch him walk away. I pick up a magazine from the seat pocket and read a bunch of facts about the train: The Channel Tunnel is fifty kilometers long. It opened in 1994 and took six years to complete. The Eurostar's top speeds are three hundred kilometers per hour, which is one hundred and eighty-six miles per hour. If I were still on the tour, this would be exactly the kind of Trivial Pursuit fodder Ms. Foley would read to us from one of her printouts. I put the magazine away.

The train starts to move, though it's so smooth that it's only when I see the platform is pulling away from us, as though it's moving, not the train, that I realize we've departed. I hear the horn blow. Out the window, the grand arches of St. Pancras glitter their farewell before we plunge into a tunnel. I look around the car. Everyone else seems happy and engaged: reading magazines or typing on laptops, texting, talking on their phones or to their seatmates. I peer over my seat back, but there is no sign of Willem. The French girls are still gone too.

I pick up the magazine again and read a restaurant review that I don't absorb at all. More minutes tick by. The train is going faster now, arrogantly bypassing London's ugly warehouses. The conductor announces the first stop, and an inspector comes through to take my ticket. "Anyone here?" he asks, gesturing to Willem's empty seat.

"Yes." Only his things aren't there. There's no evidence he ever was here.

I glance at my watch. It's ten forty-three. Almost fifteen minutes since we left London. A few minutes later, we pull into Ebbsfleet, a sleek, modern station. A crowd of people get on. An older man with a briefcase stops next to Willem's seat as if to sit there, but then he glances at his ticket again and keeps moving up the aisle. The train doors beep and then shut, and we are off again. The London cityscape gives way to green. In the distance, I see a castle. The train greedily gobbles up the landscape; I imagine it leaving a churned-up pile of earth in its wake. I grip the armrests, my nails digging in as if this were that first endlessly steep incline up one of those lunch-losing roller coasters that Melanie loves to drag me on. In spite of the blasting AC, a line of perspiration pearls along my brow.

Our train passes another oncoming train with a startling *whoomp.* I jump in my seat. After two seconds, the train is speeding past us. But I have the weirdest sensation that Willem is on it. Which is impossible. He would've had to fast-forward to another station to get that train.

But that's not to say he's on *this* train.

I look at my watch. It's been twenty minutes since he went to the café car. Our train had not yet left the platform. He might've gotten off with those girls even before we departed. Or at this last station. Maybe that's what they were saying. *Why don't you ditch that boring American girl and hang out with us?*

He is not on this train.

The certainty hits me with that same *whoomp* as the oncoming train. He changed his mind. About Paris. About me.

Taking me to Paris was an impulse buy, like all those useless gadgets grocery stores put at the checkout aisle so you're out the door before you realize what a piece of crap you just bought.

But then another thought hits me: What if this is all some sort of master plan? Find the most naïve American you can and lure her onto a train, then ditch her and send in the . . . I don't know . . . the thugs to nab her? Mom DVR'd a segment about something just like this on *20/20*. What if *that's* why he was looking at me last night, *that's* why he sought *me* out earlier today on the train from Stratford-upon-Avon? Could he have chosen easier prey? I've seen enough of those Animal Planet nature shows to know that the lions always go for the weakest gazelles.

And yet, as unrealistic as this possibility is, on a certain level, there's a nugget of cold comfort in it. The world makes sense again. *That* at least would explain why *I* am on *this* train.

Something lands on my head, soft and crackly, but in my panic, it makes me jump.

And there's another one. I pick up the projectile, a packet of Walker's salt-and-vinegar crisps.

I look up. Willem has the guilty grin of a bank robber, not to mention loot spilling out of his hands: a candy bar, three cups of assorted hot beverages, a bottle of orange juice under one armpit, a can of Coke under the other. "Sorry about the wait. The café is at the other end of the train, and they wouldn't open it until the train left St. Pancras, and there was already a queue. Then I wasn't sure if you liked coffee or tea, so I got you both. But then I remembered your Coke from earlier, so I went back for that. And then on the way back, I stumbled onto a very cranky Belgian and spilled coffee all over myself, so I had to detour to the loo, but I think I just made things worse." He plunks down two of the small cardboard cups and the can of soda on the tray table in front of me. He gestures to the front of his jeans, which now have a wet splodge on them.

I am not the sort of person to laugh at fart jokes or grossout humor. When Jonathan Spalicki let one rip in physiology last year and Mrs. Huberman had to let the hysterical class out early, she actually thanked me for being the only one to exhibit any self-control.

So it's not like me to lose it. Over a wet spot.

And yet, when I open my mouth to inform Willem that I actually don't like soda, that the Coke before was for Melanie's hangover, what comes out is a yelp. And once I hear my own laughter, it sets off fireworks. I'm laughing so hard, I am gasping for air. The panicked tears that were threatening to spill out of my eyes now have a safe excuse to stream down my face.

Willem rolls his eyes and gives his jeans a *yeah-yeah* look. He grabs some of the napkins from the tray. "I didn't think it was *so* bad." He dabs at his jeans. "Does coffee leave a stain?"

This sends me into further paroxysms of laughter. Willem offers a wry, patient smile. He is big enough to accept the joke at his expense.

"I'm. Sorry." I gasp. "Not. Laughing. At. Your. Pants."

Pants! In her tutorial of British English versus American English, Ms. Foley had informed us that the English call underwear *pants*, and pants *trousers*, and we should be mindful of announcing anything to do with pants to avoid any embarrassing misunderstandings. She went pink as she explained it.

I am doubled over now. When I manage to sit upright, I see one of the French girls coming back down the aisle. As she edges behind Willem, she rests a hand on his arm; it lingers there for a second. Then she says something in French, before slipping into her seat.

Willem doesn't even look at her. Instead, he turns back to me. His dark eyes dangle question marks.

"I thought you got off the train." The admission just slips out on the champagne bubbles of my relief.

Oh, my God. Did I actually say that? The giggles shock right out of me. I'm afraid to look at him. Because if he didn't want to leave me on the train before, I've remedied that now.

I feel the give of the seat as Willem sits down, and when I gather up the courage to peer over at him, I'm surprised to find that he doesn't look shocked or disgusted. He just has that amused private smile on his face.

He begins to unpack the junk food and pulls a bent baguette out of his backpack. After he's laid everything out over the trays, he looks right at me. "And why would I get off the train?" he asks at last, his voice light and teasing.

I could make up a lie. Because he forgot something. Or because he realized he needed to get back to Holland after all, and there wasn't time to tell me. Something ridiculous but less incriminating. But I don't.

"Because you changed your mind." I await his disgust, his shock, his pity, but he still looks amused, maybe a little intrigued now too. And I feel this unexpected rush, like I just took a hit of some drug, my own personal truth serum. So I tell him the rest. "But then for a brief minute, I thought maybe this was all some sort of scam and you were going to sell me into sex slavery or something."

I look at him, wondering if I've pushed too far. But he is smiling as he strokes his chin. "How would I do that?" he asks.

"I don't know. You'd have to make me pass out or something. What's that stuff they use? Chloroform? They put it on a handkerchief and put it up against your nose, and you fall asleep."

"I think that's just in movies. Probably easier for me to drug your drink like your friend suspected."

"But you got me three drinks, one of them unopened." I hold up the can of Coke. "I don't drink Coke, by the way."

"My plan is foiled then." He exaggerates a sigh. "Too bad. I could get good money for you on the black market."

"How much do you think I'm worth?" I ask, amazed at how quickly fear has become fodder.

He looks me up and looks me down, appraising me. "Well, it would depend on various factors."

"Like what?"

"Age. How old are you?"

"Eighteen."

He nods. "Measurements?"

"Five feet four. One hundred and fifteen pounds. I don't know metric."

"Any unusual body parts or scars or false limbs?"

"Does that matter?"

"Fetishists. They pay extra."

"No, no prosthetic limbs or anything." But then I remember my birthmark, which is ugly, almost like a scar, so I usually keep it hidden under my watch. But there's something oddly tempting about exposing it, exposing me. So I slide my watch down. "I do have this."

He takes it in, nodding his head. Then casually asks, "And are you a virgin?"

"Would that make me more or less valuable?"

"It all depends on the market."

"You seem to know a lot about this."

"I grew up in Amsterdam," he says, like this explains it.

"So what am I worth?"

"You didn't answer all the questions."

I have the strangest sensation then, like I'm holding the belt to a bathrobe and I can tie it tighter—or let it drop. "No, I'm not. A virgin."

He nods, stares in a way that unsettles me.

"I'm sure Boris will be disappointed," I add.

"Who's Boris?"

"The thuggish Ukrainian who's going to do the dirty work. You were just the bait."

Now he laughs, tilting his long neck back. When he comes up for air, he says, "I usually work with Bulgarians."

"You tease all you want, but there was a thing on TV about it. And it's not like I *know* you."

He pauses, looks straight at me, then says: "Twenty. One point nine meters. Seventy-five kilos, last time I checked. This," he points to a zigzag scar on his foot. Then he looks me dead in the eye. "And no."

It takes me a minute to realize that he's answering the same four questions he asked me. When I do, I feel a flush start to creep up my neck.

"Also, we had breakfast together. Usually the people I have breakfast with, I know very well."

Now the flush tidal-waves into a full-on blush. I try to think of something quippy to say back. But it's hard to be witty when someone is looking at you like that.

"Did you really believe I would leave you on the train?" he asks.

The question is oddly jarring after all that hilarity about black-market sex slavery. I think about it. Did I *really* think he'd do that?

"I don't know," I answer. "Maybe I was just having a minor panic because doing something impulsive like this, it's not me."

"Are you sure about that?" he asks. "You're here, after all."

"I'm here," I repeat. And I am. Here. On my way to Paris. With him. I look at him. He's got that half smile, as if there's something about me that's endlessly amusing. And maybe it's that, or the rocking of the train, or the fact that I'll never see him again after the one day, or maybe once you open the trapdoor of honesty, there's no going back. Or maybe it's just because I want to. But I let the robe drop to the floor. "I thought you got off the train because I was having a hard time believing you'd be on the train in the first place. With me. Without some ulterior motive."

And *this* is the truth. Because I may be only eighteen, but it already seems pretty obvious that the world is divided into two groups: the doers and the watchers. The people things happen to and the rest of us, who just sort of plod on with things. The Lulus and the Allysons.

It never occurred to me that by *pretending* to be Lulu, I might slip into that other column, even for just a day.

I turn to Willem, to see what he'll say to this, but before he responds, the train plunges into darkness as we enter the Channel Tunnel. According to the factoids I read, in less than twenty minutes, we will be in Calais and then, an hour later, Paris. But right now, I have a feeling that this train is not just delivering me to Paris, but to someplace entirely new.

Four

Paris

*I*mmediately, there are problems. The luggage storage place in the basement of the train station is shuttered; the workers who run the X-ray machines the bags have to pass through before they go into storage are on strike. As a result, all the automated lockers large enough for my bag are full. Willem says there's another station that's walking distance from here we might try, but if the baggage handlers are on strike, we might have the same problem there too.

"I can just drag it behind me. Or toss it into the Seine." I'm joking, though there *is* something appealing about abandoning all vestiges of Allyson.

"I have a friend who works in a nightclub not so far from here. . . ." He reaches into his backpack and pulls out a battered leather notebook. I'm about to make a joke about it being his little black book, but then I see all the names and numbers and email addresses scrawled in there, and he adds,

"She does the books, so she's usually there in the afternoons," and I realize that it actually *is* a little black book.

After finding the number he's after, he pulls out an ancient cell phone, presses the power key a few times. "No battery. Does yours work?"

I shake my head. "It's useless in Europe. Except as a camera."

"We can walk. It's close to here."

We head back up the escalators. Before we get to the automatic doors, Willem turns to me and asks, "Are you ready for Paris?"

In all the stress of dealing with my luggage, I'd sort of forgotten that the point of all this was Paris. Suddenly, I'm a little nervous. "I hope so," I say weakly.

We walk out the front of the train station and step into the shimmering heat. I squint, as if preparing for blinding disappointment. Because the truth of it is, so far on this tour, I've been let down by pretty much everywhere we went. Maybe I watch too many movies. In Rome, I really wanted an Audrey Hepburn *Roman Holiday* experience, but the Trevi Fountain was crowded, there was a McDonald's at the base of the Spanish Steps, and the ruins smelled like cat pee because of all the strays. The same thing happened in Prague, where I'd been yearning for some of the bohemianism of *The Unbearable Lightness of Being*. But no, there were no fabulous artists, no guys who looked remotely like a young Daniel Day-Lewis. I saw one mysterious-looking guy reading Sartre in a café, but then his cell phone rang and he started talking in a loud Texas twang.

And London. Melanie and I got ourselves completely lost

on the Tube just so we could visit Notting Hill, but all we found was a fancy, expensive area full of upscale shops. No quaint bookstores, no groups of lovable friends I'd want to have dinner parties with. It seemed like there was a direct link between the number of movies I'd seen about a city and the degree of my disappointment. And I've seen a lot of movies about Paris.

The Paris that greets me outside Gare du Nord is not the Paris of the movies. There's no Eiffel Tower or fancy couture stores here. It's just a regular street, with a bunch of hotels and exchange bureaus, clogged with taxis and buses.

I look around. There are rows and rows of old grayish-brown buildings. They are uniform, seeming to ripple into one another, their windows and French doors thrown open, flowers spilling out. Right across from the station are two cafés, catty-corner. Neither one is fancy, but both are packed—people clustered at round glass tables, under the awnings and umbrellas. It's both so normal and so completely foreign.

Willem and I start walking. We cross the street and pass one of the cafés. There's a woman sitting alone at one of the tables, drinking pink wine and smoking a cigarette, a small bulldog panting by her legs. As we walk by, the dog jumps up and starts sniffing under my skirt, tangling me and him in his leash.

The woman must be around my mom's age, but is wearing a short skirt and high-heeled espadrilles that lace up her shapely legs. She scolds the dog and untangles the leash. I bend over to scratch behind its ears, and the woman says something in French that makes Willem laugh.

"What did she say?" I ask as we walk away.

"She said her dog is like a truffle hog when it comes to beautiful girls."

"Really?" I feel flush with pleasure. Which is a little silly, because it was a dog, and also I'm not entirely sure what a truffle hog is.

Willem and I walk down a block full of sex shops and travel agencies and turn a corner onto some unpronounceable boulevard, and for the first time, I understand that *boulevard* is actually a French word, that all the big streets called boulevards at home are actually just busy roads. Because *here* is a boulevard: a river of life, grand, broad, and flowing, a plaza running down the middle and graceful trees arcing out toward one another overhead.

At a red light, a cute guy in a skinny suit riding a moped in the bike lane stops to check me out, looking me up and down until the moped behind him beeps its horn for him to move on.

Okay, this is, like, twice in five minutes. Granted, the first one was a dog, but it feels significant. For the past three weeks, it's been Melanie getting the catcalls—a result of her blond hair and LOOK AT ME wardrobe, I cattily assumed. Once or twice, I huffed about the objectification of women, but Melanie rolled her eyes and said I was missing the point.

As this lightness buoys me, I wonder if maybe she was right. Maybe it's not about looking hot for guys, but about feeling like a place acknowledged you, winked at you, accepted you. It's strange because, of all the people in all the cities, I'd have thought that to Parisians I'd be invisible, but apparently I'm not. Apparently, in Paris, not only can I skate, but I practically qualify for the Olympics!

"It's official," I declare. "I love Paris!"

"That was fast."

"When you know, you know. It's just become my favorite city in the whole world."

"It tends to have that effect."

"I should add that there wasn't much competition, seeing as I didn't actually enjoy most of the places on the tour."

And again, it just slips out. Apparently when you only have one day, you can say anything and live to tell. *The trip has been a bust.* How good it feels to finally admit this to someone. Because I couldn't tell my parents, who had paid for what they believed was the Trip of a Lifetime. And I couldn't tell Melanie, who really was on the Trip of a Lifetime. And not Ms. Foley, whose job it was to ensure I had the Trip of a Lifetime. But it's true. I've spent the last three weeks trying to have fun—and failing.

"I think maybe traveling is a talent, like whistling or dancing," I continue. "And some people have it—you seem to. I mean, how long have you been traveling?"

"Two years," he says.

"Two years with breaks?"

He shakes his head. "Two years since I've been back to Holland."

"Really? And you were supposed to go back today? After two years?"

He throws his arms up into the air. "What's one more day after two years?"

I suppose to him, not a lot. But to me, maybe something else. "That just proves my point. You have the talent for traveling. I'm not sure that I do. I keep hearing everyone go on about how travel broadens your horizons. I'm not even sure what that means, but it hasn't broadened anything for me, because I'm no good at it."

He's mostly silent as we walk over a long bridge spanning dozens of railroad tracks, graffiti everywhere. Then he says, "Traveling's not something you're good at. It's something you do. Like breathing."

"I don't think so. I breathe just fine."

"Are you sure? Have you ever thought about it?"

"Probably more than most people. My father's a pulmon-ologist. A lung doctor."

"What I mean is, have you ever thought about *how* it is that you do it? Day and night? While you sleep. While you eat. While you talk."

"Not so much."

"Think about it now."

"How do you think about breathing?" But then all of a sudden I do. I get tangled up in thoughts about breathing, the mechanics of it: How is it that my body knows to do it even when I'm sleeping, or crying, or hiccupping? What would happen if my body somehow forgot? And sure enough, my breath grows a little labored, as if I'm walking uphill, even though I'm walking down the slope of the bridge.

"Okay, that was weird."

"See?" Willem asks. "You thought too hard. Same with travel. You can't work too much at it, or it feels like work. You have to surrender yourself to the chaos. To the accidents."

"I'm supposed to walk in front of a bus and then I'll have a good time?"

Willem chuckles. "Not those accidents. The little things

GAYLE FORMAN

that happen. Sometimes they're insignificant; other times, they change everything."

"This all sounds very Jedi. Can you be more specific?"

"A guy picks up a girl hitchhiking in a faraway country. A year later, she runs out of money and winds up on his doorstep. Six months after that, they get married. Accidents."

"Did you marry a hitchhiker or something?"

His smile unfurls like a sail. "I'm giving examples."

"Tell me a *real* one."

"How do you know that's not real?" he teases. "Okay, this happened to me. Last year when I was in Berlin, I missed my train to Bucharest and caught a ride to Slovakia instead. The people I rode with were in a theater troupe, and one of the guys had just broken his ankle and they needed a replacement. On the six-hour ride to Bratislava, I learned his part. I stayed with the troupe until his ankle got better, and then a while after that, I met some people from Guerrilla Will, and they were in desperate need of someone who could do Shakespeare in French."

"And *you* could?"

He nods.

"Are you some kind of language savant?"

"I'm just Dutch. So I joined Guerrilla Will." He snaps his fingers. "Now I'm an actor."

This surprises me. "You seemed like you'd been doing it a lot longer."

"No. It's just accidental, just temporary. Until the next accident sends me somewhere new. That's how life works."

Something quickens in my chest. "Do you really think that's how it works? That life can change *justlikethat*?"

"I think everything is happening all the time, but if you don't put yourself in the path of it, you miss it. When you travel, you put yourself out there. It's not always great. Sometimes it's terrible. But other times . . ." He lifts his shoulders and gestures out to Paris, then sneaks me a sidelong glance. "It's not so bad."

"So long as you don't get hit by a bus," I say.

He laughs. Then gives me the point. "So long as you don't get hit by a bus," he says back.

Five

We arrive at the club where Willem's friend works; it seems completely dead, but when Willem pounds on the door, a tall man with blue-black skin opens up. Willem speaks to him in French, and after a minute, we're allowed into a huge dank room with a small stage, a narrow bar, and a bunch of tables with chairs stacked on them. Willem and the Giant confer a bit more in French and then Willem turns to me.

"Céline doesn't like surprises. Maybe it's better if I go down first."

"Sure." In the hushed dim, my voice seems to clang, and I realize I'm nervous again.

Willem heads to a staircase at the back of the club. The Giant resumes his work polishing bottles behind the bar. Obviously, he didn't get the message that Paris loves me. I take a seat on the barstool. They twirl all the way around, like the barstools at Whipple's, the ice-cream place I used to go to with my grandparents. The Giant is ignoring me, so I just sort of spin myself this way and that. And then I guess I do it a little fast, because I go spinning and the barstool comes clear off its base.

"Oh, shit! Ow!"

The Giant comes out to where I am sprawled on the floor. His face is a picture of blasé. He picks up the stool and screws it back in, then goes back behind the bar. I stay on the floor for a second, wondering which is more humiliating, remaining down here or getting back on the stool.

"You are American?"

What gives it away? Because I'm clumsy? Aren't French people ever clumsy? I'm actually pretty graceful. I took ballet for eight years. I should tell him to fix the stool before someone sues. No, if I say that, I'll definitely sound American.

"How can you tell?" I don't know why I bother to ask. Since the moment our plane touched down in London, it's like there's been a neon sign above my head, blinking: TOURIST, AMERICAN, OUTSIDER. I should be used to it. Except since arriving in Paris, it felt like it had maybe dimmed. Clearly not.

"Your friend tells me," he says. "My brother lives in Roché Estair."

"Oh?" Am I supposed to know where this is? "Is that near Paris?"

He laughs, a big loud belly laugh. "No. It is in New York. Near the big lake."

Roché Estair? "Oh! Rochester."

"Yes. Roché Estair," he repeats. "It is very cold up there. Very much snow. My brother's name is Aliou Mjodi. Maybe you know him?"

I shake my head. "I live in Pennsylvania, next to New York."

"Is there much snow in Penisvania?"

I suppress a laugh. "There's a fair amount in Penn-syl-vania," I say, emphasizing the pronunciation. "But not as much as Rochester."

He shivers. "Too cold. Especially for us. We have Senegalese blood in our veins, though we both are born in Paris. But now my brother he goes to study computers in Roché Estair, at university." The Giant looks very proud. "He does not like the snow. And he says, in summer, the mosquitoes are as big as those in Senegal."

I laugh.

The Giant's face breaks open into a jack-o'-lantern's smile. "How long in Paris?"

I look at my watch. "I've been here one hour, and I'll be here for one day."

"One day? Why are you here?" He gestures to the bar.

I point to my bag. "We need a place to store this."

"Take it downstairs. You must not waste your one day here. When the sun shines, you let it shine on you. Snow is always waiting."

"Willem told me to wait, that Céline—"

"*Pff*," he interrupts, waving his hand. He comes out from behind the bar and easily hoists my bag over his shoulder. "Come, I take it downstairs for you."

At the bottom of the stairs is a dark hallway crowded with speakers, amplifiers, cables, and lights. Upstairs, there's rapping on the door, and the Giant bounds back up, telling me to leave the bag in the office.

There are a couple of doors, so I go to the first one and knock on it. It opens to a small room with a metal desk, an old computer, a pile of papers. Willem's backpack is there, but he's not. I go back in the hall and hear the sound of a woman's rapid-fire French, and then Willem's voice, languid in response.

"Willem?" I call out. "Hello?"

He says something back, but I don't understand.

"What?"

He says something else, but I can't hear him so I crack open the door to find a small supply closet full of boxes and in it, Willem standing right up close to a girl—Céline—who even in the half darkness, I can see is beautiful in a way I can never even pretend to be. She is talking to Willem in a throaty voice while tugging his shirt over his head. He, of course, is laughing.

I slam the door shut and retreat back toward the stairs, tipping over my suitcase in my haste.

I hear something rattle. "Lulu, open the door. It's stuck."

I turn around. My suitcase is lodged underneath the handle. I scurry back to kick it out of the way and turn back toward the stairs as the door flies open.

"What are you doing?" Willem asks.

"Leaving." It's not like Willem and I are anything to each other, but still, he left me upstairs to come downstairs for a quickie?

"Come back."

I've heard about the French. I've seen plenty of French films. A lot of them are sexy; some of them are kinky. I want to be Lulu, but not *that* much.

"Lulu!" Willem's voice is firm. "Céline refuses to hold your bags unless I change my clothes," he explains. "She says I look like a dirty old man coming out of a sex shop." He points to his crotch.

It takes me a minute to understand what she means, and when I do, I flush.

Céline says something to Willem in French, and he laughs. And fine, maybe it's not what I thought it was. But it's still pretty clear that I've intruded upon *something*.

Willem turns back to me. "I said I will change my jeans, but all my other shirts are just as dirty, so she is finding me one."

Céline continues yapping away at Willem in French, and it's like I don't even exist.

Finally, she finds what she's looking for, a heather-gray T-shirt with a giant red sos emblazoned on it. Willem takes it and yanks off his own T-shirt. Céline says something else and reaches out to undo his belt buckle. He holds his hands up in surrender and then undoes the buttons himself. The jeans fall to the floor and Willem just stands there, all miles and miles of him, in nothing but a pair of fitted boxer shorts.

"*Excusez-moi,*" he says as he brushes past me so close his bare torso slides up against my arm. It's dark in here, but I'm fairly certain Céline can tell I'm blushing and has marked this as a point against me. A few seconds later, Willem returns with his backpack. He digs in it for a rumpled-but-stain-free pair of jeans. I try not to stare as he slips them on and threads his worn brown leather belt through the loops. Then he puts on the T-shirt. Céline glances at me looking at him, and I look away as though she's caught me at something. Which she has.

Watching him get dressed feels more illicit than seeing him strip.

"*D'accord?*" he asks Céline. She appraises him, her hands on her hips.

"*Mieux,*" she says back, sounding like a cat. *Mew.*

"Lulu?" Willem asks.

"Nice."

Finally, Céline acknowledges me. She says something, gesticulating wildly, then stops.

When I fail to answer, one of Céline's eyebrows shoots up into a perfect arch, while the other one stays in neutral. I've seen women from Florence to Prague do this same thing. It must be some skill they teach in European schools.

"She is asking you if you have ever heard of *Sous ou Sur,*" Willem says, pointing to the sos on the shirt. "They are a famous punk-rap band with strong lyrics about justice."

I shake my head, feeling like a double loser for not having heard of the cool French anarchist whatever justice band. "I'm sorry, I don't speak French."

Céline looks disdainful. Another stupid American who can't be bothered to learn any other languages.

"I speak a little Mandarin," I offer hopefully, but this fails to impress.

Céline deigns to switch to English: "But your name. Lulu, it is French, *non?*"

There's a small pause. Like at a concert in between songs. A perfect time to say, ever so casually, "Actually, my name is Allyson."

But then Willem answers for me. "It's short for Louise." And he winks at me.

Céline points at my suitcase with a manicured purple fingernail. "That is the bag?"

"Yes. This is it."

"It is so big."

"It's not *that* big." I think about some of the bags other girls brought on the tour, the hair dryers and adapters and three changes of clothes per day. I look at her in her black mesh tunic that stops at her thighs, a tiny black skirt that Melanie would pay too much for, and suspect this knowledge would fail to impress her.

"It can live in the storage room, not in my office."

"That's fine. Just so long as I can get it tomorrow."

"The cleaner will be here at ten o'clock. And here, we have so many extra, you can have one too," she says, handing me the same T-shirt she gave Willem, only mine is at least a size larger than his.

I'm about to open my suitcase and stuff it in, but then I visualize the contents: the sensible A-line skirts and T-shirts that Mom picked out for me. My travel journal, the entries I hoped would be breathless accounts of adventure but wound up reading like a series of telegrams: *Today we went to the Prague Castle. Stop. Then we saw* The Magic Flute *at the State Opera House. Stop. Had chicken cutlets for dinner. Stop.* The postcards from Famous European Cities, blank because after I'd mailed the obligatory few to my parents and grandmother, I'd had no one left to send them to. And then there's the Ziploc bag with one lone piece of paper inside. Before the trip, my mom made me a master inventory of all the things to bring and then she made copies, one for every stop, so each time I packed, I could check off each item, to ensure I didn't leave anything behind. There is one sheet left for my supposed last stop in London.

I stuff the T-shirt into my shoulder bag. "I'll just hang on to this. To sleep in tonight."

Céline's eyebrow shoots up again. She probably never sleeps in a T-shirt. She probably sleeps in the silky nude, even on the coldest of winter nights. I get a flash of her sleeping naked next to Willem.

"Thanks. For the shirt. For storing my bag," I say.

"*Merci,*" Céline says back, and I wonder why it is that she's thanking me, but then I realize she wants me to say thank you in French, so I do, only it comes out sounding like *mercy.*

We go upstairs. Céline is nattering away to Willem. I'm beginning to understand how his French got so fluent. As if this didn't make it clear enough that she was a dog and Willem her hydrant, when we get upstairs, she links arms with him and walks him slowly to the front of the bar. I feel like waving my arms and saying "Hello! Remember me?"

When they do that cheek-cheek-kiss-kiss thing, I feel so much of the excitement from earlier dwindle. Next to Céline, with her mile-high stilettos, her black hair, the underneath dyed blond, her perfectly symmetrical face, which is both marred and enhanced by so many piercings, I feel short as a midget and plain as a mop. And once again, I wonder, Why did he bring me here? Then I think of Shane Michaels.

All through tenth grade, I'd had a huge crush on Shane, a senior. We'd hang out, and he'd flirt with me and invite me lots of places and pay for me even, and he'd confide all kinds of personal things, including, yes, about the girls he was dating. But those relationships never lasted more than a few weeks, and I'd told myself that all the while, he and I were growing closer and that he'd eventually fall for me. When months went by and nothing happened between us, Melanie said it was never going to happen. "You have Sidekick Syndrome," she said. At the time, I thought she was jealous, but of course, she was right. It hits me that, Evan notwithstanding, it might be a lifetime affliction.

I can feel myself shriveling, feel the welcome Paris bestowed on me earlier fading away, if it even really happened. How stupid to think a dog sniffing my crotch and a quick look from some random guy meant anything. Paris adores girls like Céline. Genuine Lulus, not counterfeits.

But then, just as we're at the door, the Giant comes out from behind the bar and takes my hand and, with a jaunty "*à bientôt*," kisses both my cheeks.

A warm feeling tickles my chest. This is the first time on the trip a local has been unabashedly nice to me—because he wanted to, not because I was paying him to. And it doesn't escape my notice that Willem is no longer looking at Céline but is watching me, a curious expression lighting up his face. I'm not sure if it's these things or something else, but it makes that kiss, which I get was just platonic—a friendly, cheek-handshake thing—feel momentous. A kiss from all of Paris.

Six

"Lulu, we have something very important to discuss."

Willem looks at me solemnly, and I feel my stomach bottom out in anxiety over another unpleasant surprise.

"What now?" I ask, trying not to sound nervous.

He crosses his arms in front of his chest and then he strokes his chin. Is he going to send me back? No! I've already had that freak-out once today.

"What?" I ask again, my voice rising in spite of my best efforts.

"We lost an hour coming to France, so it's after two o'clock. Lunchtime. And this is Paris. And we just have the day. So we must consider this very seriously."

"Oh." I exhale relief. Is he *trying* to mess with me now? "I don't care. Anything except chocolate and bread, please. Those might be your staples, but they don't seem particularly French," I snap, not entirely sure why I'm so peeved except that even though we've now walked several blocks away from Céline's club, it's like she's following us somehow.

Willem feigns offense. "Bread and chocolate are not my staple foods." He grins. "Not the only ones. And they are *very* French. Chocolate croissants? We can have those for breakfast tomorrow."

Breakfast. Tomorrow. *After tonight.* Céline begins to feel a little farther away now.

"Unless, that is, you prefer crisps for breakfast," he continues. "Or pancakes. That's American. Maybe crisps with your pancakes?"

"I don't eat *chips* for breakfast. I do occasionally eat pancakes for dinner. I'm a rebel that way."

"Crêpes," he says, snapping his fingers. "We will have crêpes. Very French. And you can be rebellious."

We walk along, menu-browsing the cafés until we find one on a quiet triangle corner that serves crêpes. The menu is hand-scrawled, in French, but I don't ask Willem to translate. After that whole thing with Céline, my lack of fluency is starting to feel like a handicap. So I stumble through the menu, settling on *citron*, which I'm pretty sure means lemon, or orange, or citrus of some kind. I decide on a *citron crêpe* and a *citron pressé* drink, hoping it's some kind of lemonade.

"What are you getting?" I ask.

He scratches his chin. There is a tiny patch of golden stubble there. "I was thinking of getting a chocolate crêpe, but that is so close to chocolate and bread that I'm afraid you'll lose respect for me." He flashes me that lazy half smile.

"I wouldn't sweat it. I already lost respect for you when I found you undressing for Céline in her office," I joke.

And there's that look: surprise, amusement. "That wasn't her office," he says slowly, drawing out his words. "And I would say she was more undressing me."

"Oh, never mind, then. By all means, order the chocolate."

He gives me a long look. "No. To repent, I will order mine with Nutella."

"That's hardly repenting. Nutella is practically chocolate."

"It's made from nuts."

"And chocolate! It's disgusting."

"You just say that because you're American."

"That has nothing to do with it! You seem to have a bottomless appetite for chocolate and bread, but I don't assume it's because you're Dutch."

"Why would it be?"

"Dutch Cocoa? You guys have the lock on it."

Willem laughs. "I think you have us confused with the Belgians. And I get my sweet tooth from my mother, who's not even Dutch. She says she craved chocolate all through her pregnancy with me and that's why I like it so much."

"Figures. Blame the woman."

"Who's blaming?"

The waitress comes over with our drinks.

"So, Céline," I begin, knowing I should let this go but am somehow unable to. "She's, like, the bookkeeper? At the club."

"Yes."

I know it's catty, but I'm gratified that it's such a dull job. Until Willem elaborates. "Not the bookkeeper. She *books* all the bands, so she knows all these musicians." And if that's not bad enough, he adds, "She does some of the artwork for the posters too."

"Oh." I deflate. "She must be very talented. Do you know her from the acting thing?"

"No."

"Well, how did you meet?"

He plays with the wrapper from my straw.

"I get it," I say, wondering why I'm bothering to ask what is so painfully clear. "You guys were an item."

"No, that's not it."

"Oh." Surprise. And relief.

And then Willem says, ever so casually, "We just fell in love once."

I take a gulp of my *citron pressé*—and choke on it. It turns out it's not lemonade so much as lemon juice and water. Willem hands me a cube of sugar and a napkin.

"*Once?*" I say when I recover.

"It was a while ago."

"And now?"

"We are good friends. As you saw."

I'm not sure that's exactly what I saw.

"So you're not in love with her anymore?" I run my fingers along the rim of my glass.

Willem looks at me. "I never said I was in love with her."

"You *just* said you fell in love with her once."

"And I did."

I stare at him, confused.

"There is a world of difference, Lulu, between *falling* in love and *being* in love."

I feel my face go hot, and I'm not entirely sure why. "Isn't it just sequential—A follows B?"

"You have to fall in love to be in love, but falling in love isn't the same as being in love." Willem peers at me from under his lashes. "Have you ever fallen in love?"

Evan and I broke up the day after he mailed in his college tuition deposit. It wasn't unexpected. Not really. We had already agreed we would break up when we went to college if we didn't wind up in the same geographical area. And he was going to school in St. Louis. I was going to school in Boston. The thing I hadn't expected was the timing. Evan decided it made more sense to "rip the bandage off" and break up not in June, when we graduated, or in August, when we'd leave for school, but in April.

But the thing is, aside from being sort of humiliated by the rumor that I'd been dumped and disappointed about missing prom, I wasn't actually sad about losing *Evan*. I was surprisingly neutral about breaking up with my first boyfriend. It was like he'd never even been there. I didn't miss him, and Melanie quickly filled up whatever gaps he'd left in the schedule.

"No," I reply. "I've never been in love."

Just then the waitress arrives with our crêpes. Mine is golden brown, wafting with the sweet tartness of lemon and sugar. I concentrate on that, cutting off a slice and popping it in my mouth. It melts on the tip of my tongue like a warm, sweet snowdrop.

"That's not what I asked," Willem says. "I asked if you've ever *fallen* in love."

The playfulness in his voice is like an itch I just can't scratch. I look at him, wondering if he always parses semantics like this.

Willem puts down his fork and knife. "*This* is falling in

love." With his finger, he swipes a bit of the Nutella from inside his crêpe and puts a dollop on the inside of my wrist. It is hot and oozy and starts to melt against my sticky skin, but before it has a chance to slither away, Willem licks his thumb and wipes the smear of Nutella off and pops it into his mouth. It all happens fast, like a lizard zapping a fly. "*This* is being in love." And here he takes my other wrist, the one with my watch on it, and moves the watchband around until he sees what he's looking for. Once again, he licks his thumb. Only this time, he rubs it against my birthmark, hard, as if trying to scrub it off.

"Being in love is a birthmark?" I joke as I retract my arm. But my voice has a tremble in it, and the place where his wet thumbprint is drying against my skin burns somehow.

"It's something that never comes off, no matter how much you might want it to."

"You're comparing love to a . . . stain?"

He leans so far back in his seat that the front legs of his chair scrape off the floor. He looks very satisfied, with the crêpe or with himself, I'm not sure. "Exactly."

I think of the coffee stain on his jeans. I think of Lady Macbeth and her "Out, damned spot" stain, another speech I had to memorize for English. "*Stain* seems like an ugly word to describe love," I tell him.

Willem just shrugs. "Maybe just in English. In Dutch, it's *vlek*. In French, it's *tache*." He shakes his head, laughs. "No, still ugly."

"How many languages have you been stained in?"

He licks his thumb again and reaches across the table for my wrist, where he missed the tiniest smudge of Nutella. This time he wipes it—me—clean. "None. It always comes off."

He scoops the rest of the crêpe into his mouth, taking the dull edge of his knife to scrape the Nutella off the plate. Then he runs his finger around the rim, smearing the last of it away.

"Right," I say. "And why get stained when getting dirty is so much more fun?" I taste lemons in my mouth again, and I wonder where all the sweetness went.

Willem doesn't say anything. Just sips his coffee.

Three women wander into the café. They are all impossibly tall, almost as tall as Willem, and thin, with legs that seem to end at their boobs. They are like some strange race of human-giraffes. Models. I've never seen one in the wild before, but it is obvious what they are. One of them is wearing a tiny pair of shorts and platform sandals; she checks Willem out, and he gives her his little half smile, but then it's like he catches himself and looks back at me.

"You know what it sounds like to me?" I ask. "It sounds like you just like to screw around. Which is fine. But at least own that about yourself. Don't make up some bogus distinctions about falling in love versus being in love."

I hear my voice. I sound like Little Miss Muffet, all goody-two-shoes and sanctimonious. So not like Lulu. And I don't know why I'm upset. What is it to me if he believes in falling in love versus being in love, or if he believes that love is something the tooth fairy shoves under your pillow?

When I look up, Willem's eyes are half lidded and smiling, like I'm his court jester here to amuse him. It makes me feel covetous, a toddler about to tantrum for being refused something outrageous—a pony—she knows she can't have.

"You probably don't even believe in love." My voice is petulant.

"I do." His voice is quiet.

"Really? Define love. What would 'being stained' "—I make air quotes and roll my eyes—"look like?"

He doesn't even pause to think about it. "Like Yael and Bram."

"Who's that? Some Dutch Brangelina? That doesn't count, because who knows what it's really like for them?" I watch the herd of models sit down at a table, where they will no doubt feast on coffee and air. I imagine them one day fat and ordinary. Because nothing that beautiful lasts forever.

"Who's Brangelina?" Willem asks absently. He reaches into his pocket for a coin and balances it between two knuckles, then flips it from knuckle to knuckle.

I watch the coin, watch his hands. They are big, but his fingers are delicate. "Never mind."

"Yael and Bram are my parents," he says quietly.

"Your *parents*?"

He completes a revolution with the coin and then tosses it into the air. "Stained. I like how you put it. Yael and Bram: Stained for twenty-five years."

He says it with both affection and sadness, and something in my stomach twists.

"Are your parents like that?" he asks quietly.

"They're still married after nearly twenty-five years, but stained?" I can't help but laugh. "I don't know if they ever were. They were set up on a blind date in college. And they've always seemed less like lovebirds than like amiable business partners, for whom I'm the sole product."

"Sole. So you are alone?"

Alone? I think he must mean *only*. And I'm never alone,

not with Mom and her color-coded calendar on the fridge, making sure every spare moment of my time is accounted for, making sure every aspect of my life is happily well managed. Except when I pause for a second and think about how I feel, at home, at the dinner table with Mom and Dad talking at me, not to me, at school with a bunch of people who never really became my friends, I understand that even if he didn't mean to, he got it right.

"Yes," I say.

"Me too."

"Our parents quit while they were ahead," I say, repeating the line Mom and Dad always use when people ask if I'm an only child. We *quit while we were ahead.*

"I never understand some English sayings," Willem replies "If you're ahead, why would you quit?"

"I think it's a gambling term."

But Willem is shaking his head. "I think it's human nature to keep going when you're ahead, no matter what. You quit while you're behind." Then he looks at me again, and as if realizing that he has maybe insulted me, he hastily adds, "I'm sure with you it was different."

When I was little, my parents had tried to have more children. First they went the natural route, then they went the fertility route, Mom going through a bunch of horrible procedures that never worked. Then they looked into adoption and were in the process of filling out all the paperwork when Mom got pregnant. She was so happy. I was in first grade at the time, and she'd worked since I was a baby, but when the baby came, she was going to go on an extended leave from her job at a pharmaceutical company, then maybe only go back half time. But then in her fifth month, she lost the baby. That's when she and Dad decided to quit while they were ahead. That's what they told me. Except even back then, I think I'd recognized it as a lie. They'd wanted more, but they'd had to settle with just me, and I had to be good enough so that we could all pretend that we weren't actually settling.

"Maybe you're right," I tell Willem now. "Maybe nobody quits while they're really ahead. My parents always say that, but the truth is, they only stopped with me because they couldn't have any more. Not because I was enough."

"I'm sure *you* were enough."

"Were *you*?" I ask.

"Maybe more than enough," he says cryptically. It almost sounds like he's bragging, except it doesn't look like he's bragging.

He starts doing the thing with the coin again. As we sit silently, I watch the coin, feeling something like suspense build in my stomach, wondering if he'll let it fall. But he doesn't. He just keeps spinning it. When he finishes, he flips it in the air and tosses it to me, just like he did last night.

"Can I ask you something?" I say after a minute.

"Yes."

"Was it part of the show?"

He cocks his head.

"I mean, do you throw a coin to a girl at every performance, or was I special?"

Last night after I got back to the hotel, I spent a long time examining the coin he'd tossed me. It was a Czech koruna, worth about a nickel. But still, I'd put it in a separate corner of my wallet, away from all the other foreign coins. I pull it out now. It glints in the bright afternoon sun.

Willem looks at it too. I'm not sure if his answer is true or just maddeningly ambiguous, or maybe both. Because that's exactly what he says: "Maybe both."

Seven

---

*W*hen we leave the restaurant, Willem asks me the time. I twist the watch around my wrist. It feels heavier than ever, the skin underneath itchy and pale from being stuck under the piece of chunky metal for the past three weeks. I haven't taken it off once.

It was a present, from my parents, though it was Mom who'd given it to me on graduation night, after the party at the Italian restaurant with Melanie's family, where they told us about the tour.

"What's this?" I'd asked. We were sitting at the kitchen table, decompressing from the day. "You already gave me a graduation present."

She'd smiled. "I got you another."

I'd opened the box, seen the watch, fingered the heavy gold links. Read the engraving.

"It's too much." And it was. In every way.

"Time stops for no one," Mom had said, smiling a little sadly. "You deserve a good watch to keep up." Then she'd snapped the watch on my wrist, shown me how she had an extra safety clasp installed, pointed out that it was water-proof too. "It'll never fall off. So you can take it to Europe with you."

"Oh, no. It's way too valuable."

"It's fine. It's insured. Besides, I threw away your Swatch."

"You did?" I'd worn my zebra-striped Swatch all through high school.

"You're a grown-up now. You need a grown up watch."

I look at my watch now. It's almost four. Back on the tour, I'd be breathing a sigh of relief, because the busy part of the day would be winding down. Usually we had a rest around five, and most nights, by eight o'clock, I could be back in my hotel room watching some movie.

"We should probably start seeing some of the sights," Willem says. "Do you know what you want to do?"

I shrug. "We could start with the Seine. Isn't that it?" I point to a concrete embankment, underneath which is a river of sorts.

Willem laughs. "No, that's a canal."

We walk down the cobblestoned pathway, and Willem pulls out a thick Rough Guide to Europe. He opens to a small map of Paris, points out, more or less, where we are, an area called Villette.

"The Seine is here," he says, tracing a line down the map.

"Oh." I look out at the boat, which is stuck now between two big metal gates; the area is filling up with water. Willem explains that this is a lock, basically an elevator that lifts and drops the boats down differing depths of the canals.

"How do you know so much about everything?"

He laughs. "I'm Dutch."

"So that means you're a genius?"

"Only about canals. They say 'God made the world, but the Dutch made Holland.'" And then he goes on to tell me about how so much of the country was reclaimed from the sea, about riding your bike along the low embankments that keep the water out of Holland. How it's an act of faith to ride your bike around, with the dikes above you, knowing somehow, even though you're below sea level, you're not under water. When he talks about it, he seems so young that I can almost see him as a towheaded little kid, eyes wide, staring out at the endless waterways and wondering where they all led to.

"Maybe we can go on one of those boats?" I ask, pointing to the barge we just watched go through the lock.

Willem's eyes light up, and for a second, I see that boy again. "I don't know." He looks inside the guidebook. "It doesn't really cover this neighborhood."

"Can we ask?"

Willem asks someone in French and is given a very complicated answer full of hand gestures. He turns to me, clearly excited. "You're right. He says that they have boat rides leaving from the basin."

We go along the cobblestoned walkway until it lets out in a large lake, where people are paddling in canoes. Off to one side, next to a cement pier, a couple of boats are moored. But when we get over there, we find out that they're private boats. The tourist boats have left for the day.

"We can take a boat along the Seine," Willem says. "It's much more popular, and the boats run all day." His eyes are downcast. I can see he's disappointed, as if he let me down.

"Oh, no big deal. I don't care."

But he's staring wistfully out at the water, and I see that *he* cares. And I know I don't know him, but I swear the boy is homesick. For boats and canals and watery things. And for a second, I think of what it must be like—away from home for two years, and here he postponed his return for another day. He did that. For me.

There's a row of boats and barges tied up, bobbing in the breeze that's kicked up. I look at Willem; a melancholy expression is deepening the lines on his face. I look back at the boats.

"Actually, I do care," I say. I reach into my bag for my wallet, for the hundred-dollar bill folded inside. I hold it up in the air and call out, "I'm looking for a ride down the canals. And I can pay."

Willem's head jerks toward me. "Lulu, what are you doing?"

But I'm walking away from him. "Anyone willing to give us a lift down the canals?" I call. "I got good old-fashioned American greenbacks."

A pock-faced guy with sharp features and a scrubby goatee pops onto the side of a blue-canopied barge. "How many greenbacks?" he asks in a very thick French accent.

"All of them!"

He takes the C-note and stares at it up close. Then he smells it.

It must smell legit, because he says, "If my passengers

agree, I will take you down the canal to Arsenal, close to the Bastille. It is where we dock for the night." He gestures to the back of the boat where a quartet of gray-haired people are sitting around a small table, playing bridge or something. He calls out to one of them.

"Aye, Captain Jack," the man answers. He must be sixty. His hair is white, and his face is burnished red from the sun.

"We have some hitchhikers who want to come aboard with us."

"Can they play poker?" one of the women asks.

I used to play seven-card stud for nickels with my grandfather before he died. He said I was an excellent bluffer.

"Do not bother. She gave all her money to me," Captain Jack says.

"How much is he charging you?" one of the men asks.

"I offered him a hundred dollars," I say.

"To go where?"

"Down the canals."

"This is why we call him Captain Jack," one of the men says. "Because he's a pirate."

"No. It is because my name is Jacques, and I am your captain."

"A hundred dollars, Jacques?" a woman with a long gray braid and startlingly blue eyes asks. "That seems a little much, even for you."

"She offered this much." Jacques shrugs. "Also, now I will have more money to lose to you in poker."

"Ahh, good point," she says.

"Are you leaving now?" I ask.

"Soon."

"When is soon?" It's after four. The day is speeding by.

"You cannot rush these things." He flicks his hand in the air. "Time is like the water. Fluid."

Time doesn't seem fluid to me. It seems real and animate and hard as a rock.

"What he means," says the guy with the ponytail, "is that the trip to Arsenal takes a while and we were just about to open a bottle of claret. Come on, Captain Jack, let's shove off. For a hundred bucks, you can have your wine later."

"We'll continue with this fine French gin," the braided lady says.

He shrugs and then pockets my bill. I turn to Willem and grin. Then I nod at Captain Jack. He reaches out for my hand to escort me onboard.

The four passengers introduce themselves. They are Danish, retirees, and every year, they tell us, they rent a barge and cruise a European country for four weeks. Agnethe has the braid and Karin has short spiked hair. Bert has a shock of white hair and Gustav has the bald spot and the rat's tail of a ponytail and is sporting the ever-stylish socks-with-sandals look. Willem introduces himself, and almost automatically, I introduce *myself* as Lulu. It's almost as if I've become her. Maybe I have. Never in a million years would Allyson have done what I just did.

Captain Jack and Willem untie the line, and I'm about to say that maybe I should get some of my money back if Willem is going to play first mate but then I see that Willem is bounding about, having a blast. He clearly knows his way around a boat.

The barge chugs out of the broad basin, giving a wide view of a white-columned old building and a silver-domed modern-looking one. The Danes return to their poker game.

"Don't lose all your money," Captain Jack calls to them. "Or you won't have any left to lose to me."

I slip away to the bow of the boat and watch the scenery slip by. It's cooler down here in the canals, under the narrow arched footbridges. And it smells different too. Older, mustier, like generations of history are stored in the wet walls. If these walls could talk, I wonder what secrets they'd tell.

When we get to the first lock, Willem clambers to the side of the barge to show me how the mechanism works. The ancient-looking metal gates, rusted the same brackish color as the water, close behind us, the water drains out from beneath us, the gates reopen to a lower section.

This part of the canal is so narrow that the barge takes up almost the entire width. Steep embankments lead up to the streets, and above those, poplar and elm trees (per Captain Jack) form an arbor, a gentle respite from the hot afternoon sun.

A gust of wind shakes the trees, sending a scrim of leaves shimmying onto the deck. "Rain is coming," Captain Jack says, sniffing the air like a rabbit. I look up and then over at Willem and roll my eyes. The sky is cloudless, and there hasn't been rain in this part of Europe for ten days.

Up above, Paris carries on, doing her thing. Mothers sip coffee, keeping eyes on their kids as they scooter along the side-walks. Vendors at outdoor stalls hawk fruits and vegetables. Lovers wrap their arms around each other, never mind the heat. A clarinet player stands atop the bridge, serenading it all.

I've hardly taken any pictures on this trip. Melanie teased me about it, to which I always said I preferred to experience something rather than obsessively record it. Though, really, the truth of it was, unlike Melanie (who wanted to remember the shoe salesman and the mime and the cute waiter and all the other people on the tour), none of that really mattered to me. At the start of the trip, I took shots of the sights. The Colosseum. Belvedere Palace. Mozart Square. But I stopped. They never came out very well, and you could get postcards of these things.

But there are no postcards of this. Of life.

I snap a picture of a bald man walking four bushy-haired dogs. Of a little girl in the most absurdly frilly skirt, plucking petals off a flower. Of a couple, unabashedly making out on the fake beach along the waterside. Of the Danes, ignoring all of this, but having the time of their lives playing cards.

"Oh, let me take one of the two of you," Agnethe says, rising, a little wobbly, from the game. "Aren't you golden?" She turns to the table. "Bert, was I ever that golden?"

"You still are, my love."

"How long have you been married?" I ask.

"Thirteen years," she says, and I'm wondering if they're stained, but then she adds, "Of course, we've been divorced for ten."

She sees the look of confusion on my face. "Our divorce is more successful than most marriages."

I turn to Willem. "What kind of stain is that?" I whisper, and he laughs just as Agnethe takes the picture.

A church bell rings in the distance. Agnethe hands back the phone, and I take a picture of her and Bert. "You will send me that one? All of the ones?"

"Of course. As soon as I have reception." I turn to Willem.

"I'll text them to you too, if you give me your number."

"My phone is so old, it doesn't work with pictures."

"When I get home, then, I'll put the pictures on my computer and email them to you," I say, though I'll have to figure out a place to hide the pictures from Mom; it wouldn't be beyond her to look through my phone—or computer. Though, I realize now, only for another month. And then I'll be free. Just like today I'm free.

He looks at one of the pictures for a long time. Then he looks at me. "I'll keep you up here." He taps his temple. "Where you can't get lost."

I bite my lip to hide my smile and pretend to put the phone away, but when Captain Jack calls to Willem to take the wheel while he visits the head, I pull it back out and scroll through the photos, stopping at the one of the two of us that Agnethe took. I'm in profile, my mouth open. He's laughing. Always laughing. I run my thumb over his face, halfway expecting it to emanate some sort of heat.

I put the phone away and watch Paris drift by, feeling relaxed, almost drunk with a sleepy joy. After a while, Willem returns to me. We sit quietly, listening to the lapping of the water, the babble of the Danes. Willem pulls a coin out and does that thing, flipping it from knuckle to knuckle. I watch, hypnotized by his hand, by the gentle rocking of the water. It's peaceful until the Danes start bickering, loudly. Willem translates: Apparently they're hotly debating whether some famous French actress has ever made a pornographic film.

"You speak *Danish* too?" I ask.

"No, it's just close to Dutch."

"How many languages do you speak?"

"Fluently?"

"Oh, God. I'm sorry I asked."

"Four fluently. I get by in German and Spanish too."

I shake my head, amazed.

"Yes, but you said you speak *Chinese*."

"I wouldn't say I speak it so much as murder it. I'm kind of tone deaf, and Mandarin is all about tone."

"Let me hear."

I look at him. "*Ni zhen shuai*."

"Say something else."

"*Wo xiang wen ni*."

"Now I hear it." He covers his head. "Stop. I'm bleeding from my ears."

"Shut up or you will be." I pretend to shove him.

"What did you say?" he asks.

I give him a look. No way I'm telling.

"You just made it up."

I shrug. "You'll never know."

"What does it mean?"

I grin. "You'll have to look it up."

"Can you write it too?" He pulls out his little black book and opens to a blank page near the back. He rifles back into his bag. "Do you have a pen?"

I have one of those fancy roller balls I swiped from my dad, this one emblazoned BREATHE EASY WITH PULMO-CLEAR. I write the character for sun, moon, stars. Willem nods admiringly.

"And look, I love this one. It's double happiness."

"See how the characters are symmetrical?"

"Double happiness," Willem repeats, tracing the lines with his index finger.

"It's a popular phrase. You'll see it on restaurants and things. I think it has to do with luck. In China, it's apparently big at weddings. Probably because of the story of its origin."

"Which is?"

"A young man was traveling to take a very important exam to become a minister. On the way, he gets sick in a mountain village. So this mountain doctor takes care of him, and while he's recovering, he meets the doctor's daughter, and they fall in love. Right before he leaves, the girl tells him a line of verse. The boy heads off to the capital to take his exam and does well, and the emperor's all impressed. So, I guess to test him further, he says a line of verse. Of course, the boy immediately recognizes this mysterious line as the other half of the couplet the girl told him, so he repeats what the girl said. The emperor's doubly impressed, and the boy gets the job. Then he goes back and marries the girl. So, double happiness, I guess. He gets the job and the girl. You know, the Chinese are very big on luck."

Willem shakes his head. "I think the double happiness is the two halves finding each other. Like the couplet."

I'd never thought of it, but of course that's what it is.

"Do you remember how it goes?" Willem asks.

I nod. "Green trees against the sky in the spring rain while the sky set off the spring trees in the obscuration. Red flowers dot the land in the breeze's chase while the land colored up in red after the kiss."

— — —

The final section of the canal is underground. The walls are arched, and so low that I can reach up and touch the slick, wet bricks. It's eerie, hushed but echoey down here. Even the boisterous Danes have shushed. Willem and I sit with our legs dangling over the edge of the boat, kicking the side of the tunnel wall when we can.

He nudges my ankle with his toe. "Thank you."

"For what?"

"For arranging this." He gestures to the boat.

"My pleasure. Thank you for arranging *this*." I point above us, to where Paris is no doubt going about its business.

"Any time." He looks around. "It's nice, this. The canal." He looks at me. "You."

"I'll bet you say that to all the canals." But I flush in the musty, rich darkness.

We stay like that for the rest of the ride, swinging our legs against the side of the boat, listening as the odd bit of laughter or music from Paris seeps underground. It feels like the city is telling secrets down here, privy only to those who think to listen.

Eight

Arsenal Marina is like a parking lot for boats, tightly packed into cement piers on both sides of the water. Willem helps Captain Jack guide the barge into its narrow mooring, hopping out to tie the lines in complicated knots. We bid farewell to the Danes, who are now truly soused, and I take down Agnethe's cell phone number, promising to text her the pictures as soon as I can.

As we get off, Captain Jack shakes our hands. "I feel a little bad to take your money," he says.

"No. Don't feel bad." I think of the look on Willem's face, of being in the tunnel. That alone was worth a hundred bucks.

"And we'll take it off you soon enough," Gustav calls.

Jacques shrugs. He kisses my hand before he helps me off the boat, and he practically hugs Willem.

As we walk away, Willem taps my shoulder. "Did you see what the boat is named?"

I didn't. It's right on the back, etched in blue lettering, next to the vertical red, white, and blue stripes of the French flag. *Viola. Deauville.*

"Viola? After Shakespeare's Viola?"

"No. Jacques meant for it to be called *Voilà*, but his cousin painted it wrong, and he liked the name, so he registered her as *Viola*."

"Okaaay—that's still a little weird," I say.

As always, Willem smiles.

"Accidents?" Immediately, a strange little tremor goes up my spine.

Willem nods, almost solemnly. "Accidents," he confirms.

"But what does it mean? Does it mean we were meant to take *that* boat? Does it mean something better or worse would've happened to us if we *hadn't* taken that boat? Did taking that boat *alter* the course of our lives? Is life really that random?"

Willem just shrugs.

"Or does it mean that Jacques's cousin can't spell?" I say.

Willem laughs again. The sound is clear and strong as a bell, and it fills me with joy, and it's like, for the first time in my life, I understand that *this* is the point of laughter, to spread happiness.

"Sometimes you can't know until you know," he says.

"That's very helpful."

He laughs and looks at me for a long moment. "You know, I think you might be good at traveling after all."

"Seriously? I'm not. Today is a total anomaly. I was miserable on the tour. Trust me, I didn't flag down a single boat. Not even a taxi. Not even a bicycle."

"What about before the tour?"

"I haven't traveled much, and the kind I've done . . . not a lot of room for accidents."

Willem raises a questioning eyebrow.

"I've been places. Florida. Skiing. And to Mexico, but even that sounds more exotic than it is. Every year, we go to this time-share resort south of Cancún. It's meant to look like a giant Mayan temple, but I swear the only clue that you're not in America is the piped-in mariachi Christmas carols along the fake river waterslide thing. We stay in the same unit. We go to the same beach. We eat at the same restaurants. We barely even leave the gates, and when we do, it's to visit the ruins, but we go to the same ones every single year. It's like the calendar flips but nothing else changes."

"Same, same, but different," Willem says.

"More like same, same, but same."

"Next time when you go to Cancún, you can sneak out into the real Mexico," he suggests. "Tempt fate. See what happens."

"Maybe," I allow, just imagining my mom's response if I suggested a little freelance traveling.

"Maybe I'll go to Mexico one day," Willem says. "I'll bump into you, and we'll escape into the wilds."

"You think that would happen? We'd just randomly bump into each other?"

Willem lifts his hands up in the air. "There would have to be another accident. A big one."

"Oh, so you're saying that *I'm* an accident?"

His smile stretches like caramel. "Absolutely."

I rub my toe against the curb. I think of my Ziploc bags. I think of the color-coded schedule of all my activities that we've kept tacked to the fridge since I was, like, eight. I think of my neat files with all my college application materials. Everything ordered. Everything planned. I look at Willem, so the opposite of that, of me, today, also the opposite of that.

"I think that might possibly be one of the most flattering things anyone has ever said to me." I pause. "I'm not sure what that says about me, though."

"It says that you haven't been flattered enough."

I bow and give a sweeping be-my-guest gesture.

He stops and looks at me, and it's like his eyes are scanners. I have that same sensation I did on the train earlier, that he's appraising me, only this time not for looks and black-market value, but for something else.

"I won't say that you're pretty, because that dog already did. And I won't say you're funny, because you have had me laughing since I met you."

Evan used to tell me that he and I were "so compatible," as if being like him was the highest form of praise. *Pretty and funny*—Willem could stop right there, and it would be enough.

But he doesn't stop there. "I think you're the sort of person who finds money on the ground and waves it in the air and asks if anyone has lost it. I think you cry in movies that aren't even sad because you have a soft heart, though you don't let it show. I think you do things that scare you, and that makes you braver than those adrenaline junkies who bungee-jump off bridges."

He stops then. I open my mouth to say something, but nothing comes out and there's a lump in my throat and for one small second, I'm scared I'm going to cry.

Because I'd hoped for baubles, trinkets, fizzy things: *You have a nice smile. You have pretty legs. You're sexy.*

But what he said . . . I did once turn in forty dollars I found at the food court to mall security. I have cried in every single Jason Bourne movie. As for the last thing he said, I don't know if it's true. But I hope more than anything that it is.

"We should get going," I say, clearing my throat. "If we want to get to the Louvre. How far is it from here?"

"Maybe a few kilometers. But it's fast by bike."

"You want me to wave one down?" I joke.

"No, we'll just get a Vélib'." Willem looks around and walks toward a stand of gray bicycles. "Have you ever heard of the White Bicycle?" he asks.

I shake my head, and Willem starts explaining how for a brief time in Amsterdam in the 1960s, there used to be white bicycles, and they were free and everywhere. When you wanted a bike, you grabbed one, and when you were done, you left it. But it didn't work because there weren't enough bikes, and people stole them. "In Paris, you can borrow a bike for free for a half hour, but you have to lock it back up, or you get charged."

"Oh, I think I just read they started something like this back home. So, it's free?"

"All you need is a credit card for the deposit."

I don't have a credit card—well, not one that doesn't link back to my parents' account, but Willem has his bank card, though he says he isn't sure if there's enough. When he runs it through the little keypad, one of the bikes unlocks, but when he tries it again for a second bike, the card is declined. I'm not entirely disappointed. Cycling around Paris, sans helmet, seems vaguely suicidal.

But Willem's not replacing the bike. He's wheeling it over to where I'm standing and raising the seat. He looks at me. Then pats the saddle.

"Wait, you want *me* to ride the bike?"

He nods.

"And you'll what? Run alongside me?"

"No. I'll ride you." His eyebrows shoot up, and I feel myself blush. "On the bike," he clarifies.

I climb onto the wide seat. Willem steps in front of me. "Where exactly are you going to go?" I ask.

"Don't worry about that. You just get comfortable," he says, as if it's possible in the current situation, with his back inches from my face, so close I can feel the heat radiating off him, so close I can smell the new-clothes aroma of his T-shirt mingling with the light musk of his sweat. He puts one foot on one of the pedals. Then he turns around, an impish grin on his face. "Warn me if you see police. This isn't quite legal."

"Wait, what's not legal?"

But he's already pushed off. I shut my eyes. This is insane. We're going to die. And then my parents really will kill me.

A block later, we're still alive. I squint an eye open. Willem is leaning all the way forward over the handlebars, effortlessly standing on the pedals, while I lean back, my legs dangling alongside the rear wheel. I open my other eye, release my clammy grip on the hem of his T-shirt. The marina is well behind us, and we are on a regular street, in a bike lane, cruising along with all the other gray bicycles.

We turn onto a choked street full of construction, half the avenue blocked by scaffolding and blockades, and I'm looking at all the graffiti; the SOS, just like on the T-shirt for that band *Sous ou Sur,* is scrawled there. I'm about to point it out to Willem, but then I turn in the other direction and there's the Seine. And there's Paris. Postcard Paris! Paris from *French Kiss* and from *Midnight in Paris* and from *Charade* and every other Paris film I've ever seen. I gape at the Seine, which is rippling in the breeze and glimmering in the early-evening sun. Down the expanse of it, I can see a series of arched bridges, draped like expensive bracelets over an elegant wrist. Willem points out Notre Dame Cathedral, just towering there, in the middle of an island in the middle of a river, like it's nothing. Like it's any other day, and it's not the freaking Notre Dame! We pass by another building, a wedding-cake confection that looks like it might house royalty. But, no, it's just City Hall.

It's funny how on the tour, we often saw sights like this as we whizzed by on a bus. Ms. Foley would stand at the front of the coach, microphone in hand, and tell us facts about this cathedral or that opera house. Sometimes, we'd stop and go in, but with one or two days per city, most of the time, we drove on by.

I'm driving by them now too. But somehow, it feels different. Like, being here, outside, on the back of this bike, with the wind in my hair and the sounds singing in my ears and the centuries-old cobblestones rattling beneath my butt, I'm not missing anything. On the contrary, I'm inhaling it, consuming it, becoming it.

I'm not sure how to account for the change, for all the changes today. Is it Paris? Is it Lulu? Or is it Willem? Is it his nearness that makes the city so intoxicating or the city that makes his nearness so irresistible?

A loud whistle cuts through my reverie, and the bike comes to an abrupt halt.

"Ride's over," Willem says. I hop off, and Willem starts wheeling the bicycle down the street.

A policeman with a thin mustache and a constipated expression comes chasing after us. He starts yelling at Willem, gesticulating, wagging a finger at me. His face is turning a bright red, and when he pulls out his little book and starts pointing to me and Willem, I get nervous. I thought Willem had been joking about the illegal thing.

Then Willem says something to the cop that stops the tirade cold.

The cop starts nattering on, and I don't understand a word, except I'm pretty sure he says "Shakespeare!" while holding a finger up in an *aha* motion. Willem nods, and the cop's tone softens. He is still wagging his finger at us, but the little book goes back into his satchel. With a tip of his funny little hat, he walks away.

"Did you just quote Shakespeare to a cop?" I ask.

Willem nods.

I'm not sure what's crazier: That Willem did that. Or that the cops here know Shakespeare.

"What did you say?"

"*La beauté est une enchanteresse, et la bonne foi qui s'expose à ses charmes se dissout en sang,*" he says. "It's from *Much Ado About Nothing.*"

"What does it mean?"

Willem gives me that look of his, licks his lips, smiles. "You'll have to look it up."

We walk along the river and onto a main road full of restaurants, art galleries, and high-end boutiques. Willem parks the bike in a stand, and we take off on foot under a long portico and then make a few more turns into what, at first, seems like it should be a presidential residence or a royal palace, Versailles or something, the buildings are so huge and grand. Then I spot the glass pyramid in the middle of the courtyard, so I know we have arrived at the Louvre.

It's mobbed. Thousands of people are flooding out of the buildings, like they're evacuating it, clutching poster tubes and large black-and-white shopping bags. Some are energized, chatty, but many more look shell-shocked, weary, glazed after a day spent ingesting epic portions of Culture! I know that look. The Teen Tours! brochure bragged that it offered "young people the full-on European immersion experience! We'll expose your teen to a maximum number of cultures in a short period of time, broadening their view of history, language, art, heritage, cuisine." It was supposed to be enlightening, but it mostly felt exhausting.

So when we discover that the Louvre just closed, I'm actually relieved.

"I'm sorry," Willem says.

"Oh, I'm not." I'm not sure if this qualifies as an accident or not, but I'm happy either way.

We do an about-face and cross over a bridge and turn up the other bank of the river. Alongside the embankment there are all kinds of vendors selling books and old magazines, pristine issues of *Paris Match* with Jackie Kennedy on the cover and old pulp paperbacks with lurid covers, titled in both English and French. There's one vendor with a bunch of bric-a-brac, old vases, costume jewelry, and in a box on the side, a collection of dusty vintage alarm clocks. I paw through and find a vintage SMI in Bakelite. "Twenty euro," the kerchiefed saleslady says to me. I try to keep a poker face. Twenty euro is about thirty bucks. The clock is easily worth two hundred dollars.

"Do you want it?" Willem asks.

My mom would go nuts if I brought this home, and she'd never have to know where it was from. The woman winds the clock, to show me that it works, but hearing it tick, I'm reminded of what Jacques said, about time being fluid. I look out at the Seine, which is now glowing pink, reflecting the color of the clouds that are rolling in. I put the clock back in the box.

We head up off the embankment, into the twisty, narrow warren of streets that Willem tells me is the Latin Quarter, where students live. It's different over here. Not so many grand avenues and boulevards but alley-like lanes, barely wide enough for even the tiny, space-age two-person Smart Cars that are zooming around everywhere. Tiny churches, hidden corners, alleys. It's a whole different Paris. And just as dazzling.

"Shall we take a drink?" Willem asks.

I nod.

We cross onto a crowded avenue, full of cinemas, out-door cafés, all of them packed, and also a handful of small hotels, not too expensive judging by the prices advertised on the sandwich boards. Most of the signs say *complet*, which I'm pretty sure means full, but some don't, and some of the rooms we might be able to afford if I were to exchange the last of my cash, about forty pounds.

I haven't been able to broach tonight with Willem. Where we're staying. He hasn't seemed too worried about it, which has me worried our fallback is Céline. We pass an exchange bureau. I tell Willem I want to change some money.

"*I* have some money left," he says. "And you just paid for the boat."

"But I don't have a single euro on me. What if I wanted to, I don't know, buy a postcard?" I stop to spin a postcard caddy. "Also, there's drinks and dinner, and we'll need somewhere for, for . . ." I trail off before getting the courage to finish. "Tonight." I feel my neck go warm.

The word seems to hang out there as I wait for Willem's response, some clue of what he's thinking. But he's looking over at one of the cafés, where a group of girls at a table seem to be waving at him. Finally, he turns back to me. "Sorry?" he asks.

The girls are still waving. One of them is beckoning him over. "Do you know them?"

He looks over at the café, then back at me, then back at the restaurant. "Can you wait here for a minute?"

My stomach sinks. "Yeah, no problem."

He leaves me at a souvenir shop, where I spin the postcard caddy and spy. When he gets to the group of girls, they do the cheek-cheek-kiss-kiss thing—three times, though, instead of twice like he did with Céline. He sits down next to the girl who was gesturing to him. It's clear they know each other;

she keeps putting her hand on his knee. He throws darting glances in my direction, and I wait for him to wave me over, but he doesn't, and after an endless five minutes, the touchy girl writes something down on a bit of paper and gives it to him. He jams the slip deep into his pocket. Then he stands up, and they do another cheek-cheek-kiss-kiss thing, and he strides back to me, where I am feigning a deep interest in a Toulouse-Lautrec postcard.

"Let's go," he says as he grabs my elbow.

"Friends of yours?" I ask, jogging to keep up with his long stride.

"No."

"But you know them?"

"I knew them once."

"And you just randomly bumped into them?"

He spins toward me, and for the first time today, he's annoyed. "It's Paris, Lulu, the most touristy city in the world. It happens."

Accidents, I think. But I feel jealous, possessive, not just over the girl—whose number, I suspect, he now has in his hip pocket if he hasn't already transcribed it into his little black book—but over accidents. Because today it has felt like accidents belonged solely to us.

Willem softens. "They're just people I knew from Holland."

Something in Willem's whole demeanor has changed, like a lamp whose bulb is dimming before it burns out. And it's then that I notice the final and defeated way he says *Holland,* and it makes me realize that all day long, not once has he said he was going *home.* And then another thought hits me. Today, he was meant to be going home—or to Holland, where he's from—for the first time in two years.

In three days, I will go home, and there will be a crowd at the airport. Back at my house, there will be a welcome-home banner, a celebratory dinner I'll probably be too jet-lagged to eat. After only three weeks on a tour in which I was led around like a show pony, I'll be given a hero's welcome.

He's been gone *two years*. Why isn't Willem getting a hero's welcome? Is anyone even waiting for him?

"When we were at Céline's," I ask him now, "did you call anyone?"

He turns to me, his dark eyes furrowed and confused. "No. Why?"

Because how does anyone know you're delayed? Because how do they know to postpone your hero's welcome until tomorrow?

"Isn't anyone expecting you?" I ask.

Something happens to his face, for just the slightest of moments, a slip of his jaunty mask, which I hadn't realized was a mask until I see how tired, how uncertain—how much like me—he looks underneath it.

"You know what I think?" Willem asks.

"What?"

"We should get lost."

"I've got news for you, but I've been lost all day."

"This is different. This is getting on purpose lost. It's something I do when I first come to a new city. I'll go into the metro or on a tramline and randomly pick a stop and go."

I can see what he's doing. He's changing the scenery, changing the subject. And I get that, in some way, he needs to do this. So I let him. "Like traveler's pin the tail on the donkey?" I ask.

Willem gives me a quizzical look. His English is so good that I forget not everything computes.

"Is this about accidents?" I ask.

He looks at me, and for half a second, the mask slips again. But then just like that, it's back in place. It doesn't matter. It slipped, and I saw. And I understand. Willem is alone, like I am alone. And now this ache that I can't quite distinguish as his or mine has opened up inside of me.

"It's always about accidents," he says.

Nine

———

I pick a doozy.

Using the pin-the-tail-on-the-donkey strategy, I close my eyes and spin in front of the Metro map and land my finger on the benign-sounding Château Rouge.

When we come out of the Metro, we are in yet another Paris altogether, and there's not a chateau, rouge or otherwise, in sight.

The streets are narrow, like in the Latin Quarter, but grittier. Tinny, drum-heavy music blares out from the shop windows, and there's such an onslaught of smells, my nose doesn't know what to breathe first: curry coming out of the patisseries, the ferric tang of blood from the giant animal carcasses being trundled through the street, the sweet and exotic smell of incense smoke, exhaust from the cars and motos, the ubiquitous smell of coffee—though there aren't so many of the big cafés here, the kind that take up an entire corner, but more smaller, ad-hoc ones, bistro tables shoved onto the sidewalk. And they're all packed with men smoking and drinking coffee. The women, some wearing full black veils with only their eyes showing through the slits, others in colorful dresses, sleeping babies tied to their backs, bustle in and out of the stores. We are the only tourists in this area, and people are looking at us, not menacingly, but just curiously, like we're lost. Which we are. This is precisely why, on my own, I would never in a million years do this.

But Willem is loving it here. So I try to take a cue from him and relax, and just gape at this part of Paris meets Middle East meets Africa.

We go past a mosque, then a hulking church, all spires and buttresses, that seems like it landed in this neighborhood the same way we did. We twist and turn until we wind up in some sort of park: a quadrangle of grass and paths and handball courts sandwiched in between the apartment buildings. It's packed with girls in head scarves playing some version of hopscotch and boys on the handball courts and people walking dogs and playing chess and sitting out for a smoke at the end of a summer afternoon.

"Do you have any idea where we are?" I ask Willem.

"I am as lost as you are."

"Oh, we are *so* screwed." But I laugh. It feels kind of nice to be lost, together.

We flop down under a stand of trees in a quiet corner of the park under a mural of children playing in the clouds. I slide off my sandals. I have tan lines made from dirt and sweat. "I think my feet are broken."

Willem kicks off his flip-flops. I see the zigzag scar running up his left foot. "Mine too."

We lie on our backs as the sun throws shadows down between the clouds that are really starting to roll in on the cooling breeze, bringing with them the electric smell of rain. Maybe Jacques was right, after all.

"What time is it?" Willem asks.

I shut my eyes and stick my arm out for him to see. "Don't tell me. I don't want to know."

He takes my arm, checks the time. But then he doesn't let go. He examines my wrist, rotating it forward and back, as if it were some rare object, the first wrist he has ever seen.

"That's a very nice watch," he says finally.

"Thank you," I say dutifully.

"You don't like it?"

"No. It's not that. I mean, it was a really generous gift from my parents, who'd already given me the tour, and it's a very expensive watch." I stop myself. It's Willem, and something compels me to tell him the truth. "But, no, I don't really like it."

"Why not?"

"I don't know. It's heavy. It makes my wrist sweaty. And it ticks loudly, like it's always trying to remind me that time is passing. Like I can't ever forget about time."

"So why do you wear it?"

It's such a simple question. Why do I wear a watch that I hate? Even here, thousands of miles from home, with no one to see me wearing it, why do I still wear it? Because my parents bought it for me with the best of intentions. Because I can't let them down.

I feel the gentle pressure of Willem's fingers on my wrist again. The clasp opens, and the watch falls away, leaving a white ghost imprint. I can feel the refreshing breeze tickle against my birthmark.

Willem examines the watch, the *Going Places* engraving. "Where are you going, exactly?"

"Oh, you know. To Europe. To college. To medical school."

"Medical school?" There's surprise in his voice.

I nod. That's been the plan ever since eighth grade, when I gave the Heimlich maneuver to some guy who was choking on his lamb shank at the next table. Dad had been out front, answering a call from the service when I'd seen the guy next to us go purple. So I just got up and calmly put my arms around the guy's diaphragm and pushed until a piece of meat arced out. Mom was beyond impressed. She'd started talking about my becoming a doctor like Dad. After a while, I started talking about it too.

"So you'll take care of me?"

His voice has the usual teasing tone, so I get that he's joking, but this wave comes over me. Because who takes care of him now? I look at him, and he makes everything seem effortless, but I remember that feeling before—a certainty—that he is alone.

"Who takes care of you now?"

At first I'm not sure I said it aloud and, if I did, that he heard me, because he doesn't answer for a long time. But then finally, he says, "I take care of me."

"But what about when you can't? When you get sick?"

"I don't get sick."

"Everybody gets sick. What happens when you're on the road and you get the flu or something?"

"I get sick. I get better," he replies, waving the question away.
I prop myself up on my elbow. This weird chasm of feeling
has opened in my chest, making my breath come shallow and
my words dance like scattered leaves. "I keep thinking about
the double happiness story. That boy was traveling alone and
got sick, but someone took care of him. Is that what happens to you when you get sick? Or are you alone in some
gross hotel room?" I try to picture Willem in a mountain village, but all I get is an image of him in a dingy room. I think
of how I get when I'm sick, that deep sadness, that alone-
ness that strikes—and I have Mom to take care of me. What
about him? Does anyone bring him soup? Does anyone tell
him about the green trees against the sky in the spring rain?

Willem doesn't answer. In the distance, I can hear the pop
of the handball slamming against the wall, the coquettish
sound of women's laughter. I think of Céline. The girls on the
train. The models at the café. The slip of paper in his pocket.
There's probably no shortage of girls wanting to play nurse
with him. I get a weird feeling in my stomach. I've made a
wrong turn, like when I am skiing and I accidentally swerve
onto a black-diamond run full of moguls.

"Sorry," I say. "It's probably just the doctor in me coming
out. Or the Jewish mother."

Willem gives me a peculiar look. Another wrong turn. I
keep forgetting that in Europe, there are hardly any Jewish
people, so jokes like that don't make sense.

"I'm Jewish, and apparently that means when I get older,
I'm doomed to fuss about everyone's health," I hastily explain.
"That's what 'Jewish mother' means."

Willem lies on his back and holds my watch up to his face.

"It's strange you mention the double happiness story. Sometimes I do get sick and wind up puking into squat toilets, and it's not so nice."

I wince at the thought of it.

"But there was this one time, I was traveling from Morocco to Algeria by bus, and I got dysentery, a pretty bad case. So bad I had no choice but to get off the bus in the middle of nowhere. It was some town at the edge of the Sahara, not even mentioned in any book. I was dehydrated, hallucinating, I think, stumbling around for a place to stay when I saw a hotel and restaurant called Saba. Saba was what I used to call my grandfather. It seemed like a sign, like he was saying 'go here.' The restaurant was empty. I went straight to the toilets to throw up again. When I came out, there was a man with a short gray beard wearing a long djellaba. I asked for some tea and ginger, which is what my mother always uses for upset stomachs. He shook his head and told me I was in the desert now and had to use desert remedies. He disappeared into the kitchen and returned with a grilled lemon, cut in half. He sprinkled it with salt and told me to squeeze the juice into my mouth. I thought I would lose it again, but in twenty minutes, my stomach was okay. He gave me some terrible tea that tasted like tree bark and sent me upstairs, where I slept maybe eighteen hours. Every day, I came downstairs, and he would ask how I was feeling and then prepare me a meal specifically based on my symptoms. After that we would talk, just as I had done with Saba as a child. I stayed there for a week, in this town on the edge of the map that I am not even sure exists. So it is a lot like your story from before."

"Except he didn't have a daughter," I say. "Or you'd be married by now."

We are on our sides, facing each other, so close I can feel the warmth radiating off him, so close it's like we are breathing the same air.

"You be the daughter. Tell me that couplet again," he says.

"Green trees against the sky in the spring rain while the sky set off the spring trees in the obscuration. Red flowers dot the land in the breeze's chase while the land colored up in red after the kiss."

The last word, *kiss*, hangs in the air.

"Next time I get sick, you can tell that to me. You can be my girl in the mountains."

"Okay," I say. "I'll be your mountain girl and take care of you."

He smiles, like it's another joke, another volley in our flirtation, and I smile back, even though I'm not joking.

"And in return, I will relieve you of the burden of time." He slips my watch onto his lanky wrist, where it doesn't seem quite so much like a prison shackle. "For now, time doesn't exist. It is, what did Jacques say . . . fluid?"

"Fluid," I repeat, like an incantation. Because if time can be fluid, then maybe something that is just one day can go on indefinitely.

Ten

I fall asleep. And then I wake up, and everything feels different. The park is quiet now. The sound of laughter and echoes of handballs have disappeared into the long dusky twilight. Fat, gray rainclouds have overtaken the darkening sky.

But something else has shifted, something less quantifiable yet somehow elemental. I feel it as soon as I wake; the atoms and molecules have rearranged themselves, rendering the whole world irrevocably changed.

And that's when I notice Willem's hand.

Willem has also fallen asleep; his long body is curved in the space around mine like a question mark. We aren't touching at all except for his one hand, which is tucked into the crease of my hip, casually, like a dropped scarf, like it blew there on the soft breeze of sleep. And yet now that it's there, it feels like it belongs there. Like it's always belonged there.

I hold myself perfectly still, listening to the wind rustle

through the trees, to the soft in-out of Willem's rhythmic breathing. I concentrate on his hand, which feels like it's delivering a direct line of electricity from his fingertips into some core part of me I didn't even know existed until just now.

Willem stirs in his sleep, and I wonder if he's feeling this too. How can he not? The electricity is so real, so palpable, that if someone waved a meter around, it would spin off the dial.

He shifts again, and his fingertips dig in right there into that tender flesh in the hollow of my hip, sending a shock and a zing so deliciously intense that I buck, kicking his leg behind me.

I swear, somehow I can feel his eyelashes flutter open, followed by the heat of his breath against the back of my neck. *"Goeiemorgen,"* he says, his voice still pliant with sleep.

I roll over to face him, thankful that his hand remains slung over my hip. His ruddy cheeks bear little indentations from the grass, like tribal initiation scars. I want to touch them, to feel the grooves of his otherwise smooth skin. I want to touch every part of him. It's like his body is a giant sun, emitting its own gravitational pull.

"I think that means good morning, though technically it's still evening." My words come out sounding gaspy. I've forgotten how to talk and breathe at the same time.

"You forget, time doesn't exist anymore. You gave it to me."

"I gave it you," I repeat. There's such delicious surrender in the words, and I feel myself slipping away to him. Some small part of me warns against this. This is just one day. I am just one girl. But the part that can resist, that *would* resist, I woke up finally liberated of her.

Willem blinks at me, his eyes dark, lazy, and sexy. I can feel us kissing already. I can feel his lips all over me. I can feel the jut of his sharp hipbones against me. The park is almost deserted. There are a couple of younger girls in jeans and head scarves talking to some guys. But they are off in a corner of their own. And I don't care about propriety.

My thoughts must be like a movie projected on a screen. He watches it all. I can tell by his knowing smile. We inch closer to each other. Beneath the chirp of cicadas, I can practically hear the energy between us humming, like the power lines that buzz overhead in the countryside.

But then I hear something else. At first, I don't know how to place it, so discordant is it from the sounds in this bubble of electricity we are generating. But then I hear it a second time, cold and jagged and bracingly clear, and I know exactly what it is. Because fear needs no translation. A scream is the same in any language.

Willem jumps up. I jump up. "Stay here!" he commands. And before I know what has happened, he is striding away on those long legs of his, leaving me whiplashed between lust and terror.

There's another scream. A girl's scream. Everything seems to slow down then, like a slow-motion sequence in a movie. I see the girls, the ones with the head scarves, there are two of them, only now one isn't wearing her scarf anymore. It is on the ground, revealing a fall of black hair that is wild and staticky, as if her hair is frightened too. She is huddled with the other girl, as if trying to disappear from the boys. Who I now see aren't boys at all, but are men, the kind who sport shaved heads, and combat fatigues, and big black boots. The essential wrongness of *these* men with *these* girls in this now-quiet park hits me all at once. I pick up Willem's backpack, which he's just abandoned there, and creep closer.

I hear the soft cries of one of the girls and the men's guttural laughter. Then they speak again. I never knew French could sound so ugly.

Just as I'm wondering where he went, Willem steps between the men and the girls and starts saying something. He's speaking softly, but I can hear him all the way over here, which must be a kind of actor's trick. But he's also speaking in French, so I have no idea what he's saying. Whatever it is, it's gotten the skinheads' attention. They answer him back, in loud staccato voices that echo off the empty handball courts. Willem replies in a voice as calm and quiet as a breeze, and I strain to understand just a word of it, but I can't.

They go back and forth and as they do, the girls use the cover as it was intended and slip away. The skinheads don't even notice. Or don't care. It's Willem they are interested in now. At first, I think that Willem's powers of charm must know no bounds. That he has even made friends with skinheads. But then my ear attunes to the tone of what he is saying as opposed to the words. And I recognize the tone because it's one I've been privy to all day. He's teasing them. He is mocking them in that way that I'm not even sure they fully recognize. Because there are three of them and one of him, and if they knew what he was doing, they wouldn't still be standing there talking.

I can smell the sickly sweet odor of booze and the acrid tang of adrenaline, and all at once, I can *feel* what they are going to do to Willem. I can feel it as if they are going to do it to me. And this should paralyze me with fear. It doesn't. Instead it fills me with something hot and tender and vicious.

Who takes care of you?

Without even thinking about it, I'm reaching into Willem's bag and grabbing the thickest thing I can find—the Rough Guide—and I'm striding toward them. No one sees me coming, not even Willem, so I have the element of surprise on my side. Also, apparently, some serious fight-or-flight strength. Because when I hurl that book at that guy closest to Willem, the one holding a beer bottle, it hits him with such force that he drops the bottle. And when he raises his hand to his brow, there's a welt of blood blooming like a red flower.

I know I should be scared, but I'm not. I'm oddly calm, happy to be back in Willem's presence after those interminable seconds apart. Willem, however, is staring at me wide-eyed and slack-jawed. The skinheads are looking right past me, surveying the park, as if they can't quite believe that I could be the source of the attack.

It's their moment of confusion that saves us. Because in that moment, Willem's hand finds mine. And we run.

Out of the park, past the church, and back into that crazy mishmash neighborhood, past the tea shops and cafés and the animal carcasses. We leap over the overflowing gutters, past the congregation of motorcycles and bicycles, dodging delivery vans disgorging racks of clothing heavily bejeweled with glitter and sparkles.

The neighborhood's residents stop to watch us, parting to let us through like we are a spectator sport, an Olympic event—the Crazy-White-People Chase.

I should be scared. I am being chased by angry skinheads;

the only person who's ever run after me before is my dad when we've gone out jogging. I can hear the clomp of their boots beat in time with the heartbeat in my head. But I'm not scared. I feel my legs magically lengthen, allowing me to match Willem's long stride. I feel the ground undulating under our feet, as if it too is on our side. I feel like we are barely touching the earth, like we might just take off into the sky and run right over the Paris rooftops, where no one can ever touch us.

I hear them shouting behind us. I hear the sound of glass breaking. I hear something whizz past my ear and then something wet on my neck, as if my sweat glands have all opened up and released at once. And then I hear more laughter and the boot steps abruptly stop.

But Willem keeps going. He pulls me through the tiny jigsaw streets until they open up onto a large boulevard. We dash across as the light changes, running by a police car. It's crowded now. I'm pretty sure we aren't being chased. We are safe. But still, Willem carries on running, yanking me this way and that down a series of smaller, quieter streets until, like a bookcase revealing a secret door, a gap in the streetscape emerges. It's the keypadded opening to one of those grand apartment houses. An old man with a wheeled cart leaves the inner courtyard just as Willem skids us into the entryway. Our momentum crashes from sixty to zero as we slam together against a stone wall just as the door clicks shut behind us.

We stand there, our bodies pressed together, barely an inch of space separating us. I can feel the fast, steady thud of his heart, the sharp in-out of his breath. I can see the rivulet of perspiration trickling down his neck. I feel my blood, thrumming, like a river about to spill over its banks. It's as if my body can no longer contain me. I have become too big for it somehow.

"Willem," I begin. There is so much I need to say to him.

He puts a finger up to my neck, and I fall silent, his touch at once calming and electrifying. But then he removes his finger and it's red with blood. I reach up to touch my neck. My blood.

"*Godverdomme!*" he swears under his breath. With one hand, he reaches into his backpack for a bandanna, and with the other, he licks the blood on his finger clean.

He holds the bandanna against the side of my neck. I'm definitely bleeding, but not badly. I'm not even sure what happened.

"They threw a broken bottle at you." Willem's voice is pure fury.

But it doesn't hurt. I'm not hurt. Not really. It's just a little nick.

He's standing so close to me now, gently pressing the bandanna against my neck. And then the cut on my neck is not the point of exit for blood, but the point of entry for this weird line of electricity that is surging between us.

I want him, all of him. I want to taste his mouth, his mouth that just tasted my blood. I lean into him.

But he pushes me away, pulls himself back. His hand drops from my neck. The bandanna, now clotted with blood, hangs there limply.

I look up then, into his eyes. All the color has drained out of them, so they just seem black. But more disconcerting is what I see in them, something instantly recognizable: fear.

And more than anything, I want to do something, to take that away. Because I should be scared. But today, I'm not.

"It's okay," I begin. "*I'm* okay."

"What were you *thinking*?" he interrupts, his voice icy as a stranger's. And maybe it's that or maybe it's just relief, but now I feel like I might cry.

"They were going to hurt you," I say. My voice breaks. I look at him, to see if he understands, but his expression has only hardened, fear having been joined by its twin brother, anger. "And I promised."

"Promised what?"

An instant replay runs through my head: No punches had been exchanged. I hadn't even been able to understand what they'd been saying. But they *were* going to hurt him. I could feel it in my bones.

"That I'd take care of you." My voice goes quiet as the certainty drains out of me.

"Take care of me? How does *this* take care of me?" He opens his hand, which is stained with my blood.

He takes a step away from me, and with the twilight blinking between us now, it hits me how utterly *wrong* I have gotten this. I haven't just skied onto the diamond run; I've flown off the face of the cliff. It was a *joke*, this request to take care of him. When have I ever taken care of anybody? And he certainly never said he needed taking care of.

We stand there, the silence curdling around us. The last of the sunlight slips away, and then, almost as if waiting for cover of darkness to sneak in, the rain starts to fall. Willem looks at the sky and then looks at his watch—my watch—still snug around his wrist.

I think of those forty pounds I have left. I imagine a quiet, clean hotel room. I think of us in it, not as I imagined it an hour before in that Paris park, but just quiet, listening to the rain. *Please*, I silently implore. *Let's just go somewhere and make this better.*

But then Willem is reaching into his bag for the Eurostar schedule. And then he's unclasping my watch. And then I realize, he's giving time back to me. Which really means he's taking it away.

Eleven

There are two more trains back to London tonight. Willem tells me it's after nine, so there's probably not enough time for me to exchange my ticket and get on the next one, but I can definitely catch the last train. Because I gain an hour back going to England, I should get to London just before the Tube stops running. Willem tells me all this in a friendly helpful way, like I'm a stranger on the street who stopped him for directions. And I nod along, like I'm the kind of person who actually takes the Tube alone, day or night.

He is oddly formal as he opens the door to the apartment courtyard for me, like he's letting the dog out for its nightly pee. It's late, the night edge of the long summer twilight, and the Paris I walk out into seems wholly changed from the one I left a half hour ago, though once again, I know that it's not the rain or all the lights that have come on. Something has shifted. Or maybe shifted back. Or maybe it never shifted in the first place and I was just fooling myself.

Still, seeing this new Paris, it brings tears to my eyes that turn all the lights into a big red scar. I wipe my face with my dampening cardigan, my returned watch still grasped in my hand. Somehow I cannot bear to put it back on. It feels like it would hurt me, far more than the cut on my neck. I attempt to walk ahead of Willem, to put space between us.

"Lulu," he calls after me.

I don't answer. That's not me. It never was.

He jogs to catch up. "I think Gare du Nord is that way." He takes me by the elbow, and I steel myself against the zing, but, like tensing against a doctor's shot, that only makes it worse.

"Just tell me how to get there."

"I think you follow this street for a few blocks and then turn left. But first we have to go to Céline's club."

Right. Céline. He's acting so normal now, not normal like Willem, but normal compared to how he was twenty minutes ago, the fear gone out of his eyes, replaced with some kind of relief. The relief of unloading me. I wonder if this was always the plan. Drop me off and circle back for Céline for the evening shift. Or maybe it's the other girl, the one whose number is sitting snugly in his hip pocket. With so many options, why would he choose me?

You're a good kid. That's what my crush, Shane Michaels, had told me when I'd come as close as I ever would to admitting my feelings for him. *You're a good kid.* That's me. Shane used to hold my hand and say flirty, sweet things. I'd always thought it meant something. And then he went off with some other girl and did things that actually *did* mean something.

We follow a large boulevard back toward the station, but after a few blocks, we turn back off into the smaller streets. I look for the club, but this isn't an industrial neighborhood. It's residential, full of apartment houses, their flowering window boxes soaking up the rain, their fat cats happily dozing inside closed windows. There's a restaurant on the corner, its fogged-up windows glowing. Even from across the street, I can make out the sound of laughter and silverware clanking against plates. People, dry and warm, enjoying a Thursday-night dinner in Paris.

The rain is coming down harder now. My sweater is soaking through to my T-shirt. I pull the sleeves down over my fists. My teeth start to chatter; I clench my jaw to keep it from showing, but that just detours the shivering to the rest of my body. I pull the bandanna off my neck. The bleeding has stopped, but my neck is now grimy with blood and sweat.

Willem looks at me with dismay, or maybe it's disgust. "We need to clean you up."

"I have clean clothes in my suitcase."

Willem peers at my neck and winces. Then he takes my elbow and crosses the street and opens the door to the restaurant. Inside, candlelight flickers, illuminating the wine bottles lined up against a zinc bar and the menus scribbled on little chalkboards. I stop at the threshold. We don't belong in here.

"We can clean your cut here. See if they have an emergency kit."

"I'll do it on the train." Mom packed me a first-aid kit, naturally.

We just stand there, facing off. A waiter appears. I expect him to ream us out for letting in the chilly air, or for looking like dirty, bloodied riffraff. But he ushers me inside like he's the host to a party, and I'm the guest of honor. He sees my neck, and his eyes go wide. Willem says something in French, and he nods at once, gesturing to a corner table.

The restaurant is warm, the air tangy with onions and sweet with vanilla, and I am too defeated to resist. I slump down into a chair, covering my cut with one hand. My other hand relaxes and releases my watch onto the white cloth, where it ticks malevolently.

The waiter returns with a small, white first-aid box and a blackboard menu. Willem opens the kit and pulls out a medicated wipe, but I snatch it from him.

"I can do it myself!" I say.

I dab the wound with ointment and cover it with an oversize bandage. The waiter returns to check my work. He nods approvingly. Then he says something to me in French. "He's asking if you want to hang your sweater in the kitchen so it can dry," Willem says.

I have to fight the urge to bury my face into his long, crisp, white apron and weep with gratitude for his kindness. Instead, I hand over my soaked sweater. Underneath, my damp T-shirt clings to me; there are bloodstains on the collar. I have the T-shirt Céline gave me, the same obscure, too-cool-for-school band T-shirt Willem is wearing, but I'd rather parade around in my bra than put that on. Willem says something else in French, and moments later, a large carafe of red wine is delivered to our table.

"I thought I had a train to catch."

"You have time to eat a little something." Willem pours a glass of wine and hands it to me.

I am technically of age to drink all over Europe, but I haven't, not even when, at some of the prepaid lunches, wine was offered as a matter of course and some of the kids sneaked glasses when Ms. Foley wasn't looking. Tonight, I don't hesitate. The wine glints shades of blood in the candlelight, and drinking it is like receiving a transfusion. The warmth goes from my throat to my stomach before setting to work on the chill that has settled in my bones. I drain half a glass in one go.

"Easy there," Willem cautions.

I gulp the rest of it and thrust out my glass like a middle finger. Willem appraises me for a second, then fills the glass to the rim.

The waiter returns and makes a formal show of reading us the chalkboard menu and handing us a basket of bread with a small silver ramekin.

"*Et pour vous, le pâté.*"

"Thank you," I say. "I mean, *merci.*"

He smiles. "*De rien.*"

Willem breaks off a piece of bread and spreads it with the brown paste and offers it to me. I just glare at him.

"Better than Nutella," he teases in an almost singsong voice.

Maybe it is the wine or the prospect of getting rid of me, but Willem, the Willem I've been with all day, is back. And somehow, *this* makes me furious. "I'm not hungry," I say, even though I am, in fact, famished. I haven't eaten anything since that crêpe. "And it looks like dog food," I add for good measure.

"Just try." He holds the bread and pâté up to my mouth. I snatch it from his hand, take a tiny sample. The flavor is both delicate and intense, like meat butter. But I refuse to give him the satisfaction of seeing me enjoy it. I nibble a bite and make a face. Then I put the bread back down again.

The waiter returns, sees our emptying wine carafe, gestures to it. Willem nods. He returns with a full one. "The sole is . . . it is *finis*," he says in English, wiping the entry off the chalkboard. He looks at me. "You are cold and have lost blood," he says, as if I hemorrhaged or something. "I recommend something with *force*." He makes a fist. "The beef bourguignon is excellent. We also have a fish pot au feu, very good."

"Just keep it coming," I say, gesturing to the wine.

The waiter frowns slightly and looks to me, then Willem, like I am somehow their joint responsibility. "May I suggest to start, a salad with some asparagus and smoked salmon."

My traitorous stomach gurgles. Willem nods, then orders for both of us, the two things that the waiter recommended. He doesn't even bother to ask me what I want. Which is fine, because right now all I want is wine. I reach out for another glass, but Willem puts his hand on top of the opening of the carafe. "You have to eat something first," he says. "It's from duck, not pig."

"So?" I shove a whole piece of baguette and pâté into my mouth, defiantly and noisily chomping on it, hiding any satisfaction I'm actually taking from it. Then I hold out my glass.

Willem looks at me for a long moment. But he does oblige with a refill and then that lazy half smile. In one day, I've come to love that smile. And now I want to murder it.

We sit in silence until the waiter returns to deliver the salad with a flourish befitting the beautiful dish: a still life of pink salmon, green asparagus, yellow mustard sauce, and toast points scattered around the side of the plate like blossoms. My mouth waters, and it's like my body is waving the white flag, telling me to just give in, to quit while I'm ahead, to accept the nice day I had, which really, is far more than I had any right to hope for. But there's another part of me that is still hungry, hungry not just for food, but for everything that's been laid out in front of me today. On behalf of that hungry girl, I refuse the salad.

"You're still upset," he says. "It's not so bad as I thought. It won't even scar."

Yes, it will. Even if it heals up next week, it'll scar, although maybe not in the way he means. "You think I'm upset about *this*?" I touch the bandage on my neck.

He won't look at me. He knows damn well I'm not upset about that. "Let's just eat something, okay?"

"You're sending me back. Do what you have to do, but don't ask me to be happy about it."

Over the dancing candlelight, I see his expressions pass by like fast clouds: surprise, amusement, frustration, and tenderness—or maybe it's pity. "You were going to leave tomorrow, so what's the difference?" He brushes some bread crumbs off the tablecloth.

The difference, Willem? The difference is the night.

"Whatever," is my stellar reply.

"Whatever?" Willem asks. He runs his finger along the rim of his glass; it makes a low sound, like a foghorn. "Did you think about what would happen?"

It's all I've been thinking about, and all I've been trying not to think about: What would happen tonight.

But again, I've misunderstood him. "Did you think about what would happen if they caught us?" he continues.

I could feel what they wanted to do to him. I could taste their violence in my own mouth. "That's why I threw the book at them; they wanted to hurt you," I say. "What did you say to them to get them so angry?"

"They were already angry," he says, evading my question. "I just gave them a different reason." But by his answer and the look on his face, I can tell that I'm not wrong. That they were going to hurt him. What I felt about that, at least, was real.

"Can you imagine if they'd caught us? You?" Willem's voice is so quiet I have to lean in to hear him. "Look what they did." He reaches over as if to touch my neck, but then pulls back.

In the adrenaline of the chase and the weird euphoria that followed, I hadn't thought about them catching *me*. Maybe because it hadn't seemed possible. We had wings on our feet; they had leaden boots. But now, here, with Willem sitting across from me, wearing this strange, somber expression, with his bloody bandanna crumpled into a ball on the side of the table, I can hear those boots getting closer, can hear them stomping, can hear bones cracking.

"But they didn't catch us." I swallow the tremble in my voice with another gulp of wine.

He finishes his wine and stares at the empty glass for a moment. "This is not what I brought you here for."

"What *did* you bring me here for?" Because he never

answered that. Never said why he asked me to come to Paris with him for the day.

He rubs his eyes with the heels of his hands. When he removes his hands, he looks different somehow. Stripped bare of all the masks. "Not for things to get out of control."

"Well, a little late for that." I'm trying to be flip, to summon whatever dregs of Lulu I have left. But when I say it, the truth of it wallops me in the stomach. We, or at least, I, have long since passed the point of no return.

I look back at him. His eyes lock on mine. The current clicks back on.

"I suppose it is," Willem says.

Twelve

———

Maybe Jacques was right, and time really is fluid. Because as we eat, my watch sits there on the table and seems to bend and distort like a Salvador Dalí painting. And then at one point, somewhere between the beef bourguignon and crème brûlée, Willem reaches for it and looks at me for a long moment before slipping it back on his wrist. I feel this profound sense of relief. Not just that I'm not being sent back to London tonight, but that he is taking charge of time again. My surrender is now complete.

It is late when we spill out onto the streets, and Paris has turned into a sepia-toned photograph. It's too late to get a hotel or youth hostel, and there's no money left, anyhow. I gave the rest of my cash, my forty pounds, to Willem to help pay for dinner. The waiter protested when we paid, not because we gave him a grab-bag of euros and pounds, but because we gave him the equivalent of a twenty-five-dollar tip. "Too much," he protested. Wholly insufficient, I thought.

But now here I am: No money. No place to stay. It should be my worst nightmare. But I don't care. It's funny the things you think you're scared of until they're upon you, and then you're not.

And so we walk. The streets are quiet. It seems to be just us and street sweepers in their bright-green jumpsuits, their twig-like neon-green brooms looking like they were plucked from a magical forest. There's the flash of headlights as cars and taxis pass by, splashing through the puddles left by the earlier downpour, which has now softened to a misty drizzle.

We walk along the quiet canals and then along the park with the lake where we hitched a ride earlier in the day. We walk under the elevated railroad tracks.

Eventually, we wind up in a small Chinatown. It's closed up for the night, but the signs are all lit up.

"Look," I say to Willem, pointing to one. "It's double happiness."

Willem stops and looks at the sign. His face is beautiful, even reflected in the bright neon glow.

"Double happiness." He smiles. Then he takes my hand.

My heart somersaults. "Where are we going?"

"You never got to see any art."

"It's one in the morning."

"It's Paris!"

We wend deeper into Chinatown, cutting up and down the streets until Willem finds what he's looking for: a series of tall, dilapidated buildings with barred windows. They all look the same except for the building on the far right; it is covered in red scaffolding from which hangs a series of very modern, very distorted portraits. The front door is completely covered in colorful graffiti and flyers.

"What is this place?"

"An art squat."

"What's that?"

Willem tells me about squats, abandoned buildings that artists or musicians or punks or activists take over. "Usually, they'll put you up for the night. I haven't slept here, but I've been inside once, and they were pretty nice."

But when Willem tries the heavy steel front door, it's locked and chained from the outside. He steps back to look at the windows, but the whole place, like the surrounding neighborhood, is tucked in for the night.

Willem looks at me apologetically. "I thought someone would be here tonight." He sighs. "We can stay with Céline." But even he looks less than thrilled at that prospect.

I shake my head. I would rather walk all night in the pouring rain. And, anyway, the rain has stopped. A thin sliver of moon is dodging in and out of the clouds. It looks so fundamentally Parisian hanging over the slanting roof-tops that it's hard to believe this is the same moon that will shine in my bedroom window back home tonight. Willem follows my gaze up to the sky. Then his eyes lock on something.

He walks back toward the building, and I follow him. Along one corner, a piece of scaffolding runs up to a ledge that leads to an open window. A curtain billows in the breeze.

Willem looks at the window. Then at me. "Can you climb?"

Yesterday I would've said no. Too high. Too dangerous. But today I say, "I can try."

I sling my bag over my shoulder and step onto the ladder Willem has made with the loop of his hands. He heaves me halfway up, and I get a foothold in a groove in the plaster and use the scaffolding to get myself to the ledge. I sort of belly-slide across it and grab at the spiral railings by the window, heaving myself through headfirst.

"I'm okay!" I call. "I'm fine."

I poke my head out the window. Willem is standing just below. He has that private little half smile again. And then as effortlessly as a squirrel, he shinnies up, steps upright onto the ledge, crosses it with his arms out like a tightrope walker, bends his knees, and slips into the window.

It takes a minute for my eyes to adjust to the darkness, but once they do, I see white everywhere: white walls, white shelves, white desk, white clay sculptures.

"Someone left us a key," Willem says.

We are both quiet. I like to think it's a moment of thanksgiving for the providence of accidents.

Willem pulls out a small flashlight. "Shall we explore?"

I nod. We set off, examining a sculpture that looks like it's made of marshmallows, a series of black-and-white photos of naked fat girls, a series of oil paintings of naked skinny girls. He shines the flashlight around a giant sculpture, very futuristic, metal and tubes, all twisted and turning, like an artist's rendition of a space station.

We pad down the creaking stairs to a room with black walls and enormous photographs of people floating in deep blue water. I stand there and can almost feel the soft water, the way the waves caress when I sometimes go swimming in Mexico at night to escape the crowds.

"What do you think?" Willem asks.

"Better than the Louvre."

We go back upstairs. Willem clicks off the flashlight.

"You know? One day one of these might be in the Louvre," he says. He touches an elliptical white sculpture that seems to glow in the darkness. "You think Shakespeare ever guessed Guerrilla Will would be doing his plays four hundred years later?" He laughs a little, but there's something in his voice that sounds almost reverent. "You never know what will last."

He said that earlier, about accidents, about never knowing which one is just a kink in the road and which one is a fork, about never knowing your life is changing until it's already happened.

"I think sometimes you *do* know," I say, my voice filling with emotion.

Willem turns to me, fingers the strap on my shoulder bag. For a second, I can't move. I can't breathe. He lifts my bag and drops it to the floor. An eddy of dust flies up and tickles my nose. I sneeze.

"*Gezondheid,*" Willem says.

"*Hagelslag,*" I say back.

"You remember that?"

"I remember everything from today." There's a lump in my throat as I understand just how true this is.

"What will you remember?" He drops his backpack next to my messenger bag. They slump into each other like old war buddies.

I lean back against the worktable. The day flashes before me: From Willem's playful voice over my breakfast on the first train to the exhilaration of making my strange admission to him on the next train to the Giant's amiable kiss in the club to the cooling stickiness of Willem's saliva on my wrist at the café to the sound of secrets underneath Paris to the release I experienced when my watch came off to the electricity I felt when Willem's hand found me to the shattering fear of that girl's scream to Willem's brave and immediate reaction to it to our flight through Paris, which felt just like that, like *flight*, to his eyes: the way they watch me, tease me, test me, and, yet, somehow understand me.

That's what I see before *my* eyes when I think of this day.

It has to do with Paris, but more than that, it has to do with the person who brought me here. And with the person he allowed me to become here. I'm too overcome to explain it all, so instead I say the one word that encapsulates it: *"You."*

"And what about this?" He touches the bandage on my neck. I feel a jolt that has nothing to do with the wound.

"I don't care about that," I whisper.

"I care," he whispers back.

What Willem doesn't know—what he can't know, because he didn't know me before today—is that none of that matters. "I wasn't in danger today," I tell him in a choked voice. "I *escaped* danger today." And I did. Not just getting away from the skinheads, but I feel like the whole day has been an electrical shock, paddles straight to my heart, bringing me out of a lifelong torpor I hadn't even known I was in. "I escaped," I repeat.

"You escaped." He comes closer so he towers over me.

My back is pressed into the worktable, and my heart starts to pound because there's no escaping this. I don't want to escape this.

As if disconnected from the rest of my body, my hand raises in the air and goes to touch his cheek. But before it arrives, Willem's hand whips around and grabs my wrist. For one confused second, I think I've misread the situation again, am about to be refused.

Willem holds my wrist for a long moment, looking at that birthmark. Then he lifts it to his mouth. And though his lips are soft and his kiss is gentle, it feels like a knife jamming into the electrical socket. It feels like the moment when I go live.

Willem kisses my wrist, then moves upward, along the inside of my arm to the tickly crook of my elbow, to my armpit, to places that never seemed deserving of kisses. My breath grows ragged as his lips graze my shoulder blade now, stopping to drink at the pool of my clavicle before turning their attention to the cords of my neck, to the area around the bandage, then gently to the top of the bandage. Parts of my body I never even realized existed come alive as the circuits click on.

When he finally kisses my mouth, everything goes oddly quiet, like the moment of silence between lightning and thunder. One Mississippi. Two Mississippi. Three Mississippi. Four Mississippi. Five Mississippi.

Bang.

We kiss again. This next kiss is the kind that breaks open the sky. It steals my breath and gives it back. It shows me that every other kiss I've had in my life has been wrong.

I tangle my hands into that hair of his and pull him toward me. Willem cups the back of my neck, runs his fingers along the little outcroppings of my vertebrae. *Ping. Ping. Ping,* go the electric shocks.

His hands encircle my waist as he boosts me onto the table, so we are face-to-face, kissing hard now. My cardigan comes off. Then my T-shirt. Then his. His chest is smooth and cut, and I bury my head in it, kissing down the indentation at his centerline. I'm unbuckling his belt, tugging down his jeans with hunger I don't recognize.

My legs loop around his waist. His hands are all over me, migrating down to the crease of my hip where they'd rested during our nap. I make a sound that doesn't seem like it could come from me.

A condom materializes. My underwear is shimmied down over my sandaled feet and my skirt is bunched into a petticoat around my waist. Willem's boxers fall away. Then he lifts me off the table. And then I realize that I was wrong before. Only now is my surrender complete.

After, we fall to the floor, Willem on his back, me resting next to him. His fingers graze my birthmark, which feels like it is flashing heat, and mine tickle his wrist, the hairs so soft against the heavy links of my watch.

"So *this* is how you'd take care of me?" he jokes, pointing to a red mark on his neck where I think I bit him.

Like with everything, he's turned my promise into something funny, something to tease me with. But I don't feel like laughing, not now, not about this, not after that.

"No," I say. "That's not how." Part of me wants to disavow the whole thing. But I won't. Because he asked me if I'd take care of him, and even if it was a joke, I made a promise that I would, and that wasn't a joke. When I said I'd be his mountain girl, I knew I wasn't going to see him again. That wasn't the point. I wanted him to know that when he felt alone out there in the world . . . I was there too.

But that was yesterday. With a clench of my chest that makes me truly understand why it's called *heartbreak*, I wonder if it's not him being alone that I'm worried about.

Willem fingers the fine film of white clay dust that covers my body. "You're like a ghost," he says. "Soon you disappear." His voice is light, but when I try to catch his eye, he won't meet my gaze.

"I know." There's a lump in my throat. If we keep talking about this, it'll become a sob.

Willem wipes off a bit of the dust and my darker, tour-tanned skin reemerges. But other things, I now realize, won't come off so readily. I take Willem's chin in my hands and turn him to face me. In the wispy glow of the streetlamp, his planes and angles are both shadowed and illuminated. And then he looks at me, really looks at me, and the expression on his face is sad and wistful and tender and yearning, and it tells me everything I need to know.

My hand shakes as I raise it to my mouth. I lick my thumb and rub it against my wrist, against my birthmark. Then I rub again. I look up, look him right in his eyes, which are as dark as this night I don't want to end.

Willem's face falters for a moment, then he grows solemn, the way he did after we were chased. Then he reaches over and rubs my birthmark. *It's not coming off,* is what he is telling me.

"But you leave tomorrow," he says.

I can hear the drumbeat of my heart echo in my temples. "I don't have to."

For a second, he looks confused.

"I can stay for another day," I explain.

Another day. That's all I'm asking. Just one *more* day. I can't think beyond that. Beyond that things get complicated. Flights get delayed. Parents go ballistic. But one more day. One more day I can swing with minimal hassle, without upsetting anyone but Melanie. Who will understand. Eventually.

Part of me knows one more day won't do anything except postpone the heartbreak. But another part of me believes differently. We are born in one day. We die in one day. We can change in one day. And we can fall in love in one day. Anything can happen in just one day.

"What do you think?" I ask Willem. "One more day?"

He doesn't answer. Instead, he flips me under him. I sink into the cement floor, submitting to the weight of him. Until something sharp jabs into my rib cage.

"Ow!"

Willem reaches under me and pulls out a small metal chisel.

"We should find somewhere else to stay," I say. "*Not* with Céline."

"*Shh.*" Willem quiets me with his lips.

Later, after we have taken our time, exploring every hidden crease of each other's bodies, after we have kissed and licked and whispered and laughed until our limbs are heavy and the sky outside has started to purple with predawn light, Willem pulls a tarp over us.

"*Goeienacht*, Lulu," he says, his eyes fluttering with exhaustion.

I trace the creases of his face with my fingers. "*Goeienacht*,

Willem," I reply. I lean into his ear, push the messy bramble of his hair aside and whisper, "Allyson. My name is Allyson." But by then, he is already asleep. I rest my head in the crook between his arm and shoulder, tracing the letters of my true name onto his forearm, where I imagine their outlines will remain until morning.

Thirteen

---

*A*fter a ten-day heat wave, I'm used to waking up sweaty, but I wake up to a cool breeze gusting through an open window. I reach for a blanket, but instead of getting something warm and feathery, I get something hard and crinkly. A tarp. And in that hazy space where you can still touch your dreams, it all comes back to me. Where I am. Who I'm with. The happiness warms me from the inside.

I reach for Willem, but he's not there. I open my eyes, squinting against the gray light bouncing off the bright white of the studio walls.

Instinctively, I check my watch, but my wrist is bare. I pad over to the window, pulling my skirt around my naked chest. The streets are still quiet, the stores and cafés still shut. It's still early.

I want to call to him, but there's a church-like hush, and to disrupt it feels wrong. He must be downstairs, maybe in the bathroom. I could sort of use it myself. I pull on my clothes and tiptoe down the stairs. But Willem isn't in the bathroom, either. I quickly pee and throw water on my face and try to drink away the beginnings of my hangover.

He must be exploring the studios by daylight. Or maybe he went back up the staircase. *Calm down*, I tell myself. He's probably back upstairs right now.

"Willem?" I call.

There's no answer.

I run back upstairs to the studio we slept in. It's messy. On the floor is my bag, its contents spilling out. But his bag, his stuff, is all gone.

My hearts starts to pound. I run over to my bag and open it up, checking for my wallet and passport, my minimal cash. Immediately I feel stupid. He paid for me to come over here. He isn't going to rip me off. I remind myself of the tizzy I got myself into yesterday on the train.

I run up and down the stairs, calling his name now. But it just echoes back to me—Willem, *Willem*!—like the walls are laughing at me.

Panic is coming. I try to push it away with logic. He went out to get us something to eat. To find us somewhere to sleep.

I go stand next to the window and wait.

Paris begins to wake. Store grates go up, sidewalks are swept. Car horns start honking, bicycles chime, the sound of footfalls on the rainy pavement multiply.

If stores are open, it must be nine o'clock? Ten? Soon the artists will arrive, and what will they do when they find me squatting in their squat like Goldilocks?

I decide to wait outside. I put on my shoes and sling my

bag over my shoulder and head to the open window. But in the cold light of day, without wine emboldening me or Willem helping me, the distance between the second floor and the ground seems like an awfully long way to fall.

You got up, you can get back down, I chastise myself. But when I hoist myself onto the ledge and reach for the scaffolding, my hand slips and I feel dizzy. I imagine my parents getting the news of me falling to my death from a Paris building. I collapse back into the studio, hyperventilating into the cave of my hands.

Where is he? Where the hell is he? My mind pinballs through rationales for his delay. He went to get more money. He went to fetch my suitcase. What if he fell going out the window? I jump up, full of twisted optimism that I will find him sprawled underneath the drain pipe, hurt but okay, and then I can make good on my promise to take care of him. But there's nothing under the window except a puddle of dirty water.

I sink back down onto the studio floor, breathless with fear, which is now on an entirely different Richter scale than my little scare on the train.

More time goes by. I hug my knees, shivering in the damp morning. I creep downstairs. I try the front door, but it's locked, from the outside. I have the sense that I'm going to be trapped here forever, that I'll grow old and wither and die locked in this squat.

How late can artists sleep? What time is it? But I don't need a clock to tell me Willem has been gone too long. With each passing minute, the explanations I keep concocting ring increasingly hollow.

Finally, I hear the clank of the chain and keys jangle in the locks, but when the door swings open, it's a woman with two long braids carrying a bunch of rolled up canvases. She looks at me and starts talking to me in French, but I just spring past her.

Out on the street, I look around for Willem, but he's not here. It seems like he would never be here, on this ugly stretch of cheap Chinese restaurants and auto garages and apartment blocks, all gray in the gray rain. Why did I ever think this place was beautiful?

I run into the street. The cars honk at me, their horns strange and foreign sounding, as if even they speak another language. I spin around, having absolutely no idea where I am, no idea where to go, but desperately wanting to be home. Home in my bed. Safe.

The tears make it hard to see, but somehow I stumble across the street, down the sidewalk, ricocheting from block to block. This time no one is chasing me. But this time I am scared.

I run for several blocks, up a bunch of stairs and onto a square of sorts, with a rack of those gray-white bicycles, a real estate agency, a pharmacy, and a café, in front of which is a phone booth. Melanie! I can call Melanie. I take some deep breaths, swallow my sobs, and follow the instructions to get the international operator. But the call goes straight to voice mail. Of course it does. She left the phone off to avoid calls from my mother.

An operator comes on the line to tell me I can't leave a message because the call is collect. I start to cry. The operator asks me if she should call the police for me. I hiccup out a no, and she asks if perhaps there is someone else I might call. And that's when I remember Ms. Foley's business card.

She picks up with a brisk "Pat Foley." The operator has to ask her if she'll accept the collect call three times because I start crying harder the minute she answers, so she can't hear the request.

"Allyson. Allyson. What's the matter? Are you hurt?" she asks over the line.

I'm too scared, too numb to be hurt. That will come later. "No," I say in the tiniest of voices. "I need help."

Ms. Foley manages to pull the basics out of me. That I went to Paris with a boy I met on the train. That I'm stuck here, lost, with no money, no clue where I am.

"Please," I beg her. "I just want to go home."

"Let's work on getting you back to England, shall we?" she says calmly. "Do you have a ticket?"

Willem bought me a round trip, I think. I rifle through my bag and pull out my passport. The ticket is still folded neatly inside. "I think so," I tell Ms. Foley in a quivery voice.

"When is the return booked for?"

I look at it. The numbers and dates all swim together. "I can't tell."

"Top left corner. It'll be in military time. The twenty-four-hour clock."

And there I see it. "Thirteen thirty."

"Thirteen thirty," Ms. Foley says in that comfortingly efficient voice of hers. "Excellent. That's one thirty. It's just past noon now in Paris, so you have time to catch that train. Can you get yourself to the train station? Or to a Metro?"

I have no idea how. And no money. "No."

"How about a taxi? Take a taxi to the Gare du Nord?"

I shake my head. I don't have any euros to pay for a taxi. I tell Ms. Foley that. I can hear the disapproval in her silence. As if nothing I've told her before has lowered me in her esteem, but coming to Paris without sufficient funds? She sighs. "I can order you a taxi from here and have it prepaid to bring you to the train station."

"You can do that?"

"Just tell me where you are."

"I don't know where I am," I bellow. I paid absolutely no attention to where Willem took me yesterday. I surrendered.

"Allyson!" Her voice is a slap across the face, and it has just the intended effect. It stops my caterwauling. "Calm down. Now put the phone down for a moment and go write down the nearest intersection."

I reach into my bag for my pen, but it's not there. I put the phone down and memorize the street names. "I'm at Avenue Simon Bolivar and Rue de l'Equerre." I'm butchering the pronunciation. "In front of a pharmacy."

Ms. Foley repeats back the information, then tells me not to move, that a car will be there within a half hour and that I'm to call her back if one doesn't arrive. That if she doesn't hear from me, she will assume that I will be on the one thirty train to St. Pancras, and she will meet me in London right at edge of the platform at two forty-five. I'm not to leave the train station without her.

Fifteen minutes later, a black Mercedes cruises up to the corner. The driver holds a sign, and when I see my name— *Allyson Healey*—I feel both relieved and bereft. Lulu, wherever she came from, is truly gone now.

I slide into the backseat, and we take off for what turns out to be all of a ten-minute drive to the train station. Ms. Foley has arranged for the driver to take me inside, to show me right where to board. I'm in a daze as we make our way through the station, and it's only when I am slumped into my seat and I see people wheeling bags through the aisles that I realize that I've left my suitcase at the club. All my clothes and all the souvenirs from the trip are in there. And I don't even care. I have lost something far more valuable in Paris.

I keep it together until the train goes into the Tunnel. And then maybe it's the safety of the darkness or the memory of yesterday's underwater journey that sets everything loose, but once we leave Calais and the windows darken, I again start to quietly sob, my tears salty and endless as the sea I'm traveling through.

At St. Pancras, Ms. Foley escorts me to a café, stations me at a corner table, and buys me tea that grows cold in its cup. I tell her everything now: The underground Shakespeare play in Stratford-upon-Avon. Meeting Willem on the train. The trip to Paris. The perfect day. His mysterious disappearance this morning that I still do not understand. My panicked flight.

I expect her to be stern—disapproving, for deceiving her, for being such a not-good girl—but instead she is sympathetic.

"Oh, Allyson," she says.

"I just don't know what could've happened to him. I waited and waited for a few hours at least, and I got so scared. I panicked. I don't know, maybe I should've waited longer."

"You could've waited until next Christmas, and I scarcely

imagine it would have done a spot of good," Ms. Foley says.

I look at her. I can feel my eyes beseeching.

"He was an actor, Allyson. An *actor*. They are the worst of the lot."

"You think the whole thing was an act? Was fake?" I shake my head. "Yesterday wasn't fake." My voice is emphatic, though I'm no longer sure who I'm trying to convince.

"I daresay it was real in the moment," she says, measuring her words. "But men are different from women. Their emotions are capricious. And actors turn it on and turn it right back off."

"It wasn't an act," I repeat, but my argument is losing steam.

"Did you sleep with him?"

For a second, I can still feel him on me. I push the thought away, look at Ms. Foley, nod.

"Then he got what he came for." Her words are matter-of-fact, but not unkind. "I imagine he never planned on it being more than a one-day fling. That was exactly what he proposed, after all."

It was. Until it wasn't. Last night, we declared our feelings for each other. I am about to tell Ms. Foley this. But then I stop cold: Did we declare anything? Or did I just lick some spit on myself?

I think about Willem. Really think about him. What do I actually know about him? Only a handful of facts—how old he is, how tall he is, what he weighs, his nationality, except I don't even know that because he said his mother wasn't Dutch. He's a traveler. A drifter, really. Accidents are the defining force in his life.

I don't know his birthday. Or his favorite color, or favorite book, or favorite type of music. Or if he had a pet growing up. I don't know if he ever broke a bone. Or how he got the scar on his foot or why he hasn't been home in so long. I don't even know his last name! And that's still more than he has on me. He doesn't even know my first name!

In this ugly little café, without the romantic gleam of Paris turning everything rose-colored pretty, I begin to see things as they truly are: Willem invited me to Paris for one day. He never promised me anything more. Last night, he'd even tried to send me home. He knew Lulu wasn't my real name, and he made absolutely no attempt to ever find out who I really was. When I'd mentioned texting or emailing him the picture of the two of us, he'd cleverly refused to give out his contact details.

And it wasn't like he'd lied. He said he'd fallen in love many times, but had never been in love. He'd offered it up about himself. I think of the girls on the train, Céline, the models, the girl at the café. And that was just in a single day together. How many of us were out there? And rather than accept my lot and enjoy my one day and move on, I'd dug in my heels. I'd told him I was in love with him. That I wanted to take care of him. I'd begged for another day, assumed he wanted it too. But he never answered me. He never actually said yes.

Oh, my God! It all makes sense now. How could I have been so naïve? *Fall in love? In a day?* Everything from yesterday, it was all fake. All an illusion. As reality crystallizes into place, the shame and humiliation make me so sick, I feel dizzy. I cradle my head in my hands.

Ms. Foley reaches out to pat my head. "There, there, dear. Let it out. Predictable, yes, but still brutal. He could have at least seen you off at the train station, waved you away and then never called again. A bit more civilized." She squeezes my hand. "This too shall pass." She pauses, leans in closer. "What happened to your neck, dear?"

My hand flies up to my neck. The bandage has come off, and the scabby cut is starting to itch. "Nothing," I say. "It was an . . . " I'm about to say accident, but I stop myself. "A tree."

"And where's your lovely watch?" she asks.

I look down at my wrist. I see my birthmark, ugly, naked, blaring. I yank down my sweater sleeve to cover it. "He has it."

She clucks her tongue. "They'll do that, sometimes. Take things as a sort of trophy. Like serial killers." She takes a final slurp of her tea. "Now, shall we take you to Melanie?"

I hand Ms. Foley the scrap of paper with Veronica's address, and she pulls out a *London A–Z* book to chart our way. I fall asleep on the Tube, my tears wrung out, the blankness of exhaustion the only comfort I have now. Ms. Foley shakes me awake at Veronica's stop and leads me to the redbricked Victorian house where her flat is.

Melanie comes bounding to the door, already dressed up for tonight's trip to the theater. Her face is lit up with anticipation, waiting to hear a really good story. But then she sees Ms. Foley, and her expression skids. Without knowing anything, she knows everything: She bid Lulu farewell at the train station yesterday, and it's Allyson being returned to her like damaged goods. She gives the slightest of nods, as if none of this surprises her. Then she kicks off her heels and opens her arms to me, and when I step into them, the humiliation and heartbreak bring me to my knees. Melanie sinks to the ground alongside me, her arms hugging me tight. Behind me, I hear Ms. Foley's retreating footsteps. I let her leave without saying a word. I don't thank her. And I already know that I never will, and that is wrong considering the great kindness she's done me. But if I am to survive, I can never, ever visit this day again.

PART TWO
One Year

Fourteen

*A*llyson. Allyson. Are you *there?*"

I pull the pillow over my head and scrunch my eyes shut, faking sleep.

The key turns in the lock as my roommate Kali pushes open the door. "I wish you wouldn't *lock* the *door* when you are *here*. And I *know* you're not *asleep*. You're just playing *dead*. Like *Buster*."

Buster is Kali's dog. A Lhasa apso. She has pictures of him among the dozens tacked up on the wall. She told me all about Buster last July when we had our initial howdy-roommate phone call. Back then, I thought Buster sounded cute, and I found it quirky that Kali was named for her home state, and the way she talked—as if she were punching her words somehow—seemed sweet.

"Okaay, Allyson. *Fine*. Don't answer, but look, can you *call* your parents back? Your *mother* called *my* cell looking for *you*."

From under the pillows, I open my eyes. I'd wondered how long I could leave my phone uncharged before something would happen. Already there's been a mysterious UPS delivery. I was half expecting a carrier pigeon to arrive. But calling my roommates?

I hide under the pillow as Kali changes into going-out clothes, applying makeup and spritzing herself with that vanilla-scented perfume that gets into everything. After she leaves, I take the pillow off my head and swing my legs over the side of the bed. I push aside my chemistry textbook, the highlighter sitting in the crease, uncapped, ever hopeful it'll get used before it dries up from neglect. I locate my dead phone in my sock drawer and kick through the dirty laundry piled in my closet for the charger. When it charges back to life, the voice mail box tells me I have twenty-two new messages. I scroll through the missed calls. Eighteen are from my parents. Two from my grandmother. One from Melanie, and one from the registrar.

"Hi, Allyson, it's your mother. Just calling to check in to see how everything is going. Give me a call."

"Hi, Allyson. It's Mom. I got the new Boden catalog, and there are some cute skirts. And some warm corduroy jeans. I'll just order some and bring them up for Parents' Weekend. Call me back!"

Then there's one from my dad. "Your mother wants to know where we should make reservations for Parents' Weekend: Italian or French or maybe Japanese. I told her you'd be grateful for anything. I can't imagine dorm food has improved that much in twenty-five years."

Then we're back to Mom: "Allyson, is your phone broken?

Please tell me you did not lose that too. Can you please touch base? I'm trying to schedule Parents' Weekend. I thought I might come to classes with you. . . ."

"Hi, Ally, it's Grandma. I'm on Facebook now. I'm not sure how it works, so make me your friend. Or you could call me. But I want to do it how you kids do it."

"Allyson, it's Dad. Call your mother. Also, we are trying to get reservations at Prezzo. . . ."

"Allyson, are you ill? Because I can really think of no other explanation for the radio silence. . . ."

The messages go downhill from there, Mom acting like three months, not three days, have gone by since our last phone call. I wind up deleting the last batch without even listening, stopping only for Melanie's rambling account about school and hot New York City guys and the superiority of the pizza there.

I look at the time on my phone. It's six o'clock. If I call home, maybe Mom will be out and I'll get the machine. I'm not quite sure what she does with her days now. When I was seven, she wound up leaving her job, even though she didn't take that maternity leave after all. The plan had been to go back to work once I went to college, but it hasn't quite got off the ground yet.

She picks up on the second ring. "Allyson, where have you been?" Mom's voice is officious, a little impatient.

"I ran off to join a cult." There's a brief pause, as if she's actually considering the possibility of this. "I'm at college, Mom. I'm busy. Trying to adjust to the workload."

"If you think this is bad, wait until medical school. Wait until your residency! I hardly saw your father."

"Then you should be used to it."

Mom pauses. This snarkiness of mine is new. Dad says ever since I came back from Europe, I have come down with a case of delayed teenageritis. I never acted like this before, but now I apparently have a bad attitude and a bad haircut and an irresponsibility streak, as evidenced by the fact that I lost not just my suitcase and all its contents, but my graduation watch too, even though, according to the story Melanie and I told them, the suitcase and the watch inside it were stolen off the train. Which theoretically should make me blameless. But it doesn't. Perhaps because I'm not.

Mom changes the subject. "Did you get the package? It's one thing if you ignore me, but your grandmother would appreciate a note."

I kick through the rumpled sour clothes for the UPS box. Wrapped in bubble wrap is an antique Betty Boop alarm clock and a box of black-and-white cookies from Shriner's, a bakery in our town. The sticky note on the cookies says *These are from Grandma*.

"I thought the clock would go perfect in your collection."

"Uh-huh." I look at the still-packed boxes in my closet, where my alarm clock collection, and all my nonessential stuff from home, still remains.

"And I ordered you a bunch of new clothes. Shall I send them or just bring them up?"

"Just bring them, I guess."

"Speaking of Parents' Weekend, we're firming up plans. Saturday night we are trying to get dinner reservations at Prezzo. Sunday is the brunch, and after that, before we fly home, your father has an alumni thing, so I thought I'd splurge on spa treatments for us. Oh, and Saturday morning, before the luncheon, I'm having coffee with Kali's mother, Lynn. We've been emailing."

"Why are you emailing my roommate's mother?"

"Why not?" Mom's voice is snippy, as if there is no reason for me to be asking about this, as if there is no reason for her not to be present in every single part of my life.

"Well, can you not call Kali's cell? It's a little weird."

"It's a little weird to have your daughter go incommunicado for a week."

"Three days, Mom."

"So you were counting too." She pauses, scoring herself the point. "And if you would let me install a house phone, we wouldn't have this issue."

"No one has landlines anymore. We all have cells. Our own numbers. Please don't call me on hers."

"Then return my calls, Allyson."

"I will. I just lost my charger," I lie.

Her aggrieved sigh on the other end of the line makes me realize I've picked the wrong lie. "Must we tie your belongings to you with a rope these days?" she asks.

"I just loaned it to my roommate, and it got put away with her stuff."

"You mean Kali?"

Kali and I have barely shared a bar of soap. "Right."

"I'm looking forward to meeting her and her family. They seem lovely. They invited us to La Jolla."

I almost ask my mother if she really wants to get chummy with people who named their daughter Kali for California.

Mom has a thing about names; she hates nicknames. When I was growing up, she was kind of fascist about it, always trying to prevent anyone from shortening my name to Ally or Al. Grandma ignored her, but everyone else, even teachers at school, toed the line. I never got why, if it bothered her so much, she didn't just name me something that couldn't be truncated, even if Allyson is a family name. But I don't say anything about Kali because if I get bitchy, I'll blow my cover as Happy College Student. And my mother especially, whose parents couldn't afford to send her to the college of her choice and who had to work her way through college and later support Dad while he was in medical school, is very intent that I be a Happy College Student.

"I should go," I tell her. "I'm going out with my roommates tonight."

"Oh, how fun! Where are you going?"

"To a party."

"A keg party?"

"Maybe the movies."

"I just saw a great one with Kate Winslet. You should see that one."

"Okay, I will."

"Call me tomorrow. And leave your phone on."

"Professors tend to frown on calls in classes." The snark comes out again.

"Tomorrow's Saturday. And I know your schedule, Allyson. All your classes are in the mornings."

She *would* know my schedule. She basically created it. All those morning classes because she said they'd be less attended and I'd get more attention and then I'd have the whole rest of the day for studying. Or, as it turns out, for sleeping.

After we hang up, I shove the alarm clock into a box in my closet and take the cookies and bring them into the lounge where the rest of my roommates have started in on a six-pack. They're all dressed up and ready to go out.

When school started, the rest of them were so excited. They really were Happy College Students. Jenn made organic brownies, and Kendra drew up a little sign on our door with all our names and a moniker, the Fab Four, atop it. Kali, for her part, gave us coupons to a tanning salon to ward off the inevitable seasonal affective disorder.

Now, a month in, the three of them are a solid unit. And I'm like a goiter. I want to tell Kendra that it's okay if she takes down the little sign or replaces it with one that says something like Terrific Trio* and Allyson.

I shuffle into the lounge. "Here," I say, handing over the cookies to Kali, even though I know she watches her carbs and even though black-and-whites are my favorites. "I'm really sorry about my mom."

Kendra and Jenn cluck sympathetically, but Kali narrows her eyes. "I don't want to be a *bitch* or anything, but it's bad enough having to fend off my *own* parents, okaay?"

"She's having Empty Nest or something." That's what Dad keeps telling me. "She won't do it again," I add with more confidence than I possess.

"My mom turned my bedroom into a craft room two days after I left," Jenn says. "At least you're missed."

"Uh-huh."

"What kind of cookies are they?" Kendra asks.

"Black-and-whites."

"Just like us," Kendra jokes. She's black, or African American; I'm never sure which is right, and she uses both.

"The racial harmony of cookies," I say.

Jenn and Kendra laugh. "You should come out with us tonight," Jenn says.

"We're going to a party over at Henderson and then there's this bar over on Central that apparently has a very liberal carding policy," Kendra says, twisting her just-straightened black hair up into a bun, then thinking twice about it and pulling it down. "Lots of fine male specimen."

"And female specimen, if that's your thing," Jenn adds.

"It's not my thing. I mean, none of it is my thing."

Kali gives me a bitchy smirk. "Think you enrolled in the *wrong* school. I believe there's a *convent* in Boston."

Something twists in my stomach. "They don't take Jews."

"Back off, you two," Kendra says, ever the diplomat. She turns to me. "Why not come out for a few hours?"

"Chemistry. Physics." The room goes silent. They're all liberal arts or business majors, so invoking Science shuts them up.

"Well, I'd better get back to my room. I have a date with the Third Law of Thermodynamics."

"Sounds hot," Jenn says.

I smile to show I actually get the joke, then shuffle back to my room, where I diligently pick up *Foundations of Chemistry*, but by the time the Terrific Trio are heading out the door, my eyes have sandbags in them. I fall asleep under a mountain of unread science. And thus begins another weekend in the life of the Happy College Student.

Fifteen

I put off thinking about Parents' Weekend as long as I can and then the Thursday before they're due to arrive, I look around my dorm and see it not as I see it—walls, a bed, a desk, a dresser—but as my parents will see it. This is not the dorm of a Happy College Student. There's dirty laundry spilling out of every drawer, and my papers are everywhere. My mother despises clutter. I ditch my classes and spend the day cleaning. I haul all the dirty laundry down to the washing machines and sit with it as it turns and gyrates. I wipe down the dusty surfaces. In the closet, I hide away all my current schoolwork—the Mandarin worksheets, piling up like unread newspapers, the Scantron chemistry and physics exams with their ominously low scores scrawled in red; the lab reports with comments like "Need to be more thorough" and "Check your calculations!" and the dreaded "See me." In their place, I set out a bunch of decoy notes and graphs from early in the term, before I started obviously bombing. I unwrap the duvet cover we bought at Bed, Bath & Beyond last summer and put it over the plain quilt I've been sleeping under. I grab some of the photos from the boxes and scatter them around the room. I even drop by the U bookstore and buy one of the stupid banners with the school name on it and tack it above my bed. *Voilà.* School Spirit.

But somehow I forget the clocks. And this gives me away.

When Mom comes into the dorm, after cooing over our tiny dump of a lounge, she oohs over Kali's pictures of Buster and then looks at my relatively bare walls and gasps. By her look of horror, you'd think I'd decorated with crime-scene photos. "Where's your collection?"

I point to the boxes in the closet, unopened.

"Why are they there?"

"They're too noisy," I quickly lie. "I don't want to bother Kali with them." Never mind the fact that Kali blasts her radio at seven in the morning.

"You could put them out and not wind them," she says. "Those clocks are you."

Are they? I don't remember when I started collecting them. Mom liked to go to flea markets on weekends and then one day, I was a clock collector. I got really into it for a while, but I don't remember the moment I saw an old alarm clock and thought, *I want to collect these.*

"Your half looks terribly barren next to Kali's," Mom says.

"You should've seen my dorm," Dad says, lost in his haze of nostalgia. "My roommate put tinfoil on the windows. It looked like a spaceship. He called it the 'Future Dorm.'"

"I was going for Minimalist Dorm."

"It has a certain penitentiary charm," Dad says.

"It's like a before/after on one of those home décor shows." Mom points to Kali's half of the room, over which every inch of wall space is covered either with posters, art prints, or photos. "You're the before," she says. As if I didn't already get that.

We head off to one of the special workshops, something insanely dull on the changing face of technology in the classroom. Mom actually takes notes. Dad points out every little thing that he remembers and every little thing that is new. This is what he did when we toured the school last year; both he and Mom were so excited about the prospect of me going here. Creating a legacy. Somehow, back then, I was excited too.

After the workshop, Dad meets up with other legacy parents, and Mom has coffee with Kali's mom, Lynn. They seem to get along famously. Either Kali hasn't told her mom what a dud I am, or if she has, her mom has the good grace to shut up about it.

Before the President's Luncheon, all four members of the Fab Four and their respective families meet back at the suite and the parents all introduce themselves and cluck over the tininess of our rooms and admire what we've done with our tiny lounge and take pictures of THE FAB FOUR WELCOMES THE FAB EIGHT sign that the rest of the group made. Then we all walk out onto the quad together and tour the campus, going the long way around to point out some of the older, statelier buildings, reddening ivy creeping up old bricks. And everyone looks nice together in flannel skirts and tall black boots and cashmere sweaters and shearling jackets as we swish through the autumnal leaves. We really do look like the Happy College Students in the catalogs.

The luncheon is fine and boring, rubber chicken and rubber speeches in a big, cold echoey hall. It's only after the luncheon that the myth of the Fab Four starts to unravel. Ever so subtly, Kendra's and Jenn's and Kali's families all peel off together. I'm sure they're talking about Christmas and Thanksgiving holidays and spring breaks and potlucks and things like that. My mom gives them a look but doesn't say anything.

She and Dad go back to the hotel to get ready for dinner. Mom tells me the place is fancy and suggests I wear my black and red wrap dress. And that I wash my hair, which is looking greasy.

When they come back to pick me up, there's an awkward moment as my family meets up with the rest of the Fab Four and their Fab Families, who are all going together to a big group dinner at some famous seafood place in downtown Boston. There's a sort of standoff as my parents face the other parents. The rest of my roommates, their faces pinking, take a huge interest in the industrial gray carpeting. Finally, Jenn's dad steps in and offers a belated invitation for us to join the rest of them for dinner. "I'm sure we can squeeze three more in."

"Oh, that won't be necessary," Mom says in her haughtiest voice. "We have reservations at Prezzo in Back Bay."

"Wow! How'd you manage that?" Lynn asks. "We tried and couldn't get in until next month." Prezzo, according to Mom, is the hottest restaurant in town.

Mom smiles mysteriously. She won't tell, though Dad told me one of his golf buddies had a friend on the faculty at a hospital in Boston and he pulled some strings to get us in. Mom had been so pleased about it, but I can see now the victory is sullied.

"Enjoy your chowdah," she says. Only Dad and I catch how condescending she's being.

Dinner is painful. Even sitting at this chichi place with all the best Bostonians, I can tell Mom and, by extension, Dad feel like rejects. And they're not. It's my rejection they're feeling.

They ask me about my classes, and I dutifully tell them about chemistry, physics, biology, and Mandarin, neglecting to tell them how hard it is stay awake in class, no matter how early I go to bed, or how badly I'm doing in subjects I aced in high school. Talking about, or not talking about, all this makes me so tired I want to put my head down into my thirteen-dollar salad.

When the entrees come, Mom orders a glass of Chardonnay, Dad a Shiraz. I try not to look at the way the candlelight dances against the colors of the wine. Even that hurts. I look down at my plate of ravioli. It smells good, but I have no desire to eat it.

"Are you coming down with something?" Mom asks.

And for just the tiniest of seconds, I wonder what would happen if I told them the truth. That school is nothing like I imagined it would be. That I'm not the girl in the catalog at all. I'm not a Happy College Student. I don't know who I am. Or maybe I do know who I am and I just don't want to be her anymore.

But this is not an option. Mom would just be aggrieved, disappointed, as if my unhappiness were some personal insult to her parenting. And then she'd guilt me out about how I'm so lucky. This is college! The college experience she didn't get to have. Which was one of the reasons she spent all of high school like an army general, plotting my extracurriculars, getting me tutors for weak subjects, signing me up for SAT prep.

"I'm just tired," I say. This, at least, isn't a lie.

"You're probably spending too much time in the library," Dad interjects. "Are you getting enough sunlight? That can really affect your circadian rhythms."

I shake my head. This too is true.

"Have you been running? There are some nice tracks around here. And it's not too far to the river."

I think the last time I went running was with Dad, a couple days before I left for the tour.

"We'll go out tomorrow morning, before the brunch. Burn off dinner. Get some air in those lungs."

Just the thought of it makes me exhausted, but this isn't an invitation so much as an expectation, and the plans are being made even before I've agreed to them.

— — —

The following morning, the rest of the girls are sitting in the lounge drinking coffee, happily chattering about their dinner, which included some incident with a cute waiter and a lobster mallet that's already being mythologized into a tale called "The Hammer and the Hottie." They double-take when they see me in tracksuit bottoms and a fleece sweatshirt, looking around for my running shoes. Our dorm has a state-of-the-art gym that Kendra and Kali are addicted to and Jenn gets dragged along to, but I have yet to set foot in.

I just expect my dad, but Mom is there too, all perky in her black wool pants, a cashmere cape. "I thought we were meeting at brunch," I say.

"Oh, I just wanted to spend some time in your dorm. It'll help me to picture where you are when I'm not with you." She turns to Kali. "If that's okay with you." Her voice is so polite, Kali might never catch the bitchiness in it.

"*I* think it's *sweet*," Kali says.

"Are you ready, Allyson?" Dad asks me.

"Almost. I can't find my running shoes."

Mom gives me a look, like I obviously lose everything all the time now.

"Where's the last place you left them?" Dad asks. "Just picture it. That's how you find missing things." This is his typical advice, but it usually works. And sure enough, when I picture my shoes, still packed in the suitcase under my bed, that's where they are.

When we get downstairs, Dad does some halfhearted stretches. "Let's see if I remember how to do this," he jokes. He's not much of a runner, but he's always telling his patients to exercise, so he tries to practice what he preaches.

We take off on a path toward the river. It is a true autumn day, clear and brisk with a sharp bite of winter in the air. I don't love running, not at first, but usually after ten minutes or so, that thing kicks in and I sort of zone out and forget what I'm doing. Today, though, every time I even begin to lose myself, it's like my mind defaults to that other run, the best run, the run of my life, the run *for* my life. And then my legs turn into waterlogged tree trunks, and all the beautiful fall colors fade to gray.

After about a mile, I have to stop. I claim a cramp. I want to go back, but Dad wants to check out the downtown and see what's changed, so we do. We stop at a café for cappuccinos, and Dad asks me about my classes and waxes nostalgic for his days in organic chemistry. Then he tells me how busy he's been and that Mom is having a really hard time and I should go easy on her.

"Isn't she supposed to be going back to work?" I ask.

Dad looks at his watch. "Time to go," he says.

Dad leaves me at the dorm to change before brunch. As soon as I step inside, I know something's wrong. I hear ticking. And then I look around, and for a second, I'm confused because the dorm no longer looks like my dorm but like my bedroom at home. Mom has dug up all the posters from my closet and put them up in the exact same configuration as at home. She's moved my photos around, so they too are a mirror image of my old room. She's made the bed with a mountain of throw pillows, the throw pillows I specifically said I didn't want to bring because I hate throw pillows. You have to take them off and reorganize them every day. On top of the bed are clothes that Mom is folding into neat piles and laying out for me, just like she did when I was in fourth grade.

And along my windowsills and bookcases are all my clocks. All of them wound up and ticking.

Mom looks up from snipping the tags off a pair of pants I haven't even tried on. "You seemed so glum last night. I thought it might perk you up if it looked more like home in here. This is so much cheerier," she declares.

I begin to protest. But I'm not sure *what* to protest.

"And I spoke to Kali, and she finds the sound of the clocks soothing. Like a white-noise machine."

They don't sound soothing to me at all. They sound like a hundred time bombs waiting to explode.

Sixteen

The last time I saw Melanie, she had a fading pink streak in her blond hair and was wearing her micro-skimp Topshop uniform with some teetering platform sandals she'd picked up at the end-of-season sale at Macy's. So when she charges at me on a crowded street corner in New York's Chinatown as soon as I'm disgorged from the bus, I hardly recognize her. Now the pink streak is gone; her hair is dyed dark brown with a reddish tint. She has severe bangs cut short across her forehead, and the rest of her hair is secured back into a bun with a pair of enamel chopsticks. She's wearing this weird, funky, flowered dress and a pair of beat-up cowboy boots, and she has cat-shaped granny eyeglasses on. Her lips are painted blood red. She looks amazing, even if she looks nothing like my Melanie.

At least when she hugs me, she still smells like Melanie: hair conditioner and baby powder. "God, you got skinny," she says. "You're supposed to gain your freshman fifteen, not lose it."

"Have you had dining hall food?"

"Yeah. Hello, all-you-can-eat ice-cream bar. That alone makes the tuition worthwhile!"

I pull back. Look at her again. Everything is new. Including the eyewear. "You need glasses?"

"They're fake. Look, no lenses." She pokes through the air right to her eyes to demonstrate. "It's part of my whole punk-rock librarian look. The musician guys love it!" She pulls off her glasses, sweeps down her hair. Laughs.

"And no more blond hair."

"I want people to take me seriously." She puts her glasses back on and grabs the handle of my suitcase. "So, how's almost-Boston?"

When I chose my college, Melanie made fun of the fact it was five miles outside of Boston, like the town we grew up in was twenty miles outside of Philadelphia. She'd said I was circling urban life. She, meanwhile, dove right in. Her school is in downtown Manhattan.

"Almost good," I answer. "How's New York?"

"Beyond good! So much to do! Like tonight, we have options: There's a party at the dorm, a decent club with eighteen-and-over night on Lafayette, or a friend of a friend invited us to a loft party in Greenpoint, where this awesome band is playing. Or we could go to the last-minute tickets place in Times Square and see a Broadway show."

"I don't care. I'm just here to see you."

I feel the slightest pang when I say that. Even though it is technically true that I'm here to see her, it's not the whole story. I was going to see Melanie at home for Thanksgiving in a few days anyway, but when my parents booked my tickets, they said I had to take the train because flights were too unreliable and expensive on a holiday weekend.

When I imagined six hours on a train, I almost felt sick. Six hours of pushing back memories. Then Melanie mentioned that her parents were driving down the Tuesday before Thanksgiving to do some shopping and driving her back, so I got the brilliant idea to take the cheap Chinatown bus to New York and catch a lift back home with Melanie. I'll get the bus back to Boston too.

"Aww, I'm happy to see you as well. Have we ever gone this long without seeing each other?"

I shake my head. Not since we met.

"Okay, so dorm party, Broadway show, club, or really kick-ass band in Brooklyn?"

What I really want to do is go back to her room and watch movies and hang out like in the old days, but I suspect that if I suggested that, Melanie would accuse me of being adventure averse. The party in Brooklyn sounds the least appealing, and is probably what Melanie wants to do, so it's probably what I should choose. So I do.

It's like I picked the right answer on a test, the way her eyes light up. "Excellent! Some of my friends from school are going. We'll eat first, then go back and drop your stuff and get ready and trek out together. Sound good?"

"Great!"

"We're already in Chinatown, and my favorite Vietnamese place is nearby."

As we wind through the twisty, crowded streets, full of red

lanterns and paper umbrellas and fake pagodas, I try to keep my eyes on the sidewalk. There are signs everywhere. One of them will inevitably say double happiness. Paris is more than three thousand miles away, but the memories . . . One pops up, I push it away. But then another appears. I never know when one is going to jump out at me. They are buried everywhere, like land mines.

We go into a tiny restaurant, all fluorescent lights and Formica tables, and sit down at a corner table. Melanie orders us some spring rolls and a chicken dish and tea and then she folds up her glasses and puts them into a case (to better protect the imaginary lenses?). After she pours us each a cup of tea, she looks at me and says, "So, you're doing better?"

It's not so much a question as a command. Melanie saw me at my absolute lowest. When I got back from Paris and completely lost it, she let me cry all night long, cursing Willem for being a sleazy scoundrel just like she'd suspected all along. On the flight home, she cast scathing looks at anyone on the plane who looked at me funny when I kept crying for the entire eight-hour trip. When, somewhere over Greenland, I started hyperventilating, wondering if maybe I hadn't made an epic mistake, if maybe something hadn't happened, if maybe he hadn't got waylaid, she'd set me straight.

"Yeah. He did. He got *way laid*. By you! And then he got the hell out of Dodge."

"But what if . . . " I'd begun.

"Allyson, come on. In one day, you saw him get undressed by one girl, take a secret note from another, and God knows what happened on the train with those other girls; how do you think he really got that stain on his jeans?"

I hadn't even thought of that.

She'd taken me into the tiny airplane bathroom and shoved the Sous ou Sur T-shirt in the garbage. Then we'd flushed the coin he'd given me down the toilet, where I imagined it falling all those thousands of feet, sinking into the ocean below.

"There, we've destroyed all evidence of him," she'd said.

Well, almost. I hadn't told her about the photo on my phone, the one Agnethe took of the two of us. I still haven't deleted it, though I haven't looked at it, not even once.

When we got back home, Melanie was ready to put the trip behind her and turn her attention to our next chapter: college. I understood. I should've been excited too. I just wasn't. Every day we schlepped to IKEA and Bed, Bath & Beyond, to American Apparel and J. Crew with our moms. But it was like I had a permanent case of jet lag; all I wanted to do was take naps on the display beds. When Melanie left for school two days before me, I burst into tears. Everyone else thought I was crying for the pending separation from my best friend, but Melanie knew better, which was maybe why she sounded a little impatient when she hugged me and whispered into my ear, "It was just one day, Allyson. You'll get over it."

So when Melanie asks me now if I'm better, I can't let her down. "Yes," I tell her. "I'm great."

"Good." She claps her hands together and pulls out her phone. She fires off a text. "There's a guy going tonight, a friend of my friend Trevor. I think you'll like him."

"Oh, no. I don't think so."

"You just said you're over the Dutch dickwad."

"I am."

She stares at me. "The first three months of college are the most action you're supposed to get in your life. Have you so much as blinked at a guy?"

"I've mostly kept my eyes closed during all the wild orgies."

"Ha! Nice try. You forget I know you better than anyone. I'll bet you haven't even kissed anyone."

I pull the weird innardy parts out of the spring roll, wiping the excess grease on a paper napkin. "So?"

"So the guy I want you to meet tonight. He's way more your type."

"What's that supposed to mean?" Though I know what it means. It was absurd to think that *he* was ever my type. Or I his.

"Nice. Normal. I showed him your picture and he said you looked dark and mysterious." She reaches out to touch my hair. "Though you should cut your hair into the bob again. Right now it's more of a blob."

I haven't cut my hair since London, and it hangs down my neck in a messy curtain.

"That's the look I'm going for."

"Well, you're achieving it. But anyhow he's really nice, Mason—"

"Mason? What kind of name is that?"

"You're getting hung up on a name? You sound just like your mother."

I resist the urge to stab her through the eye with a chopstick.

"Anyhow, who cares? Maybe his name is really Jason but he just wanted to call himself Mason," Melanie continues. "Speaking of, no one calls me Melanie here. They call me Mel or Lainie."

"Two names for the price of one."

"It's college, Allyson. No one knows who you were. There's never a better time to reinvent yourself. You should try it." She gives me a pointed look.

I want to tell her that I did. It just didn't take.

— — —

Mason actually turns out to be not that bad. He's smart and slightly nerdy, and from the South, which explains the name, I guess, and he speaks in a lilting accent, which he makes fun of. When we get to the party on a desolate stretch of windblown street, miles from the subway stop, he jokes that he's from the hipster police and do I have enough tattoos to be in this part of town. At which point Trevor shows off his tribal armband and Melanie starts talking about the "tat" she's thinking of getting on her ankle or butt or other places girls get them, and Mason looks at me and rolls his eyes a little.

At the party, an elevator opens up directly into a loft, which is both huge and decrepit, with giant canvases all over the walls and the smell of oil paint and turpentine. It smelled like this in the squat. Another land mine. I kick it away before it explodes.

Melanie and Trevor are going on and on about this kick-ass band, whose grainy video they show me on Melanie's phone. They're congratulating themselves on seeing them at a place like this, before the whole world discovers them. When the band fires up, Melanie—Mel, Lainie, whoever—and Trevor hop to the front and start dancing like crazy. Mason hangs back with me. It's too loud to attempt conversation, which I'm glad about, but I'm also glad that someone stayed with me. I feel my tourist sign flashing, and I'm on native soil.

After what seems like forever, the band finally takes a break; the ringing in my ears is so loud it's like they're still playing.

"Care for a libation?" Mason asks me.

"Huh?" I'm still half deaf.

He mimes drinking something.

"Oh, no thanks."

"I'll. Be. Right. Back," he says, exaggerating the words like we're lip-reading.

Meanwhile, Melanie and Trevor are doing a kind of lip-reading of their own. They're in a corner on a couch, making out. It's like they don't notice anyone else in the room. I don't want to watch them, but I can't seem to stop myself. Seeing them kiss makes me physically ill. It's hard to push that memory down. The hardest. It's why I keep it buried the deepest.

Mason comes back with a beer for himself and a water for me. He sees Melanie and Trevor. "It was bound to happen," he tells me. "Those two have been circling each other for weeks like a pair of dogs in heat. I wondered what was going to trip the wire."

"Alcohol and 'kick-ass' music," I say, making air quotes.

"Vacations. Easier to start something up when you know you don't have to see someone for a while. Takes the pressure off." He glances at them. "I give them two weeks, tops."

"Two weeks? That's pretty generous. Some guys wouldn't give it more than a night." Even over the din, I can hear my bitterness. I can taste it in my mouth.

"I'd give you more than a night," Mason says.

And, oh, it is so the right thing to say. And who knows?

Maybe he's even sincere, though by now I know that I cannot be trusted to discern sincerity from fakery.

But still, I want to be over this. I want all those memories to disappear or to be supplanted with something else, to stop haunting me. So when Mason leans in to kiss me, I close my eyes, and I let him. I try to lose myself in it, try not to worry if the bitterness in my mouth has actually given me bad breath. I try to be kissed by someone else, try to *be* someone else.

But then Mason touches my neck, to the spot on it where the cut from that night has since healed, and I pull away.

He was right, after all; it didn't leave a scar, though part of me wishes it had. At least I'd have some evidence, some justification of this permanence. Stains are even worse when you're the only one who can see them.

Seventeen

DECEMBER
Cancún, Mexico

It has become tradition when we arrive in Cancún for Melanie and me to strip to our bathing suits as soon as we get into the condo and run to the beach for an inaugural swim. It's like our vacation baptism. We've done it for every one of the last nine years we've come down here.

But this year, when Melanie digs through her suitcase for a bikini, I go to the little desk next to the kitchen that normally holds nothing but cookbooks and prop open my textbooks. Every day, from four to six, I am to have study hall. I get New Year's Day off, but that's it. These are the terms of my parole.

I kept my grades a secret throughout the entire semester, so when the report cards showed up at the end of the term, it was kind of a shocker. I'd tried. I really had. After my midterms were so dismal, I'd tried harder, but it wasn't like my bad grades were a result of slacking off. Or skipping classes. Or partying.

But I might as well have been partying, given how tired I was all the time. It didn't matter if I got ten hours of sleep the night before—once I set foot in the lecture hall and the professor started droning on about wave motion, writing up equations on the monitor, the numbers would start dancing before my eyes and then I'd feel my lids grow heavy, and I'd wake to other students tripping over my legs to get to their next class.

During Reading Week, I drank so much espresso that I got no sleep at all, as if I was using up all the credits from the class naps. I crammed as hard as I could, but by that point, I'd fallen so behind, I was beyond help.

Given all that, I thought it was miraculous I finished the semester with a 2.7.

Needless to say, my parents thought otherwise.

When my grades came through last week, they flipped out. And when my parents flip out, they don't yell—they get quiet. But their disappointment and anger is deafening.

"What do you think we should do about this, Allyson?" they asked me as we sat at the dining room table, as if they were truly soliciting my opinion. Then they presented two options. We could cancel the trip, which would be terribly unfair for the rest of them, or I could agree to go under certain conditions.

Melanie shoots me sympathy looks as she disappears to change into her suit. Part of me wishes she'd boycott the beach in solidarity, though I know that's selfish, but it seems like something the old Melanie would've done.

But this is the new Melanie. Or the new, new Melanie. In the month since Thanksgiving, she looks totally different.

Again. She cut her hair all asymmetrical and fringy, and she got a nose ring, which her parents gave her crap about until she told them it was between that and a tattoo. Now that she's changed into a bikini, I see that she's let her armpit hair grow, though her hair is so fine and blond, it barely shows.

"Bye," she mouths as she slips out the front door, her mom, Susan, thrusting a tube of SPF-40 into her hands. My mom is digging through a suitcase for her special magnifying glass so she can check all the mattresses for bedbugs. When she finds it, she walks by me and pretends to look at my chem book with it. I snap the book shut. She gives me a pissy look.

"You think I want to be your warden? I thought I'd have all this free time now that you're in college, but it's like keeping you on track is its own full-time job."

Who asked you to keep me on track? I fume. In my head. But I bite my lip and open the chemistry textbook and dutifully reread the first chapters as Mom has instructed me to do for catch-up. They make no more sense to me now than they did the first time I attempted them.

That night, we all six go out to dinner at the Mexican restaurant, one of the eight restaurants attached to the resort. We go here every year for our first night out. The waiters wear giant sombreros, and there's a traveling mariachi band, but the food tastes the same as it does at El Torrito back home. When the waiter takes our drink orders, Melanie asks for a beer.

The parents gawk at her.

"We're legal to drink here," she says casually.

Mom gives Susan a look. "I don't think that's wise," Mom says.

"Why not?" I challenge.

"If you want my opinion, it has less to do with the age than the expectation. You've grown up with a drinking age of twenty-one, so you're not necessarily prepared for drinking now," is Susan's therapist answer.

"I'm sorry, but did you not go to college?" I ask. "I can't imagine it's changed that much. Do you not remember how all anyone does is drink?"

My parents look at each other, then at Susan and Steve.

"Is that what's going on with you? Have you been drinking too much at school?" Dad asks.

Melanie laughs so hard that the special bottled water Mom brings sprays through her nose. "I'm sorry, Frank, but do you not even know Allyson?" They continue to stare. "On the tour last summer, everyone drank." There is a moment of shocked silence. "Oh, spare me! The legal drinking age in Europe is eighteen! Anyhow, everyone drank but Allyson. She's totally straight and narrow. And you're asking if she's boozing it up at college? That's ludicrous."

My dad stares at me, then at Melanie. "We're just trying to understand what's going on with her. Why she got a two-seven GPA."

Now it's Melanie's turn to gawk. "*You got a two-seven?*" She clamps her hand over her lips and mouths, "Sorry." The look she gives me is one part surprise, one part respect.

"Melanie got a three-point-eight," Mom brags.

"Yes, Melanie is a genius, and I am an idiot. It's official."

Melanie looks wounded. "I go to the Gallatin School. Everyone gets As," she says apologetically.

"And Melanie probably drinks," I say, knowing full well she does.

She looks nervous for a second. "Of course I do. I don't pass out or anything. But it's college. I drink. Everyone drinks."

"I don't," I say. "And Melanie has the A average, and I have the C, so maybe I should go on a few benders and things will even out. Maybe that's a much better idea than this stupid study hall you have me in."

I'm really into this now, which is kind of crazy, because I don't even want a beer. One of the few things I like about this restaurant is the virgin margaritas—they're made with fresh fruit.

Mom turns to me, her mouth ready to catch some flies. "Allyson, do you have a drinking problem?"

I smack my hand to my head. "Mother, do you have a hearing problem? Because I don't know that you heard a word I said."

"I think she's saying that you might ease up a little and let them have a beer with dinner," Susan says.

"Thank you!" I say to Susan.

My mom looks to my dad. "Let the girls have a beer," he says expansively as he waves the waiter back over and asks for a couple of Tecates.

It's a victory of sorts. Except that I don't actually like beer, so in the end, I have to pretend to sip from mine as it grows sweaty on the table, and I don't order the virgin margarita I really wanted.

— — —

The next day, Melanie and I are sitting at the giant pool together. It's the first time we've managed to be alone since we got here.

"I think we should do something different," she says.

"Me too," I say. "Every year we come down here and we do the same things. We go to the same frigging ruins, even. Tulum is nice, but I was thinking we could branch out. Talk our parents into going somewhere new."

"Like swimming with the dolphins?" Melanie asks.

Dolphin swimming is different, but it's not what I'm after. Yesterday, I was looking at the map of the Yucatán Peninsula in the lobby, and some of the ruins are inland, more off the beaten path. Maybe we'd find a bit more of the real Mexico. "I was thinking we could go to Coba or Chichén Itzá. Different ruins."

"Oh, you're so wild," Melanie teases. She takes a slurp of iced tea. "Anyhow, I'm talking about New Year's Eve."

"Oh. You mean you don't want to do the Macarena with Johnny Maximo?" Johnny Maximo is this washed-up Mexican movie star who now has some job with the resort. All the mothers love him because he's handsome and macho and is always pretending to mistake them for our sisters.

"Anything but the Macarena!" Melanie puts down her book, something by Rita Mae Brown that looks like it's for school but Melanie says is not. "One of the bartenders told me about some big party on the beach in Puerto Morelos. It's a local thing, though he says lots of tourists come, but people like us. Young people. There's going to be a Mexican reggae band, which sounds bizarre. In a good way."

"You're just looking for a guy under sixty to make out with come midnight."

Melanie shrugs. "Under sixty, yes. A guy? Maybe not." She gives me a look.

"What?"

"I've sort of been doing the girl thing."

"What?!" It comes out a shout. "Sorry. Since when?"

"Since right after Thanksgiving. There was this one girl and we met in film theory class and we were friends and one night we went out and it just happened."

I look at the new haircut, the nose ring, the hairy armpits. It all makes sense. "So, are you a lesbian now?"

"I prefer not to label it," she says, somewhat sanctimoniously, the implication being that *I* need to label everything. *She's* the one who's constantly branding herself: Mel, Mel 2.0. Punk-rock librarian. I ask her girlfriend's name. She tells me they're not into defining it like that, but her name is Zanne.

"Is that with an *X*?"

"Z. Short for Suzanne."

Doesn't anybody use a real name anymore?

"Don't tell my parents, okay? You know my mom. She'd make us process it and talk about it as a phase of my development. I want to make sure this is more than a fling before I subject myself to that."

"Please, you don't have to tell me about parental over-analysis."

She pushes her sunglasses up her nose and turns to me. "Yeah, so what's that all about?"

"What do you mean? You've met my parents. Is there a part of my life they're *not* involved in? They must be freaking out to not have their fingers literally in every aspect of what I'm doing."

"I know. And when I heard about the study hall, I figured it was that. I thought maybe you had a low B average. But a two—point—seven? Really?"

"Don't *you* start on me."

"I'm not. I'm just surprised. You've always been such a kick-ass student. I don't get it." She takes a loud slurp of her mostly melted iced tea. "The Therapist says you're depressed."

"Your mom? She told you that?"

"I heard her mention it to your mom."

"What did my mom say?"

"That you weren't depressed. That you were pouting because you weren't used to being punished. Sometimes I really want to smack your mom."

"You and me both."

"Anyhow, later on my mom asked me if *I* thought you were depressed."

"And what'd you tell her?"

"I said lots of people have a hard time freshman year." She gives me a sharp look from behind her dark glasses. "I couldn't tell her the truth, could I? That I thought you were still pining for some guy you had a one-night stand with in Paris."

I pause, listening to the shriek of a little kid jumping off the high dive. When Melanie and I were little, we used to hold hands and jump together, over and over again.

"But what if it's not him? Not Willem." It's weird saying his name out loud. Here. After embargoing it for so long. *Willem.* I scarcely even allow myself to think it in my head.

"Don't tell me another guy dicked you over!"

"No! I'm talking about *me*."

"You?"

"It's, like, the me I was that day. I was different somehow."

"Different? How?"

"I was Lulu."

"But that was just a name. Just pretend."

Maybe it was. But still, that whole day, being with Willem, being Lulu, it made me realize that all my life I've been living in a small, square room, with no windows and no doors. And I was fine. I was happy, even. I thought. Then someone came along and showed me there was a door in the room. One that I'd never even seen before. Then he opened it for me. Held my hand as I walked through it. And for one perfect day, I was on the other side. I was somewhere else. Someone else. And then he was gone, and I was thrown back into my little room. And now, no matter what I do, I can't seem to find that door.

"It didn't feel pretend," I tell Melanie.

Melanie arranges her face in sympathy. "Oh, sweetie. It's because you were all hopped up on the fumes of infatuation. And Paris. But people don't change overnight. Especially you. You're Allyson. You're so solid. It's one of the things I love about you—how reliably *you* you are."

I want to protest. What about transformations? What about the reinvention she's always going on about? Are those only reserved for her? Is there a different standard for me?

"You know what you need? Some Ani DiFranco." She pulls out her iPhone and shoves the buds in my ears, and as Ani goes on about finding your voice and making it heard, I feel so frustrated with myself. Like I want to pull my skin wide open and step out of it. I scrape my feet against the hot cement floor and sigh, wishing there was someone I could explain this to. Someone who might understand what I'm feeling.

And for one small second, I do imagine the person I could talk to, about finding this door, and losing it. He would understand.

But that's the one door that needs to stay shut.

Eighteen

Somehow, using the same we're-adults-you-have-to-treat-us-that-way argument from the Beer Dinner, plus promising to hire a hotel-approved taxi for the entire night, Melanie and I manage to procure parental permission to go to that New Year's Eve party. It's being held on a narrow crescent of sand, all lit up with tiki torches, and at ten o'clock, it's already slamming. There is a low stage on which the touted Mexican reggae band will play, though right now a d.j. is playing techno.

There are several giant piles of discarded shoes. Melanie tosses off her bright-orange flip-flops. I hesitate before taking off my less conspicuous black leather sandals, hoping I'll find them again, because if I lose anything else, I swear I will never hear the end of it.

"Quite the bacchanal," Melanie says approvingly, nodding to the guys in swim trunks holding bottles of tequila by the neck, the girls in sarongs with their hair freshly corn-rowed. There are even actual Mexicans here, the guys smartly dressed in sheer white shirts, hair slicked back, and the girls in fancy party dresses, cut up to there, legs long and brown.

"Dance first or drink first?"

I don't want to dance. So I say drink. We line up at the packed bar. Behind us is a group of French-speaking people, which makes me do a double take. There's hardly anyone but Americans at our hotel, but of course people from every-where come to Mexico.

"Here." Melanie shoves a drink into my hand. It's in a hollowed-out piece of pineapple. I take a sniff. It smells like suntan lotion. It is sweet and warm and burns slightly going down. "Good girl."

I think of Ms. Foley. "Don't call me that."

"Bad girl."

"I'm not that either."

She looks peeved. "Nothing girl."

We drink our drinks in silence, taking in the growing party. "Let's dance," Melanie says, yanking me toward the ring of sand that has been allocated as the dance floor.

I shake my head. "Maybe later."

And there's that sigh again. "Are you going to be like this all night?"

"Like what?" I think of what she called me on the tour—*adventure averse*—and what she said at the pool. "So like *me*? I thought that's what you *loved* about me."

"What is your problem? You've had a stick up your ass this whole trip! It's not my fault your mom is Study-Hall Nazi."

"No, but it is your fault for making me feel like crap because I don't want to dance. I hate techno. I have *always* hated techno, so you should know that, what with me being so reliably me."

"Fine. Why don't you be reliably you and sit on the sidelines while I dance."

"Fine."

She leaves me on the perimeter of the circle and goes off and just starts dancing with random people. First she dances with some guy with dreadlocks and then turns and dances with a girl with super-short hair. She seems to be having a fine time out there, swirling, twirling, and it strikes me that if I didn't already know her, she would no longer be someone I would know.

I watch her for at least twenty minutes. In between the monotonous techno songs, she talks to other people, laughs. After a half hour, I'm getting a headache. I try to catch her eye, but I eventually give up and slip away.

The party stretches all the way down the curve of the water—and into it—where a bunch of people are skinny-dipping in the moonlit sea. A little ways farther down, it gets more mellow, with a bonfire and people around it playing guitar. I plant myself a few feet away from the bonfire, close enough to feel its heat and hear the crackle of wood. I dig my feet into the sand; the top layer is cool, but underneath it's still warm from the day's sunshine.

Down the beach, the techno stops, and the reggae band takes the stage. The more mellow *bump-bump-thump* is nice. In the water, a girl starts dancing on a guy's shoulder, pulls off her bikini top, and stands there, half naked like a moonshine mermaid, before diving in with a quiet splash. Behind me, the guys on guitars start up with "Stairway to Heaven." It mingles strangely well with the reggae.

I lie down in the sand and look up at the sky. From this vantage point, it's like I have the beach all to myself. The band finishes a song, and the singer announces that it's a half hour until the New Year. "New Year. *Año nuevo*. It's a tabula rasa. Time to *hacer borrón y cuenta nueva*," he chants. "One chance to wipe the board clean."

Can you really do that? Wipe the board clean? Would I even want to? Would I wipe all of last year away if I could?

"Tabula rasa," the singer repeats. "A new chance to start over. Start fresh, baby. Make amends. Make ch-ch-changes. To be who you want to be. Come the stroke of midnight, before you kiss your *amor,* save *un beso para tí*. Close your eyes, think of the year ahead. This is your chance. This can be the day it all changes."

Really? It's a nice idea, but why January first? You might as well say April nineteenth is the day that everything changes. A day is a day is a day. It means nothing.

"At the stroke of midnight, make your wish. *Qué es tu deseo?* For yourself. For the world."

It's New Year's. Not a birthday cake. And I'm not eight anymore. I don't believe in wishes coming true. But if I did, what would I wish for? To undo that day? To see him again?

Normally I have such willpower. Like a dieter resisting a cookie, I don't even let myself go there. But for the briefest second, I do. I picture him right here, walking down the beach, hair reflecting in the flames, eyes dark and light and full of teasing, and of so many other things. And for a second, I almost see him.

As I open myself to the fantasy, I wait for the accompanying clench of pain. But it doesn't come. Instead my breath slows and something warms inside me. I abandon caution and all good sense and wrap myself in thoughts of him. My own hands circle around my chest, as if he were holding me. For one brief moment, everything feels right.

"I thought I'd never find you!"

I look up. Melanie is striding toward me. "I've been right here."

"I've been looking for you for the last half hour! Up and down the beach. I had no idea where you were."

"I was right here."

"I looked everywhere for you. The party's getting totally out of control, like roofies-in-the-punch wild. Some girl just puked six inches from my feet, and guys are hitting on me with the worst pickup lines in the world. I've had my ass pinched more times than I can count, and one charming guy just asked me if I wanted a bite of his sandwich—and he wasn't talking about food!" She shakes her head as if trying to dislodge the memory. "We're supposed to have each other's backs!"

"I'm sorry. You were having fun, and I guess I just lost track of time."

"You lost track of time?"

"I guess so. I'm really sorry you were worried. But I'm fine. Do you want to go back to the party?"

"No! I'm over it. Let's leave."

"We don't have to." I look toward the bonfire. The flames are dancing, making it hard to pull my gaze away. "I don't mind staying." For the first time in a long while, I am having an okay time, I'm okay being where I am.

"Well, I do. I've spent the last half hour panicking, and now I'm sober, and I'm beyond over this place. It's like a Telemundo frat party."

"Oh, okay. Let's go then."

I follow her back to the shoe piles, where it takes ages for her to find her flip-flops, and then we get into our waiting taxi. By the time I think to look at the dashboard clock, it's twenty past twelve. I don't really believe what the singer said about midnight wishes, but now that I've missed mine, I feel like I should've tried before the window of opportunity closed.

We ride home in silence, save for the cab driver softly singing to his radio. When we pull into the gates of the resort, Melanie hands him some bills, and for a minute, I get an idea.

"Melanie. What if we hire this guy in a day or two and go off somewhere, away from the tourists?"

"Why would we want to do that?"

"I don't know. To see what would happen if we tried something different. Excuse me, señor, how much would it be for us to hire you for a whole day?"

"*Lo siento. No hablo inglés.*"

Melanie rolls her eyes at me. "I guess you have to be satisfied with your one big adventure."

At first I think she means this party, but then I realize she means the ruins. Because I did actually manage to get our families to visit a different ruin. We went to Coba instead of Tulum. And just as I'd hoped, we stopped at a small village along the way, and for a moment there, I'd gotten excited, thinking this was it, I had actually escaped into the real Mexico. Okay, my whole family was in tow, but it was a Mayan village. Except then Susan and my mom went crazy buying beaded jewelry, and the villagers came out and played drums for us, and we all were invited to dance in a circle and then there was even a traditional spiritual cleansing. But everyone was videoing everything, and after his cleansing, my dad "donated" ten dollars to a hat that was conspicuously put in front of us, and I realized that this was no different from being on the tour.

The condo is quiet. The parents are all in bed, though as soon as the door closes, Mom pops out of her bedroom. "You're early," she says.

"I was tired," Melanie lies. "Good night. Happy New Year." She pads off toward our room, and Mom gives me a New Year's kiss and goes back to hers.

I'm nowhere near tired, so I sit out on the balcony and listen to the dwindling sounds of the hotel's party. On the horizon, a lightning storm is brewing. I reach into my purse for my phone and, for the first time in months, open the photo album.

His face is so beautiful, it makes my stomach twist. But he seems unreal, not someone I would ever know. But then I look at me, the me in the photo, and I hardly recognize her, either, and not just because the hair is different, but because she seems different. That's not me. That's Lulu. And she's just as gone as he is.

Tabula rasa. That's what the reggae singer said. Maybe I can't get my wish, but I can try to wipe the slate clean, try to get over this.

I allow myself to look at the picture of Willem and Lulu in Paris for a long minute.

"Happy New Year," I tell them.

And then I erase them.

Nineteen

*T*wo feet of snow fall in Boston while I'm in Mexico, and the temperature never rises above freezing, so when I get back two weeks later, campus looks like a depressing gray tundra. I arrive a few days before classes start, with excuses of getting prepped for the new semester, but really because I could not handle being at home, under the watchful eye of the warden, one day longer. It had been bad enough in Cancún, but home, without Melanie to distract me—she took off for New York City the day after we got back, before we got a chance to ever resolve the weirdness that had settled between us—it was unbearable.

The Terrific Trio comes back from break full of stories and inside jokes. They spent New Year's together at Kendra's family's Virginia Beach condo and went swimming in the snow, and now they are ordering themselves Polar Bear T-shirts. They're nice enough, asking about my trip, but I find it hard to breathe with all that bonhomie, so I pile on my sweaters and parkas and trudge over to the U bookstore to pick up a new Mandarin workbook.

I'm in the foreign languages section when my cell phone rings. I don't even need to look at the caller ID. Mom has been calling at least twice a day since I got back.

"Hey, Mom."

"Allyson Healey." The voice on the other end is high and winsome, the opposite of Mom.

"Yes, this is Allyson."

"Oh, hello, Allyson. This is Gretchen Price from the guidance office."

I pause, breathing through the sickening feeling in my stomach. "Yes?"

"I'm wondering if you might like to stop by my office. Say hello."

Now I feel like I'm going to throw up right on the stacks of *Buon Giorno Italiano*. "Did my mother call you?"

"Your mother? I don't think so." I hear the sound of something knocking over. "Damn. Hang on." There's more shuffling and then she's back on the line. "Look, I apologize for the last-minute notice, but that seems to be my MO these days. I'd love for you to come in before the term starts."

"Umm, the term starts the day after tomorrow."

"So it does. How about today, then?"

They are going to kick me out. I've blown it in one term. They know I'm not a Happy College Student. I don't belong in the catalog. Or here. "Am I in some kind of trouble?"

That tinkling laugh again. "Not with me. Why don't you

come by—hang on." There's more shuffling of paper. "How about four?"

"You're sure my mother didn't call?"

"Yes, Allyson, I'm quite sure. So four?"

"What's it about?"

"Oh, just getting-to-know-you stuff. I'll see you at four."

Gretchen Price's office is in a crowded corner of the ivy-covered administration buildings. Stacks of books and papers and magazines are scattered everywhere, on the round table and chairs by the window, on the love seat, on her messy desk.

She is on the phone when I'm ushered in, so I just stand there in the doorway. She gestures for me to come inside. "You must be Allyson. Just move a pile off the chair and take a seat. I'll be with you in a second."

I move a dirty Raggedy Ann doll with one of the braids chopped off and a stack of folders from one of the chairs. Some of the folders have sticky notes on them: *Yes. No. Maybe.* Paperwork slips out of one. It's a printout of a college application, like the one I sent in a year ago. I shove it back into the folder and put it on the next chair.

Gretchen hangs up the phone. "So, Allyson, how's it going?"

"It's going fine." I glance at all the applications, all the comers who want a spot like mine. "*Great* in fact."

"Really?" She picks up a file, and I have the distinct impression my goose is cooked.

"Yep," I say with all the chipperness I can muster.

"See, the thing is, I've been looking at your first-term grades."

I feel tears spring to my eyes. She lured me here under false pretenses. She said I wasn't in trouble, it was just a getting-to-know-you session. And I didn't fail. I just got Cs!

She looks at my stricken face and motions for me to calm down with her hands. "Relax, Allyson," she says in a soothing voice. "I'm not here to bust you. I just want to see if you need some help, and to offer it if that's the case."

"It's my first term. I was adjusting." I've used this excuse so much I've almost come to believe it.

She leans back in her chair. "You know, people tend think that college admissions is inherently unfair. That you can't judge people from paper. But the thing is, paper can actually tell you an awful lot." She takes a gulp from one of those coffee cups that kids paint. Hers is covered in smudgy pastel thumbprints. "Having never met you before, but judging just from what I'm seeing on paper, I suspect that you're struggling a bit."

She's not asking me *if* I'm struggling. She's not asking *why* I'm struggling. She just knows. The tears come, and I let them. Relief is more powerful than shame.

"Let me be clear," Gretchen continues, sliding over a box of tissues. "I'm not concerned about your GPA. First-term slides are as common as the freshman fifteen. Oh, man, you should've seen my first-semester GPA." She shakes her head and laughs. "Generally, struggling students here fall into two categories: Those getting used to the freedom, maybe spending a little too much time at the keg parties, not enough time in the library. They generally straighten out after a term or two." She looks at me. "Are you pounding too many shots of Jägermeister, Allyson?"

I shake my head, even though by the tone of her question, it seems like she already knows the answer.

She nods. "So the other pattern is a bit more insidious. But it's actually a predictor for dropouts. And that's why I wanted to see you."

"You think I'm going to drop out?"

She stares hard at me. "No. But looking at your records from high school and your first term, you fit a pattern." She waves around a file, which obviously contains my whole academic history. "Students like you, young women, in particular, do extraordinarily well in high school. Look at your grades. Across the board, they're excellent. AP, science classes, humanities classes, all As. Extremely high SAT scores. Then you get into college, which is supposedly why you've been working so hard, right?"

I nod.

"Well you get here, and you crumple. You'd be surprised how many of my straight-A, straight-and-narrow students wind up dropping out." She shakes her head in dismay. "I hate it when that happens. I help choose who goes here. It reflects badly on me if they crash and burn."

"Like a doctor losing a patient."

"Great analogy. See how smart you are?"

I offer a rueful smile.

"The thing is, Allyson, college is supposed to be . . ."

"The best years of my life?"

"I was going to say nourishing. An adventure. An exploration. I'm looking at you, and you don't seem nourished. And I'm looking at your schedule. . . ." She peers at her computer screen. "Biology, chemistry. Physics. Mandarin. Labs. It's very ambitious for your first year."

"I'm pre-med," I say. "I have to take those classes."

She doesn't say anything. She takes another gulp of coffee. Then she says. "Are those the classes you *want* to take?"

I pause. Nobody has ever asked me that. When we got the course catalog in the mail, it was just assumed I'd tackle all the pre-med requirements. Mom knew just what I should take when. I'd looked at some electives, had mentioned that I thought pottery sounded cool, but I may as well have said I was planning on majoring in underwater basket weaving.

"I don't know what I want to take."

"Why don't you take a look and see about switching things up a bit. Registration is still in flux, and I might be able to pull some strings." She stops and pushes the catalog clear across the desk. "Even if you do wind up pre-med, you have four years to take these classes, and you have a lot of humanities requisites to get in too. You don't need to jam everything together all at once. This isn't medical school."

"What about my parents?"

"What *about* your parents?"

"I can't let them down."

"Even if it means letting yourself down? Which I doubt they'd want for you."

The tears come again. She hands me another tissue.

"I understand about wanting to please your parents, to make them proud. It's a noble impulse, and I commend you for it. But at the end of the day, it's your education, Allyson. You have to own it. And you should enjoy it." She pauses, slurps some more coffee. "And somehow I imagine that your parents will be happier if they see your GPA come up."

She's right about that. I nod. She turns to her computer

screen. "So, let's just pretend we're going to jiggle some classes around. Any idea of what you might like to take?"

I shake my head.

She grabs the course catalog and flips through it. "Come on. It's an intellectual buffet. Archaeology. Salsa dancing. Child development. Painting. Intro to finance. Journalism. Anthropology. Ceramics."

"Is that like pottery?" I interrupt.

"It is." She widens her eyes and taps on her computer. "Beginning Ceramics, Tuesdays at eleven. It's open. Oh, but it conflicts with your physics lab. Shall we postpone the lab, and maybe physics, for another term?"

"Cut them." Saying it feels wonderful, like letting go of a bunch of helium balloons and watching them disappear into the sky.

"See? You're already getting the hang of it," Gretchen says. "How about some humanities, to balance you out? You're going to need those to graduate anyway as part of your core curriculum. Are you more interested in ancient history or modern history? There's a wonderful European survey. And a great seminar on the Russian Revolution. Or a fascinating American Pre-Revolution class that makes excellent use of our being so close to Boston. Or you could get started on some of your literature classes. Let's see. Your AP exams tested you out of the basic writing requirement. You know, we could be devilish and slip you into one of the more interesting seminar classes." She scrolls down her computer. "Beat Poetry. Holocaust Literature. Politics in Prose. Medieval Verse. Shakespeare Out Loud."

I feel something jolt up my spine. An old circuit-breaker

long since forgotten being tested out and sparking in the darkness.

Gretchen must see my expression, because she starts telling me about how this isn't just any Shakespeare class, how Professor Glenny has very strong opinions on how Shakespeare should be taught, and how he has a cult following on campus.

I can't help but think of *him*. And then I think of the tabula rasa. The resolution I made on New Year's. The fact that I am pre-med. "I don't think I'm supposed to take this class."

This makes her smile. "Sometimes the best way to find out what you're supposed to do is by doing the thing you're *not* supposed to do." She taps on her keyboard. "It's full, as usual, so you'll have to fight your way in off the wait list. Why not give it a shot? Leave it up to the fates."

The fates. I think that's another word for accidents.

Which I don't believe in anymore.

But I let her register me for the class just the same.

Twenty

Stepping into the classroom for Shakespeare Out Loud is like stepping into an entirely different school than the one I've attended for the past four months. Instead of a giant lecture hall, which is where all my science courses were located, or even a large classroom like Mandarin, it's in a tiny, intimate classroom, the kind we had in high school. There are maybe twenty-five desks arced into a U, around a lectern in the middle. And the students sitting at them, they look different too. Lip rings and hair dyed colors not found naturally on the human head. It's a sea of well-manicured alienation. The arty crowd, I guess. When I come in and look for a seat—they're all taken—no one looks at me.

I take a seat on the floor, near the door, for an easier escape. I may not belong in chemistry, but I don't belong here either. When Professor Glenny strides in five minutes late and looking like a rock star—shaggy graying hair, beat-up leather boots, he even has pouty Mick Jagger lips—he steps on me. As in, literally treads on my hand. As bad as my other classes have been, no one has ever stepped on me. Not an auspicious start, and I almost leave right then and there, but my way is now blocked by the overflow of other students.

"Show of hands," Professor Glenny begins after he has dropped his artfully worn leather satchel on top of the lectern. "How many of you have ever read a Shakespeare play for the sheer pleasure of it?" He has a British accent, though not the Masterpiece Theatre kind.

About half the hands in the class shoot up. I almost consider raising mine, but it's just too much of a lie, and there's no point in brown-nosing if I'm not staying.

"Excellent. Ancillary question: How many of you have fallen asleep while attempting to read a Shakespeare play by yourself?"

The class goes silent. No hands go up. Then Professor Glenny looks right at me, and I'm wondering how he knows, but then I realize he's not looking at me but the guy behind me, who is the only person who's raised a hand. Along with everyone else in the class, I turn and stare at him. He's one of two African American students in the room, though he's the only one sporting a huge halo of an afro covered in bejeweled barrettes, and bubble-gum-pink gloss on his lips. Otherwise, he's dressed like a soccer mom, in sweats and pink Uggs. In a field of carefully cultivated weirdness, he's a wildflower, or maybe a weed.

"Which play bored you to sleep?" Professor Glenny asks.

"Take your pick. *Hamlet. Macbeth. Othello.* I napped to the best of them."

The class titters, as if falling asleep while studying is so déclassé.

Professor Glenny nods. "So why, then, please—sorry, your name . . . ?"

"D'Angelo Harrison, but my friends call me Dee."

"I'll be presumptuous and call you Dee. Dee, why take this class? Unless you're here to catch up on your sleep."

Again, the class laughs.

"By my count, this class costs about five grand a semester," Dee says. "I can sleep for free."

I attempt the math. Is that how much one class costs?

"Quite prudent," Professor Glenny says. "So, again, why take this class, given the expenditure and given Shakespeare's soporific track record?"

"Well, I'm not actually in the class yet. I'm on your wait list."

At this point, I can't tell if he's stalling or parrying with the professor, but either way, I'm impressed. Everyone else here seems eager to give the right answer, and this guy is stringing the professor along. To his credit, Professor Glenny seems more amused than annoyed.

"My point is, Dee, why attempt it even?"

There's a long pause. You can hear the fluorescent lights humming, the throat-clearing of a few students who clearly have a ready answer. And then Dee says, "Because the movie of *Romeo and Juliet* makes me cry harder than just about anything else. Every damn time I see it."

Again, the class laughs. It's not a kind laugh. Professor Glenny turns back toward the lectern and pulls a paper and pen out of his satchel. It's a list. He stares at it ominously and then checks off a name—and I wonder if this Dee just got himself kicked off the wait list. What kind of class did Gretchen Price put me in? Gladiator Shakespeare?

Then Professor Glenny turns to a girl with weird pink Tootsie Roll twists who has her nose in a copy of the collected works of Shakespeare, the kind of girl who probably never deigned to watch Leo and Claire's version of *Romeo and Juliet* or fall asleep while reading *Macbeth*. He looms over her for a moment. She looks up at him and smiles bashfully, like, oh-you-caught-me-reading-my-book. He flashes a thousand-watt smile back at her. And then he slams her book shut. It's a big book. It makes a loud noise.

Professor Glenny returns to the lectern. "Shakespeare is a mysterious character. There is so much written about this man about whom we truly know so little. Sometimes I think only Jesus has had more ink spilled with less fruitful result. So I resist making any characterizations about the man. But I will go out on a limb and say this: Shakespeare did not write his plays so that you could sit in a library carrel and read them in silence." He pauses, lets that sink in before continuing. "Playwrights are not novelists. They create works that need to be performed, interpreted. To be reinterpreted through the ages. It is credit to Shakespeare's genius that he gave us such great raw material that really could survive the ages, withstand the myriad reinterpretations we throw at it. But to truly appreciate Shakespeare, to understand why he has endured, you must hear it out loud, or better yet, see it performed, whether you see it performed in period costume or done naked, a dubious pleasure I've had. Though a good film production can do the trick, as our friend Dee has so aptly demonstrated. And Mr. Harrison." He looks at Dee again. "Thank you for your honesty. I too have fallen asleep while reading Shakespeare. My college textbook still bears some drool marks. You're off the wait list."

Striding back to the whiteboard, Professor Glenny scrawls *English 317—Shakespeare Out Loud* on it. "The name of this class is not accidental. It is quite literal. For in this class, we do not *read* Shakespeare quietly to ourselves or in the privacy of our bedrooms or libraries. We *perform* it. We *see* it performed. We read it aloud, in class or with partners. Every last one of us will become actors in this class, interpreters for one another, in front of one another. For those of you not prepared for this or who prefer a more conventional approach, this fine institution offers plenty of Shakespeare survey courses, and I suggest you avail yourself of one of them."

He pauses, as if to give people a chance to escape. Here would be my chance to go, but something roots me in place.

"If you know anything about this class, it's that I coordinate our readings to go with whatever Shakespeare is being performed during the term, be it by a community group or professional theater company. I expect attendance at all the plays, and I get us excellent group rates. As it happens, this winter and spring bring a delightful selection of plays."

He starts handing out the syllabus, and before one gets to me, before he finishes writing the order of plays on the board, I know it will be among them, even though Shakespeare wrote more than thirty plays, I know this one will be on our list.

It's midway through the syllabus, after *Henry V* and *The Winter's Tale* and before *As You Like It* and *Cymbeline* and

Measure for Measure. But there on the page, it seems to jump out at me like a billboard. *Twelfth Night*. And whether I want to take this class or not is irrelevant. I can't stand up here and read those lines. That is the opposite of tabula rasa.

Professor Glenny goes on for a while about the plays, pointing to them one by one with his hand, erasing the ink in his enthusiasm. "My absolute favorite thing about this class is that we, in effect, let the themes choose us by letting the plays choose us. The dean was skeptical at first of this academia via serendipity, but it always seems to work out. Take this sampling." He points to the list of plays again. "Can anyone surmise this semester's theme based on these particular plays?"

"They're all comedies?" the girl up front with the Tootsie Roll twists asks.

"Good guess. *The Winter's Tale, Measure for Measure*, and *Cymbeline*, though all have much humor, are not considered comedies so much as problem plays, a category we shall discuss later. And *Henry V*, though it has many funny bits, is quite a serious play. Any other takers?"

Silence.

"I'll give you a hint. It's most obvious in *Twelfth Night* or *As You Like It*, which *are* comedies—which isn't to say they're not also quite moving plays."

More silence.

"Come now. Some of you fine scholars must have seen one of these. Who here has seen *As You Like It* or *Twelfth Night*?"

I don't realize I've raised my hand until it's too late. Until Professor Glenny has seen me and nodded to me with those bright, curious eyes of his. I want to say that I've made a mistake, that it was some other version of Allyson who used to raise her hand in class who temporarily reappeared. But I can't, so I blurt out that I saw *Twelfth Night* over the summer.

Professor Glenny stands there, as if waiting for me to finish my thought. But that was it; that's all I have to say. There's an awkward silence, like I just announced I was an alcoholic—at a Daughters of the American Revolution meeting.

But Professor Glenny refuses to give up on me: "And . . . what was the main source of tension and humor in that particular play?"

For the briefest of seconds, I'm not in this overheated classroom on a winter's morning. It's the hot English night, and I'm at the canal basin in Stratford-upon-Avon. And then I'm in a Paris park. And then I'm back here. In all three places, the answer remains the same: "No one is who they pretend to be."

"Thank you. . . . ?"

"Allyson," I finish. "Allyson Healey."

"Allyson. Perhaps a slight overgeneralization, but for our purposes, it hits the nail right on the head." He turns to the board and scrawls *Altering Identity, Altering Reality* on it. Then he checks something else off on his sheet of paper.

Professor Glenny continues, "Now, before we part ways, one last piece of housekeeping. We won't have time to read each play completely in class, though we will make quite a dent. I believe I've made my point about reading alone to yourselves, so I'd like you to read the remaining sections aloud with partners. This is not optional. Please pair up now. If you're on the wait list, find a partner also on the wait list.

Allyson, you're no longer on the wait list. As you can see, class participation is rewarded in here."

There's bustle as everyone pairs off. I look around. Next to me is a normalish-girl with cat-eye glasses. I could ask her.

Or I could get up and walk out of the class. Even though I'm off the wait list, I could just drop the class, leave my spot for someone else.

But for some reason, I don't do either of those things. I turn away from the girl in the glasses and look behind me. That guy, Dee, is sitting there, like the unpopular and unathletic kid who always wound up the remainder during team picking for grade-school kickball games. He's wearing a bemused look, as if he knows no one will ask him and he's saving everyone the trouble. So when I ask him if he wants to be partners, his arch expression falls away for a moment and he appears genuinely surprised.

"Just so happens my dance card is none too full at the moment."

"Is that a yes?"

He nods.

"Good. I do have one condition. It's more of a favor. Two favors, actually."

He frowns for a moment, then arches his plucked eyebrow so high, it disappears into the halo of hair.

"I don't want to read *Twelfth Night* out loud. You can do all the parts, if you want, and I'll listen, and then I'll read one of the other plays. Or we can rent a movie version and read along. I just don't want to have to say it. Not a word of it."

"How you gonna get away with that in class?"

"I'll figure it out."

"What you got against *Twelfth Night*?"

"That's the other thing. I don't want to talk about it."

He sighs as if considering. "Are you a flake or a diva? Diva I can work with, but I got no time for flakes."

"I don't think I'm either." Dee looks skeptical. "It's just that one play, I swear. I'm sure there's a DVD for it."

He looks at me for a long minute, as if trying to X-ray my true self. Then he either decides I'm okay or recognizes he has no other options, because he rolls his eyes and sighs loudly. "There are several versions of *Twelfth Night*, actually." Suddenly, his voice and diction have completely changed. Even his expression has gone professorial. "There's a film version with Helena Bonham Carter, who is magnificent. But if we're going to cheat like this, we should rent the stage version."

I stare at him a moment, baffled. He stares back, then his mouth cracks into the smallest of grins. And I realize what I said before was right: *No one is who they pretend to be.*

Twenty-one

*F*or the first few weeks of class, Dee and I tried meeting in the library, but we got dirty looks, especially when Dee broke out into his voices. And he has lots of voices: a solemn English accent when doing Henry, a weird Irish brogue—his take on a Welsh accent, I guess—as Fluellen, exaggerated French accents when doing the French characters. I don't bother with accents. It's enough for me to get the words right.

After getting shushed in the library one too many times, we switched to the Student Union, but Dee couldn't hear me over the din. He projected so well, you'd think he was a theater major or something. But I think he's history or political science. Not that he's told me this; we don't talk aside from the reading. But I've glimpsed his textbooks, and they're all tomes about the history of the labor movement or treatises on government.

So right before we start reading the second play, *The Win-*

ter's Tale, I suggest that we move to my dorm, where it's generally quiet in the afternoons. Dee gives me a long look and then says okay. I tell him to come over at four.

That afternoon, I lay out a plate of the cookies that Grandma keeps sending me, and I make tea. I have no idea what Dee expects, but this is the first time I've ever entertained in my room, though I'm not sure what I'm doing qualifies as entertaining or if Dee is company.

But when Dee sees the cookies, he gives me a funny little smile. Then he takes off his coat and hangs it in the closet, even though mine is tossed over a chair. He kicks off his boots. Then he looks around my room.

"Do you have a clock?" he asks. "My phone's dead."

I get up and show him the box of alarm clocks, which I have since put back in the closet. "Take your pick."

He takes a long time choosing, finally settling on a 1940s mahogany deco number. I show him how to wind it. He asks how to set the alarm. I show him. Then he sets it for five fifty, explaining he has to be at his job at the dining hall at six. The reading usually doesn't take more than a half hour, so I'm not sure why he sets the alarm. But I don't say anything. About that. Or about his job, even though I'm curious about it.

He sits down on my desk chair. I sit on my bed. He picks up a tube of fruit flies from the desk, examining it with a slightly amused expression. "They're *Drosophila*," I explain. "I'm breeding them for a class."

He shakes his head. "If you run out, you can come get more in my mama's kitchen."

I want to ask him where that kitchen is. Where he's from.

But he seems guarded. Or maybe it's me. Maybe making friends is a specific skill, and I missed the lesson. "Okay, time for work. See you later, my dropsillas," he says to the bugs. I don't correct his pronunciation.

We read a really good scene at the beginning of *The Winter's Tale*, when Leontes freaks out and thinks that Hermione is cheating on him. When we get to the end point, Dee packs up his Shakespeare textbook, and I think he's going to leave, but instead he pulls out a book by someone called Marcuse. He gives me the quickest of looks.

"I'll make more tea," I say.

We study together in silence. It's nice. At five fifty, the alarm goes off and Dee packs up to go to work.

"Wednesday?" he says.

"Sure."

Two days later, we go through the same routine, cookies, tea, hello to the "dropsillas," Shakespeare out loud, and silent study. We don't talk. We just work. On Friday, Kali comes into the room. It's the first time she's seen Dee, seen anyone, in the room with me, and she looks at him for a long moment. I introduce them.

"Hi, *Dee*. Pleasure to *meet* you," she says in a strangely flirty voice.

"Oh, the pleasure is all mine," Dee says, his voice all exaggeratedly animated.

Kali looks at him and then smiles. Then she goes to her closet and pulls out a camel coat and a pair of tawny suede boots. "Dee, can I *ask* you something? What do you think of *these* boots with this jacket? Too *matchy matchy*?"

I look at Dee. He is wearing sky-blue sweats and a T-shirt

with sparkly lettering spelling out I BELIEVE. I'm not clear how this reads Fashion Expert to Kali.

But Dee gets right into it. "Oh, girl, those boots are fine. I might have to take them from you."

I look at him, sort of shocked. I mean I figured Dee was gay, but I've never heard him talk all sassy-gay-sidekick before.

"Oh, no, you won't," Kali replies, her strange ways of KO'ing words now blending with some latent Valley Girl tendencies. "They cost me, like, *four hundred* dollars. You can *borrow* them."

"Oh, you're a doll baby. But you got Cinderella feet, and ole Dee's like one of them ugly stepsisters."

Kali laughs, and they go on like this for some time, talking about fashion. I feel kind of bad. I guess I never realized Dee was so into this kind of thing. Kali got it right away. It's like she has some radar, the one that tells you how to pick up on things with people, how to be friends. I don't really care about fashion, but that night, when the alarm goes off and Dee packs up to leave, I show him the latest skirt my mom sent me and ask if he thinks it's too preppy. But he barely gives it half a glance. "It's fine."

After that, Kali starts showing up more often, and she and Dee go all *Project Runway*, and Dee always switches into that voice. I write it off as just a fashion thing. But then a few days after that, as we're leaving, Kendra walks in, and I introduce them. Kendra sizes Dee up, like she does with people, and puts on her flight-attendant smile and asks Dee where he's from.

"New York," he says. I make a note of that. I've known

him for almost three weeks, and I'm just now finding out the basics.

"Where in New York?"

"The city."

"Where?"

"The Bronx."

The flight attendant smile is gone, replaced by a tight line that looks penciled on.

"Oh, like the South Bronx? Well. You must be so glad to be living here."

Now it's Dee who gives Kendra the once-over. They're eyeing each other like dogs, and I wonder if it's because they're both black. Then, he switches to a different voice from the one he talks to Kali or me in. "You from the South Bronx?"

Kendra recoils a little. "No! I'm from Washington."

"Like where they got all the rain and shit?"

Rain and shit?

"No, not state. DC."

"Oh. I got some cousins in DC. Down in Anacostia. Shit, those are some nasty-ass projects. Even worse than where I came up. There's a shooting at their school every damn week."

Kendra looks horrified. "I've never even been to Anacostia. I live in Georgetown. And I went to Sidwell Friends, where the Obama girls go."

"I went to South Bronx High. Most wack school in America. Ever heard of it?"

"No, I'm afraid I haven't." She gives me a quick look. "Well, I have to go. I'm meeting Jeb soon." Jeb is her new boyfriend.

"Catch you later, homegirl," Dee calls as Kendra disappears into her room. As Dee picks up his backpack to leave, he is quaking with laughter.

I decide to walk him to the dining hall, maybe eat there for a change. Eating alone sucks, but there are only so many microwave burritos a girl can stomach. When we get downstairs, I ask him if he really went to South Bronx High School.

When he speaks again, he sounds like Dee. Or the Dee I know. "They closed South Bronx High School a year ago, not that I ever went there. I went to a charter school. Then I got snagged in Prep for Prep—scholarship thing—by a private school that's even more expensive than Sidwell Friends. Take that, Miss Thang."

"Why didn't you just tell her where you went?"

He looks at me and then, reverting to the voice he'd used with Kendra, says, "If homegirls wanna see me as ghetto trash"—he stops and switches to his lispy, sassy voice—"or big-ass queer"—now he switches to his deepest Shakespeare voice—"I shall not take it upon myself to disabuse them."

When we reach the dining hall, I feel like I should say something to him. But I'm not sure what. In the end, I just ask him if he wants chocolate chip or butter cookies next time. Grandma sent me both.

"I'll supply cookies. My mama sent up some homemade molasses spice ones."

"That's nice."

"Nothin' nice about it. She's throwing down. She wasn't about to be outdone by somebody's grandma."

I laugh. It's a strange sound, like an old car being started after a long time in the garage. "We won't tell my grandma that. If she accepts the challenge and bakes her own cookies, we might get food poisoning. She's the worst cook in the world."

— — —

It becomes a routine then. Every Monday, Wednesday, and Friday: cookies, tea, alarm clock, Shakespeare, study. We still don't talk much about ourselves, but little things slip through the cracks. His mother works at a hospital. He has no siblings, but five zillion cousins. He's on a full scholarship. He has a rather huge crush on Professor Glenny. He is double-majoring in history and literature, and maybe a minor in political science. He hums when he's bored, and when he's really into his reading, he twists his hair around his index finger so tight, it turns pink. And just as I suspected from that first day in class, he's smart. That he doesn't tell me, but it's obvious. He's the only one in the entire class to get an A on Glenny's first assignment, a paper on *Henry V*; Professor Glenny announces it to the class and reads snippets of Dee's paper to the class as an example of what the rest of us should strive for. Dee looks mortified, and I feel sort of bad, but the Glenny groupies regard Dee with such looks of naked envy that it's almost worth it. I, meanwhile, get a very solid B on my paper about Perdita and themes of lost and found.

I tell Dee little things about me too, but half the time, I find myself censoring what I want to say. I like him. I do. But I'm trying to make good on my tabula-rasa promise. Still, I sort of wish I could ask Dee's opinion about Melanie. I sent her the very first piece I made from ceramics class, along with a note about how I'd completely upended my schedule. I sent it Priority Mail, and then a week went by, and I didn't hear anything. So I'd called her up to make sure she'd gotten it—it was just a crappy, handmade bowl, but it had a beautiful crackly turquoise glaze—and she apologized for not responding, saying she was busy.

I told her all about my new classes, and about the crazy lengths I was going to so my parents wouldn't find out: sending them biology tests with improving scores (Dee's and my lengthy study sessions are paying off) but also sending them my old chemistry lab partner's tests, with my name on them. I figured she'd get a good laugh about this, but instead her voice had stayed flat, and she'd warned me about the kind of trouble I'd be in if I got caught—as if I didn't already know that. Then I'd switched gears, telling her all about Professor Glenny and Dee and reading out loud and how mortifying I'd thought it would be to read in front of the class but how everyone does it and it isn't so bad. I'd expected her to be excited for me, but her voice had been practically monotone, and I'd found myself getting so angry. We haven't talked or emailed in a couple of weeks, and I'm both upset about it and relieved too.

I'd kind of like to tell Dee about this, but I'm not sure how to do it. Aside from Melanie, I've never had a really close friend, and I'm unclear how you make one. It's silly, I know. I've seen other people do it. They make it seem so easy: Have fun, open up, share stories. But how am I supposed to do that when the one story I really want to tell is the very one I'm supposed to be wiping clean? And besides, the last time I did open up to somebody . . . well, that's precisely why I'm in need of a tabula rasa in the first place. It just seems safer to keep it like it is—friendly, cordial, nice and simple.

— — —

At the end of February, my parents come up for Presidents' Weekend. It's the first time they've been up since Parents' Weekend, and having learned my lesson, I go to elaborate lengths to keep up the image they expect of me. I put my clocks back out. I highlight pages in my unused chemistry textbook and copy labs out of my old lab partner's book. I make us lots of plans in Boston to keep us off campus, away from incriminating evidence and the Terrific Trio (who now have become more of a Dynamic Duo anyway because Kendra's always with her boyfriend). And I tell Dee, with whom I now study on weekends sometimes, that I won't be around and that I can't get together Friday and Monday.

"You throwing me over for Drew?" Drew is the second best Shakespeare reader in the class.

"No. Of course not," I reply, my voice all pinched and panicked. "It's just I have one of those trips with my ceramics class Friday." This isn't entirely untrue. My ceramics class does go on field trips occasionally. We're experimenting with glazes, using different kinds of organic materials in the kiln, and sometimes even firing our pottery outside in earthen furnaces we build. I *do* have field trips, just not in the next couple of days.

"And I'll probably work on a paper this weekend." Another lie; the only class I have papers for is Shakespeare. It's amazing how good at lying I've become. "I'll see you Wednesday, okay? I'll bring the cookies."

"Tell your grandma to send some more of those twisty ones with the poppy seeds."

"Rugelach."

"I can't say it. I just eat it."

"I'll tell her."

— — —

The weekend with my parents goes decently enough. We go to the Museum of Fine Arts, the Museum of Science. We go ice skating (I can't keep my blades straight). We go to the movies. We take tons of pictures. There's an awkward moment or two when Mom pulls out next year's course catalog and starts going over class schedules with me and then asks me about my summer plans, but I just listen to her suggestions like I always have and don't say anything. By the end of the weekend, I feel drained in the same way that I do after a marathon session of reading Shakespeare aloud and trying to be all those different people.

On Sunday afternoon, we're back at my dorm before dinner when Dee pops by. And though I haven't told him one single thing about my family, not even that they were coming, let alone what they believe about me, what they expect of me, he still shows up in a pair of plain jeans and a sweater, something I've never seen him wear before. His hair is pulled back into a cap and he's not wearing lip gloss. I almost don't recognize him.

"So, how do you two know each other?" Mom asks after I nervously introduce them.

I freeze, in a panic.

"We're biology lab partners," Dee says, not missing a

beat. "We're raising the *Drosophila* together." It's the first time I've ever heard him pronounce it correctly. He picks up the tube. "Breeding all kinds of genetic abnormalities here."

My dad laughs. "They had us do the same experiment when I went here too." He looks at Dee. "Are you pre-med also?"

Dee's eyebrows flicker up, the slightest ripple of surprise. "I'm still undeclared."

"Well, there's no rush," Mom says. Which almost makes me laugh out loud.

Dad turns to puts the tube back next to a cylinder of pottery I forgot to hide away. "What's this?"

"Oh, *I* made that," Dee says, picking up the piece. And then he starts explaining how he's taking a pottery class, and this year's class is experimenting with different kinds of glazes and firing methods, and for these pieces, they fired everything in an earthen kiln fueled by cow patties.

"Cow patties?" Mom asks. "As in . . . *feces?*"

Dee nods. "Yes, we went to local farms and asked if we could collect their cow manure. They actually don't smell that bad. They're grass-fed cows."

And it hits me then that Dee is using another voice, but this time, the person he's playing is me. I had told him all about the cow patties, the earthy smell, collecting them from the farms . . . though when I'd done it, he'd laughed his head off at the thought of all us rich kids at our forty-thousand-dollar-a-year school paying for a class in which we went to farms and picked up after cows. I've told Dee more about myself than I guess I realized. And he listened.

He paid attention, absorbed a bit of me. And now he's saving my ass with it.

"Cow feces. How fascinating," my mother tells him.

— — —

The next day, my parents leave, and on Wednesday, our Shakespeare class starts on *Twelfth Night*. Dee has checked out two different versions from the media center for us to watch. He feels that as penance for not doing our homework, we should at least watch several. He hands me the stage version as I fire up my laptop.

"Thank you for getting these," I say. "I would have done it."

"I was at the media center anyway."

"Well, thank you. Also, thank you for how completely awesome you were with my parents." I pause for a second, more than a little embarrassed. "How'd you know they were coming?"

"My girlfriend Kali. She tell me. She tell me *everything*, because we be *besties*." He narrows his eyes. "See? Wasn't no need to hide Miss Dee from the folks. I clean up real nice."

"Oh, right. I'm sorry about that."

Dee stares at me, waiting for more.

"Really. It's just my parents. There's a lot . . . well, it's complicated."

"Ain't so complicated. I gets it just fine. Okay to slum with Dee but not to bring out the good silver."

"No! You've got it wrong!" I exclaim. "I'm not slumming. I really like you."

He crosses his arms and stares at me. "How was your *field trip*?" he asks acidly.

I want to explain, I do. But how? How do I do that without giving myself away? Because I'm trying. I'm trying to be a new person here, a different person, a tabula rasa. But if I explain about my parents, about Melanie, about Willem, if I show who I really am, then aren't I just stuck back where I started?

"I'm sorry I lied. But I swear, it's not about you. I can't tell you how much I appreciate what you did."

"Ain't no *thang*."

"No, I *really* mean it. You were great. My parents loved you. And you were so smooth, about everything. They didn't suspect a thing."

He whips the lip gloss out of his pocket and, with painstaking precision, applies it first to his top lip, then his bottom. Then he smacks them together, noisily like some kind of rebuke. "What's to suspect? I don't know nothin' 'bout nobody. I just be the help."

I want to make it right. For him to know that I care about him. That I'm not ashamed of him. That he is safe with me. "You know," I begin, "you don't have to do that with me. The voices. You can just be yourself."

I mean it as a compliment, so he'll know that I like him as is. But he doesn't take it that way. He purses his lips and shakes his head. "This *is* myself, baby. All of my selves. I own each and every one of them. I know who I'm pretending to be and who I am." The look he gives me is withering. "Do you?"

I purposely tried to keep all of that from him, but Dee—smart, sharp Dee—he got it. All of it. He knows what a big fat fake I am. I'm so ashamed I don't even know what to say.

After a while, he slips *Twelfth Night* into my computer. We watch the entire thing in silence, no voices, no commentary, no laughing, just four eyeballs staring at a screen. And that's how I know I've blown it with Dee.

I'm so miserable about this that I forget to be upset about Willem.

Twenty-two

*T*he winter drags on, no matter what the groundhog says. Dee stops coming over in the afternoons, ostensibly because we're not reading *Twelfth Night* aloud, but I know that's not really it. The cookies from my grandmother pile up. I get a bad cold, which I can't seem to shake, though it does have the side benefit of getting me out of reading any of *Twelfth Night* in front of the class. Professor Glenny, who is stuffy himself, gives me a packet of something called Lemsips and tells me to get in shape so I can pull a double shift as Rosalind in *As You Like It*, one of his favorite plays.

We finish *Twelfth Night*. I thought I'd feel relieved, as if I'd dodged a bullet. But I don't. With Dee out of my life, I feel like I took the bullet, even without reading the play. Tabula rasa was the right move. Taking this class was the wrong move. Now I just have to buckle down and push through. I'm getting used to that.

We move on to *As You Like It*. In his introductory spiel, Professor Glenny goes on about how this is one of Shakespeare's most romantic plays, his sexiest, and this gets all the Glenny groupies up front swooning. I take vacant notes as he outlines the plot: A deposed duke's daughter named Rosalind and a gentleman named Orlando meet and fall in love at first sight. But then Rosalind's uncle kicks her out of his house, and she flees with her cousin Celia to the Forest of Arden. There, Rosalind takes on the identity of a boy named Ganymede. Orlando, who has also fled to Arden, meets Ganymede, and the two strike up a friendship. Rosalind as Ganymede uses her disguise and their friendship to test Orlando's proclaimed love for Rosalind. Meanwhile, all sorts of people take on different identities and fall in love. As always, Professor Glenny tells us to pay attention to specific themes and passages, specifically how emboldened Rosalind becomes when she is Ganymede and how that alters both her and the courtship with Orlando. It kind of all sounds like a sitcom, and I have to work hard to keep it straight.

Dee and I start reading together again, but now we're back in the Student Union, and he packs up as soon as we finish our assignment. He's stopped doing all the crazy voices, which makes me realize just how helpful they were in "interpreting" the plays because now, with both of us reading in monotones, the words sort of drift over me like a foreign language. We may as well be reading it to ourselves for how boring it has become. The only time Dee uses his voices now is when he has to speak to me. I get a different voice, or two, or three, every day. The message is clear: I've been demoted.

I want to undo this. To make it right. But I have no idea how. I don't seem to know how to open up to people without getting the door slammed in my face. So I do nothing.

— — —

"Today we will read one of my favorite scenes in *As You Like It*, the beginning of act four," Professor Glenny says, one bone-chillingly cold March day that makes it seem like we're heading into winter, not out of it. "Orlando and Ganymede/Rosalind are meeting again in the Forest of Arden, and the chemistry between them reaches its boiling point. Which is kind of confusing and amusing, given that Orlando believes himself to be speaking to Ganymede, who is male. But it's equally confusing for Rosalind, who is in a kind of delicious torment, torn between two identities, the male and the female, and two desires: a desire to protect herself and remain Orlando's equal, and the exquisite desire to simply submit." Up in the front of the classroom, the groupies seem to emit a little joint sigh. If Dee and I were still friends, it would be the kind of thing that would make us look at each other and roll our eyes. But we're not, so I don't even look at him.

"So, Orlando comes to Ganymede in the forest, and the two perform a sort of Kabuki theater together, and in doing so, they fall deeper in love, even as they don't entirely know *whom* they're falling in love with," Professor Glenny continues. "The line between true self and feigned self is blurred on all sides. Which I think is a rather handy metaphor for falling in love. So, it's a good day to read. Who's up?" He scans the class. People are actually raising their hands. "Drew, why don't you read Orlando." There's a smattering of applause as Drew walks up to the front of the room. He's one of the best readers in the class. Normally, Professor Glenny pairs him with Nell or Kaitlin, two of the best girls. But not today. "Allyson, I believe you owe me a Rosalind."

I shuffle up to the front of the room, along with the other readers he's chosen. I've never loved this part of the class, but at least before, I could feel Dee cheering me on. Once we're assembled, Professor Glenny turns into a director, which apparently is what he used to do before becoming an academic. He offers us notes: "Drew, in these scenes, Orlando is ardent and steadfast, completely in love. Allyson, your Ganymede is torn: smitten, but also toying with Orlando, like a cat with a mouse. What makes this scene so fascinating to me is that as Ganymede questions Orlando, challenges him to prove his love, you can feel the wall between Rosalind and Ganymede drop. I love that moment in Shakespeare's plays. When the identities and false identities become a morass of emotion. Both characters feel it here. It gets very charged. Let's see how you two do."

The scene opens with Rosalind/Ganymede/me asking Orlando/Drew where he's been, why he's taken so long to come see me—I'm "pretending" to be Rosalind. That's the gimmick. Rosalind has been pretending to be Ganymede, who must now pretend to be Rosalind. And she tries to talk Orlando out of loving Rosalind, even though she really *is* Rosalind and even though she really does love him back. Trying to keep track of all the pretending makes my head spin.

Drew/Orlando replies that he came within an hour of his promised time. I say to be even an hour late when you've made a promise in love's name puts in question whether you're truly in love. He begs my forgiveness. We banter a bit more, and then I, as Rosalind as Ganymede feigning Rosalind, ask, "What would you say to me now, an I were your very very Rosalind?"

Drew pauses, and I find that I'm waiting, holding my breath, even, for his answer.

And then he replies, "I would kiss before I spoke."

Drew's eyes are blue, nothing like *his*, but for a second, it's his dark eyes I see. Electric and charged, right before he kissed me.

I'm kind of rattled as I deliver my next lines, advising Orlando that he should speak before he kisses. We go back and forth, and when we get to the part when Orlando says he would marry me—her—I don't know about Rosalind, but I'm feeling dizzy. Luckily, Rosalind has more grit than I do. She, as Ganymede, says, "Well, in her person, I say I will not have you."

Then Drew says, "Then in mine own person I die."

And then something in me just comes undone. I can't find the right line or the right page. And I seem to have lost something else too. My grip on myself, on this place. On time. I'm not sure how much of it elapses while I stand there frozen. I hear Drew clear his throat, waiting for me to say my next line. I hear Professor Glenny shift in his chair. Drew whispers my line to me, and I repeat it and somehow manage to regain my bearings. I continue to question Orlando. Continue to ask him to prove his love. But I am no longer acting, no longer pretending.

"Now tell me how long you would have her after you have possessed her?" I ask as Rosalind. My voice no longer sounds like mine. It is rich and resonant with emotion—full of the questions I should've asked back when I had the chance.

He answers, "For ever and a day."

All the breath whooshes out of me. This is the answer that I need. Even if it doesn't happen to be true.

I try to read the next line, but I can't speak. I can't breathe. I hear a roar of wind in my ears and blink to stop the words from dancing all over the page. After a few moments, I manage to choke out the next sentence, "Say 'a day' without the 'ever,'" before my voice breaks.

Because Rosalind understands. *Say a day without the ever.* That after the one day comes heartbreak. No wonder she won't tell him who she truly is.

I feel the hot tears in my eyes and through their veil see the class, silent, gaping at me. I drop my book to the floor and bolt toward the door. I run out into the hallway, past the classrooms, and into the ladies' room. Crouching in a corner stall, I gulp deep breaths and listen to the hum of the fluorescent lights, trying desperately to push back against this hollowness that threatens to swallow me alive.

I have a full life. How can I be this empty? Because of *one* guy? Because of *one* day? But as I hold back my tears, I see the days before Willem. I see myself with Melanie at school, feeling all cocooned and smug, gossiping about girls we didn't bother to get to know or, later on, on the tour, pantomiming a friendship sputtering on fumes. I see myself with my parents, at the dinner table, Mom with her ever-present calendar, scheduling dance class or SAT prep or some other enrichment activity, leafing through catalogs for a new pair of snow boots, talking at each other but not to each other. I see myself with Evan, after we slept together for the first time and he said something about how this meant we were the closest people to each other, and it had been a sweet thing to say, but it felt like something he'd gotten out of a book. Or maybe it was that I hadn't felt it because I'd begun to suspect that we'd only gotten together because Melanie had started dating his best friend. When I'd started to cry, Evan had mistaken my tears for joy, which had only made it worse. And, yet, I'd stayed with him.

I have been empty for a long time. Long before Willem entered and exited my life so abruptly.

I'm not sure how long I'm in there before I hear the squeak of the door. Then I see Dee's pink Ugg knockoffs under the stall.

"You in here?" he asks quietly.

"No."

"Can I come in?"

I unlock the stall. There's Dee, holding all my stuff.

"I'm so sorry," I tell him.

"Sorry? You were stupendous. You got a standing ovation."

"I'm sorry I didn't tell you my parents were coming. I'm sorry I lied to you. I'm sorry I bungled everything. I don't know how to be a friend. I don't know how to be anything."

"You know how to be Rosalind," he says.

"That's because I'm an expert faker." I swipe a tear with my hand. "I'm so good at faking I don't even know when I'm doing it."

"Oh, honey, have you learned nothing from these plays? Ain't such a line between faking and being." He opens his arms, and I step into them. "I'm sorry too," he says. "I might've overreacted a hair. I can be dramatic, in case you haven't noticed."

I laugh. "Really?"

Dee holds my coat, and I slip into it. "I don't like being lied to, but I do appreciate what you tried to say to me. People have never known what to make of me—not in my neighborhood, not at high school, not here—so they're always trying to figure it out and tell me what I am."

"Yeah, I know something about that."

We look at each other for a long minute. A whole lot gets said in that silence. Then Dee asks, "You wanna tell me what all that was about in there?"

And I do. So much it's squeezing my chest. I've been wanting to tell him this, everything about me, for weeks now. I nod.

Dee offers me his arm, and I loop mine through it, and we leave the bathroom as a pair of girls come in, giving us a strange look.

"Well, there was this guy . . ." I begin.

He shakes his head and gently clucks his tongue like a sweetly scolding grandmother. "There always is."

———

I take Dee back to my dorm. I serve him a backlog of cookies. And I tell him everything. When I finish, we've munched our way through black-and-whites and peanut butter. He wipes the crumbs off his lap and asks me if I ever thought about *Romeo and Juliet*.

"Not *everything* tracks back to Shakespeare."

"Yes it does. Did you ever think what might've happened if

they weren't so damn impatient? If maybe Romeo had stopped for a second and gotten a doctor, or waited for Juliet to wake up? Not jumped to conclusions and gone and poisoned himself thinking she was dead when she was *just sleeping*?"

"I can see you have." And I can. He's pretty worked up.

"I've seen that movie so many times, and every damn time, it's like screaming at the girl in the horror movie. *Stop. Don't go in the basement. The killer's down there*. With Romeo and Juliet, I yell, 'Don't jump to conclusions.' But do those fools ever listen to me?" He shakes his head in dismay. "I always imagine what might've happened if they'd waited. Juliet would've woken up. They'd already be married. They might've moved away, far away from the Montagues and the Capulets, gotten themselves a cute castle of their own. Deco rated it up nice. Maybe it would've been like *The Winter's Tale*. By thinking Hermione was dead, Leontes had time to stop acting like a fool and then later he was so happy to find out she was alive. Maybe the Montagues and Capulets would find out later that their beloved kids weren't dead, and wasn't it stupid to feud, and everyone would be happy. Maybe it would've turned the whole tragedy into a comedy."

"*The Winter's Tale* isn't a comedy; it's a problem play."

"Oh, you hush up. You see where I'm going with this."

And I do. And maybe I hadn't thought about this with *Romeo and Juliet*, but I had briefly gone to the what-if place with me and Willem. On the train back to England and then on the flight home, I'd had second thoughts. What if something had happened to him? But both times, I'd voiced my doubts—first to Ms. Foley and then to Melanie—and both times I'd been set straight. Willem wasn't Romeo. He was *a* romeo. And I'm no Juliet. I tell Dee this. I enumerate all the examples of him being a player, beginning with the fact that he picked up a random girl on a train and, an hour later, invited her to Paris for the day.

"Normal people don't do that," I say.

"Who said anything about normal? And maybe you weren't random. Maybe you were something to him too."

"But he didn't even know *me*. I was someone else that day. I was Lulu. That's who he liked. And besides, let's pretend something did happen, he didn't ditch me. I only know his first name. He doesn't even know my name. He lives a continent away. He's irretrievably lost. How do you find someone like that?"

Dee looks at me as if the answer is obvious. "You look."

Twenty-three

NAME: Willem
NATIONALITY: Dutch
AGE: 20 as of last August
GREW UP IN AMSTERDAM.
PARENTS: Yael and Bram. Mom isn't Dutch
Mom is a naturopathic doctor
1.9 meters, which is about 6'3"; 75 kilos,
    which is about 165 pounds.
Acted with the theater troupe Guerrilla Will
    last summer

*T*his is the complete list of hard biographical facts that I have on Willem. It takes up barely a third of a page in one of my abandoned lab notebooks. When I finish, the list is like a taunt, reality's bitchslap. *You think you fell in love with someone, and* this *is what you know about him? Eight things?* And how would I find him with these eight things? Forget looking for a needle in a haystack. That's easy. At least it would stand out. I'm looking for one specific needle in a needle factory.

Eight things. It's humiliating. I stare at the page and am about to tear it out and crumple it up.

But instead, I turn the page and start writing a different list. Random things. Like the amused look on his face when I admitted I'd thought he was a kidnapper. And the way he looked at the café when he found out I was an only child and asked if I was alone. The goofy happiness as he bounded around the barge with Captain Jack. How good it felt to know that I was responsible for him looking that way. The way Paris sounded under the canal. The way it looked from the back of the bike. The way his hand felt in the crook of my hip. The fierceness in his eyes when he jumped up to help those girls in the park. The reassurance of his hand, grasping mine as we ran through the streets of Paris. The raw expression on his face at the dinner table when I'd asked him why he'd brought me there. And later, at the squat, how he looked at me and I felt so big and strong and capable and brave.

I let the memories flood me as I fill one page. Then another. And then I'm not even writing about him anymore. I'm writing about me. About all the things I felt that day, including panic and jealousy, but more about feeling like the world was full of nothing but possibility.

I fill three pages. None of what I'm writing will help me find him. But in writing, I feel good—no, not just good, but full. Right, somehow. It's a feeling I haven't experienced in a long, long time, and it's this more than anything that convinces me to look for him.

—— —— ——

The most concrete thing on the list is Guerrilla Will, so I start there. They have a bare-basics website, which gets me pretty excited—until I see how out of date it is. It's advertising plays from two summers ago. But still, there's a contact tab with an email address. I spend hours composing ten different emails and then finally just delete them in favor of a simple one:

Hello:
I am trying to find a Dutch guy named Willem, age 20, who performed in last summer's run of Twelfth Night. I saw it and met him, in Stratford-upon-Avon, and went to Paris with him last August. If anyone knows where he is, please tell him that Lulu, also known as Allyson Healey, would like him to get in touch with her. This is very important.

I list all my contact info and then I pause there for a moment, imagining the ones and zeros or whatever it is that emails are made of, traveling across oceans and mountains, landing somewhere in someone's inbox. Who knows? Maybe even his.

And then I press Send.

Thirty seconds later, my inbox chimes. Could it be? Could it be that fast? That easy? Someone knows where he is. Or maybe he's been looking for me all this time.

My hand shakes as I go to my inbox. Only all that's there is the message I just sent, bounced. I check the address. I send it again. It bounces again.

"Strike one," I tell Dee before class the next day. I explain about the bounced email.

"I don't do sports metaphors, but I'm pretty sure baseball games are generally nine innings."

"Meaning?"

"Dig in for the long haul."

Professor Glenny sweeps in and starts talking about *Cymbeline*, the play we're about to start, and announcing last call for tickets for *As You Like It* before giving a brief warning to start thinking about oral presentations at the end of the year. "You can either work alone or with your partners, do a regular presentation or something more theatrical."

"We'll do theatrical," Dee whispers.

"It's the Glenny way."

And then we look at each other as if both getting the same idea. After class, we go up to the lectern where the usual coterie of groupies are simpering.

"Well, Rosalind, here to buy your *As You Like It* tickets?"

I blush. "I already bought mine. I'm actually trying to get ahold of someone I lost touch with, and I don't have very many leads, but the one I do have is through this Shakespeare troupe that I saw in Stratford-upon-Avon last year, and they have a website, but the email bounced, but I saw them do a play less than a year ago . . ."

"In Stratford-upon-Avon?"

"Yeah. But not at a theater. It was sort of an underground thing. It was called Guerrilla Will. They performed at the canal basin. They were really good. I actually ditched the RSC's *Hamlet* to watch them do *Twelfth Night*."

Professor Glenny likes this. "I see. And you've lost a Sebastian, have you?" I gasp and I blush but then I realize he's just referring to the play. "I have an old mate in the tourist bureau there. Guerrilla Will, you say?"

I nod.

"I'll see what I can dig up."

The following week, right before spring break, Professor Glenny hands me an address. "This is what my friend found. It's from police records. Apparently your Guerrilla Will friends have a habit of performing without permits, and this is from an old arrest. Not sure how current it is." I look at the address. It's for a city in England called Leeds.

"Thank you," I say.

"You're welcome. Let me know how it ends."

That night, I print out the copy of the email I sent to Guerrilla Will but then I change my mind and write a handwritten letter to Willem.

> *Dear Willem:*
>
> *I've been trying to forget about you and our day in Paris for months now, but as you can see, it's not going all that well. I guess more than anything, I want to know, did you just leave? If you did, it's okay. I mean it's not, but if I can know the truth, I can get over it. And if you didn't leave, I don't know what to say. Except I'm sorry that I did.*
>
> *I don't know what your response will be at getting this letter, like a ghost from your past. But no matter what happened, I hope you're okay.*

I sign Lulu and Allyson and leave all my various contact details. I put it inside an envelope and write Forward to Willem, in care of Guerrilla Will. The night before I leave for spring break, I mail it.

— — —

I spend a boring break at home. Melanie's vacation doesn't coincide with mine, and I both miss her and feel relieved not to have to see her. I hole up in my room and prop my old science books all around me and spend the time doing Facebook searches and Twitter searches and every imaginable social networking search, but it turns out, only having a first name is kind of a problem. Especially because Willem is a pretty common Dutch name. Still, I go through hundreds of pages, staring at pictures of all different Willems, but none of them are him.

I post a Facebook page as Lulu with pictures of Louise Brooks and of me. I change the status every day, to something only he'd understand. *Do you believe in accidents of the universe? Is Nutella chocolate? Is falling in love the same as being in love?* I get friend requests from New Age freaks. I get requests from perverts. I get requests from a Nutella fan club in Minnesota (who knew?). But nothing from him.

I try searching for his parents. I do combination searches: Willem, Bram, Yael and then just Bram, Yael. But without a last name, I get nothing. I search every Dutch naturopathic site I can find for a Yael but come up with nothing. I Google the name Yael, and it's a Hebrew name. Is his mom Jewish? Israeli? Why didn't I think to ask him any of these questions when I had the chance? But I know why. Because when I was with him, I felt like I already knew him.

Twenty-four

Spring break ends, and in Shakespeare class we start reading *Cymbeline*. Dee and I are halfway through, at the really juicy part where Posthumus, Imogen's husband, sees Iachimo with the secret bracelet that he gave Imogen and decides this is proof that she cheated on him, though of course, the bracelet was stolen by Iachimo, precisely so he could win his bet with Posthumus that he could get Imogen to cheat.

"Another jumped conclusion," Dee says, looking at me pointedly.

"Well, he did have good reason to suspect," I say. "Iachimo totally knew things about her, what her bedroom looked like, that she had a mole on her boob."

"Because he spied on her when she was sleeping," Dee says. "There was an explanation."

"I know. I know. Just like you say there might be a good explanation for Willem disappearing. But you know, sometimes you do have to accept the evidence at face value. In one day, I saw Willem flirt with, get undressed by, and get a telephone number from a minimum of three girls, not counting me. That says 'player' to me. And I got played."

"For a player, boy talked a lot about falling in love."

"Falling in love, not being in love," I say. "And with Céline." Though when he spoke of his parents, of being stained, I recall the look on his face, one of unmasked yearning. And then I feel the heat on my wrist, as if his saliva were still wet there.

"Céline," Dee says, snapping his fingers. "The hottie French girl."

"She wasn't *that* hot."

Dee rolls his eyes. "Why didn't we think of this? What's the name of the club she worked at? Where you left your bag?"

"I have no idea."

"Okay. Where was it?"

"Near the train station."

"Which train station?"

I shrug. I've sort of blocked it all out.

Dee grabs my laptop. "Now you're just being ornery." He taps away. "If you came from London, you arrived at Gare du Nord." He pronounces it Gary du Nord.

"Aren't you clever?"

He pulls up Google Maps and then types something in. A cluster of red flags appear. "There."

"What?"

"Those are the nightclubs near Gare du Nord. You call them. Presumably Céline works in one of them. Find her, find him."

"Yeah, maybe in the same bed."

"Allyson, you just said you had to have your eyes wide open."

"I do. I just don't ever want to see Céline again."

"How bad do you want to find him?" Dee asks.

"I don't know. I guess, more than anything, I want to find out what happened."

"All the more reason to call this Céline person."

"So I'm supposed to call all these clubs and ask for her? You forget, I don't speak French."

"How hard can it be?" He stops and arranges his face into a puckered expression. "*Bon lacroix monsoir oui, tres, chic chic croissant French Ho-bag.*" He smirks. "See? Easy peasy lemon squeezy."

"Is that French too?"

"No, that's Latin. And you can ask for the other guy too, the African."

The Giant. Him I wouldn't mind talking to, but of course, I don't even know his name.

"You do it. You're better at all that than me."

"What you on about? I studied Spanish."

"I just mean you're better at voices, pretending."

"I've seen you do Rosalind. And you spent a day playing Lulu, and you're currently masquerading as a pre-med student to your parents."

I look down, pick at my nail. "That just makes me a liar."

"No it doesn't. You're just trying on different identities, like everyone in those Shakespeare plays. And the people we pretend at, they're already in us. That's why we pretend them in the first place."

— — —

Kali is taking first-year French, so I ask her, as casually as possible, how one might ask for Céline or a Senegalese bartender whose brother lives in Rochester. At first she looks at me, shocked. It's probably the first time I've asked her something more involved than "Are these socks yours?" since school started.

"Well, that would *depend* on lots of *factors*," she says. "Who *are* these people? What is your *relationship* to them? French is a language of *nuance*."

"Um, can't they just be people I'm wanting to get on the phone?"

Kali narrows her eyes at me, turns back to her work. "Try an *online* translation program."

I take a deep breath, sigh out a gust. "Fine. They are, respectively, a total bitchy beauty and a really nice guy I met once. They both work at some Parisian night club, and I feel like they might hold the key to my . . . my happiness. Does that help you with your nuance?"

Kali closes her textbook and turns to me. "Yes. And no." She grabs a piece of paper and taps it against her chin. "Do you happen to *know* the brother from *Rochester*'s name?"

I shake my head. "He told it to me once, really fast. Why?"

She shrugs. "Just seems if you *had* it, you could *track* him down in Rochester and *then* find his brother."

"Oh, my God, I didn't even think of that. Maybe I can remember it and try that too. Thank you."

"*Amazing* things happen when you *ask* for help." She gives me a pointed look.

"Do you want to know the whole story?"

Her raised eyebrow says *Do pigs like mud?*

So I tell her, Kali, the unlikeliest of confidantes, a brief version of the saga.

"Oh. My. God. So *that* explains it."

"Explains what?"

"Why you have been such a *loner*, always saying *no* to us. We thought you *hated* us."

"What? No! I don't hate you. I just felt like a reject and felt so bad you guys got stuck with me."

Kali rolls her eyes. "I broke up with my *boyfriend* right before I *got* here, and Jenn split with her *girlfriend*. Why do you think I have so many pictures of *Buster*? *Everyone* was feeling sad and homesick. That's why we *partied* so much."

I shake my head. I didn't know. I didn't think to know. And then I laugh. "I've had the same best friend since I was seven. She's the only girlfriend I've ever really hung out with, so it's like I missed the integral years of learning how to be friends with people."

"You missed *nothing*. Unless you missed *kindergarten* too."

I stare at her helplessly. Of course I went to kindergarten.

"If you went to *kindergarten*, you learned how to make *friends*. It's like the *first* thing they teach you." She stares at me. "To *make* a friend . . ." she begins.

"You have to *be* a friend," I finish, remembering the saying I was taught in Mrs. Finn's class. Or maybe it was from *Barney*.

She smiles as she picks up the pen. "I think it'll be *simpler* if you just ask for this *Céline* chick and the *bartender* from Senegal, leave out the *brother*, because how many Senegalese *bartenders* are there? Then if you get the *bartender*, you can ask if he has a *brother* in Rochester."

"Roché Estair," I correct. "That's what he called it."

"I can *see* why. It sounds much *classier* that way. Here." She hands me a piece of paper. *Je voudrais parler à Céline ou au barman qui vient du Sénégal, s'il vous plaît.* She has written both the French and the phonetic translations. "That's how you ask for them in *French*. If you want *help* making the calls, let me *know. Friends* do that."

Je voudrais parler à Céline ou au barman qui vient du Sénégal, s'il vous plaît. One week later, I've uttered this phrase so many times—first to practice, then in a series of increasingly depressing phone calls—that I swear I'm saying it in my sleep. I make twenty-three phone calls. *Je voudrais parler à Céline ou au barman qui vient du Sénégal, s'il vous plaît.* . . . That's what I say. And then one of three things happens: One, I get hung up on. Two, I get some form of *non*—and then hung up on. Those I cross off the list, a definitive no. But three is when the people launch into turbo-French, to which I am helpless to respond. *Céline? Barman? Sénégal?* I repeat into the receiver, the words sinking like defective life rafts. I have no idea what these people are saying. Maybe they're saying Céline and the Giant are at lunch but will be back soon. Or maybe they're saying that Céline is here but she's downstairs having sex with a tall Dutchman.

I take Kali up on her offer of help, and sometimes she can suss out that there is no Céline, no Senegalese bartender, but more often than not, she's as baffled as I am. Meanwhile, she and Dee start Googling every potential Senegalese name in Rochester. We make a few embarrassing calls but come up empty.

After the twenty-fourth miserable phone call, I run out of nightclubs anywhere in the vicinity of Gare du Nord. Then I remember the name of the band on the T-shirt Céline had in the club, the one she gave to Willem—and me. I Google Sous ou Sur and look up all their tour dates. But if they played at Céline's nightclub, it was a long time ago, because now they're apparently broken up.

By this point, more than three weeks have passed since I mailed my letter, so I'm losing hope on that front too. The chances of finding him, never all that great, dim. But the strangest thing is, that feeling of rightness, it doesn't. If anything, it grows brighter.

—

"How's your search for Sebastian going?" Professor Glenny calls after class one day as we're lining up to get our *Cymbeline* papers back. The groupies all look at me with envy. Ever since I told him about Guerrilla Will, he has a newfound respect for me. And, of course, he's always loved Dee.

"Sort of dried up," I tell him. "No more leads."

He grins. "Always more leads. What is it the detectives in film always say? 'Gotta think outside the box.'" He says the last part in a terrible New York accent. He hands me my paper. "Nice work."

I look at the paper, at the big red A minus on it, and feel a huge rush of pride. As Dee and I walk to our next classes, I keep peeking at it, to make sure it doesn't shape-shift into a C, though I know it won't. I still can't stop looking. And grinning. Dee catches me and laughs.

"For some of us, these A grades are novel," I say.

"Oh, cry me a river. See you at four?"

"I'll be counting the moments."

When Dee comes in at four, he's bouncing off the walls. "Never mind thinking outside the box—we got to look inside the box." He holds up two DVDs from the media center. The title on one reads *Pandora's Box,* and there's a picture of a beautiful woman with sad, dark eyes and a sleek helmet of black hair. I immediately know who she is.

"How are these going to help us?"

"I don't know. But when you open up Pandora's Box, you never know what's gonna fly out. We can watch them tonight. After I get off work."

I nod. "I'll make popcorn."

"I'll take some leftover cakes from the dining hall."

"We know how to party on a Friday night."

Later, as I'm getting ready for Dee, I see Kali in the lounge. She looks at the popcorn. "Having a *snack attack*?"

"Dee and I are watching some movies." I've never invited Kali anywhere. And she almost always goes out on weekend nights. But I think of the help she's offered, and what she said about being a friend, and so I invite her to join us. "It's sort of a movie/fact-finding mission. We could use your help. You were so smart with your idea of trying to find the brother in Rochester."

Her eyes widen. "I'd *love* to help. I'm so *over* keg parties. Jenn, wanna watch a *movie* with *Allyson* and *Dee*?"

"Before you say yes, be warned, they're silent movies."

"Cool," Jenn says. "I've never seen one before."

Neither have I, and turns out to be a little like watching Shakespeare. You have to adjust to it, to get into a rhythm.

There are no words, but it's not like a foreign film, either, where all the dialogue is subtitled. Only major pieces of dialogue are shown with words. The rest you sort of have to figure out from the actors' expressions, from the context, from the swell of the orchestral music. You have to work a little bit.

We watch all of *Pandora's Box*, which is about a beautiful party girl named Lulu, who goes from man to man. First she marries her lover, then shoots him on the eve of her wedding. She's tried for murder but escapes jail, going into exile with her murdered husband's son. She winds up sold into prostitution. It ends with her getting killed on Christmas Eve, by Jack the Ripper, no less. We all watch it like you'd watch a slow-motion train wreck.

After we finish, Dee pulls out the next one, *Diary of a Lost Girl*. "This one's a comedy," he jokes.

It's not quite as bad. Lulu, though she's not called that in this one, doesn't die in the end. But she does get seduced, have a baby out of wedlock, get the baby taken away from her, wind up cast out and dumped in a horrible reform school. She too dabbles in prostitution.

It's almost two in the morning when we flick on the lights. We all look at each other, bleary-eyed.

"So?" Jenn asks.

"I like her *outfits*," Kali says.

"The outfits were indeed extraordinary, but not exactly enlightening." Dee turns to me. "Any clues?"

I look around. "I got nothin'." And really, I don't. All this time, I've been thinking I was like Lulu. But I'm *nothing* like the girl in those movies. I wouldn't want to be.

Jenn yawns and opens a laptop and pulls up a page on

Louise Brooks, who apparently had a life as tumultuous as Lulu's, going from A-list movie star to a shopgirl at Saks, winding up a kept woman, and finally a recluse. "But it says here she was always a rebel. She always did things her own way. And she had a lesbian affair with Greta Garbo!" Jenn smiles at that.

Kali grabs the computer and reads. "Also, she *pioneered* the short bobbed haircut."

"My hair was cut into a bob when we met. I probably should've mentioned that."

Kali puts the computer down and takes my hair out of its ponytail and folds it up to my chin. "Hmm. With your hair *bobbed*, you *do* sort of look like her."

"Yeah, that's what he said. That I looked like her."

"If he saw you that way," Jenn says, "it means he thought you were very beautiful."

"Yeah. Maybe. Or maybe this is all some game to him. Or calling me Lulu was a way to distance me, so he never had to learn anything about me." But as I throw out the less romantic scenarios—and let's be honest, the more likely ones—I don't feel that usual clutch of shame and humiliation. With these guys at my back, nothing feels quite so fraught.

Kendra's staying over at Jeb's, so Kali offers her bed to Dee, and she crashes on Kendra's bed. When all of us nestle under our covers, we call out good night to each other, like we're in summer camp or something, and I feel that sense of rightness, stronger than ever.

Dee starts snoring straightaway, but it takes me a long time to drift off, because I'm still wondering about Lulu. Maybe it was just a name. Maybe it was just pretend. But at some point, it stopped being pretend. Because for that day, I really did become Lulu. Maybe not the Lulu from the film or the real Louise Brooks, but my own idea of what Lulu represented. Freedom. Daring. Adventure. Saying yes.

I realize it's not just Willem I'm looking for; it's Lulu, too.

Twenty-five

*M*om and Dad are waiting for me at my gate in the Miami airport, Mom having arranged for their flight to get in a half hour before mine. I'd hoped I might have gotten out of this year's Passover Seder. I just saw Mom and Dad for spring break a few weeks ago, and coming down for Seder means taking a day off from school. But no such luck. Tradition is tradition, and Passover is the one time of year we go to Grandma's.

I love Grandma, and even if the Seders are always mind-numbingly dull and you take your life in your own hands eating so much of Grandma's home cooking, that's not why I dread them.

Grandma makes Mom crazy, which means that whenever we're visiting, Mom makes *us* crazy. When Grandma visits us at home, it's dealable. Mom can get away, go vent to Susan, play tennis, organize the calendar, go to the mall to buy me a new wardrobe I don't need. But when we're at Grandma's old-people condo in Miami Beach, it's like being trapped on a geriatric island.

Mom starts in on me at the baggage claim, sniping at me for not sending thank-you notes out for my birthday presents, which means she must have asked Grandma and Susan if they'd gotten theirs. Because other than Jenn and Kali—who baked me a cake—and Dee—who took me out to his favorite food truck in Boston for dinner—and Mom and Dad, of course, there was no one else to send thank-you cards to this year. Melanie didn't send anything. She just posted a greeting on my Facebook page.

Once we get into a cab (the second one, Mom having rejected the first one because the AC was too weak—no one is safe from Mom when she's on a Grandma trajectory)—she starts in on me about my summer plans.

Back in February, when she first brought this up, asking what I was going to do over the summer, I told her I had no idea. Then, a few weeks later, at the end of spring break, she announced that she had made some inquiries on my behalf and used some connections and now had two promising offers. One is working in a lab at one of the pharmaceutical companies near Philadelphia. The other is working in one of Dad's doctor friend's offices, a proctologist named Dr. Baumgartner (Melanie used to call him Dr. Bum-Gardner). Neither job would be paid, she explained, but she and Dad had discussed it and decided they'd counter the loss with a generous allowance. She looked so pleased with herself. Both jobs would look excellent on my résumé, would go a long way toward offsetting what she referred to as the "debacle" of my first term.

I'd been so irritated, I'd almost told her that I couldn't

take those internships because I wasn't qualified; I wasn't pre-med. Just to spite her. Just to see the look on her face. But then I'd gotten scared. I was getting an A in Shakespeare Out Loud. An A minus in Mandarin, which was a first for me. A solid B in my biology class and labs, and an A in ceramics. I realized I was actually proud of how well I was doing in my classes and I didn't want Mom's inevitable and perennial disappointment to poison that. But that was going to happen no matter what, though I was sticking to my plan A—to show her my final grades when I made the announcement.

But finals are still three weeks away, and Mom is breathing down my neck right now about these jobs. So as we pull into Grandma's high-rise, I tell her that I'm still mulling it over and then I skip out of the cab to help Dad with the bags.

It's so strange. Mom is the most formidable person I know, but when Grandma opens the door, Mom seems to shrink, as if Grandma is some ogre instead of a five-foot bottle blonde in a yellow tracksuit and a KISS THE MESHUGGENEH COOK apron. Grandma grabs me in a fierce hug that smells of Shalimar and chicken fat. "*Ally!* Let me look at you! You're doing something different with your hair! I saw the pictures on Facebook."

"You're on Facebook?" Mom asks.

"Ally and I are friends, aren't we?" She winks at me.

I see Mom wince. I'm not sure if it's because Grandma and I are FB friends or because Grandma insists on shortening my name.

We step inside. Grandma's boyfriend, Phil, is asleep on the big floral couch. A basketball game blares from the giant television.

Grandma touches my hair. It's to my shoulders now. I haven't cut it since last summer. "It was shorter before," I say. "It's sort of in between."

"It's better than it was. That bob was awful!" Mom says.

"It was a bob, Mom. Not a Mohawk."

"I know what it was. But it made you look like a boy."

I turn to Grandma. "Was she traumatized by a bad haircut in her youth? Because she seems unwilling to let this go."

Grandma claps her hands. "Oh, Ally, you might be right. When she was ten, she saw *Rosemary's Baby* and begged me to take her to the children's beauty parlor. She kept making the lady go shorter until it was all off, and as we were leaving the salon, another mother pointed Ellie out to her son and said, 'Why don't you get a haircut like that nice little boy?'" She looks at Mom, smiling. "I didn't realize that still upset you, Ellie."

"It doesn't upset me, because it never happened, Mother. I never saw *Rosemary's Baby*. And if I had, at ten, that would've been entirely inappropriate, by the way."

"I can show you the pictures!"

"That won't be necessary."

Grandma eyes Mom's hair. "You might think of trying that pixie again now. I think you've been wearing the same style since Bill Clinton was president." Grandma gives another wicked grin.

Mom seems to shrink another inch as she touches her hair—straight, brown, in a low ponytail. Grandma leaves her like that, pulling me into the kitchen. "You want some cookies? I have some macaroons."

"Macaroons are not cookies, Grandma. They're coconut cookie substitutes. And they're disgusting." Grandma doesn't keep anything in the house with flour during Passover.

"Let's see what else I have." I follow Grandma into the kitchen. She pours me some of her diet lemonade. "Your mom is having such a hard time," Grandma says. When Mom's out of sight, she's sympathetic, almost defending her, like I was the one who riled her up.

"I don't see why. She has a charmed life."

"Funny, that's what she says about you whenever she thinks you're being ungrateful." Grandma opens the oven door to check on something. "She's having a hard time adjusting, with you being gone. You're all she's got."

I feel a pit in my stomach. Another way I've let Mom down.

Grandma puts out a plate of those gross jelly candies I can never resist. "I told her she should have another child, give her something to do with herself."

I spit out my lemonade. "She's forty-seven."

"She could adopt." Grandma waves her hand. "One of those Chinese orphans. Lucy Rosenbaum got a cute one as a granddaughter."

"They're not dogs, Grandma!"

"I know that. Still, she could get an older one. It's a real mitzvah then."

"Did you tell Mom that?"

"Of course I did."

Grandma always brings up things the rest of us don't. Like she lights a memorial candle on the anniversary of when Mom had her miscarriage all those years ago. This, too, drives Mom crazy.

"She needs to do something if she's not going back to work." She glances out toward the living room. I know Mom and Grandma fight about Mom not working. Once, Grandma sent a clipping from a news magazine about how badly the ex-wives of doctors fared financially in the event of divorce. They didn't speak for months after that.

Mom comes into the kitchen. She glances at the jelly candy. "Mother, can you feed her some real food, please?"

"Oh, cool your jets. She can feed herself. She's nineteen now." She winks at me, then turns to Mom. "Why don't you take some cold cuts out?"

Mom pokes in Grandma's refrigerator. "Where's the brisket? It's almost two now. We should put it in soon."

"Oh, it's already cooking," Grandma says.

"What time did you put in?"

"Don't you worry. I got a nice recipe from the paper."

"How long has it been in?" Mom peeks in the oven. "It's not that big. It shouldn't take longer than three hours. And you have to cover it in foil. Also you have the heat way up. Brisket's meant to slow-cook. We're starting the Seder at five? When did it go in?"

"Never you mind."

"It'll be like leather."

"Do I tell you how to cook in your kitchen?"

"Yes. All the time. But I don't listen. And we've dodged many a case of food poisoning because of it."

"Enough of your smart mouth."

"I think I'll go change," I announce. But neither one is paying attention to me anymore.

I go into the spare room and find Dad hiding in there, looking wistfully at a golf shirt. "What are the chances I can escape for a round?"

"You'd have to throw down some plagues at the Pharaoh first." I look out the window to the silver-blue strip of sea.

He puts the golf shirt back in the suitcase. How quickly we all give in to her. This Seder means nothing to him. Dad's not even Jewish, though he celebrates all the holidays with Mom. Grandma was supposedly furious when Mom got engaged to him, though after Grandpa died, she took up with Phil, who's not Jewish, either.

"I was just kidding," I say, even though I wasn't. "Why don't you just go?"

Dad shakes his head. "Your mom needs backup."

I scoff, as if Mom needs anything from anyone.

Dad changes the subject. "We saw Melanie last weekend."

"Oh, really?"

"Her band had a gig in Philadelphia, so she made a rare appearance."

She's in a *band* now? So she can become Mel 4.0—and I'm supposed to stay reliably me? I smile tightly at my dad, pretending like I know this.

"Frank, I can't find my Seder plate," Grandma calls. "I had it out for a polish."

"Just visualize the last place you had it," Dad says. Then he gives me a little shrug and heads off to help. After the Seder plate is located, he helps Grandma get down serving bowls, and then I hear Mom tell him to keep Phil company, so he sits and watches the basketball with napping Phil. So much for golf. I go out onto the balcony and listen to the competing sounds of Mom and Grandma's bickering and the game on the TV. My life feels so small it itches, like a too-tight wool sweater.

"I'm going for a walk," I announce, even though there's no one on the balcony but me. I put on my shoes and slip out the door and walk down to the beach. I take off my shoes and run up and down the shore. The rhythmic beat of my feet on the wet sand seems to churn something out of me, pushing it through the sweat on my sticky skin. After a while, I stop and sit down and look out over the water. On the other side is Europe. Somewhere over there is him. And somewhere over there, a different version of me.

— — —

When I get back, Mom tells me to shower and set the table. At five, we sit down, settling in for a long night of reenacting the Jews' escape from slavery in ancient Egypt, which is supposed to be an act of liberation, but somehow with Mom and Grandma glowering at each other, it always winds up feeling just like more oppression. At least the adults can get drunk. You have to down, like, four glasses of wine during the night. I, of course, get grape juice, in my own crystal carafe. At least I usually do. This time when I go to drink my first sip of juice after the first blessing, I almost choke. It's wine. I think it's a mistake, except Grandma catches my eye and winks.

The Seder carries on as usual. Mom, who, in every other part of her life, is respectful, assumes the mantle of rebellious teenager. When Grandma reads the part about the Jews wandering through the desert for forty years, Mom cracks it's because Moses was a man who refused to ask for directions. When the talk turns to Israel, Mom harps on about politics, even though she knows this gets Grandma crazy. When we eat matzo-ball soup, they argue about the cholesterol content of matzo balls.

Dad knows enough to keep quiet. And Phil plays with his hearing aids and dozes in and out of consciousness. I refill my "juice" glass many, many times.

After two hours, we get to the brisket, which means we get to stop talking about Exodus for a while, which is a relief, even if the brisket isn't. It's so dry it looks like beef jerky and tastes charred. I move it around my plate, while Grandma chitchats about her bridge club and the cruise she and Phil are taking. Then she asks about our annual summer trip to Rehoboth Beach, which she usually comes up for a portion of.

"What else do you have planned for the summer?" she asks me casually.

It's a throwaway question, really. Along the lines of *how are you*? Or *what's new*? I'm about to say, "Oh, this and that," when Mom interrupts to say that I'm working in a lab. Then she tells Grandma all about it. A research lab at a pharmaceutical company. Apparently, I accepted the position just today.

It's not like I didn't know she would do this. It's not like she hasn't done this my entire life. It's not like I haven't let her.

The fury that fills me feels hot and cold, liquid and metal, coating my insides like a second skeleton, one stronger than my own. Maybe this is what allows me to say, "I'm not working in a lab this summer."

"Well, it's too late," Mom snaps back. "I already called Dr. Baumgartner to decline his offer. If you'd had a preference, you had three weeks to make it known."

"I'm not working at Dr. Baumgartner's, either."

"Did you line up something else?" Dad asks.

Mom scoffs, as if that's unthinkable. And maybe it is. I've never had a job. Never had to get one. Never had to do anything for myself. I am helpless. I am a void. A disappointment. My helplessness, my dependency, my passivity, I feel it whorling into a little fiery ball, and I harness that ball, somewhere wondering how something made of weakness can feel so strong. But the ball grows hotter, so hot, the only thing I can do with it is hurl it. At her.

"I don't think your lab would want me anymore, given that I've dropped most of my science courses and am going to drop the rest of them come fall," I say, spite dripping from my voice. "See, I'm not pre-med anymore. So sorry to *disappoint* you."

My sarcasm hangs in the humid air—and then, like a vapor, it floats away as I realize that, for the first time in my life, I'm *not* sorry to disappoint her. Maybe it's the spite talking, or maybe Grandma's secret wine, but I'm almost glad of it. I'm so tired of avoiding the unavoidable, because I feel like I've been disappointing her for such a long time.

"You've dropped pre-med?" Her voice is quiet, that lethal mix of fury and woundedness that could always take me down like a bullet to the heart.

"That was always *your* dream, Ellie," Grandma says, shielding me. She turns to me. "You still haven't answered my question, Ally. What are *you* doing this summer?"

Mom is looking so fragile and so angry, and I feel my will starting to break, feel myself starting to give in. But then I hear a voice—my voice—announcing this:

"I'm going back to Paris."

It comes out, as if the idea were fully formed, something plotted for months, when in fact, it just slipped out, the same way all those admissions to Willem did. But when it does, I feel a thousand pounds lighter, my anger now fully dissipated, replaced by exhilaration flowing through me like sunlight and air.

This is how I felt that day in Paris with Willem. And *this* is how I know that it's the right thing to do.

"Also, I'm learning French," I add. And for some reason, this announcement makes the table erupt into pandemonium. Mom starts screaming at me about lying to her and throwing my whole future away. Dad is yelling about switching majors and who's going to pay for my exchange program to Paris. Grandma is yelling at Mom for ruining yet another Seder.

So with all the commotion, it's a little strange that anyone can hear Phil, who has barely said a word since the soup, when he pipes up, "*Back* to Paris, Ally? I thought Helen said your trip to Paris got canceled because they were striking." He shakes his head. "They always seem to be striking over there."

The table goes silent. Phil picks up a piece of matzo and starts munching on it. Mom, Dad, and Grandma all stare at me.

I could so easily cover this up. Phil's hearing aid was turned down. He heard wrong. I could say that I want to go *to* Paris because I never made it there on the last trip. I've told so many lies. What's one more?

But I don't want to lie. I don't want to cover up. I don't want to pretend anymore. Because that day with Willem, I may have pretended to be someone named Lulu, but I had never been more honest in my life.

Maybe that's the thing with liberation. It comes at a price. Forty years wandering through the desert. Or incurring the wrath of two very pissed-off parents.

I take a breath. I brave up.

"*Back* to Paris," I say.

Twenty-six

MAY

Home

I make a new list.
- Airfare to Paris: $1200
- French class at community college:
  $400
- Spending money for two weeks in
  Europe: $1000.

All together that's $2,600. That's how much money I'll need to save to get to Europe. Mom and Dad are not helping with the trip, obviously, and they're refusing to let me use any of the money in my savings account, from gifts through the years, because that's supposed to be for educational purposes, and they're the trustees on the account, so I can't argue. Besides, it's only through Grandma's intervention, coupled with my threat to go live at Dee's for the summer, that Mom has even agreed to let me live at home. She's that mad. She's that mad without even knowing the entire story. I told them

I went to Paris. I didn't tell them why. Or with whom. Or why I need to go back, except that I left something important there—they think it's the suitcase.

I'm not sure what infuriates her more. Last summer's deceit or the fact that I won't tell her everything about it. She refused to speak to me after the Seder and then four weeks went by with barely a word from her. Now that I'm back home for the start of the summer she basically avoids me. Which is both a relief and also kind of scary, because she's never done anything like this before.

Dee says that twenty-six hundred dollars is a lot for two months, but not impossible. He suggests skipping the French class. But I feel like I need to do that. I've always wanted to learn French. And I'm not going back to Paris—not facing down Céline—without it.

So, twenty-six hundred bucks. Doable. If I get a job. But the thing is, I've never had a job before. Nothing remotely job-like, beyond babysitting and filing at Dad's office, which hardly fills the spiffy new résumé that I've printed on beautiful card stock. Maybe this explains why, after dropping it off at every business in town with a job opening, I get zero response.

I decide to sell my clock collection. I take them to an antique dealer in Philadelphia. He offers me five hundred bucks for the lot. I've easily spent double that on the clocks over the years, but he just looks at me and says that maybe I'll do better on eBay. But that would take months, and I just want to be rid of them. So I hand over the clocks, except for a Betty Boop one, which I send to Dee.

When Mom finds out what I've done, she shakes her head

with such profound disgust, like I have just sold my body, not my clocks. The disapproval intensifies. It wafts through the house like a radiation cloud. Nowhere is safe to hide.

I *have* to get a job. Not just to earn the money but to get out of this house. Escaping to Melanie's isn't an option. Number one, we're not speaking, and number two, she's at a music program in Maine for the first half of summer—this according to my dad.

"You just gotta keep trying," Dee advises when I call him for job advice from our landline. As part of my punishment, my cell phone has been turned off, and the family Internet password protected, so I have to ask them to log me onto the web or else go to the library. "Drop your résumé at every business in town, not just the ones saying they're hiring, 'cause usually places that are desperate enough to hire someone like you don't have time to advertise."

"Thanks a lot."

"You want a job? Swallow your pride. And drop off a résumé everywhere."

"Even the car wash?" I joke.

"Yeah. Even the car wash." Dee isn't kidding. "And ask to speak to the manager of the car wash and treat him like the King of All Car Washes."

I imagine myself scrubbing hubcaps. But then I think of Dee, working in a pillow factory this summer or hosing off dishes in the dining hall. He does what he has to do. So the next day, I print out fifty new résumés and just go door to door, from bookstore to sewing shop to grocery store, CPA firm to the liquor store to, yes, the car wash. I don't just drop my résumé. I ask to speak to managers. Sometimes the managers come out. They ask me about my experience. They ask me how long I want to be employed for. I listen to my own answers: No real job experience to speak of. Two months. I get why nobody's hiring me.

I'm almost out of résumés when I pass by Café Finlay. It's a small restaurant on the edge of town, all done up in 1950s décor, with black-and-white-checked floors and a mishmash of Formica tables. Every other time I've gone past, it seemed to be closed.

But today music is blasting from inside so loud the windows are vibrating. I push the door, and it nudges open. I shout "hello." No one replies. The chairs are all stacked up on the tables. There's a pile of fresh linens on one of the booths. Yesterday's specials are scrawled on a chalkboard on the wall. Things like halibut with an orange tequila jalapeño beurre blanc with kiwi fruit. Mom calls the food here "eclectic," her code for weird, which is why we've never eaten here. I don't know anyone who eats here.

"You here with the bread?"

I spin around. There's a woman, Amazon tall and just as broad, with wild red hair poking out from under a blue bandanna.

"No," I say.

"Mother*fucker*!" She shakes her head. "What do you want?" I hold out a résumé. She waves it away. "Ever work in a kitchen?" I shake my head.

"Sorry. No," she says.

She looks at the Marilyn Monroe wall clock. "I'm going to kill you, Jonas!" She shakes her fist at the door.

I turn to leave, but then I stop. "What's the bread order?" I ask. "I'll run and get it for you."

She glances at the clock again and sighs dramatically. "Grimaldi's. I need eighteen French baguettes, six loaves of the Harvest. And a couple of day-old brioche. You got that?"

"I think so."

"*Think so*'s not gonna butter the bread, honey."

"Eighteen baguettes. Six loaves of Harvest and a couple of day-old brioche."

"Make sure it's *stale* brioche. Can't make bread pudding with fresh bread. And ask for Jonas. Tell him it's for Babs and tell him he can throw in the brioche for free and knock twenty percent off the rest because his damn delivery guy was a no-show again. Also, make sure I don't get any sourdough. I hate that shit."

She grabs a wad of cash from the vintage register. I take it from her and sprint to the bakery as fast as I can, get Jonas, bark the order, and run back with it, which is harder than it sounds, carrying thirty loaves of bread.

I pant as Babs looks over the bread order. "You know how to wash dishes?"

I nod. That much I can do.

She shakes her head in resignation. "Go to the back and ask Nathaniel to introduce you to Hobart."

"Hobart?"

"Yep. You two'll be getting intimate."

Hobart turns out to be the name of the industrial dish washer, and once the restaurant opens, I spend hours with it, rinsing dishes with a giant hose, loading them in Hobart, unloading them while they're still scalding hot, and repeating the whole enterprise. By some miracle, I manage to stay on top of the never-ending flow of dishes and not drop anything or burn my fingers too badly. When there's a lull, Babs orders me to cut bread or whip cream by hand (she insists it tastes better that way) or mop the floor or find the tenderloins from one of the walk-in coolers. I spend the night in an adrenaline panic, thinking I'm about to screw up.

Nathaniel, the prep cook, helps me as much as he can, telling me where things are, helping me scrub sauté pans when I get too slammed. "Just wait till the weekend," he warns.

"I thought no one ever ate here." I put my hand over my mouth, instinctually knowing Babs would be mad to hear that.

But Nathaniel just laughs. "Are you kidding? Babs is worshipped by the Philadelphia foodies. They make the trek out here just for her. She'd make way more money if she moved to Philly, but she says her dogs would hate it in the city. And by dogs, I think she means us."

When the last of the diners leave, the kitchen staff and the waiters seem to all exhale at once. Someone blasts some old Rolling Stones. A bunch of tables are pushed together and everyone sits down. It's well past midnight, and I have a long walk home. I start to pack up my things, but Nathaniel motions for me to join them. I sit at the table, feeling shy even though I've been bumping hips with these people all night.

"You want a beer?" he asks. "We have to pay for them, but only cost."

"Or you can have some of the reject wine the distributors bring by," a waitress named Gillian says.

"I'll take some wine."

"It looks like someone died on you," says one of the waiters. I look down. My nice skirt and top—my good job-hunting outfit—are covered in sauces that look vaguely like bodily fluids.

"I feel like I'm the one who died," I say. I don't think I've ever been this tired. My muscles ache. My hands are red from the near-scalding water. And my feet? Don't get me started.

Gillian laughs. "Spoken like a true kitchen slave."

Babs appears with the big bowls of steaming pasta and small chunks of leftover fish and steak. My stomach lets out a gurgle. The platters get passed around. I don't know if her cooking is "eclectic," but the food is amazing, the orange tequila jalapeño sauce is only faintly orange, and it's smoky rather than spicy. I clear my plate, and then sop up any remaining sauce with a hunk of Jonas's not-sourdough bread.

"So?" Babs asks me when I've finished.

All eyes turn to me. "It's the second best meal I've ever had," I say. Which is the truth.

Everyone else oohs, like I've just insulted Babs. But she just smirks. "I'll bet your first best was with a lover," she says, and I go as red as her hair.

Babs instructs me to return the next day at five, and the routine starts all over again. I work harder than I ever have, eat an amazing meal, and pour myself into bed. I have no idea if I'm filling in for someone or maybe being auditioned. Babs screams at me constantly, for using soap on her cast-iron sauté pan or not getting the lipstick off the coffee cups before they go into Hobart or making the whipped cream too stiff or not stiff enough or not adding the exact right amount of vanilla extract. But by the fourth night, I'm learning not to take it so personally.

On the fifth night, before the dinner rush, Babs calls me to the back near the walk-in refrigerator. She's sucking on a bottle of vodka, which is what she does before the rush begins. Her lipstick leaves smudges on the rim. For a second, I think this is it, that she's going to fire me. But instead she hands me a sheaf of documents.

"Tax forms," she explains. "I pay minimum wage, but you'll get tips. Which reminds me. You keep forgetting to collect yours." She reaches under the counter for an envelope with my name on it.

I open up the envelope. There's a wad of cash in there. Easily a hundred dollars. "This is *mine*?"

She nods. "We pool tips. Everyone gets a cut."

I run my fingers over the money. The bills snag on my ragged hangnails. My hands are beyond thrashed, but I don't care because they're thrashed from my job. Which has earned me this money. I feel something well up inside me that has nothing to do with airplane tickets or Paris trips or money at all, really.

"It'll go up in the fall," Babs says. "Summer's our slow season."

I hesitate. "That's great. Except I won't be here in the fall."

She wrinkles her red brows. "But I just broke you in."

I feel bad, guilty, but it was right there on my résumé, the first line—Objective: To obtain short-term employment. Of course, Babs never read my résumé.

"I go to college," I explain.

"We'll work around your schedule. Gillian's a student too. And Nathaniel, on and off."

"In Boston."

"Oh." She pauses. "Oh, well. I think Gordon's coming back after Labor Day."

"I'm hoping to leave by the end of July. But only if I can save two thousand dollars by then." And as I say it, I do the math. More than a hundred bucks a week in tips, plus wages—I actually might be able to pull it off.

"Saving for a car?" she asks absentmindedly. She takes another swig of her vodka. "You can buy mine. That beast'll be the death of me." Babs drives an ancient Thunderbird.

"No. I'm saving for Paris."

She puts her bottle down. "Paris?"

I nod.

"What's in Paris?"

I look at her. I think of him for the first time in a while. In the craziness of the kitchen, he became a little abstract. "Answers."

She shakes her head with such vehemence her auburn curls come loose from her bandanna. "You can't go to Paris looking for answers. You have to go looking for questions—or, at the very least, macarons."

"Macaroons? The coconut things?" I think of the gross cookie replacements we eat on Passover.

"Not macaroons. Macarons. They're meringue cookies in pastel colors. They are edible angel's kisses." She looks at me. "You need two thousand bucks by when?"

"August."

She narrows her eyes at me. They're always a little bit bloodshot, though, oddly, more so at the beginning of a shift than at the end, when they take on a sort of manic gleam. "I'll make you a deal. If you don't mind working some doubles for weekend brunch, I'll make sure you earn your two grand by July twenty-fifth, which is when I close the restaurant for two weeks for *my* summer vacation. On one condition."

"Which is?"

"Every day in Paris, you eat a macaron. They have to be fresh, so no buying a pack and eating one a day." She stops and closes her eyes. "I ate my first macaron in Paris on my honeymoon. I'm divorced now, but some loves are enduring. Especially if they happen in Paris."

A tiny chill prickles up my neck. "Do you really believe that?" I ask her.

She takes a slug of vodka, her eyes glinting knowingly. "Ahh, it's those kind of answers you're after. Well, I can't help you with that, but if you hustle into the walk-in and find the buttermilk and the cream, I can give you the answer to the proverbial question of how to make the perfect crème fraîche."

Twenty-seven

JUNE
Home

Intro to French runs three days a week for six weeks, from eleven thirty to one, giving me yet another reason to be out of the House of Disapproval. Though I'm at Café Finlay five nights a week these days, and all day on weekends, on weekdays, I still don't go in until five. And the restaurant is closed on Monday and Tuesday, so there's a lot of dead time for Mom and me to avoid each other in.

On the first day of class, I arrive a half hour early and grab an iced tea from the little kiosk and find the classroom and start looking through my book. There's lots of pictures of France, many from Paris.

The other students start to filter in. I expected college kids, but everyone except me is my parents' age. One woman with frosted blond hair plops down at the desk next to mine and introduces herself as Carol and offers me a piece of gum. I gladly accept her handshake but decline the gum—it doesn't seem very French to chew gum in class.

A birdlike woman with cropped gray hair strides in. She looks like she stepped out of a magazine in her tight linen pencil skirt and little silk blouse, both perfectly pressed, which seems impossible, given the ninety percent humidity outside. Plus, she's wearing a scarf, also strange, given the ninety percent humidity.

Clearly, she is French. And if the scarf wasn't a giveaway, then there's the fact that she marches up to the front of the room and starts speaking. In French.

"*Are we in the wrong class?*" Carol whispers. Then the teacher goes to the board and writes her name, Madame Lambert, and the name of the class, Intro to French. She also writes it in French. "Oh, no such luck," Carol says.

Madame Lambert turns to us and in the thickest accent imaginable tells us in English that this is beginning French, but that the best way to learn French is to speak and hear it. And that is about the only English I hear for the next hour and a half.

"*Je m'appelle Thérèse Lambert,*" she says, making it sound like this: Teh-rez. Lomb-behr. "*Comment vous appelez-vous?*"

The class stares at her. She repeats the question, gesturing to herself, then pointing to us. Still no one answers. She rolls her eyes and does this clicking with her teeth. She points to me. Clicks again, gestures for me to stand up. "*Je m'appelle Thérèse Lambert,*" she repeats, enunciating slowly and tapping her chest. "*Comment t'appelles-tu?*"

I stand there for a second frozen, feeling like it's Céline again jabbering away at me disdainfully. Madame Lambert repeats the question. I get that she's asking me my name. But I don't speak French. If I did, I wouldn't be here. In *Intro* to French.

But she's just waiting now. She's not letting me sit down.

"Je m'appelle Allyson?" I try.

She beams, as though I've just explained the origins of the French Revolution, in French. *"Bravo! Enchantée, Allyson."*

And she goes around the class asking everyone else's name the same way.

That was round one. Then comes round two: *"Pourquoi voulez-vous apprendre le français?"*

She repeats the question, writing it down on the board, circling certain words and writing their English translations. *Pourquoi*: why. *Apprendre*: learn. *Voulez-vous*: do you want. Oh, I see. She's asking why we want to learn French.

I have no clue how to begin to answer that. That's why I'm here.

But then she continues.

"Je veux apprendre le français parce que . . ." She circles *Je veux*: I want. *Parce que*: because. She repeats it three times. Then points to us.

"I can do this one. I know this word from the movie," Carol whispers. She raises her hand. *"Je veux apprendre le français parce que,"* she stumbles over the words and her accent is awful, but Madame just watches her expectantly. *"Parce que le divorce!"*

"Excellent," Madame Lambert says, only she says it in the French way, which makes it sound even more excellent. *Le divorce,* she writes on the board. *"Divorce. La même,"* she says. *The same,* she writes. Then she writes down *le mariage* and explains that this is the antonym.

Carol leans in. "When I divorced my husband, I told myself I was going to let myself get fat and I was going to learn French. If I do as well with the French as I'm doing with the fat, I'll be fluent by September!"

Madame Lambert goes around the room, and people stumble to explain why they want to learn French. Two of the people are going on vacation in France. One is going to study art history and needs some French. One thinks it's pretty. In each case, Madame writes down the word, its translation, and its opposite. Vacation: *vacances*. Work: *travail*.

I went first last time, and this time I'm last. I'm in a bit of panic by then, trying to think of what to say. How do you say *accidents* in French? Or because I think I might have made a mistake. Or *Romeo and Juliet*. Or to find a lost thing. Or because I don't want to compete, I just want to speak French. But I don't know how to say that in French. If I did, I wouldn't be here.

Then I remember Willem. The Nutella. Falling in love versus being in love. How did he say it? *Stain* in French? *Sash*? *Tache*?

"Allyson," she says. *"Pourquoi veux-tu apprendre le français?"*

"Je veux apprendre le français," I begin, mimicking what I've just heard everyone else say. I've got that part down. *"Parce que . . ."* I stop to think. *"Le tache,"* I say finally.

It's such a weird thing to say, if that's what I've said. A stain. It doesn't make any sense. But Madame Lambert gives a stern nod and writes *la tâche* on the board. Then she writes *task*. I wonder if I remembered the word wrong. She looks at me, at my confusion. And then she writes another word on the board. *La tache*: stain.

I nod my head. Yes, that's it. She doesn't write down an opposite. There is no opposite of stain.

When we're all done, Madame smiles and claps. *"C'est courageux d'aller dans l'inconnu,"* she says, writing it down on the board. She has us write it down and deconstruct it with a dictionary. *Courageux* we get is courageous. *Dans* is into. *L'inconnu* is the unknown. *D'aller.* It takes us twenty minutes, but we finally get it: It's courageous to go into territory unknown. When we figure this out, the class is as proud as Madame.

Still, I spend the first week of class living in a state of half terror of being called on—because everyone gets called on a lot; there are only six of us, and Madame is a big fan of class participation. Whenever we get shy, she reminds us, *"C'est courageux d'aller dans l'inconnu."* Eventually, I just sort of get over myself. I blunder every time I speak, and I know I'm butchering the grammar, and my pronunciation is awful, but then we're all in the same boat. The more I do it, the less self-conscious I get and the easier it is to just try.

"I feel like a damn fool, but it might just be working," Carol says one afternoon after class.

She and I and a few of the other students have started getting together for coffee or lunch after class to practice, to recover from Madame Lambert's verbal barrages, and to deconstruct what she really means when she goes "pff" and blows air through her lips. There's a whole language in her *pff*s.

"I think I had a dream in French," Carol says. "I was telling my ex terrible things in perfect French." She grins at the memory.

"I don't know if I'm that advanced, but I'm definitely getting the hang of it," I reply. "Or maybe I'm just getting the hang of feeling like an idiot."

"*Un idiot.*" Carol says it in French. "Half the time, you add a French accent and it works. But getting over feeling like *un idiot* might just be half the battle."

I imagine myself, alone in Paris. There are so many battles I'm going to have to fight, traveling alone, facing Céline, speaking French all of it is so daunting, some days I can't believe I'm actually even attempting it. But I think Carol might be right about this, and the more I flub and get over it in class, somehow, the better prepared I feel for the trip. Not just the French. All of it. *C'est courageux d'aller dans l'inconnu.*

— — —

At the restaurant, Babs blabs to the entire staff that I'm saving to go to Paris to meet my lover, and I'm learning French because he speaks no English, so now Gillian and Nathaniel have taken it upon themselves to tutor me. Babs is doing her part by adding a bunch of French items to the specials menu, including macarons, which apparently take hours to make, but when I eat them—oh, my God, I get what all the fuss is about. Pale pink, hard outside, but spongy and light and delicate inside, with a raspberry deliciousness filling.

In between classes, hanging with my fellow students, and being at work, I'm spending a fair amount of time, if not speaking French, then thinking about it. When Gillian buses plates into the kitchen, she'll drill me on verbs. "Eat," she'll call out. *"Je mange, tu manges, il mange, nous mangeons, vous mangez, ils mangent,"* I'll call back. Nathaniel, who doesn't actually speak French but used to have a French girlfriend, teaches me how to swear. Specifically, how to fight with your girlfriend.

T'es toujours aussi salope? Are you always such a bitch?

T'as tes règles ou quoi? Are you on the rag or what?

And *ferme ta gueule!* Which he claims means: Shut your piehole!

"They can't say 'shut your piehole' in France," I say.

"Well, maybe it's not a direct translation, but it's pretty damn close," he replies.

"But it's so crass. The French are tasteful."

"Dude, those people sainted Jerry Lewis. They're human just like you and me." He pauses, then grins. "Except for the women. They're superhuman."

I think of Céline and get a bad feeling in my stomach.

Another one of the waiters loans me his Rosetta Stone CDs, and I start practicing with those too. After a few weeks, I start to notice that my French is improving, that when Madame Lambert calls on me to describe what I'm eating for lunch, I can handle it. I start to speak in phrases, then sentences, sentences I don't have to map out beforehand like I do with Mandarin. Somehow, it's happening. I'm doing it.

— — —

One morning, toward the end of the month, I come downstairs to find Mom at the kitchen table. In front of her is the catalog from the community college and her checkbook. I say good morning and go the fridge for some orange juice. Mom just watches me. I'm about to take my juice out to the back patio, which is sort of what we've done if Dad's not home as a buffer—if she's in one room, I go into another—when she tells me to sit down.

"Your father and I have decided to reimburse you for your French class," she says, ripping off the check. "It doesn't mean we condone any part of this trip. Or condone your duplicity. We absolutely don't. But the French class is part of your education, and you're obviously taking it seriously, so you shouldn't have to pay for it."

She hands me the check. It's for four hundred dollars. It's a lot of money. But I've already saved nearly a thousand dollars, even with the money I paid for my class, and I just put a deposit down on an airplane ticket to Paris, and Babs is advancing me a week's wages so I can buy it next week. And I have a month yet to save. The four hundred dollars would take the edge off. But the thing is, maybe I don't need the edge to be off.

"It's okay," I tell Mom, handing back the check. "But thank you."

"What, you don't want it?"

"It's not that. I don't need it."

"Of course you need it," she retorts. "Paris is expensive."

"I know, but I'm saving a lot of money from my job, and I'm hardly spending anything this summer. I don't even have to pay for gas." I try to make a joke out of it.

"That's another thing. If you're going to be working until all hours, you should take the car at night."

"That's okay. I don't want to leave you stranded."

"Well, call me for a ride."

"It's late. And I usually get a lift home from someone."

She takes the check back and with a violence that surprises me, rips it up. "Well, I can't do anything for you anymore, can I?"

"What does that mean?"

"You don't want my money or my car or my ride. I tried to help you get a job, and you don't need me for that."

"I'm nineteen," I say.

"I am aware of how old you are, Allyson. I did give birth to you!" Her voice cracks like a whip, and the snap of it seems to startle even her.

Sometimes, you can only feel something by its absence. By the empty space it leaves behind. As I look at Mom, all pissed and pinched, I finally get that she's not just angry. She's hurt. A wave of sympathy washes over me, taking away a bit of my anger. Once it's gone, I realize how much of it I have. How angry I am at her. Have been for this past year. Maybe a lot longer.

"I know you gave birth to me," I tell her.

"It's just I've spent nineteen years raising you, and now I'm being shut out of your life. I can't know anything about you. I don't know what classes you're taking. I don't know who you're friends with anymore. I don't know why you're going to Paris." She lets out something between a shudder and a sigh.

"But *I* know," I tell her. "And for now, can't that be enough?"

"No, it can't," she snaps.

"Well, it'll have to be," I snap back.

"So you dictate the rules now, is that it?"

"There aren't any rules. I'm not dictating anything. I'm just saying you have to trust the job you did raising me."

"*Did*. Past tense. I wish you'd stop talking like you're laying me off from my job."

I'm startled by that, not by her thinking of me as a job, so much as by the implication that I am in a position to do the firing. "I thought you were going to go back to some kind of PR job."

"I was, wasn't I?" She guffaws. "I said I'd do it when you started middle school. When you started high school. When you got your driver's license." She rubs her eyes with the heels of her hands. "Don't you think if I'd wanted to go back, I'd have done it by now?"

"So why haven't you?"

"It wasn't what I wanted."

"What *do* you want?"

"For things to be how they were."

For some reason, this makes me angry. Because it's both true—she wants to keep me fossilized—and such a lie. "Even when things were 'how they were,' it was never enough. I was never enough."

Mom looks up, her eyes tired and surprised at the same time. "Of course you were," she says. "You are."

"You know what bothers me? How you and Dad always say you quit while you were ahead. There's *no such thing* as quitting while you're ahead. You quit while you were *behind*. That's *why* you quit!"

Mom frowns, exasperated; it's her dealing-with-a-crazy-teenager look, one I've gotten to know well this past year, my last year of actually being a teenager. Oddly enough, it wasn't something she had to zing me with much before. Which I now realize was maybe part of the problem.

"You wanted more kids," I continue. "And you had to settle for just me. And you've spent my whole life trying to make me be enough."

That gets her attention. "What are you talking about? You are enough."

"No, I'm not. How can I be? I'm the one shot, the heir *and* the spare, so you have to make damn sure your one investment pays off because there's no backup."

"That's ridiculous. You're not an investment."

"You treat me like one. You've poured all your expectations into me. It's like I have to carry the load of hopes and dreams for all the kids you didn't get to have."

She shakes her head. "You don't know what you're talking about," she says in a quiet voice.

"Really? Medical school at thirteen. *Come. On!* What thirteen-year-old wants to go to medical school?"

For a moment, Mom looks like she's been punched in the gut. Then she places her hand on her stomach, as if covering the place of impact. "*This* thirteen-year-old."

"*What?*" I'm totally confused now. But then I remember how in high school, Dad always sent me to Mom when I needed help with chem or bio, even though he was the doctor. And I can hear Mom reciting the pre-med requisites by heart when the college catalog came. And I think about the job she once had, doing public relations, but for a drug company. Then I remember what Grandma said to her at the disastrous Seder: *That was always your dream.*

"You?" I ask. "*You* wanted to be a doctor."

She nods. "I was studying for the MCATs when I met your father. He was just in his first year of medical school and somehow found the time to tutor in his spare time. I took the tests, applied to ten schools, and didn't get into one. Your father said it was because I didn't have any lab experience. So I went to work at Glaxo, and I thought I'd apply again, but then your father and I got married, and I wound up moving over to PR, and then a few years went by, and we decided to start a family, and I didn't want your father and me to both be in the midst of school and residencies with a small baby and then we had all the fertility issues. When we gave up on having another child, I quit working—because we could afford to live on your father's income. I thought about applying again, but then I discovered I liked spending time with you. I didn't want to be away from you."

My head is spinning. "You always said you and Dad were set up."

"We were. By the campus tutoring center. I never told you everything because I didn't want you to feel like I'd given up on account of you."

"You didn't want me to know you'd quit when you were behind," I clarify. Because isn't that exactly what she did do?

Mom reaches out to grab my wrists. "No! Allyson, you're wrong about quitting while you're ahead. It means being grateful. Stopping when you realize what you have is enough."

I don't entirely believe her. "If that's true, maybe you should quit while you're ahead now—before things between us get really messed up."

"Are you asking me to quit being your mother?"

At first I think the question is rhetorical, but then I see her looking at me, her eyes wide and fearful, and a little bit of my heart breaks to think she'd ever truly think that.

"No," I say quietly. There's a moment of silence as I steel myself to say the next thing. Mom stiffens, like she's maybe steeling herself too. "But I am asking you to be a different kind of mother."

She slumps back in her chair, I can't tell if it's in relief or defeat. "And what do I get out of this?"

For a brief second, I can picture us one day, having tea, me telling her all about what happened in Paris last summer, what will happen on this trip I'm about to take. One day. Just not yet.

"A different kind of daughter," I say.

Twenty-eight

JULY
Home

I've bought my airplane ticket. I've paid for my French class, and even with both of those expenditures, I still have five hundred dollars saved by the end of a surprisingly busy and lucrative July Fourth weekend. Café Finlay closes on July 25, but unless things go disastrously in the next three weeks, I should have enough money saved by then.

Right after the Fourth of July, Melanie comes home. My parents told me she'd be back from camp for a week before heading off to a rafting trip in Colorado. By the time she gets back from that, I'll be gone. And by the time I come back from Europe, it'll be time for school. I wonder if the entire summer is going to pass, as the last six months have, as if our friendship never existed. When I see Melanie's car in her driveway, I don't say anything. Mom doesn't either, which is how I know that she and Susan have discussed our falling-out.

French class comes to an end. During the last week, each

of us has to give an oral presentation about something particularly French. I give mine on macarons, explaining their origins and how they're made. I dress up in one of Babs's chef aprons and wear a beret, and when I'm done, I hand out macarons that Babs made special for the class, along with Café Finlay postcards.

I am coming home from class in Mom's car, which I've borrowed to lug all my presentation stuff, when I see Melanie in her driveway. She sees me too, and we look at each other for a moment. It's like we're asking each other, Are we both going to pretend the other doesn't exist? That *we* don't exist?

But we do exist. At least we used to. And so I wave to her. Then I walk toward the neutral territory of the sidewalk. Melanie does too. When she gets closer, her eyes widen. I look at my silly costume.

"French class," I explain. "Here, do you want a macaron?" I pull out one of the extras that I was bringing home for Mom and Dad.

"Oh, thanks." She takes a bite, and her eyes widen. I want to say, *I know*. But with all the months gone by, I don't. Because maybe I don't know. Not anymore.

"So French class?" she says. "We both did the summer-school thing this year, huh?"

"Right, you were in Portland. At a music program?"

Her eyes light up. "Yeah. It was intense. Not just playing, but composing and learning about different facets of the industry. We had these professionals come in to work with us. I composed an experimental piece that I'm going to produce at school next year." Her whole face glows. "I think I'm going to major in music theory. What about you?"

I shake my head. "I'm not sure. I think I like languages." In addition to Mandarin, this fall, I'll take French, along with another Shakespeare class with Professor Glenny. Intro to Semiotics. And African Dance.

She looks up, hesitates for a second. "So, no Rehoboth Beach this summer?"

We've gone to the same summer house since I was five. But not this year. "Dad was invited to a conference in Hawaii, and he convinced Mom to go with him. As a personal favor to me, I think."

"Because you're going to Paris."

"Right. I'm going to Paris."

There's a pause. In the background, I can hear the neighbor kids splashing around in the sprinklers. Just like Melanie and I used to.

"To find him."

"I have to know. If something happened. I just need to find out."

I brace myself for Melanie's derision, for her to scoff or laugh at me. But she just considers what I've said. And when she says the next thing, it's not snide so much as matter-of-fact: "Even if you find him. Even if he didn't leave you on purpose, he can't possibly live up to the person you've built him into."

It's not like the thought hasn't occurred to me. I get that the chances of finding him are small, but the chances of finding him as I remember him are even smaller. But I just keep going back to what my dad always says, about how when you lose something, you have to visualize the last place you had it. And I found—and then lost—so many things in Paris.

"I know," I tell Melanie. And it's weird because I don't feel defensive. I feel a little bit relieved because it almost seems like Melanie is worrying about me again. And also relieved because I'm *not* worrying about me. Not about this, anyhow. "I don't know that it matters."

Her eyes widen at that. Then she narrows them, looks me up and down. "You look different."

I laugh. "No. I still look like me. It's just this outfit."

"It's not the outfit," Melanie says, almost harshly. "You just seem different."

"Oh. Well . . . *thanks?*"

I look at Melanie, and for the first time, I notice how she seems. Which is utterly familiar. Like Melanie again. Her hair is growing out and is back to its natural color. She's wearing cutoff shorts, a cute embroidered tee. No nose rings. No tats. No multicolored hair. No slutty-chic outfits. Of course, just because she looks the same has no bearing on whether she actually is the same. It hits me that Melanie's year was probably was just as tumultuous as mine in ways that I didn't understand, either.

Melanie is still staring at me. "I'm sorry," she says at last.

"For what?" I ask.

"For forcing you to cut your hair in London when you weren't ready. I felt so bad when you cried like that."

"It's okay. And I'm glad I did it." And I am. Maybe he never would've stopped me had I not had the Louise Brooks hair. Or maybe he would've, and we would've exchanged actual names. I'll never know. Once accidents happen, there's no backtracking.

We both just stand there on the sidewalk, hands at our

sides, unsure of what to say. I hear the neighbor kids yelp in the sprinklers. I think of me and Melanie when we were younger, on the high dive at the pool in Mexico. We would always hold hands as we jumped, but by the time we swam back up to the surface, we'd have let go. No matter how we tried, once we started swimming, we always let go. But after we bobbed to the surface, we'd climb out of the pool, clamber up the high-dive ladder, clasp hands, and do it again.

We're swimming separately now. I get that. Maybe it's just what you have to do to keep above water. But who knows? Maybe one day, we'll climb out, grab hands, and jump again.

Twenty-nine

*M*y parents want to drive me to JFK, but I've made plans to spend the day with Dee before I go, so they drop me off at 30th Street Station in Philadelphia. I'm going to take the train—my first train in a year—to Manhattan, and Dee will meet me at Penn Station. Tomorrow night, I catch my flight to London and then onward to Paris.

When my train is announced, we walk toward the platform. Dad taps his toes impatiently, visions of Maui golf courses dancing through his head. They leave on Monday. Mom just paces. Then when my train's headlights are visible in the distance, she pulls a box out of her purse.

"I thought we weren't doing presents this time." Last year, there'd been the big dinner out, lots of little last-minute gadgets. Last night was more low-key. Homemade lasagna in the dining room. Both Mom and I pushed it around our plates.

"It's less for you than for me."

I open the box. Inside is a small cell phone with a charger and a plug adapter.

"You got me a new phone?"

"No. I mean yes. I mean, your old phone, we'll unfreeze the plan when you get back. But this is a special quad-band phone. It *definitely* works in Europe. You just have to buy a . . . what are they called?" she asks Dad.

"SIM card."

"Right." She fumbles to flick open the back. "They're very inexpensive, apparently. So you can get a local number anywhere you go and have a phone if you need one, and you can call us in an emergency or text us—but only if you choose to. It's more for you, so you have a way to reach us. If you need to. But you don't have to—"

"Mom," I interrupt, "it's okay. I'll text you."

"Really?"

"Well, yeah! And you can text me back from Hawaii. And does this thing have a photo function?" I peer at the camera. "I'll send you pictures."

"You will?"

"Of course I will."

By the look on her face, you'd think I'd given her the present.

———

Penn Station is mobbed, but I find Dee right away, under the departure board, wearing a pair of lemon-lime paneled nylon shorts and a tank top with UNICORNS ARE REAL emblazoned on it. He scoops me up in a big hug.

"Where's your suitcase?" he asks.

I turn around, show off the olive backpack I got from the Army-Navy surplus store in Philadelphia.

Dee whistles. "How'd you fit your ball gown?"

"It folds down really small."

"I thought you'd have a bigger bag, and I told Mama we'd come back home before we went out exploring, so she made lunch."

"I like lunch."

Dee throws up his hands. "Actually, Mama planned a surprise party for you. Don't tell her I told."

"A party? She doesn't even know me."

"She thinks she does by how much I talk about you, and she'll use any excuse to cook. My family's coming, including my cousin Tanya. I told you about her?"

"The one who does hair?"

Dee nods. "I asked her if she'd do yours. She does white-girl hair too, works in a fancy salon in Manhattan. I thought maybe you could get a bob again, go all Louise Brooks. Look just like you did when you met. You gotta do something with that mop." He fingers my hair, up, as usual, in a clip.

We take the subway all the way uptown, to the last stop on the train. We get out and transfer to a bus. I look out the window, expecting the rough-and-tumble streets of the South Bronx, but the bus passes a bunch of pretty brick buildings all shaded by mature trees.

"*This* is the South Bronx?" I ask Dee.

"I never said I lived in the South Bronx."

I look at him. "Are you serious? I've heard you say a bunch of times that you're from the South Bronx."

"I only said that I was from the Bronx. This is the Bronx, technically. It's Riverdale."

"But you told Kendra you were from the South Bronx. You told her you went to South Bronx High School. . . ." I pause, remembering that first conversation. "Which does not even exist."

"I left the girl to her own jumped conclusions." He gives me a knowing smirk. He rings the bell to get off the bus. We exit onto a busy street full of tall apartment buildings. It's not fancy, but it's nice.

"You are a master pretender, D'Angelo Harrison."

"Takes one to know one. I *am* from the Bronx. And I *am* poor. If people want to translate that as ghetto boy, that's their choice." He smiles. "Especially if they want to throw scholarship money my way."

We arrive at a pretty brick building with cracked gargoyles hanging over the front entrance. Dee rings the buzzer—"so they know we're coming"—and then we take one of those ancient caged-in elevators to the fifth floor. Outside the front door, he looks at me and tucks some strands of stray hair behind my ear.

"Act surprised," he whispers and opens the door.

We step into a party, about a dozen people crowded into the small living room where there's a BON VOYAGE ALLYSON sign tacked up over a table laden with food. I look at Dee, eyes wide in shock.

"Surprise!" he says, twinkling jazz hands.

Dee's mother, Sandra, comes up to me and wraps me in a gardenia-scented bear hug. "He told you, didn't he? That was the worst look of surprise I ever saw. My baby couldn't keep a secret if it was stapled to him. Well, come on, then, meet the folk, have some food."

Sandra introduces me to various aunts and uncles and cousins and gives me a plate of barbecued chicken and mac and cheese and some greens and sits me down at a table. "Now you hold court."

Dee has pretty much told everyone about Willem, so they all have advice on how to track him down. Then they start peppering me with questions about the trip. How I'm getting there—a flight from New York to London and then on to Paris—and where I'm staying—a youth hostel in the Villette area Willem and I hung out in, twenty-five bucks a night for a dorm—and how I'll get around—with the help of a guidebook, and I will brave the Metro. And they ask about Paris, and I tell them about what I saw last year, and they're very interested to hear how diverse it was, about the sections that were full of Africans and then this starts a big debate about which African countries France colonized until someone goes for a map to figure it out.

While everyone pores over the atlas, Sandra comes up with a plate of peach cobbler. "I got you a little something," she says, handing me a thin package.

"Oh, you shouldn't—"

She waves away my objections like stale air. I open the package. Inside is a laminated map of Paris. "The man at the store said this would be 'indispensable.' It has all the subway stops and an index of major streets." She opens the map to show me. "And D'Angelo and I spent so many hours looking at it, it has our good blessings coursing through it."

"Then I'll never get lost again."

She folds the map up and puts it in my hands. She has the same eyes as Dee. "I want to thank you for helping my boy this year."

"Me helping Dee?" I shake my head. "I think you have it the other way around."

"I know exactly the way I have it," she says.

"No, seriously. All Dee has done is help me. It's almost embarrassing."

"Stop with such nonsense. D'Angelo is both brilliant and blessed with the road life has taken him on. But it's not been easy for him. In his four years of high school and one year of college, you are the first friend from school he's ever talked about, much less brought home."

"You two are talking about me, aren't you?" Dee asks. He puts an arm around each of us. "Extolling my brilliance?"

"Extolling your something," I say.

"Don't either of you believe a word!" He turns around to introduce a tall, regal girl with a head full of intricate twists. "I was telling you about Tanya."

We exchange hellos, and Sandra goes off to fetch some more cobbler. Tanya reaches out to free my hair from its clip. She fingers the ends and shakes her head, clucking her tongue the same disapproving way Dee so often does.

"I know. I know. It's been a year," I say. And then I realize it has. A year.

"Was it short or long?" Dee asks. He turns to Tanya. "You have to make her look just the same. For when she finds him."

"*If* I find him," I clarify. "It was to here." I point to the base of my skull, where the stylist in London had cut my hair to last year. But then I drop my hand. "You know, though. I don't think I want the bob."

"You don't want a haircut?" Tanya asks.

"No, I would *love* a haircut," I tell her. "But not a bob. I want to try something totally new."

Thirty

Paris

---

*I*t takes approximately thirteen hours and six time zones for me to freak out.

It happens when I stumble into the arrivals hall of Charles de Gaulle airport. All around me, other passengers are being greeted by hugging relatives or drivers with signs. I'm not being met by anyone. No one is expecting me. No one is watching out for me. I know I have people out there in the world who love me, but right now, I've never felt so alone. I feel that flashing sign click on over my head, the one that used to read TOURIST. Only now it also reads WHAT HAVE YOU DONE?

I pull my backpack straps tighter around my chest, like they could hug me. I take a deep breath. I pick up one leg and put it in front of the other. A step. I take another. And another. I pull out the to-do list I made on the plane. Number one: exchange money.

I go to one of the many foreign exchange bureaus and in

halting French ask if I can exchange my dollars. "Of course. This is a bank," the man behind the counter answers in French. I hand over a hundred dollars and am too relieved to bother to count the euros I get in return.

Next on the list: find youth hostel. I've mapped the route, a train to the city, then a Metro to the Jaurès stop. I follow the signs for the RER, the train to central Paris, but it turns out I have to take an airport train to get to the RER station, and I go the wrong way and wind up at a different terminal and have to double back around, so it takes me almost an hour just to get to the airport train station.

When I get up to the automated ticket machines, it's like facing off against an enemy. Even with choosing English as the language, the instructions are bewildering. Do I need a Metro ticket? A train ticket? Two tickets? I feel that neon sign over my head flash brighter. Now it says WHAT THE *HELL* HAVE YOU DONE?

I open the guidebook again to the section about getting into Paris. Okay, one ticket will get me into Paris and transfer to the Metro. I look at the map of the Paris Metro. The different lines knot together like snakes. Finally, I locate my stop, Jaurès. I trace the RER line to the airport to the transfer point and realize with a start that it's at Gare du Nord. Someplace familiar, someplace to tie me to that day.

"Okay, Allyson, no way through it but through it," I tell myself. And then I face the ticket machine, shoulders back, like we are competitors in a duel. I punch the touch screen, feed it a ten-euro note and then it spits me back some change and a tiny ticket. A small victory against an impassive opponent, but I am flush with satisfaction.

I follow the throngs to the gates, which work like the Tube gates, though it turns out, it's much easier to get through them when you're not lugging a giant suitcase. Ha! Another enemy foiled.

In the Metro/RER interchange beneath Gare du Nord, I get lost again trying to find the right Metro line, and then I misplace my little ticket, which you need not only to get out of RER but into the Metro. Then I almost get on the Metro going the wrong direction but figure it out right before the doors close and jump off. When I finally arrive at my stop, I'm completely exhausted and totally disoriented. It takes about fifteen minutes poring over the map just to figure where I am. I take a half dozen more wrong turns until I hit the canals, which is the first sign that I'm in the right area.

But I still have no idea where the hostel is, and I'm exhausted, frustrated, and near tears. I can't even find the hostel. And I have an address. And a map. What in the world makes me think I can find him?

But then just when I'm about to lose it, I stop, look out at the canals, and I just breathe. And my panic subsides. Because this place, it feels familiar. It *is* familiar, because I've been here before.

I fold up my map and put it away. I breathe some more. I look around. There are the same gray bicycles. There are the same stylish women, teetering across the cobblestones on heels. The cafés, crowded, as though no one ever has to work. I take another deep breath, and a sort of sense memory takes over. And somehow I just know where I am. To the left is the park with the lake where we met Jacques and the Danes. To my right, a few blocks back, is the café where we had crêpes.

I take the map out again. I find myself. Five minutes later, I'm at the youth hostel.

My room is on the sixth floor, and the elevator is out of order, so I walk up a winding stairway. A guy with a tattoo of some sort of Greek god on his arm points out the breakfast room, the communal bathrooms (coed), and then my room, with seven beds. He gives me a lock and shows me where I can store my stuff when I go out. Then he leaves me with a *bonne chance*, which means good luck, and I wonder if he says that to everyone or if he senses that I'll need it.

I sit down on the bed and unhook the sleeping bag from the top of my backpack, and as I slump into the springy mattress, I wonder if Willem has stayed here. Has slept in this very bed. It's not likely, but it's not impossible either. This is the neighborhood he introduced me to. And everything seems possible right now, this feeling of rightness, throbbing right alongside my heartbeat, soothing me to sleep.

I wake up a few hours later with drool on my pillow and static in my head. I take a lukewarm shower, shampooing the jet lag out of my hair. Then I towel it dry and put in the gel like Tanya showed me—wash and wear, she said. It's very different, all chunks and layers, and I like it.

Downstairs, the clock on the lobby wall behind the giant spray-painted peace sign reads seven o'clock; I haven't eaten anything since the hard roll and yogurt they gave me on the plane over from London, and I'm woozy with hunger. The little café in the lobby only serves drinks. I know that part of traveling alone means eating alone and ordering in French, and I practiced that a lot with Madame Lambert. And it's not like I haven't eaten alone plenty of times in the dining hall this past year. But I decide I've conquered enough things for one day. Tonight, I can get a sandwich and eat in my room.

In front of the hostel, a bunch of people are hanging out in the drizzle. They're speaking English in what I think are Australian accents. I take a breath and walk over and ask them if they know of a place to get a good sandwich nearby.

One muscular girl with streaky brown hair and a ruddy face turns to me and smiles brightly. "Oh, there's a place over the canal that makes gorgeous smoked salmon sandwiches," she says. She points out the way and then she resumes talking to her friend about a bistro that supposedly sells a prix fixe for twelve euro, fifteen with a glass of wine.

My mouth waters at the mere thought of it, the food, the company. It seems incredibly presumptuous to invite myself, the kind of thing I would never do.

But then again, I'm alone in Paris, so this is all virgin territory. I tap the Australian girl on her sunburnt shoulder and ask if I can tag along with them for dinner. "It's my first day traveling, and I'm not sure where to go," I explain.

"Good on you," she replies. "We've all been at it for ages. We're on our OAs."

"OAs?"

"Overseas Adventures. It's so bloody expensive to get out of Australia that once you go, you stay gone. I'm Kelly, by the way. This is Mick, that's Nick, that's Nico, short for Nicola, and that's Shazzer. She's from England, but we love her anyway."

Shazzer sticks her tongue out at Kelly, smiles at me.

"I'm Allyson."

"That's my mum's name!" Kelly says. "And I was just saying I was missing my mum! Wasn't I? It's karma!"

"Kismet," Nico corrects.

"That too."

Kelly looks at me, and for half a second, I stand there, because she hasn't said yes and I'm going to feel like an idiot if she says no. Still, maybe it's all that prep in French class, but I'm kind of okay with feeling like an idiot. The group starts to walk off, and I start to turn toward the sandwich place. Then Kelly turns around.

"Come on, then," she says to me. "Don't know about you, but I could eat a horse."

"You might do. They eat those here," Shazzer says.

"No they don't," one of the guys says. Mick or Nick. I'm not quite sure who's who.

"That's Japan," Nico says. "It's a delicacy there."

We start walking, and I listen as the rest of them argue over whether or not the French eat horse meat, and as I amble along, it hits me that I'm doing it. Going to dinner. In Paris. With people I met five minutes ago. Somehow, more than anything else that's happened in the last year, this blows my mind.

On the way to the restaurant, we stop so I can get a SIM card for my phone. Then, after getting slightly lost, we find the place and wait for a table big enough to seat us all. The menu's in French, but I can understand it. I order a delicious salad with beets that's so beautiful I take a picture of it to text my mom. She immediately texts me back the less artful looking loco moco that Dad is having for breakfast. For my entrée, it's some kind of mystery fish in a peppery sauce. I'm having such a nice time, mostly listening to their outrageous travel tales, that it's only when it's time for dessert that I remember my promise to Babs. I check out the menu, but there are no macarons on it. It's already ten o'clock, and the shops are closed. Day one, and I've already blown my promise.

"Shit," I say. "Or make that *merde!*"

"What's wrong?" Mick/Nick asks.

I explain about the macarons, and everyone listens, rapt.

"You should ask the waiter," Nico says. "I used to work at a place in Sydney, and we had a whole menu that wasn't on the menu. For VIPs." We all give her a look. "It never hurts to ask."

So I do. I explain, in French that would make Madame Lambert proud, about *ma promesse de manger des macarons tous les jours*. The waiter listens intently, as though this is serious business and goes into the kitchen. He returns with everyone else's dessert—crèmes brûlées and chocolate mousse—and, miraculously, one perfect creamy macaron just for me. The inside is filled with brown, sweet, gritty paste, figs I think. It's dusted with powdered sugar so artfully it's like a painting. I take another picture. Then I eat it.

By eleven o'clock, I'm falling asleep into my plate. The rest of the group drops me off back at the hostel before going out to hear some French all-girl band play. I fall into a dead sleep and wake up in the morning to discover that Kelly, Nico, and Shazzer are my dorm mates.

"What time is it?" I ask.

"Late! Ten o'clock," says Kelly. "You slept ages. And through such a racket. There's a Russian girl who blow-dries her hair for an hour every day. I waited for you to see if you wanted to come with us. We're all going to Père Lachaise Cemetery today. We're going to have a picnic. Which sounds bloody morbid to me, but apparently French people do it all the time."

It's tempting: to go with Kelly and her friends and spend my two weeks in Paris being a tourist, having fun. I wouldn't have to go to dank nightclubs. I wouldn't have to face Céline. I wouldn't have to risk getting my heart broken all over again.

"Maybe I'll meet up with you later," I tell her. "I've got something to do today."

"Right. You're on an epic quest for macarons."

"Right," I say. "That."

At breakfast, I spend a little time with my map, figuring out the route between the hostel and Gare du Nord. It's walking distance, so I set out. The route seems familiar, the big wide boulevard with the bike paths and sidewalks in the middle. But as I get closer to the station, I start to feel sick to my stomach, the tea I had a while ago coming back to my mouth, all acidic with fear.

At Gare du Nord, I stall for time. I go in the station. I wander over to the Eurostar tracks. There's one there, like a horse waiting to leave the gate. I think of when I was here a year ago, broken, scared, running back to Ms. Foley.

I force myself to leave the station, letting my memory guide me again. I turn. I turn again. I turn once more. Over the train tracks and into the industrial neighborhood. And then, there it is. It's kind of shocking, after all that searching online, how easy it is to find. I wonder if this one wasn't listed on Google, or if it was and maybe my French was so mangled that no one understood me.

Or maybe that's not it at all. Maybe I was perfectly understood and Céline and the Giant simply don't work here anymore. A year is a long time. A lot can change!

When I open the door and see a younger-looking man

with hair in a ponytail behind the bar, I almost cry out in disappointment. Where is the Giant? What if he's not here? What if she's not here?

"*Excusez-moi, je cherche Céline ou un barman qui vient du Sénégal.*"

He says nothing. Doesn't even respond. He just continues washing glasses in soapy water.

Did I speak? Was it in French? I try again: I add a *s'il vous plaît* this time. He gives me a quick look, pulls out his phone, texts something, and then goes back to dishes.

Con, I mutter in French, another of Nathaniel's teachings. I shove open the door, adrenaline pushing through me. I'm so angry at that jerk behind the counter who wouldn't even answer me, at myself, for coming all this way for nothing.

"You came back!"

And I look up. And it's him.

"I knew you would come back." The Giant takes my hand and kisses me on each cheek, just like the last time. "For the suitcase, *non?*"

I'm speechless. So I just nod. Then I throw my arms around him. Because I'm so happy to see him again. I tell him so.

"As am I. And so happy I save your suitcase. Céline insist to take it away, but I say no, she will come back to Paris and want her things."

I find my voice. "Wait, how'd you know I was here? I mean, today?"

"Marco just text me an American girl was looking for me. I knew it had to be you. Come."

I follow him back inside the club, where this Marco is now mopping the floor and refusing to look at me. I have a hard time looking at him after calling him an asshole in French.

"*Je suis très désolée,*" I apologize as I shuffle past him.

"He's Latvian. His French is new, so he's timid to speak," the Giant says. "He is the cleaner. Come downstairs, that is where your suitcase is." I glance at Marco and think of Dee, and Shakespeare, and remind myself that things are rarely what they appear. I hope he didn't understand my French curses, either. I apologize again. The Giant beckons downstairs to the storeroom. In a corner, behind a stack of boxes, is my suitcase.

Everything is as I left it. The Ziploc with the list. The souvenirs. My travel diary with the bag of blank postcards inside. I half expect it to all be covered in a layer of dust. I finger the diary. The souvenirs from last year's trip. They're not the memories that matter, the ones that lasted.

"It is very nice suitcase," the Giant says.

"You want it?" I ask. I don't want to lug it around with me. I can ship the souvenirs home. The suitcase is just extra baggage.

"Oh, no, no, no. It is for you."

"I can't take it. I'll take the important things, but I can't carry all this with me."

He looks at me seriously. "But I save it for you."

"The saving is the best part, but I really don't need it anymore."

He smiles, the whites of his teeth gleaming. "I *am* going to Roché Estair in the spring, to celebrate my brother's graduation."

I fish out the important things—my diary, my favorite

T-shirt, earrings I've missed—and put them in my bag. I put all the souvenirs, the unwritten postcards in a cardboard box to ship home. "You take this to Roché Estair for the graduation," I tell him. "It would make me happy."

He nods solemnly. "You did not come back for your suitcase."

I shake my head. "Have you seen him?" I ask.

He looks at me for a long moment. He nods again. "One time. The day after I meet you."

"Do you know where I might find him?"

He strokes the goatee on his chin and looks at me with a sympathy I could really do without. After a long moment, he says, "Maybe you should better speak with Céline."

And the way he says it, it implies all the things I already know. That Willem and Céline have a history. That I might've been right to doubt him all along. But if the Giant knows any of that, he's not saying. "She is off today, but sometimes she comes to the shows at night. Androgynie is playing, and she is very good friends with them. I will see if she is coming and let you know. Then you can find out what you need. You can call me later, and I will let you know if she will be here."

"Okay." I pull out my Paris phone, and we exchange numbers. "You never told me your name, by the way?"

He laughs at that. "No, I didn't. I am Modou Mjodi. And I never learned your name. I looked on the suitcase but there was nothing."

"I know. My name is Allyson, but Céline will know me as Lulu."

He looks perplexed. "Which is correct?"

"I'm beginning to think they both are."

He shrugs a little, takes my hand, kisses my cheeks twice, and then he bids me adieu.

— — —

It's only lunchtime when I leave Modou, and with no idea when I will see Céline, I feel oddly relieved, like I've been given a reprieve. I hadn't really planned on being a tourist in Paris, but I decide to do it. I brave the Metro and get off in the Marais quarter and go to one of the cafés along the beautiful Place des Vosges, where I order a salad and a *citron pressé*, adding plenty of sugar this time. I sit there for hours, waiting for the waiter to kick me out, but he leaves me alone until I ask for my check. At a patisserie, I get a ridiculously expensive macaron—this one a pale tangerine, like the last whispers of a sunset. I eat it and walk, in and out of the narrow streets, through a lively Jewish section, full of Orthodox men with black hats and stylish skinny suits. I snap a few pictures for my mom and text them to her and tell her to forward them to Grandma, who'll get a kick out of it. Then I wander around looking at the boutiques, gazing at clothing I can barely afford to touch. When the salesladies ask me in French if I need help, I answer in French that I am just browsing.

I buy some postcards and go back to Place des Vosges and sit down in the park inside the square. Amid the mothers playing with their babies and the old men reading their newspapers, puffing away on cigarettes, I write them out. I have a lot to send. One to my parents, one to my grandmother, one to Dee, one to Kali, one to Jenn, one to Café Finlay, one to Carol. And then, at the last minute, I decide to write one to Melanie too.

It's kind of a perfect day. I feel totally relaxed, and though I'm undoubtedly a tourist, I also feel like a Parisian. I'm almost relieved that I haven't heard from Modou. Kelly sends me a text about meeting up for dinner, and I'm getting ready to make my way back to the hostel when my phone chirps. It's from Modou. Céline will be at the club after ten o'clock.

I feel like the mellow relaxing vibe of the afternoon disappears behind a storm cloud. It's only seven. I have several hours to kill, and I could go meet the Oz gang for dinner, but I'm too nervous. So, I walk the city in my nervousness. I get to the club at nine thirty and stand outside, the heavy bass thump of live music making my heart pound. She's probably already there, but it feels like being early is some kind of faux pas. So I linger outside, watching the stylishly edgy Parisians with razored haircuts and angular clothes filter into the club. I look down at myself: khaki skirt, black T-shirt, leather flip-flops. Why didn't I dress for battle?

At ten fifteen, I pay my (ten-euro) entry and go in. The club is packed, and there's a band on the stage, all heavy guitars and a violin screeching feedback, and the tiniest Asian girl singing in this high, squeaky voice. All alone, surrounded by these hipsters, I don't think I've ever felt so out of place, and every part of me is telling me to leave before I make a fool of myself. But I don't. I haven't come this far to chicken out. I fight my way to the bar, and when I see Modou, I greet him like a long-lost brother. He smiles at me and pours me a glass of wine. When I try to pay, he waves the bill away, and immediately, I feel better.

"Ahh, Céline is there," he says, pointing to a table up front. She sits, alone, watching the band with a strange intensity, the smoke from her cigarette curling witchily around her.

I walk over to her table. She doesn't acknowledge me, though I can't tell if it's because she's snubbing me or concentrating on the band. I stand next to the open chair waiting for her to invite me to sit down, but then I just give up. I pull the chair out and sit. She gives me the slightest of nods, takes a puff of the cigarette, and blows smoke all over me, which I suppose counts as a greeting. Then she turns back to the band.

We sit there, listening. We are sitting right up close to the speakers, so the sound is extra deafening; my ears are already beginning to ring. It's hard to tell if she's enjoying the music. She doesn't tap her toes or sway or anything. She just stares and smokes.

Finally, when the band takes a break, she looks at me. "Your name is Allyson." She pronounces it *Aleeseesyoohn*, which makes it sound ridiculous somehow, an SUV of an American name with too many syllables.

I nod.

"So, not French at all?"

I shake my head. I never claimed it was.

We stare at each other, and I realize she won't give me a thing. I have to take it. "I'm looking for Willem. Do you know where I can find him?" I'd meant to come in guns blazing, French spouting, but my nerves have sent me scurrying back to the comforts of my mother tongue.

She lights a new cigarette and blows more smoke on me. "No."

"But, but he said you were good friends."

"He said that? No. I am just like you."

I cannot imagine in what way she would think she is even remotely like me, aside from us both possessing two X chromosomes. "How, how are we anything alike?"

"I am just one of the girls. There are many of us."

It's not like I didn't know this about him. Not like he hid it. But hearing it out loud, from her, I feel exhausted, jet lag dropping me like a plummeting elevator.

"So you don't know where he is?"

She shakes her head.

"And you don't know where I can find him?"

"No."

"And would you even tell me if you did?"

Her eyebrow goes up into that perfect arch as smoke curls out of her mouth.

"Can you even tell me his last name? Can you tell me that much?"

And here she smiles. Because in this little game we are playing, have been playing since last summer, I just showed my hand. And what a rotten hand it is. She takes a pen and a scrap of paper and writes something down. She slides the paper over to me. His name is on there. His full name! But I won't give her the satisfaction of my eagerness, so I casually tuck it in my pocket without even glancing at it.

"Do you need anything else?" Her tone, haughty and gloating, manages to carry over the sounds of the band, who have started playing again. I can already hear her laughing about me with all her hipster pals.

"No, you've done quite enough."

She eyes me for a long second. Her eyes aren't so much blue as violet. "What will you do now?"

I force a bitchy smile, which I expect doesn't look bitchy so much as constipated. "Oh, you know, see the sights."

She blows more smoke on me. "Yes, you can be a *touriste*," she says, as though tourist were an epithet. Then she begins ticking off all the places lowly people like us go. The Eiffel Tower. Sacré-Coeur. The Louvre.

I search her face for hidden meaning. Did he tell her about our day? I can just picture them laughing about me throwing the book at the skinheads, telling Willem I'd take care of him.

Céline is still talking about all the things I can do in Paris. "You can go shopping," she is saying. Buy a new handbag. Some jewelry. Another watch. Some shoes. I can't quite fathom how someone spouting off Ms. Foley–like advice can be so condescending.

"Thank you for your time," I say. In French. Annoyance has made me bilingual.

Thirty-one

---

*W*illem de Ruiter.

His name is Willem de Ruiter. I rush to an Internet café and start Googling him. But Willem de Ruiter turns out to be a popular name in Holland. There's a Dutch cinematographer with that name. There's some famous diplomat with that name. And hundreds of other nonfamous people who nevertheless have some reason to be on the Internet. I go through hundreds of pages, in English, in Dutch, and I find not one link to him, not one piece of evidence that he actually exists. I Google his parents' names. Bram de Ruiter. Yael de Ruiter. Naturopath. Actor. Anything I can think of. All these combinations. I get vaguely excited when some weird theater thing comes up, but when I click through, the website is down.

How can it be this hard to find someone? It occurs to me that maybe Céline intentionally gave me the wrong name.

But then I Google myself, "Allyson Healey," and I don't come up, either. You have to add the name of my college before you get my Facebook page.

I realize then it's not enough to know what someone is called.

You have to know who they are.

Thirty-two

The next morning, Kelly and her friends ask me if I want to join them for a trip to the Rodin Museum, followed by some shopping. And I almost say yes. Because that's what I would like. But there is still one more stop. It's not even that I think I'll find anything; it's just that, if I'm facing down demons, I have to go there too.

I'm not sure where it is, exactly, but I do know the intersection where Ms. Foley had me picked up. It is seared into my brain. Avenue Simon Bolivar and Rue de l'Equerre, the cross streets of Humiliation and Defeat.

When I get out of the Metro, nothing seems familiar. Maybe because the last time I was here, I was flipping out in such a panic. But I know I didn't run that far before finding the pay phone, so I know it can't be that far to the art squat. I methodically go up one block. Down the next. Up and back. But nothing seems familiar. I attempt to ask directions, but how do you say "art squat" in French? Old building with artists? That doesn't work. I remember the Chinese restaurants in the vicinity and ask for them. One young guy gets really excited and, I think, offers a recommendation to one supposedly good place across on Rue de Belleville. I find it. And from there, I find a sign for double happiness. It could be one of many, but I have a feeling it's the one.

I wander around for fifteen more minutes and, on a quiet triangle of streets, find the squat. It has the same scaffolding, same distorted portraits, maybe a little more weather-beaten. I knock on the steel door. No one answers, but there are obviously people inside. Music wafts out from the open windows. I give the door a push. It creaks open. I push it farther. I walk inside. No one pays me any notice. I go up the creaking staircase, to the place where it all happened.

I see the clay first, bright white, yet at the same time, golden and warm. Inside, a man is working. He is petite, Asian, a study in contrasts: His hair white with black roots, his clothes all black and strangely antiquated, like he stepped out of a Charles Dickens novel, and all covered in the same white dust that covered me that night.

He is carving at a piece of clay with a scalpel, his attention so focused I'm afraid he'll startle with the merest sound. I clear my throat and knock quietly on the door.

He looks up and rubs his eyes, which are bleary with concentration. "*Oui.*"

"*Bonjour,*" I begin. And then I sputter. My limited French is no match for what I need to explain to him. I crashed your squat, with a guy. I had the most intimate night of my life, and I woke up utterly alone. "Umm, I'm looking for a friend who I think you might know. Oh, I'm sorry—*parlez-vous anglais?*"

He lifts his head and nods, slightly, with the delicacy and control of a ballet dancer. "Yes," he says.

"I'm looking for a friend of mine, and I wonder if you might know him. His name is Willem de Ruiter. He's Dutch?" I watch his face for a flicker of recognition, but it remains impassive, as smooth as the clay sculptures that surround us.

"No? Well, he and I stayed here one night. Not exactly *stayed* here . . ." I trail off, looking around the studio, and it all comes back to me: the smell of the rain against the thirsty pavement, the swirl of dust, the smooth wood of his work-table pressing into my back. Willem towering over me.

"What did you say your name was?"

"Allyson," I hear myself say as if from a distance away.

"Van," he says, introducing himself while fingering an old pocket watch on a chain.

I'm staring at the table, remembering the intense sharpness of it against my back, the ease with which Willem hoisted me onto it. The table is, as it was then, meticulously clean, the neat pile of papers, the half-finished pieces in the corner, the mesh cup of charcoals, and pens. Wait, what? I grab for the pens.

"That's my pen!"

"I'm sorry?" Van asks.

I reach over to grab the pen out of the cup. The "roller ball," inscribed BREATHE EASY WITH PULMOCLEAR. "This is my pen! From my dad's practice."

Van is looking at me, perplexed. But he doesn't understand. The pen was in my bag. I never took it out. It just went missing. I had it on the barge. I wrote double happiness with it. And then the next day, when I was on the phone with Ms. Foley, it was gone.

"Last summer, my friend Willem and I, well, we came here hoping someone might put us up for the night. He said that squats will do that." I pause. Van nods slightly. "But no one was here. Except a window was open. So we slept here, in your studio, and when I woke up the next morning, my friend, Willem, he was gone."

I wait for Van to get upset about our trespassing, but he is looking at me, still trying to understand why I'm gripping the Pulmoclear pen in my hand like it's a sword. "This pen was in my purse and then it was gone and now it's here, and I'm wondering, maybe there was a note or something. . . ."

Van's face remains blank, and I'm about to apologize, for trespassing before, and now again, but then I see something, like the faint glimmers of light before a sunrise, as some sort of recognition illuminates his face. He taps his index finger to the bridge of his nose.

"I did find something; I thought it was a shopping list."

"A shopping list?"

"It said something about, about . . . I don't recall, perhaps chocolate and bread?"

"Chocolate and bread?" Those were Willem's staple foods. My heart starts to pound.

"I don't remember. I thought it came in from the garbage. I had been away for holiday, and when I came back, everything was disarrayed. I disposed of it. I'm so sorry." He looks stricken.

We snuck into his studio, made a mess of it, and *he* looks guilty.

"No, don't be sorry. This is so helpful. Would there have been any reason for a shopping list to be in here? I mean, might you have written it?"

"No. And if I did, it would not have contained bread and chocolate."

I smile at that. "Could the list have been, maybe, a note?"

"It is possible."

"We were supposed to have bread and chocolate for breakfast. And my pen is here."

"Please, take your pen."

"No, you can *have* the pen," I say, and out escapes a whoop of laughter. A note. Could he have left me a note?

I throw my arms around Van, who stiffens for a moment in surprise but then relaxes into my embrace and reaches around to hug me back. It feels good, and he smells nice, like oil paint and turpentine and dust and old wood—smells that, like everything from that day, are stitched into the fabric of me now. For the first time in a long time, this doesn't seem like a curse.

— — —

When I leave Van, it's mid-afternoon. The Oz crew is probably still at the Rodin Museum; I could meet up with them. But instead, I decide to try something else. I go to the nearest Metro station and close my eyes and spin around and then I pick a stop. I land on Jules Joffrin and then I figure out the series of trains that will take me there.

I wind up in a very Parisian-seeming neighborhood, lots of narrow, uphill streets and everyday shops: shoe stores, barbershops, little neighborhood bars. I meander a ways, no idea where I am, but surprisingly enjoying the feeling of being lost. Eventually, I come across a broad staircase, carved into the steep hillside, forming a little canyon between the apartment buildings and green foliage hanging down on either side. I have no idea where the stairs lead. I can practically hear Willem's voice: *All the more reason to take them.*

So I do. And take them, and take them. No sooner do I reach one landing than I find another set of stairs. At the top of the stairs, I cross a small cobblestoned medieval street and then, *boom*, it's like I'm back in the world of the tour. There are idling coaches and sardine-packed cafés, and an accordion player doing Edith Piaf covers.

I follow the crowds around the corner, and at the end of a street full of cafés advertising menus in English, Spanish, French, and German is a huge white-domed cathedral.

"Excusez-moi, qu'est-ce que c'est?" I ask a man standing outside of one of the cafés.

He rolls his eyes. *"C'est Sacré-Coeur!"*

Oh, Sacré-Coeur. Of course. I walk closer and see three domes, two smaller ones flanking the big one in the middle, reigning regal over the rooftops of Paris. In front of the cathedral, which is glowing golden in the afternoon sun, is a grassy hillside esplanade, bisected by marble staircases leading down the other side of the hill. There are people everywhere: the tourists with their video cameras rolling, backpackers lolling in the sun, artists with easels out, young couples leaning into each other, whispering secrets. Paris! Life!

At the end of the tour, I'd sworn off setting foot in another moldering old church. But for some reason, I follow the crowds inside. Even with the golden mosaics, looming statues and swelling crowds, it somehow still manages to feel like a neighborhood church, with people quietly praying, fingering rosaries, or just lost in thought.

There's a stand of candles, and you can pay a few euros and light one yourself. I'm not Catholic, and I'm not entirely clear on this ritual, but I feel the need to commemorate this somehow. I hand over some change and am given a candle, and when I light it, it occurs to me that I should say a prayer. Should I pray for someone who's died, like my grandfather? Or should I pray for Dee? For my mom? Should I pray to find Willem?

But none of that feels right. What feels right is just *this*. Being here. Again. By myself, this time. I'm not sure what the word for *this* is, but I say a prayer for it anyway.

I'm getting hungry, and the long twilight is starting. I decide to go down the back steps into that typical neighborhood and try to find an inexpensive bistro for dinner. But first, I need to get a macaron before all the patisseries close for the day.

At the base of the steps, I wander for a few blocks before I find a patisserie. At first I think it's closed because a shade is drawn down the door, but I hear voices, lots and lots of voices, inside, so hesitantly, I push the door open.

It seems like a party is going on. The air is humid with so many people crammed together, and there are bottles of booze and bouquets of flowers. I begin to edge back out, but there is a huge booming protest from inside, so I open it up again, and they wave me in. Inside, there are maybe ten people, some of them still in bakers' aprons, others in street clothes. They all have cups in hands, faces flushed with excitement.

In halting French, I ask if it might be possible to buy a macaron. There is much shuffling, and a macaron is produced. When I reach for my wallet, my money is refused. I start to head for the door, but before I get to it, I'm handed some champagne in a paper cup. I raise the cup and everyone clinks with me and drinks. Then a burly guy with a handlebar mustache starts to cry and everyone pats him on the back.

I have no idea what's going on. I look around questioningly, and one of the women starts talking very fast, in a very strong accent, so I don't catch much, but I do catch *bébé*.

"Baby?" I exclaim in English.

The guy with the handlebar mustache hands me his telephone. On it is a photo of a puckered, red-faced thing in a blue cap. "Rémy!" he declares.

"Your son?" I ask. "*Votre fils?*"

Handlebar Mustache nods, then his eyes fill with tears.

"*Félicitations!*" I say. And then Handlebar Mustache embraces me in a huge hug, and the crowd claps and cheers.

A bottle of amber booze is passed around. When all our paper cups have been filled, people hold them up and offer different toasts or just say some version of cheers. Everyone takes a turn, and when it gets to me, I shout out what Jewish people say at times like this: "*L'chaim!*"

"It means 'to life,'" I explain. And as I say it, I think that maybe this is what I was saying a prayer for back in the cathedral. To life.

"*L'chaim,*" the rowdy bakers repeat back to me. And then we drink.

Thirty-three

The next day, I accept Kelly's invitation to join the Oz crew. Today they're going to brave the Louvre. Tomorrow they're going to Versailles. The day after that, they're taking the train to Nice. I'm invited to come with them for all of it. I have ten days left on my ticket, and it feels like I've found as much as I'm going to find. I found out that he left me a note. Which is almost more than I could've hoped for. I am considering going with them to Nice. And, after my wonderful day yesterday, I'm also considering going off on my own somewhere.

After breakfast, we all get onto the Metro toward the Louvre. Nico and Shazzer are showing off some of their new clothes, which they got from a street market, and Kelly is making fun of them for coming to Paris to buy clothes made in China. "At least I got something local." She thrusts out her wrist to show off her new high-tech digital Frenchmanufactured watch. "There's this huge store near Vendôme, all they sell is watches."

"Why do you need a watch when you're traveling?" Nick asks.

"How many bloody trains have we missed because someone's phone alarm failed to go off?"

Nick gives her that one.

"You should see this place. It's bloody enormous. They sell watches from all over; some of them cost a hundred thousand euros. Imagine spending that on a watch," Kelly goes on, but I've stopped listening because I'm suddenly thinking of Céline. About what she said. About how I could get *another* watch. Another. Like she knew I lost my last one.

The Metro is pulling into a station. "I'm sorry," I tell Kelly and the gang. "I've gotta go."

— — —

"Where's my watch? And where's Willem?"

I find Céline in the club's office, surrounded by stacks of paperwork, wearing a thick pair of eyeglasses that somehow makes her both more and less intimidating.

She looks up from her papers, all sleepy-eyed and, maddeningly, unsurprised.

"You said I could get *another* watch, which means you knew Willem had *my* watch," I continue.

I expect her to deny it, to shoot me down. Instead, she gives me a dismissive little shrug. "Why would you do that? Give him such an expensive watch after one day? It is a little desperate, no?"

"As desperate as lying to me?"

She shrugs again, lazily taps on her computer. "I did not lie. You asked if I knew where to find him. I do not."

"But you didn't tell me everything, either. You saw him, after . . . after he, he left me."

She does this thing, neither a nod nor a shake of the head, somewhere in between. A perfect expression of ambiguity. A diamond-encrusted stonewall.

And at just that moment, another one of Nathaniel's French lessons comes back to me: *"T'es toujours aussi salope?"* I ask her.

One eyebrow goes up, but her cigarette goes into the ashtray. "You speak French now?" she asks, in French.

"Un petit peu." A little bit.

She shuffles the paperwork, stubs out the smoldering cigarette. *"Il faut mieux être salope que lâche,"* she says.

I have no idea what she said. I do my best to keep a straight face as I try to find keywords to unlock the sentence like Madame taught us, *salope*, bitch; *mieux*, better. *Lâche*. Milk? No, that's *lait*. But then I remember Madame's refrain about venturing into the unknown being an act of bravery and her teaching us, as always, the opposite of *courageux*: lâche.

Did Céline just call me a coward? I feel the indignation travel from the back of my neck up to my ears to the top of my head. "You can't call me that," I sputter in English. "You don't *get* to call me that. You don't even know me!"

"I know enough," she replies in English. "I know that you forfeited." Forfeit. I see myself waving a white flag.

"Forfeit? How did I forfeit?"

"You ran away."

"What did the note say?" I am practically screaming now.

But the more excited I become, the more aloof she becomes. "I don't know anything about it."

"But you know *something*."

She lights another cigarette and blows smoke on me. I wave it away. "Please, Céline, for a whole year, I've assumed the worst, and now I'm wondering if I assumed the wrong worst."

More silence. Then "He had the, how do you say it, sue-tours."

"Sue-tours?"

"Like with sewing on skin." She points to her cheek.

"Sutures? Stitches? He had stitches?"

"Yes, and his face was very swollen, and his eye black."

"*What happened?*"

"He would not tell me."

"Why didn't you tell me this yesterday?"

"You did not ask me this yesterday."

I want to be furious with her. Not just for this, but for being such a bitch that first day in Paris, for accusing me of cowardice. But I finally get that none of this is about Céline; it never was. I'm the one who told Willem I was in love with him. I'm the one who said that I'd take care of him. I'm the one who bailed.

I look up at Céline, who is watching me with the cagey expression of a cat eyeing a sleeping dog. *"Je suis désolée,"* I apologize. And then I pull the macaron out of my bag and give it to her. It's raspberry, and I was saving it as a reward for confronting Céline. It is cheating Babs's rule to give it to someone else, but somehow, I feel she'd approve.

She eyes it suspiciously, then takes it, pinching it between her fingers as though it were contagious. She gingerly lays it on a stack of CD cases.

"So, what happened?" I ask. "He came back here all banged up?"

She nods, barely.

"Why?"

She frowns. "He would not say."

Silence. She looks down, then quickly glances at me. "He looked through your suitcase."

What was in there? A packing list. Clothes. Souvenirs. Unwritten postcards. My luggage tag? No, that snapped off in the Tube station back in London. My diary? Which I now have. I grab it out of my bag, leaf through a few entries. There's something about Rome and feral cats. Vienna and the Schönbrunn Palace. The opera in Prague. But there is nothing, nothing of me. Not my name. My address. My email address. Not the addresses of any of the people I met on the tour. We didn't even bother with the pretense of keeping in touch. I shove the diary back in my bag. Céline is peering through narrowed eyes, watching while pretending not to.

"Did he take anything from my bag? Find anything?"

"No. He only smelled. . . ." She stops, as if in pain.

"He smelled what?"

"He smelled terrible," she says solemnly. "He took your watch. I told him to leave it. My uncle is a jeweler, so I know it was expensive. But he refused."

I sigh. "Where can I find him, Céline? Please. You can help me with that much."

"*That much?* I help you with so much already," she says, all huffy with her own indignation. "And I don't know where to find him. I don't lie." She looks hard at me. "I tell you the truth, and that is that Willem is the kind of man who comes when he comes. And mostly, he doesn't."

I wish I could tell her that she's wrong. That with us, it was different. But if he didn't stay in love with Céline, what makes me think that after one day, even if he did like me, I haven't been completely licked clean?

"So you did not have any luck? On the Internet?" she asks.

I start to gather my things. "No."

"Willem de Ruiter is a common name, *n'est-ce pas?*" she says. Then she does something I wouldn't have thought her capable of. She blushes. And that is how I know she's looked for him too. And she didn't find him, either. And all at once, I wonder if I haven't gotten Céline, if not altogether wrong, then a little bit wrong.

I take one of my extra Paris postcards. I write my name, address, all my details on it, and hand it to her. "If you see Willem. Or if you're ever in Boston and need a place to crash—or store your stuff."

She takes the postcard and looks at it. Then she shoves it in a drawer. "Boss-tone. I think I prefer New York," she sniffs. I'm almost relieved that she's sounding like her haughty self again.

I think of Dee. He could handle Céline. "That can probably be arranged."

When I get to the door, Céline calls out my name. I turn around. I see that she's taken a bite of the macaron, the round cookie now a half moon.

"I am sorry I called you a coward," she says.

"That's okay," I say. "I am sometimes. But I'm trying to be braver."

"*Bon.*" She pauses, and if I didn't know better, I'd think she maybe almost was considering a smile. "If you find Willem again, you will need to be brave."

———

I go sit down on the edge of a fountain to consider what Céline said. I can't quite make out if it was meant in support or warning, or maybe both. But it all seems academic, anyhow, because I've reached a dead end. She doesn't know where he is. I can try some more Internet searching and send another letter to Guerrilla Will, but other than that, I'm tapped.

You will need to be brave.

Maybe it's all for the best. Maybe I end here. Tomorrow I will go to Versailles with the Oz crew. And that feels okay. I pull out the map Dee and Sandra gave me to plot my route back to the hostel. It's not too far. I can walk. I trace the route with my finger. When I do, my finger runs over not one but two big pink squares. The big pink squares on this map are hospitals. I pull the map closer to my face. There are pink squares all over the place. Paris is crazy with hospitals. I run my finger to the art squat. There are several hospitals within a thumb's width of the squat too.

If Willem got hurt near the art squat, and he got stitches, there's a good chance it happened at one of these hospitals. "Thank you, Dee!" I call out into the Paris afternoon. "And thank you, Céline," I add a bit more quietly. And then I get up and go.

———

The next day, Kelly greets me coolly, which I can tell is hard work for her. I apologize for going MIA yesterday.

"S'okay," she says, "but you're coming with us today to Versailles?"

I grimace. "I can't."

Her face hardens into hurt. "If you don't want to hang with us, it's fine, but don't make plans to spare our feelings."

I'm not sure why I haven't told her. It feels sort of silly, being over here, going to all this trouble, for a guy I knew for a day. But as I tell Kelly a short version of the long story, including today's mad quest, her face grows serious. When I'm done, she just gives a little nod of her head. "I understand," she says solemnly. "I'll see you down at brekkie."

When I get down to the breakfast room, Kelly and the group are huddled around one of the big wooden tables, maps spread out in front of them. I take my croissant and tea and yogurt and join them.

"We're coming with you," she declares. "All of us."

"What? Why?"

"Because you need an army for this." The rest of the group sloppily salute me, and then they all start talking at once. Very loudly. People look over at us, but these guys are irrepressible. Only the pale petite girl at the edge of our table ignores us, keeping her nose in a book.

"Are you sure you guys want to miss Versailles?"

"Versailles is a relic," Kelly insists. "It's not going anywhere. But this is real life. Real romance. What could be more French than that?"

"We're coming with you, like it or not. If we have to follow you to every French hospital between here and Nice," Shazzer says.

"I don't think that'll be necessary," I say. "I've looked on the map. I've narrowed it down to three likely hospitals."

The elfin girl looks up. Her eyes are so pale they seem to be made of water. "I'm sorry, but did you say you were going to a hospital?" she asks.

I look at the Australians, my ragtag army, all of them gung ho. "Apparently so."

The elfin girl looks at me with a weird intensity. "I know hospitals," she says in a quiet voice.

I look back at her. Really, I can't think of anything more boring than this, except maybe a visit to a French unemployment office. I can't imagine that she would want to come along. Except maybe she's lonely. And that I understand.

"Do you, do you want to go with us?" I ask.

"Not particularly," she says. "But I think I should."

The first hospital on the map turns out to be some sort of private hospital, where, after an hour of being sent from one office to the next, we find out that, while there is an emergency room, it does not take most cases off the street, but rather sends them to the public hospitals. They send us to Hôpital Lariboisière. We head straight for the *urgences*, the French version of the emergency room, and after being given a number and told to wait, we sit for ages in uncomfortable chairs, along with all the people with broken elbows and coughs that sound really ugly and contagious.

The initial enthusiasm of the group starts to flag when they realize that going to an emergency room is as boring in

France as it is anywhere else. They are reduced to entertaining themselves with spitballs and card games of War, which does not endear them to the nurses. Wren, the strange, pale, pixie girl we've picked up, participates in none of the silliness. She just keeps reading her book.

By the time we are called to the front counter, the nurses are hating us, and the feeling is pretty much mutual. Shazzer, who apparently speaks the best French, is anointed ambassador, and I don't know if it's her French skills or her diplomatic ones that are lacking, but within five minutes, she is heatedly arguing with the nurse, and within ten, we are being escorted to the street.

It's now three o'clock. The day is half gone, and I can see the group is antsy, tired, hungry, wishing that they'd gone to Versailles. And now that I think about it, I realize how ridiculous this is. The front desk at my father's practice is manned by a nurse named Leona, who won't let even me go back into the office unless my father is in there and waiting for me. Leona would never give out a record to me—her boss's daughter, who speaks the same language as she does—let alone a foreign stranger.

"That was a bust," I tell them when we come out onto the pavement. The cloud layer that has been sitting over Paris for the last few days has burned off while we were waiting inside, and the day has turned hot and clear. "At least you can salvage the rest of the afternoon. Get some food and have a picnic in the Luxembourg Gardens."

I can see the idea is tempting. No one rebuffs it. "But we promised we'd be your wingmen," Kelly says. "We can't let you do this alone."

I hold up my hands in surrender. "You're not. I'm done. This is a lost cause."

Maps are taken out. Metro routes are debated. Picnic items are discussed.

"People mix up their patron saints, you know?" I look up. Wren, our pixie tagalong, who has been all but silent all day, has finally spoken.

"They do?"

She nods. "Saint Anthony is the patron saint of lost things. But Saint Jude is the patron saint of lost causes. You have to make sure you ask the right saint for help."

There's a moment as everyone looks at Wren. Is she some kind of religious nut?

"Who would be in charge of a lost person?" I ask.

Wren stops to consider. "That would depend. What kind of lost?"

I don't know. I don't know if he's lost at all. Maybe he's exactly where he wants to be. Maybe I'm the lost one, chasing someone who has no desire to be found. "I'm not sure."

Wren twirls her bracelet, fingering the charms. "Perhaps you should just pray to both." She shows me the little charms with each patron saint. There are many more charms, one with a date, another with a clover, one with a bird.

"But I'm Jewish."

"Oh, they don't care." Wren looks up at me. Her eyes don't seem blue so much as the absence of blue. Like the sky just before dawn. "You should ask the saints for help. And you should go to that third hospital."

— — —

Hôpital Saint-Louis turns out to be a four-hundred-year-old hospital. Wren and I make our way into the modern wing that sits adjacent. I've sent the others on to Luxembourg Gardens without much of an argument. Sunlight filters in through the glass atrium, throwing prisms of light onto the floor.

It's quiet in the ER, only a few people sitting among rows of empty chairs. Wren goes right up to the two male nurses behind the desk and that weirdly mellifluous voice of hers breaks out in perfect French. I stand behind her, catching enough of what she says to get that she is telling my story, mesmerizing them with it. Even the people in the chairs are leaning in to hear her quiet voice. I have no idea how Wren even knows the story; I didn't tell her. Maybe she picked it up at breakfast or among the others. She finishes, and there is silence. The nurses stare at her, then look down and start typing.

"*How do you speak French so well?*" I whisper.

"I'm from Quebec."

"Why didn't you translate at the other hospital?"

"Because it wasn't the right one."

The nurses ask me his name. I say it. I spell it. I hear the tap of the computer keys as they input it.

"*Non,*" one nurse says. "*Pas ici.*" He shakes his head.

"*Attendez,*" the other says. *Wait.*

He types some more. He says a bunch of things to Wren, and I lose track, but then one phrase floats to the top: a date. The day after the day Willem and I spent together. The day we got separated.

My breath stops. He looks up, repeats the date to me.

"Yes," I say. That would've been when he was here. "*Oui.*"

The nurse says something and something else I don't understand. I turn to Wren. "Can they tell us how to find him?"

Wren asks a question, then translates back. "The records are sealed."

"But they don't have to give us anything written. They must have something on him."

"They say it's all in the billing department now. They don't keep much here."

"There has to be something. Now's the time to ask Saint Jude for help."

Wren fingers the charm on her bracelet. A pair of doctors in scrubs and lab coats come through the double doors, coffee cups in hand. Wren and I look at each other, Saint Jude apparently deciding to bestow twin inspiration.

"Can I speak to a doctor?" I ask the nurses in my horrible French. "Maybe the . . ." I turn to Wren. "How do you say 'attending physician' in French? Or the doctor who treated Willem?"

The nurse must understand some English because he rubs his chin and goes back to the computer. "Ahh, Dr. Robinet," he says, and picks up a phone. A few minutes later, a pair of double doors swing open, and it's like this time Saint Jude decided to send us a bonus, because the doctor is TV-handsome: curly salt-and-pepper hair, a face that's both delicate and rugged. Wren starts to explain the situation, but then I realize that, lost cause or not, I have to make my own case. In the most labored French imaginable, I attempt to explain: *Friend hurt. At this hospital. Lost friend. Need to find.* I'm frazzled, and with my bare-basics phrases, I must sound like a cavewoman.

Dr. Robinet looks at me for a while. Then he beckons for us to follow him through the double doors into an empty examination room, where he gestures for us to sit on the table while he settles on a rolling stool.

"I understand your dilemma," he replies in perfect British-accented English. "But we can't just give out files about a patient." He turns to look directly at me. His eyes are bright green, both sharp and kind. "I understand you've come all the way from America, but I am sorry."

"Can you at least *tell* me what happened to him? Without actually looking into his chart? Would that be breaking protocol?"

Dr. Robinet smiles patiently. "I see dozens of patients a day. And this was, you say, a year ago?"

I nod. "Yes." I bury my head in my hands. The folly of it hits me anew. One day. One year.

"Perhaps if you described him." Dr. Robinet feeds me some rope.

I snatch it up. "He was Dutch. Very tall, six foot three—it's one point nine in metric. Seventy-five kilos. He had very light hair, almost like straw, but very dark eyes, almost like coals. He was skinny. His fingers were long. He had a scar, like a zigzag, right on the top of his foot." As I continue to describe him, details I thought I'd forgotten come back to me, and an image of him emerges.

But Dr. Robinet can't see it. He looks puzzled, and I realize that from his point of view, I've described a tall blond guy, one person among thousands.

"Perhaps if you had a photograph?"

I feel as if the image I've created of Willem is alive in the room. He'd been right about not needing a camera to record the important things. He'd been there inside me all this time.

"I don't," I say. "Oh, but he had stitches. And a black eye."

"That describes a majority of the people we treat," Dr. Robinet says. "I am very sorry." He stands up off the stool; something clinks to the ground. Wren retrieves a euro coin off the floor and starts to hand it back to him.

"Wait! He did this thing with coins," I say. "He could balance a coin along his knuckles. Like this. May I?" I reach out for the euro and show how he flipped a coin across his knuckles.

I hand Dr. Robinet back his euro, and he holds it in his hand, examining it as if it were a rare coin. Then he flips it up in the air and catches it. "*Commotion cérébrale!*" he says.

"What?"

"Concussion!" Wren translates.

"Concussion?"

He holds up his index finger and turns it around slowly, like he's spooling information from a deep well. "He had a concussion. And if I recall, a facial laceration. We wanted him to stay for observation—concussions can be serious—and we wanted to report it to the police because he'd been assaulted."

"*Assaulted?* Why? By whom?"

"We don't know. It is customary to file a police report, but he refused. He was very agitated. I remember now! He wouldn't stay beyond a few hours. He wanted to leave straight away, but we insisted he stay for a CT scan. But as soon as we stitched him up and saw there was no cerebral bleeding, he insisted he had to go. He said it was very important. Someone he was going to lose." He turns to me, his eyes huge now. "*You?*"

"You," Wren says.

"Me," I say. Black spots dance in my vision, and my head feels liquid.

"I think she's going to faint," Wren says.

"Put your head between your legs," Dr. Robinet advises. He calls out into the hall, and a nurse brings me a glass of water. I drink it. The world stops spinning. Slowly, I sit back up. Dr. Robinet is looking at me now, and it's like the shade of professionalism has dropped.

"But this was a year ago," he says in a blanket-soft voice. "You lost each other a year ago?"

I nod.

"And you've been looking all this time?"

I nod again. In some way, I have.

"And do you think he's been looking for you?"

"I don't know." And I don't. Just because he tried to find me a year ago doesn't mean he wants to find me now. Or wants me to find him.

"But you *must* know," he replies. And for a minute I think he's reprimanding me that I ought to know, but then he picks up the phone and makes a call. When he's done, he turns to me. "You must know," he repeats. "Go to window two in the billing office now. They cannot release his chart, but I have instructed them to release his address."

"They have it? They have his address?"

"They have *an* address. Go collect it now. And then find him." He looks at me again. "No matter what, you must know."

— — —

I walk out of the hospital, past where the cancer patients are taking their chemotherapy treatments in the late afternoon sun. The printout with Willem's address is clenched in my fist. I haven't looked at it yet. I tell Wren that I need a moment alone and make my way toward the old hospital walls.

I sit down on a bench alongside the quadrangle of grass, between the old brick buildings. Bees dance between the flower bushes, and children play—there's so much life in these old hospital walls. I look at the paper in my hand. It could have any address. He could be anywhere in the world. How far am I willing to take this?

I think of Willem, beaten—*beaten!*—and still trying to find me. I take a deep breath. The smell of fresh-cut grass mingles with pollen and the fumes from trucks idling on the street. I look at the birthmark on my wrist.

I open the paper, not sure where I'm going next, only sure that I'm going.

Thirty-four

*M*y guidebook has all of two pages on Utrecht, so I expect it to be tiny or ugly or industrial, but it turns out to be a gorgeous, twisting medieval city full of gabled row houses and canals with houseboats, and tiny little alley streets that look like they might house humans or might house dolls. There aren't many youth hostels, but when I turn up at the only one I can afford, I learn that before it was a hostel, it was a squat. And I get that sense, almost like a radar communicating from some secret part of the world just to me: *Yes, this is where you're meant to be.*

The guys at the youth hostel are friendly and helpful and speak perfect English, just like Willem did. One of them even looks like him—that same angular face, those puffy red lips. I actually ask him if he knows Willem; he doesn't and when I explain that he looks like someone I'm looking for, he laughs and says he and half of Holland. He gives me a map of Utrecht and shows me how to get to the address the hospital gave me, a few kilometers from here, and suggests I rent a bike.

I opt for the bus. The house is out of the center, in an area full of record stores, ethnic restaurants with meat turning on spits, and graffiti. After a couple of wrong turns, I find the street, opposite some railroad tracks, on which sits an abandoned freight car, almost completely graffitied over. Right across the street is a skinny town house, which according to my printout, is the last known address of Willem de Ruiter.

I have to push my way past six bikes locked to the front rail to get to the door, which is painted electric blue. I hesitate before pressing the doorbell, which looks like an eyeball. I feel strangely calm as I press. I hear the ring. Then the heavy clump of feet. I've only known Willem for a day, but I recognize that those are not his footsteps. His would be lighter, somehow. A pretty, tall girl with a long brown braid opens the door.

"Hi. Do you speak English?" I ask.

"Yes, of course," she answers.

"I'm looking for Willem de Ruiter. I'm told he lives here." I hold up the piece of paper as if in proof.

Somehow I knew he wasn't here. Maybe because I wasn't nervous enough. So when her expression doesn't register, I'm not all that surprised. "I don't know him. I'm just renting here for the summer," she says. "I'm sorry." She starts to close the door.

By now, I've learned *no* or *sorry* or *I can't help you*—these are opening offers. "Is there someone else here who might know him?"

"Saskia," she calls. From the top of a stairway so narrow it looks like a ladder, a girl appears. She climbs down. She has blond hair and rosy cheeks and blue eyes, and there's something vaguely farm-fresh about her, as though she just this minute finished riding a horse or plowing a field, even though her hair is cut in spikes and she's dressed in a woven black sweater that is anything but traditional.

Once again I explain that I'm looking for Willem de Ruiter. Then, even though she doesn't know me, Saskia invites me in and offers me a cup of coffee or tea.

The three of us sit down at a messy wooden table, piled high with stacks of magazines and envelopes. There are clothes strewn everywhere. It's clear a lot of people live here. But apparently not Willem.

"He never really lived here," Saskia explains after she serves me tea and chocolates.

"But you know him?" I ask.

"I've met him a few times. I was friends with Lien, who was the girlfriend of one of Robert-Jan's friends. But I don't really know Willem. Like Anamiek, I just moved in over the summer."

"Do you know why he would use this as his address?"

"Probably because of Robert-Jan," Saskia says.

"Who's Robert-Jan?"

"He goes to the University of Utrecht, same as me. He used to live here," Saskia explains. "But he moved out. I took over his room."

"Of course you did," I mutter to myself.

"In student houses, people come and go. But Robert-Jan will be back to Utrecht. Not here but to a new flat. Unfortunately, I don't know where that will be. I just took over his room." She shrugs as if to say, that's all.

I drum my fingers on the old wooden table. I look at the pile of mail. "Do you think maybe I could look through the mail? See if there's anything with a clue?"

"Go ahead," Saskia says.

I go through the piles. They are mostly bills and magazines and catalogs, addressed to various people who live or have lived at this address. I count at least a half dozen names, including Robert-Jan. But Willem doesn't have a single piece of mail.

"Did Willem *ever* get mail here?"

"There used to be some," Saskia replies. "But someone organized the mail a few days ago, so maybe they threw his away. Like I said, he hasn't been around in months."

"Wait," Anamiek says. "I think I saw some new mail with his name on it. It's still in the box by the door."

She returns with an envelope. This one isn't junk mail. It's a letter, with the address handwritten. The stamps are Dutch. I want to find him, but not enough to open his personal correspondence. I put the envelope down on the piles, but then I double-take. Because the return address in the upper left-hand corner, written in a swirling unfamiliar script, is mine.

I take the envelope and hold it up to the lamp. There's another envelope inside. I open the outer envelope and out of that spills my letter, the one I sent to Guerrilla Will in England, looking for Willem. From the looks of the stamps and crossed-out addresses and tape on the envelope, it's been forwarded a few times. I open up the original letter to see if anyone has added anything to it, but they haven't. It's just been read and passed on.

Still, I feel overjoyed somehow. All this time, my scrappy

little letter has been trying to find him too. I want to kiss it for its tenacity.

I show the letter to Saskia and Anamiek. They read it and look at me confused. "I wrote this letter," I say. "Five months ago. When I first tried to find him. I sent it to an address in England, and somehow it found its way here. Same as me." As I say it, I get that sense again. I'm on the right path. My letter and I landed in the same place, even if it's the wrong place.

Saskia and Anamiek look at each other.

"We will make some calls," Saskia says. "We can certainly help you find Robert-Jan."

The girls disappear up the stairs. I hear a computer chime on. I hear the sounds of one-sided conversations, Saskia on the phone. About twenty minutes later, they come back down. "It's August, so almost everyone is away, but I am sure I can get you contact information for Robert-Jan in a day or two."

"Thank you," I say.

Her eyes flicker up. I don't like the way they look at me. "Though I might have found a faster way to find Willem."

"Really? What?"

She hesitates. "His girlfriend."

Thirty-five

Ana Lucia Aureliano. That's her name. Willem's girlfriend. She goes to some honors college connected to the University of Utrecht.

In all the time I've been looking, I never dreamed of getting this far. So I didn't let myself imagine actually finding him. And while I have imagined him having *lots* of girls, I hadn't thought of him having just one. Which, in retrospect, seems awfully stupid.

It's not like I'm here to get back together. It's not like there's a together to get back to. But if I came this close, only to leave, I think I'd regret it for the rest of my life.

Ironically, it's Céline's words that finally convince me to go find the girlfriend: *You will need to be brave.*

University College's campus is small and self-contained, unlike the University of Utrecht, which sprawls through the city center, Saskia explained. It's on the outskirts of town, and as I ride out there on a pink bike that Saskia insisted I borrow, I practice what I'm going to say if I find her. Or find him.

The school has very few students, and they all live on campus, and it's also an international school, drawing students from all over the world, with all the classes taught in English. Which means it only takes asking two people about Ana Lucia before I'm given directions to her dorm.

A dorm that seems less like a college residence than an IKEA showroom. I peer inside the sliding-glass door; it's all sleek wood and modern furniture, a million miles away from the industrial blah of the room I shared with Kali. The lights are out, and when I knock, no one answers. There's a little cement landing outside the door that has some embroidered cushions, so I sit down and wait.

I must have dozed off because I wake up falling backward. Someone has opened the door behind me. I look up. The girl—Ana Lucia, I assume—is beautiful, with long wavy brown hair and rosebud lips, accentuated with red lipstick. Between her and Céline, I should feel flattered to be in such company, but that's not what I'm feeling at the moment.

"Can I help you?" she asks, hovering over me, eyeing me as you might eye a vagrant you caught sleeping on your stoop.

The sun has come out from behind the clouds and it reflects off the glass window, creating a glare. I shield my eyes with my hands and heave myself up. "I'm sorry. I must've fallen asleep. I'm looking for Ana Lucia Aureliano."

"I'm Ana Lucia," she says, emphasizing the correct pronunciation with the strength of her Spanish lisp: *Ana Lu-thee-uh*. She squints her eyes, studying me. "Have we met before?"

"Oh, no. I'm Allyson Healey. I'm . . . I'm sorry. This is weird. I'm from America, and I'm trying to find someone."

"Is this your first term here? There is an online student directory."

"What? Oh, no. I don't go here. I go to school in Boston."

"Who do you search for?"

I almost don't want to say his name. I could make up a name and then she'd be none the wiser. I wouldn't have to hear her ask in that adorable accent of hers why I want to know where her boyfriend is. But then I would go home, and I'd have come this far and would never know. So I say it.

"Willem de Ruiter."

She looks at me for a long moment and then her pretty face puckers, her cosmetic-ad lips part. And then out of those perfect lips comes a spew of what I assume is invective. I can't be sure. It's in Spanish. But she's waving her arms and talking a mile a minute, and her face has gone red. *Vate! Déjame, puta!* And then she picks me up by my shoulders and throws me off the stoop, like a bouncer ejecting a drunk. She throws my backpack after me, so that everything spills out. Then she slams the door shut, as much as you can slam a sliding-glass door. Locks it. And draws the shades.

I sit there agape for a moment. Then, in a daze, I start putting my things back in my bag. I examine my elbow, which has a scrape from where I landed, and my arm, which bears the half-moons of her nail marks.

"Are you okay?" I look up and see a pretty girl with dreadlocks who has bent down beside me and is handing me my sunglasses.

I nod.

"You don't need ice or anything? I have some in my room." She starts to walk back to her stoop.

I touch my head. There's a bump there too, but nothing serious. "I think I'm okay. Thanks."

She looks at me and shakes her head. "You were not, by any chance, asking about Willem?"

"You know him?" I ask. "You know Willem?" I come over to her stoop. There's a laptop and a textbook sitting there. It's a physics book. She has it open to the section on quantum entanglement.

"I've seen him around. This is only my second year, so I didn't know him when he went here. But only one person makes Ana Lucia crazy like that."

"Wait. *Here?* He went to college? Here?" I try to reconcile the Willem I met, the itinerant traveling actor, with an honors college student, and it hits me again how little I know this person.

"For one year. Before I got here. He studied economics, I think."

"So what happened?" I meant with the college, but she starts telling me about Ana Lucia. About how she and Willem got back together last year but then how she found out that he'd been cheating on her with some French girl the whole time. She's very casual about it, like none of it is all that surprising.

But my head is reeling. Willem went *here*. He studied *economics*. So it takes a minute to finally digest the last part. The cheating-on-Ana-Lucia-with-a-French-girl part.

"A French girl?" I repeat.

"Yes. Apparently, Willem was going to meet her for some secret tryst, in Spain, I think. Ana Lucia saw him shopping for flights on her computer, and thought he was planning to take her as a surprise because she has relatives there. So she canceled her vacation to Switzerland, and then told her family all about it, and they planned a big party, only to discover that the tickets were never for her. They were for the French girl. She freaked out, confronted him right in the middle of the campus—it was quite a scene. He hasn't been around since, obviously. Are you sure you don't need some ice for your head?"

I sink onto the stoop next to her. Céline? But she claimed she hadn't seen him since last year. But then she'd said a lot of things. Including that we were both just ports that Willem visited. Maybe there were a bunch of us out there. A French girl. Or two or three. A Spaniard. An American. A whole United Nations of girls waving from their ports. I think of Céline's parting words to me, and now they seem ominous.

I always knew that Willem was a player and that I was one of many. But now I also know that he didn't ditch me that day. He wrote me a note. He tried, however halfheartedly, to find me.

I think of what my mom said. About being grateful for what you have instead of yearning for what you think you want. Standing here, on the campus where he once walked, I think I finally get what she was talking about. I think I finally understand what it truly means to quit while you're ahead.

Thirty-six

*F*orward momentum. That's my new motto. No regrets.
And no going back.

I cancel the Paris–London portion of my flight home so I
can fly home straight from London. I don't want to go back
to Paris. I want to go somewhere else. I have five more days
in Europe, and there are all these low-cost airlines. I could go
to Ireland. Or Romania. I could take a train to Nice and hook
up with the Oz crew. I could go anywhere.

But to get to any of those places, I have to go to Amsterdam. So that's where I'm going first. On the pink bike.

When I went to deliver the bike to Saskia, along with a
box of chocolates to say thank you, I told her that I didn't
need her to find me Robert-Jan's contact information.

"You found what you needed?" she asked.

"Yes and no."

She seemed to understand. She took the chocolates but

told me to keep the bike. It didn't belong to anyone, and I'd need it in Amsterdam, and I could take it with me on the train or pass it along to someone else.

"The pink White Bicycle," I said.

She smiled. "You know about the White Bicycle?"

I nodded.

"I wish it still existed."

I thought about my travels, about all the things that people had passed on to me: friendship, help, ideas, encouragement, macarons. "I think it still does," I told her.

Anamiek has written me instructions on biking from Utrecht to Amsterdam. It's only twenty-five miles, and there are bike paths the whole, flat way. Once I get to the eastern end of the city, I'll hook up with the tram line nine, and I can just follow that all the way to Centraal Station, which is where most of the budget youth hostels are.

Once out of Utrecht, the landscape turns industrial and then to farms. Cows lolling in green fields, big stone windmills—I even catch a farmer in clogs. But it doesn't take long for the bucolic to meld with office parks and then I'm on the outskirts of Amsterdam, going past a huge stadium that says Ajax and then the bike path dumps me onto the street and things get a little confusing. I hear the *bring-bring* of a tram, and it's the number nine, just as Anamiek promised. I follow it up the long stretches past the Oosterpark and what I assume is the zoo—a flock of pink flamingos in the middle of the city—but then things get even more confusing at an intersection by a big flea market and I lose the tram. Behind me, motos are beeping, and the traffic of bicycles seems twice that of cars, and I keep trying to find the tram, but the canals all seem to go in circles, each one looking like the last, with tall stone banks and every kind of boat—from houseboat to rowboat to glass-domed tour boat—on its brackish waters. I pass by improbably skinny gabled row houses and cozy little cafés, doors flung open to reveal walls a hundred years' worth of brown. I turn right and wind up at a flower market, the colorful blooms popping in the gray morning.

I pull out my map and turn it around. This whole city seems to turn in circles, and the names of the streets read like all the letters in the alphabet got into a car accident: Oudezijds Voorburgwal. Nieuwebrugsteeg. Completely lost, I pedal up next to a tall guy in a leather jacket who's strapping a blond toddler into a bike seat. When I see his face, I do another double take because he's another, albeit older, Willem clone.

I ask him for directions, and he has me follow him to Dam Square and from there points me around the dizzying traffic circle to the Warmoesstraat. I pedal up a street full of sex shops, brazen with their lurid window displays. At the end of the block is one of the city's cheaper youth hostels.

The lobby is boisterous with activity: people are playing pool and Ping-Pong, and there's a card game going, and everyone seems to have a beer in hand, even though it's barely lunchtime. I ask for a dormitory room, and wordlessly, the dark-eyed girl at the desk takes my passport info and money. Upstairs in my room, in spite of the NO DRUG USE IN THE DORMS sign, the air is thick with hash smoke, and a bleary-eyed guy is smoking something through a tube on a piece of tinfoil, which I'm pretty sure is neither hash nor legal. I lock my backpack in the locker and head back downstairs and out onto the street to a crowded Internet café.

I pay for a half hour and check out the budget airline sites. It's Thursday now. I fly home out of London on Monday. There's a flight to Lisbon for forty-six euros. One to Milan, and one to somewhere in Croatia! I Google Croatia and look at pictures of rocky beaches and old lighthouses. There are even cheap hotels in the lighthouses. I could stay in a lighthouse. I could do anything!

I know almost nothing about Croatia, so I decide to go there. I pull out my debit card to pay for the ticket, but I notice a new email has popped up in the other window I have open. I toggle over. It's from Wren. The subject line reads WHERE ARE YOU?

I quickly write back that I'm in Amsterdam. When I said good-bye to Wren and the Oz gang in Paris last week, she was planning on catching a train to Madrid, and Kelly and the crew were heading to Nice, and they were talking about maybe meeting up in Barcelona, so I'm a little surprised when, thirty seconds later, I get an email back from her that reads NO WAY. ME TOO!!!! The message has her cell number.

I'm grinning as I call her. "I knew you were here," she says. "I could feel it! Where are you?"

"At an Internet café on the Warmoesstraat. Where are you? I thought you were going to Spain!"

"I changed my plans. Winston, how far is Warmoesstraat?" she calls. "Winston's the cute guy who works here," she whispers to me. I hear a male voice in the background. Then Wren squeals. "We're, like, five minutes from each other. Meet me at Dam Square, in front of the white tower thing that looks like a penis."

I close the browser window, and ten minutes later, I'm hugging Wren like she's a long-lost relative.

"Boy, that Saint Anthony works fast," she says.

"I'll say!"

"So what happened?"

I give her the quick rundown about finding Ana Lucia, almost finding Willem, and deciding not to find him. "So now I'm going to Croatia."

She looks disappointed. "You are. When?"

"I was going to fly out tomorrow morning. I was just booking my ticket when you called."

"Oh, stay a few more days. We can explore together. We can rent bikes. Or rent one bike and have the other ride side-saddle like the Dutch girls do."

"I already *have* a bike," I say. "It's pink."

"Does it have a rack on the back where I can sit?"

Her grin is too infectious to resist. "It does."

"Oh. You have to stay. I'm at a hostel up near the Jordaan. My room is the size of a bathtub, but it's sweet and the bed's a double. Come share with me."

I look up. It is threatening rain again, and it's freezing for August, and the web said Croatia was mid-eighties and sunny. But Wren is here, and what are the chances of that? She believes in saints. I believe in accidents. I think we basically believe in the same thing.

We get my stuff out of my room at the hostel, where that one guy is now passed out, and move it to her hostel. It's much cozier than mine, especially since tall-dark-and-grinning Winston is there checking in on us. Upstairs, her bed is covered with guidebooks, not just from Europe but from all over the world.

"What's all this?"

"Winston loaned them to me. They're for my bucket list."

"Bucket list?"

"All the things I want to do before I die."

That curious cryptic thing Wren said when we first met in Paris comes back to me: *I know hospitals.* I've only known Wren a day and a half, but that's enough for the thought of losing her to be inconceivable. She must see something on my face, because she gently touches my arm. "Don't worry, I plan on living a long time."

"Why are you making a bucket list, then?"

"Because if you wait until you're really dying, it's too late."

I look at her. *I know hospitals.* The saints. "Who?" I ask softly.

"My sister, Francesca." She pulls out a piece of paper. It has a bunch of titles and locations, *La Belle Angèle* (Paris), *The Music Lesson* (London), *The Resurrection* (Madrid). It goes on like that.

"I don't get it." I hand back the paper.

"Francesca didn't have much of a chance to be good at a lot of things, but she was a totally dedicated artist. She'd be in the hospital, a chemo drip in one arm, a sketchpad in the other. She made hundreds of paintings and drawings, her legacy, she liked to say, because at least when she died, they'd live on—if only in the attic."

"You never know," I say, thinking of those paintings and sculptures in the art squat that might one day be in the Louvre.

"Well, that's exactly it. She found a lot of comfort in the fact that artists like Van Gogh and Vermeer were obscure in life but famous in death. And she wanted to see their paintings in person, so the last time she was in remission, we made a pilgrimage to Toronto and New York to see a bunch of them. After that, she made a bigger list."

I glance at the list again. "So which painting is here? A Van Gogh?"

"There was a Van Gogh on her list. *The Starry Night*, which we saw together in New York, and she has some Vermeers on here, though the one she loved best is in London. But that's *her* list, which has been back-burnered since Paris."

"I don't understand."

"I love Francesca, and I *will* see those paintings for her, one day. But I've spent a lot of my life in her shadow. It had to be that way. But now she's gone—and it's like I'm still in her shadow, you know?"

Strangely, I sort of do. I nod.

"There was something about seeing you in Paris. You're just this normal girl who's doing something kind of crazy. It inspired me. I changed my plans. And now I've started to wonder if meeting you isn't the whole reason I'm on this trip. That maybe Francesca, the saints, they wanted us to meet."

I get a chill from that. "You really think so?"

"I think I do. Don't worry, I won't tell my parents you're the reason I'm coming home a month later. They're a tad upset."

I laugh. I understand that too. "So what's on your list?"

"It's far less noble than Francesca's." She reaches into her travel journal and pulls out a creased piece of paper. *Kiss a boy on top of the Eiffel Tower. Roll in a field of tulips. Swim with dolphins. See the northern lights. Climb a volcano. Sing in a rock band. Cobble my own boots. Cook a feast for 25 friends. Make 25 friends.* "It's a work in progress. I keep adding to it, and already I've had some hiccups. I came here for tulip fields, but they only bloom in the springtime. So now I'll have to figure something else out. Oh, well. I think I can catch the northern lights in this place called Bodø in Norway."

"Did you manage to kiss a boy on top of the Eiffel Tower?"

Her lips prick up into a slightly wicked pixie elf grin. "I did. I went up the morning you left. There was a group of Italians. They can be very obliging, those Italians." She lowers her voice to a whisper. "I didn't even get a name."

I whisper back, "Sometimes you don't need to."

Thirty-seven

*W*e go to a late lunch at an Indonesian restaurant that serves one of those massive *rijsttafel* meals, and we stuff ourselves silly, and as we're wobbling along on the bike, I get an idea. It's not quite the flower fields at Keukenhof, but maybe it'll do. I get us lost for about twenty minutes until I find the flower market I passed this morning. The vendors are closing up their stalls and leaving behind a good number of throwaways. Wren and I steal a bunch of them and lay them out on the crooked sidewalk above the canal bank. She rolls around in them, happy as can be. I laugh as I snap some pictures with her camera and with my phone and text them to my mom.

The vendors look at her with mild amusement, as if this type of thing happens at least twice a week. Then a big bearded guy wearing suspenders over his butte of a belly comes over with some wilting lavender. "She can have these too."

"Here, Wren." I throw the fragrant purple blooms her way.

"Thanks," I say to the guy. Then I explain to him about Wren and her bucket list and the big fields of tulips being out of season so we had to settle for this.

He looks at Wren, who's attempting to extract the petals and leaves from her sweater. He reaches into his pocket and pulls out a card. "Tulips in August is not so easy. But if you and your friend don't mind to wake up early, I can maybe get you a small field of them."

— — —

The next morning, Wren and I set our alarm for four, and fifteen minutes later, go downstairs to the deserted street to find Wolfgang waiting with his mini truck. Every warning I've ever had from my parents about not getting into cars with strangers comes to me, but I realize, as improbable as it is, Wolfgang isn't a stranger. We all three squeeze into the front seat as we trundle toward a greenhouse in Aalsmeer. Wren is practically bouncing with excitement, which seems unnatural for four fifteen in the morning, and she hasn't even had any coffee yet, though Wolfgang has thoughtfully brought a thermos of it along with some hard-boiled eggs and bread.

We spend the drive listening to cheesy europop and Wolfgang's tales of spending thirty years in the merchant marines before moving to the Jordaan neighborhood in Amsterdam. "I'm German by birth, but I'll be an Amsterdammer by death," he says with a big toothy grin.

By five o'clock, we pull up to Bioflor, which hardly looks like the pictures of Keukenhof Gardens, with its carpets of color, but instead looks like some kind of industrial farm. I look at Wren and shrug. Wolfgang pulls in and stops alongside a football-field-sized greenhouse with a row of solar panels on top. A rosy-faced guy named Jos greets us. And then he unlocks the door, and Wren and I gasp.

There are rows and rows of flowers in every color. Acres of them. We walk down the tiny paths in between the beds, the air thick with humidity and manure until Wolfgang points out a section of tulips in fuchsia, sunburst, and one explosive citrusy combo that looks like a blood orange. I walk away, leaving Wren to her flowers.

She just stands there for a while. Then I hear her call out: "This is *incredible*. Can you *see* this?" Wolfgang looks at me but I don't answer because I don't think it's us she's talking to.

Wren runs around this greenhouse, and another one full of fragrant freesia, and I snap a bunch of pictures. And then Wolfgang has to get back. We belt Abba songs all the way, Wolfgang saying Abba is Esperanto for happiness, and the United Nations should play their songs at general assemblies.

It's only when we get to a warehouse outside Amsterdam that I notice that the back of Wolfgang's truck is still empty. "Didn't you buy flowers for your stall?"

He shakes his head. "Oh, I don't buy flowers directly from the farms. I buy at auction via wholesalers who deliver here." He points to where people are loading up their trucks with flowers.

"So you just went all the way out there for us?" I ask.

He gives me a little shrug, like, of course, why else? And at this point, I really have no right to be surprised by people's capacity for kindness and generosity, but still, I am. I'm floored every time.

"Can we take you out to dinner tonight?" I ask.

He shakes his head. "Not tonight. I'm going to see a play in Vondelpark." He looks at us. "You should come. It's in English."

"Why would a play in Holland be in English?" Wren asks.

"That's the difference between the Germans and the Dutch," Wolfgang replies. "The Germans translate Shakespeare. The Dutch leave him in English."

"*Shakespeare?*" I ask, feeling every hair on my body rise. "Which play?"

And before Wolfgang finishes telling me the title, I just start laughing. Because it's simply not possible. It's less possible than finding that one needle in a needle factory. Less possible than finding a lone star in the universe. It's less possible than finding that one person in all the billions who you might love.

Because tonight, playing in Vondelpark, is *As You Like It*. And I know with a certainty I cannot explain but that I would stake my life on, that he will be in it.

Thirty-eight

*A*nd so, after a year, I find him as I first found him: In a park, in the sultry dusk, speaking the words of William Shakespeare.

Except tonight, after this year, everything is different. This is no Guerrilla Will. This is a real production, with a stage, with seats, with lights, with a crowd. A large crowd. Such that by the time we get there, we are shunted off to a low wall on the edge of the small amphitheater.

And this year, he is no longer in a supporting role. This year, he is a star. He is Orlando, as I knew he would be. He is the first actor to take the stage, and from that moment on, he owns it. He is riveting. Not just to me. To everyone. A hush falls over the crowd as soon as he delivers the first soliloquy and continues for the rest of the performance. The sky darkens, and the moths and mosquitoes dance in the spotlights, and Amsterdam's Vondelpark is transformed into the Forest of Arden, a magical place where that which was lost can be found.

As I watch him, it's as though it is only us two. Just Willem and me. Everything else disappears: The sound of bicycle bells and tram chimes disappears. The mosquitoes buzzing around the fountain in the pond disappear. The group of rowdy guys sitting next to us disappears. The other actors disappear. The last year disappears. All my doubts disappear. The feeling of being on the right path fills every part of me. I have found him. Here. As Orlando. Everything has led me to this.

His Orlando is different from the way we played it in class or from the way the actor in Boston played it. His is sexy and vulnerable, the yearning for Rosalind so palpable it becomes physical, a pheromone that wafts off him and drifts through the swirl of floodlights, where it lands on my damp and welcoming skin. I feel my lust, my yearning and, yes, my love, coming off me in pulses, swimming toward the stage, where I imagine them being fed to him, like lines.

He can't know I'm here. But as crazy as it sounds, I feel like he does. I sense he feels me somewhere in the words he speaks, the same way I felt him when I first spoke them in Professor Glenny's class.

I remember so many of Rosalind's lines, of Orlando's too, that I can mouth them along with the actors. It feels like a private call-and-response chorus between me and Willem.

> *The little strength that I have, I would it were*
> *with you.*
> *Fare you well: pray heaven I be deceived in you!*
> *Then love me, Rosalind.*

And wilt thou have me?
Are you not good?
I hope so.
Now tell me how long you would have her after
you have possessed her?
For ever and a day.

For ever and a day.

I hold Wren's hand in one of my hands and Wolfgang's with the other. We make a chain, us three. Standing there like that until the play is over. Until everyone gets their happy endings: Rosalind marries Orlando, and Celia marries Oliver, who reconciles with Orlando, and Phoebe marries Silvius, and the bad duke is redeemed, and the exiled duke is returned home.

After Rosalind gives her final soliloquy, it's over, and people are going crazy, just nuts, clapping and whistling, and I'm turning and throwing my arms around Wren and then Wolfgang, pressing my cheek against the broadcloth of his cotton shirt, inhaling the smoky tobacco scent mingled with flower nectar and dirt. And then someone is hugging Wren and me, the rowdy guys from next to us. "That's my best friend!" one of the guys shouts. He's got impish blue eyes, and he's a head shorter than the others, more Hobbit than Dutchman.

"Who?" Wren asks. She's now being passed around in hugs by the rowdy, and it appears, drunk, Dutch guys.

"Orlando!" the Hobbit answers.

"Oh," Wren says, her eyes so wide and pale they gleam like pearls. "*Oh,*" she says to me.

"You wouldn't be Robert-Jan, by any chance?" I ask.

The Hobbit looks surprised for a second. Then he just grins. "Broodje to my friends."

"Broodje," Wolfgang chuckles. He turns to me. "It's a kind of sandwich."

"Which Broodje loves to eat," one of his friends says, patting his belly.

Broodje/Robert-Jan pushes the hand away. "You should come to our party tonight. It's going to be the party to end all parties. He was fantastic, was he not?"

Wren and I both nod. Broodje/Robert-Jan goes on about how great Willem was and then his friend says something to him in Dutch, something, I think, about Willem.

"What did he say?" I whisper to Wolfgang.

"He said he hasn't seen him, Orlando, I think, so happy, since, I didn't hear it all, something about his father."

Wolfgang takes out a packet of tobacco from a leather pouch and begins to roll a cigarette. Without looking at me, he says in his rumbly voice, "I think the actors come out over there." He points to the little metal gate on the far side of the stage.

He lights his cigarette. His eyes flash. He points to the gate again.

My body feels like it's no longer solid matter. It is particle dust. It is pure electricity. It dances me across the theater, toward the side of the stage. There is a crowd of well-wishers awaiting the actors. People holding bouquets of flowers, bottles of champagne. The actress who played Celia comes out to whoops and hugs. Next comes Adam, then Rosalind, who gets a heap of bouquets. My heart starts to thunder. Could I have come this close only to miss him?

But then I hear him. He is, as always, laughing; this time at something the guy who played Jaques said. And then I see his hair, shorter than it was, his eyes, dark and light all at once, his face, a small scar on his cheek, which only makes him more strikingly handsome.

My breath catches in my throat. I'd thought I'd embellished him. But really, if anything, the opposite is true. I'd forgotten how truly beautiful he is. How intrinsically Willem.

Willem. His name forms in my throat.

"Willem!" His name rings out loud and clear.

But it's not my voice that said it.

I touch my fingers to my throat to be sure.

"Willem!"

I hear the voice again. And then I see the blur of movement. A young woman races out from the crowd. The flowers she is carrying drop to the ground as she hurls herself into his arms. And he takes her in. He lifts her off the ground, holds her tight. His arms clutch into her auburn hair, laughing at whatever it is she's whispering into his ear. They spin around, a tangle of happiness. Of love.

I stand there rooted, watching this very private public display. Finally, someone comes up to Willem and taps him on the shoulder, and the woman slides to the ground. She picks up the flowers—sunflowers, exactly what I would've chosen for him—and dusts them off. Willem slides an easy arm around her and kisses her hand. She snakes her arm around his waist. And I realize then that I wasn't wrong about the love wafting off him during the performance. I was just wrong about who it was for.

They walk off, so close I can feel the breeze as he passes by. We are so close, but he's looking at her, so he doesn't see me at all. They go off, hand in hand, toward a gazebo, away from the fray. I just stand there.

I feel a gentle tap on my shoulder. It's Wolfgang. He looks at me, tilts his head to the side. "Finished?" he asks.

I look back at Willem and the girl. Maybe this is the French girl. Or someone altogether new. They are sitting facing each other, knees touching, talking, holding hands. It's like the rest of the world doesn't exist. That's how it felt when I was with him last year. Maybe if an outsider saw us then, that's exactly how we would've looked. But now I'm the one who's the outsider. I look at them again. Even from here, I can tell she is someone special to him. Someone he loves.

I wait for the fist of devastation, the collapse of a year's worth of hopes, the roar of sadness. And I do feel it. The pain of losing him. Or the idea of him. But along with that pain is something else, something quiet at first, so I have to strain for it. But when I do, I hear the sound of a door quietly clicking shut. And then the most amazing thing happens: The night is calm, but I feel a rush of wind, as if a thousand other doors have just simultaneously flung open.

I give one last glance toward Willem. Then I turn to Wolfgang. "Finished," I say.

But I suspect the opposite is true. That really, I'm just beginning.

Thirty-nine

I wake up to bright blinking sunlight. I squint at the travel alarm. It's almost noon. In four hours, I'm leaving. Wren has decided to stay on a few more days. There's a bunch of weird museums she just found out about that she wants to see, one devoted to medieval torture, another to handbags, and Winston has told her that he knows someone who can teach her how to cobble shoes, which might keep her here another week. But I have three days left, and I've decided to go to Croatia.

I won't get there till tonight, and I'll have to leave first thing Monday morning to make my flight back home. So I'll have just one full day there. But I now know what can happen in just one day. Absolutely anything.

Wren thinks I'm making a mistake. She didn't see Willem with the redhead, and she keeps arguing that she could be anyone—his sister, for instance. I don't tell her that

Willem, like me, like Wren herself now, is an only child. All last night, she begged me to go to the party, to see how it played out. "I know where it is. Robert-Jan told me. It's on, oh, I can't remember the street name, but he said it means 'belt' in Dutch. Number one eighty-nine."

I'd held up my hand. "Stop! I don't want to go."

"But just imagine," she'd said. "What if you'd never met Willem before, and Broodje invited us to the party, and we went, and you two met there for the first time and fell in love? Maybe that's what happens."

It's a nice theory. And I can't help but wonder if that *would've* happened. Would we fall in love if we met today? Had I really fallen in love with him in the first place? Or was it just infatuation fueled by mystery?

But I'm also starting to wonder something else. If maybe the point of this crazy quest I'm on wasn't to help me find Willem. Maybe it was to help me find someone else entirely.

I'm getting dressed when Wren opens the door, clutching a paper bag. "Hi, sleepyhead. I made you some breakfast. Or rather Winston did. He said it's very Dutch."

I take the bag. "Thanks." I look at Wren, who's grinning like crazy. "Winston, huh?"

Now she's blushing. "He just got off work and he's going to take me for a bike ride and introduce me to his cobbler friend as soon as you leave," she says, her grin now threatening to split her face. "And tomorrow he says I have to go to an Ajax football game with him." She pauses to consider. "It wasn't on my list, but you never know."

"No, you don't. Well, I should go soon. Let you get to your, um, cobbling."

"But your flight's not for ages yet."

"That's okay. I want to leave enough time, and I hear the airport is amazing."

I pack up the rest of my things and go downstairs with Wren. Winston points me toward the train station.

"Are you sure you don't want me to come with you to the station or the airport?" Wren asks.

I shake my head. I want to see Wren ride away on the pink bike as if I'll see her again tomorrow. She hugs me tight and then kisses me three times like the Dutch do. *"Tot ziens,"* she calls. "It means 'see you later' in Dutch, because we aren't saying good-bye." I swallow the lump in my throat. And then Winston gets on his big black bike and Wren gets on the little pink bike, and they pedal away.

I hoist my backpack up and make the short walk to the train station. There are trains every fifteen minutes or so to Schiphol, and I buy a ticket and a cup of tea and go sit under the clattering destination board to eat my breakfast. When I see what's inside, I have to laugh. Because Winston has made me a *hagelslag* sandwich. For all our talk, I never did get to try this particular delicacy.

I take a bite. The *hagelslag* crunches, then melts into the butter and still-warm bread. And what's left over tastes just like him.

All at once, I finally understand what it means for time to be fluid. Because suddenly the entire last year flows before me, condensing and expanding, so that I'm here in Amsterdam eating *hagelslag,* and at the same time, I'm in Paris, his hand on my hip, and at the same time, I'm on that first train to London, watching the countryside whiz by, and at the same time, I'm in the line for *Hamlet*. I see Willem. At the canal basin, catching my eye. On the train, his jeans still unstained, me still unstained. On the train to Paris, his thousand shades of laughter.

The destination board shuffles, and I look up at it, and as I do, imagine a different version of time. One in which *Willem* quits while he's ahead. One in which he never makes that remark about my breakfast. One in which he just says good-bye on that platform in London instead of inviting me to Paris. Or one in which he never stops to talk to me in Stratford-upon-Avon.

And that's when I understand that I *have* been stained. Whether I'm still in love with him, whether he was *ever* in love with me, and no matter who he's in love with now, Willem changed my life. He showed me how to get lost, and then I showed myself how to get found.

Maybe accident isn't the right word after all. Maybe miracle is.

Or maybe it's not a miracle. Maybe this is just life. When you open yourself up to it. When you put yourself in the path of it. When you say yes.

How can I come this far and not tell him—he, who would understand it best—that by giving me that flyer, by inviting me to skip *Hamlet*, he helped me realize that it's not *to* be that matters, but *how* to be?

How can I come this far and not be brave?

"Excuse me," I say to a woman in a polka-dot dress and cowboy boots. "Is there a street in Amsterdam named after a belt?"

"Ceintuurbaan," she answers. "Tram line twenty-five. Right outside the station."

I race out of the train station and jump onto the tram, asking the driver where to get off for Ceintuurbaan number one eighty-nine. "Near Sarphatipark," he replies. "I'll show you."

Twenty minutes later, I get off at the park. Inside, there's a small playground with a large sandpit, and I go sit down under a tree to summon my bravery. A couple of children are putting the finishing touches on an elaborate sand castle, several feet high, with towers and turrets and moats.

I stand up and make my way to the building. I don't even know for sure that he lives here, except that the feeling of rightness, it has never been stronger. There are three bells. I ring the bottom one. An intercom squawks with a woman's voice.

"Hello," I call. Before I say anything else, the door clicks open.

I walk inside the dark, musty hallway. A door swings open, and my heart skips a beat, but it's not him. It's an older woman with a yappy dog at her heels.

"Willem?" I ask her. She points a thumb up and shuts her door.

I climb the steep stairs to the second floor. There are two other flats in the building, so this could be his, or the one upstairs. So I just stand there on the doorstep for a moment, listening for sounds inside. It is quiet, save for the faint strains of music. But my heart is beating fast and strong, like a radar pinging: *Yes, yes, yes.*

My hand shakes a little bit as I knock, and at first the sound is faint, as if I'm knocking on a hollowed-out log. But then I tighten my grip, and I knock again. I hear his footsteps. I remember the scar on his foot. Was it on the right foot or the left? The footsteps come closer. I feel my heart speed up, in double time to those footsteps.

And then the door swings open, and he's there.

Willem.

His tall body casts a shadow over me, just like it did that first day, that only other day, really, when we met. His eyes, those dark, dark eyes, hiding a spectrum of hidden things, they widen, and his mouth drops. I hear his gasp of breath, the shock of it all.

He just stands there, his body taking up the doorway, looking at me like I am a ghost, which I suppose I am. But if he knows anything at all about Shakespeare, it's that the ghosts always come haunting.

I look at him as the questions and answers collide all over his face. There is so much I want to tell him. Where do I even begin?

"Hello, Willem," I say. "My name is Allyson."

He says nothing in response. He just stays there for a minute, looking at me. And then he steps to the side, opens the door wider, wide enough for me to walk through.

And so I do.

ACKNOWLEDGMENTS

This book begins with Shakespeare, and so my thank-yous begin with Tamara Glenny, who, when I told her I was writing something with some Shakespeare in it, promptly wrote me up notes on plays to look at, got us tickets to a number of those plays—including that fateful production of *As You Like It*—and answered dozens of ridiculously obscure questions with her usual enthusiasm and good humor.

The book then moves on to France, and I would like to thank Céline Faure and Philippe Robinet, for helping me discover Allyson and Willem's Paris, and for not blinking when I asked for such translations as: "shut your piehole." Laurence Checler graciously helped with so many more of the translations in the book. Marie-Elisa Gramain helped me find the perfect French band name. Also thank you to Taly Meas for the hospital tour, Willy Levitanus, Patricia Roth, and Julie Roth for orchestrating it all.

We move on to Holland then, and to Heleen Buth and Emke Spauwen who gave me such a fantastic tour of Utrecht and provided me with so many details that sparked so much of Allyson's and Willem's stories. My brother-in-law, Robert Schamhart, helped me with many of the Dutch subtleties, and allowed me to steal a few key aspects of his identity, down to his nickname. *Hartelijk bedankt*!

Back stateside, my inimitable editor, Julie Strauss-Gabel, once again, helped me figure out the book I *meant* to write and remained a steady, optimistic force whenever I became discouraged that I'd ever actually write it. "I'm not worried about you," she frequently says, such reassuring words, when I'm in a tizzy. Thank you for not worrying—and for worrying. Thank you also to the other extraordinary member of Team Dutton: Liza Kaplan, as well as to Scottie Bowditch, Danielle Delaney, Eileen Kreit, Deborah Kaplan, Kristin Gilson, Rosanne Lauer, Elyse Marshall, Emily Romero, Don Weisberg; and the entire staff of Penguin Young Readers Group: the amazing sales and marketing team, the wonderful school and library department, the ever-brilliant online department, and all the fantastic field reps—who give so much heart to the authors they publish.

Sarah Burnes is my agent, my advocate, my reality check, my Mama Bear, and above all, my wise and generous friend. I feel thankful to have someone who understands all the sides of me—and by extension, my characters and books—in my corner. The powerhouse team of Logan Garrison, Rebecca Gardner, and Will Roberts have propelled my books to places I never dreamed of. You couldn't imagine a nicer, smarter group of bulldogs!

I would like to thank Isabel Kyriacou for, among many other things, helping me curse more proficiently in Spanish. I would like to thank my YA cohorts, particularly Libba Bray and Stephanie Perkins, who provided the writerly equivalent of therapy: lots of listening, combined with the occasional, laser-beam insightful question or comment. (I believe they accept most insurance.) Thank you also to Nina LaCour, E. Lockhart, Sandy London, Margaret Stohl, Courtney Sheinmel, Robin Wasserman, and whoever else might've listened to me jabber about complicated plot threads. Thank you Onome Edodi-Disowe, Victoria Hill, and all the ladies of the BK/BNS crews, for taking hold of the reins so that I might let them go. Thank you to Veronica Brodsky, for helping me understand what this book is truly about. And to Rebecca Haworth for taking that first trip with me. We had our Melanie moments—and came out the other side. Thank you, Marjorie Ingall, for reading, hand-holding, and geeking out with me about Shakespeare.

Speaking of, I know he is long dead and there's no collecting royalty or praise from the grave, but I must thank Shakespeare anyway, for giving me the surprise of this book, and for providing me a play that keeps working on so many levels. Thank you Royal Shakespeare Company, for bringing As You Like It to New York City just as I was starting this book. Thank you Fiasco Theater Company for turning me onto Cymbeline—and for all your help with this book, and the next.

Thank you to my parents, for passing on their love of travel, for being proud when, the week after high-school graduation, I took off on a one-way ticket to Europe to attend "The University of Life," and for teaching me to be self-sufficient enough to travel on my own, and on my own dime, for the next several years. Thank you to my siblings, Tamar and Greg, for being such cheerleaders and supporters of their little sister and for, each in their own way, showing me how to say yes. Thank you to Karen and Detta, Rebecca, Hannah, Liam, Lucy, and all of my extended brood.

Thank you to all the people I've met in my travels over the years—some of whom I kept in touch with, some of whom I put into this book, and some of whom have changed the trajectory of my life. Without you, I would not be here now, writing these words.

Thank you to my readers, for packing their mental suitcases and coming off on another trip with me. Without you, I would not be here now, writing these words.

Finally, thank you to Nick, Willa, and Denbele: You are the ones I travel with now. And how wild and wonderful the journey is.

JUST ONE **YEAR**

GAYLE FORMAN

JUST ONE **YEAR**

SPEAK
An imprint of Penguin Random House LLC
375 Hudson Street
New York, New York 10014

USA * Canada * UK * Ireland * Australia
New Zealand * India * South Africa * China

penguin.com
A Penguin Random House Company

First published in the United States of America by Dutton Books, 2013
Published by Speak, an imprint of Penguin Group (USA) LLC, 2014,
This omnibus edition published by Speak,
an imprint of Penguin Random House LLC, 2017

THE LIBRARY OF CONGRESS HAS CATALOGED THE DUTTON BOOKS EDITION AS FOLLOWS:
Forman, Gayle.
Just one year / by Gayle Forman.
pages cm
Sequel to: Just one day.
Summary: "After spending an amazing day and night with a nameless girl in Paris, Willem
embarks on his own transformative journey to find her once again"—Provided by the pub-
lisher.
ISBN 978-0-525-42592-2 (hardback)
[1. Voyages and travels—Fiction. 2. Self-actualization (Psychology)—Fiction. 3. Love—Fic-
tion.]
I. Title.
PZ7.F75876Jw 2013
[Fic]—dc23
2013022976

Speak ISBN 9780142422960
This omnibus edition ISBN 9780451478795

Designed by Danielle Delaney
Printed in the United States of America

For Marjorie, Tamara,

and Libba

Double, double, toil and trouble . . .

WHEN I WAS AT HOME, I WAS IN A BETTER PLACE:
BUT TRAVELLERS MUST BE CONTENT.

From William Shakespeare's *As You Like It*

PART ONE

One Year

One

AUGUST

Paris

---

*I*t's the dream I always have: I'm on a plane, high above the clouds. The plane starts to descend, and I have this sudden panic because I just know that I'm on the wrong plane, am traveling to the wrong place. It's never clear where I'm landing—in a war zone, in the midst of an epidemic, in the wrong century—only that it's somewhere I shouldn't be. Sometimes I try to ask the person next to me where we are going, but I can never quite see a face, can never quite hear an answer. I wake in a disoriented sweat to the sound of the landing gear dropping, to the echo of my heart beating. It usually takes me a few moments to find my bearings, to locate where it is I am—an apartment in Prague, a hostel in Cairo—but even once that's been established, the sense of being lost lingers.

I think I'm having the dream now. Just as always, I lift

the shade to peer at the clouds. I feel the hydraulic lurch of the engines, the thrust downward, the pressure in my ears, the ignition of panic. I turn to the faceless person next to me—only this time I get the feeling it's not a stranger. It's someone I know. Someone I'm traveling with. And that fills me with such intense relief. We can't *both* have gotten on the wrong plane.

"Do you know where we're going?" I ask. I lean closer. I'm just about there, just about to see a face, just about to get an answer, just about to find out where it is I'm going—

And then I hear sirens.

— — —

I first noticed the sirens in Dubrovnik. I was traveling with a guy I'd met in Albania, when we heard a siren go by. It sounded like the kind they have in American action movies, and the guy I was traveling with commented on how each country had its own siren sound. "It's helpful because if you forget where you are, you can always close your eyes, let the sirens tell you," he told me. I'd been gone a year by then, and it had taken me a few minutes to summon the sound of the sirens at home. They were musical almost, a down-up-down-up la, *la*, la, *la*, like someone absentmindedly, but cheerfully, humming.

That's not what *this* siren is. It is monotonous, a *nyeah-nyeah, nyeah-nyeah*, like the bleating of electric sheep. It doesn't become louder or fainter as it comes closer or gets farther away; it's just a wall of wailing. Much as I try, I cannot locate this siren, have no idea where I am.

I only know that I am not home.

I open my eyes. There is bright light everywhere, from over-head, but also from my own eyes: tiny pinprick explosions that hurt like hell. I close my eyes.

Kai. The guy I traveled with from Tirana to Dubrovnik was called Kai. We drank weak Croatian pilsner on the ram-parts of the city and then laughed as we pissed into the Adri-atic. His name was Kai. He was from Finland.

The sirens blare. I still don't know where I am.

The sirens stop. I hear a door opening, I feel water on my skin. A shifting of my body. I sense it is better to keep my eyes closed. None of this is anything I want to witness.

But then my eyes are forced open, and there's another light, harsh and painful, like the time I spent too long looking at a solar eclipse. Saba warned me not to, but some things are impossible to tear yourself away from. After, I had a head-ache for hours. Eclipse migraine. That's what they called it on the news. Lots of people got them from staring at the sun. I know that, too. But I still don't know where I am.

There are voices now, as if echoing out from a tunnel. I can hear them, but I cannot make out what they're saying.

"*Comment vous appelez-vous?*" someone asks in a lan-guage I know is not mine but that I somehow understand. *What is your name?*

"Can you tell us your name?" The question again in an-other language, also not my own.

"Willem de Ruiter." This time it's my voice. My name.

"Good." It is a man's voice. It switches back to the other

language. French. It says that I got my own name right, and I wonder how it is he knows this. For a second I think it is Bram speaking, but even as muddled as I am, I realize this is not possible. Bram never did learn French.

———

"Willem, we are going to sit you up now."

The back of my bed—*I think I'm on a bed*—tilts forward. I try to open my eyes again. Everything is blurry, but I can make out bright lights overhead, scuffed walls, a metal table.

"Willem, you are in the hospital," the man says.

Yes, I was just sussing that part out. It would also explain my shirt being covered in blood, if not the shirt itself, which is not mine. It is gray and says sos in red lettering. What does sos mean? Whose shirt is this? And whose blood is on it?

I look around. I see the man—a doctor?—in the lab coat, the nurse next to him, holding out an ice compress for me to take. I touch my cheek. The skin is hot and swollen. My finger comes away with more blood. That answers one question.

"You are in Paris," the doctor says. "Do you know where Paris is?"

I am eating tagine at a Moroccan restaurant in Montorgueil with Yael and Bram. I am passing the hat after a performance with the German acrobats in Montmartre. I am thrashing, sweaty, at a Mollier Than Molly show at Divan du Monde with Céline. And I'm running, running through the Barbès market, a girl's hand in mine.

Which girl?

"In France," I manage to answer. My tongue feels thick as a wool sock.

"Can you remember what happened?" the doctor asks.

I hear boots and taste blood. There is a pool of it in my mouth. I don't know what to do with it, so I swallow.

"It appears you were in a fight," the doctor continues. "You will need to make a report to the police. But first you will need sutures for your face, and we must take a scan of your head to make sure there is no subdural hematoma. Are you on holiday here?"

Black hair. Soft breath. A gnawing feeling that I've misplaced something valuable. I pat my pocket.

"My things?" I ask.

"They found your bag and its contents scattered at the scene. Your passport was still inside. So was your wallet."

He hands it to me. I look at the billfold. There are more than a hundred euros inside, though I seem to recall having a lot more. My identity card is missing.

"We also found this." He shows me a small black book. "There is still quite a bit of money in your wallet, no? It doesn't suggest a robbery, unless you fought off your attackers." He frowns, I assume at the apparent foolishness of this maneuver.

Did I do that? A low fog sits overhead, like the mist coming off the canals in the morning that I used to watch and will to burn off. I was always cold. Yael said it was because though I looked Dutch, her Mediterranean blood was swimming in me. I remember that, remember the scratchy wool blanket I would wrap myself in to stay warm. And though

I now know where I am, I don't know why I'm here. I'm not supposed to be in Paris. I'm supposed to be in Holland. Maybe that explains that niggling feeling.

Burn off. Burn off, I will the fog. But it is as stubborn as the Dutch fog. Or maybe my will is as weak as the winter sun. Either way, it doesn't burn off.

"Do you know the date?" the doctor asks.

I try to think, but dates float by like leaves in a gutter. But this is nothing new. I know that I never know the date. I don't need to. I shake my head.

"Do you know what month it is?"

Augustus. Août. No, English. "August."

"Day of the week?"

Donderdag, something in my head says. Thursday. "Thursday?" I try.

"Friday," the doctor corrects, and the gnawing feeling grows stronger. Perhaps I am supposed to be somewhere on Friday.

The intercom buzzes. The doctor picks it up, talks for a minute, hangs up, turns to me. "Radiology will be here in thirty minutes." Then he begins talking to me about *commotions cérébrales* or concussions and temporary short-term memory loss and cats and scans and none of it is making a lot of sense.

"Is there someone we can call?" he asks. And I feel like there is, but for the life of me, I can't think who. Bram is gone and Saba is gone and Yael might as well be. Who else is there?

The nausea hits, fast, like a wave I had my back to. And then there's puke all over my bloodied shirt. The nurse is quick with the basin, but not quick enough. She gives me a towel to clean myself with. The doctor is saying something about nausea and concussions. There are tears in my eyes. I never did learn to throw up without crying.

The nurse mops my face with another towel. "Oh, I missed a spot," she says with a tender smile. "There, on your watch."

On my wrist is a watch, bright and gold. It's not mine. For the quickest moment, I see it on a girl's wrist. I travel up the hand to a slender arm, a strong shoulder, a swan's neck. When I get to the face, I expect it to be blank, like the faces in the dream. But it's not.

Black hair. Pale skin. Warm eyes.

I look at the watch again. The crystal is cracked but it's still ticking. It reads nine. I begin to suspect what it is I've forgotten.

I try to sit up. The world turns to soup.

The doctor pushes me back onto the bed, a hand on my shoulder. "You are agitated because you are confused. This is all temporary, but we will need to take the CT scan to make sure there is no bleeding on the brain. While we wait, we can attend to your facial lacerations. First I will give you something to make the area numb."

The nurse swabs off my cheek with something orange. "Do not worry. This won't stain."

It doesn't stain; it just stings.

——— ——— ———

"I think I should go now," I say when the sutures are done.

The doctor laughs. And for a second I see white skin

covered in white dust, but warmer underneath. A white room. A throbbing in my cheek.

"Someone is waiting for me." I don't know who, but I know it's true.

"Who is waiting for you?" the doctor asks.

"I don't remember," I admit.

"Mr. de Ruiter. You must have a CT scan. And, after, I would like to keep you for observation until your mental clarity returns. Until you know who it is who waits for you."

Neck. Skin. Lips. Her fragile-strong hand over my heart. I touch my hand to my chest, over the green scrub shirt the nurse gave me after they cut off my bloody shirt to check for broken ribs. And the name, it's almost right there.

Orderlies come to wheel me to a different floor. I'm loaded into a metal tube that clatters around my head. Maybe it's the noise, but inside the tube, the fog begins to burn off. But there is no sunshine behind it, only a dull, leaden sky as the fragments click together. "I need to go. Now!" I shout from the tube.

There's silence. Then the click of the intercom. "Please hold still," a disembodied voice orders in French.

—— —— ——

I am wheeled back downstairs to wait. It is past twelve o'clock.

I wait more. I remember hospitals, remember exactly why I hate them.

I wait more. I am adrenaline slammed into inertia: a fast car stuck in traffic. I take a coin out of my pocket and do the trick Saba taught me as a little boy. It works. I calm down, and when I do, more of the missing pieces slot into place. We came together to Paris. We *are* together in Paris. I feel her hand gentle on my side, as she rode on the back of the bicycle. I feel her not-so-gentle hand on my side, as we held each other tight. Last night. In a white room.

The white room. She is in the white room, waiting for me.

I look around. Hospital rooms are never white like people believe. They are beige, taupe, mauve: neutral tones meant to soothe heartbreak. What I wouldn't give to be in an actual white room right now.

— — —

Later, the doctor comes back in. He is smiling. "Good news! There is no subdural bleeding. Only a concussion. How is your memory?"

"Better."

"Good. We will wait for the police. They will take your statement and then I can release you to your friend. But you must take it very easy. I will give you an instruction sheet for care, but it is in French. Perhaps someone can translate it, or we can find you one in English or Dutch online."

"*Ce ne sera pas nécessaire,*" I say.

"Ahh, you speak French?" he asks in French.

I nod. "It came back to me."

"Good. Everything else will, too."

"So I can go?"

"Someone must come for you! And you have to make a report to the police."

Police. It will be hours. And I have nothing to tell them, really. I take the coin back out and play it across my knuckle. "No police!"

The doctor follows the coin as it flips across my hand. "Do you have problems with the police?" he asks.

"No. It's not that. I have to find someone," I say. The coin clatters to the floor.

The doctor picks it up and hands it to me. "Find who?"

Perhaps it's the casual way he asked; my bruised brain doesn't have time to scramble it before spitting it out. Or perhaps the fog is lifting now, and leaving a terrific headache behind. But there it is, a name, on my lips, like I say it all the time.

"*Lulu*."

"Ahh, Lulu. *Très bien*!" The doctor claps his hands together. "Let us call this Lulu. She can come get you. Or we can bring her to you."

It is too much to explain that I don't know where Lulu is. Only that she's in the white room and she's waiting for me and she's been waiting for a long time. And I have this terrible feeling, and it's not just because I'm in a hospital where things are routinely lost, but because of something else.

"I have to go," I insist. "If I don't go now, it could be too late."

The doctor looks at the clock on the wall. "It is not yet two o'clock. Not late at all."

"It might be too late for me." *Might be*. As if whatever is going to happen hasn't already happened.

The doctor looks at me for a long minute. Then he shakes

his head. "It is better to wait. A few more hours, your memory will return, and you will find her."

"I don't have a few hours!"

I wonder if he can keep me here against my will. I wonder if at this moment I even have a will. But something pulls me forward, through the mist and the pain. "I have to go," I insist. "Now."

The doctor looks at me and sighs. "*D'accord.*" He hands me a sheaf of papers, tells me I am to rest for the next two days, clean my wound every day, the sutures will dissolve. Then he hands me a small card. "This is the police inspector. I will tell him to expect your call tomorrow."

I nod.

"You have somewhere to go?" he asks.

Céline's club. I recite the address. The Métro stop. These I remember easily. These I can find.

"Okay," the doctor says. "Go to the billing office to check out, and then you may go."

"Thank you."

He touches me on the shoulder, reminds me to take it easy. "I am sorry Paris brought you such misfortune."

I turn to face him. He's wearing a name tag and the blurriness in my vision has subsided so I can focus on it. DOCTEUR ROBINET, it reads. And while my vision is okay, the day is still muddy, but I get this feeling about it. A hazy feeling of something—not quite happiness, but solidness, stepping on earth after being at sea for too long—fills me up. It tells me that whoever this Lulu is, something happened between us in Paris, something that was the opposite of misfortune.

TWO

At the billing office, I fill out a few thousand forms. There are problems when they ask for an address. I don't have one. I haven't for such a long time. But they won't let me leave until I supply one. At first, I think to give them Marjolein, my family's attorney. She's who Yael has deal with all her important mail, and whom, I realize too late, I was supposed to meet with today—or was it tomorrow? Or yesterday now?—in Amsterdam. But if a hospital bill goes to Marjolein, then all of this goes straight back to Yael, and I don't want to explain it to her. I don't want to *not* explain it, either, in the more likely event she never asks about it.

"Can I give you a friend's address?" I ask the clerk.

"I don't care if you give me the Queen of England's address so long as we have somewhere to mail the bill," she says.

I can give them Broodje's address in Utrecht. "One moment," I say.

"Take your time, *mon chéri*."

I lean on the counter and rifle through my address book, flipping through the last year of accumulated acquaintances. There are countless names of people I don't remember, names I didn't remember even before I got this nasty bump on my head. There's a message to *Remember the caves in Matala*. I do remember the caves, and the girl who wrote the message, but not why I'm supposed to remember them.

I find Robert-Jan's address right at the front. I read it to the clerk, and as I close the book it falls open to one of the last pages. There's all this unfamiliar writing, and at first I think my eyesight must really be messed up, but then I realize it's just that the words are not English or Dutch but Chinese.

And for a second, I'm not here in this hospital, but I'm on a boat, with her, and she's writing in my notebook. I remember. She spoke Chinese. She showed it to me. I turn the page, and there's this.

There's no translation next to it, but I somehow know what that character means.

Double happiness.

I see the character here in the book. And I see it larger, on a sign. Double happiness. Is that where she is?

"Is there maybe a Chinese restaurant or store nearby?" I ask the clerk.

She scratches her hair with a pencil and consults a colleague. They start to argue about the best place to eat.

"No," I explain. "Not to eat. I'm looking for this." I show them the character in my book.

They look at each other and shrug.

"A Chinatown?" I ask.

"In the thirteenth arrondissement," one replies.

"Where's that?"

"Left Bank."

"Would an ambulance have brought me here from there?" I ask.

"No, of course not," she answers.

"There's a smaller one in Belleville," the other clerk offers.

"It is a few kilometers from here, not far," the first clerk explains and tells me how to get to the Métro.

I put on my rucksack, and leave.

I don't get far. My rucksack feels like it's full of wet cement. When I left Holland two years ago, I carried a big pack with many more things. But then it got stolen and I never replaced it, instead making do with a smaller bag. Over time, the rucksacks kept getting smaller and smaller, because there's so little a person actually needs. These days, all I keep is a few changes of clothes, some books, some toiletries, but now even that feels like too much. When I go down the stairs into the Métro, the bag bounces with each step, and pain knifes deep into me.

"Bruised, not broken," Dr. Robinet told me before I left. I thought he was talking about my spirit, but he'd been referring to my ribs.

On the Métro platform, I pull everything out of the rucksack except for my passport, wallet, address book, and toothbrush. When the train comes, I leave the rest on the platform. I'm lighter now, but it's not any easier.

The Belleville Chinatown begins right after the Métro stop. I try to match the signs from her character in my book, but there are so many signs and the neon lettering looks nothing like those soft ink lines she wrote. I ask around for double happiness. I have no idea if I'm asking for a place, a person, a food, a state of mind. The Chinese people look frightened of me and no one answers, and I begin to wonder if maybe I'm not really speaking French, only imagining I do. Finally one of them, an old man with grizzled hands clutching an ornate cane, stares at me and then says, "You are a long way from double happiness."

I am about to ask what he means, where it is, but then I catch a glimpse of my reflection in a shop window, my eye swelling purple, the bandage on my face seeping blood. I understand he isn't talking about a place.

But then I do glimpse familiar letters. Not the double happiness character, but the SOS letters from the mysterious T-shirt I was wearing earlier at the hospital. I see it now on another T-shirt, worn by a guy my age with jagged hair and an armful of metal cuffs. Maybe he's connected to double happiness somehow.

It winds me to catch up with him, a half block away. When I tap him on the shoulder, he turns around and steps back. I point to his shirt. I'm about to ask him what it means when he asks me in French, "What happened to you?"

"Skinheads," I reply in English. It's the same word all over. I explain in French that I was wearing a T-shirt like his before.

"Ahh," he says, nodding. "The racists hate Sous ou Sur. They are very anti-fascist."

I nod, though I remember now why they beat me up, and I'm pretty certain it had little to do with my T-shirt.

"Can you help me?" I ask.

"I think you need a doctor, my friend."

I shake my head. That's not what I need.

"What do you want?" the guy asks me.

"I'm looking for a place around here with a sign like this."

"What is it?"

"Double happiness."

"What's that?"

"I'm not sure."

"What is it you're looking for?"

"Maybe a store. Restaurant. Club. I don't know, really."

"You don't know shit, do you?"

"I know that I don't know shit. That counts for something." I point to the egg on my head. "Things got scrambled."

He peers at my head. "You should have that looked at."

"I already did." I point to the bandage covering the stitches on my cheek.

"Shouldn't you be resting or something?"

"Later. After I find it. The double happiness."

"What's so important about this double happiness?"

I see her then, not just see her, but *feel* her, soft breath against my cheek as she whispered something to me just as I was falling asleep last night. I didn't hear what she said. I only remember I was happy. To be in that white room. "Lulu," I say.

"Oh. A girl. I'm on my way to see *my* girl." He pulls out his phone and texts something. "But she can wait; they always do!" He grins at me, showing off a set of defiantly crooked teeth.

He's right. They do. Even when I didn't know they would, even when I'd been gone a long time, the girls, they waited. I never cared one way or another.

We take off, walking up and down the narrow blocks, the air thick with the smell of stewed organs. I feel like I'm running to keep up with him, and the exertion sets my stomach churning again.

"You don't look so pretty, friend," he tells me right as I retch bile into the gutter. He looks vaguely alarmed. "Are you sure you don't want a doctor?"

I shake my head, wipe my mouth, my eyes.

"Okay. I think maybe I should take you to meet my girl, Toshi. She works in this area, so she might know this double happiness place."

I follow him a few blocks. I'm still trying to find the double happiness sign, but it's even harder now because I got some sick on my address book and the ink's smeared. Also, there are black spots dancing before my eyes making it hard to see where the pavement really is.

When we finally stop, I almost cry in relief. Because we've found it, the double happiness place. Everything is familiar. The steel door, the red scaffolding, the distorted portraits, even the faded name on the facade, Ganterie, after the glove factory it must have once been. This is the place.

Toshi comes to the door, a tiny black girl with tight dreadlocks, and I want to hug her for delivering me to the white room. I want to march straight to the white room and lie down next to Lulu, to have everything feel right again.

I try to say this, but I can't. I can't even really get my legs to move because the ground beneath me has turned liquid and wavy. Toshi and my samaritan, whose name is Pierre, are arguing in French. She wants to call the police and Pierre says they have to help me find double happiness.

It's okay, I want to tell him. *I've found it*. This is the place. But I can't quite make the words come out straight. "Lulu," I manage to say. "Is she here?"

A few more people crowd around the door. "Lulu," I say again. "I left Lulu here."

"Here?" Pierre asks. He turns to Toshi and points to his head and then to my head.

I keep repeating her name: *Lulu, Lulu*. And then I stop but her name continues, like in an echo chamber, like my pleas are traveling deep into the building and will bring her back from wherever it is she's gone.

When the crowd parts, I think it really has worked. That my words dredged her up, returned her to me. That the one time I wanted one to wait, one did.

A girl steps out from the crowd. "*Oui, Lulu, c'est moi*," she says delicately.

But that's not Lulu. Lulu was willowy with black hair and eyes as dark. This girl is a petite china doll, and blonde. She is not Lulu. Only then do I remember that Lulu is not Lulu either. Lulu was the name I gave her. I don't know her real name.

The crowd stares at me. I hear myself babbling about needing to find Lulu. The other Lulu. I left her in the white room.

They look at me with odd expressions on their faces and then Toshi pulls out her mobile phone. I hear her talking; she is requesting an ambulance. It takes me a minute to realize it's for me.

"No," I tell her. "I already have been to the hospital."

"I would hate to see you before," Wrong Lulu says. "Were you in an accident?"

"He got beaten up by skinheads," Pierre tells her.

But Wrong Lulu is right. Accident—how I found her. Accident—how I lost her. You have to give the universe credit, the way it evens things out like that.

Three

I take a taxi to Céline's club. The fare eats into the last of my money but it doesn't matter. I just need enough to get back to Amsterdam, and I already have a train ticket. On the short ride over, I nod off in the backseat and it's only when we pull up outside La Ruelle that I remember we left Lulu's suitcase here.

The bar is dark and empty, but the door is unlocked. I hobble down to Céline's office. It's dark inside there, too, only the grayish glow of her computer monitor lighting her face. At first, when she looks up and sees me, she smiles that smile of hers, like a lion waking from a nap, refreshed but hungry. Then I click on the light.

"*Mon dieu!*" she exclaims. "What did she do to you?"

"Was she here? Lulu?"

Céline rolls her eyes. "Yes. Yesterday. With you."

"Since then?"

"What happened to your face?"

"Where is the suitcase?"

"In the storage room, where we left it. What happened to you?"

"Give me the keys."

Céline narrows her eyes with one of her looks, but she opens a desk drawer and tosses me the keys. I unlock the door, and there's the suitcase. She hasn't come back for it, and for a moment I feel happy because it means she must still be here. Still be in Paris, looking for me.

But then I think about what the woman from Ganterie said, the one who came downstairs after my vision went all black and Toshi threatened again to call an ambulance and I begged for a taxi instead. This woman said that she saw a girl race out of the doors when she unlocked them this morning. "I called after her to come back, but she just ran away," she told me, in French.

Lulu didn't speak French. And she didn't know her way around Paris. She didn't know how to get to the train station last night. She didn't know how to get to the club, either. She wouldn't know where her suitcase is. She wouldn't know where I was—even *if* she wanted to find me.

I take the suitcase, search for a luggage tag, and find nothing: not a name tag or an airplane baggage claim. I try to open it, but it's locked. I pause for all of a second before yanking off the flimsy padlock. As soon as I open the bag, I'm hit with the familiar. Not the contents— clothes and souvenirs I've never seen before—but the smell. I pick up a neatly folded T-shirt, put it to my face, and inhale.

"What are you doing?" Céline asks, suddenly appearing in the doorway.

I slam the door shut in her face and continue going through Lulu's things. There are souvenirs, including one of those wind-up clocks like one we looked at together at one of the stalls on the Seine, some plug adapters, chargers, toiletries, but nothing that tracks back to her. There is a sheet of paper in a plastic bag, and I pick that up, hopeful, but it only contains an inventory of sorts.

Tucked underneath a sweater is a travel journal. I finger the cover. I was on a train to Warsaw more than a year ago when my rucksack got nicked. I had my passport, money, and address book on me, so all the thieves got was a half-broken backpack with a bunch of dirty clothes, an old camera, and a diary inside of it. They had probably just thrown everything away once they'd realized there was nothing to sell. Maybe they got twenty euros for the camera, though it was worth a lot more to me. As for the diary, worthless; I prayed they tossed it. I couldn't bear the idea of anyone reading it. It was the only time in the last two years I'd considered going home. I didn't. But when I bought new things, I didn't replace the diary.

I wonder what Lulu would think of me reading her journal. I try to imagine how I'd have felt had she read all my raw rantings about Bram and Yael from my stolen journal. When I do, it's not the usual embarrassment or shame or the disgust that washes over me. Instead, it's something quiet, familiar. Something like relief.

I open her journal, flipping through the pages, knowing I shouldn't. But I'm looking for a way to contact her, though maybe, I'm just looking for more of her. A different way to breathe her in.

But I find no scent of her. Not a single name or address: not hers, not anyone's she met. There are only a few vague entries, nothing telling, nothing Lulu.

I flip to the end of the journal. The spine is stiff and cracks. Behind the back cover is a deck of postcards. I search them for addresses, but they're blank.

I reach for a pen on one of the shelves and start writing my name, phone number, email address, and Broodje's address for good measure, on each of the postcards. I write myself into Rome, Vienna, Prague, Edinburgh. London. All the while, I'm wondering why. *Keep in touch.* It's like a mantra on the road. This act you do. But it rarely happens. You meet people, you part ways, sometimes you cross paths again. Mostly, you don't.

The last postcard is of William Shakespeare from Stratford-upon-Avon. I'd told her to skip *Hamlet* and come see us instead. I'd told her the night was too nice for tragedy. I should have known better than to say a thing like that.

I flip Shakespeare over. "Please," I begin. I'm about to write something else: *Please get in touch. Please let me explain. Please tell me who you are.* But my cheek is throbbing and my vision has gone all soft-focus again and I'm exhausted and weighted with regret. So I bookend the "please" with that regret. "I'm sorry," I write.

I tuck all the postcards back in the bag and then back in the journal. I zip up the suitcase and put it back in the corner. I shut the door.

Four

The last time I was in Céline's flat, more than a year ago, she hurled a vase of dead flowers at my head. I'd been staying with her about a month, and I told her it was time for me to move on. It had been unseasonably warm and I'd stayed unusually long. But then the weather had turned cold and I felt the claustrophobia return. Céline accused me of being a fair-weather boyfriend, and she wasn't entirely wrong about the weather, but I'd never actually been her boyfriend, never promised to stay. There was screaming, curses, then the vase sailing through the air, missing my head but smashing into the faded blue wall. I tried to help with the mess before I left, but she refused to let me.

I don't think either of us expected me ever to set foot in here again. I don't think we ever thought we'd see each other again. But then I bumped into her at La Ruelle a few months later. She had recently been made booking manager, and she seemed happy enough to see me. She gave me free drinks all night and invited me down to her office to show me the roster of bands she had scheduled in the coming months. I went with her, even though I was pretty certain that the calendar was not what she wanted to show me, and sure enough, as soon as we got to the office, she locked the door, and never turned on her computer.

There was an unspoken agreement that I'd never go back to her flat. I had a place to stay, anyway, and I was leaving the next morning. After that, I saw her whenever I came through Paris. Always at the club, in the office, with the door locked.

So I think we are both surprised when I ask if I can stay at her place.

"Really? You want to?"

"If you don't mind. You can give me the keys and meet me later. I know you have to work. I'll leave tomorrow."

"Stay as long as you like. Let me come with you. I can help you."

My fingers absently touch the watch, still on my wrist. "You don't have to. I just need to rest."

Céline sees the watch. "Is that hers?" she asks.

I run my finger along the cracked crystal.

"Are you going to keep it?" she asks, her tone gone sour.

I nod. Céline starts to protest, but I hold up my hand to stop her. I barely have the energy to stand. But I am keeping this watch.

Céline rolls her eyes, but she also shuts down her computer and helps me up the stairs. She calls out to Modou, who is now digging around behind the bar, that she is taking me home for the night.

"What happened to your friend?" Modou asks, popping back up.

I turn back toward him. The lights are dim and Céline's arm is around me for support. I can hardly see him. "Tell her I'm sorry. Her suitcase is in the closet. If she comes back. Tell her that." I want to tell him to make sure she looks at the postcards, but Céline is yanking me out the door. Outside, I was expecting darkness, but, no, it's still daytime. Days like these go on for years. It's the ones you want to last that slip away—one, two, three—in seconds.

— — —

The watermark from where the vase smashed into the wall is still there. So are the piles of books, magazines, CDs, and precarious towers of vinyl records. The picture windows, which she never bothers to cover, even at night, are wide open, letting in the endless, endless daytime.

Céline gives me a glass of water, and at last I take the painkillers Dr. Robinet gave me before I left the hospital. He advised me to take them *before* the pain came on, and to keep taking them until it subsided. But I was afraid taking them earlier would dull whatever wits I had left about me.

The instructions on the bottle say one pill every six hours. I take three.

"Lift up your hands," Céline instructs. And it's like yesterday, when she was making me change my clothes and Lulu walked in on us, and I'd thought it cute that she tried to hide her jealousy. And then Modou had kissed her and I'd had to hide mine.

I can't lift my arms over my head, so Céline helps me off with the hospital scrubs. She stares at my chest a long time. She shakes her head.

"What?"

She clucks her tongue. "She should not have left you like this."

I start to explain that she didn't leave me like this, not knowingly. Céline dismisses me with a wave of her hands. "No matter. You are here now. Go into the bathroom and clean yourself up. I will cook something."

"You?"

"Do not laugh. I can make eggs. Or soup."

"Don't trouble yourself. I have no appetite."

"Then I will make you a bath."

She draws me a bath. I hear it running and think of rain, which has stopped. I feel the drugs starting to work, the soft tentacles of sleep slowly tugging me under. Céline's bed is like a throne and I collapse onto it, thinking of my airplane dream earlier today and how it felt slightly different from the usual nightmare. Right before I fall asleep, one of my lines—Sebastian's lines—from *Twelfth Night* pops into my head: "If it be thus to dream, still let me sleep!"

———

At first, I think I'm dreaming again. Not the airplane dream, a different one, a good one. A hand trailing up and down my back, slipping lower, lower. She kept her hand on my heart. All morning as we slept on that hard floor. This hand tickles toward my waist and then goes lower. *Bruised, not broken*, the doctor said. In my sleep, I feel my strength returning.

My own hand finds her warm body, so soft, so inviting. I slip my hand between her legs. She groans.

"Je savais que tu reviendrais."

And then it's the nightmare all over again. Wrong place. Wrong person. Wrong plane. I jolt up in bed, push her away so hard she tumbles to the floor.

"What are you doing?" I shout at Céline.

She stands up, unapologetically naked in glow of the streetlight. "You are in *my* bed," she points out.

"You're supposed to be taking care of me," I say. This sounds all the more pathetic because we both know I don't want her to.

"I thought I was," she says, attempting a smile. She sits down on the edge of the bed, pats the sheet next to her. "You don't have to do anything but lie back and relax."

I am wearing nothing but my boxers. When did I take off my jeans? I see them folded neatly on the floor, along with the shirt from the hospital. I reach for the shirt. My muscles protest. I stand up. They howl.

"What are you doing?" Céline asks.

"Leaving," I say, panting with the exertion. I'm not entirely sure I can get out of here, but I know I cannot stay.

"Now? It is late." She looks incredulous. Until I step in my jeans. It is a painstakingly slow process, and it gives her time to digest the fact that I am, in fact, going. I can see what will happen: the reprise of the last time I was here. A stream of cursing, in French. I am a prick. I have humiliated her.

"I offered you my bed, me, and you push me out. Literally." She is laughing, not because it's funny but because it's inconceivable.

"I'm sorry about that."

"But you came to *me*. Yesterday. Again today. You *always* come back to me."

"It was only for a place to leave the suitcase," I explain. "It was for Lulu."

The look on her face is different from what it was last time, when she threw the vase at me, after I told her it was time for me to go. That was fury. This is fury before it's had time to set, raw and bloody. How foolish it was to visit Céline. We could've found another place for that suitcase.

"Her?" Céline yells. "Her? She was just some girl. Nothing special! And look at you now! She left you like this. I am always the one you come running to, Willem. That means something."

I hadn't taken Céline for one of the ones who wait. "I shouldn't have come here. I won't do it again," I promise. I gather the rest of my things and hobble out of her flat, down the stairs to the street.

A police car flies by, its lights flashing through the finally dark streets, its siren whining: *nyeah-nyeah, nyeah-nyeah.*

Paris.

Not home.

I need to get home.

Five

SEPTEMBER
Amsterdam

*M*arjolein's office is in a narrow canal house off of the Brouwersgracht, the inside of it all white and modern. Bram designed it, calling it one of his "vanity projects." But there was nothing vain about Bram; that was just his code for not getting paid.

Bram's day job was designing temporary crisis shelters for refugees, something he believed in but that didn't challenge his creative side. So he was always on the lookout for ways to exercise his modern sensibilities—like transforming a tired transport barge into a three-story glass, wood, and steel floating palace that was once described as "Bauhaus on the Gracht" in a design journal.

Sara, Marjolein's assistant, sits behind a clear Lucite table, a vase of white roses on the desk. When I come in, she gives me a nervous smile and slowly rises to take my coat. I lean in to kiss her hello. "Sorry I'm late," I apologize.

"You're *three weeks* late, Willem," she says, as she ushers me in, accepting a kiss but not eye contact.

I give my best rogue's grin, even though it pulls at the now-itchy wound on my cheek. "But worth waiting for?"

She doesn't answer. It was more than two years ago that Sara and I had our moment. I was spending a lot of time in this office then, and she was there, our family attorney's assistant. When it had first happened, I'd been besotted, Sara the older woman with the doleful eyes and the blue-painted bed. But it didn't last. It never does.

"Technically, I was only a few days late," I tell her now. "Marjolein's the one who delayed us by two weeks."

"Because she went on holiday," Sara says, strangely huffy. "Which she had purposely booked for after the closing."

"Willem." Marjolein towers in the doorway, naturally tall, and taller yet in the stiletto heels she always wears. She beckons me into her office where Bram's modern sensibility is everywhere. The messy papers and folders in precarious piles are Marjolein's contributions.

"So you threw me over for a girl," Marjolein says, shutting the door behind her.

I wonder how it is that Marjolein can possibly know this. She stares at me, clearly amused by something. "I called back, you know?"

On the train from London to Paris, I'd tried to text Marjolein about my delay, but my phone wouldn't get a signal and was about to die anyway, and for some reason, I didn't want to tell Lulu about any of it. So when I'd seen one of the

Belgian backpacker girls in the café, I'd borrowed her phone. I'd had to fumble in my backpack for Marjolein's number in my address book and had wound up spilling coffee all over me and the Belgian girl.

"She sounded pretty," Marjolein says, with a grin that is both mischievous and scolding at the same time.

"She was," I say.

"They always are," Marjolein says. "Well, come give us a kiss." I step forward to be kissed but before I do, she stops me. "What happened to your face?"

One upside to our meeting being postponed is that it's given the bruises time to fade. The sutures have dissolved, too. All that's left now of that day is a thick raised welt that I'd hoped would go unnoticed.

When I don't answer, Marjolein does. "Tangled with the wrong girl, eh? One with an angry boyfriend?" She gestures to the reception area. "Speaking of, Sara has a nice Italian bloke, so lay off. She moped for months after you left last time. I almost had to fire her."

I hold up my hands and feign innocence.

Marjolein rolls her eyes. "Was that really because of a girl?" She points to my cheek.

Put that way, the story skirts a little close to the truth. "Bicycle. Beer. Dangerous combination." I cheerfully mime falling off a bike.

"My God. Have you been gone so long you've forgotten how to drink and ride a bike?" she asks. "How can you even call yourself Dutch anymore? We got you back just in time."

"So it appears."

"Come. Let me get you a coffee. And I have some excellent chocolate hiding around here somewhere. And then we'll sign the papers."

She calls to Sara, who brings in two demitasses of coffee. Marjolein rifles around in her drawers until she pulls out a box of hard, chewy chocolates. I take one and let it melt on my tongue.

She starts explaining what I'm signing, though it doesn't matter because my signature is only required due to some bureaucratic formality. Yael never took Dutch citizenship, and Bram, who used to say, "God is in the details," when it came to the meticulousness of his designs, apparently held the opposite view when it came to his personal affairs.

All of which means my presence is necessary to finalize the sale and set up the various trusts. Marjolein prattles on as I sign and sign and sign again. Apparently Yael's not being Dutch, and no longer residing here or in Israel either, but floating around like some stateless refugee, is actually a big tax boon for her. She sold the boat for seven hundred and seventeen thousand euros, Marjolein explains. A chunk goes to the government, but a much larger sum goes to us. By the end of business day tomorrow, one hundred thousand euros will be deposited into my bank account.

As I sign, Marjolein keeps looking at me.

"What?" I ask.

"It's just I forgot how much you look like him."

I pause, the pen poised over another line of legalese. Bram always used to say that though Yael was the strongest woman in the world, somehow his mild mannered genes clobbered her dark Israeli stock.

"Sorry," Marjolein says, back to business. "Where have you been staying since you got back? With Daniel?"

Uncle Daniel? I haven't seen him since the funeral, and before that only a handful of times. He lives overseas and rents out his flat. Why would I stay there?

No, since I've been back it's almost been like I am still on the traveler circuit. I've stuck to the tight radius around the train station, near the budget youth hostels and the disappearing red-light district. Partly this was a matter of necessity. I wasn't sure I'd have enough money to last the few weeks, but somehow, my bank account hasn't hit zero. I could've gone to stay with old family friends, but I don't want anyone to know I'm back; I don't want to revisit any of those places. I certainly haven't gone anywhere near Nieuwe Prinsengracht.

"With a friend," I say vaguely.

Marjolein misreads it. "Oh, with *a friend*. I see."

I give a half-guilty smile. Leaving people to jumped conclusions is sometimes simpler than explaining a complicated truth.

"Be sure this friend doesn't have an angry boyfriend."

"I'll do my best," I say.

I finish signing the papers. "That's that then," she says. She opens her desk and pulls out a manila folder. "Here's some mail. I've arranged for anything that goes to the boat to be forwarded here until you give me a new address."

"It might be a while."

"That's okay. *I'm* not going anywhere." Marjolein opens a cabinet and pulls out a bottle of Scotch and two shot glasses. "You just became a man of means. This deserves a drink."

Bram used to joke that as far as Marjolein was concerned, every time the minute hand of the clock passed twelve, it was cause for a drink. But I accept the shot glass.

"What shall we toast?" she asks. "To new ventures? A new future."

I shake my head. "Let's drink to the accidents."

I see the shock in her face, and I realize belatedly that this sounds like I'm talking about what happened to Bram, though that wasn't so much an accident as a freak occurrence.

But that's not what I'm talking about. I'm talking about *our* accident. The one that created our family. Surely Marjolein must've heard the story. Bram loved to tell it. It was like a family origin myth, fairy tale, and lullaby all wrapped together:

Bram and Daniel, driving through Israel in a Fiat that broke down constantly. It was broken down one day outside of the seaside town of Netanya and Bram was trying to fix it, when a soldier, rifle slung over the shoulder, cigarette dangling, ambled over. "Scariest sight you could ever imagine," Bram would say, smiling at the memory.

Yael. Hitching her way back to her army base in Galilee after a weekend's leave spent in Netanya, at a friend's house, or maybe a guy's, anywhere but at the apartment she'd grown up in with Saba. The brothers were driving to Safed, and after she reconnected their radiator hose, they offered her a ride.

Bram gallantly offered her the front seat; after all, she'd fixed the car. But Yael, seeing the cramped backseat said, "Whoever's shortest should sit in back." She claimed to have meant herself, and to not have known which brother was taller, because Daniel had been in the passenger seat, rolling a joint with the Lebanese hash he'd bought off a surfer in Netanya.

But Bram had misunderstood, and so after a needless measuring decided Bram was taller by about three centimeters, Daniel took the back.

They drove the soldier back to her base. Before they parted ways, Bram gave her his address in Amsterdam.

A year and a half later, Yael finished her military service and, determined to put as much distance as she could between herself and everything she grew up with, took what little money she'd saved and began hitching her way north. She lasted four months and got all the way to Amsterdam before she ran out of money. So she knocked on a door. Bram opened it, and even though he hadn't seen her in all that time, and even though he didn't know why she was there, and even though it wasn't really his way, he surprised himself and he kissed her. "Like I'd been expecting her all that time," he'd say in a voice full of wonder.

"See how funny life is," Bram used to say as the epilogue to their epic love story. "If the car hadn't broken down just there, or if she'd run out of money in Copenhagen, or if Daniel were the taller one, none of this might ever have happened."

But I knew what he was really saying was: *Accidents. It's all about the accidents.*

Six

Two days later, one hundred thousand euros appears in my bank account, as if by magic. But of course, it's not magic. It's been a long time since I was kicked off my economics course, but I've since come to understand that the universe operates on the same general equilibrium theory as markets. It never gives you something without making you pay for it somehow.

I buy a beat-up bike off a junkie and another change of clothes from the flea market. I may have money now, but I've grown used to living simply, to owning only what I can carry. And besides, I'm not staying long, so I may as well leave as few fingerprints as possible.

I wander up and down the Damrak looking at travel agencies, trying to decide where to go next: Palau. Tonga. Brazil. Once the options increase, settling on one becomes harder. Maybe I'll track down Uncle Daniel in Bangkok, or is it Bali now?

At one of the student agencies, a dark-haired girl behind the desk sees me peering at the ads. She catches my eye, smiles, and gestures for me to come inside.

"What are you looking for?" she asks in slightly accented Dutch. She sounds Eastern, maybe Romanian.

"Somewhere that isn't here."

"Can you be more specific?" she says, laughing a little.

"Somewhere warm, cheap, and far away." *Somewhere that with one hundred thousand euros, I can stay lost as long as I want to*, I think.

She laughs. "That describes about half the world. Let's narrow it down. Do you want beaches? There are some fantastic spots in Micronesia. Thailand is still quite cheap. If you're into a more chaotic cultural affair, India is fascinating."

I shake my head. "Not India."

"New Zealand? Australia? People are raving about Malawi in Central Africa. I'm hearing great things about Panama and Honduras, though they had that coup there. How long do you want to go for?"

"Indefinitely."

"Oh, then you might look into a round-the-world ticket. We have a few on special." She types away on her computer. "Here's one: Amsterdam, Nairobi, Dubai, Delhi, Singapore, Sydney, Los Angeles, Amsterdam."

"You have one that doesn't stop in Delhi?"

"You really don't want India, huh?"

I just smile.

"Okay. So what part of the world *do* you want to see?"

"I don't care. Anywhere will work, really, so long as it's warm, cheap, and far away. And not India. Why don't you pick for me?"

She laughs, like it's a joke. But I'm serious. I've been stuck in a kind of sluggish inertia since coming back, spending whole days in sad hostel beds waiting for my meeting with Marjolein. Whole days, lots of empty hours, holding a broken-but-still-ticking watch, wondering useless things about the girl whom it belongs to. It's all doing a bit of a number on my head. All the more reason for me to get back on the road.

She taps her fingers against her keyboard. "You have to help me out. For starters, where have you already been?"

"Here." I push my battered passport across the desk. "This has my history."

She opens it. "Oh it does, does it?" she says. Her voice has changed, from friendly to coy. She flips through the pages. "You get around, don't you?"

I'm tired. I don't want to do this dance, not right now. I just want to buy my airplane ticket and go. Once I'm out of here, away from Europe, somewhere warm and far, I'll get back to my old self.

She shrugs and returns to leafing through my passport. "Uh-oh. You know what? I can't book you anywhere yet."

"Why not?"

"Your passport's about to expire." She closes the passport and slides it back. "Do you have an identity card?"

"It got stolen."

"Did you file a report?"

I shake my head. Never did call the French police.

"Never mind. You need a passport for most of these places anyhow. You just have to get it renewed."

"How long will that take?"

"Not long. A few weeks. Go to City Hall for the forms." She rattles off some of the other paperwork I'll need, none of which I have here.

Suddenly I feel stuck, and I'm not sure how that happened. After managing for two entire years not to set foot in Holland? After going to some absurd lengths to bypass this small-but-central landmass—for instance convincing Tor, Guerrilla Will's dictatorial director, to forgo performing in Amsterdam and to hit Stockholm instead, with some half-baked story about the Swedes being the most Shakespeare-loving people in Europe outside the UK?

But then last spring Marjolein had finally cleared up Bram's messy estate and the deed of the houseboat transferred to Yael. Who celebrated by immediately putting the home he'd built for her up for sale. I shouldn't have been surprised, not at that point.

Still, to ask me to come and sign the papers? That took gall. *Chutzpah*, Saba would call it. I understood for Yael it was a matter of practicality. I was a train ride, she was a plane ride. It would only be a few days for me, a minor inconvenience.

Except I delayed for one day. And somehow, that's changed everything.

Seven

*I*t occurs to me, belatedly, that maybe I should've called. Maybe last month, when I first got back. Certainly before now, before showing up at his house. But I didn't. And now it's too late. I'm just here. Hoping to make this as painless as possible.

At the house on Bloemstraat, someone has swapped out the old doorbell for one in the shape of an eyeball that stares reproachfully. This feels like a bad omen. Our correspondence, always irregular, has been nonexistent in the last few months. I can't remember the last time I emailed or texted him. Three months ago? Six months? It occurs to me, also belatedly, that he might not even live here anymore.

Except, somehow, I know he does. Because Broodje wouldn't have left without telling me. He wouldn't have done that.

Broodje and I met when we were eight. I caught him spying on our boat with a pair of binoculars. When I asked what he was doing, he explained that he wasn't spying on *us*. There'd been a rash of break-ins in our neighborhood, and his parents had been talking about leaving Amsterdam for somewhere safer. He preferred to stay put in his family's flat, so it was up to him to find the culprits. "That's very serious," I'd told him. "Yes, it is," he'd replied. "But I have this." Out of his bike basket he'd pulled the rest of his spy kit: decoder scope, noise-enhancing ear buds, night-vision goggles, which he'd let me try on. "If you need help finding the bad guys, I can be your partner," I'd offered. There were not many children in our neighborhood on the eastern edge of Amsterdam's center, no children at all on the adjacent houseboats on the Nieuwe Prinsengracht where our boat was moored, and I had no siblings. I spent much of my time kicking balls off the pier against the hull of the boat, losing most of them to the murky waters of the canals.

Broodje accepted my help, and we became partners. We spent hours casing the neighborhood, taking pictures of suspicious-looking people and vehicles, cracking the case. Until an old man saw us, and, thinking we were working with the criminals, called the police on us. The police found us crouched next to my neighbor's pier, looking through the binoculars at a suspicious van that seemed to appear regularly (because, we later found out, it belonged to the bakery around the corner). We were questioned and we both started crying, thinking we were going to jail. We stammered our explanations and crime-fighting strategies. The police listened, trying hard not to laugh, before taking us home and explaining everything to Broodje's parents. Before they left, one of the detectives gave each of us a card, winked, and said to call with any tips.

I threw away my card, but Broodje kept his. For years. I spotted it when we were twelve, tacked to the bulletin board in his bedroom in the suburbs where he wound up moving after all. "You still have this?" I'd asked him. He'd moved two years before and we didn't see each other frequently. Broodje had looked at the card, and then looked at me. "Don't you know, Willy?" he'd said. "I keep things."

—— —— ——

A lanky guy in a PSV soccer jersey, his hair stiff with gel, opens the door. I feel my stomach plummet, because Broodje used to live here with two girls, both of whom he was constantly, and unsuccessfully, trying to sleep with, and a skinny guy named Ivo. But then the guy's eyes spark open with recognition and I realize it's Henk, one of Broodje's friends from the University of Utrecht. "Is that you, Willem?" he asks, and before I can answer he's calling into the house, "Broodje, Willem's back."

I hear scrambling and the creak of the scuffed wood floorboards and then there he is, a head shorter and a shoulder wider than me, a disparity that used to prompt the old man on the houseboat next to ours to call us Spaghetti and Meatball, a moniker Broodje quite liked, because wasn't a meatball so much tastier than a noodle?

"Willy?" Broodje pauses for a half second before he

launches himself at me. "Willy! I thought you were dead!"

"Back from the dead," I say.

"Really?" His eyes are so round and so blue, like shiny coins. "When did you get back? How long are you here for? Are you hungry? I wish you'd told me you were coming, I would've made something. Well, I can pull together a nice *borrelhapje*. Come in. Henk, look, Willy's back."

"I see that," Henk says, nodding.

"W," Broodje calls. "Willy's back."

I walk into the lounge. Before, it was relatively neat, with feminine touches around like flower-scented candles that Broodje used to pretend to dislike but would light even when the girls weren't home. Now, it smells of stale socks, old coffee, and spilled beer, and the only remnant of the girls is an old Picasso poster, askew in its frame above the mantel. "What happened to the girls?" I ask.

Broodje grins. "Leave it to Willy to ask about the girls first." He laughs. "They moved into their own flat last year, and Henk and W moved in. Ivo just left to do a course in Estonia."

"Latvia," Wouter, or W, corrects, coming down the stairs. He's even taller than me, with short, unintentionally spiky hair and an Adam's apple as big as a doorknob.

"Latvia," Broodje says.

"What happened to your face?" W asks. W never was one for social pleasantries.

I touch the scar. "I fell off my bike," I say. The lie I told Marjolein comes out automatically. I'm not sure why, except for a desire to put as much distance as possible between myself and that day.

"When did you get back?" W asks.

"Yeah, Willy," Broodje says, panting and pawing like a puppy. "How long ago?"

"A bit ago," I say, treading water between hurtful truth and balls-out lies. "I had to deal with some things in Amsterdam."

"I've been wondering where you were," Broodje says. "I tried calling you a while back but got a strange recording, and you're shit about email."

"I know. I lost my phone and all my contacts, and some Irish guy gave me his, including his SIM card. I thought I texted you the new number."

"Maybe you did. Anyhow, come in. Let me go see what I have to eat." He turns right into the galley kitchen. I hear drawers opening and closing.

Five minutes later Broodje returns with a tray of food and beers for all of us. "So tell us everything. The glamorous life of a roving actor. Is it a girl every night?"

"Jesus, Broodje, let the guy sit down," Henk says.

"Sorry. I live vicariously through him; it was like having a movie star in the house having him around. And, it's been a little dry these past few years."

"And by past few years, you mean twenty?" W says drolly.

"So you've been in Amsterdam?" Broodje asks. "How is your ma?"

"I wouldn't know," I say lightly. "She's in India."

"Still?" Broodje asks. "Or there and back?"

"Still. This whole time."

"Oh. I was in the old neighborhood recently and the boat

was all lit up and there was furniture inside, so I thought she might be back."

"Nope, they must've put furniture in there to make it look lived in, but it's not. Not by us, anyhow," I say, rolling up a piece of *cervelaat* and shoving it in my mouth. "It's been sold."

"You sold Bram's boat?" Broodje says incredulously.

"My mother sold it," I clarify.

"She must've made a boatload," Henk jokes.

I pause for a second, somehow unable to tell them that I did, too. Then W starts talking about a piece he read in *De Volkskrant* recently about Europeans paying top dollar for the old houseboats in Amsterdam, for the mooring rights, which are as valuable as the boats themselves.

"Not this boat. You should've seen it," Broodje says. "His father was an architect, so it was beautiful, three floors, balconies, glass everywhere." He looks wistful. "What did that magazine call it?"

"Bauhaus on the Gracht." A photographer had come and taken pictures of the boat, and us on it. When the magazine had come out, most of the shots had been of just the boat, but there had been one of Yael and Bram, framed by the picture window, the trees and canal reflecting like a mirror behind them. I'd been in the original of that shot but had been cropped out. Bram explained that they'd used this one because of the window and the reflection; it was a representation of the design, not our family. But I'd thought it had been a fairly accurate depiction of our family, too.

"I can't believe she sold it," Broodje says.

Some days I can't believe it and other days I can absolutely believe it. Yael is the sort to chew off her own hand if she needs to escape. She'd done it before.

The boys are all looking at me now, their faces blanking out with a kind of concern that I'm unaccustomed to after two years of anonymity.

"So, Holland-Turkey tonight," I begin.

The guys look at me for a moment. Then nod.

"I hope things go better for us," I say. "After the sad offerings during Euro Cup, I don't know if I can take it. Sneijder . . ." I shake my head.

Henk takes the bait first. "Are you kidding? Sneijder was the only striker who proved his mettle."

"No way!" Broodje interrupts. "Van Persie scored that beautiful goal against Germany."

Then W jumps in with math talk, something about regression toward the mean guaranteeing improvement after the last lousy year, and now there's nowhere to go but up, and I relax. There's a universal language of small talk. On the road, it's about travel: some unknown island, or a cheap hostel, a restaurant with a good fixed-price menu. With these guys, it's soccer.

"You gonna watch the game with us, Willy?" Broodje asks. "We were going to O'Leary's."

I didn't come to Utrecht for small talk or for soccer or for friendship. I came for paperwork. A quick visit to University College for some papers to get my passport. Once I get that, I'll go back to the travel agent, maybe ask her for a drink this time, and figure out where to go. Buy my ticket. Maybe take a trip to The Hague to pick up some visas, a visit to the travel clinic for some shots. A trip to the flea market for new clothes. A train to the airport. A thorough body search by immigration officials, because a lone man with a one-way ticket is always an object of suspicion. A long flight. Jetlag. Immigration. Customs. And then finally, that first step into a new place, that moment of exhilaration and disorientation, each feeding the other. That moment when anything can happen.

I have only one thing to do in Utrecht, but suddenly the rest of the things I'll need to accomplish to get myself out of here feels endless. Stranger yet, nothing about it excites me. Not even arriving somewhere new, which used to make all the hassle worthwhile. It all just seems exhausting. I can't summon the energy for the slog it'll take me to get out of here.

But O'Leary's? O'Leary's is right around the corner, not even a block away. That I can manage.

Eight

October turns cold and wet, as if we used up our quota of clear, hot days during the summer's heat wave. It's especially cold in my attic room on Bloemstraat, making me wonder if moving in had been the right call. Not that it had been a call. After I woke up on the downstairs sofa for the third morning in a row, having accomplished little during my days in Utrecht, Broodje had suggested I move into the attic room.

The offer wasn't so much enticing as a *fait accompli*. I was already living here. Sometimes the wind blows you places you weren't expecting; sometimes it blows you away from those places, too.

— — —

The attic room is drafty, with windows that rattle in the wind. In the morning, I see my breath. Staying warm becomes my main vocation. On the road, I often spent whole days in libraries. You could always find magazines or books, and respite from the weather or whatever else needed escaping.

The Central University library offers all the same comforts: big sunny windows, comfortable couches, and a bank of computers I can use to browse the Internet. The last is a mixed blessing. On the road, my fellow travelers were obsessive about keeping up with email. I was the opposite. I hated checking in. I still do.

Yael's emails come like clockwork, once every two weeks. I think she must have it on her calendar, along with all the other chores. The notes never say much, which makes answering them next to impossible.

One came yesterday, a bit of fluff about taking a day off to go to a pilgrim festival in some village. She never tells me what she's taking a day off from, never elaborates about her actual work there, her day-to-day life, which is a bleary mystery, the contours filled in only by offhanded remarks from Marjolein. No, Yael's emails to me are all in a sort of postcard language. The perfect small talk, saying little, revealing less.

"Hoi Ma," I begin my reply. And then I stare at the screen and try to think of what to say. I'm so conversant in every kind of small talk, but I find myself at a loss for words when it comes to my mother. When I was traveling, it was simpler because I could just send a sort of postcard. *In Romania now at one of the Black Sea resorts, but it's off season and quiet. Watched the fishermen for hours.* Although even those had addendums in my mind. How watching the fishermen one blustery morning reminded me of our family trip to Croatia when I was ten. Or was it eleven? Yael slept late, but Bram and I woke early to go down to the docks to buy the day's catches from the just-returning fishermen, who all smelled of salt and vodka. But following Yael's lead, I excise those bits of nostalgia from my missives.

"Hoi Ma." The cursor blinks like a reprimand and I can't get past it, can't think of what to say. I toggle back to my in-box, scrolling backward in time. The last few years and their occasional notes from Broodje, and the notes from people I met on the road—vague promises to meet up in Tangiers, in Belfast, in Barcelona, in Riga—plans that rarely material-ized. Before that, there's the flurry of emails from various professors on the economics faculty, warning me that unless I appealed "special circumstances," I was in danger of not be-ing asked back next year. (I didn't, and I wasn't.) Before that, condolence emails, some of them still unopened, and before that, notes from Bram, mostly silly things he liked to forward to me, a restaurant review of a place he wanted to try out, a photo of a particularly monstrous piece of architecture, an invitation to help on his latest fix-it project. I scroll back now four years and there are the emails from Saba, who, in the two years between discovering email and getting too sick to use it, had delighted in this instant form of communication, where you could write pages and pages and it didn't cost any more to send.

I return to the note to Yael. "Hoi Ma, I'm back in Utrecht now, hanging out with Robert-Jan and the boys. Nothing much to report. It's pissing down rain every day; no sign of the sun for a week now. You're glad not to be here for it. I know how you hate the gray. Talk soon. Willem."

Postcard Language, the smallest of small talk.

Nine

The boys and I are going to a movie, along with W's new girlfriend. Some Jan de Bont thriller at the Louis Hartlooper. I haven't liked a de Bont film since—I can't even remember—but I've been outvoted because W has a girlfriend, and this is a big thing, and if she wants explosions, we will watch explosions.

The theater complex is packed, people spilling out the front doors. We fight our way through the crowds to the box office. And that's when I see her: Lulu.

Not my Lulu. But the Lulu I named her for. Louise Brooks. The theater has lots of old movie posters in the lobby, but I've never seen this one, which isn't on the wall but is propped up on an easel. It's a still shot from *Pandora's Box*, Lulu, pouring a drink, her eyebrow raised in amusement and challenge.

"She's pretty." I look up. Behind me is Lien, W's punked-out math major girlfriend. No one can quite get over how he did it, but apparently they fell in love over numbers theory.

"Yeah," I agree.

I look closer at the poster. It is advertising a Louise Brooks film retrospective. *Pandora's Box* is on tonight.

"Who was she?" Lien asks.

"Louise Brooks," Saba had said. "Look at those eyes, so much delight, you know there's sadness to hide." I was thirteen, and Saba, who hated Amsterdam's mercurial wet summers, had just discovered the revival cinemas. That summer was particularly dreary, and Saba had introduced me to all the silent film stars: Charlie Chaplin, Buster Keaton, Rudolph Valentino, Pola Negri, Greta Garbo, and his favorite, Louise Brooks.

"Silent film star," I tell Lien. "There's a festival on. Unfortunately it's tonight."

"We could see that instead," she says. I can't tell if her tone is sarcastic; she's as dry as W is. But when I get to the front of the line to buy the tickets, I find myself asking for five to *Pandora's Box*.

At first, the boys are amused. They think I'm joking, until I point to the poster and explain about the retrospective. Then they are not so amused.

"There's a live piano player," I say.

"Is that supposed to make us feel *better*?" Henk asks.

"No way I'm seeing this," W adds.

"What if *I* wanted to see it?" Lien interjects.

I offer her a silent thank-you and she gives me a perplexed eyebrow raise in return, showing off her piercing. W acquiesces and the rest follow suit.

Upstairs, we take our seats. In the quiet, you can hear the explosions from the adjacent theater and I can see Henk's eyes go wistful.

The lights go down and the piano player starts in with the overture and Lulu's face fills the screen. The movie starts, all scratchy and black and white; you can almost hear it crackle like an old LP. But there is nothing old about Lulu. She's timeless, flirting gaily in the nightclub, being caught with her lover, shooting her husband on their wedding night.

It's strange because I've seen this film before, a few times. I know exactly how it ends, but as it goes on, a tension starts to build, a suspense, churning uncomfortably in my gut. It takes a certain kind of naiveté, or perhaps just stupidity, to know how things will end and still hope otherwise.

Fidgety, I shove my hands into my pockets. Though I try not to, my mind keeps going to the other Lulu on that hot August night. I tossed her the coin, as I'd done to so many other girls. But unlike the other girls who always came back— lingering by our makeshift stage to return my very valuable worthless coin and to see what it might buy—Lulu didn't.

That should've been my first sign that the girl could see through my acts. But all I'd thought was: *Not to be*. It was just as well. I had an early train to catch the next day, and a big, shitty day after that, and I never slept well with strangers.

I hadn't slept well anyhow, and I'd been up early, so I'd caught an earlier train down to London. And there she was, on that train. It was the third time in twenty-four hours that I'd seen her and when I walked into that train's café car, I remember feeling a jolt. As if the universe was saying: *pay attention.*

So I'd paid attention. I'd stopped and we'd chatted, but then we were in London and about to go our separate ways. By that point, the knot of dread that had been building in me since Yael's request that I return to Holland to sign away my home had solidified into a fist. The banter with Lulu on the way down to London had made it unravel, somehow. But I knew that once I got on that next train to Amsterdam, it would grow, it would take over my insides, and I wouldn't be able to eat or do anything except nervously roll a coin along my knuckles and focus on the next *next*—the next train or plane I'd be boarding. The next departure.

But then Lulu started talking about wanting to go to Paris, and I had all this money from the summer's worth of Guerrilla Will, cash I wouldn't be needing much longer. And in that train station in London, I'd thought, okay, maybe *this* was the meant to be: The universe, I knew, loved nothing more than balance, and here was a girl who wanted to go to Paris and here was me who wanted to go anywhere but back to Amsterdam. As soon as I'd suggested we go to Paris together, balance was restored. The dread in my gut disappeared. On the train to Paris, I was as hungry as ever.

On-screen, Lulu is crying. I imagine my Lulu waking up the next day, finding me gone, reading a note that promised a quick return that never materialized. I wonder, as I have so many times, how long it took her to think the worst of me when she already *had* thought the worst of me. On the train from London to Paris, she'd started laughing uncontrollably, because she'd thought I'd left her there. I'd made a joke of it; and of course, it wasn't true. I wasn't planning that. But it had got to me because it was my first warning that somehow, this girl saw me in a way I hadn't intended to be seen.

As the movie goes on, desire and longing and regret and second-guessing of everything about that day start building in me. It's all pointless, but somehow knowing that only makes it worse, and it builds and builds and has nowhere to go. I shove my hands deeper into my pockets and punch a hole right through.

"Damn!" I say, louder than I mean to.

Lien looks at me, but I pretend to be absorbed in the movie. The piano player is building to a crescendo as Lulu flirts with Jack the Ripper and, lonely and defeated, invites him up to her room. She thinks she has found someone to love, and he thinks that he has found someone to love, and then he sees the knife, and you know what will happen. He'll just revert to his old ways. I'm sure that's what she thinks of me, and maybe she's right to think it. The film ends with a frenzied flourish of the piano. And then there's silence.

The boys sit there for a minute and then all start talking at once. "That's it? So he killed her?" Broodje asks.

"It's Jack the Ripper and he had a knife," Lien responds. "He wasn't carving her a Christmas turkey."

"What a way to go. I'll give you one thing, it wasn't boring," Henk says. "Willem? Hey, Willem, are you there?"

I startle up. "Yeah. What?"

The four of them all look at me for what feels like a while. "Are you okay?" Lien asks at last.

"I'm fine. I'm great!" I smile. It feels unnatural. I can almost feel the scar on my face tug like a rubber band. "Let's go get a drink."

We all make our way to the crowded café downstairs. I order a round of beers and then a round of *jenever* for good measure. The boys give me a look, though if it's for the booze or for paying for it all, I don't know. They know about my inheritance now, but they still expect the same frugality from me as always.

I drain my shot and then my beer.

"Whoa," W says, passing me his shot. "No *kopstoot* for me."

I knock his shot back, too.

They're quiet as they look at me. "Are you sure you're okay?" Broodje asks, strangely hesitant.

"Why wouldn't I be?" The *jenever* is doing its job, heating me up and burning away the memories that came alive in the dark.

"Your father died. Your mother left for India," W says bluntly. "Also, your grandfather died."

There's a moment of awkward silence. "Thanks," I say. "I'd forgotten all about that." I mean it to come out as a joke, but it just comes out as bitter as the booze that's burning its way back up my throat.

"Oh, don't mind him," Lien says, tweaking his ear affectionately. "He's working on human emotions like sympathy."

"I don't need anyone's sympathy," I say. "I'm fine."

"Okay, it's just you haven't really seemed yourself since . . ." Broodje trails off.

"You spend a lot of time alone," Henk blurts.

"Alone? I'm with you."

"Exactly," Broodje says.

There's another moment of silence. I'm not quite sure what I'm being accused of. Then Lien illuminates.

"From what I understand, you always had a girl around, and now the guys are worried because you're always alone," Lien says. She looks at the boys. "Do I have that right?"

Kind of sort of yeah, they all mumble.

"So you've been discussing this?" This should be funny, except it's not.

"We think you're depressed because you're not having sex," W says. Lien smacks him. "What?" he asks. "It's a viable physiological issue. Sexual activity releases serotonin, which increases feelings of well-being. It's simple science."

"No wonder you like me so much," Lien teases. "All that simple science."

"Oh, so I'm depressed now?" I try to sound amused but it's hard to keep that tinge of something else out of my voice. No one will look at me except for Lien. "Is that what you think?" I ask, trying to make a joke of it. "I'm suffering from a clinical case of blue balls?"

"It's not your balls I think are blue," she says coolly. "It's your heart."

There's a beat of silence, and then the boys erupt into raucous laughter. "Sorry, *schatje*," W says. "But that would be anomalous behavior. You just don't know him yet. It's much more likely a serotonin issue."

"I know what I know," Lien says.

They all argue over this and I find myself wishing for the anonymity of the road, where you had no past and no future either, just that one moment in time. And if that moment happened to get sticky or uncomfortable, there was always a train departing to the next moment.

"Well, if he does have a broken heart or blue balls, the cure is the same," Broodje says.

"And what's that?" Lien asks.

"Getting laid," Broodje and Henk crow together.

It's too much. "I've gotta piss," I say, standing up.

In the bathroom, I splash water on my face. I stare in the mirror. The scar is still red and angry, aggravated, as though I've been picking at it.

Outside, the corridor is crowded, another film having just let out, not the de Bont but one of those treacly British romantic comedies, the kind that promise an everlasting love in two hours.

"Willem de Ruiter, as I live and breathe."

I turn around, and coming out of the cinema, her eyes misty with fabricated emotion, is Ana Lucia Aureliano.

I stop, letting her catch up. We kiss hello. She gestures for her friends, people I recognize from University College, to go on ahead. "You never called me," she says, adjusting her face into a little-girl pout that somehow looks charming on her, though almost anything would.

"I didn't have your number," I say. I have no reason to be sheepish, but it's like a reflex.

"But I gave it to you. In Paris."

Paris. Lulu. The feelings from the movie start to come back, but I push back against them. Paris was make-believe. No different from the romantic movie Ana Lucia just saw.

Ana Lucia leans in. She smells good, like cinnamon and smoke and perfume.

"Why don't you give me your number again," I say, pulling out my phone. "So I *can* call you later."

"Why bother?" she says.

I shrug. I'd heard rumors she wasn't too happy when things ended last time. I put my phone away.

But then she grabs my hand in hers. Mine is cold. Hers is hot. "I mean why bother calling me *later* when I'm right here, right *now*?"

And she is. Here now. And so am I.

The cure is the same, I hear Broodje say.

Maybe it is.

Ten

*A*na Lucia's dorm is like a cocoon, thick feather quilts, radiators hissing full blast, endless cups of custard-like hot chocolate. For the first few days, I am content just to be here, with her.

"Did you ever think we'd get back together?" she coos, snuggling up to me like a warm little kitten.

"Hmm," I say, because there's no right way to answer that. I never thought we'd get back together because I never considered us together in the first place. Ana Lucia and I had a three, maybe four-week fling in that hazy spring after Bram died, when I was spectacularly floundering in school but also spectacularly succeeding with women. Though succeeding isn't the right word, exactly. It implies a kind of effort, when really, it was the one thing in my life that was effortless.

"*I* did," she says, nibbling my ear. "I thought about you so much these past few years. And then we bumped into each other in Paris, and it felt like it meant something, like fate."

"Hmmm," I repeat. I remember bumping into her in Paris and also feeling like it meant something, but not fate. More like the encroachment, a day too soon, of a world I'd left behind.

"But then you didn't call me," she says.

"Oh, you know. Something came up."

"I'm sure *something* did." Her hand drifts between my legs. "I saw you with that girl. In Paris. She was pretty."

She says it offhandedly, dismissively even, but something skitters to life in my gut. A kind of warning. Ana Lucia's hand is still between my legs and it's having the intended effect, but now Lulu's somewhere in the room, too. Just like that day in Paris, when I ran into Ana Lucia and her cousins while I was in the Latin Quarter with Lulu, I want nothing but distance between these two girls.

"She was pretty, but *you're* beautiful." I say it, trying to steer the conversation away. My words are true, but meaningless. Though Ana Lucia is probably technically prettier than Lulu, such contests are rarely won on technicalities.

Her grip tightens. "What was her name?" she asks.

I don't want to say her name. But Ana Lucia has me firmly in hand and if I don't say it, I'll arouse suspicion. "Lulu," I say into the pillow. It's not even her real name, but it feels like a betrayal.

"Lulu," Ana Lucia says. She lets go of me and sits up in the bed. "A French girl. Was she your girlfriend?"

Morning light is filtering through the window, pale and gray and tinting everything in here slightly greenish. Somehow, the gray dawn light had made Lulu glow in that white room.

"Of course not."

"Just another one of your flings then?" Ana Lucia's laughter answers her own question; the knowingness irks me.

That night in the art squat, after everything, Lulu had smudged her finger against her wrist, and I'd done the same. A kind of code for *stain*, for something that lasts, even if you might not want it to. It had meant something, in that moment at least. "You know me," I say lightly.

Ana Lucia laughs again, the sound of it throaty and full, rich and indulgent. She climbs on top of me, straddling my hips. "I *do* know you," she says, her eyes flashing. She runs a finger down my center line. "I know what you've been through now. I didn't understand before. But I've grown up. You've grown up. I think we're both different people, with different needs."

"My needs haven't changed," I tell her. "They're the same as they ever were. Very basic." I yank her toward me. I'm still angry at her, but her invoking of Lulu's name has riled me up. I finger the lace along the trim of her camisole. I dip a finger under the straps.

Her eyes flutter closed for a minute and I close mine, too. I feel the give of the bed and the trail of her waxy kisses on my neck. "*Dime que me quieres,*" she whispers. "*Dime que me necesitas.*" *Tell me you want me. Tell me you need me.*

I don't tell her because she's speaking Spanish, which she

doesn't realize I now understand. I keep my eyes closed, but even in darkness I hear a voice telling me she'll be my mountain girl.

"I'll take care of you," Ana Lucia says, and I jump in the bed at hearing Lulu's words come out of Ana Lucia's mouth.

But as Ana Lucia's head dips under the covers, I realize it's a different kind of taking care she's talking about. It's not the kind I really need. But I don't refuse it.

Eleven

After two weeks ensconced in Ana Lucia's dorm, I make my way back to Bloemstraat. It's quiet, a welcome change from the constant hubbub in and around the University College campus, everyone in everyone's business.

In the kitchen, I open the cupboards. Ana Lucia has been bringing me back cafeteria food or ordering takeout, charging it away on her father's credit cards. I crave something real.

There's not much here, a couple of bags of pasta and some onions and garlic. There's a can of tomatoes in the pantry. Enough for a sauce. I start to chop the onions and my eyes immediately tear. They always do this. Yael's too. She never cooked much, but occasionally she'd get homesick for Israel, and she'd play bad Hebrew pop music and make *shakshouka*. I might be all the way upstairs in my room and I'd feel the burn. I'd gravitate down to the kitchen. Bram would find us sometimes, together and red-eyed, and he'd laugh and ruffle my hair and kiss Yael and joke that chopping onions was the only time you'd ever catch Yael Shiloh crying.

Around four, I hear the key click in the lock. I call out a hello.

"Willy, you're back. And you're cook—" Broodje says as he turns the corner into the kitchen. Then he stops mid-sentence. "What's wrong?"

"Huh?" And then I realize he means my tears. "Just the onions," I explain.

"Oh," Broodje says. "Onions." He picks up the wooden spoon and swirls it in the sauce, blows, then tastes. Then he reaches into the pantry for several dried herbs and rubs them between his fingers before sprinkling them in. He gives a few shakes of salt and several turns of the pepper mill. Then he turns the flame down low and puts on the lid. "Because if it's not the onions . . ." he says.

"What else would it be?"

He shuffles his foot against the floor. "I've been worried about you since that night," he says. "What happened after the movie."

"What about it?" I say.

He starts to say something. Then stops. "Nothing," he says. "So, Ana Lucia? Again."

"Yeah. Ana Lucia. Again." I can think of nothing else to add so I revert to small talk. "She sends her greetings."

"I'm sure she does," Broodje says, not buying it for a minute.

"You want to eat?"

"I do," he says. "But the sauce isn't ready."

Broodje goes up to his room. I'm perplexed. It's unlike him to turn down food, no matter how cooked it is. I've seen him eat raw hamburger meat. I let the sauce simmer. The aroma fills up the house and he still doesn't come down. So I go up and tap on his door. "Hungry yet?" I ask.

"I'm always hungry."

"Do you want to come down? I can make some pasta."

He shakes his head.

"Are you on a hunger strike?" I joke. "Like Sarsak."

He shrugs. "Maybe I will go on a hunger strike."

"What will you strike for?" I ask. "It would have to be very important for you to go without food."

"*You* are very important."

"*Me?*"

Broodje swivels in his desk chair. "Didn't we used to tell each other things, Willy?"

"Of course."

"Haven't we always been good friends? Even when I moved away we stayed close. Even when you were gone and you didn't ever contact me, I thought we were good friends, and now you're back, what if we're not really friends at all?"

"What are you talking about?"

"Where have you been, Willy?"

"Where have I been? With Ana Lucia. Jesus, you were the one who said I needed to get laid to get over it."

His eyes flash. "Get over *what*, Willy?"

I sit down on the bed. Get over what? That's the question, right there.

"Is it your pa?" Broodje asks. "It's okay if it still is. It's only been three years. It took me that long to get over Varken, and he was a dog."

Bram's death gutted me. It did. But that was then and I've been okay so I'm not sure why it feels so raw again *now*. Maybe because I'm back in Holland. Maybe it was a mistake to stay.

"I don't know what it is," I tell Broodje. It's a relief to admit this much.

"But it is *something*," he says.

I can't really explain it, because it makes no sense. One girl. One day.

"It is something," I tell Broodje.

He doesn't say anything, but the silence is like an invitation, and I'm not sure why I'm keeping this a secret. So I tell him: About meeting Lulu in Stratford-upon-Avon. About seeing her again on the train. About our flirtation on the train about *hagelslag* of all things. About calling her Lulu, a name that seemed to fit her so well that I forgot she wasn't actually called that.

I tell him some of the highlights of a day that seems so perfect in retrospect, I sometimes think I invented it: Lulu marching up and down the Bassin de la Villette with a hundred-dollar bill, bribing Jacques to take us down the canal. The two of us almost getting arrested by that gendarme for illegally riding two people on a single Vélib' bike, but then when the gendarme asked me why I'd done something so stupid, I'd quoted that Shakespeare line about beauty being a witch, and he recognized it, and let us off with a warning. Lulu blindly picking a Métro stop to go to and us winding up in Barbès Rochechouart, and Lulu, who claimed to be uncomfortable with traveling, seeming to love the randomness of it all. I tell him about the skinheads, too. About how I didn't really think about it when I intervened and tried to stop them from hassling those two Arab girls about their headscarves. I didn't really think about what they might do to *me*, and just as it was starting to dawn on me that I might have really screwed myself, there was Lulu, hurling a book at one of them.

Even as I explain it, I realize I'm not doing it justice. Not the day. Not Lulu. I'm not telling the whole story, either, because there are things I just don't know how to explain. Like how when Lulu bribed Jacques to give us that ride on the canal, it wasn't her generosity that got to me. I never told her I'd grown up on a boat, or that I was one day away from signing it all away. But she seemed to know. How did she know? How do I explain that?

When I'm done with my story, I'm unsure if I've made any sense. But I feel better somehow. "So," I say to Broodje. "Now what?"

Broodje sniffs the air. The smell of the sauce has infiltrated the entire house. "Sauce is ready. Now we eat."

Twelve

"I've been thinking," Ana Lucia says. It's sleeting outside but it's toasty in her dorm, with our little feast of Thai food on her bed.

"Always dangerous words," I joke.

She throws a sachet of duck sauce at me. "I've been thinking about Christmas. I know you don't really celebrate it, but maybe you should come with me to Switzerland next month. So you're among family."

"I didn't realize I had relatives in Switzerland," I tease, popping a spring roll in my mouth.

"I meant my family." She looks at me, her eyes uncomfortably intense. "They want to meet you."

Ana Lucia belongs to a sprawling Spanish clan, the heirs to a shipping company that was sold to the Chinese before the recession crippled their economy. She has endless relatives, siblings and cousins, living all over Europe and the U.S., Mexico, and Argentina, and she speaks to them in a kind of round-robin on the phone each night. "You never know what might happen. One day, you might think of them as your family, too."

I want to say I already have a family, but it hardly seems true anymore. Who's left? Yael and me. And Uncle Daniel, but he barely counted in the first place. The roll sticks in my throat. I wash it down with a gulp of beer.

"It's beautiful there," she adds.

Bram took Yael and me skiing once in Italy. We both stayed huddled in the lodge, freezing. He learned his lesson. The next year we went to Tenerife. "Switzerland's too cold," I say.

"And it's so nice here?" she asks.

Ana Lucia and I have been together for three weeks. Christmas is in six weeks. You don't need to be W to figure out the math on that one.

When I don't answer, Ana Lucia says, "Or maybe you want me to go, so you can have someone else keep you warm?" Just like that, her tone changes, and the suspicion that I now realize has been lurking outside all along comes rushing in.

— — —

The next afternoon, when I head back to Bloemstraat, I find the boys at the table, papers sprawled out all over the place. Broodje looks up wearing the expression of a guilty dog who stole the dinner.

"I'm sorry," he says straightaway.

"About what?" I ask.

"I may have told them a little bit about our conversation," he stammers. "About what you said."

"It wasn't much of a surprise," W says. "It was obvious *something* has been wrong since you came back. And I *knew* that scar wasn't from a bicycle accident. It doesn't look like something you'd get from a fall."

"My story was I got hit by a tree branch."

"But you got beaten up by skinheads," Henk tells me. "The same ones the girl threw the book at the day before."

"I think he knows what happened to him," Broodje says.

"Crazy that you saw the same guys," Henk says.

"More like bad luck," Broodje says.

I don't say anything

"We think you have that post-traumatic thing," Henk says. "That's why you've been so depressed."

"So you've scrapped the celibacy theory?"

"Well, yeah," Henk says. "Because you're getting laid now and you're still depressed."

"You think it's because of this," I say, tapping the scar. "Not because of the girl?" I look at W. "You don't think maybe Lien was right?"

The three of them try not to laugh. "What's so funny?" I ask, feeling irritated and defensive all of a sudden.

"This girl didn't break your heart," W says. "She just broke your streak."

"What's that supposed to mean?" I ask.

"Willy, come on," Broodje says, waving his arms to calm us all down. "I know you. I know how you are with girls. You fall in love and then it disappears like snow in the sun.

If you'd had another few weeks with this girl you'd get tired of her, just like you do all the others. But you didn't. It was almost like she dumped you. So you're pining."

You're comparing love to a stain? Lulu had asked. She'd been skeptical at first.

Something that never comes off, no matter how much you might want it to. Yes, stain had seemed about right.

"Okay," W says, clicking his pen. "Let's start at the beginning, with as much detail as you can muster."

"The beginning of what?"

"Your story."

"Why?"

W starts to explain about the Principle of Connectivity and how police use that to track down criminals, via who they associate with. He is always talking about theories like this. He believes that all of life boils down to mathematics, that there's a numeric principle or algorithm to describe every event, even the random ones (chaos theory!). It takes me a while to understand that he means to use the Principle of Connectivity to solve the mystery of Lulu.

"Again, why? The mystery's solved," I snap. "I'm pining over the girl who got away, because she got away." I'm not sure if I'm irritated because I think this is true or because I think it's not.

W rolls his eyes, as if this is beside the point. "But you want to find her, don't you?"

———   ———   ———

By that night, W has spreadsheets and graphs and on the mantel, below the fading Picasso poster, an empty poster board. "Principle of Connectivity. Basically, we track down the people we can find and see what connections they have back to your mystery girl," W says. "Our best bet is to start with Céline. Lulu may have gone back for the suitcase." He writes Céline's name and draws a circle around it.

The thought has crossed my mind a number of times, and each time, I've been tempted to contact Céline. But then I think back to that night, the raw, wounded look on her face. In any case, it doesn't matter. Either the suitcase is at the club, and Lulu hasn't gone back for it, or it's not there and she did somehow retrieve it and she found my notes inside and chose not to respond. Knowing does nothing to change the situation.

"Céline is off the table," I say.

"But she's the strongest connection," W protests.

I don't tell them about Céline and what happened at her flat that night, or what I promised her. "She's out."

W makes a rather dramatic X through Céline's name. Then he draws a circle. Inside he writes "barge."

"What about it?" I ask.

"Did she fill out any paperwork?" W says. "Pay with a card?"

I shake my head. "She paid with a hundred-dollar bill. She basically bribed Jacques."

He writes "Jacques." Circles it.

I shake my head again. "I spent more time with him than she did."

"What do you know about him?"

"He's a typical sailor. Lives on the water all year round. Sails in warm weather, kept the barge anchored in a marina, in Deauville he said, I think."

W writes "Deauville" and puts a circle around it. "What about other passengers?"

"They were older. Danish. One married couple, one divorced couple that seemed married. They were all drunk off their heads."

W writes "Drunk Danes" in a circle way off on the side of the poster board.

"We'll consider them last resorts," W says, moving to the next line. "I think the strongest lead is probably the most time-consuming." Small grin there. Then on the bottom of the poster he writes "TOUR COMPANY" in large block letters.

"Only problem is I don't know which one it was."

"Odds are, it's one of these seven," W says, reaching for a computer printout.

"You found the tour company? Why didn't you say so to begin with?"

"I didn't find it. But I did narrow down the seven companies that do tours for American students that had a tour operating in Stratford-upon-Avon on the nights in question."

"Nights in question," Henk jokes. "This is starting to sound like a detective program."

I stare at the printout. "How did you do that? In one night?"

I expect some complicated mathematical theorem, but he just shrugs and says: "The Internet." He pauses. "There may be more than seven tours, but these are seven that I've confirmed as possibilities."

"More?" Broodje says. "Seven already seems like a lot."

"There was a music festival that week," I explain. It was why Guerrilla Will had gone to Stratford-upon-Avon in the first place. Tor generally avoided it; she had a poisonous grudge against the Royal Shakespeare Company, related to her even more toxic grudge against the Royal Academy of Dramatic Art, which had denied her admission twice. It was after that that she'd gone all anarchist and started Guerrilla Will.

W writes and circles the names of the tours on the poster: "Wide Horizons," "Europe Unlimited," "It's a Small World," "Adventure Edge," "Go Away," "Teen Tours!" and "Cool Europa." "My guess is that your mystery girl was on one of these."

"Okay, but there's seven tours," Henk says. "Now what?"

"I call them?" I guess.

"Exactly," W says.

"Looking for . . . damn." Once again, it comes back to me: I don't even know her name.

"What identifying details *do* you know?" W asks.

I know the timbre of her laugh. I know the heat of her breath. I know the cast of moonlight against her skin.

"She was traveling with her friend," I say, "who was blonde, and Lulu had black hair, cut short, in a bob, like Louise Brooks." The boys all exchange a look. "She had a birthmark right here." I touch my wrist. Since she first showed it to me on the train, I'd wondered what it would taste like. "She mostly kept it covered with a watch. Oh, right, she had an expensive gold watch. Or did have. I have it now."

"That's hers?" Broodje asks.

I nod.

W scribbles this down. "This is good," W says. "The watch, especially. It identifies her."

"Also, it gives you a cover," Broodje says. "A reason to be tracking her down other than wanting to bone her a few more times to get her out of your system. You can say you want to return the watch."

A half hour ago the poster board was empty, but now it's half filled, all these circles, these tenuous connections, linking me to her. W turns toward it, too.

"Principle of Connectivity," he says.

———

Over the next week, one by one, the circles on W's connectivity board become Xs, as connections that I understand never actually existed are severed. It's a Small World is for teens and their parents, so that one's out. Go Away doesn't have any record of anyone with a black bob and a watch on that tour. Adventure Edge refuses to divulge information about their clients and Cool Europa appears to have gone out of business. Teen Tours! doesn't pick up the phone, though I've left several messages and emails.

It's a dispiriting process, this. And complicated, too, because I have to dodge time zones and callbacks and the ever-more-suspicious Ana Lucia. She's not pleased with my more frequent absences, which I've attributed to the soccer league I've supposedly joined.

One night the phone rings past eleven. "Your girlfriend?" Ana Lucia says, her voice flat. *Girlfriend* is what she calls Broodje these days, because she thinks I spend more time with him than her. It's a joke, but it gives my stomach a guilty twist every time.

I pick up the phone and cross to the other side of her room.

"Hi. I'm looking for a Willem de Ruiter?" The voice, in English, butchers the pronunciation of my name.

"Yes, hello," I respond, trying to stay businesslike because Ana Lucia is right there.

"Hi Willem! This is Erica from Teen Tours! I'm responding to your email about trying to return a missing watch."

"Oh, good," I say, keeping it breezy, though Ana Lucia is now looking at me with narrowed suspicious eyes and I realize it's because I'm speaking in English, and though I speak English with her, on the phone, with the boys, I always speak Dutch.

"We provide loss and theft insurance for all our travelers so if she'd lost something of value, there'd be a claim."

"Oh," I say.

"But I've checked all the claims for that time period, and all I've found is a claim for a stolen iPad from Rome and a bracelet that was recovered. But if you have a name, I can double check."

I look at Ana Lucia, who's decidedly not looking at me now, so I know she's listening. "I can't give you that now."

"Oh. Okay. Well, maybe you can call me back with that later?"

"I can't really do that either."

"Oh. You sure it was a Teen Tours! tour?"

I now see how the missing-watch story is as cracked as

the watch itself. Even if this was the right tour, there's no way the tour operators would know Lulu lost the watch because she lost it after the tour. It's a fiction. This is *all* a fiction. The truth is, I'm looking for a girl whose name I don't know, who bears a passing resemblance to Louise Brooks. None of which I can say out loud. Nor do I want to. This is absurd.

Erica goes on, "You know, one of our veterans led that tour. She'd know if anything went amiss. Do you want her number?"

I turn to the bed. Ana Lucia is up, throwing off the covers.

"Her name is Patricia Foley," Erica continues. "Would you like her number?"

Ana Lucia walks across the room and stands in front of me, totally naked, like she knows she's offering a choice. But it's not really a choice, when the other option doesn't actually exist.

"That won't be necessary," I say to Erica.

———

I wake up the next morning to knocking. I squint at the sliding glass door. There's Broodje, holding a bag, and putting a finger to his lips.

I crack open the door. Broodje pops his head in and hands me the bag.

From the bed, Ana Lucia rubs her eyes, looking grumpy.

"Sorry to wake you," he calls to Ana Lucia. "I need to steal him. We have a soccer match. Lapland forfeited so now we're playing Wiesbaden."

Lapland and Wiesbaden? Ana Lucia is ignorant about

all things soccer, but this is pushing it. But her face registers no suspicion about the pairing, only sourness about Broodje's untimely arrival.

In the bag is someone's old soccer kit, jersey, shorts, cleats, and a thin tracksuit to wear on top. I look at Broodje. He gives me a look. "Better go change now," he says.

"When will you be back?" she asks me when I return. The tracksuit is several centimeters too short for me. I can't tell if she notices.

"Late," Broodje answers. "It's an away game. In France." He turns to me. "In Deauville."

Deauville? No. The search is over. But Broodje is halfway out the door and Ana Lucia already has her hands crossed over her chest. I'm already paying the price, so I may as well do the crime.

I go to give her a kiss good-bye. "Wish me luck," I say, forgetting for a second that there is no game, no soccer game at least, and that she's the last person who should be wishing me luck.

Anyway, she doesn't. "I hope you lose," she says.

Thirteen

Deauville

---

*I*t's off season in Deauville, and the seaside resort is buttoned up tight, a cold wind whipping in off the Channel. From a distance, I can see the marina, rows of sailboats in drydock, on their stands, their masts unstepped. As we get closer, the whole marina appears shut down, hibernating for the winter. Which seems about the right idea.

On the drive down in Lien's car, which had smelled of lavender when we left and now smells of wet, dirty laundry somehow, the boys had been ebullient. W had located a barge called *Viola* late last night and had then decided we should take a road trip to France. "Wouldn't it be easier to call?" I'd asked after the plan had been explained to me. But no. They seemed to think we should just go. Of course, they were properly dressed for it, and I was in nothing but a thin track-suit. And they had nothing to lose, except a day's worth of studies. Me, I had even less, but it felt like more somehow.

We drive around the labyrinthine marina, finally reaching the main office only to find it closed. Of course. It's now four o'clock on a dark November day; anyone in their right mind is holed up somewhere warm.

"Well, we'll just have to find it ourselves," W says.

I look around. As far as I can see in every direction are masts. "I don't see how."

"Are marinas organized by type of vessel?" W asks.

I sigh. "Sometimes."

"So there might be a section for barges?" he prompts.

I sigh again. "Possibly."

"And you said this Jacques lives on his boat year-round so it wouldn't be drydocked?"

"Probably not." We had to pull our houseboat out of the water every four years for service overhauls. Drydocking for a vessel that size is a massive undertaking. "Probably anchored."

"To what?" Henk asks.

"Probably to a pier."

"There. We walk around until we find the barges," W says, as if it's all that easy.

But it's not easy at all. It's raining hard now, wet below us and above us. And it seems deserted around here, no sound except the steady pounding of rain, the waves against the sides of the hulls, and the clang of the halyards.

A cat streaks out across one of the piers, and behind it, a barking dog, and behind the dog, a man in a yellow slicker, one dot of color in all the gloom. I watch them go and wonder if I'm like that dog, chasing a cat because it's what a dog does.

The boys take shelter under an awning. I'm shivering now, ready to pack it in. I turn around to suggest a warm bistro, a nice meal, and some drinks before the long drive home. But the boys are all pointing behind me. I turn back around.

The *Viola*'s blue steel shutters are closed, making her look lonely out here strapped alongside the cement slips and the massive wooden posts. She looks cold, too, like she also wishes she were back in the hot Paris summer.

I step on the pier, and for a second, I can almost feel the rays of sunlight on my skin, can hear Lulu introducing me to double happiness. It was right there we'd sat, by the railing. Right there we'd disagreed about what double happiness meant. *Luck*, she'd said. *Love*, I'd countered.

"What the hell are you doing here?"

Striding toward us is the man in the yellow slicker, the runaway mutt now leashed and shivering.

"Many a thief has underestimated Napoleon and has paid for it in a pound of flesh, haven't they?" the man says to his dog. He pulls at the leash and Napoleon barks pitifully.

"I'm not a thief," I say in French.

The man wrinkles his nose. "Worse! You are a foreigner. I knew you were too tall. German?"

"Dutch."

"No matter. Get out of there before I call the gendarme or let Napoleon loose on you."

I hold up my hands. "I'm not here to steal anything. I'm looking for Jacques."

I'm not sure if it's the dropping of Jacques's name or the fact that Napoleon has started licking his balls, but the man backs down. "You know Jacques?"

"A little."

"If you know Jacques even a little, you know where to find him when he's not on the *Viola*."

"Maybe less than a little. I met him last summer."

"You meet lots of people. You don't board a man's vessel without an invitation. That is the ultimate violation of his kingdom."

"I know. I just want to find him, and this is the only place I can think of."

He squints. "Does he owe you money?"

"No."

"You're sure? This isn't about the races? He always backs the wrong horses."

"Nothing to do with that."

"Did he sleep with your wife?"

"No! Last summer he took four passengers through Paris."

"The Danes? Bastards! He lost almost his whole charter fee right back to them. He's a terrible poker player. Did he lose money to you?"

"No! He got money off us. A hundred dollars. Me and this American girl."

"Terrible, those Americans. They never speak French."

"She spoke Chinese."

"What good does *that* do you?"

I sigh. "Look, this girl . . ." I start to explain. But he waves me away.

"If you want Jacques, go to Bar de la Marine. When he's not on the water, he's in the drink."

— — —

I find Jacques at the long wooden bar, slung over a near-empty glass. As soon as we walk in, he waves at me, though whether it's because he recognizes me or because this is just his standard greeting, I'm not sure. He is carrying on an in-depth conversation about new slip fees with the bartender. I buy the boys a round of beers, settle them into a corner table, and sit down next to Jacques.

"Two of what he's having," I tell the bartender, and he pours us each a glass of teeth-achingly sweet brandy on the rocks.

"Good to see you again," Jacques tells me.

"So you remember me?"

"Of course I remember you." He squints, placing me. "Paris." He belches and then pounds his chest with his fist. "Don't look so surprised. It was only a few weeks ago."

"It was three months ago."

"Weeks, months. Time is so fluid."

"Yes, I remember you saying that."

"You want to charter the *Viola*? She's dry for the season but we get wet again in May."

"I don't need a charter."

"So what can I do for you?" He downs the rest of his drink and crunches hard on the ice. Then he starts in on the fresh one.

I don't really have an answer for him. What *can* he do for me?

"I was with that American girl and I'm trying to get in touch with her. She didn't by any chance get in touch with you?"

"The American girl. Oh yes, she did."

"Really?"

"Yeah. She said to tell that tall bastard I'm done with him 'cause I've found myself a new man." He points to himself. Then he laughs.

"So she didn't get in touch with you?"

"No. Sorry, boy. She leave you high and dry?"

"Something like that."

"You could ask those bastard Danes. One of them keeps texting me. Let me see if I can find it." He pulls out a smartphone and starts fumbling with it. "My sister got me this, said it would help with navigation, bookings . . . but I can't figure it out." He hands it to me. "You try."

I check his text queue and find a note from Agnethe. I open the text and there are several more before it, including pictures from last summer when they were cruising on the *Viola*. Most are of Jacques, in front of fields of yellow safflower, or cows, or sunsets, but there's one shot I recognize: a clarinet player on a bridge over Canal Saint Martin. I'm about to hand the phone back when I see it: in the corner, a sliver of Lulu. It's not her face, it's the back of her—shoulders, neck, hair—but it's her. A reminder that she's not some fiction of my own making.

I've often wondered how many photos I've been accidentally captured in. There was another photo that day, not accidental at all. An intentional shot of Lulu and me that she'd asked Agnethe to take with her phone. Lulu had offered to send it to me. And I'd said no.

"Can I forward this to myself?" I ask Jacques.

"As you wish," he says, with a wave of the hand.

I forward the shot to Broodje's phone because it was true that mine won't accept photo texts, though that wasn't the reason I didn't want the shot of Lulu and me when she offered it. It was automatic, that denial, a reflex almost. I had almost no pictures from the last year of my traveling. Though I'm sure I am in many people's photos, I'm in none of my own.

In my rucksack, the one that got stolen on that train to Warsaw, had been an old digital camera. And on that camera were photographs of me and Yael and Bram from my eighteenth birthday. They were some of the last photos I had of the three of us together, and I hadn't even discovered them until I was on the road, bored one night and going through all the shots on my memory stick. And there we were.

I should've had those pictures emailed somewhere. Or printed. Done something permanent. I planned to, I did. But I put it off and then my rucksack got nicked and it was too late.

The devastation caught me off guard. There's a difference between losing something you knew you had and losing something you discovered you had. One is a disappointment. The other is truly a loss.

I didn't realize that before. I realize it now.

Fourteen

Utrecht

On the ride back to Utrecht, I call Agnethe the Dane to see if Lulu sent her any photographs, if there had been any correspondence. But she hardly remembers who I am. It's depressing. This day, so seared in my memory, is just another day to everyone else. And in any case, it was just one day, and it's over now.

It's over now with Ana Lucia, too. I can feel it, even if she can't. When I come back, defeated, telling her soccer season is over, she is sympathetic, or maybe victorious. She's full of kisses and *cariños*.

I accept them. But I know now it's just a matter of time. In three weeks, she leaves for Switzerland. By the time she gets back, four weeks later, I will be gone. I make a mental note to get on that passport renewal.

It's as if Ana Lucia senses all this. Because she starts pushing harder for me to join her in Switzerland. Every day, a new appeal. "Look how nice the weather is," she says one morning as she gets ready for class. She opens her computer and reads me the weather report from Gstaad. "Sunny skies every day. Not even so cold."

I don't answer. Just force a smile.

"And here," she says, clicking over to a travel site she likes and tilting the laptop toward me to show me pictures of snowy alps and painted nutcrackers. "Here it shows you all the things you can do besides skiing. You don't have to sit at the lodge. We're close to Lausanne or Bern. Geneva's not even so far. We can go shopping there. It's famous for watches. I know! I'll buy you a watch."

My whole body stiffens. "I already have a watch."

"You do? I never see you wear it."

It's back at Bloemstraat, in my rucksack. Still ticking. I can almost hear it from here. And suddenly, three weeks feels too long.

"We should talk." The words trip out before I know what to follow them with. Breaking up is not something I've done in a while. So much easier to kiss good-bye and catch a train.

"Not now," she says, rising to apply lipstick in the mirror. "I'm already late."

Okay. Not now. Later. Good. It will give me time to find the right words. There are always right words.

— — —

After she leaves, I get dressed, make a coffee, and sit down at her computer to check my email before I leave. The travel page she was on is still open, and I'm about to close the window when I see one of the banner ads. MEXICO!!! it screams. Outside, it's cold and gray, but the pictures promise only warmth and sunshine.

I click on the link, and it takes me to a page listing several package holiday specials, not the kind of thing I'd ever do, but I feel warmer just looking at the beaches. And then I see some ads for trips to Cancún.

Cancún.

Where Lulu goes every year.

Where she has gone with her family to the same place every year. Her mother's predictability, so exasperating to her, is now my best hope.

I pull up the details. Like everything from that day, they're as fresh as wet paint. A resort fashioned like a Mayan temple. Like America behind walls with Christmas carols mariachi-style. Christmas. They went for the holidays. Christmas. Or was it New Year's? I can just go for both!

Channeling W, I start searching for resorts in Cancún. One crystalline-water beach after the other flashes across the screen. There is no end to them, these megaresorts like Mayan fortresses and temples. She said it had some kind of river. I'd remembered wondering about that, a resort with a river. There aren't any natural rivers running through Cancún. There are golf courses and swimming pools and diving cliffs, and waterslides. But rivers? I'm looking at the listing for Palacio Maya when I stumble across it. A *lazy* river, a kind of fake stream you ride on in an inflatable tube.

I narrow my search. There don't seem to be *that* many resorts that look like Mayan temples and have lazy rivers.

Four, that I can see. Four that Lulu might be staying at some time between Christmas and New Year's.

Outside it's pouring, but the sites brag that the weather in Mexico is hot, endless blue skies and sunshine. All this time, I've been stuck, trying to figure out where to go next. Why not here? To find her? I click over to an airline consolidator and look up the prices for two tickets to Cancún. Expensive, but then again, I can afford it.

I snap the computer shut, a list forming in my head. It seems so simple.

Get my passport.

Invite Broodje.

Buy the tickets.

Find Lulu.

Fifteen

By six o'clock that night, I've bought Broodje's and my plane tickets and reserved us a room at a cheap hotel in Playa del Carmen. I feel flush with satisfaction, having accomplished more in this single day than I have in the last two months. There's only one thing left to do.

"We need to talk," I text Ana Lucia. She texts me right back, "I know what you want to talk about. Come by at 8." I am limber with relief. Ana Lucia is smart. She knows, like I know, that whatever this is, it's not a stain.

I buy a bottle of wine on my way over. No reason this can't be civilized.

She greets me at the door, wearing a red bikini and redder lips. Taking the wine from my hand, she pulls me inside. There are lit votive candles everywhere, like a cathedral on a saint's day. I get a bad feeling.

"Cariño, I understand it now. All that talk about how much you hate the cold. I should've guessed."

"You should've guessed?"

"Of course you want to go somewhere warm. And you know my aunt and uncle are in Mexico City but what I can't figure out is how you know about the villa on Isla Mujeres?"

"Isla Mujeres?"

"It's beautiful. Right on the beach, with a pool and servants. They have invited us to stay there if we want, or we can stay on the mainland, though not at one of those cheap places." She wrinkles her nose. "I insist to pay for the hotel, no arguments. Because it's only fair you bought the tickets."

"Bought the tickets." All I can do is repeat.

"Oh cariño," she coos. "You'll meet my family, after all. They are going to throw us a party. My parents were upset about me canceling Switzerland but they understand the things you do for love."

"For love," I repeat although with a sickening feeling I'm starting to piece together what has happened. Her Internet browser. My entire search history. Tickets for two. The hotel. My smile is pulled taut, full of false sweetness. How can I find the words for this? A misunderstanding, I will tell her; the tickets are for a boys' holiday, for me and Broodje, which *is* true.

"I know you wanted it to be a surprise," she continues. "Now I know why you have been sneaking off on the telephone, but *amor*, we leave in three weeks, when did you plan to tell me?"

"Ana Lucia," I begin. "There's been a misunderstanding."

"What do you mean?" she says. And the hope is still there, as if the misunderstanding is about a minor detail, like the hotel.

"Those tickets. They're not for you. They're for—"

She cuts me off. "It's that other girl, isn't it? The one from Paris?"

Maybe I'm not so good an actor as I think. Because the way her expression has tectonically shifted from adoration to suspicion shows me that she's probably always known. And I must be a terrible actor now, because even as my mouth starts to form a plausible explanation, my face must be giving it all away. I can tell it is by what's happening to Ana Lucia's face—her pretty features puckering into disbelief, and then into belief.

"*Hijo de la gran puta!* It's the French girl? You've been with her all this time, haven't you?" Ana Lucia screams. "*That's* why you went to France?"

"It's not what you think," I say, holding up my hands.

She flings open the sliding-glass door leading onto the quad. "It's exactly what I think," she says, shoving me out the door. I just stand there. She reaches for a candle and hurls it at me. It flies past me and lands on one of the throw pillow she keeps on the cement stoop. "You've been sneaking around all this time with that French whore!" Another candle whizzes by, landing in the shrubbery.

"You're going to start a fire."

"Good! I'll burn the memory of you, *culero*!" She flings another candle at me.

The rain has stopped, and though it's a chilly night, it

seems as if half the college has now gathered around us. I try to bring her back inside, to calm her down. I am unsuccessful at both.

"I canceled my trip to Switzerland for you! My relatives arranged a party for you. And all along, you were sneaking off to see your French whore. In my land. Where my family lives." She pounds on her bare chest, as if she's claiming ownership not just of Spain but of all of Latin America.

She hurls another candle. I catch this one, and it explodes, spilling glass and hot wax down my hand. My skin bubbles to a blister. I wonder, vaguely, if it'll scar. I suspect it won't.

Sixteen

DECEMBER
Cancún

The height of the Mayan civilization was more than a thousand years ago, but it's hard to imagine the holiest of temples back then were as well guarded as the Maya del Sol is now.

"Room number?" The guards ask Broodje and me as we approach the gate in the imposing carved wall that seems to stretch a kilometer in each direction.

"Four-oh-seven," Broodje says before I have a chance to speak.

"Key card," the guard says. There are sweat patches all down the side of his sweater vest.

"Um, I left it in the room," Broodje replies.

The guard opens a binder and looks through a sheaf of papers. "Mr. and Mrs. *Yoshimoto*?" he asks.

"Uh-huh," Broodje replies, linking arms with me.

The guard looks annoyed. "Guests only." He snaps the binder shut and goes to close the little window.

"We're not guests," I say, smiling conspiratorially. "But we're trying to *find* a guest."

"Name?" He picks up the binder again.

"I don't know, exactly."

A black Mercedes with tinted windows glides up and barely stops before the guards lift the gate and wave it through. The guard turns back to us, weary, and for a second I think we've won. But then he says, "Go now, before I have to call the police."

"The police?" Broodje exclaims. "Whoa, whoa, whoa. Let's just all cool down a minute. Take off our sweater vests. Maybe have a drink. We can go to the bar; the hotel must have some nice bars. We'll bring you back a beer."

"This is not a hotel. It's a vacation club."

"What does that mean, exactly?" Broodje asks.

"It means you can't come in."

"Have a heart. We came from Holland. He's looking for a girl," Broodje says.

"Aren't we all?" the guard behind him asks, and they both laugh. But they still don't let us in.

I give the moped a good frustrated kick, which at least means it sputters to life. Nothing so far is going quite how I'd expected it to, not even the weather. I'd thought Mexico would be warm, but it's like being in an oven all day long. Or maybe it only feels that way because instead of spending our first day on a breeze-cooled beach as Broodje had the good sense to do, I spent yesterday at the Tulum ruins. Lulu had mentioned her family went to the same ruins every year and Tulum is the closest one, so I'd thought I might just catch her there. For four hours I watched thousands of people as they belched out of tour buses and minivans and rental cars. Twice, I thought I saw her and ran after a girl. Right hair, wrong girl. And I realized she might not even have that haircut anymore.

I'd come back to our little hotel with a sunburn and a headache, the optimism I'd had about this trip souring into a sinking feeling. Broodje cheerfully suggested we try the hotels, a more contained environment. And if that didn't work out, he'd pointed toward the beach. "There are so many girls here," he'd said in a hushed, almost reverent tone, gesturing out to the sand, which was covered, every square yard of it, with bikinis.

So many girls, I'd thought. *Why am I trying to find just one?*

—— —— ——

Palacio Maya, another of the faux-Mayan resorts on my hit list, is a few kilometers north of here. We putter up the highway, breathing in the fumes of the passing tour buses and trucks. This time, we stash the moped in some flowering shrubs along the winding manicured road that leads to the front gates. Palacio Maya looks a lot like the Maya del Sol, only instead of a monolithic wall, it is fronted by a giant pyramid, with a guard gate in the middle. This time, I'm ready. In Spanish, I tell the guard I'm trying to find a friend of mine who's staying here but I want to surprise her. Then I slip him a twenty-dollar bill. He doesn't say a word—he just opens the gates.

"Twenty dollars," Broodje says, nodding his head. "Much classier than a couple of beers."

"It's probably what a couple of beers go for in a place like this."

We walk along the paved roadway, expecting to find a hotel, or some evidence of one, but what we find is another guard gate. The guards smile at us and call *buenos días*, as if they're expecting us, and by the way they're appraising us, like they're cats and we're mice, I see the other guards have called ahead. Without saying a word, I reach into my wallet and hand over another ten.

"Oh *gracias, señor*," the guard says. "*Que generoso!*" But then he looks around. "Only there are two of us."

I reach back into my wallet. The well's dry. I show my empty wallet. The guard shakes his head. I realize I over-played it back at the first gate. I should've offered up the ten first.

"Come on," I say. "It's all I have left."

"Do you know how much rooms here are?" he asks. "Twelve hundred dollars a night. If you want me to let you in, and your friend, to enjoy the pools, the beaches, the ten-nis, the buffets, you have to pay."

"*Buffets?*" Broodje interrupts.

"Shh!" I whisper. To the guard I say, "We don't care about any of that. We're just trying to find a guest here."

The guard raises his eyebrow. "If you know guests, why you sneak in like a thief? You think just because you have white skin, and a ten-dollar bill, we think you are rich?" He laughs. "It's an old trick, amigo."

"I'm not trying to sneak anything. I'm trying to find a girl. An American girl. She might be staying here."

This makes the guard laugh even harder. "An American girl? I'd like one of those, too. They cost more than ten dollars."

We glare at each other. "Give me my money back," I say.

"What money?" the guard asks.

I'm furious when we get back to the bike. Broodje, too, is muttering about getting ripped off that thirty dollars. But I don't care about the money, and it's not the guards I'm mad at.

I keep replaying a conversation with Lulu in my head. The one when she'd told me about Mexico. About how frustrating it was to go to the same resort with her family every year. I'd told her maybe she should go off the grid next time she went to Cancún. "Tempt fate," I'd said. "See what happens." Then I'd joked that maybe I'd go to Mexico one day, too, bump into her, and we'd escape into the wilds, having no idea at the time that this silly aside would become a mission of sorts. "You think that would happen?" she'd asked. "We'd just randomly bump into each other?" I'd told her it would have to be another big accident and she'd teased back: "So you're saying *I'm* an accident?"

After I told her that she was, she'd said something strange. She'd said that me calling her an accident might be the most flattering thing anyone has ever said about her. She wasn't simply fishing for compliments. She was revealing something with that honesty of hers, so completely disarming it was like she was stripping not just herself bare but me, too. When she said that, it had made me feel as if I'd been entrusted with something very important. And it also made me sad, because I sensed it was true. And if it was, it was wrong.

I've flattered lots of girls, many who deserved it, many who didn't. Lulu deserved it, she deserved so much more flattery than being called an accident. So I opened my mouth to say something nice. What came out, I think, surprised us both. I told her that she was the sort of person who found money and returned it, who cried in movies you weren't meant to cry in, who did things that scared her. I wasn't even sure where these things were coming from, only that as I said them, I was certain that they were true. Because improbable as it was, I *knew* her.

Only now it strikes me how wrong I was. I didn't know her at all. And I didn't ask the simplest of questions, like where she stayed in Mexico or when she visited or what her last name was, or what her first name was. And as a result, here I am, at the mercy of security guards.

We ride back to our hostel in the dusty part of Playa del Carmen, full of stray dogs and rundown shops. The cantina next door serves cheap beer and fish tacos. We order several of each. A couple of travelers from our hostel roll in. Broodje waves them over, and he starts telling them about our day, embellishing it so that it almost sounds fun. It's how all good travel stories are born. Nightmares spun into punch lines. But my frustration is too fresh to make anything seem funny.

Marjorie, a pretty Canadian girl, clucks sympathetically.

A British girl named Cassandra, with short spiky brown hair, laments the state of poverty in Mexico and the failures of NAFTA, while T.J., a sunburnt guy from Texas, just laughs. "I seen that place Maya del Sol. It's like Disneyland on the Riviera."

At the table behind us, I hear someone snicker. "*Más como Disneyland del infierno.*"

I turn around. "You know the place?" I ask in Spanish.

"We work there," the taller one answers in Spanish.

I put out my hand. "Willem," I say.

"Esteban," he answers.

"José," says the shorter. They're a bit of a spaghetti-and-meatball pair, too.

"Any chance you can sneak me in?"

Esteban shakes his head. "Not without risking my job. But there's an easy way to get in. They'll pay you to visit."

"Really?"

Esteban asks me if I have a credit card.

I pull out my wallet and show him my brand-new Visa, a gift from the bank after my large deposit.

"Okay, good," Esteban says. Then he looks at my outfit, a T-shirt and a beat-up pair of khakis. "You'll also need better clothes. Not these surfer things."

"No problem. Then what?"

Esteban explains how Cancún is full of sales reps trying to get people into those resorts to buy a timeshare. They hang out at car-rental places, in the airports, even at some of the ruins. "If they think you *have* money, they'll invite you to take a tour. They'll even pay *you* for your trouble, money, free tours, massages."

I explain this all to Broodje.

"Sounds too good to be true," he says.

"It's no too good, and it is true," José answers in English. "So many people buy, make such a big decision after just one day." He shakes his head, in wonderment, or disgust, or both.

"Fools and their money," T.J. says, laughing. "So y'all gotta look like you're loaded."

"But he *is* loaded!" Broodje says. "What does it matter what he looks like?"

José says, "No matter what you is; only matter what you seem."

— — —

I buy Broodje and myself some linen pants and button-up shirts for next to nothing and spend a ridiculous amount on a couple of pairs of Armani sunglasses from one of the stalls in the touristy section of town.

Broodje is aghast at the cost of the glasses. But I tell him they're necessary. "It's the little details that tell the big story." That was what Tor always said, to explain why we had such minimal costumes in Guerrilla Will.

"What's the big story?" he asks.

"We're slacker playboys with trust funds, renting a house on Isla Mujeres."

"So, aside from the house, you're pretending to be you?"

— — —

The next day is Christmas so we wait until the day after to set off. At the first car rental agency, we've practically rented a car by the time we realize that there's no one there offering us a tour. At the second car rental agency, we're met by a smiling, big-toothed American blonde who asks us how long we're in town for and where we're staying.

"Oh, I love the Isla," she purrs after we tell her about our villa. "Have you eaten at Mango yet?"

Broodje looks mildly panicked but I just give a little smile. "Not yet."

"Oh," she says. "Does your villa come with a cook?"

I just continue to smile, a little bashfully this time, as if the largesse embarrasses me.

"Wait. Are you renting the white adobe place with the infinity pool?"

Again, I smile. Little nod.

"So Rosa is the cook there?"

I don't answer, I don't need to. An embarrassed shrug will do.

"Oh, I *love* that place. And Rosa's mole is divine. Just thinking about it makes me hungry."

"I'm always hungry," Broodje says, leering. She looks at him quizzically. I give him a discreet kick.

"That place is very expensive," she says. "Have you ever considered buying something down here?"

I chuckle. "Too much responsibility," says Willem, Millionaire Playboy.

She nods, as if she too understands the burdens of juggling multiple properties. "Yes. But there is another way. You can own, and have someone else take care of it for you, even rent it out for you." She pulls out glossy brochures of several different hotels—including the Maya del Sol.

I glance at the brochures, scratching my chin. "You know, I heard about such an investment for tax-sheltering purposes," I say, channeling Marjolein now.

"Oh, fantastic moneymaker and money saver. You really should see one of these properties."

I pretend to casually glance at the brochures. "This one looks nice," I say, flicking a finger at the Maya del Sol brochure.

"It's sinfully decadent." She starts telling me all the things I know about the place, about the beach and the pools and the restaurants and the movie theater and the golf. I feign disinterest.

"I don't know," I say.

"Oh, at least take a tour!" She's practically pleading now. "You could even do one today."

I heave a big sigh and allow my eyes to flicker toward her for a brief minute. "We'd planned to see the ruins. That's why we're renting a car."

"I can arrange a free tour of the ruins for you." She reaches for another brochure. "This one goes to Coba, and you swim in a cenote and go on a zip line. I can throw that in for you two. Gratis."

I pause, as if considering it.

"Look, you can go, spend the day." She beckons me closer. "Don't tell them I told you but you could even spend the night. Once you get past the gates, you're in."

I look at Broodje, as if seeking his permission to do the girl this favor and take her tour. He gamely plays along, giving me a put-upon look that says, *well, if you must.*

I crack a smile at the girl and she positively beams in return. "Oh, fantastic!" She starts to write us up the paperwork, all the while chatting about the tour we'll go on. "And when you get back on the Isla, you must go to Mango. The brunches are to die for." She looks up from her paperwork. "Maybe I can take you."

"Maybe," I allow.

"Will you still be here for New Year's?"

I nod.

"What are you doing?"

I shrug, open my hands, as if to suggest so many, many options.

"There's this great party on the beach at Puerto Morelos. Las Olas de Molas, this wild reggae band, are playing. It's usually the best thing going in all of the Playa. A lot of us dance all night, and sometimes catch a ferry to the Isla for hangover brunch."

"Maybe I'll see you there."

She grins. "I'll cross my fingers. Here's everything you need for your tours," she says, handing me some paperwork, as well as a card with her personal cell phone number on it. "I'm Kayla. Call me if you need anything. *Anything* at all."

— — —

The same sweating, sweater-vested security guards are manning the gate to Maya del Sol, but they don't recognize us. Or they don't care. In the backseat of a taxi, with official paperwork in triplicate in hand, I am transformed.

We are deposited in the front lobby, an enormous atrium

full of bamboo, flowers, and tropical birds tied to perches. We sit down on a wicker loveseat while a burnished Mexican woman takes our IDs and makes copies of my credit card. Then we are delivered to an older Mexican man with a flip of golden hair held back by a pair of tortoiseshell Ray-Bans.

"Welcome!" he says. "My name is Johnny Maximo, and I'm here to tell you that at Maya del Sol, fantasy becomes reality."

"That's just what he's hoping for," Broodje says.

Johnny grins. He glances at the piece of paper in his hand. "So, William, Robert. Is it Robert or Bob?"

"Robert-Jan, actually," Broodje says.

"Robert then. Have you ever owned a vacation property?"

"I can't say that I have."

"What about you, William?"

"I'm more of a see-the-world kind of guy."

Johnny laughs. "Me, too. See all the ladies of the world. So I take it you two bachelors have never to been to a vacation club before."

"Can't say that I have, Johnny," Broodje says.

"I am telling you: this is the life. Why rent your vacation when you can own it? Why live half a life when you can live a whole one?"

"Or two lives, even," Broodje says.

"Here is one of our pools. We have six of them," Johnny brags. It's surrounded by chaise longues and flowering shrubs. Beyond, the Caribbean glitters as if its sole purpose is to be a backdrop. "The view is nice, no?" Johnny laughs, pointing to a row of sunbathing women.

"Very," I say, scanning them, one by one.

"So, what do you do, William?"

"Real estate," I say.

"Ahh, so you already know how lucrative it is. You know . . ." He motions me closer. "I used to be a big movie star in Mexico," he says in an exaggerated whisper. "But now—"

"You were an actor?" I interrupt.

This catches him off guard. "Before. But I make more money as an owner here than I ever did in the film business."

"What films were you in?" I ask.

"Oh, nothing you'd ever hear of."

"We get lots of foreign films in Holland. Try me."

"Really, I don't think you'd hear of them. I was in a film with Armand Assante. Mostly I was in the telenovelas."

"Soap operas? Like *Good Times, Bad Times*," Broodje says, scoffing a little.

"Here, they are taken very seriously," Johnny says with a sniff.

"That's cool," I say. "That you made your living like that."

For a second, Johnny's face flattens out. Even his tan seems to fade. And then he snaps to. "That was then. I make so much more money now." He claps his hands together and turns toward me. "So, William, what would you like to see?" He gestures out toward the grounds, and I have this first inkling, tiny but real, that she might be here. It's a small thing, but somehow it's the happiest I've felt in months.

"Every single centimeter of the resort," I say.

"Well, we are more than one square kilometer so that might take a while, but I am glad to see you are so motivated."

"Oh, you have no idea how motivated I am." Which is a funny thing to say because I wasn't that motivated yesterday. But now it's like I've switched into character.

"Why don't we start with one of our world-class restaurants. We have eight. Mexican, Italian, burger bar, sushi . . ."

"Yes," Broodje says.

"Why don't you show us the one that is the most popular for guests having lunch at this time," I suggest. "I'd like to see the makeup of the crowds."

"Oh, that would be Olé, Olé, our open-air cantina. It has a lunch buffet."

Broodje grins. Lunch buffet. Magic words.

———

Lulu is not at the lunch buffet, or any of the seven other restaurants we visit during our five-hour tour. She's not at any of the six pools or the two beaches or the twelve tennis courts or the two nightclubs or the three lobbies or the Zen day spa or the endless gardens. She's not at the petting zoo, either.

As the day lags on, I realize there are just too many variables. Maybe this is the wrong place. Or maybe this is the right place, but it's the wrong time. Or maybe it's the right place and the right time but she was watching TV in her room when I was at the pool. Maybe right now she is sitting by one of the pools while I'm looking at one of the model rooms.

Or maybe I walked right past her and I didn't even know it.

The good feeling from earlier begins to collapse in on itself. She could be anywhere. She could be nowhere. And worst of all, she could be right here and I didn't even recognize her.

A couple of girls in bikinis sashay past me, laughing. Broodje nudges me but I barely look at them. I'm beginning to think that I've talked myself into a lie of my own telling. Because the truth is I don't know her. All I know is that she's a girl who bears a passing resemblance to Louise Brooks. But what is that? The contours of a person, but really no more real than a fantasy projected onto a screen.

Seventeen

"Cheer up, hombre, it's almost a new year."

Esteban hands me a bottle. He, José, Broodje, Cassandra, and I are crammed into a taxi, crawling through holiday traffic as we head north to that party in Puerto Morelos, the one Kayla told me about. José and Esteban know about it, too, so apparently it really is the place to be.

"Yeah, come on. It's New Year's," Cassandra says.

"And you won't go home empty-handed if you don't want to," Broodje says. "Unlike some of us," he adds, full of exaggerated self-pity.

"Poor Broodje," Cassandra says. "Am I saying it right?"

"Bro-djuh," Broodje corrects, adding, "it means sandwich."

Cassandra smiles. "Don't worry, Sandwich Boy. We'll make sure somebody takes a bite out of you tonight."

"*I think she wants a bite of my sandwich,*" Broodje says in Dutch, grinning at the prospect. I attempt a smile back. But really, I'm done. I've been done since Maya del Sol, though I have dutifully checked out a few other resorts, thanks to José and Esteban, who told me how to get into Palacio Maya and got me wristbands for Maya Vieja. But it's felt like going through the motions. I don't even know who I'm looking for, so how am I going to find her?

The taxi skids onto a strip of undeveloped beach. We pay the driver and emerge onto a scene. Music throbs from huge speakers, and hundreds of people are scattered up and down the beach. Everyone seems to be barefoot, judging by the enormous piles of shoes right at the entrance to the party.

"Maybe you can find by her shoe," Cassandra says. "Like Cinderella. What would a glass slipper for the modern girl look like? How about this?" She holds up a pair of shiny orange flip-flops. She tries them on. "Too big," she says, flinging them back onto the piles.

"Would beautiful lady like to dance?" José asks Cassandra.

"Sure," she says, grinning. They walk away, José already with a hand on her hip.

Broodje's face falls. "I guess his taco was more appetizing than my sandwich."

"As you keep reminding me, there are lots of girls. I'm sure one of them will want a bite of your sandwich."

And there are so many girls. Hundreds of them, in all shapes and colors, perfumed and primed for partying. On any other New Year's, it would be a promising start.

The line for the bar snakes all the way around the palm trees and hammocks. We're inching our way forward when a girl wearing a sarong, a smile, and not much else stumbles into me.

"Steady there," I say, righting her by the elbow. She holds up a half-empty bottle of tequila, curtseys, and takes a long slug.

"You might want to pace yourself," I say.

"Why don't *you* pace me?"

"Okay." I take the bottle from her and swig. I hand it to Broodje, who does the same. He gives the bottle back to her.

She holds it up, swishes it around so the larva inside somersaults. "You can have the worm, if you want to," she says in a slurry voice. "Worm, worm, can the hottie eat you?" She holds the bottle up to her ear. "The worm says yes." She leans in closer, and in a hot whisper adds, "So do I."

"It's not really a worm," Broodje says. "It's an agave larva." José is a bartender and he explained this all to us.

Her eyes roll unfocused in her head. "What's the diff? Worm, larva. You know what they say? The early bird gets the worm." She hands Broodje the bottle, then puts both arms on my shoulder and kisses me, fast, wet, and boozy, on the mouth. She reels back, grabbing her tequila bottle. "Gets the kiss, too," she says, laughing. "Happy New Year."

Broodje and I watch her stumble through the sand. Then he turns to me. "I forgot what it's like, being out with you. What you're like."

Six months ago, I'd have kissed the girl back, and the night would be set. Broodje may know what I'm like, but I don't.

When we get our drinks, Broodje makes his way toward the dance area. I tell him I'll meet up with him later. Up the beach, away from the stage and dance area, I spot a small bonfire with a group of people sitting around it, strumming on guitars. I start off in that direction, but then I see someone walking toward me. Kayla of the car rental agency, waving tentatively, as if she's not sure it's really me.

I pretend to not be me, and pivot toward the shoreline. As crowded and chaotic as the party is, the water is surprisingly quiet. There are a few people splashing about. Farther out, it's empty, just moonlight reflecting on the water. Even at night, the water is bluer than I imagined it; it's the only part of this trip that is coming close to meeting expectations.

I strip down to my boxers and dive in, swimming far out, until I reach a floating raft. I grip the splintering wood. The sounds of the guitars strumming "Stairway to Heaven" and the heavy bass of a reggae band reverberate through the water. It's a good party, on a beautiful beach, on a soft, warm night. All the things that used to be enough.

I swim out a little farther and duck back under. Tiny silvery fish zip by. I reach out to touch them, but they whip out of reach so fast it's like they're leaving contrails behind. When I can't hold my breath any longer, I come up for air to hear the reggae singer announce: "Half hour until the New Year. Until it all starts again. *Año nuevo*. It's a tabula rasa."

I take a breath and go back under. I scoop up a handful of

sand and let it go, watching the grains disperse in the water. I come back up.

"Come the stroke of midnight, before you kiss your *amor*, save *un beso para tí*."

A kiss for you.

Moments before I'd kissed her for the first time, Lulu had said another one of her strange things: *I escaped danger*. She was emphatic about it, her eyes had a fire to them, just as they had when she'd come between me and the skinheads. It had seemed a peculiar thing to say. Until I'd kissed her. And then I felt it, as visceral and all-encompassing as the water around me now. Escaping danger. I'm not sure what danger she'd been referring to. All I knew was that kissing Lulu made me feel relief, like I'd landed somewhere after a long journey.

I turn onto my back, looking at the canvas of a star-spangled sky.

"Tabula rasa . . . time to *hacer borrón y cuenta nueva*, wipe the board clean," the singer chants.

Wipe the board clean? I feel like my board is too clean, perpetually wiped bare. What I want is the opposite: a messy scrawl, constellations of indelible things that can't ever be washed away.

She *must* be here. Maybe not at this party, or on this beach, or at the resorts I visited, but *somewhere* here. Swimming in *this* water, the same water I'm in now.

But it's a big ocean. It's an even bigger world. And maybe we've gotten as close as we're supposed to get.

Eighteen

*T*he bus is shaped like a monkey, it's full of old people, and I don't want to be on it. But Broodje does, and after dragging him to half the resorts on the Mayan Riviera, I'm not one to argue.

"First stop, Coba, then we go to a Mayan village. Then a zip line—not sure about these folks and a zip line," Broodje says, nodding to our mostly gray-haired tour mates. "Then swimming in a cenote—it's a kind of underground cave lake—then Tulum." He flips the brochure around. "This tour costs a hundred and fifty dollars per person and we got it for free."

"Hmm," I say.

"I don't get it. You're Dutch on one side, Israeli on the other. By all rights, this should make you the cheapest bastard alive."

"Uhh-huh."

"Are you listening?"

"Sorry. I'm tired."

"Hungover more like. When we stop for lunch, we'll get some tequila. Hair of the dog is what T.J. calls it."

I bunch my rucksack into a makeshift pillow and lean my head against the window. Broodje pulls out a copy of *Voetbal International*. The bus chugs off. I fall asleep, waking when we arrive at Coba. We plod off the bus, standing in a little clump as the guide tells us about the ancient Mayan ruins, a series of isolated temples and pyramids half overtaken by the trees and vines of the jungle. "It's very unique," she says. "This is one of the few ruins you can still climb. And you'll also be interested in the lagoon, La Iglesia, or church, and of course, the ball courts."

Behind us, a girl, the only other person our age, asks, "Ball courts? What kind of ball did they play?"

"A sort of basketball," the guide answers.

"Oh." She sounds disappointed.

"You don't like basketball?" Broodje asks her. "I thought Americans loved basketball."

"She's a soccer player," an older woman says. "She was all-state in high school."

"Nana!"

"Really? What position?" Broodje asks.

"Striker."

"Midfield." He taps his chest.

They look at each other. "Wanna go check out the ball courts?" she asks.

"Sure."

"Be back in a half hour, Candace," the older lady says.

"Okay."

Broodje looks at me to come, but I nod for him to go alone. When the rest of the tour sets off toward the lagoon, I turn straight for the Nohoch Mul pyramid, climbing the 120 near-vertical steps to the top. It's midday and hot so there's hardly anyone up here, just a family taking pictures. It's still enough for the quiet to be loud: the rustle of the breeze in the trees, the squawk of tropical birds, the metallic chirp of crickets. A gust of hot wind picks up a dry leaf and carries it over the jungle canopy.

The stillness is interrupted by a couple of kids, who have started shouting each other's names in bird chirps. *"Josh!"* the girl squawks, as her brother laughs.

"Allie!" the boy, Josh, presumably, chirps back.

"Joshua, Allison, *shh*," their mother chides, gesturing to me. "You're not the only ones up here."

The kids look at me, cocking their heads, as if inviting me to call out a name, too. I hold up my hands and shrug because I don't actually know the name I want to yell. I'm not even sure I want to yell it anymore.

Back at the Monkey Bus, I find Broodje and Candace sharing a Coke, one bottle, two straws. When we lumber back on board, I slip into a seat next to an older man traveling solo, allowing Broodje and Candace to sit together in our row. When I hear them arguing about whether Van Persie or Messi is the best striker, I smile, and my gentleman seatmate smiles back.

After lunch, we stop at a traditional Mayan village and are given the option of a ten-dollar spiritual cleansing by a Mayan priest. I stay off to the side as the others take turns standing under a smoking canopy. Then we're herded back on the bus. The doors wheeze open. Broodje climbs on, Candace climbs on, my seatmate with the sandals and the socks climbs on, the guide climbs on. Everyone climbs on, except me.

"Willy, you coming?" Broodje calls.

He sees me hesitating by the door and comes back down the aisle to talk to me. "Willy, all is good? Are you mad that I'm sitting with Candace?"

"Of course not. I think it's great."

"Come on."

I do the calculations in my mind. Candace said she was in town until the eighth, longer than we are. Broodje will have company.

"I'm getting off here." As soon as I say it, I feel that familiar relief. When you're on the road, there is always the promise of the next stop being better than the last.

His face goes serious. "Are you staying away because of what I said before, about you getting all the girls? Don't worry. I think one actually likes me."

"I'm sure of it. So you should make the most of it. I'll see you back at the airport for the flight home."

"*What?* That's in four days. And you don't have your things."

"I have what I need. Just bring the rest to the airport."

The bus driver guns the engine. The guide taps her watch. Broodje looks panicked.

"It's okay," I reassure him, tightening the straps on my rucksack.

"You won't get lost?" he asks.

I paste on a reassuring smile. But of course, the truth is, that is exactly what I intend to do.

Nineteen

Valladolid, Mexico

*T*wo hitched truck rides later, I find myself on the outskirts of Valladolid, a small colonial town. I wander around the central square, full of low-rise, pastel colonial buildings reflecting in a large fountain. Soon I stumble upon a cheap hotel.

It feels a world away from the Mayan Riviera here. Not just the lack of megaresorts or partying tourists, but how I got here. Not looking, just finding.

I have no schedule. I sleep when I'm tired, eat when I'm hungry, grabbing something hot and spicy from one of the food carts. I linger late into the night. I don't look for anyone. I don't talk to anyone. After the last few months on Bloemstraat, the boys always around, or if not them, Ana Lucia, I'm not used to being alone.

I sit at the edge of the fountain and watch people and, for a minute, indulge myself imagining Lulu being one of them, imagining that we really had escaped into the wilds of Mexico. Is this where we'd go? Would we sit at a café, our ankles intertwined, our heads close, like that couple over there under the umbrella? Would we walk all night, ducking into the alleyways to steal a kiss? Would we wake up the next morning, untangle our bodies, pull out a map, close our eyes, and decide where to go next? Or would we just never get out of bed?

No! Stop it! This is pointless. A road nowhere. I get up, brush off my pants, and return to the hotel. Lying in bed, I spin a twenty-peso coin around my knuckles and ponder what to do next. When the coin falls to the floor, I reach for it. And then I stop. Heads, I'll stay in Valladolid another day. Tails, I'll move on. Tails.

It's not pointing at the map. But it'll do.

———

The next morning I go downstairs in search of coffee. The worn dining room is practically empty—one Spanish-speaking family at one table, and in the corner by the window, a pretty woman about my age with hair the color of rust.

"I was wondering about you," she calls in English. She sounds American.

I pour some coffee from the samovar. "I often wonder about me, too," I reply.

"I saw you last night at the food carts. I've been trying to brave up to eat at them, but I wasn't sure what they were serving or if it would kill a gringo like me."

"I think it was pork. I don't ask too many questions."

"Well, it didn't kill you." She laughs. "And whatever doesn't kill you makes you stronger."

We stand there for a second. I gesture to join her at the same time she gestures for me to take a seat. I sit down across from her. A waiter in a tired tuxedo drops off a plate of Mexican sweet bread.

"Careful there," she says, flicking at her own stale bread with a turquoise-painted nail. "I almost chipped a tooth."

I knock at it. It sounds like a hollow log. "I've had worse."

"What are you, some kind of a professional adventure eater?"

"Something like that."

"Where are you from?" She holds up a hand. "No, wait, let me guess. Say something else."

"Something else?"

She taps a finger to her temple, then snaps her fingers. "You're Dutch."

"Good ear."

"Not much of an accent, though."

"Very good ear. I grew up speaking English."

"Did you live in England?"

"No, it was just my mother didn't like speaking Dutch, thought it sounded too much like German. So at home, it was English."

She glances at the phone on the table. "Well, I suspect there is a fascinating story behind that, but I'm afraid it'll have to remain a mystery." She pauses. "I'm a day late already."

"Late for what?"

"For Mérida. I was supposed to be there yesterday, but my car broke down, and, well, it's been a cascading comedy of errors. What about you? Where are you headed?"

I pause. "Mérida—if you'll give me a ride."

"I wonder what would piss off David more—driving alone or giving a ride to strangers."

"Willem." I hold out my hand. "Now I'm not a stranger."

She narrows her eyes at my outstretched hand. "You'll need to do better than that."

"Sorry. I'm Willem de Ruiter." I reach into my backpack for my stiff new passport and hand it over. "Here's some identification."

She flips through it. "Nice picture, Willem. I'm Kate. Kate Roebling. And I'm not showing you my passport because the picture is very unfortunate. You'll just have to trust me on that."

She smiles and slides my passport back across the table. "Okay, then, Willem de Ruiter, traveling adventure-eater. The garage just opened so I'm grabbing the car. Assuming it's actually ready, I'll be hitting the road in about a half hour. Does that give you time to get packed and ready to go?"

I point to my rucksack on the floor next to me. "I'm always packed and ready to go."

— — —

Kate picks me up in a sputtering Volkswagen jeep, the seats torn, the foam stuffing coming out. "*This* is fixed?" I ask, climbing in.

"That's just cosmetic. You should've seen it before. The

muffler was falling out, literally dragging behind the car, sparking. The whole rainforest could've gone up in flames because of this baby. No offense. Who's a pretty girl?" She pats the dashboard and turns to me, whispering. "You have to be nice to her. Or she won't go."

I tip an imaginary hat to the car. "My apologies."

"This is actually a great car. Appearances can be quite deceiving, you know." She guns the engine.

"Yes, I've noticed."

"Thank God, or I'd be out of a job."

"Bank robber?"

"Ha! I'm an actor."

"*Really*?"

She turns to me. "Why? Are you of the tribe?"

"Not really."

She raises an eyebrow. "'Not really'? That's like being 'a little' pregnant. You either are or you're not."

"How about I was, not seriously, and now I'm not."

"Oh, did you need to get a 'real job'?" she asks sympathetically.

"No. I don't have one of those, either."

"So you just travel and eat dangerously?"

"More or less."

"Nice life."

"More or less." The car hits a pothole and my stomach seems to smack against the roof and then just as abruptly, plummet back to the floor. "What kind of acting do you do?" I ask when I've regained my equilibrium.

"I'm a cofounder and artistic director of a small theater

company in New York called Ruckus. We do productions, but also training and teaching programs."

"That's not impressive at all."

"I know, right? I never meant to be quite so ambitious, but when my friends and I moved to New York, we couldn't get the kind of roles we wanted, so we started our own company. And it's just kind of grown. We produce our own plays and we teach, and now we've started this overseas initiative. That's why we're in Mexico. We're running a workshop on Shakespeare in Mérida in conjunction with Universidad Autónoma de Yucatán."

"You're teaching Shakespeare in Spanish?"

"Well, *I'm* not, because I don't speak a lick of Spanish. I'll work with the English speakers. David, my fiancé, he speaks Spanish. Though the funny thing is, even when we do the Shakespeare in translation, I somehow know where we are in the plays. Maybe because I know them so well. Or because Shakespeare transcends language."

I nod. "The first time I did Shakespeare, I did it in French."

She turns to me. Her eyes are green, bright as autumn apples, and there's a smattering of freckles across the bridge of her nose. "You did Shakespeare then? And in French?"

"Mostly in English, of course."

"Oh, *of course*." She pauses. "That's pretty good for a not-serious actor."

"I never said I was any good."

She laughs. "Oh, I can tell you were good."

"Really?"

"Yep. I have a Spidey-sense for these things." She pulls

out a package of gum, takes a stick, and offers me a piece. It tastes like talcum powder and coconuts and makes my still-churning stomach rebel a little bit more. I spit it out.

"Vile, right? Yet strangely addictive." She pops a second piece. "So how in the world did a Dutchman wind up doing Shakespeare in French?"

"I was traveling. I was broke. I was in Lyon. I met this Shakespeare troupe called Guerrilla Will. They mostly performed in English but the director is a little . . . eccentric and she thought the way to one-up the other street performers was to do Shakespeare in the native language. She'd cobbled together a cast of French speakers to do *Much Ado About Nothing* in France, in French. But the guy who'd been playing Claudio ran off to be with some Norwegian guy he'd met; everyone was already doubling up parts so they just needed someone who could get by in French. And I could."

"You'd never done Shakespeare before?"

"I'd never acted before. I'd been traveling with an acrobatic troupe. So when I tell you it was all by accident, I'm not kidding."

"But you did other plays?"

"Yeah, *Much Ado* was a disaster but we ran it for four nights before Tor realized it. Then Guerrilla Will switched back to English and I stayed on. It was decent money."

"Oh, you're one of *those*. Doing Shakespeare just for the money," she jokes. "You whore."

I laugh.

"So what other plays did you do?"

"*Romeo and Juliet*, of course. *A Midsummer Night's Dream. All's Well That Ends Well. Twelfth Night.* All the crowd-pleasers."

"I love *Twelfth Night*; we're talking about doing that next year when we have time. We just closed a two-year off-Broadway run of *Cymbeline* and we've been touring it. Do you know it?"

"I've heard of it, but I've never seen it."

"It's a lovely, funny, romantic play and there's lots of music in it. At least the way we do it."

"Us, too. We had a drum circle in our *Twelfth Night*."

She glances at me sidelong as she keeps her eyes on the road. "*Our Twelfth Night?*"

"Theirs. Guerrilla Will's."

"Sounds like the whore fell in love with the john."

"No. No falling in love," I say.

"But you miss it?"

I shake my head. "I've moved on."

"I see." We're quiet for a while. Then she says, "Do you do that a lot? Move on?"

"Maybe. But only because I travel a lot."

She taps out a beat on the steering wheel, audible only to herself. "Or maybe you travel a lot because it lets you move on."

"Perhaps."

She's quiet again. Then: "So are you moving on now? Is that what brought you to the grand metropolis of Valladolid?"

"No. The wind just blew me there."

"What? Like a plastic bag?"

"I prefer to think of myself as a ship. Like a sailboat."

"But sailboats aren't steered by the wind; they're powered by it. There's a difference."

I look out the window. The jungle is everywhere. I look back at her. "Can you move on from something when you're not sure what it is you're moving on from?"

"You can move on from absolutely anything," she replies. "But that does sound a little complicated."

"It is," I say. "Complicated."

Kate doesn't answer, and the silence stretches out, shimmery, like the road ahead of us.

"And a long story," I add.

"It's a long drive," she replies.

There's something about Kate that reminds me of Lulu. Maybe it's just that they're both American or how we met: during journeys, talking food.

Or maybe it's because in a few hours, I'll never see her again. There's nothing to lose. So as we drive, I tell Kate the story of that day, but it's a different version from the one I told Broodje and the boys. You play to your audience, Tor always said. Which is maybe why I can tell Kate the parts of the story that I didn't—couldn't—tell Broodje and the boys. "It was like she knew me," I tell her. "Straightaway, she knew me."

"How?"

I tell Kate about Lulu thinking I'd deserted her on the train when I'd spent too long in the café. Hysterically laughing, and then out of the blue—my glimmer of her strange honesty—telling me she'd thought I'd got off the train.

"Were you going to?" Kate asks, her eyes wide.

"No, of course not," I answer. And I wasn't, but the memory of it still shames me because of what I was going to do later.

"So how did she *see* you, exactly?"

"She said she couldn't understand why I invited her without an ulterior motive."

Kate laughs. "I hardly think you wanting to sleep with a pretty girl qualifies as an ulterior motive."

I wanted to sleep with her, of course. "But that wasn't the ulterior motive. I invited her to Paris because I didn't want to go back to Holland that day."

"Why not?"

My stomach lurches again. Bram, gone. Yael, all but gone. The houseboat, a signature away from gone. I force a smile. "That is a much longer story and I'm not done with this one."

I tell Kate the double happiness story Lulu told me. About the Chinese boy traveling to take some important exam, and along the way, falling sick. About the mountain doctor taking care of him. About the doctor's daughter telling him this strange line of verse. About the emperor who, after the boy does well on the exam, recites a mysterious line to him. About the boy immediately recognizing the line as the other half of what the girl told him, and repeating the line the girl had told him, pleasing the emperor, getting the job, going back, and marrying the girl. About double happiness.

"*Green trees against the sky in the spring rain while the sky set off the spring trees in the obscuration. Red flowers* dot the land in the breeze's chase while the land colored up in red after the kiss." That had been the couplet. As soon as Lulu told it to me, there had been something instantly familiar about it, even though I'd never heard it before, never heard the story before. Unknown and familiar. Which, by that point, was how Lulu was seeming.

I tell Kate about Lulu asking who took care of me—as if she knew the answer—and then doing it herself. Stepping between me and the skinheads. Throwing that book. Distracting them so we could get away before we got hurt. Only she got hurt. Even now, the memory of the blood on her neck from when one of the skinheads threw the bottle at her, after all these months, it makes me sick. And ashamed. I don't tell Kate that.

"That was very brave of her," Kate says when I tell her what Lulu did.

Saba used to say there was a difference between bravery and courage. Bravery was doing something dangerous without thinking. Courage was walking into danger, knowing full well the risks.

"No," I tell Kate. "It was courageous."

"You both were courageous."

But I wasn't. Because I tried to send Lulu back. Cowardly. And then I didn't manage to. Cowardly. I don't tell Kate this part either.

"So you're here in Mexico to do what?" she asks.

I think of the boys. They think I'm here to inoculate myself. To find Lulu, sleep with her a few more times, and get on with things.

"I don't know . . . find her. At the very least, set the record straight."

"What record? You left a note."

"Yes, but . . ." I almost say it. Then I stop myself.

"But what?" Kate asks.

"But . . . I didn't come back," I finish.

Kate looks at me for a long moment. The car starts to drift off the road before she returns her attention to driving.

"Willem, in case you haven't noticed, Cancún is back that way?" She points in the reverse direction. I nod. "The chances of you finding this girl seem unfavorable enough without you going to an entirely different city."

"It wasn't going to happen. I could tell."

"How could you tell?"

"Because you don't ever find things when you're looking for them. You find them when you're not."

"If that were true, nobody would ever find their keys."

"Not keys. The bigger things."

She sighs. "I don't get it. On one hand, you put all this faith into these accidents of yours, and on the other hand, you write off the chance of one even happening."

"I didn't write it off. I came all the way to Cancún."

"And promptly went to Mérida."

"I wasn't going to find her. By looking." I shake my head. It's hard to explain this part. "It wasn't meant to be."

"Meant to be," Kate scoffs. "Excuse me but I'm having a hard time buying all this woo-woo stuff." She waves her arms in the air and I have to reach out for the steering wheel until she takes it again. "Nothing happens without intention,

Willem. Nothing. This theory of yours—life is ruled by accidents—isn't that just one huge excuse for passivity?"

I start to disagree, but then the image of Ana Lucia flits through my head. Right place at the right time. It had seemed like a fortuitous accident back then. Now, it feels more like surrender.

"How do you explain us?" I point back and forth to me and her. "Right now, right here, having this conversation, if not for accidents? If not because your car muffler broke and put you in Valladolid, where I wasn't even meant to be?" I don't mention the flipped coin being a deciding factor, even though it would seem to support my case.

"Oh, no, don't go falling in love with me." She laughs and taps the ring on her finger. "Look, I don't discount a magical hand of fate. I am an actor, after all, and a Shakespearian, no less. But it can't be the ruling force of your life. You have to be the driver. And by the way, yes, we are having this conversation because my car— lovely, sweet car that you are," she baby talks, stroking the dashboard, "had some mechanical issues. But *you* were the one who asked *me* for a ride, persuaded me to give you a ride, so you discredit your own theory right there. That was pure will, Willem. Sometimes fate or life or whatever you want to call it, leaves a door a little open and you walk through it. But sometimes it locks the door and you have to find the key, or pick the lock, or knock the damn thing down. And sometimes, it doesn't even show you the door, and you have to build it yourself. But if you keep waiting for the doors to be opened for you. . . ." she trails off.

"What?"

"I think you'll have a hard time finding single happiness, let alone that double portion."

"I'm beginning to doubt that double happiness even exists," I say, thinking of my parents.

"That's because you're looking for it. Doubt is part of searching. Same as faith."

"Aren't those opposites?"

"Maybe they're just two parts of the couplet."

It reminds me of something Saba used to say: *A truth and its opposite are flip sides of the same coin.* It never quite made sense to me before.

"Willem, I suspect deep down you know *exactly* why you're here, *exactly* what you want, but you're unwilling to commit to it, unwilling to commit to the wanting, let alone the having. Because both of those propositions are terrifying."

She turns to me and gives me a long, searing look. It goes on a while, and the car starts to drift. Again, I take the wheel to right us. She lets go of the wheel entirely and I grasp it with both hands.

"Look there, Willem. You grabbed the wheel."

"Only to keep us from crashing."

"Or, you might say, to keep us from having an accident."

Twenty

Mérida, Mexico

*M*érida is a bigger version of Valladolid, a colonial pastel-painted city. Kate drops me off in front of a historic peach-colored building that she has heard is a decent hostel. I book myself a room with a balcony overlooking the square and I sit out and watch people taking shelter from the afternoon sun. Shops are closing up for siesta and though I'd planned to scout out the area and find some lunch, I'm not actually hungry. I'm a little wrung out from the morning's drive and my stomach still feels as if it's on the bumpy highway. I decide to take a siesta, too.

— — —

I wake up covered in sweat. It's dark outside, the air in my room still and stale. I sit up to open my window or the balcony door, but when I do, my stomach heaves. I flop back down on the bed and close my eyes, willing myself back to sleep. Sometimes I can trick my body into righting itself before it realizes something's wrong. Sometimes that works.

But not tonight. I think of the pork in the brown sauce I ate for dinner last night and the memory of it makes my stomach wave and flutter, like there's a small feral animal trapped inside.

Food poisoning. It must be. I sigh. Okay. A few hours discomfort, and then sleep. Then it will be over. It's all about getting to the sleep.

I'm not sure of the time so I don't know how long it takes for the sun to come up, but when it does, I haven't even touched sleep. I've puked so many times the plastic wastebin is almost full. I tried, a few times, to crawl to the shared bathroom down the hall, but I couldn't make it past my door. Now that the sun is up, the room is heating up. I can almost see the toxic fumes from the wastebin spreading out, poisoning me all over again.

I keep throwing up. There's no respite or relief in between bouts. I puke until there's nothing left: no food, no bile, none of me left, it seems.

That's when the thirst hits. I've long since drunk the rest of the water in my bottle, and thrown that up too. I start to fantasize about mountain streams, waterfalls, rain showers, even the Dutch canal; I'd drink from those if I could. They sell bottled water downstairs. And there's a tap in the bathroom. But I can't sit up, let alone stand up, let alone make it to water.

Is anyone there? I call. In Dutch. In English. I try to remember the Spanish but the words get jumbled. I think I'm talking but I can't tell and it's noisy in the square and my weak voice stands no chance.

I listen for a knock at the door, praying for an offering of water, clean sheets, a cool compress, a soft hand on my forehead. But none comes. This is a hostel, bare bones, no housekeeping, and I prepaid two nights.

I retch again. Nothing comes out except my tears. I am twenty-one years old and I still cry when I puke.

Finally, sleep comes to rescue me. And then I wake up, and I see her, so close. And all I can think is: *It was worth it if it brought you.*

Who takes care of you now? she whispers. Her breath feels like a cooling breeze.

You, I whisper back. *You take care of me.*

I'll be your mountain girl.

I try to reach for her, but now she's gone and the room is full of the others: Céline and Ana Lucia and Kayla and Sara and the girl with the worm, and there's more yet—a Franke in Riga, a Gianna in Prague, a Jossra in Tunis. They all start talking at me.

We'll take care of you.

Go away, I want Lulu back. Tell her to come back.

Green turtles, red blood, blue sky, double happiness, la-lala, they singsong.

No! That's not how it goes. That's not how double happiness goes.

But I can't remember how it goes either.

She left you like this.

I'll take care of you.

French whore.

Call me if you need anything.

Wanna share with me?

Stop it! I yell.

Take the wheel! Now it's Kate yelling. Only I can't see any wheel and I have the awful feeling, like in the dreams, that I'm going to crash.

No! Stop. Go away! All of you! You're not real. None of you! Not even Lulu. I screw my eyes shut and cover my ears with the sweat-soaked pillow and curl up into a fetal ball. And finally, finally, like this, I fall asleep.

— — —

I wake up. My skin is cool. The sky is purple. I'm not sure if it's twilight or dawn, how long I've been out. I'm coherent enough to know that I'm supposed to be back in Cancún soon to meet Broodje and fly back to Holland, and I need to get word to him somehow, that he might have to leave without me. I swing my legs over the side of the bed. The room teeters before my eyes, but it doesn't totter over. I plant my feet. I pull to a stand. Like a toddler or a very old man, I take the steps, one at a time, to the lobby.

In the corner is an Internet café where you can make long-distance phone calls. I feel like I've been in the dark for months, the lights from all those monitors hurt my eyes so. I hand over some money and ask for a phone and am guided to a bank of computers with a telephone handset. I open my address book. Kate's card, RUCKUS THEATER

COMPANY splashed across the top in red lettering, falls out.

I start to dial. The digits swim on the page and I'm not sure if I have the country code right or if I dialed correctly.

But there's a tinny ring. And then a voice: faraway, tunnel-like, but unmistakably hers. As soon as I hear it, my throat closes.

"Hello. Hello? Who is this?"

"Ma?" I manage to croak out.

Silence. And when she says my name I want to cry.

"Ma," I say again.

"Willem, where are you?" Her voice is crisp, officious, businesslike as always.

"I'm lost."

"You're *lost?*"

I've been lost before, in new cities with no familiar landmarks to set me straight, waking up in strange beds, unsure of where I was or who was next to me. But I realize now, *that* wasn't lost. It was something else. This . . . I may know exactly where I am—in a hostel, in the central square, in Mérida, Mexico—but I have never been so utterly unmoored.

There's a long silence on the line and I'm afraid the call has dropped. But then Yael says: "Come to me. I'll send you a ticket. Come to me."

It's not what I really want to hear. What I want—what I ache—to hear is *come home.*

But she can't tell me to come to a place that no longer exists, any more than I can go to that place. For now, this is the best either of us can do.

Twenty-one

FEBRUARY
Mumbai, India

Emirates 148
13 Feb: Departure 14:40 Amsterdam—00:10 Dubai
Emirates 504
14 Feb: Departure 03:55 Dubai—08:20 Mumbai
Have a safe trip.

This email, containing my itinerary, comprises the bulk of the communication between Yael and me since I returned from Mexico last month. When I got back from Cancún, a friendly travel agent named Mukesh called to request a copy of my passport. A week later, I got the itinerary from Yael. I've heard little else since.

I try not to read too much into it. This is Yael. And this is me. The most charitable explanation is that she's hoarding the small talk so we will have something to say to each other for the next . . . two weeks, month, six weeks? I'm not sure. We haven't discussed it. Mukesh told me that the ticket was valid for three months and that if I wanted help booking flights within India, or out of India, I should contact him. I try not to read too much into that, either.

In the immigration line, I'm jangly with nerves. The bar of duty-free Toblerone (meant for Yael) that I wound up eating as the plane descended into Mumbai probably didn't help matters. As the line lurches forward, an impatient Indian woman pushes into me with her prodigious sari-wrapped belly, as if that will make us go faster. I almost switch places with her. To stop the pushing. And to make us go slower.

When I exit into the airport arrivals hall, the scene is both space age and biblical. The airport is modern and new, but the hall is thronged with people who seem to be carrying their entire lives on metal trolleys. The minute I get out of customs, I know that Yael is not here. It's not that I don't see her, though I don't. It's that I realize, belatedly, she never specifically said she'd meet me. I just assumed. And with my mother, you never assume.

But it's been almost three years. And she invited me here. I go back and forth through the hall. All around me, people swarm and push and shove, as if racing for some invisible finish line. But there's no Yael.

Ever optimistic, I go outside to see if she's waiting there. The bright morning light hurts my eyes. I wait ten minutes. Fifteen. There's no sign of my mother.

There's a gladiator match of taxi drivers and porters vying for passengers. *Psst,* they hiss at me. I stare at the itinerary now gone limp in my hand, as if it will somehow impart critical new information.

"Are you being met?"

In front of me is a man. Or a boy. Somewhere in between. He seems about my age, except for his eyes, which are ancient.

I give the area one more sweep. "It appears I'm not."

"Do you need a driver?"

"It appears I do."

"Where are you going?"

I recall the address from the immigration forms I just filled out in triplicate. "The Bombay Royale. In Colaba. Do you know it?"

He gives his head a half nod, half shake that isn't exactly reassuring. "I take you there."

"Are you a driver?"

He wags his head again. "Where is your suitcase?"

I point to the small rucksack on my back.

He laughs. "Like Kurma."

"The food?"

"No. That is korma. Kurma is one of Vishnu's incarnations, a tortoise, carries his home on his back. But if you like korma, I can show you a good place."

The boy introduces himself as Prateek and then confidently threads us through the crowd past the airport garage and to a dusty lot. On one side are the runways, the other, high-rise buildings and even higher cranes, swinging in the wind. Prateek locates the car—something that back home might be called vintage, but when I compliment it, he makes a face and tells me it belongs to his uncle and one day, he will buy his own car, a good one made abroad, a Renault, or a Ford, not a Maruti or a Tata. He pays the skinny dusty boy who was guarding the car a few coins and opens the backseat. I toss my rucksack there and try to open the front door. Prateek tells me to wait, and with a complicated sequence of rattles and twists, opens it from the inside, sweeping a pile of magazines from the passenger seat.

The car shudders to life and the little brass statue cemented to the dash—a tiny elephant with a sort of smile of the perpetually amused—starts to dance.

"Ganesha," Prateek says. "Remover of obstacles."

"Where were you last month?" I ask the statue.

"He was right here," Prateek answers solemnly.

We drive out of the airport complex, past a bunch of ramshackle houses, before climbing onto an elevated expressway. I tilt my head out the window. It's pleasantly hot, but not as hot as it will be, Prateek warns. It's still winter; it will get warmer until the monsoons come in June.

As we drive, Prateek points out landmarks. A famous temple. A spidery suspension bridge crossing Mahim Bay. "Many Bollywood stars live in this area. Closer to the studios, which are near the airport." He thumbs behind us. "Though some live in Juhu Beach, and some in Malabar Hill. Some even in Colaba where you are staying. Taj Mahal Hotel is there. Angelina Jolie, Brad Pitt, Roger Moore, Double-Oh Seven. Also American presidents all stayed there."

Traffic starts to back up. We slow down and Ganesha stops his dance. "What is your favorite movie?" Prateek asks me.

"Hard to pick just one."

"What is the last movie you saw?"

I flipped through a half dozen of them on the flights over, but was too antsy to focus on any one. I suppose the last movie I watched in full was *Pandora's Box*. That was the movie that started it all, that led to the disastrous trip to Mexico, which funnily enough, has now landed me here. Lulu. If she was far away before, she's farther now. Not one but two oceans between us now.

"Never heard of that movie," Prateek says, wagging his head. "My favorite movie of the last year is a tie. *Gangs of Wasseypur*. Thriller. And *London, Paris, New York*. Do you know how many films Hollywood studios produce a year?"

"No idea."

"Take a guess."

"A thousand."

He frowns. "I speak of the studios, not an amateur with a camera. One thousand, that would be impossible."

"A hundred?"

His smile flips on like a switch. "Wrong! Four hundred. Now do you know how many films Bollywood produces a year? I won't make you guess because you will be wrong." He pauses for dramatic effect. "Eight hundred!"

"Eight hundred," I repeat because it's clear he thinks the number warrants repeating.

"Yes!" He's smiling broadly now. "Twice the number of Hollywood. Do you know how many people in India go to the movies every single day?"

"I have a feeling you're going to tell me."

"Fourteen million. Do fourteen million people go to the movies every day in Germany?"

"I wouldn't know. I'm from Holland. But given that the entire population isn't much more than sixteen million, I doubt it."

He beams with pride now.

We exit the expressway onto the streets of what must be colonial Mumbai and turn into an area with an arbor of trees and a line of idling double-decker buses belching out black exhaust.

"There is the Gateway of India," Prateek says, pointing out a carved arch monument on the edge of the Arabian Sea. "The Taj Mahal Hotel I told you about," he says, pulling past a massive confection of a hotel, all domes and cornices. A group of Arab men in billowing white robes are piling into a series of window-tinted SUVs. "Inside is a Starbucks." He lowers his voice to a whisper. "Have you ever had a Starbucks coffee?"

"I have."

"My cousin said that in America they drink it with every meal." He pulls up in front of another graying building, Victorian, and it seems, almost sweating in the heat. The sign, in fading elaborate cursive, reads BO BAY RO AL. "Here you are. Bombay Royale."

I follow Prateek into a darkened, cool lobby, quiet except for the whoosh and squeak of ceiling fans and the faint chirping of crickets nesting somewhere in the walls. Behind a long mahogany desk, a man so old he seems original to the building is napping. Prateek loudly rings the bell and he startles awake.

Immediately, the two start arguing, mostly in Hindi but with a few English words thrown in here and there. "Regulations," the old man keeps saying.

Eventually, Prateek turns to me. "He says you can't stay here."

I shake my head. *Why did she bring me here? Why did I come?*

"It's a private residence club, not a hotel," Prateek explains.

"Yes. I've heard of those."

Prateek frowns. "There are other hotels in Colaba."

"But this must be the place." This is the address I've had for her for the last few years. "Look under my mother's name. Yael Shiloh."

At the mention of her name, the old man's head whips up. "Willem saab?" he asks.

"Willem. Yes, that's me."

He squints his eyes and grasps my hands. "You are nothing like the memsahib," he says.

I don't have to know what that means to know who he's talking about. It's what everyone says.

"But where is she?" he asks.

There's a kernel of comfort. I'm not the only one in the dark. "Oh, you know her," I say.

"Yes, yes, yes," he says, doing the same head nod/shake as Prateek.

"So can I go to her flat?" I ask the old man.

He considers it, scratching the gray stubble on his chin. "Regulations say only members can stay here. When memsahib makes you a member, you will be a member."

"But she's not here," Prateek points out helpfully.

"Regulations," the old man says.

"But you knew I was coming," I say.

"But you are not with her. What if you are not really you? Do you have proof?"

Proof? Like what. A surname? Mine is different. Photos? "Here," I say, pulling out the email, now damp and creased.

He squints at it with dark eyes that have gone filmy with age. He must decide it's enough. Because he gives two quick nods of his head and says, "Welcome, Willem saab."

"At last," Prateek says.

"I am Chaudhary," the old man says, ignoring Prateek and handing me a sheaf of papers to fill out. When I finish, he heaves at the opening to the front desk and creaks out from behind. He shuffles down the scuffed wooden hallway. I follow him. Prateek trails behind me. When we reach the elevators, Chaudhary makes a tick-tock gesture to Prateek with his fingers. "Members only in the elevator," he tells him. "You may take the stairs."

"But he's with me," I say.

"Regulations, Willem saab."

Prateek shakes his head. "I should probably get the car back to my uncle," he says.

"Okay, let me pay you." I pull out a wad of filthy rupees.

"Three hundred rupees for no AC. Four hundred with," Chaudhary says. "That's the law."

I hand Prateek five hundred rupees, about the price of a sandwich back home. He backs up to leave. "Hey, what about that korma?" I ask him.

His smile is goofy, a little like Broodje's. "I will be in touch," he promises.

The elevator lurches to the fifth floor. Chaudhary opens the gate onto a light-filled corridor, smelling of floor wax and incense. He leads me past a series of slatted wood doors, stopping at the farthest one, and pulls out a master key.

At first, I think the old man got the wrong room. Yael has lived here for two years, but this is an empty suite of rooms. Anonymous bulky wood furniture, generic paintings on the wall of desert forts and Bengal tigers. A small round table against a pair of French doors.

And then I smell it. Beneath the competing scents of onion and incense and ammonia and wax, is the undeniable smell of citrus and wet earth. The scent, I realize with the clarity of something you've always known, but never needed to recognize before, of my mother.

I take a tentative step into the hallway and another blast hits me. And just like that, I'm not in India. I'm back in Amsterdam, at home, a long summer twilight. It had finally stopped raining, so Yael and Bram were outside, celebrating the minor miracle of sunshine. Still cold from the rain, I stayed huddled inside under a scratchy wool blanket and watched them through the big picture window. Some students who lived in one of the flats across the canal were blasting music. A song came on, something old and New Wave from when Yael and Bram were younger, and he grabbed her and they danced, head to head, even though it wasn't a slow song. I watched them through the glass, fixed on the sight of them, pretending not to be. I must've been eleven or twelve, an age when such displays should've embarrassed me, but didn't. Yael saw me watching, and—this is what surprised me then, still surprises me now as I remember it—she came inside. She didn't exactly drag me out or invite me to dance with them, as Bram might've. She just folded up the blanket and pulled me up by the elbow. I was enveloped by her smell, oranges and leaves, that ever-present loamy tang of her tinctures, and the canals and all their murky secrets. I tried to make it like I was acquiescing, allowing myself to be led, giving no trace of how happy I was. But I must not have been able to fully contain it because she smiled back at me and said, "We have to snatch the sun when we have it, don't we?"

She could be warm like that. But it came and went with as much regularity as the Dutch sun. Except with Bram. But maybe it was reflected warmth—he was her sun, after all.

After Chaudhary leaves, I lie down on the sofa. My head rests uncomfortably against the heavy wood arm but I don't move, because I'm in the sunlight and the heat feels necessary, like a transfusion of sorts. *I should probably get in touch with Yael*, I think, but drowsiness and jetlag and a certain kind of relief are pulling me under, and before I can do so much as remove my shoes, I am asleep.

———   ———   ———

I'm flying again. Back on a plane, which feels wrong because I just got off a plane. But it's so vivid and real it takes a beat longer than usual to recognize it as the dream; and then it warps and becomes lurid and surreal, heavy and slow, the way dreams do when your mind is rebelling against a betrayed body clock. Maybe that's why in this dream, there is no landing. No illumination of the seatbelt sign, no inaudible announcement from the captain. Just the buzz of the engines, the feeling of being aloft. Just flying.

But there is someone next to me. I turn and try to ask, *Where are we?* But everything is heavy, lugubrious, I can't get my mouth to work right because what comes out is, *Who are you?*

"Willem," a voice in the distance calls.

The person in the dream turns. Still faceless. Already familiar.

"Willem." The voice again. I don't answer it. I don't want out of the dream quite yet, not this time. Again, I turn toward my seatmate.

"Willem!" The voice is sharp this time and it pulls me out of the honey stickiness of sleep.

I open my eyes. I sit up and for a second, we just look at each other, blinking.

"What are you doing here?" she asks.

I've been wondering that myself for the past month, after my initial optimism about this trip faded to ambivalence and then curdled into pessimism and now has withered into regret. *What* am *I doing here?*

"You sent me a ticket." I try to make it seem like a joke, but my head is cloudy with the dream, and Yael only frowns.

"I mean what are you doing *here*? We've been looking everywhere for you at the airport."

We? "I didn't see you."

"I was needed at the clinic. I sent a driver and he was running a bit late. He said he sent you several texts."

I take out my phone and turn it on. Nothing happens. "I don't think it works here."

She looks, disgusted, at my phone, and I feel a sudden and fierce loyalty to it. Then she sighs. "The important thing is you made it," she says, which seems both obvious and optimistic.

I stand up. My neck has a crick and when I circle it, it gives off a loud pop that makes Yael frown again. I stand up, stretch, and look around the room.

"Nice place," I say, continuing the small talk that has sustained us for the past three years. "I like what you've done with it."

It's like a reflex, trying to make her smile. It never worked for me before and it doesn't work now. She walks away, opening the French doors leading to the balcony, overlooking the Gateway, the water beyond. "I should probably get something closer to Andheri, but I seem to have grown too accustomed to living on the water."

"Andheri?"

"Where the *clinic* is," she says, as if I should know this. But how, exactly? Talk of her work has been strictly off limits in our casual chit-chat emails. The weather. The food. The myriad Indian festivals. Postcards, without the pretty pictures.

I know that Yael came to India to study Ayurvedic medicine. It was what she and Bram had intended to do once I left for university. Travel more. For Yael to study traditional healing methods. India was to be the first stop. The tickets were booked before Bram died.

After he died, I expected Yael to fall apart. Only this time, I would be there. I would put aside my own grief and I would help her. Finally, instead of me being an interloper into her great love affair, I would be the product of it. I would be a comfort to her. What she wasn't as a mother, I would be as a son.

For two weeks, she locked herself in the top-floor room, the one Bram had built for her, shutters closed, door locked, ignoring most of the visitors who'd stopped by. In life, Bram had been all hers, and in death, that hadn't changed.

Then, six weeks later, she'd left for India as scheduled, as if nothing had happened. Marjolein said Yael was just licking her wounds. She'd be back soon.

Two months later, though, Yael sent word that she wasn't coming back. Long ago, before she studied naturopathic medicine, she'd had a nursing degree, and now she was going back to that, working in a clinic in Mumbai. She said she was closing down the boat; she'd already boxed up the important things and everything else was being sold. I should take what I wanted. I packed up a few boxes and stored them in my uncle Daniel's attic. Everything else, I left. Not long after that, I got kicked off of my program. Then I packed up my own rucksack and took off.

"You're just like your mother," Marjolein had said, somewhat mournfully, when I told her I was leaving.

But we both knew that wasn't true. I am nothing like my mother.

— — —

The same emergency that kept Yael from the airport is apparently pulling her back to the clinic after all of an hour in my company. She invites me to come with her, but the invitation is halfhearted and rote, a lot like this invitation to come to India, I suspect. I politely decline, with excuses of jetlag.

"You should be out in the sunshine; it's the best cure." She looks at me. "Though make sure you cover this." She touches the mirror image on her face where my scar is. "It looks fresh."

I touch the scar. It's six months old now. And, for a minute, I imagine telling Yael about it. It would infuriate her if she knew what I said to the skinheads to take their attention off the girls and onto me. *A one four six oh three*—the identification number the Nazis tattooed on Saba's wrist—but at least I would get a reaction.

But I don't tell Yael. This goes way beyond small talk. It goes to painful things we never mention: Saba. The war. Yael's mother. Yael's entire childhood. I touch the scar. It feels hot, as if merely thinking about that day has inflamed it. "It's not that fresh," I tell her. "It's just not healing right."

"I can mix you up something for that." Yael brushes the scar. Her fingers are rough and callused. Workers' hands, Bram used to say, though he was the one who should've had the rougher hands. I realize then we haven't embraced or kissed or done any of the things one might expect for a re-union.

Still, when she takes her hand away, I wish she hadn't. And when she starts packing up with promises of things we will do when she has a day off, I'm wishing I had told her about the skinheads, about Paris, about Lulu. Except even if I'd tried, I wouldn't have known how. My mother and I, we both speak Dutch and English. But we never could speak the same language.

Twenty-two

I am awoken by the ringing of a phone. I reach for my mobile, remember it doesn't work here. The phone keeps ringing. It's the house line. It doesn't stop. Finally, I pick it up.

"Willem saab. Chaudhary here." He clears his throat. "On the line for you, Prateek Sanu," he continues formally. "Would you like me to ask the nature of his business?"

"No, that's okay. You can put him through."

"One moment." There is a series of clicks. Then Prateek's voice echoing hellos, interrupted by Chaudhary, declaring. "Prateek Sanu calling for Willem Shiloh."

It's funny to be called by Yael and Saba's surname. I don't correct him. After a moment of silence, Chaudhary clicks off.

"Willem!" Prateek booms, as if it's been months, not hours, since we last spoke. "How are you?"

"I'm good."

"And what do you think of the Maximum City?"

"I haven't seen much of it," I admit. "I've been asleep."

"You are awake now. What are your plans?"

"Haven't worked that out yet."

"Let me make a proposal: Pay a visit to me at Crawford Market."

"Sounds good."

Prateek gives me instructions. After a cold shower, I head outside, Chaudhary trailing behind me with dire warnings of "pickpockets, thieves, prostitutes, and roving gangs." He ticks off the threats on his thick fingers. "They will accost you."

I assure him I can take it, and in any case the only people to accost me are begging mothers, who congregate in the grassy medians in the center of the shady streets, asking for money to buy formula for the sleeping babies in their arms.

This part of Mumbai reminds me a bit of London with its decaying colonial buildings, except it's supersaturated with color: the women's saris, the marigold-festooned temples, the crazily painted buses. It's like everything absorbs and reflects the bright sun.

From the outside, Crawford Market seems like another building plucked out of old England, but inside it is all India: bustling commerce and yet more surreally bright colors. I walk around the fruit stalls, the clothing stalls, making my way toward the electronics stalls where Prateek told me to find him. I feel a tap on my shoulder.

"Lost?" Prateek asks, a grin splitting his face.

"Not in a bad way."

He frowns at that, confounded. "I was worried," he says. "I wanted to call you but I don't have your mobile."

"My mobile doesn't work here."

The smile returns. "As it happens, we have many mobile phones at my uncle's electronics stall."

"So that's why you lured me here?" I tease.

Prateek looks insulted. "Of course not. How did I know you lacked a phone?" He gestures to the stalls around us. "You can buy from another stall."

"I'm joking, Prateek."

"Oh." He takes me to his uncle's stall, crammed to the ceiling with cellphones, radios, computers, knockoff iPads, televisions, and more. He introduces me to his uncle and buys us all cups of tea from the chai-wallah, the traveling tea salesman. Then he takes me to the back of the stall and we sit down on a couple of rickety stools.

"You work here?"

"On Mondays, Tuesdays, and Fridays."

"What do you do the other days?"

He does the head nod/wag thing. "I'm studying accounting. I also work for my mother some days. And I help my cousin sometimes to find *goreh* for movies."

"*Goreh.*"

"White people, like you. It's why I was at the airport today. I had to drive my cousin."

"Why didn't you ask *me*?" I joke.

"Oh, I am not a casting director, or even an assistant to an assistant. I just drove Rahul to the airport to look for backpackers needing money. Do you need money, Willem?"

"No."

"I did not think so. You are staying at the Bombay Royale. Very high class. And visiting your mother. Where is your father?" he asks.

It's been a while since anyone asked me that. "He's dead."

"Oh, mine, too," Prateek says almost cheerfully. "But I have many uncles. And cousins. You?"

I almost say yes. I have an uncle. But how do you explain Daniel? Not so much a black sheep as an invisible one, eclipsed by Bram. And Yael. Daniel, the footnote to Yael and Bram's story, the small print that nobody bothers to read. Daniel, the younger, scragglier, messier, less directed—and not to forget, shorter—brother. Daniel, the one relegated to the backseat of the Fiat, and consequently, it seemed, the backseat of life.

"Not much family," is all I say in the end, bookending my vagueness with a shrug, my own version of the head wag.

Prateek presents me a choice of phones. I choose one and buy a SIM card. He immediately programs his number and, for good measure, his uncle's into it. We finish our tea and then he announces, "Now I think you must go to the movies."

"I just got here."

"Exactly. What is more Indian than that? Fourteen million people—"

"A day go to the movies here," I interrupt. "Yes, I've been told."

He pulls a heap of magazines out of his bag, the same ones I'd seen in the car. *Magna. Stardust.* He opens one and shows me pages of attractive people, all with extremely white teeth. He rattles off a bunch of names, dismayed that I know none of them.

"We will go now," he declares.

"Don't you have to work?"

"In India, work is the master, but the guest is god," Prateek says. "Besides, between the phone and taxi . . ." He smiles. "My uncle will not object." He opens a newspaper. "*Dil Mera Golmaal* is on. So is *Gangs of Wasseypur.* Or *Dhal Gaya Din.* What do you think, Baba?"

Prateek and his uncle carry on a spirited conversation in a mix of Hindi and English, debating the merits and deficits of all three films. Finally they settle on *Dil Mera Golmaal.*

The theater is an art deco building with peeling white paint, not unlike the revival houses Saba used to take me to when he visited. I buy our tickets and our popcorn. Prateek promises to translate in return.

The film—a sort of convoluted take on *Romeo and Juliet,* involving warring families, gangsters, a terrorist plot to steal nuclear weapons, plus countless explosions and dance numbers—doesn't require much translation. It is both nonsensical and oddly self-explanatory.

Still, Prateek gives it a shot. "That man is that one's brother but he doesn't know it," he whispers. "One is evil, the other is good, and the girl is engaged to the bad one, but she loves the good one. Her family hates his family and his family hates her family but they don't really because the feud has to do with the other one's father, who engineered the feud when he stole the baby at birth, you see. He is also a terrorist."

"Right."

Then there's a dance number and a fight scene and then suddenly we are in the desert. "Dubai," Prateek whispers.

"Why, exactly?" I ask.

Prateek explains that the oil consortium is there. As are the terrorists.

There are several scenes in the desert, including a duel between two monster trucks that Henk would appreciate.

Then the film switches abruptly to Paris. One moment, there's a generic shot of the Seine. And then, a second later, a shot down the banks of the river. Then we see the heroine and the good twin brother, who, Prateek explains, have gotten married and fled together. They break out into song. But they're no longer on the Seine; now they are on one of the arched bridges that span the canals in Villette. I recognize it. Lulu and I cruised under it, sitting side by side, our legs knocking against the hull. Occasionally, we'd accidentally knock ankles and there had been something electric about it, a turn-on, just in that.

I feel it now in this musty theater. Almost like a reflex, my thumb goes to the inside of my wrist, but the gesture is meaningless, here in the dark.

Soon the song is over and we're back in India for the grand finale when the families reunite and reconcile and there's another wedding ceremony and a big dance number. Unlike Romeo and Juliet, these lovers get a happy ending.

After the movie, we walk through the crowded streets. It's dark now, and the heat's gone wavy. We meander our way to a wide crescent of sand. "Chowpatty Beach," Prateek tells me, pointing out the luxury highrises on Marine Drive. They sparkle like diamonds against the slender curving wrist of the bay.

It's a carnival atmosphere with all the food vendors and clowns and balloon shapers and the furtive lovers taking advantage of the darkness to steal kisses behind a palm tree. I try not to watch them. I try not to remember stealing kisses. I try not to remember that first kiss. Not her lips, but that birthmark on her wrist. I'd been wanting to kiss it all day. Somehow, I knew exactly what it would taste like.

The water laps against the shore. The Arabian Sea. The Atlantic Ocean. Two oceans between us. And still not enough.

Twenty-three

After four days, Yael finally has a day off. Instead of waking up from my fold-up bed to find her rushing out the door, I see her in her pajamas. "I've ordered up breakfast," she says in that crisp voice of hers, the gutturalness of her Israeli accent ironed out from all the years of speaking English.

There's a knock at the door. Chaudhary, who seems to always work and to do every single job here, shuffles in, pushing a trolley. "Breakfast, Memsahib," he announces.

"Thank you, Chaudhary," Yael says.

He studies the two of us. Then shakes his head. "He is nothing like you, Memsahib," he says.

"He looks like his baba," Yael replies.

I know it's true, but it's strange to hear her say it. Though not as strange, I'd imagine, as seeing the face of her dead husband staring back at her. Sometimes when I'm feeling charitable, I'll justify this as the reason she's put such distance between us these last three years. Then the less charitable side of me will ask, *What about the eighteen years before that?*

With a dramatic flourish, Chaudhary sets out toast, coffee, tea, and juice. Then he backs out of the door.

"Does he ever leave?" I ask.

"No, not really. His children are all overseas and his wife passed. So he works."

"Sounds miserable."

She gives me one of her inscrutable looks. "At least he has a purpose."

She flips open the newspaper. Even that is colorful, a salmony shade of pink. "What have you been doing the last few days?" she asks me as she eyes the headlines.

I went back to Chowpatty Beach, the markets around Colaba, the Gateway. I went to another movie with Prateek. I've wandered mostly. Without purpose. "This and that," I say.

"So today we do that and this," she replies.

Downstairs, we are besieged by the usual congregation of beggars. "Ten rupees," a woman carrying a sleeping baby says. "For formula for my baby. You come with me to buy it."

I start to pull out money, but Yael snaps at me to stop and then snaps at the woman in Hindi.

I don't say a word. But my expression must give me away, because Yael gives an exasperated explanation. "It's a scam, Willem. The babies are props. The women are part of begging rings, run by organized crime syndicates."

I look at the woman, now standing across from the Taj Hotel, and shrug. "So? She still needs the money."

Yael nods and frowns. "Yes, *she* does. And the *baby* needs food, no doubt, but neither of them will get what they need. If you bought milk for that woman, you'd pay an inflated price, and you'd get an inflated sense of goodwill. You helped a mother feed her baby. What could be better?"

I don't say anything, because I've been giving them money every day and now I feel foolish for it.

"As soon as you walk away, the milk's returned to the shop. And your money? The shopkeeper gets a cut; the crime bosses get a cut. The women, the women are indentured, and they get nothing. As for what happens to the babies . . ." She trails off ominously.

"What happens to the babies?" The question pops out before I realize I might not want to know the answer.

"They die. Sometimes of malnutrition. Or sometimes of pneumonia. When life is so tenuous, something small might do it."

"I know," I say. *Sometimes even when life isn't that tenuous*, I think and I wonder if she's thinking the same thing.

"In fact, the day you arrived, I was late because of an emergency with one of those very children." She doesn't elaborate, leaving it for me to put the pieces together.

Yael's non-admission manages to make me feel retroactively guilty for faulting her—there was something more important—and bitter—there always is something more important. But mostly it makes me tired. Couldn't she have just told me and saved me the trouble of my guilt and bitterness?

Then again, sometimes I think that guilt and bitterness may be Yael's and my true common language.

— — —

Our first stop is the Shree Siddhivinayak Temple, an ornate wedding cake of a temple that is being attacked by a tourist horde of ants. Yael and I take our place among the masses and push into a stuffy gold hall, wending our way to a flower-covered statue of the elephant god. He's beet-red, as if embarrassed, or maybe he's just hot, too.

"Ganesha," Yael tells me.

"The remover of obstacles."

She nods.

All around us, people are laying garlands around the shrine or singing or praying.

"Do you have to make an offering?" I ask. "To get your obstacles removed?"

"You can," she replies. "Or just chant a mantra."

"What mantra?"

"There are several." Yael doesn't say anything else for a while. And then, in a low and clear voice, she chants: "*Om gam ganapatayae namaha.*" She gives me a look, like that's enough of that.

"What does it mean?"

She cocks her head. "Roughly I've heard it translated as: 'Wake up.'"

"Wake up?"

She looks at me for a second, and though we have the same eyes, I really have no idea what she sees through hers.

"It's not the translation that matters with a mantra. It's the intention," she says. "And this is what you say when you want a new beginning."

— —— —

After the temple, we hail a rickshaw. "Where to now?" I ask.

"We are meeting Mukesh for lunch."

Mukesh? The travel agent who booked my flights?

We spend the next half hour in silence as we weave through more traffic and dodge more cows, finally arriving at a sort of dusty shopping center. As we're paying the driver, a tall, broad, smiling man in a voluminous white shirt comes barreling out of a place called Outbound Travels.

"Willem!" he says, greeting me warmly, grasping both my hands. "Welcome."

"Thank you," I say, looking back and forth between him and Yael, who's decidedly not looking at him, and I wonder what exactly is going on. Are they together? It would be just her way, introduce the idea of a boyfriend by not introducing him as her boyfriend and leaving me to figure it out.

Mukesh tells our driver to wait and then goes back into the travel agency to pick up a plastic bag, and then we climb back in and drive through fifteen more minutes of traffic to the restaurant.

"It's Middle Eastern," Mukesh says proudly. "Like Mummy."

Mukesh pushes the menu aside and calls over the waiter, ordering platters of hummus and grape leaves, baba ghanoush and tabouli.

When the first platter of hummus arrives, Mukesh asks me how I'm liking Indian food so far.

I explain about the dosas and the pakoras I've been eating off the stands. "I still haven't had a proper curry."

"We will have to arrange that for you," he says. "Which is why I'm here." He reaches into the plastic bag and pulls out a number of glossy brochures. "You don't have so much time here, so I suggest you pick one region—Rajasthan, Kerala, Uttar Pradesh—and explore that. I have taken the liberty of coming up with a few sample itineraries." He slides me over a computer printout. One is for Rajasthan. It has everything. Return flights to Jaipur, transfers to Jodhpur, Udaipur and Jaisalmer. There's even a camel trip. There's a similar packed itinerary for Kerala, flights, transfers, river cruises.

I'm confused. "Are we taking a trip?" I ask Yael.

"Oh, no, no," Mukesh answers for her. "Mummy has to work. This is a special trip for you, to make sure your time in India is tip-top."

And then I understand the guilty look. Mukesh isn't the boyfriend. He's the travel agent. The one enlisted to bring me here. The one enlisted to send me away.

At least I know why I'm here. Not for new beginnings. A hasty invitation that was foolish to issue, foolish to accept—and most foolish of all to solicit.

"Which trip do you prefer?" Mukesh asks. He seems unaware of the thorny dynamic he's stumbled into.

My anger feels hot and bilious but I keep it bottled until it doubles back and I'm mad at myself. What's the definition of insanity? Doing the same thing over and over and expecting different results.

"This one," I say, flicking the brochure on top of the pile. I don't even look where it goes to. It hardly seems the point.

Twenty-four

MARCH
Jaisalmer, India

---

*I*t's ten o'clock in Jaisalmer and the desert sun is beating down on the sand-colored stones of the fortress city. The narrow alleys and staircases are thick with heat and smoke from the early morning dung fires, and that, along with the ever-present camels and cows, gives the city a particular aroma.

I skirt past a group of women, their eyes kohl-dipped, downturned, shy it seems, though they manage to flirt in other ways, with the swoosh of their electric-colored saris, the tinkle of their ankle bracelets.

At the bottom of the hill, I pass several stalls hawking local textiles. I stop at one of them, peering at a purple-mirrored wall-hanging.

"You like what you see?" the young man behind the counter asks casually, no sign that he knows me except for the twinkle in his eye.

"Perhaps," I say noncommittally.

"Is there something particular you like?"

"I have my eye on something."

Nawal nods solemnly, no hint of a smile, no hint that we have had almost this exact same conversation for the past four days. It's like a game. Or a play we started acting in when I first found the tapestry I want. Or rather, Prateek wants.

Two days into my tour of Rajasthan, when I was still full of bitterness and bile and of half a mind to just fly back to Amsterdam early, Prateek sent me a text about his "grand proposal!!!!!!!!!!!!" Turned out to be not so grand. He wanted me to shop for Rajasthani handicrafts that he'd sell back in Mumbai for a markup. He'd reimburse me for what I spent and we'd split the profit. At first I told him no, especially after he texted the shopping list. But then one day in Jaipur I wound up in the Bapu Bazaar with nothing much to do, so I started looking for the kind of leather sandals he wanted. And from there, I kept going. Combing the markets for spices and bangles and a very particular kind of slipper has given the trip a sort of shape, allowing me to forget that it's actually an exile. And because of that, I've extended the exile, having Mukesh lengthen it by a week. I've now been gone three weeks, and I'll get back to Mumbai with only a handful of days before my return flight to Amsterdam.

In Jaisalmer, Prateek has instructed me to buy a particular kind of tapestry that the area is known for. It must be silk, and I will know it is silk because I must burn a thread, and it will give off the odor of burnt hair. It should be embroidered, sewn, not glued, and I will know it's sewn because I must turn it over and yank the thread, which also must be silk and must be tested with a match. And it's to cost no more than two thousand rupees, and I must bargain, hard. Prateek had grave doubts about my bargaining ability, because he claims I overpaid him for the taxi, but I assured him that I'd seen my grandfather barter down a wheel of cheese by half in the Albert Cuyp market, so it was in me.

"Some tea, perhaps, while you look?" Nawal asks. I look under the counter and see that, like yesterday, the tea is already prepared.

"Why not?"

At which point, the script ends and conversation takes over. Hours of it. I sit down in the canvas chair next to Nawal's, and as we have done for the past four days, we talk. When it gets too hot, or when Nawal gets a serious customer, I leave. Before I do, he will drop the price of the tapestry by five hundred rupees, insuring that I'll come back and do the whole thing again the next day.

Nawal pours the spicy tea from the ornate metal pot. His radio is playing the same crazy Hindi pop that Prateek loves. "Cricket game on later. If you want to listen," he informs me.

I take a sip of the tea. "Cricket? Really? The only thing duller than watching cricket is listening to it."

"You only say that because you don't understand the particulars of the game."

Nawal enjoys schooling me about all the things that I don't understand. I don't understand cricket, or soccer for that matter, and I don't understand the politics between India and Pakistan, and I don't understand the truth about global

warming, and I certainly don't understand why love marriages are inferior to arranged marriages. Yesterday, I made
the mistake of asking what was so wrong with love marriages, and I got quite a lecture.

"The divorce rate in India is the lowest in the world. In
the West, it's fifty percent. And that's if they even get married," Nawal had said, disgusted. "Here, I tell you a story:
All my grandparents, my aunties, my uncles, my parents, my
brothers, all had arranged marriages. Happy. Long lives. My
cousin, he chose a love marriage, and after two years, no
children, the wife leaves him in disgrace."

"What happened?" I'd asked.

"What happened is they were not compatible," he'd said.
"They were driving without a map. You cannot do that. You
must have it arranged properly. Tomorrow I will show you."

So today, Nawal has brought a copy of the astrological
chart that was drawn up to decide if he and his fiancée, Geeta,
are compatible. Nawal insists it shows his and Geeta's happy
future, ordained by the gods. "With matters such as these,
you have to rely on forces larger than the human heart," he
says.

The chart looks not unlike one of W's mathematical
equations, with the paper divided into sections and different symbols in each one. I know W believes that all of life's
questions can be solved through mathematical principle, but
I think even he would find this a stretch.

"You don't believe in it?" Nawal challenges. "Name me
one good love marriage that lasts."

Lulu had asked me a similar question. Sitting at that café,
arguing about love, she'd demanded to know one couple

who'd stayed in love, who'd stayed stained. And so I'd said *Yael and Bram*. Their names had just popped out. And it was so strange because in two years on the road, I had never told anyone about them, not even people I'd traveled with for a long time. As soon as I said that, I'd wanted to tell her *everything* about them, the story of how they met, how they seemed like interlocking puzzle pieces and how sometimes I didn't seem to fit into the equation. But it had been so long since I'd spoken of them, I hadn't known how to do it. Though in some strange way, it seemed like another unsaid thing she already knew. Still, I wish I'd told her everything. Add it to my list of regrets.

I'm about to tell Nawal about them. My parents, who had a pretty spectacular love marriage, but then again, maybe it was there, in the charts all along, how it would end. I have wondered: If you could know going in that twenty-five years of love would break you in the end, would you risk it? Because isn't it inevitable? When you make such a large withdrawal of happiness, somewhere you'll have to make an equally large deposit. It all goes back to the universal law of equilibrium.

"I think this whole falling in love business is a mistake," Nawal continues. "I mean look at *you*." He says it like an indictment.

"What about *me*?"

"You are twenty-one and you are all alone."

"I'm not all alone. I'm here with you."

Nawal eyes me pityingly, reminding me that, pleasant as these days have been, he is here to sell something and I am here to buy something.

"You have no wife. And I'll wager you have been in love. I'll wager you have been in love many times like they always seem to be in Western films."

"Actually, I have never been in love." Nawal looks surprised at that, and I'm about to explain that while I haven't been in love, I've fallen in love many times. That they're separate entities entirely.

But then I stop. Because once again, I'm transported from the deserts of Rajasthan to that Paris café. I can almost hear the skepticism in Lulu's voice when I'd told her: *There's a world of difference between* falling *in love and* being *in love.* Then I'd dabbed the Nutella on her wrist, supposedly to demonstrate my point, but really because it had given me an excuse to see what she tasted like.

She'd laughed at me. She'd said the distinction between falling in love and being in love was false. *It sounds like you just like to screw around. At least own that about yourself.*

I smile at the memory of it, although Lulu, who had been right about me so much that day, was wrong about this. Yael had trained as a paratrooper in the Israel Defense Forces, and she once described how it felt to jump out of a plane: hurtling through the air, the wind everywhere, the exhilaration, the speed, your stomach in your throat, the hard landing. It always seemed the exact right way to describe how things felt with girls—that wind and the exhilaration, the hurtling, the wanting, the freefall. The abrupt end.

Oddly enough, though, that day with Lulu, it didn't feel anything like falling. It felt like arriving.

Nawal and I drink our tea and listen to music, talk about upcoming elections in India and upcoming soccer tournaments. The sun blazes through the canopy roof and we go quiet in the heat. No customers come this time of day.

The ringing of my phone disturbs the idyll. It'll be Mukesh. He is the only one who calls me here. Prateek texts. Yael does neither.

"Willem, is everything tip-top?" he asks.

"A-okay," I say. In Mukesh's hierarchy, A-okay is one step above tip-top.

"Excellent. Not to worry you but I call with a change in plans. Camel tour is canceled."

"Canceled? Why?"

"Camels got sick."

"Sick?"

"Yes, yes, vomiting, diarrhea, terrible, terrible."

"Can't we book another one?" The three-night desert camel tour was the one part of his planned itinerary I was actually looking forward to. When I extended my trip a week, I'd asked Mukesh to reschedule the camel trip for me.

"I tried. But unfortunately, next tour I could get you on was not for another week, and if you take that, you miss your flight to Dubai next Monday."

"Is there a problem?" Nawal asks.

"My camel tour was canceled. The camels are sick."

"My cousin runs a tour." Nawal is already picking up his mobile. "I can arrange it for you."

"Mukesh, I think my friend here can book me on a different tour."

"Oh, no! Willem. That will be most unacceptable." His ever-friendly tone goes brusque. Then, in a milder voice he continues: "I already booked your train back to Jaipur tonight, and a flight back to Mumbai tomorrow."

"Tonight? What's the rush? I don't leave for a week." When I asked Mukesh to extend my Rajasthan trip by a week, I also asked him to book my return flight to Amsterdam for a few days after I am due to get back to Mumbai. I had it all timed out perfectly so I'd only have to see Yael for a couple of days at the tail end. "Maybe I could stay here another few days?"

Mukesh clucks his tongue, which, in his particular argot, is the exact opposite of A-okay. He starts rattling on about flight schedules and change fees and warnings of me being stuck in India unless I come back to Mumbai now, and finally there is nothing to do but give in. "Good, good. I'll email you the itinerary," he says.

"My email's not working right. I got locked out of it and had to reset the password and then a whole bunch of recent messages disappeared," I say. "Apparently there's a virus going around."

"Yes, that would be the Jagdish virus." He tsks again. "You must set up a new account. In the meantime, I will text you your train and flight itinerary."

I get off the phone with Mukesh and reach into my backpack for my wallet. I count out three thousand rupees, the last price Nawal had dropped to. His face falls.

"I have to leave," I explain. "This evening."

Nawal reaches behind the counter for a thick square

wrapped up in brown paper. "I set it aside on day one so no one else would get it." He peels back the paper, showing me the tapestry. "I put a little something extra in it for you."

We say good-bye. I wish him luck with his marriage. "I don't need luck; it's in the stars. You, I think, are the one who needs luck."

It makes me think of something Kate said when she dropped me off in Mérida. "I'd wish you luck, Willem, but I think you need to stop relying on that."

I'm not sure which one of them is right.

I pack up my things and then walk to the train station through the late afternoon heat. The city looks golden up the hills, the sand dunes rippling behind it, and it all makes me feel wistful, nostalgic already.

The train gets me into Jaipur at six the next morning. My flight to Mumbai is at ten. I haven't had a chance to set up a new email, and Mukesh has texted nothing about a ride from the airport. I text Prateek. He hasn't replied to any of my texts in the last two days. So I try ringing him.

He answers, distracted.

"Prateek, hey, it's Willem."

"Willem, where are you?"

"On a train. I've got your tapestry here." I rattle the package.

"Oh, good." For all his manic enthusiasm about this latest venture, he seems oddly blasé.

"Everything okay?"

"Better than okay. Very good. My cousin Rahul, he is sick with influenza."

"That's terrible. Is he okay?"

"Fine. Fine. But bed rest for him," Prateek says cheerfully. "I am helping him out." He lowers his voice to a whisper. "With the movies."

"The movies?"

"Yes! I find the *goreh* to act in the movies. If I can get ten, they will put my name in the credits. Assistant to assistant director of casting."

"Congratulations."

"Thank you," he says formally. "But only if I find four more. Tomorrow, I return to Salvation Army and maybe to the airport."

"Actually, if you're coming to the airport, that's perfect. I need a ride."

"You return on Saturday, I thought."

"Change of plans. I'm coming back tomorrow now."

There's a silence, during which Prateek and I have the same idea. "Do you want to be in?" he asks at the same time I offer, "Would you want me to be in . . . ?"

The line echoes with our laughter. I give him my flight information and hang up. Outside, the sun is setting; a bright flame behind the train, and darkness in front of us. A short while later, it's all dark.

Mukesh has booked me a sleeper seat in an air-conditioned car, which India Rail chills like a meat locker. The bed has nothing but a sheet. I shiver, and then think of the tapestry, thick and warm. I unwrap the paper; out tumbles something small and hard.

It's a small statue of Ganesha, holding his ax and his lotus, smiling his smile, like he knows something the rest of us haven't figured out yet.

Twenty-five

Mumbai

The movie is called *Heera Ki Tamanna*, which translates, roughly, as *Wishing for a Diamond*. It is a romance starring Billy Devali—big star—and Amisha Rai—big, big star— and is directed by Faruk Khan, who apparently is so big, he needs no further description. Prateek tells me all this in a breathless monologue; he has hardly stopped talking since he swooped me out of the arrivals hall and rushed me to the car, barely glancing at the various Rajasthani goods I painstakingly shopped and bargained for over the past three weeks.

"Oh, Willem, that was the last plan," he says, shaking his head, dismayed that he must explain such things. "I am working in Bollywood now." Then he tells me that yesterday, Amisha Rai swept by him so close that the edge of her sari brushed his arm. "Can I tell you what it felt like?" he asks, not waiting for me to answer. "It felt like a caress from the gods. Can I tell you what she smelled like?" He closes his eyes and inhales. Apparently, her odor defies words.

"What exactly do I do?"

"Do you remember in *Dil Mera Golmaal*, the scene after the shootout?"

I nod. It was like *Reservoir Dogs*, but on a ship. With dancing.

"Where do you think all those white people came from?"

"From the same magical place as the go-go dancers?"

"From casting directors like me." He pounds his chest.

"Casting director? So it's official. You're up to ten?"

"You make eight. But I will get there. You are so tall and handsome and . . . white."

"Maybe I can count for two?" I joke.

Prateek looks at me like I'm an idiot. "No, you count for one. You are only one man."

We arrive in Film City, the suburb that houses many of the studios, and then we pull into the complex and then into what looks like a large airplane hangar.

"Oh, by the way, the payment," Prateek says nonchalantly. "I must tell you, it's ten dollars a day."

I don't answer. I hadn't planned on being paid anything.

He mistakes my silence. "I know for Westerners it is not much," he explains. "But you get meals, and also lodging so you do not need to commute back to Colaba each night. Please, please tell me you'll agree to it."

"Of course. I'm not in it for the money." Which is exactly what Tor used to say about Guerrilla Will. *We're not in it for the money.* But half the time she would say this as she was carefully counting the night's take or checking weather reports in the *International Herald Tribune* to determine the sunniest—and most lucrative—places to hit next.

Back then, I was very much in it for the money. Even the little I earned from Guerrilla Will kept me from having to return to an unwelcoming home.

Funny that, how little things have changed.

———

On the set, Prateek introduces me to Arun, the assistant casting director, who takes a brief pause from his mobile phone conversation to appraise me. He says something to Prateek in Hindi and then nods at me and barks, "Costume."

Prateek squeezes my arm, as he leads me to the costume room, which is a series of rolling racks full of suits and dresses, tended to by a harried woman with glasses. "Find something that fits," she orders.

Everything is at least a head too short for me. Which is about the amount by which I tower over most Indians. Prateek looks worried. "Do you have a suit?" he asks.

The last time I wore a suit was to Bram's funeral. No, I don't have a suit.

"What seems to be the problem?" Neema, the wardrobe lady, snaps.

Prateek grovels, apologizing for my height, as if it were a personality defect.

She sighs impatiently. "Wait here."

Prateek looks at me in alarm. "I hope they do not send you back. Arun just told me that one of the ashram people left this morning and now I am back down to seven."

I slouch, make myself shorter. "Does that help?"

"The suit still will not fit," he says, shaking his head as if I'm an imbecile.

Neema returns with a garment bag. Inside is a suit, freshly pressed, shiny blue, sharkskin. "This is from the actors' wardrobe, so don't mess it," she warns, shoving me into a curtained area to try it on.

The suit fits. When Prateek sees me, he grins. "You look so first-class," he says, amazed. "Come, walk by Arun. Casual, casual. Oh, yes, he sees. Very good. I think I am almost assured a spot in the credits. To think, one day, I might be like Arun."

"Dare to dream."

I'm teasing, but I keep forgetting that Prateek takes everything literally. "Oh, yes. To dream is the ultimate dare, is it not?"

— — —

The film set is a faux cocktail lounge, with a grand piano right in the middle. The Indian stars circle the area around the bar, and then deeper into the set mill the fifty or so extras. The majority of them are Indians, but there are about fifteen or twenty Westerners. I go stand next to an Indian in a tux, but he narrows his eyes at me and scoots away.

"They're such snobs!" a skinny, tan girl in a sparkly blue dress says, laughing. "They won't talk to us."

"It's like reverse colonialism or something," says a guy with dreadlocks tied back into a band. "Nash," he says, sticking out a hand.

"Tasha," says the girl.

"Willem."

"Willem," they repeat, dreamily. "You at the ashram?"

"No."

"Oh. We didn't think so. We'd have recognized *you*," Tasha says. "You're so tall. Like Jules."

Nash nods his head. I do too. We all nod at this Jules's height.

"What brings you to India?" I ask, slipping easily back into Postcard Language.

"We are refugees," Tasha says. "From the fame-and-celebrity-obsessed materialistic world in the States. We are here to cleanse ourselves."

"Here?" I gesture to the set.

Nash laughs. "Enlightenment ain't free. It's kind of expensive, actually. So we're here trying to buy some more time. What about you, dude? What brings you to Bollywoodland?"

"The fame, of course."

They both laugh. Then Nash asks, "Wanna go get baked? They aren't doing anything except making us wait." He pulls out a fat joint. "I wait just as well stoned."

I shrug. "Why not?"

We sneak off outside where half of the extras seem to be smoking cigarettes in the shade of the overhang. Nash lights up and takes a hit, passes it to Tasha, who takes a long, deep drag and passes it to me. The hash is strong and it's been a while, so it hits me immediately. We pass the joint around a few more times.

"You're really . . . tall, Willem," Tasha says.

"Yes, I think you mentioned that."

"We really have to introduce him to Jules," Tasha drawls. "She's tall. And Canadian."

"Totally," Nash says. "Righteous idea."

The world's gone a bit washed out, overbright and spinny. "Who's Jules?" I ask.

"She's a girl," Nash answers. "Cute. Ginger hair. She's at the ashram but she might come out in a day or two. She's tall. Oh, Tasha already said that. Shit, here comes the assistant director dude. Hide the joint."

Tasha pinches the joint between her fingers just as a bird-like man comes and looks at us. Even though Tasha is holding the joint, it's me he focuses on. He takes out his phone and snaps a picture, and then disappears without saying a word.

"Oh. Shit," Tasha says, giggling. "We got caught."

"*He* got caught," Nash says. "They only took his picture." He sounds a bit insulted.

"If there's hash, you always blame the Dutchman," I say.

"Oh, right," Nash says, nodding.

"I'm paranoid now," Tasha says.

"Let's get back. Save the rest of that for later," Nash says.

With the hash buzzing around my head, the waiting on set goes slower, not faster. I spend a few minutes twirling a rupee coin across my hand but I keep dropping it. I turn on my phone to play some solitaire, but then, on a strange stoned whim, use my phone for its intended purpose. I make a call.

"Hello . . . this is Willem," I say when she picks up.

"I know who this is." I can hear fury in her voice. Even calling her gets me in trouble? "Where are you?" she asks.

"I'm on a film set. I'm acting in a Bollywood movie for the next few days."

Silence. Yael never had much patience for "low" culture, outside of the cheesy Israeli pop music she couldn't resist. She didn't like movies or TV shows. She surely thinks all this is a waste of time.

"And when did you decide to do this?" she says at last. Her voice is flinty enough to spark a fire.

"Yesterday. This morning officially."

"And when did you think to tell me?"

Maybe it's the hash, but I actually laugh out loud. Because it's just funny—in the way that absurd things are.

Yael doesn't think so. "What's so amusing?"

"What's so amusing?" I ask. "You wanting to know my itinerary, that's pretty amusing. When you haven't given a thought to my whereabouts, my well-being for the last three years. When you brought me over to India and then a week later shipped me right back off again and didn't bother to call once. You couldn't even be bothered to come to the airport to pick me up. Oh, I know there was an emergency, something more important, but there always is, isn't there? So why would you need to know that I was acting in a Bollywood movie?"

I stop. And it's like the effects of the hash have worn off, taking my anger—or my bravery—with them.

"The reason I would need to know," she says, her voice

measured, infuriatingly so, "is so I would know not to come to the airport this time to pick you up."

After she hangs up, I turn my phone over. I see the half dozen missed calls, the *Where are you?* texts.

Another missed connection. Story of my life these days.

Twenty-six

*T*hat night, we finish up at eight and pile into a rickety bus for an hour-long ride to a squat cement hotel where we're put four to a room. I wind up with Nash and Tasha and Argin, another acolyte from their ashram. The three of them pass a joint around and tell repeating stories about reaching enlightenment. They offer the joint to me, but after the afternoon's hash-fueled debacle with Yael, I don't trust myself. Eventually, I fall asleep, but I'm woken up in the middle of the night to the enthusiastic squeaking of the bedframe. Nash and Tasha. Or maybe all three of them. It is extremely unpleasant—and it's pathetic because I can't think of anywhere else I'd rather be.

The next day, on set, it's more of the same. After I put on my suit, I see Prateek for half a second before he dashes off. "Must find more people," he calls to me. "Three left yesterday. I need four today!" Neema evil-eyes me. The assistant director snaps another picture. They really are serious about the suit.

Late that afternoon Prateek returns with new recruits, including a leggy woman with reddish hair streaked through with pink.

"Jules!" Nash and Tasha scream when she arrives. They all hug and dance in a small circle and then Tasha waves me over.

"Jules," she says. "This is Willem. We've decided he's perfect for you."

"Oh have you?" Jules rolls her eyes a bit. She is tall, not quite as tall as me, but nearly. "I'm Jules, but apparently you already know that," she says.

"I'm Willem."

"I like your suit, Willem."

"You should. It's a very special suit. So special they keep snapping my picture to make sure I don't mess it up."

"Clearly you're a man who knows his way around a closet. I'm supposed to get into wardrobe. Show me where to go?"

"Glad to."

She links an arm around mine as we walk to the racks. "So you met Nash and Tash, I see?"

"I had the pleasure of spending the night with them."

She makes a face. "They had sex, didn't they?"

I nod.

She shakes her head. "My condolences."

I laugh at that.

"Well, I'm staying in the room with you tonight. I'll try to even things out." She gives me a look. "Not like that, if that's what you're thinking."

"All I'm thinking about is getting you into a dress," I say.

"Really?" she asks. "Getting me *into* a dress?"

I laugh again. Jules has got her arm wrapped around mine, which is a pleasant distraction from the hangover I've had since yesterday's fight with Yael. Girls have always been the best distractions.

Until a girl became the thing I needed distraction from.

Twenty-seven

It's after five when we finally get around to shooting. Our scene is a song, the moment when Billy Devali's character first meets Amisha Rai's and is so besotted he breaks out singing and playing the piano. We are all supposed to watch, mesmerized by this authentic display of love at first sight. At the end, we clap.

We spend the rest of the day shooting. When we break for the day, the assistant director tells us to plan on staying at least two more days. Prateek takes me aside to say it'll probably be more than that and would I mind staying? I don't mind. I'm quite happy to stay until I fly back to Holland.

We're lining up for the bus again, when the assistant director snaps yet another picture of me. "Man, they're building a serious case against you," Nash says.

"I don't understand," I say. "I'm not even wearing the suit right now."

That night in the hotel, there are five of us. Nash, Ta-sha, Argin, me, and Jules. Jules and I share a mattress on the floor. Nothing happens. Not with us, anyhow. Her presence does little to stop Nash and Tasha from their late-night cal-isthenics, but when it happens, I can see Jules quaking with laughter, and then I am, too.

She rolls over on her side to face me. "Misery loves com-pany," she whispers.

―― ― ―

The next day, I'm in the lunch queue for some dal and rice when the assistant director taps me on the back. I even pose this time for the anticipated photo, but there's no camera. Instead he instructs me to come with him.

"Did you stain the suit?" Jules calls after me.

Arun trots up behind us, followed by Prateek, who looks stricken. How much can this suit be worth?

"What's going on?" I ask Prateek as we walk past the set and toward the row of trailers.

"Faruk! Khan!" He sputters the name like a cough.

"What about Faruk Khan?" But before Prateek can an-swer, I'm pulled up the stairs and pushed into one of the trailers. Inside, Faruk Khan, Amisha Rai, and Billy Devali are sitting in a huddle. They all stare at me for what seems like an eternity, until Billy finally booms, "There! Did I not tell you?"

Amisha lights another cigarette and kicks up her bare feet, which are covered with vinelike henna tattoos. "You are absolutely right," she says in a lilting accent. "He looks like an American movie star."

"Like that one." Billy snaps his fingers. "Heath Ledger."

"Only not dead," Faruk says.

They cluck in agreement.

"I think Heath Ledger was from Australia," I say.

"Never mind that," Faruk says. "Where are you from? America? UK?"

"Holland."

Billy wrinkles his nose. "You don't have an accent."

"You almost sound British," Amisha says. "Close enough to South African."

"This is closer to South African," I say in a clipped Afrikaans accent.

Amisha claps her hands. "He can do accents."

"Afrikaans is close to Dutch," I explain.

"Have you ever acted before?" Faruk asks.

"Not really."

"Not really?" Amisha asks, arching an eyebrow.

"A little Shakespeare."

"You cannot say 'not really' and then say you've done William Shakespeare," Faruk says scornfully. "What is your name? Or should we call you Mr. Not Really?"

"I prefer Willem. Willem de Ruiter."

"Bit of a mouthful," Billy says.

"Not a good stage name," Amisha says.

"He can change it," Billy says. "All the Americans do."

"Like the Indians don't," Amisha says. "*Billy.*"

"I'm not American," I interrupt. "I'm Dutch."

"Oh, yes. Mr. de . . . Willem," Faruk says. "No matter. We have a problem. One of our Western actors, an American named Dirk Digby, he lives in Dubai, perhaps you've heard of him?"

I shake my head.

"Never mind. It appears Mr. Digby had some last-minute problems with the contract and had to make other plans, and this leaves us with a small part open. It's a South African diamond dealer, shady character, who tries to woo our Miss Rai while also trying to steal her family's Shakti Diamond. Not a large part, but significant, and we find ourselves in a bit of a bind. We were looking for someone who can look the part and who can manage a few lines of Hindi and a few lines of English. How are you with languages?"

"Pretty good," I say. "I grew up speaking several."

"Okay, try this line," Faruk says, and he reads me something.

"Tell me what it means."

"You see?" Amisha says. "A natural actor would want to know. I don't think Dirk ever knows what he's saying."

Faruk waves her off. He turns to me. "You are trying to keep Amisha's character, Heera, from marrying Billy here, but really, you only want her family's diamonds. It's in English with some Hindi. This is the part where you tell Heera you know who she is, and that her name means diamond. I'll say it, you repeat?"

"Okay."

"*Main jaanta hoon tum kaun ho*, Heera Gopal. Heera, it means diamond, doesn't it?" Faruk says.

"*Main jaanta hoon tum kaun ho*, Heera Gopal. Heera, it means diamond, doesn't it?" I repeat.

They all stare at me.

"How did you do that?" Amisha asks.

"Do what?"

"You sounded as if you spoke Hindi fluently," Billy says.

"I don't know. I've always had an ear for languages."

"Incredible, really." Amisha turns to Faruk. "You wouldn't have to cut the dialogue."

Faruk stares at me. "We shoot next week. Here in Mumbai. You will have to learn lines. I can have someone help you with the Hindi pronunciation and translations, but there is a good bit of English." He strokes his beard. "I can pay you thirty thousand rupees."

I pause, trying to do the conversions.

Faruk takes my silence for bargaining. "Okay," he counters. "Forty thousand rupees."

"How long would I have to stay?"

"Shoot starts Monday, maybe three more days after that." Faruk says.

Monday is when I'm meant to fly back to Amsterdam. Do I want to stay three more days? But then Faruk continues. "We would put you up in the cast hotel. It's on Juhu Beach."

"Juhu Beach is very nice," Billy says.

"I'm meant to leave on Monday. I have a flight."

"Can't you change your flight?" Faruk asks.

I'm sure Mukesh can. And if they're putting me up in a hotel, it would keep me from having to go back to the Bombay Royale.

"Fifty thousand," Faruk says. "But that's my final offer."

"That's more than a thousand dollars, Mr. de Ruiter," Amisha informs me with a husky laugh and a billowing exhale of cigarette smoke. "Too good to turn down, I think."

Twenty-eight

---

*T*he production immediately relocates me to a posh hotel in Juhu Beach. The first thing I do is shower. Then I plug in my phone, which has been dead for the past day. I half expect a text or call from Yael, but there isn't one. I consider telling her I'm staying longer, but after our last conversation, after the last three weeks—three years—I feel like she has no right to this information. Instead, I text Mukesh, asking him to bump my departure date by another three days.

Immediately, he calls back. "You've decided to stay with us longer!" he says. He sounds delighted.

"Just a few days." I explain to him about being an extra and now being cast in a small part.

"Oh, that is most exciting," he says. "Mummy must be thrilled."

"*Mummy* doesn't know, actually."

"Doesn't know?"

"I haven't seen her. I've been staying out by the studios, and now I'm in a hotel in Juhu Beach."

"Juhu Beach. Very classy," Mukesh says. "But you haven't seen Mummy since you came back from Rajasthan? I thought she picked you up at the airport."

"Change of plans."

"Oh. I see." There's a pause. "When do you want to leave?"

"I'm supposed to start shooting on Monday, and it's meant to take three days."

"Safer to assume it'll take double," Mukesh says. "I'll see what I can do."

We hang up and I pick up my script. Faruk has written English translations above the Hindi and someone has made me a tape recording of the Hindi. I spend the afternoon repeating the lines.

When I'm done, I pace the room for a bit. It's all modern and posh, with a bathtub and a shower and a wide double bed. I haven't slept somewhere this nice in ages, and it's a little too quiet, a little too pristine. I sit on the bed, watch Hindi TV just to have some company. I order dinner in my room. That night when I go to bed, I find I can't sleep. The bed is too soft, too big, after so many years of sleeping on trains, in cars, on bunkbeds, sofas, futons, Ana Lucia's cramped bed. Now I'm like one of those rescued shipwrecked men who, once rescued and back in civilization, can only sleep on the floor.

———

Friday I wake up and practice my lines again. The shoot doesn't start for three more days, and they stretch in front of me, endlessly, like the gray-blue sea out my window. When my phone rings, I am embarrassed by my relief.

"Willem, Mukesh here. I have news about your flights."

"Great."

"So, soonest I can get you out is April." He tells me some dates.

"*What?* Why so long?"

"What can I say? All the flights are booked until then. Easter."

Easter? In a Hindu/Muslim country? I sigh. "You're sure there's nothing sooner? I don't mind paying a bit extra."

"Nothing to be done. I did the best I could." He sounds a bit insulted when he says the last bit.

"What about booking me a new flight?"

"Really, Willem, it is only a matter of weeks, and flights are expensive this time of year, and also full." His voice has gone scolding. "It is just a few extra days."

"Can you keep looking? See if any seats open up?"

"Certainly! Will do."

I hang up and try to fight off the sense of impending doom. I'd thought the film would keep me here a few extra days, all of them in a hotel. Now I'm stuck. I remind myself that I don't need to stay in Mumbai past the shoot. Nash and Tasha and Jules are going to Goa for a few days if they can cobble the cash together. Maybe I'll go with them. Maybe I'll even pay.

I send Jules a text: *Is Goa still a go?*

She texts back: *Only if I don't kill N&T. Last night unbearably loud. You are a traitor for deserting.*

I look around my hotel room where last night it was un-bearably quiet. I take a shot of the view from the balcony and send it to Jules. *It's quiet here. And there's room for two if you want to desert*, I write.

I like dessert, she texts back. *Tell me where you are.*

A few hours later, there's a knock at the door. I open it and Jules comes in. She admires the view and hops on the bed. She picks up the script from the coffee table.

"Want to run lines?" I ask. "There's English transla-tions."

She smiles. "Sure."

I show her where to start. She clears her throat and ar-ranges her face. "And who do you think you are?" she asks in a haughty voice, her attempt, I think, to mimic Amisha.

"Sometimes I wonder," I reply. "The name on my birth certificate reads Lars Von Gelder. But I know who *you* are, Heera Gopal. Heera, it means diamond, doesn't it? And you glitter as brightly as your name."

"I don't care to discuss my name with you, Mr. Von Gelder."

"Oh, so you know me after all?"

"I know all I care to."

"Then you know I am the top exporter of diamonds in South Africa, so I know a thing or two about precious gems. I can see more with my naked eye than most jewelers can with a loupe. And looking at you, I can tell that you are a million carats. And flawless."

"Word has it that you're after my family's diamond, Mr. Von Gelder."

"Oh, I am, Miss Gopal. I am." I pause for a beat. "But perhaps not the Shakti Diamond."

At the end of the section, Jules puts down the script. "This is quite cheesy, Mr. Van Gelder."

"It's Von Gelder, actually."

"Oh. Sorry. Mr. *Von* Gelder."

"It's very important, you know? Names," I say.

"Oh, yeah? What's Jules short for?"

"Juliana?" I try. "Like the Dutch queen?"

"Nope." Jules stands up from her chair and walks toward me, smiling as she folds herself into my lap. Then she kisses me.

"Juliet," I try.

She shakes her head, smiling as she unbuttons her shirt. "Not Juliet. But you're welcome to be my Romeo tonight."

Twenty-nine

The next morning, Jules leaves, back to Pune and the ashram with Nash and Tasha. We make vague plans to meet up in Goa the following week. I never do find out what Jules is short for.

I feel hungover even though we didn't drink, and lonely even though I'm used to being on my own. I call Prateek to see what he's doing this weekend, but he's helping his mother at home today and tomorrow he is going to a big family dinner with his uncle. I spend the day wandering Juhu Beach. I watch a bunch of men play soccer on the sand and it all makes me miss the boys in Utrecht. And then all the missing congeals, and it's Lulu I miss, and I know it must be displaced, my loneliness a heat-seeking missile, her the heat. Only I can't seem to find a new source of heat. I don't miss Jules at all.

— — —

By Sunday, I'm going stir-crazy. I decide to take a train out of the city, a day trip somewhere. I've just opened my guidebook to figure out where to go when my phone rings. I practically leap on it.

"Willem!" Mukesh's jovial voice echoes through the line. I don't think I've ever been happier to hear from him. "What are you doing today?"

"I'm just trying to suss that out. I was thinking of making a day trip to Khandala."

"Khandala is very nice, but far for one day so you must leave early. If you like, I can arrange a driver for you another day. I have a different proposal for you. How about I take you around?"

"Really?"

"Yes. There are some very lovely temples in Mumbai, smaller temples tourists so rarely see. My wife and daughters are away, so I have the day free."

I gratefully accept, and at noon, Mukesh picks me up in a small battered Ford and proceeds to speed me around Mumbai. We stop at three different temples, watching young men do yoga-like calisthenics, watching old Sadhus meditating in prayer. The third stop is a Jain temple, the acolytes all hold small brooms sweeping in front of them as they walk. "To brush any living creatures out of their way so not to inadvertently take a life," Mukesh explains. "Such care for life," he says. "Just like Mummy."

"Right. Mummy is practically a Jain," I say. "Or maybe she's aiming to be the next Mother Teresa?"

Mukesh gives me a sympathetic look that makes me want to break something. "You know how I met Mummy, do you not?" he asks as we walk through a breezeway in the temple.

"I assume it had something to do with the fascinating world of air travel." I'm being unfair to Mukesh, but such is the price for making himself her emissary.

He shakes his head. "That came later. I was with my own mummy who had the cancer." He clucks his tongue. "She was having her treatments, tip-top doctor, but it was in the lungs, so not much to be done. We were coming from the specialist one day, waiting for a taxi, but Amma, that's my mummy, was quite weak and dizzy and she fell on the street. Your mummy happened to be nearby and she rushed up to ask if she could help. I explained to her about Amma's condition—it was terminal," he lowers his voice to a whisper. "But your mummy told me about different things that could help, not to cure her, but to make the dizziness and the weakness better. And she came, every week, to my home, with her needles and her massages and it helped so much. When my amma's time came, her journey to the next life was so much more peaceful. Thanks to your mummy."

I see what he's doing. Mukesh is attempting to interpret my mother to me much in the way Bram used to do when he'd explain why Yael seemed so gruff or distant. He was the one to quietly tell me stories about Saba, who, after the death of Yael's mother, Naomi, came undone by one tragedy too many. He turned overprotective, paranoid, or more overprotective and paranoid, Bram said, not allowing Yael to do the simplest things—swim in a public pool, have a friend over—and forcing her to keep disaster preparation checklists for any kind of emergency. "She promised she would do everything differently," he said. "So it would be different for you. So it wouldn't be oppressive."

As if there's only one kind of oppressive.

———

After the temples, we have lunch. I'm feeling bad about how I acted toward Mukesh, so when he tells me he has something extra special he wants to show me—something very few tourists ever see—I paste on my smile and act excited. As we bump across Mumbai, the streets become more dense: bicycles, rickshaws, cars, donkey-pulled carts, cows, women with bundles on their heads, all converge onto choked streets that don't seem built for such traffic. The buildings themselves suffer from the same syndrome; the mix of high-rises and shacks are all overflowing with rivers of people, sleeping on mats, hanging laundry on lines, cooking on small fires outside.

We turn down a dank narrow alley, shrouded somehow from the bright sunlight. Mukesh points to the row of young girls in tattered saris, standing. "Prostitutes," he says.

At the end of the alley we stop. I look back at the prostitutes. Some are younger than me, and their eyes look blank, and it all makes me feel ashamed somehow. Mukesh points to a squat cement building with a name written on it in both swirly Hindi and block English. "Here we are," he says.

I read the sign. MITALI. It's vaguely familiar.

"What is this?" I ask.

"Why, Mummy's clinic, of course," he says.

"Yael's clinic?" I ask in alarm.

"Yes, I thought we might pay her a visit."

"But, but . . ." I sputter for excuses. "It's Sunday," I finish, as if the day of the week is the problem.

"Sickness does not take a Sabbath." Mukesh points to a small teashop on the corner. "I will wait for you there." And then he's gone.

I stand in front of the clinic for a minute. One of the prostitutes—she looks no older than thirteen—starts to walk toward me and I can't stand the thought that she thinks I'm a client, so I shove open the door to the clinic. The door swings open, right onto an old woman crouched just inside. There are people everywhere, with homemade bandages, and listless babies, napping on pallets on the floor. They're camped all up the cement stairs and all around the waiting room, giving new meaning to the term.

"Are you Willem?" From behind the glass partition a no-nonsense Indian woman in a lab coat is looking at me. Two seconds later, she opens the door to the waiting room. I feel all the eyes turn to me. The woman says something in Hindi or Marathi and there is much silent nodding, giving new meaning to the term *patient*, too.

"I'm Doctor Gupta," she says, her voice brisk, efficient but warm. "I work with your mother. Let me go find her. Would you like some tea?"

"No thank you." I have the sickening feeling that everyone else is in on a joke but me.

"Good, good. Wait here."

She leads me to a small windowless room with a ripped gurney, and a rush of memory overtakes me. The last time I was in a hospital: Paris. The time before that: Amsterdam. Yael had called me at my dorm, very early that morning, telling me to come. Bram was sick.

I couldn't understand the urgency. I'd seen him not a week before. He'd been a little off his game, a sore throat, but Yael was tending to him with her usual teas and tinctures. I had an exam that day. I asked if I could come after.

"Come now," she said.

At the hospital, Yael had stood in the corner while three doctors—the traditional kind, with stethoscopes and guarded expressions—surrounded me in a grim little circle and explained to me that Bram had contracted a rare strain of strep that had sent his body into septic shock. His kidneys had already failed and now his liver was going, too. They were doing everything they could, putting him on dialysis and pumping him full of the most powerful antibiotics, but so far, nothing had been effective. I should brace myself for the worst.

"I don't understand," I said.

Neither did they, really. All they could say was, "It's one of those one-in-a-million cases." Such comforting odds, except when you were the one.

It was like finding out the world was made of gossamer and could be so easily ripped apart. To be so solely at the mercy of fate. Even with all Bram's talk of accidents, it seemed inconceivable.

I looked to Yael, mighty Yael, to intervene, to swoop in, to take care of Bram like she always had. But she just shrank into that corner, not saying a word.

"Do something, goddammit!" I screamed at her. *"You have to do something."*

But she didn't. Couldn't. And two days later, Bram was gone.

— — —

"Willem."

I turn around and there's Yael. I always think she's so frightening, but she's actually tiny, barely reaching my shoulder.

"You're crying," she says.

I reach out and touch my face and I find it wet with tears. I'm mortified to be doing this. In front of her. I turn away. I want to run. Out of this clinic. Out of India. Forget the shoot. Forget the flight delay. Buy a new ticket. It doesn't have to be back to Amsterdam. Anywhere that's not here.

I feel her hands on me, turning me back around. "Willem?" she asks. "Tell me why you're lost."

It's shocking to hear her words, my words. That she remembered.

But how can I answer her? How can I answer when I've been nothing but lost these last three years? So much more than I ever anticipated. I keep thinking of another one of the stories Bram used to tell, a horror story really, about when Yael was a girl. She was ten and Saba had taken her camping in the desert. Just the two of them. As the sun started to set, Saba said he'd be right back, and then left her alone with one of those disaster preparation checklists that he was always having her make. Yael, terrified, but capable because of those very disaster preparation checklists, made a fire, made dinner, made camp, fended. When Saba showed up the next day, she screamed at him, *How could you leave me alone?* And Saba had said, *I wasn't leaving you alone. I was watching the whole time. I was preparing you.*

Why didn't she prepare me? Why didn't she teach me about the universal law of equilibrium before I had to find it out for myself? Maybe then I wouldn't miss everything so much.

"I miss . . ." I start to say, but I can't get the words out.

"You miss Bram," she says.

And yes, of course I do. I miss my father. I miss my grandfather. I miss my home. And I miss my mother. But the thing is, for almost three years, I managed not to miss any of them. And then I spent that one day with that one girl. One day. One day of watching the rise and fall of her sleep under the rolling clouds in that park and feeling so peaceful that I fell asleep myself. One day of being under her protection—I can still feel the grasp of her hand as we flew through the streets after she threw the book at the skinheads, her grip so strong that it felt like we were one person, not two. One day of being the beneficiary of her strange generosity—the barge ride, the watch, that honesty, her willingness to show fear, her willingness to show courage. It was like she gave me her whole self, and somehow as a result, I gave her more of myself than I even realized there was to give. But then she was gone. And only after I'd been filled up by her, by that day, did I understand how empty I really was.

Yael watches me a moment longer. "Who else do you miss?" she asks, like she already knows the answer.

"I don't know," I say, and for a minute she looks frustrated, like I'm keeping it from her, but that's not it, and I don't want to keep things from her anymore. So I clarify. "I don't know her name."

Yael looks up, surprised, and not. "Whose name?"

"Lulu."

"Isn't *that* her name?"

So I tell my mother. About finding this girl, this strange and nameless girl, whom I showed nothing but who saw everything. I tell her how since losing her, I have felt bereft. And the relief at telling my mother this is almost as profound as the relief of finding Lulu was.

When I finish telling Yael the story about that day in Paris, I look at her. And I'm shocked all over again because she's doing something I've only seen her do in the kitchen while cutting onions.

My mother is crying.

"Why are *you* crying?" I ask her, now crying again myself.

"Because it sounds just like how I met Bram," she says, laughing on a sob.

Of course it does. I've thought about that every single day since I met Lulu. Wondered if that's not why I'm stuck on her. Because the story is so much like Yael and Bram's.

"Except for one thing," I say.

"What's that?" she asks, swiping at her eyes.

The most important detail. And you'd think I would've known better, having heard Bram's story so many times.

"You give the girl your address."

Thirty

APRIL
Mumbai

As Mukesh expected, the shoot goes over schedule by double, so for six days I have the pleasure of becoming Lars Von Gelder. And it is. A pleasure. A surprising one. On set, in costume, with Amisha and the other actors across from me, Lars Von Gelder's cheesy Hindi lines cease to feel cheesy. They don't even feel like another language. They roll off my tongue and I feel like I am him, the calculating operator who says one thing and wants another.

In between takes, I hang out in Amisha's trailer, playing games of hearts with her and Billy. "We're all impressed with your abilities," Amisha tells me. "Even Faruk, though he'll never say so."

He doesn't. Not exactly. But at the end of each day, he pats me on the back and says, "Not bad, Mr. Not Really." And I feel proud.

But then it's the last day and I know it's over, because

instead of saying "not bad," Faruk says "good work," and thanks me.

And that's it. Next week, Amisha and the principals are packing for Abu Dhabi, where they will shoot the final scenes of the film. And me? Yesterday I got a text from Tasha. She and Nash and Jules are in Goa. I'm invited to go with them. But I won't.

I have a couple more weeks here. And I'm spending them with my mother.

My first night back at the Bombay Royale, I get in late. Chaudhary is snoring behind the desk, so I take the stairs up to the fifth floor rather than wake him. Yael has left the door propped open, but she's also asleep when I get in. I'm both relieved and disappointed. We haven't really spoken since that day at the clinic. I don't quite know what to expect between us. Have things changed? Do we speak a common language now?

The next morning she shakes me awake.

"Hey," I say, blinking my eyes.

"Hey," she says back, almost shyly. "I wanted to know, before I leave for work, if you wanted to join me tonight for a Seder. It's the first night of Passover."

I almost think she's joking. When I was growing up, we only celebrated the secular holidays. New Year's. Queen's Day. We never once had a Seder. I didn't even know what they were until Saba started visiting and told me about all the holidays he celebrated, that Yael used to celebrate when she was a child.

"Since when do you go to Seders?" I ask. My question is hesitant, because the mere asking of it touches on the tender spot of her childhood.

"Two years now," she answers. "There's an American family that started a school near the clinic, and they wanted to have one last year and I was the only Jew they knew, so they begged me to come, because they said they'd feel funny having one without a Jew."

"They're not Jewish then?"

"No. They're Christians. Missionaries, even."

"You're kidding?"

She shakes her head, but she's smiling. "I have discovered that no one likes a Jewish holiday quite like a Christian fundamentalist." She laughs, and I can't remember the last time I heard her do that. "There might be a Catholic nun there, too."

"A nun? This is starting to sound like one of Uncle Daniel's jokes. A nun and a missionary walk into a Seder."

"You need three. A nun, a missionary, and an imam walk into a Seder," Yael says.

Imam. I think of the Muslim girls in Paris, and I'm reminded, again, of Lulu. "She was Jewish, too," I say. "My American girl."

Yael's eyebrows go up. "Really?"

I nod.

Yael raises her hands into the air. "Well, maybe she's having her own Seder tonight."

The thought hadn't occurred to me, but as soon as she says it, I get a strange feeling that it's true. And for a second, even with those two oceans and everything else between us, Lulu doesn't feel quite so far away.

Thirty-one

*T*he Donnellys, the family hosting tonight's Seder, live in a large sprawling white stucco house with a makeshift soccer pitch out front. When we arrive, several blond people spill out the front door, including three boys who Yael has told me she can't tell apart. I can see why. Aside from their height, they are identical, all tousled hair and gangly limbs and knobby Adam's apples. "One's Declan, one's Matthew, and the little one, I think, is Lucas," Yael says, not so helpfully.

The tallest one bounces a soccer ball in his hand. "Time for a quick game?" he asks.

"Don't get too muddy, Dec," the blonde woman says. She smiles. "Hi, Willem. I'm Kelsey. This is Sister Karenna," she says, gesturing to a weathered old smiling woman in a full Catholic habit.

"Welcome, welcome," the nun says.

"And I'm Paul," a mustached man in a Hawaiian shirt says, bundling me into a hug. "And you look just like your mama."

Yael and I stare at each other. No one ever says that.

"It's in the eyes," Paul says. He turns to Yael. "You hear about the cholera outbreak in the Dharavi slum?"

They immediately start talking about that, so I go play some soccer with the brothers. They tell me how they've been discussing Passover and the Exodus all week long as part of their studies. They are homeschooled. "We even made matzo over a campfire," the smallest one, Lucas, tells me.

"Well, you know more than me," I say.

They laugh, like I'm joking.

After a while, Kelsey calls us inside. The house reminds me of a flea market, a little of this, a little of that. A dining table on one side, a chalkboard on the other. Chore charts on the wall, alongside pictures of Jesus, Gandhi, and Ganesha. The entire house is fragrant with roasting meat.

"It smells wonderful," Yael says.

Kelsey smiles. "I made roast leg of lamb stuffed with apples and walnuts." She turns to me. "We tried to get a brisket, but it's impossible here."

"Holy cow and all," Paul says.

"This is an Israeli recipe," Kelsey continues. "At least that's what the website said."

Yael is quiet for a minute. "It's what my mother would've made."

Yael's mother, Naomi, who escaped the horrors Saba had lived through only to be struck by a delivery truck on the way back from walking Yael to school. Universal law of equilibrium. Escape one horror, get hit by another.

"What else do you remember?" I ask hesitantly. "About Naomi." She was another unmentionable when I was growing up.

"She sang," Yael says quietly. "All the time. At the Seders too. So there was lots of singing at the Seders—before. And people. When I was a child, we had a full house. Not after. Then it was just us. . . ." She trails off. "It wasn't as joyful."

"So tonight, there will be singing," Paul says. "Someone get my guitar."

"Oh, no. Not the guitar," Matthew jokes.

"I like the guitar," Lucas says.

"Me, too," Kelsey says. "Reminds me of when we met." Her and Paul's eyes meet and tell a quiet story, the way Yael and Bram's used to, and I feel a longing pull at me.

"Shall we sit down?" Kelsey asks, gesturing to the table. We take our seats.

"I know I railroaded you into this again, but Yael, would you mind being the leader?" Paul asks. "I've been studying up since last year and I'll chime in, but I feel you're better qualified. Otherwise we can ask Sister Karenna to do it."

"What? I do it?" Sister Karenna jerks up.

"She's a little deaf," Declan whispers to me.

"You don't have to do anything, Sister, but relax," Kelsey says in a loud voice.

"I'll do it," Yael tells Paul. "If you help."

"We'll tag-team it," Paul says, winking at me.

But Yael hardly seems like she needs the help. She says

an opening prayer over the wine in a clear strong voice, as if she's done this every year. Then she turns to Paul. "Maybe you might explain the point of the Seder."

"Sure." Paul clears his throat and starts a long meandering explanation about how a Seder is meant to commemorate the Jews' exodus from Egypt, their escape from slavery and their return to the Promised Land, the miracles that ensued to make this happen. "Though this happened thousands of years ago, Jews today retell the story every year to rejoice in the triumphant history, to remember it. But here's why I wanted to jump on the bandwagon. Because it's not just a retelling or a celebration of history. It's also a reminder of the price and the privilege of liberation." He turns to Yael. "That sound right?"

She nods. "It's a story we repeat because it's a history we want to see repeated," she says.

The Seder continues. We say blessings over the matzo, we eat the vegetables in salt water, and then the bitter herbs. Kelsey serves soup. "Not matzo ball, mulligatawny," she says. "I hope lentils are okay."

While we're eating our soup, Paul suggests that since the point of the Seder is to retell a story of liberation, we all take a turn and talk about a time in our lives when we escaped some sort of oppression. "Or escaped anything really." He goes first, talking about his life as it used to be, drinking, drugs, aimless and sad before he found God, and then found Kelsey and then found meaning.

Sister Karenna goes next, talking about escaping the brutality of poverty when she was taken in by a church school, and going on to become a nun to serve others.

Then it's my turn. I pause. My first instinct is to tell about Lulu. Because really that was a day I felt like I escaped danger.

But I decide to tell a different story, in part because I don't think this one has been told out loud since he died. The story of one hitchhiking girl and two brothers and the three centimeters that sealed all our fates. It's not really my escape. It's hers. But it is my story. The founding tale of my family. And as Yael said about the Seder, it's a story I repeat because it's a history I want to see repeated.

Thirty-two

The night before I fly back to Amsterdam, Mukesh calls to go over all my flight details. "I got you an exit row seat," he says. "You'll be more comfortable, with all your height. Though maybe if you tell them you are a Bollywood star, you'll get business class."

I laugh. "I'll do my best."

"When does the film come out?"

"I'm not sure. They just finished shooting."

"Funny how it all worked out."

"Right place, right time," I tell him.

"Yes, but you wouldn't have been in the right place in the right time had we not canceled your camel trip."

"You mean it got canceled. Because the camels got sick."

"Oh, no, camels just fine. Mummy asked me to bring you back early." He lowers his voice. "Also, plenty of flights back to Amsterdam before tomorrow, but when you disappeared to the movie, Mummy asked me to keep you here a little bit longer." He chuckles. "Right place, right time."

— — —

The next morning, Prateek comes to drive us to the airport. Chaudhary shuffles to the curb to see us off, wagging his fingers and reminding us of the legally mandated taxi fares.

I sit in the backseat this time, because this time Yael is coming with us. On the ride to the airport, she is quiet. So am I. I don't quite know what to say. Mukesh's confession last night has rattled me, and I want to ask Yael about it, but I don't know if I should. If she'd wanted me to know, she would've told me.

"What will you do when you get back?" she asks me after a while.

"I don't know." I really have no idea. At the same time, I'm ready to go back.

"Where will you stay?"

I shrug. "I can stay on Broodje's couch for a few weeks."

"On the couch? I thought you were living there."

"My room's been rented." Even if it hadn't, everyone is moving out at the end of the summer. W is moving in with Lien in Amsterdam. Henk and Broodje are going to get their own flat together. *It's the end of an era, Willy,* Broodje wrote me in an email.

"Why don't you go back to Amsterdam?" Yael asks.

"Because there's nowhere to go," I say.

I look straight at her and she looks straight at me and it's like we're acknowledging that. But then she raises her eyebrow. "You never know," she says.

"Don't worry. I'll land somewhere." I look out the window. The car is climbing onto the expressway. I can already feel Mumbai falling away.

"Will you keep looking for her? That girl?"

The way she says it, *keep looking*, as if I haven't stopped. And I realize in some way, I haven't. Which is maybe the problem.

"What girl is this?" Prateek asks, surprised. I never told him of any girl.

I look at the dashboard, where Ganesha is dancing away just as he did on that first drive from the airport. "Hey, Ma. What was that mantra? The one from the Ganesha temple?"

"*Om gam ganapatayae namaha*?" Yael asks.

"That's the one."

From the front seat, Prateek chants it. "*Om gam ganapatayae namaha*."

I repeat it. "*Om gam ganapatayae namaha*." I pause as the sound floats through the car. "That's what I'm after. New beginnings."

Yael reaches out to touch the scar on my face. It's faded now, thanks to her ministrations. She smiles at me. And it occurs to me that I might have already gotten what I asked for.

Thirty-three

A week after I get back from India, while I'm still camped out at the couch on Bloemstraat trying to get over my jetlag and figure out what my next move is, I get an unlikely call.

"Hey, little man. You coming to clear your shit out of my attic?" There's no introduction, no preamble. Not that I need one. Even though we have not spoken in years, I know the voice. It's so much like his brother's.

"Uncle Daniel," I say. "Hey. Where are you?"

"Where am I? I'm in my flat. With my attic. That has your shit in it."

This is a surprise. All the years I grew up, I have never actually seen Daniel in the flat he owns. It's the same flat on the Ceintuurbaan that he and Bram used to live in. Back then, it was a squat. It's where they were living when Yael came and knocked on the door and changed everything.

Within six months, Bram had married Yael and moved them into their own flat. Within another year, he'd cobbled together the funds to buy a broken-down old barge on the Nieuwe Prinsengracht. Daniel stayed in the squat, eventually getting a lease for it and then buying it from the city government for a pittance. Unlike Bram, who went on to fix up his boat, floorboard by floorboard, until it was the "Bauhaus on the Gracht," Daniel left the flat in its state of anarchist disrepair and rented it out. He got almost nothing for it. "But nothing is enough to live like a king in Southeast Asia," Bram used to say. So that's where Daniel stayed, riding the ups and down of the Asian economy with a series of business ventures that mostly went nowhere.

"Your ma called," Daniel continues. "Told me you were back. Said you might need a place to stay. I told her you needed to come get your shit out of my attic."

"So I have shit in the attic?" I ask him, stretching out from the too-short sofa and trying to digest my surprise. Yael called Daniel? For me?

"*Everyone* has shit in the attic," Daniel says, laughing a huskier, smokier version of Bram's laugh. "When can you come over?"

We arrange for me to come over the next day. Daniel texts me the address, though that's hardly necessary. I know his flat better than I know him. I know the stuck-in-time furniture—the zebra-striped egg chair, the 1950s lamps that Bram used to find at flea markets and rewire. I even know the smell, patchouli and hash. "It's how this place has smelled for twenty years," Bram would say when he and I would visit the flat together to fix a faucet or deliver keys to a new tenant. When I was younger, the lively multi-ethnic area where Daniel lived, right across from the treasures of the Albert Cuyp street market, seemed like another country from the quiet outer canal where we lived.

Over the years, the neighborhood has changed. The once working-class cafés around the market now serve things with truffles, and in the market, alongside the stalls hawking fish and cheese, there are designer boutiques. The houses have smartened up, too. You can see them through picture windows, the sparkling kitchens, the expensive clean-lined furniture.

Not Daniel's place, though. As his neighbors renovated and upgraded, his flat dug into its time warp. I suspect that's still the case, especially after he warns me that the buzzer doesn't work and instructs me to call upon arrival so he can throw down the keys. So I'm caught a little off guard when he opens the door to the flat and I'm ushered into a lounge, all wide-plank bamboo floors, sage-colored walls, low, modern sofas. I look around the room. It's unrecognizable, except for the egg chair, and even that's been reupholstered.

"Little man," Daniel says, though I am not little at all, a few fingers taller than him. I look at Daniel. His reddish hair is maybe a little shot through with gray, the smile lines cut a little deeper, but otherwise he's the same.

"Little uncle," I joke back, patting him on the head as I hand him back the keys. I walk around. "You've done something to the place," I say, tapping a finger to my chin.

Daniel laughs. "Oh. I'm only halfway there, but that's halfway farther than no way."

"True enough."

"I've got big plans. Actual plans. Where are my plans?" Out the window, there's the roar of a jet rumbling through the clouds. Daniel watches it, then he resumes his search, spinning around peering at the crowded bookshelves. "It's a little slow going because I'm doing the work myself, though I can afford to hire it out, but it just seemed like I should do it this way."

Afford it? Daniel has always been broke; Bram used to help him out. But Bram's not here. Maybe one of his Asian business ventures finally hit. I watch Daniel skitter around the room in search of something, finally locating a set of blueprints shoved halfway under the coffee table.

"I wish he was here to help me; I think he'd be happy that I'm finally making this place mine. But in a way I feel like he is here. Also, he's footing the bill," he says.

It takes me a minute to understand who he's talking about, what he's talking about. "The boat?" I ask.

He nods.

Back in India, Yael barely spoke of Daniel. I figured that they weren't in touch anymore. With Bram gone, why would they be? They never liked each other. At least that's how it seemed to me. Daniel was flakey, messy, a spendthrift—all the things that Yael loved in Bram in less extreme form—and Yael was the person who swept in and upended Daniel's life. If there wasn't much room for me, I can only imagine how it felt for him. It made sense to me why Daniel moved half a world away a few years after Yael showed up.

"There wasn't a will," Daniel says. "She didn't have to do that, but of course she did. That's your ma for you."

Is it? I think about my trip to Rajasthan, an exile that turned out to be what I needed. Then I think about Mukesh, not just canceling the camel tour and delaying my return flight at Yael's behest, but also dropping me off at the clinic that day, when everyone seemed to be expecting me. I'd always assumed my mother was so hands off, taking care of everyone but me. But I'm starting to wonder if perhaps I misunderstood her brand of caretaking.

"I'm beginning to get that," I tell Daniel.

"Good timing, too," he says. He scratches his beard. "I didn't offer you coffee. You want coffee?"

"I wouldn't say no to a coffee."

I follow him into the kitchen, which is the old kitchen, all chipped cupboards, cracked tiles, ancient tiny gas range, cold-water-only sink.

"Kitchen's next. And the bedrooms. Maybe halfway was a bit optimistic. I'd better get on it. You should come live with me. Help me out," he says with a loud clap of his hands. "Your pa always said you were handy."

I'm not sure if I'm handy, but Bram was always drafting me for help with some home-improvement project or another.

He puts the coffee on the stove. "I gotta get into gear. I've got two months now, so tick-tock, tick-tock."

"Two months until what?"

"Oh, shit. I didn't tell you. I only just told your ma." His face breaks out into a smile that looks so much like Bram's it hurts.

"Told her what?"

"Well, Willem, I'm going to be a father."

——— —— ———

As we drink coffee, Daniel fills me on the big news. At the age of forty-seven, the perennial bachelor has at last found love. But, because apparently the de Ruiter men can never do things the simple way, the mother of Daniel's child is Brazilian. Her name is Fabiola. They met in Bali. She lives in Bahia. He shows me a picture of a doe-eyed woman with a lit-from-within smile. Then he shows me an accordion folder, several centimeters thick, his correspondence with the various government agencies to prove the legitimacy of their relationship so she can get a visa and they can be married. In July, he is going to Brazil in preparation for the birth in September, and, he hopes, the wedding soon after. All going well, they'll be in Amsterdam in the fall, and return to Brazil for the winter. "Winters there, summers here, and when he is old enough for school, we'll reverse it."

"He?" I ask.

Daniel smiles. "It's a boy. We know. We already have a name for him. Abraão."

"Abraão," I say, rolling it over my tongue.

Daniel nods. "It's Portuguese for Abraham."

We both are silent for a moment. Abraham, Bram's full name.

"You'll move in, help, won't you?" He points to the blueprints, the one bedroom that will be made into two, the flat that once housed the two brothers, and for a spell housed all three of them before it was just Daniel all on his own. And then, not even him.

But now we are two here. And soon there will be more. After so much contracting, somehow, inexplicably, my family is growing again.

Thirty-four

JUNE
Amsterdam

Daniel and I are on the way to the plumbing supply shop to pick up a shower body when his bike gets a flat tire.

We stop to inspect. There's a nail lodged deep into the tube. It's four thirty. The plumbing store closes at five. And then it's closed for the weekend. Daniel frowns and throws his arms in the air like a frustrated child.

"Goddammit!" he curses. "The plumber's coming tomorrow."

We did the bedrooms first, a mess of studs and drywall and plaster, neither of us knowing exactly what we were doing, but between books and some old friends of Bram's, we managed to make a tiny "master" bedroom, with a loft bed, and a tinier nursery, which is where I'm now living.

But the learning curve was high and it took longer than we'd expected, and then the bathroom, which Daniel thought would be simple—swapping out seventy-year-old fixtures for modern ones—turned out to be anything but. All the pipes had to be replaced. Coordinating the arrival of the tub and the sink and the plumber—another of Bram's friends, who is doing the job on the cheap but also on his off hours, nights and weekends—has challenged Daniel's already limited logistical skills, but he soldiers on. He keeps saying that if Bram built a *boat* for his family, dammit, he's going to build a flat for his. And it's such a strange thing to hear, because I'd always thought Bram built the boat for Yael.

The plumber came last night, we thought, to finish the bath and shower installations, only to tell us he couldn't install the new tub that had finally arrived until we had a shower body. And we can't finish tiling the bathroom and move on to the kitchen—which the plumber said will probably also need all new pipes—until we have a shower.

For the most part, Daniel has approached the renovation with the sheer enthusiasm of a child building a sand castle at the beach. Every other night, when he and Fabiola Skype, he lugs his battered laptop around the flat, showing off all the latest modifications, discussing furniture placement (she's big into feng shui) and colors (pale blue for their room; butter yellow for the baby's).

But during those semi-nightly calls, you can see the bump is growing. After the plumber left, Daniel admitted he could almost hear the baby inside, ticking like one of those old alarm clocks. "Ready or not, here he comes," he'd said, shaking his head. "Forty-seven years, you'd think I'd be ready."

"Maybe you're never ready until it's upon you," I'd said.

"Very wise, little man," he'd said. "But goddamn it, if *I'm* not ready, I'm going to have the *flat* ready."

"Go on ahead, take mine," I tell Daniel now, swinging off my bike. It's the same beat-up old workhorse I bought off a junkie when I first came back to Amsterdam last year. It stayed locked up outside Bloemstraat all those months I was in India, no worse for wear. When I started working on the flat, I brought it back to Amsterdam, along with the rest of my things, all of which fit on the bottom two shelves of the bookshelf in the baby's room. I don't have much: Some clothes. A few books. The Ganesha statue Nawal gave me. And Lulu's watch. It still ticks. I hear it in the night sometimes.

Problem solved, Daniel is bright sunshine again. With a gappy grin, he hops onto my bike, and takes off pedaling, waving behind him, almost slamming into an oncoming moto. I wheel his bike off the narrow alley and turn onto the wide canal of the Kloveniersburgwal. I'm in an area sandwiched between the shrinking Red Light District and the university. I head in the direction of the university, more likely to find bike repair shops there. I pass an English-language bookstore I've ridden by a few times before, always somewhat curious. On the stoop is a box of one-euro books. I poke through—it's mostly American paperbacks, the kind of thing I read in a day and traded when I was traveling. But at the bottom of the box, like a displaced refugee, is a copy of *Twelfth Night*.

I know I probably won't read it. But I have a bookshelf now for the first time since college, even if it's only temporary.

I go inside to pay. "Do you know of a bike repair place nearby?" I ask the man behind the counter.

"Two blocks down, on Boerensteeg," he says, without looking up from his book.

"Thanks." I slide over the Shakespeare.

He glances at the cover, then looks up. "You're buying this?" He sounds skeptical.

"Yeah," I say, and then by way of an explanation I don't need to give, I tell him I was in the play last year. "I played Sebastian."

"You did it in English?" he asks, in English, with that strange hybrid accent of someone who's lived abroad a long time.

"Yeah," I say.

"Oh." He goes back to his book. I hand him a euro.

I'm almost out the door when he calls out: "If you do Shakespeare, you should check out the theater down the way. They put on some decent Shakespeare plays in English in Vondelpark in the summer. I saw that they're holding auditions this year."

He says it casually, dropping the suggestion like a piece of litter. I ponder it there, on the ground. Maybe it's worthless, maybe not. I won't know unless I pick it up.

Thirty-five

*N*ame."

"Willem. De Ruiter." It comes out a whisper.

"Come again."

I clear my throat. Try again. "Willem de Ruiter."

Silence. I can feel my heartbeat, in my chest, my temple, my throat. I can't remember ever being nervous like this before and I don't quite understand it. I've never had stage fright. Not even that first time with the acrobats, not even going on with Guerrilla Will, in French. Not even the first time Faruk shouted action and the cameras rolled and I had to speak Lars Von Gelder's lines, in Hindi.

But now, I can barely say my name out loud. It's as if, unbeknownst to me, there is a volume switch on me and someone has turned it all the way down. I squint my eyes and try to peer into the audience, but the bright lights are rendering whoever is out there invisible.

I wonder what they're doing. Are they looking at the ridiculous head shot I scrambled to put together? Daniel took it of me in the Sarphatipark. And then we'd printed my Guerrilla Will stats on the back. It doesn't look half bad from a distance. I have several plays to my credit, all of them Shakespearian. It's only if you inspect it closely you see that the picture is shitty quality, pixelated to the extreme, taken on a phone and printed at home. And my acting credentials, well, Guerrilla Will isn't exactly repertory theater. I'd seen some of the headshots of the other actors. They came from all over Europe—the Czech Republic, Germany, France and the UK, as well as here—and had real plays under their belts. Better photos, too.

I take a deep breath. At least I *have* a head shot. Thanks to Kate Roebling. I called her at the last minute for advice because I've never auditioned before. With Guerrilla Will, Tor decided what role you'd play. There was some sniping about this, but I didn't care. The money was split equally, no matter how many lines you had.

"Ahh, yes, Willem," a disembodied voice says. It sounds bored before I've even begun. "What will you be reading for us today?"

The play being produced this summer is *As You Like It*, one I've never seen or heard much about. When I stopped in the theater last week, they told me I could prepare any Shakespearian monologue. In English. Obviously. Kate had told me to take a look at *As You Like It*. That I might find something really meaty in it.

"Sebastian, from *Twelfth Night*," I say. I decided to put together three shorter Sebastian speeches. Easiest to do that.

It was the last part I played. And I still remembered most of the lines.

"Whenever you're ready."

I try to remember Kate's words, but they swirl in my head like a foreign language I barely know. *Choose something you feel? Be who you are, not who they want you to be? Go big or go home?* And there was something else, something she told me before she rang off. It was important. But I can't remember it now. At this point, it'll be enough to remember my lines.

A throat clears. "Whenever you're ready." It's a woman's voice this time, in a tone that says: *Get on with it.*

Breathe. Kate said to breathe. That much I remember. So I breathe. And then I begin:

"By your patience, no. My stars shine darkly over me: the malignancy of my fate might perhaps distemper yours."

The first lines come out. Not too bad. I continue.

"Therefore I shall crave of you your leave that I may bear my evils alone."

The words start to flow out of me. Not as they did last summer in that endless array of parks and squares and plazas. Not haltingly, as they did in Daniel's bathroom, where I practiced them all weekend, to the mirror, to the tiles, and on occasion, to Daniel himself.

"If the heavens had been pleased, would we had so ended!"

The words come differently now. Understood in a fresh way. Sebastian is not just some aimless drifter, going where the wind blows him. He's someone recovering, rubbed raw and unsure by his spate of bad fortune, by the malignancy of his fate.

"She bore a mind that envy could not but call fair," I say and it's Lulu I see, on that hot English night, the last time I spoke these words in front of an audience. The faint smile on her lips.

"She is drowned already sir, with salt water, though I seem to drown her remembrance again with more."

And then it's over. There's no applause, only a loud silence. I can hear my breathing, my heartbeat, still hammering. Aren't the nerves supposed to go away once you are on stage? Once you've finished?

"Thank you," the woman says. Her words are clipped, generic, no actual gratitude in them. For a second, I think perhaps I should thank them.

But I don't. I leave the stage in a bit of a daze wondering what just happened. As I walk up the aisle, I see the director and producer and stage manager (Kate told me whom to expect) already conferring about someone else's headshot. Then I'm squinting in the bright light of the lobby. I rub my eyes. I'm unsure of what to do next.

"Glad that's over?" a skinny guy asks me in English.

"Yeah," I say reflexively. Only it's not true. Already, I'm starting to feel this melancholy set in, like the first cold fall day after a hot summer.

"What brought about the change of mind?" Kate had asked me on the phone. We hadn't been in any kind of contact since Mexico, and when I told her my plans, she sounded surprised.

"Oh, I don't know." I'd explained to her about finding *Twelfth Night* and then being told about the auditions, about being in the right place at the right time.

"So how'd it go?" the skinny guy asks me now. He has a copy of *As You Like It* in his hand, and his knee is thumping, up-down-up-down.

I shrug. I have no idea. Truly. I don't.

"I'm going for Jaques. What about you?"

I look at the play, which I haven't even read. I just figured I'd get what they gave me, as it always was with Tor. With a sinking feeling, I begin to suspect that wasn't the right way to go.

And it's then I remember what Kate said on the phone, after I explained the roundabout way I'd come to audition.

"*Commit*, Willem. You have to *commit*. To something."

Like so many of the important things these days, the memory comes too late.

Thirty-six

A week goes by, I hear nothing. The skinny guy I'd spoken to, Vincent, had said there'd be a series of callbacks before final casting. I don't get called. I put it behind me and get back to work on Daniel's flat, channeling so much energy into my tiling that Daniel and I finish the bathroom a couple of days ahead of schedule and get started on the kitchen. We take the metro out to IKEA to pick cabinets. We're in a showcase kitchen with cabinets the color of red nail varnish when my phone rings.

"Willem, this is Linus Felder from the Allerzielentheater."

My heart thuds like I'm on stage all over again.

"I need you to learn Orlando's opening speech and come in tomorrow morning at nine. Can you manage that?" he asks.

Of course I can manage it. I want to tell him that I'll more than manage it. "Sure," I say. And before I have a chance to ask any particulars, Linus hangs up.

"Who was that?" Daniel asks.

"The stage manager from that play I auditioned for. He wants me to come back in. To read for Orlando. The lead."

Daniel jumps up and down like an excited child, knocking over the prop mixer in the show kitchen. "Oh, shit." He pulls us away, whistling innocently.

I leave Daniel in IKEA and spend the rest of the day in the drizzle at the Sarphatipark, memorizing the speech. When it's a decent hour in New York, I call Kate for more advice but I wake her up because it turns out she's in California now. Ruckus is about to start a six-week tour of *Cymbeline* on the West Coast before coming to the UK in August for various festivals. When I hear this, I'm almost embarrassed to ask her for help. But, generous as always, she takes a few minutes to tell me what to expect on a callback. I might read a bunch of scenes and a bunch of parts, opposite several actors, and even though they've asked me to read Orlando, I shouldn't assume that's the role I'm up for. "But it's promising they've asked you to read him," she says. "It's quite a role for you."

"How do you mean?"

She sighs, noisily. "You *still* haven't read the play?"

I'm embarrassed all over again. "I will, I promise. Later today."

We talk a little more. She says she's planning on spending nonfestival weekends traveling out of the UK, so maybe she'll come to Amsterdam. I tell her she's welcome any time. And then she reminds me again to read the play.

Late that night, after I've read the opening monologue so many times I could recite it in my sleep, I start on the rest of the play. I'm falling asleep at this point and it's a little difficult to get into. I try to see what Kate means about Orlando. I suppose it's that he meets a girl and falls in love with her and then meets her again but she's disguised. Except Orlando gets a happy ending.

———

When I arrive at the theater the next morning, it's almost empty, and dark except for a single lamp burning on the stage. I sit down in the last seat, and a short while later, the house lights flicker on. Linus strolls in, clipboard in hand, and behind him, Petra, the diminutive director.

There are no pleasantries. "Whenever you're ready," Linus says.

This time, I am ready. I'm determined to be.

Except I'm not. I get the lines right, but as I say one, then the next, I can hear myself say them and then I wonder how they sounded, did I hit the right beat? And the more I do that, the stranger the words start to sound, in the way that a perfectly normal word can start to sound like gibberish. I try to focus, but the harder I try, the harder it becomes, and then I hear a cricket chirping somewhere backstage and it sounds like the lobby of the Bombay Royale, and then I'm thinking about Yael and Prateek and I'm everywhere in the world except in this theater.

By the time I finish, I'm furious with myself. All that practice, and it was for shit. The Sebastian monologue, which

I didn't even care that much about, was infinitely better than this.

"Can I try that again?" I ask.

"No need," Petra says. I hear her and Linus murmuring.

"Really. I know I could do better." There's a jaunty smile on my face, which may be my finest acting of the day. Because really, I don't know that I could do better. This *was* me trying.

"It was fine," Petra barks. "Come back Monday at nine. Linus will get your paperwork before you leave."

Is that it? Did I just get the part of Orlando?

Maybe I shouldn't be so surprised. After all, it *was* that easy with the acrobats and with Guerrilla Will and even with Lars Von Gelder. I should be elated. I should be relieved. But, weirdly, all I feel is let down. Because this matters to me now. And something tells me if it matters, maybe it shouldn't be easy.

Thirty-seven

JULY
Amsterdam

---

*H*ey, Willem, how are you feeling today?"

"I'm fine, Jeroen. How are you?"

"Oh, you know, the gout is acting up." Jeroen pounds his chest and heaves a cough.

"Gout is in your leg, you twat," Max says, sliding into the seat next to me.

"Oh, right." Jeroen flashes her his most charming smile as he limps away, laughing.

"What a tosser!" Max says, dropping her bag at my feet. "If I have to kiss him, I swear, I might puke on the stage."

"Pray for Marina's health then."

"Wouldn't mind kissing her though." Max grins and looks at Marina, the actress who plays Rosalind opposite Jeroen's Orlando. "Ahh, lovely Marina, self-serving though it is, wouldn't want her to fall ill. She's so lovely. And besides, if

- 241 -

she couldn't go on, I'd have to kiss that git. *He's* the one who I want to get sick."

"But he doesn't get sick," I tell Max, as though she needs reminding. Since being cast as his understudy, I have heard, endlessly, relentlessly, how in his dozen years of doing theater, Jeroen Gosslers has never, ever missed a performance, not even when he was throwing up with the flu, not even when he had lost his voice, not even when his girlfriend went into labor with their daughter hours before curtain. In fact, Jeroen's spotless record is apparently why I was given this shot in the first place, after the actor originally cast as an understudy booked a Mentos ad that would've required him missing three rehearsals to shoot the commercial. Three rehearsals, for an understudy who will never go on. Petra demands everything of her understudies, while at the same time demanding nothing of them.

As required, I've been at the theater every day since that very first table read, when the cast sat around a long wooden scuffed table on the stage, going through the text line by line, parsing meaning, deconstructing what this word meant, how that line should be interpreted. Petra was surprisingly egalitarian, open to almost anyone's opinions about what Sad Lucretia meant or why Rosalind persisted in keeping up her disguise for so long. If one of Duke Frederick's men wanted to interpret an exchange between Celia and Rosalind, Petra would entertain it. "If you are at this table, you have a right to be heard," she said, magnanimously.

Max and I, however, were conspicuously not at the table, but rather seated a few paces away, near enough to hear, but far enough that for us to participate in the discussion made us feel like interlopers. At first, I wondered if this was unintentional. But after hearing Petra repeat, several times, that "performing is so much more than speaking lines. It's about communicating with your audience through every gesture, every word unsaid," I understood it was completely intentional.

It seems almost quaint now, that I worried about it being *too* easy. Though it has turned out to be easy, only not in the way I thought. Max and I are the only understudies who don't have any actual roles in the play. We occupy a strange place in the cast. Semi-cast members. Shadow-cast members. Seat warmers. Very few people in the cast speak to us. Vincent does. He got his Jaques after all. And Marina, who plays Rosalind, does as well, because she is uniquely gracious. And of course Jeroen makes it a point to talk to me every day, though I wish he wouldn't.

"So, what we got on today?" Max asks in her London cockney. Like me, she's a mutt; her father is Dutch from Surinam and her mother is from London. The cockney gets stronger when she drinks too much, though when she reads Rosalind, her English goes silky as the British Queen's.

"They're going over the fight scene choreography," I tell her.

"Oh, good. Maybe that ponce will actually get hurt." She laughs and runs a hand through her spiky hair. "Wanna run lines later? Won't be much of a chance once we start tech."

Soon, we move the set out of the theater for the final five days of tech rehearsals and dress rehearsals at the amphitheater in Vondelpark where the show will go up for six weekends. In two Fridays, we'll have our soft opening, and then Saturday, the hard opening. For the rest of the cast, this is the payoff for all the work. For Max and me, it's when we cash out, when any semblance of us being in the cast disappears. Linus has told us to make sure we know the entire play, all the blocking, by heart, and we're to trail Jeroen and Marina through the first tech rehearsal. This is as close to the action as we get. Not once has Linus or Petra given us any direction or asked us to run lines or gone over any aspect of the play. Max and I run lines incessantly, the two of us. I think it's how we make ourselves feel like we're actually a part of the production.

"Can we do the Ganymede parts? You know I like those best," Max says.

"Only because you get to be a boy."

"Well, natch. I prefer Rosalind when she's channeling her man. She's such a simp in the beginning."

"She's not a simp. She's in love."

"At first sight." She rolls her eyes. "A simp. She's ballsier when she's pretending to have balls."

"Sometimes it's easier to be someone else," I say.

"I should think so. It's why I became a bleeding actor." And then she looks at me and snorts with laughter. We may memorize the lines. We may know the blocking. We may show up. But neither one of us is an actor. We are seat warmers.

Max sighs and kicks her feet up onto the chair, daring a wordless reprimand from Petra and a follow-up telling off from Linus, or, as Max calls him, the Flunky.

Up on stage, Jeroen is arguing with the choreographer. "That's not really working for me. It doesn't feel authentic," he says. Max rolls her eyes again but I sit up to listen. This happened about every other day during the blocking, Jeroen not "feeling" the movements and Petra changing them, but Jeroen not feeling the new blocking either, so most of the time, she changed it back. My script is a crosshatch of scribbles and erasures, a road map of Jeroen's quest for authenticity.

Marina is sitting on the cement pilings on the stage next to Nikki, the actress playing Celia. They both look bored as they watch the fight choreography. For a second Marina catches my eye and we exchange a sympathetic smile.

"I saw that," Max says.

"Saw what?"

"Marina. She wants you."

"She doesn't even know me."

"That may be the case, but she was giving you fuck-me eyes at the bar last night."

Every night after rehearsal, most of the cast goes to a bar around the corner. Because we are either provocative or masochistic, Max and I go along with them. Usually we wind up sitting at the long wooden bar on our own or at a table with Vincent. There never seems to be room at the big table for Max and me.

"She was not giving me fuck-me eyes."

"She was giving *one* of us fuck-me eyes. I haven't gotten any Sapphic vibes off her, though you never can tell with Dutch girls."

I look at Marina. She's laughing at something Nikki said, as Jeroen and the actor playing Charles the wrestler work some fake punches with the fight choreographer.

"Unless you don't like girls," Max continues, "but I'm not getting that vibe off you either."

"I like girls just fine."

"Then why do you leave the bar with me every night?"

"Are you not a girl?"

Max rolls her eyes. "I am sorry, Willem, but charming as you are, it's not going to happen with us."

I laugh and give Max a wet kiss on the cheek, which she wipes off, with excess drama. Up on stage, Jeroen attempts a false punch at Charles and stumbles over himself. Max claps. "Mind that gout," she calls.

Petra swerves around, her sharp eyes full of disapproval. Max pretends to be absorbed in her script.

"Fuck running lines," Max whispers when Petra's attention is safely returned to the stage. "Let's get drunk."

——— ——— ———

That night, over drinks at the bar, Max asks me, "So why don't you?"

"Why don't I what?"

"Get off with a girl. If not Marina, one of the civilians at the bar."

"Why don't *you*?" I ask.

"Who's to say I don't?"

"You leave with me every night, Max."

She sighs, a big deep sigh that seems a lot older than Max,

who is only a year older than me. Which is why she doesn't mind seat-warming, she says. *My time will come.* She makes a slash mark over her chest. "Broken heart," she says. "Dykes take dog-years to heal."

I nod.

"So what about you?" Max says. "Broken heart?"

At times, I'd thought it was something like that—after all, I'd never been quite so strung out about a girl. But it's a funny thing because since that day with Lulu in Paris, I've reconnected with Broodje and the boys, I've visited my mother and have been talking to her again, and now I'm living with Uncle Daniel. And I'm acting. Okay, perhaps not acting, exactly. But not accidentally acting, either. And just in general, I'm better. Better than I've been since Bram died, and in some ways, better than I was even before that. No, Lulu didn't break my heart. But I'm beginning to wonder if in some roundabout way, she fixed it.

I shake my head.

"So what are you waiting for?" Max asks me.

"I don't know," I answer.

But one thing I do know: Next time, I'll know it when I find it.

Thirty-eight

---

*B*efore Daniel leaves, we hang the last of the kitchen cabinets. The kitchen is almost finished. The plumber will come to install the dishwasher and we'll put in the backsplash and then that's that. "We're nearly there," I say.

"Just have to fix the buzzer and tackle your shit in the attic," Daniel says.

"Right. The shit in the attic. How much is there?" I ask. I don't remember putting that many boxes up there.

But Daniel and I lug down at least a dozen boxes with my name on them. "We should just throw it all away," I say. "I've gone this long without."

He shrugs. "Whatever you want."

Curiosity gets me. I open one box, papers and clothes from my dorm, not sure why I kept them. I put them in the garbage. I go through another and do the same. But then I come upon a third box. Inside are colored folders, the kind Yael used to keep patient records in, and I think the box must be mislabeled with my name. But then I see a sheet of paper sticking out of one of the folders. I pick it up.

> *The wind in my hair*
> *Wheels bounce over cobblestones*
> *As big as the sky*

A memory rushes back: "It doesn't rhyme," Bram had said when I'd showed it to him, so full of pride because the teacher had asked me to read it to the entire class.

"It's not supposed to. It's a haiku," Yael had said, rolling her eyes at him and bestowing upon me a rare conspiratorial smile.

I pull out the folder. Inside is some of my old schoolwork, my early writing, math tests. I look in another folder: not schoolwork but drawings of a ship, a Star of David that Saba taught me to do with two triangles. Pages and pages of this stuff. Unsentimental Yael and clutter-phobic Bram never displayed things like this. I assumed they threw it away.

In another box, I find a tin full of ticket stubs: airplane tickets, concert tickets, train tickets. An old Israeli passport, Yael's, full of stamps. Beneath that, I uncover a couple of very old black-and-white photos. It takes me a moment to recognize that they're of Saba. I've never seen him this young before. I hadn't realized any of these photos had survived the war. But it's unmistakably him. The eyes, they are Yael's. And mine, too. In one photo, he has his arm slung over a pretty girl, all dark hair and mystery eyes. He looks at her adoringly. She looks vaguely familiar, but it can't be Naomi, whom he didn't meet until after the war.

I look for more old photos of Saba and the girl, but find just an odd newspaper clipping of her in a plastic liner. I peer closer. She's wearing a fancy dress and is flanked by two men in tuxedoes. I hold it up to the light. The faded writing is in Hungarian, but there's a caption with names: Peter Lorre, Fritz Lang—Hollywood names I recognize—and a third name, Olga Szabo, which I don't.

I set the photos aside and keep digging. In another box, there are endless keepsakes. More papers. And then in another box, a large manila envelope. I open it up and out tumbles more photos: me, Yael, and Bram, on holiday in Croatia. I remember again how Bram and I walked to the docks every morning to buy fresh fish that no one really knew how to cook. There's another photo: us bundled up for skating the year the canals froze over and everyone took to their skates. And another: celebrating Bram's fortieth birthday with that massive party that spilled off the boat, onto the pier, onto the street, until all the neighbors came and it became a block party. There are the outtakes from the architectural magazine shoot, the shot of the three of us before I was cropped out. When I get to the bottom of the pile, there's one photo left, stuck to the envelope. I have to gently pry it away.

The breath that comes out of me isn't a sigh or a sob or a shudder. It's something alive, like a bird, wings beating, taking flight. And then it's gone, off into the quiet afternoon.

"Everything okay?" Daniel asks me.

I stare at the shot. The three of us, from my eighteenth birthday, not the photo I lost, but a different picture, taken from a different perspective, from someone else's camera. Another accidental picture.

"I thought I'd lost this," I say, gripping the picture.

Daniel cocks his head to the side and scratches at his temple. "I'm always losing things, and then I find them again in the strangest places."

Thirty-nine

A few days later, I leave for rehearsal and Daniel leaves for the airport. It's strange to think that when I come back that night, Daniel will be gone. Though I won't have the flat to myself for long. Broodje has been in The Hague for most of the summer on an internship, and now he's in Turkey visiting Candace, who's on a two-week trip there with her grandparents. When he comes back, he'll stay here with me until he and Henk move into their new flat in Utrecht in the fall.

Rehearsal today is frenzied and frenetic. The set is being broken down, transported to the park for tomorrow's tech, and the lack of scenery seems to have unhinged everyone. Petra is a whirlwind of terror, yelling at the actors, yelling at the tech guys, yelling at Linus, who looks like he would like to take cover under his clipboard.

"Poor Flunky," Max says. "For someone menopausal,

Petra seems like she's on the rag. She smashed Nikki's mobile."

"Really?" I ask Max, sliding into our usual seats.

"Well, you know how she is if you put your phone on in the 'sacred rehearsal room.' But I heard she's extra uppity because Geert said 'Mackers' in the theater earlier."

"Mackers?"

"The Scottish Play," she says. When I fail to understand she mouths *Macbeth*. "Very bad mojo to say it in a theater."

"You believe that?"

"I believe you don't mess with Petra the day before the first tech."

Jeroen walks by. He looks at me and feigns a cough.

"That the best you can do?" Max calls after him. She turns to me. "And he calls himself an actor."

Linus has the cast do an entire run-through. It's a mess. Lines are forgotten. Cues are missed. Blocking is flubbed. *"The curse of Mackers,"* Max whispers.

———

By six o'clock, Petra is in such a state that Linus lets us all go early. "Get a good night's sleep," he says. "Tomorrow is a long day. Call is at ten."

"It's too early to go to the bar," Max says. "Let's go eat and then go dancing or hear a band play. We can see who's on at Paradiso or Melkweg."

We ride over to the Leidseplein. Max is beside herself because some musician who was once in a famous band is playing solo tonight at the Paradiso and there's still tickets left. We buy a pair. Then we wander around the square, which this time of year is ground zero for tourists. There's a crowd of them surrounding some street performers.

"It's probably just those bloody Peruvian musicians," Max says. "Do you know, when I was little, I thought it was the same troupe, following me. Took me ages to work out they were clones." She laughs and knocks her head with her knuckles. "I can be right thick sometimes."

It's not the Peruvians. It's a group of jugglers. They're not bad, juggling all kinds of typically spiked flaming things. We watch for a while, and when the hat passes, I toss in a handful of coins.

We turn to leave and Max pokes me in the side. "Now's the real show," she says. I turn around and see who she's talking about: a woman has her legs wrapped around one of the jugglers' hips, her arms tangled in his hair. "Get a room," Max jokes.

I watch them a moment longer than I ought to. And then the girl drops down and turns around. She spots me and I spot her, and we do a double take.

"Wills?" she calls.

"Bex?" I call.

"*Wills*?" Max repeats.

Dragging the juggler behind her, Bex comes up to me and gives me a big theatrical hug and kiss. It's quite a change since the last time I saw her when she would barely shake my hand. She introduces me to Matthias. I introduce her to Max. "Your girlfriend?" Bex asks, sending Max into a theatrical howl of protestation.

After a bit of chit-chat, we run out of things to say, because we never really did have that much to say even when we were sleeping together. "We should go. Matthias needs lots of *rest* before so he can *perform*." Bex gives an obvious wink in case anyone wasn't clear about what kind of resting and what kind of performing she was referring to.

"Okay then." We kiss, kiss, kiss good-bye.

We're walking away when Bex calls out. "Hey, did Tor ever find you?"

I stop. "Tor was looking for me?"

"She was trying to track you down. Apparently some letter came for you at Headingley."

It's like a switch is thrown, the way my body surges. "At Headingley?"

"Tor's place in Leeds," Bex says.

I know where Headingley is. But I rarely gave anyone a mailing address at all, and I don't remember ever giving anyone Tor's home address, which was the occasional Guerrilla Will headquarters, where we'd go to rehearse or recuperate. There's no reason on earth to think she'd send me a letter there, that she'd know to send me a letter there. But still, I walk back toward Bex. "A letter? From whom?"

"Dunno. But Tor was quite keen to get it to you. She said she tried emailing you but you were unresponsive. Imagine that?"

I ignore the dig. "When?"

She scratches her brow, trying to dislodge the memory. "I can't remember. It was a bit ago. Wait, when were we in Belfast?" she asks Matthias.

He shrugs. "Around Easter, wasn't it?"

"No. I think it was earlier. Around Shrove Tuesday," Bex says. She throws up her hands. "Some time around February. I remember pancakes. Or March. Or maybe it was April. Tor said she tried emailing you and got no reply so she wanted to know if *I* knew how to reach you." She widens her eyes, to show the absurdity of such a notion.

March. April. When I was in India, traveling, and my email account got infected with that virus. I switched to a new address after that. I haven't checked the old account in months. Maybe it's right there. Maybe it's been there all along.

"Don't suppose you know who the letter was from?"

Bex looks peeved, bringing back a bunch of memories. When it didn't last between us, and Bex had been nasty the rest of the season, Skev had made fun of me: "Didn't you ever hear? Don't shit where you eat, man."

"No idea," Bex tells me in a bored tone that seems practiced, so I'm unsure whether she doesn't know or does but won't say. "If you're so interested, you can just ask Tor." She laughs then. It's not friendly. "Though good luck getting her before fall."

Part of Tor's "method" was to try to live as close to Shakespearian times as possible while she was on the road. She refused to use a computer or a phone, though she would sometimes borrow someone else's to send an email or make a call if it was important. She didn't watch TV or listen to an iPod. And though she obsessively checked the weather reports, which seemed a rather modern innovation, she checked them in the newspapers, which somehow made it fair game because newspapers were around in seventeenth-century England, so she said.

"Don't suppose you have any idea what she did with it?" My heart has sped up, as if I've been running, and I feel breathless, but I force myself to sound as bored as Bex, for fear that if I make the letter sound important, she won't tell me anything.

"She might've sent it to the boat."

"The boat?"

"The one you used to live on."

"How'd she even know about the boat?"

"Good Christ, Wills, how should I know? Presumably you told someone about it. You did live with everyone for a year, more or less."

I told one person about the boat. Skev. He was going to Amsterdam and asked if I could hook him up with any free places to stay. I mentioned a few squats and also said if the key was still in its hiding place, and no one else was there, he could camp on the boat.

"Yeah, but I haven't lived on that boat for years."

"Well, it's obviously not that important," Bex says. "Otherwise whoever wrote it would have known where to find you."

Bex is wrong but she's also right. Because Lulu should've known where to find me. And then I stop myself. Lulu. After all this time? The letter's more likely from a tax collector.

"What was all that about?" Max asks after Bex and Matthias have gone.

I shake my head. "I'm not sure." I look across the square. "Do you mind? I need to duck into an Internet café for a second."

"Okay," she says. "I'll grab a coffee."

I log onto my old email account. There's not much there but junk. I go back to the spring, when it got infected with that virus, and there's a pocket of nothing. Four weeks of messages that have just vanished. I try the bulk bin. Nothing there. Out of habit before I sign off, I scroll back for the emails from Bram and Saba, relieved to find them still there. Tomorrow, I'm going to print them out and also forward them to my new account. In the meantime, I change the settings on my old account to forward all new mail to my current address.

I check my current email account, even though Tor wouldn't have known about it because I only told a handful of people the new address. I search the inbox, the junk mail. There's nothing.

I send Skev a quick note, asking him to ring me. Then I send a note to Tor as well, asking about the letter, what it said, where she sent it. Knowing Tor, I won't get a response until the fall. By that point, it'll have been more than a year since I met Lulu. Any sane person would say it's too late. It already felt too late that first day, when I woke up in the hospital. But even so, I've kept looking.

I'm still looking.

Forty

The tech rehearsal is a monster. Aside from lines, plenty of which get forgotten in the new environment, everything has to be relearned and reblocked on the amphitheater stage. All day long, I stand behind Jeroen, Max behind Marina, as they fumble through their various scenes. Once again we're like their shadows. Except none of us has a shadow because there's no sun today, just a steady drizzle that has put everyone in a sour mood. Jeroen hasn't even made a joke about his malady of the day.

"It makes you wonder whose brilliant idea this was," Max says. "Outdoor bloody Shakespeare. In Holland, where English isn't even the language and it rains all the time."

"You forget, the Dutch are the eternal optimists," I tell her.

"Is that true?" she asks me. "I thought they were the eternal pragmatists."

I don't know. Maybe *I'm* the optimist. I checked my email when I got back from the Paradiso last night and again before I left this morning for rehearsal. There was an email from Yael, and a forwarded joke from Henk, and a bunch of the usual junk, but nothing from Skev or Tor. What exactly did I expect?

I'm not even sure what there is to be optimistic about. If the letter is from her, what's to say it's not a long-distance piss off? She'd have every right.

We break for lunch and I check my phone. Broodje's texted to say he's heading off on some wooden sailing boat and he'll be incommunicado for a few days, but he'll be back in Amsterdam next week. Daniel's also texted to let me know he's arrived safely in Brazil, and forwarded a photo of Fabiola's belly. Tomorrow, I vow, I'm getting a phone that accepts pictures.

Petra forbids mobile phones in rehearsal. But when she's talking to Jeroen, I put my ringer to vibrate and slip my phone into my pocket anyway. Optimist indeed.

Around five o'clock, the drizzle lets up and Linus resumes the rehearsal. We're having trouble with the light cues, which we can't see. Because the show starts at dusk and goes into the night, the lights come up halfway through, so tomorrow's rehearsal will be from two in the afternoon to midnight, so we can make sure the second half, the in-darkness part, is properly lit.

At six, my phone vibrates. I pull it out of my pocket. Max widens her eyes at me. "Cover me," I whisper, and scuttle off to the wings.

It's Skev.

"Hey, thanks for getting back to me," I whisper.

"Where are you?" he asks, his voice dropped to a whisper, too.

"Amsterdam? You?"

"Back in Brighton. Why are we whispering?"

"I'm in a rehearsal."

"For what?"

"Shakespeare."

"In Amsterdam. Fuck, that's cool. I gave that shit up. I'm working at a Starbucks now."

"Oh, shit, sorry."

"Nah, it's all good, man."

"Listen, Skev, I can't talk long but I ran into Bex."

"Bex." He whistles. "How is that sweet thing?"

"Same as always, hooked up with a juggler. She mentioned a letter Tor was trying to get to me. Earlier in the year."

There's a pause. "Victoria. Man. She is something else."

"I know."

"I asked if I could come back and she said no. Just that one time. Off season. Don't shit where you eat."

"I know. I know. About that letter . . ."

"Yeah, man, I don't know anything about it."

"Oh."

"Victoria wouldn't tell me. Said it was personal. You know how she gets." He sighs. "So I just told her to send it to you. I gave her the address on the boat. I didn't know if you could get mail on the boat."

"You could. We could. We did."

"So you got the letter?"

"No, Skev. That's why I'm calling."

"Well, it must be at the boat, man."

"But we don't live there anymore. Haven't done for a while."

"Oh, shit. Forgot it was empty. Sorry about that."

"No worries, man."

"Break a leg with your Shakespeare and shit."

"Yeah, you too—with your cappuccinos and all."

He laughs. Then we say good-bye.

I go back to the rehearsal. Max is looking crazed. "I told them you had to puke. The Flunky is mad you didn't ask first. I wonder if he calls Petra for permission before he makes love to his wife."

It's an image I do my best not to conjure. "I owe you. I'll tell Linus it was a false alarm."

"You gonna tell me what this is about?"

I think of Lulu, all the wild-goose chases this year that have led nowhere. Why would this be anything else?

"Probably just what I said: a false alarm," I tell Max.

———

Except that *probably* becomes a pebble in my shoe, aggravating me for the rest of the day, making it hard to keep from thinking about the letter, where it is, what it says, who it's from. By the time rehearsal ends, I feel this sort of urgency to know; so even though the rain has returned, and even though I'm bone tired, I decide to try Marjolein. She doesn't answer her phone and I don't want to wait until tomorrow. She lives close by, on the ground floor of a wide house in a posh neighborhood at the south end of the park. She's always told me to drop by any time.

"Willem," she says, opening the door. She has a glass of wine in one hand, a cigarette in the other, and she doesn't seem so happy that I've dropped by. I'm dripping wet, and she doesn't invite me in. "What brings you here?"

"Sorry to bother you but I'm trying to find a letter."

"A letter?"

"That was sent to the boat, some time in the spring."

"Why are you still getting mail at the boat?"

"I'm not. Someone just sent it there."

She shakes her head. "If it went to the boat, it would've been forwarded to the office and then on to the address you provided us."

"In Utrecht?"

She sighs. "Probably. Can you call me in the morning?"

"It's important."

She sighs. "Try Sara. She handles the mail."

"Do you have Sara's number?"

"I'd have thought *you'd* have Sara's number," she says.

"Not for a long time now."

She sighs. Then reaches for her mobile. "Don't start anything up with her."

"I won't," I promise.

"Right. You're a changed man." I can't quite get whether she's being sarcastic or not.

Inside, the music changes, from mellow jazz to something

wilder with screaming trumpets. Marjolein looks longingly inside. I realize that she's not alone.

"I'll let you go," I say.

She leans forward to kiss good-bye. "Your mother will be pleased I saw you."

She starts to close the door. "Can I ask you something? About Yael?"

"Sure," she says absently, her attention already back in the warm house and on whoever's waiting in there.

"Did she, I don't know, do things, to help me, that I didn't know about?"

Her face is half hidden in shadows, but her toothy smile shines in the reflected light. "What did she say?"

"She didn't *say* anything."

Marjolein shakes her head. "Then neither can I." She starts to close the door. Then she stops. "But did you consider in all those months you were gone, why your bank account never ever went to zero?"

I hadn't considered it, not really. I rarely used my bank card but when I did, it usually worked.

"Someone was always watching," Marjolein says. When she shuts the door, she's still smiling.

Forty-one

Utrecht

---

*E*verything takes too long. The train is late. The bike share line is too long. So I catch a bus instead and it stops to pick up every old lady in town. I shouldn't have left so late, but it was already late when I got hold of Sara this morning. Then it took a bit of cajoling before she finally remembered there was a letter. No, she didn't read it. No, she didn't remember where it came from. But she thinks she forwarded to the address on file. The one in Utrecht. Not that long ago.

By the time I get to Bloemstraat, it's almost noon. The second tech rehearsal is at 2:00 back in Amsterdam. I have nothing but time in my life, but never enough of it when I need it.

I ring the eyeball bell. There's no answer. I have no idea who lives here anymore. I texted Broodje on the train over but he didn't answer. Then I remembered that he's in the middle of the Aegean somewhere. With Candace. Whose name he knows, whose telephone number and email address he got before he left Mexico.

The front door is locked but I still have my key and it still works. The first good sign.

"Hello," I call, my voice echoing through the empty house. It no longer looks like the place I lived in. No more lumpy sofa. No more boy smell. Even the Picasso flowers are gone.

There's a dining room table, with the post scattered all over it. I rifle through the stacks as quickly as possible, but I see nothing, so I make myself slow down and methodically go through each piece of mail, dividing it into neat piles: for Broodje, for Henk, for W, even some for Ivo, who's still getting letters here, for a couple of unfamiliar girls who must be living here now. There is some mail for me, mostly dead letters from the university and a travel catalog from the agency I used to book our Mexico tickets.

I look up the stairs. Perhaps the letter is up there. Or in the attic in my old room. Or in one of the cabinets. Or maybe it isn't the one Sara forwarded. Maybe it's still back on the Nieuwe Prinsengracht. Or somewhere in Marjolein's office.

Or maybe there is no letter from her. Maybe it's just another false hope I've conjured for myself.

I hear ticking. On the mantel, where the Picasso used to hang, there's an old-fashioned wooden clock, like the kind Saba once had in his Jerusalem apartment. It was one of the few pieces Yael kept after he died. I wonder where it is now.

It's half past twelve. If I want to get the train back in time for the tech rehearsal, I have to leave now. Otherwise, I'll be late. And being late for tech? The only thing worse in Petra's book would be not showing for a performance. I think of the original understudy, replaced because he had to miss three rehearsals. It's too late for her to replace me, but that's not to say she can't fire me. I'm nothing but a shadow, anyhow.

Being fired won't make any material difference in my life right now. Except I don't *want* to be fired. And more than that, I don't want to hand over that decision to Petra. If I'm late, that's exactly what will happen.

The house seems huge all of a sudden, like it would take years to search all the rooms. The moment seems even bigger.

I've given up on Lulu before. In Utrecht. In Mexico. But that felt like surrendering. Like it was *me* I was really giving up on. This feels different, somehow. Like maybe Lulu brought me to this place, and for the first time in a long time, I'm on the cusp of something real. Maybe *this* is the point of it all. Maybe this is where the road is meant to end.

I think of the postcards I left in her suitcase. I'd written *sorry* on one of them. Only now do I understand what I really should've written was *thank you.*

"Thank you," I say quietly to the empty house. I know she'll never hear it, but somehow that seems beside the point.

Then I drop my mail in the recycling and head back to Amsterdam, closing the door behind me.

PART TWO

One Day

Forty-two

AUGUST
Amsterdam

$\mathcal{T}$he phone is ringing. And I'm sleeping. Two things that shouldn't be happening at the same time. I open my eyes, fumble for the phone, but the ringing continues, crying out into the still night.

A light flicks on. Broodje, naked as a newborn, stands in front of me squinting in the yellow light of the lamp, and the lemony walls of the nursery. He holds out my phone. "It's for you," he mumbles, and then he flicks off the light and sleep-walks back to bed.

I put the phone to my ear and I hear the exact four words you don't want to hear on the other end of a middle-of-the-night phone call.

"There's been an accident."

My stomach plummets and I hear a whistling in my ears as I wait to hear who. Yael. Daniel. Fabiola. The baby. Some subtraction in my family that I can no longer bear.

But the voice continues talking and it takes me a minute to slow my breathing and hear what is being said. *Bicycle* and *moto* and *ankle* and *fracture* and *performance* and *emergency* and it's then that I understand that it's not that kind of accident.

"Jeroen?" I say at last, though who else can it be? I want to laugh. Not because of the irony, but because of the relief.

"Yes, Jeroen," Linus snaps. Jeroen the invincible, felled by a drunken moto driver. Jeroen insistent he can go on anyhow, with his foot in a cast, and maybe he can, for next weekend's performances. But this weekend's? "We might have to cancel," Linus says. "We need you at the theater as soon as possible. Petra wants to see what you can do."

I rub my eyes. Light is peeking through the shades. It's not the middle of the night after all. Linus tells me to be at the theater—the actual theater, not the stage in Vondelpark—at eight.

"It's going to be a long day," he warns.

———

Petra and Linus hardly look up when I arrive at the theater. A sloe-eyed Marina offers a tired, sympathetic look. She's holding a roll and breaks off half and hands it to me. "Thank you," I say. "I didn't have time to eat."

"I figured as much," she says.

I sit down on the edge of the stage, alongside her. "So what happened?"

She arches her eyebrow. "Karma happened." She tucks

a piece of hair behind her ear. "I know it's his joke to brag about his perfect record, and I've heard him do it many times before and nothing's come of it." She pauses to dust the crumbs off her lap. "But you don't laugh at fate like that without fate eventually having the last laugh. The only problem is, it doesn't just affect him. It might shut down the remaining run."

"Shut it down? I thought it was just tonight's."

"Jeroen won't be able to perform either of this weekend's performances, and even if he can actually manage it in the boot cast he's apparently going to have to wear for the next six weeks, they'll have to reblock the whole thing. Plus, there are questions of insurance." She sighs. "It might be easier to just cancel."

My shoulders slump with the weight of that statement. So it falls to me. "I think I'm starting to believe in the Mackers curse," I tell Marina.

She looks at me, the worry in her eyes mixed with sympathy. She seems about to say something when Petra orders me to the stage.

Linus looks miserable. But Petra, she of the thousand tantrums, is actually calm, cigarette smoke swirling around her like a statue on fire. It takes me a minute to realize she's not calm. She's resigned. She's already written tonight off.

I climb onto the stage. I take a breath. "What can I do?" I ask her.

"We have the cast on standby for a full run-through later," Linus answers. "Right now, we'd like to run your scenes with Marina. See how those go."

Petra stubs out her cigarette. "We'll skip ahead to Act

One, Scene Two with Rosalind. I will read Celia. Linus will read Le Beau and the Duke. Let's start just before the fight with Le Beau's line."

"'Monsieur the challenger, the princesses call for you?'" Linus asks. Petra nods.

"I attend them with all respect and duty," I say, jumping right in with Orlando's next line.

There's a moment of surprise as they all look at me

"Young man, have you challenged Charles the wrestler?" Marina asks as Rosalind.

"No, fair princess; he is the general challenger: I come but in, as others do, to try with him the strength of my youth," I reply, not boastfully, as Jeroen does, but tempering the bravado with a little uncertainty, which I somehow now know is what Orlando must feel.

I've said these words hundreds of times in readings with Max, but they were just lines in a script, and I never stopped to figure out what it all meant because I never really had to. But just as Sebastian's monologue came alive during my audition months ago, the words seem charged with meaning all of a sudden. They become a language I know.

We go back and forth and then I get to Orlando's line: "I shall do my friends no wrong, for I have none to lament me, the world no injury, for in it I have nothing." As I say the words, I feel a tiny catch of emotion in the back of my throat. Because I know what he means. For a minute, I think to swallow the emotion down, but I don't. I breathe into it, letting it carry me through the scene.

I'm feeling loose and good as we move onto the fight scene, in which I pantomime fighting an invisible opponent.

I know this part well. Orlando wins the fight, but he loses anyway. He is cast out of the Duke's kingdom and warned that his brother wants to kill him.

We reach the end of the scene. Petra, Linus, even Marina, they all stare at me, not saying a thing.

"Shall we continue?" I ask. "On to Act Two?" They nod. I run that scene with Linus reading the part of Adam, and when I finish that, Petra clears her throat and asks me to take it from the beginning, Orlando's opening monologue, the one I flubbed so badly during my callback.

I don't flub it this time. When I finish, there is more silence. "So you're off book, that is clear," Linus says finally. "And the blocking?"

"Yes, that too," I say.

They look so incredulous. What do they think I've been doing all this time?

Warming a seat, comes my own answer. And maybe I shouldn't be so surprised by their surprise. Because isn't that exactly what I'd thought I'd been doing, too?

Petra and Linus excuse Marina and me. They have some things to discuss. If they decide to proceed with tonight's performance, there will be an all-cast rehearsal at the theater at noon, and I'll have to do an additional tech run-through at the amphitheater later in the day with just Linus.

"Sit tight. Keep your phone on," Linus says and he pats my back and gives me a look that's almost fatherly. "We'll speak soon."

Marina and I head to a nearby café for coffee. It's raining, and inside the windows are fogged up. We sit down at a table. I rub a circle of condensation off the window. Across the canal is the bookstore where I first found the copy of *Twelfth Night*. It's just opening up for the day. I tell Marina about the flat tire and stopping at the shop, the strange chain of events that led to me being Jeroen's understudy, and now possibly, playing Orlando.

"None of that has anything to do with that performance you just gave." She shakes her head and smiles, a private smile, and it's this, more than anything else, that makes me stop feeling like a member of the shadow cast. "You were holding out on us."

I don't know how to answer. Maybe I've been holding out on myself, too.

"You should tell him," she says, gesturing to the bookstore. "The guy who sold you the book and told you about the play. If you go on, you should tell him it's partly because of him."

If I go on, there are lots of people I'll have to tell.

"Wouldn't you want to know?" Marina continues. "That in some little way, something random you did had such an impact on someone's life? What do they call that? The Butterfly Effect?"

I watch the man open the bookstore. I should tell him. Though the person I really want to tell, the person who is somehow intricately tied up in all this, who has really led me to this, I can't tell.

"While we're confessing," Marina says, "I should tell you that I've been a little intrigued by you from the start, this mysterious actor who keeps to himself, whom no one has ever heard of, but who is good enough to get cast as the understudy."

Good enough? That surprises me. I'd thought it was the opposite.

"I have a strict policy of no showmances," she continues. "Nikki keeps saying you can be an exception because you're an understudy and not in the show, but now that you maybe are, I'm even more intrigued." She gives me that private smile again. "Either we close tonight or we close in three weeks, but either way, after it's over, maybe we can spend some time together?"

That surge of longing for Lulu is still in my bloodstream, like a drug wearing out its half life. Marina is not Lulu. But Lulu is not even Lulu. And Marina is amazing. Who knows what might happen?

I'm about to tell her yes, after we close, I'd like that, but I'm interrupted by the ringing of my phone. She glances at the number and smiles at me. "That's your fate calling."

Forty-three

So much to do. There's an all-cast rehearsal at noon. Then a tech run-through. I need to run back to the flat, grab some things, tell the boys. And Daniel. Yael.

Broodje is only waking up. Breathlessly, I tell him the news. By the time I've finished, he's already on his phone, calling the boys.

"Did you tell your ma?" he asks when he hangs up.

"I'm calling her now."

I calculate the time difference. It's not quite five o'clock in Mumbai, so Yael will still be working. I send her an email instead. While I'm at it, I send one to Daniel. At the last minute, I send one to Kate, telling her about Jeroen's accident, inviting her to tonight's show if she's at all in the area. I even invite her to stay with me and give her the address of the flat.

I'm about to log off when I do a quick scan of my inbox. There's a new message from an unfamiliar address and I think it's junk. Until I see the subject line: Letter.

My hand's shaking a bit as I click on the message. It's from Tor. Or relayed from Tor via some Guerrilla Will player who doesn't abide by the email ban as she does.

> *Hi Willem:*
>
> *Tor asked me to email you to say that she ran into Bex last week and Bex told her that you hadn't gotten that letter. Tor was pretty upset because the letter was important and she'd gone to a lot of trouble to try to get it to you. She wanted you to know it was from a girl you'd met in Paris who was looking for you because you'd dicked her over and pulled a runner. (Tor's words, not mine.) She said that you ought to know that actions have consequences. Again, Tor's words. Don't shoot the messenger. ☺ You know how she is.*
>
> *Cheers! Josie*

I sink down onto my bed as very different emotions battle it out. *Dicked her over, pulled a runner.* I feel Tor's anger. And Lulu's too. Shame and regret well up but then just stop there, held at bay by some invisible force. Because she's looking for me. Lulu is looking for me, too. Or she was. Maybe just to tell me to piss off. But she was looking for me like I was looking for her.

I don't know what to feel as I wander into the kitchen. It's all just too much for one day.

I find Broodje cracking eggs into a frying pan. "Want an *uitsmijter*?" he asks.

I shake my head.

"You should eat something. Keep your strength up."

"I have to go."

"Now? Henk and W are on their way over. They want to see you. Will you be around at all before your big debut?"

The rehearsal starts at noon and will take at least three hours, and then Linus said I'd have a break before I go for a run-through at the amphitheater at six. "I can probably get back here around four or five?"

"Great. We should have the party plans well under way by then."

"Party plans?"

"Willy, this is big." He pauses to look at me. "After the year you've had—the *years* you've had—we should celebrate this."

"Okay, fine," I say, still half dazed.

I go back into my room to pack up a change of clothes for under the costume, shoes to wear. I'm about to leave when I see Lulu's watch sitting on my shelf. I hold it in my hand. After all this time, it's still ticking. I hold it in my hand a moment longer. Then I slip it into my pocket.

Forty-four

At the theater, the rest of the cast has assembled. Max comes up behind me. *"I've got your back,"* she whispers.

I'm about to ask her what she means, and then I see what she means. For the better part of three months, I have been mostly invisible to many of these people, a shadow-cast member. And now, the spotlight is glaring and there's no safety in the shadows anymore. People are looking at me with a particular mix of suspicion and condescension, a familiar feeling from when I was traveling and walked through certain neighborhoods where my kind didn't tend to wander. As I did when I was traveling, I just act like I don't notice and carry on. Soon enough Petra is clapping her hands, gathering us together.

"We have no time to lose," Linus says. "We will do a modified run-through, skipping over scenes that Orlando is not in."

"So why did you call *all* of us in?" mutters Geert, who plays the swing roles of one of Frederick's men and Silvius; he has almost no scenes with Orlando.

"I know. Sitting around watching other people act is such a bloody waste of time," Max says, her voice so sincere that it takes Geert a few seconds to have the good sense to look chastened.

Max gives me a crooked smile. I'm glad she's here.

"I called everyone in," Petra says, with an exaggerated patience that lets you know she's reaching the end of her supply, "so you could all accustom yourself to the different rhythms of a new actor, and so we could all of us help Willem ensure that the transition between him and Jeroen is as seamless as possible. Ideally, you won't even be able to tell the difference."

Max rolls her eyes at this and once again I'm glad she's here.

"Now from the top, please," Linus says, tapping his clipboard. "There's no set and no marks so just do your best."

As soon as I step onto the stage, I feel relieved. This is where I'm meant to be. In Orlando's head. As we move through the play, I discover more things about Orlando. I discover how key that first scene when he and Rosalind meet is. It's just for a few moments, but they see something in each other, recognize something. And that the spark sustains the passion, for both of them, for the rest of the play. They don't see each other—knowingly see each other—again until the very end.

Such a dance that Shakespeare wrote into a handful of

pages of text. Orlando's about to fight a man far stronger than he is, but he peacocks in front of Rosalind and Celia to impress them. He's scared, he must be, but instead of showing it, he bluffs. He flirts. "Let your fair eyes and gentle wishes go with me to my trial," he says.

The world pivots on moments. And in this play, it's the moment when Rosalind says, "The little strength that I have, I would it were with you."

That one line. It cracks open his facade. It reveals what's underneath. Rosalind sees Orlando. He sees her. That's the whole play, right there.

I feel the lines like I haven't before, like I'm truly understanding Shakespeare's intentions. I feel as if there really was a Rosalind and an Orlando and I'm here to represent them. It isn't acting in a play. It goes back further than that. It's much bigger than me.

"Ten-minute break," Linus calls at the end of Act One. Everyone heads out for a smoke or a coffee. But I am reluctant to leave the stage.

"Willem," Petra calls to me. "A word."

She's smiling, which she rarely does, and at first I read it for pleasure, because isn't that what a smile communicates?

The theater empties out. It's just the two of us now. Not even Linus. "I want to tell you how impressed I am," she begins.

Inside I'm a little boy grinning on a birthday morning, about to get the presents. But I try to keep my face professional.

"With so little experience, to know the language so well.

We were taken with your ease with the language at your audition, but this . . ." She smiles again, only now I notice that it looks a bit like a dog baring its fangs. "And the blocking, you have it cold. Linus tells me that you even learned some of the fight choreography."

"I observed," I tell her. "I paid attention."

"Excellent. That's just what you needed to do." And there's that smile again. Only now do I begin to doubt it reflects any pleasure. "I spoke to Jeroen today," she continues.

I don't say anything but my gut twists. All this, and now Jeroen is going to lumber back with his cast.

"He's terribly embarrassed by what happened, but most of all he's disappointed to have let down his company."

"There's no one to blame. He was in an accident," I say.

"Yes. Of course. An accident. And he very much wants to be back for the last two weeks of the season and we will do our best to adapt to meet his needs, because that is what you do when you are part of a cast. Do you understand?"

I nod, even though I don't really understand what she's on about.

"I understand what you were trying to do up there with your Orlando."

Your Orlando. Something about the way she says that makes me feel like it won't be mine for much longer.

"But the role of the understudy is not to bring his own interpretation to the part," she continues. "It is to play the part as the actor you're replacing played it. So in effect, you aren't playing Orlando. You are playing Jeroen Gosslers playing Orlando."

But Jeroen's Orlando *is all wrong*, I want to say. It's all machismo and prancing and no revealing; and without vulnerability, Rosalind wouldn't love him, and if Rosalind doesn't love him, why should the audience care? I want to say: *Let me do this. Let me do it right this time.*

But I don't say any of that. And Petra just stares at me. Then, finally she asks: "Do you think you can manage that?"

Petra smiles again. How foolish of me—of all people— not to recognize her smile for what it was. "We can still cancel for this weekend," she says, her voice soft, the threat clear. "Our star has had an accident. No one would fault us."

Something given, something taken away. Does it always have to work like that?

The cast starts to drift back into the theater, the ten-minute break over, ready to get back to work, to make this happen. When they see me and Petra talking, they go quiet.

"Are we understood?" she asks, her voice so friendly it's almost singsong.

I look at the cast again. I look at Petra. I nod. We're understood.

Forty-five

*W*hen Linus releases us for the afternoon, I bolt for the door. "Willem," Max calls.

"Willem," Marina calls behind her.

I wave them off. I have to be fitted for my costume and then I have only a couple hours until Linus will meet me to go through my marks on the amphitheater stage. As for what Marina and Max have to say: if it's compliments of my performance, so Jeroen-like even Petra was impressed, I don't want to hear it. If it's questions about why I'm playing it like this, when I played it so differently before, then I really don't want to hear it.

"I have to go," I tell them. "I'll see you tonight."

They look wounded, each in their own way. But I just walk away from them.

Back at the flat, I find W, Henk, and Broodje busy at work, pages of yellow pad on the coffee table. "That's Femke in," Broodje is saying. "Hey, it's the star."

Henk and W start to congratulate me. I just shake my head. "What's all this?" I gesture to the project on the table.

"Your party," W says.

"My party?"

"The one we're throwing tonight," Broodje says.

I sigh. I forgot all about that. "I don't want a party."

"What do you mean you don't want a party?" Broodje asks. "You said it was okay."

"Now it's not. Cancel it."

"Why? Aren't you going on?"

"I'm going on." I go into my room. "No party," I call.

"Willy," Broodje yells after me.

I slam the door, lie down on the bed. I close my eyes and try to sleep, but that's not happening. I sit up and flip through one of Broodje's copies of *Voetbal International* but that's not happening either. I toss it back on my bookshelf. It lands next to a large manila envelope. The package of photos I unearthed from the attic last month.

I open the envelope, thumb through the pictures. I linger on the one of me and Yael and Bram from my eighteenth birthday. It's like an ache, how much I miss them. How much I miss her. I'm so tired of missing things I don't have.

I pick up the phone, not even calculating the time difference.

She answers straight away. And just like that time before, I'm at a loss for words. But not Yael. Not this time.

"What's wrong? Tell me."

"Did you get my email?"

"I haven't checked it. Is something wrong?"

She sounds panicked. I should know better. Out-of-the-blue phone calls. They require reassurance. "It's nothing like that."

"Nothing like what?"

"Like before. I mean, nobody is sick, though someone did break an ankle." I tell her about Jeroen, about my taking on his part.

"But shouldn't this make you happy?" she asks.

I thought it would make me happy. It did make me so happy this morning. Hearing about Lulu's letter made me happy this morning. But now that's worn off and all I feel is her recrimination. How far the pendulum can swing in one day. You'd think I'd know that by now. "It appears not."

She sighs. "But Daniel said you seemed so energized."

"You spoke to Daniel? About me?"

"Several times. I asked his advice."

"You asked *Daniel* for advice?" Somehow this is even more shocking than her asking him about me.

"I wondered if he thought I should ask you to come back here." She pauses. "To live with me."

"You want me to come back to India?"

"If you want to. You might act here. It seemed to go well for you. And we could find a bigger flat. Something big enough for both of us. But Daniel thought I should hold off. He thought you seemed to have found something."

"I haven't found anything. And you might've asked *me*." It comes out so bitter.

She must hear it, too. But her voice stays soft. "I *am* asking you, Willem."

And I realize she is. After all this time. Tears well up in

my eyes. I'm grateful, in that small moment, for the thousands of kilometers that separate us.

"How soon could I come?" I ask.

There's a pause. Then she gives the answer I need: "As soon as you want."

The play. I'll have to do it this weekend, and then Jeroen will come back or I can quit. "Monday?"

"Monday?" She sounds only a little bit surprised. "I'll have to ask Mukesh what he can do."

Monday. It's in three days. But what is there to stay for? The flat is finished. Soon enough Daniel and Fabiola will be back with the baby, and there won't be room for me.

"It's not too soon?" I ask.

"It's not too soon," she says. "I'm just grateful it's not too late."

There's a hitch in my throat and I can't speak. But I don't need to. Because Yael starts speaking. In torrents, apologizing for keeping me at arm's length, telling me what Bram always said, that it wasn't me, it was her, Saba, her childhood. All the things I already knew but just didn't really understand until now.

"Ma, it's okay." I stop her.

"It's not, though," she says.

But it is. Because I understand all the ways of trying to escape, how sometimes you escape one prison only to find you've built yourself a different one.

It's a funny thing, because I think that my mother and I may finally be speaking the same language. But somehow, now words don't seem as necessary.

Forty-six

I hang up the phone with Yael, feeling as though someone has opened a window and let the air in. This is how it is with traveling. One day, it all seems hopeless, lost. And then you take a train or get a phone call, and there's a whole new map of options opening up. Petra, the play, it had seemed like something, but maybe it was just the latest place the wind blew me. And now it's blowing back to India. Back to my mother. Where I belong.

I'm still holding the envelope of photos. Once again, I forgot to ask Yael about them. I look at the one of Saba and mystery girl and realize now why she looked familiar to me the first time I saw her. With her dark hair and playful smile and bobbed hair, she looks quite a bit like Louise Brooks, this . . . I grab the newspaper clipping . . . this Olga Szabo. Who was she? Saba's girlfriend? Was she Saba's one that got away?

I'm not quite sure what to do with them now. The safest thing would be to put them back in the attic, but that feels a little like imprisoning them. I could make copies of them and take the originals with me, but they still might get lost.

I stare at the picture of Saba. I flip to one of Yael. I think of the impossible life those two had together because Saba loved her so much and tried so hard to keep her safe. I'm not sure it's possible to simultaneously love something and keep it safe. Loving someone is such an inherently dangerous act. And yet, love, that's where safety lives.

I wonder if Saba understood this. After all, he's the one who always said: *The truth and its opposite are flip sides of the same coin.*

Forty-seven

It's half past four. I'm not due to meet Linus until six for a quick tech run through before the curtain. Out in the lounge, I hear Broodje and the boys. I don't want to face them. I can't imagine telling them I'm going back to India in three days.

I leave my phone on the bed and slip out the door, saying good-bye to the boys. Broodje gives me such a mournful look. "Do you even want us to go tonight?" he asks.

I don't. Not really. But I can't be that cruel. Not to him. "Sure," I lie.

Downstairs, I bump into my neighbor Mrs. Van der Meer, who's on her way out to walk her dog. "Looks like we're getting some sun finally," she tells me.

"Great," I say, though this is one time I'd prefer rain. People will stay away in the rain.

But, sure enough, the sun is fighting its way through the

stubborn cloud cover. I make my way over to the little park across the street. I'm almost through the gates when I hear someone calling my name. I keep going. There are a thousand Willems. But the name gets louder. And then it yells in English. "Willem, is that you?"

I stop. I turn around. It can't be.

But it is. Kate.

"Jesus Christ, thank God!" she says, running up to me. "I've been calling you and there's no answer and then I came over but your stupid bell doesn't work. Why didn't you pick up?"

It feels like I sent her that email a year ago. From a different world. I'm embarrassed by it now, to have asked her to come all this way. "I left it in the flat."

"Good thing I saw your dog-walking neighbor and she said she thought you went this way. It's like one of your little accidents." She laughs. "It's a day of them. Because your email came at the most serendipitous moment. David was intent on dragging me to the most hideous-sounding avant-garde *Medea* in Berlin tonight and I was desperately trying to find an excuse not to go, and then this morning I got your email so I came here instead. And I was on the plane when I realized I had no idea where you were performing. And you didn't answer your phone and I got a little panicky, so I thought I'd track you down. But now here we are and everything's good." She exaggeratedly wipes a hand across her brow. "Phew!"

"Phew," I say weakly.

Kate's radar goes up. "Or maybe not phew."

"Perhaps not."

"What is it?"

"Can I ask you to do something?" I've asked Kate so much already. But having her there? Broodje and the boys, they may not know any better. But Kate will. She can see through all the bullshit.

"Of course."

"Will you not go tonight?"

She laughs. As if this is a joke. And then she realizes it's not a joke "Oh," she says, turning serious. "Are they not putting you on? Did the other Orlando's ankle mysteriously heal?"

I shake my head. I look down and see that Kate is holding her suitcase. She literally did come straight from the airport. To see me.

"Where are you staying?" I ask Kate.

"The only place I could find at the last minute." She pulls out a slip of paper from her bag. "Major Rug Hotel?" she says. "I have no idea how to pronounce it, let alone where it is." She hands me the paper. "Do you know it?"

Hotel Magere Brug. I know exactly where it is. I rode past it almost every day of my life. On weekends they used to serve homemade pastries in the lobby, and Broodje and I would sneak in sometimes to take some. The manager pretended not to notice.

I take her suitcase. "Come on. I'll take you home."

———

The last time I was at the boat, it was September; I got as far as the pier before I rode away. It looked so empty, so haunted, like it was mourning his loss, too, which made a certain sense because he built it. Even the clematis that Saba had planted—"because even a cloud-soaked country needs shade"—which had once run riot over the deck, had gone shriveled and brown. If Saba had been here, he would've cut it back. It's what he always did when he came back in the summer and found the plants ailing in his absence.

The clematis is back now, bushy and wild, dropping purple petals all over the deck. The deck is full of other blooms, trellises, vines, arbors, pots, viny flowering things.

"This was my home," I tell Kate. "It's where I grew up."

Kate was mostly quiet on the tram ride over. "It's beautiful," she says.

"My father built it." I can see Bram's winked smile, hear him announce as if to no one: *I need a helper this morning.* Yael would hide under the duvet. Ten minutes later, I'd have a drill in my hand. "I helped, though. I haven't been here in a long time. Your hotel is just around the corner."

"What a coincidence," she says.

"Sometimes I think everything is."

"No. Everything isn't." She looks at me. Then she asks, "So what's wrong, Willem? Stage fright?"

"No."

"Then what is it?"

I tell her. About getting the call this morning. About that moment in the first rehearsal, finding something new, finding something real in Orlando, and then having it all go to hell.

"Now I just want to get up there, get through it, get it over with," I tell her. "With as few witnesses as possible."

I expect sympathy. Or Kate's undecipherable yet somehow

resonant acting advice. Instead, I get laughter. Snorts and hiccups of it. Then she says, "You have got to be kidding me."

I am not kidding. I don't say anything.

She attempts to contain herself. "I'm sorry, but the opportunity of a lifetime drops into your lap—you finally get one of your glorious accidents—and you're going to let a lousy piece of direction derail you."

She is making it seem so slight, a bad piece of advice. But it feels like so much more. A wallop in the face, not a piece of bad direction, but a redirection. *This is not the way.* And just when I thought I had really found something. I try to find the words to explain this . . . this betrayal. "It's like finding the girl of your dreams," I begin.

"And realizing you never caught her name?" Kate finishes.

"I was going to say finding out she was actually a guy. That you had it so completely wrong."

"That only happens in movies. Or Shakespeare. Though it's funny you mention the girl of your dreams, because I've been thinking about your girl, the one you were chasing in Mexico."

"Lulu? What does she have to do with this?"

"I was telling David about you and your story and he asked this ridiculously simple question that I've been obsessing about ever since."

"Yes?"

"It's about your backpack."

"You've been obsessing about my *backpack*?" I make it sound like a joke, but all of a sudden, my heart has sped up.

Pulled a runner. Dicked her over. I can hear Tor's disgust, in that Yorkshire accent of hers.

"Here's the thing: If you were just going out for coffee or croissants or to book a hotel room or whatever, why did you take your backpack, with all your things in it, with you?"

"It wasn't a big backpack. You saw it. It was the same one I had in Mexico. I always travel light like that." I'm talking too fast, like someone with something to hide.

"Right. Right. Traveling light. So you can move on. But you were going back to that squat, and you had to climb, if I recall, out of a second-story building. Isn't that right?" I nod. "And you brought a backpack with you? Wouldn't it have been easier to leave most of your things there? Easier to climb. At the very least, it would've been a sure sign that you intended to return."

I was there on that ledge, one leg in, one leg out. A gust of wind, so sharp and cold after all that heat, knifed through me. Inside, I heard rustling as Lulu rolled over and wrapped herself in the tarp. I'd watched her for a moment, and as I did, this feeling had come over me stronger than ever. I'd thought, *Maybe I should just wait for her to wake up.* But I was already out the window and I could see a patisserie down the way.

I'd landed heavily, in a puddle, rainwater sloshing around my feet. When I'd looked back up at the window, the white curtain flapping in the gusty breeze, I'd felt both sadness and relief, the oppositional tug of heaviness and lightness, one lifting me up, one pushing me down. I understood then, Lulu and I had started something, something I'd always wanted, but also something I was scared of getting. Something I wanted more of. And, also, something I wanted to get away from. The truth and its opposite.

I set off for the patisserie not quite knowing what to do, not quite knowing if I should go back, stay another day, but knowing if I did, it would break all this wide open. I bought the croissants, still not knowing what to do. And then I turned a corner and there were the skinheads. And in a twisted way, I was relieved: They would make the decision for me.

Except as soon as I woke up in that hospital, unable to remember Lulu, or her name, or where she was, but desperate to find her, I understood that it was the wrong decision.

"I *was* coming back," I tell Kate. But there's a razor of uncertainty in my voice, and it cuts my deception wide open.

"You know what I think, Willem?" Kate says, her voice gentle. "I think acting, that girl, it's the same thing. You get close to something and you get spooked, so you find a way to distance yourself."

In Paris, the moment when Lulu had made me feel the safest, when she had stood between me and the skinheads, when she had taken care of me, when she became my mountain girl, I'd almost sent her away. That moment, when we'd found safety, I'd looked at her, the determination burning in her eyes, the love already there, improbably after just one day. And I felt it all—the wanting and the needing—but also the fear because I'd seen what losing this kind of thing could do. I wanted to be protected by her love, and to be protected from it.

I didn't understand then. Love is not something you protect. It's something you risk.

"You know the irony about acting?" Kate muses. "We wear a thousand masks, are experts at concealment, but the one place it's impossible to hide is on stage. So no wonder you're freaked out. And Orlando, well now!"

She's right, again. I know she is. Petra didn't do anything today except give me an excuse to pull another runner. But the truth of it is I didn't really want to pull a runner that day with Lulu. And I don't want to pull one now, either.

"What's the worst that happens if you do it your way tonight?" Kate asks.

"She fires me." But if she does, it'll be my action that decides it. Not my inaction. I start to smile. It's tentative, but it's real.

Kate matches mine with a big American version. "You know what I say: Go big or go home."

I look at the boat; it's quiet, but the garden is so lush and well-tended in a way that it never was with us. It is a home, not mine, but someone else's now.

Go big or go home. I heard Kate say that before and didn't quite get it. But I understand it now, though I think on this one, Kate has it wrong. Because for me, it's not go big or go home. It's go big *and* go home.

I need to do one to do the other.

Forty-eight

*B*ackstage. It's the usual craziness, only I feel strangely calm. Linus hustles me to the makeshift dressing room where I change out of my street clothes into Orlando's clothes, hastily altered to fit me. I put on my makeup. I fold my clothes into the lockers behind the stage. My jeans, my shirt, Lulu's watch. I hold it in my hand one second longer, feel the ticking vibrate against my palm, and then I put it in the locker.

Linus gathers us into a circle. There are vocal exercises. The musicians tune their guitars. Petra barks last-minute direction, about finding my light and keeping the focus and the other actors supporting me, and just doing my best. She is giving me a piercing, worried look.

Linus calls five minutes and puts on his headset, and Petra walks away. Max has come backstage for tonight's performance and is sitting on a three-legged stool in the wings.

She doesn't say anything, but just looks at me and kisses two fingers and holds them up in the air. I kiss the same two on my hand and hold them up to her.

"*Break a leg*," someone whispers in my ear. It's Marina, come up behind me. Her arms quickly encircle me from behind as she kisses me somewhere between my ear and my neck. Max catches this and smirks.

"Places!" Linus calls. Petra is nowhere to be seen. She disappears before curtain and won't reappear until the show is over. Vincent says she goes somewhere to pace, or smoke, or disembowel kittens.

Linus grabs my wrist. "Willem," he says. I spin to look at him. He gives a small squeeze and nods. I nod back. "Musicians, go!" Linus commands into his headset.

The musicians start to play. I take my place at the side of the stage.

"Light cue one, go," Linus says.

The lights go up. The audience hushes.

Linus: "Orlando, go!"

I hesitate a moment. *Breathe*, I hear Kate say. I take a breath.

My heart hammers in my head. *Thud, thud, thud.* I close my eyes and can hear the ticking of Lulu's watch; it's as if I'm still wearing it. I stop and listen to them both before I walk onto the stage.

And then time just stops. It is a year and a day. One hour and twenty-four. It is time, happening, all at once.

The last three years solidify into this one moment, into me, into Orlando. This bereft young man, missing a father, without a family, without a home. This Orlando, who happens upon this Rosalind. And even though these two have known each other only moments, they recognize something in each other.

"The little strength that I have, I would it were with you," Rosalind says, cracking it all wide open.

Who takes care of you? Lulu asked, cracking me wide open.

"Wear this for me," Marina says as Rosalind, handing me the prop chain from around her neck.

I'll be your mountain girl and take care of you, Lulu said, moments before I took the watch from her wrist.

Time is passing. I know it must be. I enter the stage, I exit the stage. I make my cues, hit my marks. The sun dips across the sky and then dances toward the horizon and the stars come out, the floodlights go on, the crickets sing. I sense it happening as I drift above it somehow. I am only here, now. This moment. On this stage. I am Orlando, giving myself to Rosalind. And I am Willem, too, giving myself to Lulu, in a way that I should've done a year ago, but couldn't.

"You should ask me what time o' day: there's no clock in the forest," I say to my Rosalind.

You forget, time doesn't exist anymore. You gave it to me, I said to my Lulu.

I feel the watch on my wrist that day in Paris; I hear it ticking in my head now. I can't tell them apart, last year, this year. They are one and the same. Then is now. Now is then.

"I would not be cured, youth," my Orlando tells Marina's Rosalind.

"I would cure you, if you would but call me Rosalind," Marina replies.

I'll take care of you, Lulu promised.

"By my troth, and in good earnest, and so God mend me, and by all pretty oaths that are not dangerous," Marina's Rosalind says.

I escaped danger, Lulu said.

We both did. Something happened that day. It's still happening. It's happening up here on this stage. It was just one day and it's been just one year. But maybe one day is enough. Maybe one hour is enough. Maybe time has nothing at all to do with it.

"Fair youth, I would I could make thee believe I love," my Orlando tells Rosalind.

Define love, Lulu had demanded. *What would "being stained" look like?*

Like this, Lulu.

It would look like this.

— —— —

And then it's over. Like a great wave crashing onto a shore, the applause erupts and I'm here, on this stage, surrounded by the shocked and delighted smiles of my castmates. We are grasping hands and bowing and Marina is pulling me out front for our curtain call and then stepping to the side and gesturing for me to walk ahead and I do and the applause grows even louder.

Backstage, it is madness. Max is screaming. And Marina is crying and Linus is smiling, although his eyes keep darting to the side entrance that Petra left from hours ago. People are surrounding me, patting me on the back, offering congratulations and kisses and I'm here but I'm not—I'm still in some strange limbo where the boundaries of time and place and person don't exist, where I can be here and in Paris, where it can be now and then, where I'm me and also Orlando.

I try to stay in this place as I change out of my clothes, scrub the makeup off my face. I look at myself in the mirror and try to digest what I just did. It feels completely unreal, and like the truest thing I have ever done. The truth and its opposite. Up on stage, playing a role, revealing myself.

People gather round me. There is talk, of parties, celebration, a cast party tonight, even though the show doesn't wrap for two more weeks and to celebrate now is technically bad luck. But it seems like everyone has given up on luck tonight. We make our own.

Petra comes backstage, stone-faced and not saying a word. She walks right past me. Goes straight to Linus.

I leave the backstage and go out the gate that serves as a stage door. Max is at my side, jumping up and down like an exuberant puppy. "So was Marina a decent kisser?" she asks me.

"I'm sure she was glad not to be kissing Jeroen," Vincent says, and I laugh.

Outside, I scan the area for my friends. I'm not quite sure who will be here. And then I hear her call my name.

"Willem!" she says again.

It's Kate, charging toward me, a blur of gold and red. My heart seems to expand as she leaps into my arms and we spin around.

"You did it. You did it. You did it!" she murmurs in my ear.

"I did it. I did it. I did it," I repeat, laughing with joy and relief and awe at the direction this day has taken.

Someone taps me on the shoulder. "You dropped something."

"Oh, right. Your flowers," Kate says, leaning over to pick up a bouquet of sunflowers. "For your stunning debut."

I take the flowers.

"How do you feel?" she asks.

I have no answer, no words. I just feel full. I try to explain it but then Kate interrupts: "Like you just had the best sex in the world?" And I laugh. Yeah, something like that. I take her hand and kiss it. She twines an arm around my waist.

"Ready to meet your adoring public?" she asks.

I'm not. Right now, I just want to savor this. With the person who helped make it happen. Leading her by the hand, I take us over to a quiet bench under a nearby gazebo and attempt in some way to articulate what just happened.

"How did that happen?" is all I can think to ask.

She holds my hands in hers. "Do you really need to ask that?"

"I think I do. It felt like something otherworldly."

"Oh, no," she says, laughing. "I believe in the muse and all, but don't go attributing that performance to one of your accidents. It was all you up there."

It was. And it wasn't. Because I wasn't alone up there.

We sit there for a little while longer. I feel my whole body buzzing, humming. This night is perfect.

"I think your groupies are waiting," Kate says after a while, gesturing behind me. I turn around and there are Broodje, Henk, W, Lien, and a few other people, watching us curiously. I take Kate by the hand and introduce her to the boys.

"You're coming to our party, aren't you?" Broodje asks.

"*Our* party?" I ask.

Broodje manages to look a tiny bit sheepish. "It's hard to un-throw a party at short notice."

"Especially since he has now invited the cast, and about half the audience," Henk says.

"That's not true!" Broodje says. "Not half. Just a couple of Canadians."

I roll my eyes and laugh. "Fine. Let's go."

Lien laughs and takes my hand. "I'm going to say good-night. One of us should be coherent tomorrow. It's moving day." She kisses W. Then me. "Well done, Willem."

"I'm going to follow her out of the park," Kate says. "This city confounds me."

"You're not coming?" I ask.

"I have some things I need to do first. I'll come later. Prop the door open for me."

"Always," I say. I go to kiss her on the cheek and she whispers into my ear, "I knew you could do it."

"Not without you," I say.

"Don't be silly. You just needed a pep talk."

But I don't mean the pep talk. I know Kate believes that I have to commit, to not rely on the accidents, to take the wheel. But had we not met in Mexico, would I be here now? Was it accidents? Or will?

For the hundredth time tonight, I'm back with Lulu, on Jacques's barge, the improbably named *Viola*. She'd just told me the story of double happiness and we were arguing over the meaning. She'd thought it meant the luck of the boy getting the job and the girl. But I'd disagreed. It was the couplet fitting together, the two halves finding each other. It was love.

But maybe we were both wrong, and both right. It's not either/or, not luck *or* love. Not fate *or* will.

Maybe for double happiness, you need both.

Forty-nine

*I*nside the flat, it is complete mayhem. More than fifty people, from the cast, from Utrecht, even old school friends from my Amsterdam days. I have no idea how Broodje dug everyone up so fast.

Max pounces on me as soon as she comes in the door, followed by Vincent. "Holy. Shit," Max says.

"You might've mentioned you could act!" Vincent adds.

I smile. "I like to preserve a bit of mystery."

"Yeah, well, everyone in the cast is bloody delighted," says Max. "Except Petra. She's pissy as ever."

"Only because her understudy just completely cockblocked her star. And now she has to decide whether to put up a lame, and I mean that both literally and figuratively, star, or let you carry us home," Vincent says.

"Decisions, decisions," Max adds. "Don't look now but Marina is giving you the fuck-me eyes again."

We all look. Marina is staring right at me and smiling.

"And don't even deny it, unless it's *me* she wants to shag," Max says.

"I'll be right back," I tell Max. I go over to where Marina's standing by the table Broodje has turned into the bar. She has a glass of something in her hand. "What do you have there?" I ask.

"Not entirely sure. One of your mates gave it to me, promised me no hangover. I'm taking him at his word."

"That's your first mistake right there."

She runs a finger along the top of the rim. "I have a feeling I'm long past making my first mistake." She takes a gulp of her drink. "Aren't you drinking?"

"I already feel drunk."

"Here. Catch up with yourself."

She hands me her glass and I take a sip. I taste the sour tequila that Broodje now favors, mixed with some other orange-flavored booze. "Yeah. No hangover from this. Definitely not."

She laughs, touches my arm. "I'm not going to tell you how fantastic you were tonight. You're probably sick of hearing it."

"Do you *ever* get sick of hearing it?"

She grins. "No." She looks away. "I know what I said earlier today, about after the show, but all the rules seem to be getting broken today. . . ." She trails off. "So really, can three weeks make much of a difference?"

Marina is sexy and gorgeous and smart. And she's also wrong. Three weeks can make all the difference. I know that because one day can make all the difference.

"Yes," I tell Marina. "They can."

"Oh," she says, sounding surprised, a little hurt. Then: "Are you with someone else?"

Tonight on that stage, it felt like I was. But that *was* a ghost. Shakespeare's full of them. "No," I tell her.

"Oh, I just saw you, with that woman. After the show. I wasn't sure."

Kate. The need to see her feels urgent. Because what I want is so clear to me now.

I excuse myself from Marina and poke through the flat, but there's no sign of Kate. I go downstairs to see if the door is still propped open. It is. I bump into Mrs. Van der Meer again, out walking her dog. "Sorry about all the noise," I tell her.

"It's okay," she says. She looks upstairs. "We used to have some wild parties here."

"You lived here back when it was a squat?" I ask, trying to reconcile the middle-aged *vrouw* with the young anarchists I've seen in pictures.

"Oh, yes. I knew your father."

"What was he like then?" I don't know why I'm asking that. Bram was never the hard one to crack.

But Mrs. Van der Meer's answer surprises me. "He was a bit of a melancholy young man," she says. And then her eyes flicker up to the flat, like she's seeing him there. "Until that mother of yours showed up."

Her dog yanks on the leash and she sets off, leaving me to ponder how much I know, and don't know, about my parents.

Fifty

*T*he phone is ringing. And I'm sleeping.

I fumble for it. It's next to my pillow.

"Hello," I mumble.

"Willem!" Yael says in a breathless gulp. "Did I wake you?"

"Ma?" I ask. I wait to feel the usual panic but none comes. Instead, there's something else, a residue of something good. I rub my eyes and it's still there, floating like a mist: a dream I was having.

"I talked to Mukesh. And he worked his magic. He can get you out Monday but we have to book now. We'll do an open-ended ticket this time. Come for a year. Then decide what to do."

My head is hazy with lack of sleep. The party went until four. I fell asleep around five. The sun was already up. Slowly, yesterday's conversation with my mother comes back to me. The offer she made. How much I wanted it. Or thought I did. Some things you don't know you want until they're gone. Other things you think you want, but don't understand you already have them.

"Ma," I say. "I'm not coming back to India."

"You're not?" There's curiosity in her voice, and disappointment, too.

"I don't belong there."

"You belong where I belong."

It's a relief, after all this time, to hear her say so. But I don't think it's true. I'm grateful that she has made a new home for herself in India, but it's not where I'm meant to be.

Go big and go home.

"I'm going to act, Ma," I say. And I feel it. The idea, the plan, fully formed since last night, maybe since much longer. The urgency to see Kate, who never did show up at the party, courses through me. This is one chance I'm not going to let slip through my fingers. This *is* something I need. "I'm going to act," I repeat. "Because I'm an actor."

Yael laughs. "Of course you are. It's in your blood. Just like Olga."

The name is instantly familiar. "Olga Szabo, you mean?"

There's a pause. I can feel her surprise crackle through the line. "Saba told you about her?"

"No. I found the pictures. In the attic. I meant to ask you about them but I didn't, because I've been busy . . ." I trail off. "And because we never really talked about these things."

"No. We never did, did we?"

"Who was she? Saba's girlfriend?"

"She was his sister," she replies. And I should be surprised, but I'm not. Not at all. It's like the pieces of a puzzle slotting together.

"She would have been your great-aunt," Yael continues. "He always said she was an incredible actress. She was meant to go to Hollywood. But then the war came and she didn't survive."

She didn't survive. Only Saba did.

"Was Szabo her stage name?" I ask.

"No. Szabo was Saba's surname before he emigrated to Israel and Hebreified it. Lots of Europeans did that."

To distance himself, I think. I understand that. Though he couldn't really distance himself. All those silent films he took me to. The ghosts he held at bay, and held close.

Olga Szabo, my great-aunt. Sister to my grandfather, Oskar Szabo, who became Oskar Shiloh, father of Yael Shiloh, wife of Bram de Ruiter, brother of Daniel de Ruiter, soon to be father of Abraão de Ruiter.

And just like that, my family grows again.

Fifty-one

When I emerge from my bedroom, Broodje and Henk are just waking up and are surveying the wreckage like army generals who have lost a major ground battle.

Broodje turns to me, his face twisted in apology. "I'm sorry. I can clean it all later. But we promised we'd meet W at ten to help him move. And we're already late."

"I think I'm going to be sick," Henk says.

Broodje picks up a beer bottle, two-thirds full of cigarette butts. "You can be sick *later*," he says. "We made a promise to W." Broodje looks at me. "And to Willy. I'll clean the flat later. And Henk's vomit, which he's going to keep corked for now."

"Don't worry about it," I say. "I'll clean it all. I'll fix everything!"

"You don't have to be so cheerful about it," Henk says, wincing and touching his temples.

I grab the keys from the counter. "Sorry," I say, not sorry at all. I head to the door.

"Where are you going?" Broodje asks.

"To take the wheel!"

———

I'm unlocking my bike downstairs when my phone rings. It's her. Kate.

"I've been calling you for the last hour," I say. "I'm coming to your hotel."

"My hotel, huh?" she says. I can hear the smile in her voice.

"I was worried you'd leave. And I have a proposition for you."

"Well, propositions *are* best proposed in person. But sit tight because I'm actually on my way to you. That's why I'm calling. Are you home?"

I think of the flat, Broodje and Henk in their boxers, the unbelievable mess. The sun is out, really out, for the first time in days. I suggest we meet at the Sarphatipark instead. "Across the street. Where we were yesterday," I remind her.

"Proposition downgraded from a hotel to a park, Willem?" she teases. "I'm not sure whether to be flattered or insulted."

"Yeah, me neither."

I go straight to the park and wait, sitting down on one of the benches near the sandpit. A little boy and girl are discussing their plans for a fort.

"Can it have one hundred towers?" the little boy asks. The girl says, "I think twenty is better." Then the boy asks,

"Can we live there forever?" The girl considers the sky a moment and says, "Until it rains."

By the time Kate shows up, they've made significant progress, digging a moat and constructing two towers.

"Sorry it took so long," Kate says, breathless. "I got lost. This city of yours, it runs in circles."

I start to explain about the concentric canals, the Ceintuurbaan being a belt that goes around the waist of the city. She waves me off. "Don't bother. I'm hopeless." She sits down next to me. "Any word from Frau Directeur?"

"Total silence."

"That sounds ominous."

I shrug. "Maybe. Nothing I can do. Anyway, I have a new plan."

"Oh," Kate says, widening her already big green eyes. "You do?"

"I do. In fact, that's what my proposition is about."

"The thick plottens."

"What?"

She shakes her head. "Never mind." She crosses her legs, leans in toward me. "I'm ready. Proposition me."

I take her hand. "I want you." I pause. "To be my director."

"Isn't that a little like shaking hands after making love?" she asks.

"What happened last night," I begin, "it happened because of you. And I want to work with you. I want to come study with Ruckus. Be an apprentice."

Kate's eyes slit into smiles. "How do you know about our apprenticeships?" she drawls.

"I may have looked at your website one or a hundred

times. And I know you mostly work with Americans, but I grew up speaking English, I act in English. Most of the time, I dream in English. I want to do Shakespeare. In English. I want to do it. With you."

The grin has disappeared from Kate's face. "It wouldn't be like last night—Orlando on a main stage. Our apprentices do everything. They build sets. They work tech. They study. They act in the ensemble. I'm not saying you wouldn't play principal roles one day—I would not rule that out, not after last night. But it would take a while. And, there are visa issues to consider, not to mention the union, so you couldn't come over expecting the spotlight. And I've told David he needs to meet you."

I look at Kate and am about to say that I wouldn't expect that, that I'd be patient, that I know how to build things. But I stop myself because it occurs to me that I don't need to convince *her* of anything.

"Where do you think I was last night?" she asks. "I was waiting for David to get back from his *Medea*, so I could tell him about you. Then I arranged for him to get his ass on a plane so he could see you tonight before that invalid comes back. He's on his way, and in fact, I have to leave soon to go to the airport to meet him. After all this trouble, they'd better put you on again, otherwise you're going to have to do it solo for him."

She laughs. "I'm kidding. But Ruckus is a small operation so we make decisions like this communally. That's another thing you have to be prepared for, how dysfunctionally codependent we all are." She throws up her arms. "But every family is like that."

"So, wait? You were going to ask me?"

The grin is back. "Was there any doubt? But it pleases me no end, Willem, that *you* asked *me*. It shows you've been paying attention, which is what a director wants in an actor." She taps her temple. "Also, very clever of you to move to the States. Good for your career but also it's where your Lulu is from."

I think of Tor's letter, only today the regret and recrimination is gone. She looked for me. I looked for her. And last night, in some strange way, we found each other.

"That's not why I want to go," I tell Kate.

She smiles. "I know. I'm just teasing. Though I think you'll really take to Brooklyn. It has a lot in common with Amsterdam. The brownstones and the rowhouses, the loving tolerance of eccentricity. I think you'll feel right at home."

When she says that a feeling comes over me. Of pausing, of resting, of all the clocks in the world going quiet.

Home.

Fifty-two

*B*ut Daniel's home. That is a mess.

When I get back, the boys have left, and there is crap everywhere. It looks like how Bram used to describe it in the old days, before Yael arrived and asserted her brand of order.

There are bottles and ashtrays and plates and pizza boxes and every dish seems dirty and out. The whole place smells like cigarettes. It's certainly not a place that a baby should live. I'm momentarily paralyzed, not sure where to start.

I put on a CD of Adam Wilde, that singer-songwriter Max and I went to see a few weeks ago. And then I just go. I empty out the beer and wine bottles and put them in a box for recycling. Next, I dump the ashtrays and rinse them out. Even though there's a dishwasher now, I fill the sink with hot, soapy water and clean all the dirty dishes, then dry them. I throw open the windows to air out the place, and sunshine and fresh air come blowing in.

By noon, I've collected the bottles, tossed the cigarette butts, washed and dried the dishes, dusted and vacuumed. It's about as clean as it was on its best day with Daniel, though when he comes home with Abraão and Fabiola, I'll have it spotless. Ready.

I make a coffee. I check my phone to see if there's any word from Linus, but it's sitting on my bed, dead. I plug it in to charge, setting the coffee on my shelf. The envelope is still there, with the photos of me, Yael, Bram, Saba, Olga. I run my finger along the crease of the envelope, feel the weight of history inside. Wherever I'm going next, these are coming with me.

I glance at my phone. It's still dead, but soon there will be some word from Linus and Petra. Part of me thinks that I must be fired. That has to be the price to pay for last night's triumph, and it's okay because it's a price I'm willing to pay. But another part of me is losing faith that the universal law of equilibrium operates that way.

I go back into the lounge. The Adam Wilde CD has been repeating and the songs are starting to become familiar enough that I know I will be able to hear them when I'm not listening to them.

I look around the room. I fluff the cushions and lie down on the sofa. I should be in suspense, waiting for word about tonight, but I feel the opposite. It's like that moment of pause when I step out of a train station or bus station or airport into a new city and it's nothing but possibility.

Through the open window, the dissonant sounds of the city—of tram chimes and bicycle bells and the occasional jet roaring overhead—drift in and mingle with the music and lull me to sleep.

For the third time in one day, I'm woken up by the ringing of a phone. Like this morning when Yael called, I have that same feeling, of being somewhere else, somewhere right.

The ringing stops. But I know it must be Linus. *My fate*, Marina had called it. But it's not my fate; it's just about tonight. My fate is up to me.

I go into my room and pick up the phone. Out the window, climbing through the clouds, I make out the blue-and-white underbelly of a KLM jet. I picture myself on a plane, flying out of Amsterdam, over the North Sea, over England and Ireland, past Iceland and Greenland and down Newfoundland and along the Eastern Seaboard, into New York. I feel the jerk, hear the skid of the tires touching down, the explosion of applause from the passengers. Because we are all of us, so grateful for having at last arrived.

I glance at my phone. It's full of congratulatory texts from last night, and a voicemail from Linus. "Willem, can you please call in as soon as possible," he says.

I take a deep breath, prepare myself for whatever he has to say. It doesn't really matter. I went big and now I'm going home.

Just as Linus answers there's a faint knock at the front door.

"Hello, hello . . ." Linus's voice echoes.

There's another knock, louder this time. Kate? Broodje?

I tell Linus I'll call him right back. I put the phone down. I open the door. And once again, time stops.

I'm shocked. And I'm not. She is just as I remember her. And completely transformed. A stranger. And someone I know. *The truth and its opposite are flip sides of the same coin*, I hear Saba say.

"Hello Willem," she says. "My name is Allyson."

Allyson. I say the name in my head and a year's worth of memories and fantasies and one-sided conversations are revised and updated. Not Lulu. Allyson. A strong name. A solid name. And somehow, a familiar name. Everything about her seems familiar. I know this person. I'm known to this person. It's then I understand what I was dreaming about this morning, who it is that's been sitting next to me on that plane all this time.

Allyson walks in.

The door clicks shut behind her. And for a minute, they're in the room with us too. Yael and Bram, thirty years ago. Their entire story rushes through my head, because it's our story, too. Only now, I realize, it was an incomplete story. Because no matter how many times he told it, Bram never told me the important part. What happened during those first three hours together in the car.

Or maybe he did, only without words. With his action.

"And so I kissed her. Like I'd been expecting her all that time," my previously melancholy father would say, always with wonder in his voice.

I'd thought the wonder was for the accidents. But maybe it wasn't. Maybe the wonder was for the stain. Three hours in a car, that was all it took. And two years later, there she was.

Maybe he was overwhelmed, like I am overwhelmed, by

that mysterious intersection where love meets luck, where fate meets will. Because he'd been waiting for her. And there she was.

So he'd kissed her.

I kiss Allyson.

I complete the history that came before us, and in doing so, begin one all of our own.

Double happiness: I get it now.

ACKNOWLEDGMENTS

A novelist is a thief by necessity. I would first like to apologize to and then thank all of the people I've met over the years in my travels and in my life, whose bits and pieces I've stolen, disguised, and put in this book. There are too many of you to list, and I don't even know if I remember everyone's names. But I remember them just the same. People you meet for a day really can inspire you in ways you might not recognize until, decades later, a tiny piece of them gets plunked into a novel.

For all those who knowingly helped me with this great big hodgepodge of an internationally globetrotting book, a heartfelt thank you, merci, bedankt, gracias, הדות, धन्यवाद, köszönöm, and obrigada. Specifically to: Jessie Austrian, Fabiola Bergi, Michael Bourret, Libba Bray, Sarah Burnes, Heleen Buth, Mitali Dave (and parents), Danielle Delaney, Céline Faure, Fiasco Theater Company, Greg Forman, Lee and Ruth Forman, Rebecca Gardner, Logan Garrison, Tamara Glenny, Marie-Elisa Gramain, Tori Hill, Ben Hoffman, Marjorie Ingall, Anna Jarzab, Maureen Johnson, Deborah Kaplan, Isabel Kyriacou, E. Lockhart, Elyse Marshall, Tali Meas, Stephanie Perkins, Mukesh Prasad, Will Roberts, Philippe Robinet, Leila Sales, Tamar and Robert Schamhart,

William Shakespeare, Deb Shapiro, Courtney Sheinmel, *Slings & Arrows*, Andreas Sonju, Emke Spauwen, Margaret Stohl, Julie Strauss-Gabel, Alex Ulyett, Robin Wasserman, Cameron and Jackie Wilson, Ken Wright, and the whole team at Penguin Young Readers Group. It takes a village—in this case, a global one.

And finally, thank you to Nick, Willa, and Denbele: My family. My home.

JUST ONE **NIGHT**

GAYLE FORMAN

JUST ONE **NIGHT**

SPEAK
An imprint of Penguin Random House LLC
375 Hudson Street
New York, New York 10014

First published in the United States of America by Viking,
an imprint of Penguin Group (USA) LLC, 2014
Published by Speak, an imprint of Penguin Group (USA) LLC, 2015
This omnibus edition published by Speak,
an imprint of Penguin Random House LLC, 2017

Speak ISBN 9780147518156
This omnibus edition ISBN 9780451478795

Designed by Danielle Delaney
Printed in the United States of America

*I*t isn't a first kiss. It isn't even *their* first kiss. But it feels like one.

Not because it is fumbling or awkward. Not because she doesn't know where to put her hand, or he doesn't know where to put his nose. None of those. They slot together like puzzle pieces. As Allyson and Willem kiss for the first time in a year, both are thinking the same thing: *This feels new.*

Though perhaps *thinking* is not the right term, because with a kiss like this, thinking goes out the window and something more instinctual takes over: inner voices, gut instincts. "Knowing it in your *kishkes*" is how Willem's saba would've described it.

In his *kishkes*, Willem is marveling that Allyson found him, as Yael found Bram. He doesn't know how it happened, only that it did happen and that it means something.

Allyson is doing a mental fist pump and an *I told you so.*

She'd spent a year looking for him, looking for the girl she was with him. And then last night, watching Willem perform Orlando in Vondelpark, she'd been certain she'd found them both, certain the words he was speaking were meant for her. *For ever and a day.* She'd felt it. Right in her gut. But listening to that inner voice was new to Allyson. She'd spent nineteen years of her life ignoring it, listening to pretty much everything *but* it. So when she'd seen Willem with another woman, looking luminously happy with another woman, she'd gone away.

Only not really. Because here she is, at his flat, where he is kissing her, and she is kissing him right back. And the kiss feels like something completely new. But it also feels like something deeply known. Which would seem to be a contradiction. Only it's not. *The truth and its opposite are flip sides of the same coin*, Saba always said.

Nothing goes on forever. Not even second first kisses. Not even those as hard-won as this. Outside the window, a tram bell chimes. It is like an alarm clock, crystallizing the moment from fuzzy to real. Allyson and Willem break apart.

Allyson isn't quite sure what to do next. She is supposed to be catching a flight to Croatia. This stop at Willem's flat was a detour, the kiss a happy surprise. But now what?

Willem takes her backpack, as if answering the question, as if completing the transaction. Then he offers her a coffee.

He would like to kick himself. This girl he has not seen in a year, this girl he's thought about, dreamed about, looked for, for a year, this girl he just kissed (he's still a bit dazed from that kiss) . . . and his first words to her are those of a waiter.

But then he remembers something. "Or a tea. You like tea, don't you?"

It is the smallest thing. She likes tea. She drank tea on the train to London, when they'd first started talking, about *hagelslag* of all things. She drank it again on the train they'd taken to Paris together, later that morning.

Tea. One day. A year ago. He remembered.

A little voice in Allyson's gut (it's her *kishkes*, only she doesn't know that word yet) is yelling: *See?*

"Yes," Allyson says. "I would love some tea." She's not really thirsty. Five minutes ago, nerves had left her with a mouth as dry as paper, but the kiss has taken care of that. But this feels like more than a beverage being offered.

"Tea," Willem says. He can see that the offer has unfastened something in her face, as when she'd jokingly solicited a compliment from him last year, and he'd told her she was brave and generous and openhearted. Back then he'd been guessing. Now he is remembering. He remembers it all. He wants to tell her. He *will* tell her.

But first, tea.

Willem starts toward the kitchen. Allyson isn't sure whether to follow him, but then he turns around and says, "Wait here," and then a few steps later adds, "Don't go anywhere."

She sits down on the low leather couch. It is a nice apartment, all bright and sunny and modern. Does he live here? She hasn't thought about where he might live. About him living anywhere. When she'd met him, he'd lived out of a backpack.

In the kitchen, Willem tries to collect himself as he makes drinks. (He watches the kettle; the adage is true, it refuses to boil.) He digs through the cabinets for the tea that he recalls his uncle Daniel saying he kept for Fabiola, his soon-to-be wife, the soon-to-be mother of his child, whom he is now with in Brazil. Willem makes himself a coffee—using the instant because it is faster and it has already taken too long for the water to boil.

He puts it all on a tray and returns to the lounge. Allyson is sitting on the sofa, her sandals off, neatly placed under the coffee table. (The sight of her bare feet. What this is doing to Willem's blood pressure. She might as well have taken off all her clothes.)

He puts the tray down on the coffee table and sits on the couch, but on the opposite side from Allyson. "I hope chamomile is okay," he says. "It's all my uncle has."

"It's fine," Allyson says. Then, "Your uncle?"

"Daniel. This is his flat. I'm staying here while he's in Brazil."

Allyson almost tells him she thought he lived in Utrecht, that was where she'd tracked him down before the trail went cold. Or she'd thought it went cold. Until she'd accidentally heard about *As You Like It* being performed in Vondelpark last night and she somehow *knew* that Willem would be in it.

Accidents. All about the accidents. She wants to tell Willem this, is working out how to start without sounding like a complete lunatic, when he says: "Daniel used to share this flat with my father, Bram. When they were young. And then my father met a girl while he was traveling. They spent a day together. Not even a day, a few hours, and a year later, she showed up here. She knocked on the door."

Like you just did, Willem thinks, but he doesn't say that. He doesn't want to sound like a complete lunatic.

"Your mother," Allyson says.

"Yes. My mother. She's in India right now." He thinks of

her. He cannot wait to tell her this. He takes a small moment to savor that, being eager to tell his mother something. Then he goes back to savoring Allyson, and her bare feet, which are *right here*. He never thought he had a thing for feet, but he is beginning to reconsider.

Allyson remembers Willem talking about his mother and father. It was during their conversation—argument? debate?—about love when Willem had smeared the Nutella on her wrist and licked it off. Allyson had challenged Willem to name one couple who hadn't just fallen in love but had remained in love, had stayed stained. *Yael and Bram*, he had said.

"Yael and Bram," Allyson says now, not even having to reach for the names.

She remembers Willem's sadness last summer. And immediately she knows, maybe she knew then, that there is no more Bram. Which isn't to say there is no more stain.

Yael and Bram. Something in Willem's chest catches. He'd been right. He is known to this person. Has been from the very start.

He looks at her. She looks at him. "I told you I would remember," Allyson says.

Before he'd kissed her that night in the art squat, she had told him that she'd remember everything about their day in Paris. That she would remember *him*.

Willem had made no such promises. But he can taste, touch, hear, and smell every last detail of that day together. "I remember, too," he says.

There is so much to say. It is like shoving all the sand of the world into an hourglass. Or trying to get it out.

But Willem's phone keeps ringing. He keeps ignoring it, until he remembers he promised he'd call Linus back right before he opened the door to her.

"Oh, shit. Linus." He goes to fetch his mobile. Five missed calls.

Allyson looks curious. He tells her, "I have to make a call."

She thinks he will go into the other room to do it, but he doesn't. He sits down next to her.

The conversation is in Dutch so Allyson doesn't understand what he's saying, anyway. She can't really make much out from the look on his face, either: a half smile. A shoulder shrug. She's not sure if the news is good or bad.

Willem hangs up the phone. "I'm the understudy for Orlando in a play. Shakespeare again. *As You Like It*," he begins.

"Understudy?" Allyson asks. "I thought you *were* Orlando."

Only for last night's performance. And tonight's. That's what Petra had decreed, Linus has just told him. Next week Jeroen, the actor Willem replaced, will come back, ankle cast and all, for a final weekend of performances. After this evening, Willem's services will no longer be needed, as actor or understudy. But he's on for tonight. In fact, they need him to come listen to notes before the 7:00 call. He is about to explain this all to Allyson, but then he stops himself.

"You knew?" he asks.

And then she says, "I was there."

He shouldn't be surprised. Hadn't he felt her there? Hadn't he spoken his lines to her? But after all the false hopes of the last year, and after that letter Tor had told him about, he'd thought he had conjured her. Maybe he had. Maybe he had done such a fine job of it, he'd conjured her right into existence, into his uncle's flat, where she is now sitting, with her feet resting in his lap.

How did that happen? He vaguely remembers grabbing her ankles and laying her feet across his legs, casually, as if they were a blanket, but he can't be sure. It all feels like a dream and yet as natural as breathing. This is what you do. Put Allyson's feet into your lap.

"You were fantastic," Allyson tells him. "Magnetic. It was like you *were* Orlando."

Willem had felt a kinship with Orlando, a bereaved young man inexplicably fallen in love with a girl who came and disappeared like a wisp of smoke. But the girl came back. (*The girl came back.*)

"I always thought you were good," she continues. "Even when I saw you perform last year, the night we met, but it was nothing like last night."

The night they met. He'd been doing *Twelfth Night* with Guerrilla Will, playing Sebastian. They hadn't spoken, but he'd tossed her a coin at the end of the play. It was a flirtation, an invitation. God, he'd had no idea then.

"A lot has happened this year," Willem tells her.

When Allyson smiles, Willem is reminded of a sunrise. A bit of light, then more of it, then a burst of brightness. A sunrise is something you can see all the time and still marvel at. Maybe that is why her smile feels so familiar. He has seen many sunrises.

No, that is not why it feels familiar.

Allyson meanwhile is remembering. *Why this person?* All the things she has told herself, or other people have told her—

infatuation or Paris or good acting or lust—no longer hold water, because she remembers so viscerally and feels it anew. It's not any of that. It's not even him. Or all him. It's her. The way she can be with him.

It was so new that day: the liberation of being honest, of being brave, maybe a little stupid. She's had a bit more practice at it now, the past few weeks alone in Europe, a lot of practice. She knows this girl pretty well now.

"A lot has happened to me too," she tells Willem.

They tell the story in bits, in tandem. The parts already known: Willem being concussed. The parts guessed: Willem being beaten by the skinheads; Allyson fleeing back to London in misery. They share the frustration of never finding out each other's true names, their whole names, email addresses. They remedy that. (Willem Shiloh De Ruiter. Allyson Leigh Healey, etc. etc.) Allyson tells Willem about the letter she wrote him last March, when she finally allowed herself to wonder if maybe the worst hadn't happened, if maybe Willem hadn't abandoned her.

Willem tells Allyson about only just finding out about the letter's existence last month, trying to track it down, and only yesterday finding out what it said.

"How is that possible?" Allyson asks. "I got the letter back four days ago."

"*You* got it back?" Willem asks. "How?"

"When I went to your house. Your old house, in Utrecht."

Broodje's place, on Bloemstraat, where he'd spent the dark days following his return from Paris, healing from the beating, from everything, really.

"How did you know to go there?" he asks. "To Bloemstraat." He hadn't lived there when they'd met, and he hadn't
given her any contact information. This was something he had
regretted.

Allyson is embarrassed now, at the lengths she went through
to find him. She doesn't regret going through them, but she understands how overzealous it might look. In her discomfort, she
starts to pull her feet away. But Willem won't let her. He holds
them fast. And this small gesture gives her the courage to tell
him. About venturing to Paris. About tracking down Céline.
About going to the Hôpital Saint-Louis. About Dr. Robinet and
his kindness. The address, which led her back to the house in
Utrecht. And to the letter.

"I kept the letter. I actually have it in my backpack."

She leans over and pulls out a creased envelope. She hands
it to Willem. There are generations of addresses here. Tor's
house in Leeds, the original Guerilla Will headquarters (how
had she found that?), forwarded to Willem's former houseboat
in Amsterdam, since sold, and forwarded on to Bloemstraat.

"You can read it if you want," Allyson offers.

"Seems beyond the point," Willem says. Though that isn't
why he doesn't want to read it. Tor had instructed someone to
email him and tell him what the letter said. He doesn't have the
stomach to read the whole letter in front of Allyson.

But Allyson takes the envelope back, unfolds the letter inside of it, and hands it to him.

>*Dear Willem:*
>*I've been trying to forget about you*
>*and our day in Paris for nine months now,*

but as you can see, it's not going all that well.
I guess more than anything, I want to know,
did you just leave? If you did, it's okay. I
mean it's not, but if I can know the truth,
I can get over it. And if you didn't leave,
I don't know what to say. Except I'm sorry
that I did.
* I don't know what your response will*
be at getting this letter, like a ghost from
your past. But no matter what happened,
I hope you're okay.

The letter is not what he thought it would be. Not what Tor suggested it was. It takes Willem a moment to find his voice again, and when he does, he speaks to the Allyson who wrote the letter as much as to the girl sitting here. "I didn't just leave," he says. "I'm glad you didn't forget. And I wasn't okay."

"I know that now," she says. "I think part of me knew it then, too but I wasn't brave enough to believe it. I was okay that day but I wasn't okay generally. I am now."

Willem folds the letter, carefully, like it is sacred text. "I am, too."

He hands the letter back to Allyson. She shakes her head. "I wrote it to you."

He knows exactly where he will keep it. With the photo of him and Yael and Bram from his eighteenth birthday. With the photo of Saba and Saba's sister, Willem's great aunt Olga, who, like this letter, he only recently discovered had existed. This letter from Allyson will join the important things, thought lost, now found.

"I still don't understand," Willem says. "I went to the house on Bloemstraat last month and the letter wasn't there."

"That's weird," Allyson says. "Saskia and Anamiek never mentioned seeing you."

"Who are they?" Willem asks.

"They live there."

"Ahh. Well, I didn't meet them. I let myself in with my key."

Allyson laughs. "That explains it. They didn't know you, either, though they knew of you. And also . . ." She pauses and then forces herself to finish. "Ana Lucia."

"Ana Lucia?" Willem asks. He has not thought much about her since their spectacular blowout before Christmas last year. "What about Ana Lucia?"

"I met her."

"*You met Ana Lucia?*"

Allyson remembers the girl's fury. Another student at Ana Lucia's college had told Allyson that Willem had been cheating on Ana Lucia with a French girl all along. When she'd heard that, it had seemed to confirm everything bad Allyson suspected about him.

"How did *that* go?" Willem asks.

"Well, she didn't punch me."

Willem winces. "She wasn't so happy to see you," he says.

"I didn't get it. I'd never even met her before."

"You have. A bit."

Allyson shakes her head. "No. I think I'd remember."

"In Paris. In the Latin Quarter."

Allyson's mind spins and lands on the carousel of postcards that she had pretended to look at while Willem chatted with some girls he'd known from home. Ana Lucia was one of them?

"But why would she hate me?" Allyson asks, remembering her own jealousy at any girl Willem seemed vaguely interested in. But jealousy was one thing. Ana Lucia had literally thrown Allyson out of her dorm room.

"Because she caught me buying the airplane tickets to find you."

Airplane tickets? Find me where? Allyson's mind scrambles to incorporate this new information. It still doesn't make sense. Willem had gone to Spain to meet the French girl he'd been cheating on Ana Lucia with. Allyson had suspected it was Céline, even though Céline had told Allyson she had not seen Willem since the day he was with Allyson in Paris. At the time, Allyson had believed her.

And just like that, Allyson understands it. How jealousy contorts things. She thinks of Céline, how jealous she had been of her, and how wrong about her. *She* was Ana Lucia's Céline.

There was no *French* girl. There was an American girl he met in *France*.

"So you didn't go to Spain?" Allyson asks.

"Spain?" Willem says. "No. I went to Mexico."

The more questions are answered, the more are asked. But now Willem has to leave to meet Petra and Linus. Neither Allyson nor Willem wants to part. For now, they wish they could both stay like this, talking.

He would like to bring her with him now, to put her in his pocket. Except he must face Petra, his cantankerous director, who he knows is furious with him about last night's performance. He ignored her direction to play the part safe, to play it as Jeroen had played it. Instead, he had done what his friend

Kate had suggested. He'd done it his way, found his own Orlando and in doing so, opened up a vein of himself on that stage. It had been the most exhilarating experience of his life. Well, until the knock at the door today.

Much as he would like to keep Allyson close by, he knows it is unwise to parade her in front of Petra. Though he cannot wait to introduce her to Kate. He will introduce her to Kate tonight. And Broodje. And W and Henk and Max. All the people who led him back to her.

"I am in trouble with the director," Willem explains. "Maybe it's better if we meet later."

There is something then that hangs between them. Meeting later is what got them into this predicament in the first place. Willem stepping out for a bit. Accidents happening. And a year before they found each other again.

They both seem to recognize the moment. But they also know now is not then. And as if to prove it, Willem slides a key off a ring and gives it to Allyson. She stares at it in her palm. So does he.

A year ago I had a backpack, and now I have a key, he thinks.

A year ago we didn't give each other our names, and now he gave me a key, she thinks.

(Also, Willem has just glanced at the birthmark on Allyson's wrist, giving himself an urgent desire to taste it again. Between her feet and her wrist, he is having a hard time getting out the door.)

(Speaking of feet, Allyson is looking at the zigzag scar on Willem's foot—left foot—and remembering she wanted to find out how he got it. Along with his birthday and his favorite ice cream flavor and ten thousand other things there don't seem to be enough time for.)

So for now Willem tells her to make herself at home. Eat what is in the kitchen. Use the computer. There is WiFi. Skype. Have a rest. His bedroom is the yellow one. He likes to picture her in his flat.

"Here is my cellphone number," he tells her. He writes it on a pad. He resists the urge to write it on her arm, to tattoo it there.

He is about to leave, but stops in the doorway. They are now mirror images of how they were a few hours ago, Willem in the flat, Allyson in the hall. Neither is sure what this means.

What they are sure is that they want to kiss. Both of them do. There is a pull, it feels almost like a chain, linking them.

"I'll be back here at six," Willem promises.

"Six," she repeats. It's after four now. She has officially missed her flight to Croatia.

He starts to close the door behind him. Then opens it again. "You'll be here?" He is nervous now about leaving. He can't help it. The mirror images. The Universal Law of Equilibrium. Last year, he vanished. This year, it could be her.

Except he thinks he has stopped believing in this universal register of deposits and debits, of good things coming at a cost. And when Allyson closes the door, promising that she will be there, he allows himself to believe it.

There is news to share. They each share it.

Willem, in a rush, texts Kate, whom he just saw a few hours ago when she was on her way to meet her fiancé at the airport. She was bringing him to meet Willem so Willem could get his seal of approval to join their theater group.

I have big news, he writes. *I'm Orlando tonight.*

He writes a version of the same to Broodje, who, along with

Henk is helping W move into a new flat with his girlfriend, Lien. He knows all of them will get the message and all of them will come, even though they all came last night, because that is how his friends are.

He is riding his bike to the theater when he realizes that they will all think the big news is that he was given one more chance to do Orlando. Though in reality, he was fired. He is going on tonight out of necessity. He can almost taste Petra's disgust at having to put him back on the stage.

That isn't the news. The news is Lulu, of course. Allyson. But tonight, they will all come. And they will find out.

Then he thinks of Yael. His mother, so far away from him these past few years, until that day in Paris last year that set everything in motion. It's the middle of the night in Mumbai, so Willem texts her.

I found her. He stops. Maybe it is more accurate to say she found him. But that is not what he is feeling. He is feeling that he found her. So that is what he writes.

He doesn't elaborate. He knows his mother will understand.

Back in Willem's flat, Allyson has texted Wren. *CALL ME ASAP!!!* And then she decides to be nosy. Not to snoop exactly, but to look around.

The living room does not offer clues. Even had Allyson not been told this apartment belonged to Willem's uncle, she would've been able to tell it was not Willem's. She goes into the bedroom in the back. The yellow one. The bed is unmade, and it smells of Willem. Somehow she knows this.

She feels shy, tentative, as if she is invading. But she remembers Willem telling her, exhorting her, as much as someone as

Willem exhorts, to make herself at home. The key to the flat is still in her pocket.

She sits down on the bed. It's low to the ground, the view looking up out the window. There's a small bookshelf. She smiles when she sees a copy of *Twelfth Night* there. She leafs through it, remembering how she avoided reading it in her Shakespeare Out Loud class. She thinks of Dee. She hasn't talked with him since Paris. She calculates the time difference. It's a little past 8:00 a.m. in New York. Maybe she can Skype him.

The laptop is on the bookshelf. When she takes it, she accidentally knocks over a large envelope. Out spill several photographs, newspaper clippings, some of them very old. There's also a picture of Willem, a younger Willem, his face slightly less chiseled, but still Willem. He is flanked by a man and a woman. The woman is small, dark, intense, and the man is her opposite, all tall golden smiles. These must be Yael and Bram.

She feels a little as if she knows them. And sorry she never did.

She carefully puts the photographs back in the envelope and puts the envelope in a safe corner of the bookshelf. That is when she hears the sound, instantly familiar. It takes her a moment to locate it, inside the pocket of the jacket she saw Willem wearing after the play last night.

She pulls it out. Her old gold watch, last year's high-school graduation gift. She'd hated it, so heavy and perfect, but it's kind of endearing now, all scuffed up, the face of it cracked. She turns it over. The GOING PLACES engraving had seemed so burdensome when her mother had given it to her, but now it seems kind of prophetic, like the most perfect thing to have wished for her. She wants to tell her mother about this revelation and stops for a moment to savor that, wanting to tell her mother something.

That said, she doesn't want the watch back.

In that Paris park, she'd given it to Willem, given time to him, and in exchange she became the girl in the Double Happiness story. His mountain girl, he'd called her.

She'd known he kept the watch. Céline had told her as much when she'd confronted her in Paris last week. But she'd made it sound as though Willem had kept it to pawn it. But he'd kept it to keep. To keep her.

Allyson holds the watch in her hand. She feels the vibration of its ticking and is full in a way she can't really explain.

Willem is trying hard not to laugh.

Petra is berating him, telling him he made a mockery of the company last night. This might be true, but Willem also knows the performance was a triumph. Which is perhaps the real mockery. But he lets Petra give him all her notes. Tell him all the beats he got wrong, how he mangled the language, how he confused the audience.

"Tonight you will play the part as Jeroen plays it, as an understudy must play it," she commands. It is the same direction she'd given him yesterday, when he was called up to step in for Jeroen after the lead actor broke his ankle. It was the direction that had almost derailed him, until Kate had persuaded him to take the risk. "Go big or go home" was how Kate put it. But Willem had come to understand it as "Go big *and* go home." That's how it had felt. Last night he had thought the going home was to acting, to a new home in New York City, to an apprenticeship with Ruckus Theater Company, which Kate runs with her fiancé. But today it feels as though home has come to him.

"Are we clear?" Petra asks after she has smoked her way through two cigarettes worth of criticisms. "You will do as your director tells you."

He *would* do as his director told him, but Kate was his director now. "I will perform the role as I did last night," he tells Petra.

Petra's face goes purple. It doesn't bother Willem one bit. What can she do? Fire him?

She stomps her feet. She seems like a little girl denied her dessert. He tries to keep a straight face, tries not to laugh, tries not to notice that Linus appears to be holding in a chuckle of his own.

Dee is laughing, too.

At the story his girl has just finished telling him. It's almost too crazy to believe, which is how you know it's true.

"Too bad Shakespeare's dead," Dee tells Allyson. "Because that's a story he'd wanna steal."

"I know, right?" Allyson says.

Dee's mama drops a cup of coffee onto the desk. He can smell bacon frying in the kitchen. "That our girl?" she asks.

Dee isn't sure when Allyson went from being his girl to *their* girl, but he opens the screen so his mama can say hello, too.

"Hey, baby," she says. "How you doin'? Want some waffles?"

"Hi, Mrs. Harri—"

Dee's warning face travels four thousand miles in a split second.

"I mean, Sandra," Allyson corrects. "I'd love some. Not sure you can Skype food."

"Someday, I wouldn't put it past them," she says.

Dee angles the computer away. "Mama, I haven't talked to my girl in a week. You can have her when she comes home." Dee turns back to the screen. "Am I still picking you up at the airport?"

"You can. I think my mom was going to drive down, too. She said you could come back with us."

"When's this party starting?" Dee asks.

"I'm meant to be flying home tomorrow afternoon. I'm actually meant to be in Croatia right now."

"You got a lotta 'meant to' going on," he says.

"I know." Allyson laughs. "Truth is I don't have a clue what I'm doing."

She might not have a clue but Dee knows the signs and symptoms of a girl in love. She's practically glowing, and without the benefit of the cucumber-and-yogurt facial he has planned as part of his welcome-home pampering spa day. He's got a whole list of activities, but mostly he just wants to sit in the same room and talk. He misses her. Dee didn't know you could miss a friend as much as he's missed Allyson this summer, but then again, he's never had a friend like her.

"You never did have a clue. At least now you're owning your ignorance," Dee teases.

"You know me so well!" Allyson jokes, but she touches her hand to the camera so it appears on the screen and Dee knows she's not joking, not really. He reciprocates by putting his hand on her screen. They let the gesture say the unspoken things: Thank you for getting me here. Thank you for understanding me.

"I miss you," Allyson says.

It's just what Dee needs to hear. "I miss you, too, baby."

Mama swoops back behind him, forcing herself back into the screen. She blows Allyson kisses. "He does. My boy is pining."

"I miss him, too."

Sandra sticks her head right in front of the camera. "How's that map working out?"

She had bought Allyson a laminated map of Paris as a bon voyage present. The gesture had embarrassed Dee at first, along with the bon voyage party his mama had insisted on throwing for Allyson, even though she'd never met her. "Feels more like what you're really doin' is throwing me a hooray-you-finally-done-made-a-friend party," Dee had said. His mama had raised one formidable eyebrow and retorted, "And why can't I do both?" (Dee lost the argument. The party had been delightful.)

"Mama, she ain't in Paris anymore. She's in Amster—" Dee starts to say.

But Allyson cuts him off. "The map was perfect," she says. She explains how the map had given her the idea to check the Paris hospitals, which had led her to Wren and to Dr. Robinet and to the house on Bloemstraat and now here. "So you see, I wouldn't have found my way here without it."

Broodje is shattered. He was up most of the night drinking, celebrating Willem's debut as Orlando. He woke up after three hours of sleep with a Queen's-Day-level hangover, only to remember he and Henk had promised W they'd help him move.

They'd spent the day lugging boxes up four flights of steep stairs. (W would have to be moving into the top-floor flat. Broodje had remarked that if they weren't hungover, the flat would've been garden level. W spent fifteen long minutes poking holes in the logic of such a statement.)

Now Broodje is back at his flat. Not his, exactly. His for the next two weeks until he moves back to Utrecht with Henk. He doesn't really want to go to Willy's show again tonight, but he will because it's Willy. At least he has a few hours free to rest. All he wants to do is take off his dusty, sweaty clothes and climb into bed.

He is already pulling off his shirt when he walks in the door. And then he screams.

"Oh, shit, sorry," he says, putting the shirt back on. "I didn't know Willy had company."

It's a bit of a déjà vu this, walking in on one of Willy's girls. It used to be like this all the time. But not for a while. Not for a really long while.

"Sorry," the girl says. "I didn't know anyone was coming."

Then Broodje looks at the girl for a longer moment. "Wait, I know you. You were at the play last night. In the park." He'd invited her and her friend to come to the party. He'd talked more to the friend, who was very cute, though he still missed Candace, his sort-of girlfriend, but she lived in America so they were trying to figure things out. When did Willy hook up with the friend?

"You're Broodje," the girl says.

"Yeah, that's right," Broodje says. He is tired and hungover and his muscles ache and he doesn't want to entertain one of Willy's girls. "Who are you?"

"I'm Allyson," she says. Then she seems to reconsider. "But you might know me as Lulu."

Broodje looks at her for a minute. And then he tackles her in a hug.

––––––

When Willem comes home, he finds his best friend and the girl his best friend tried to help him track down sitting together, eating. Broodje has emptied the kitchen, it seems: cheese, crackers, sausage, herring, beer. He is feeding Allyson, which is what Broodje does with people he loves. Willem sees Allyson has received a fast pass to his best friend's heart.

"Willy!" Broodje calls. "We were just talking about you."

"You were?" Willem says. He steps forward and his instinct is to kiss Allyson. He does not want to enter or leave a room without kissing her. This, too, is something new. But he doesn't because this is all so new, even though the way Broodje and Allyson are sitting there, smearing cheese on crackers, it seems like they've been doing this for decades.

"I was telling Lulu, sorry, Allyson, what a sad sack you've been all year."

"Not *all* year," Willem says. (Though, really, it was almost all year.)

"Okay. Maybe not in India. I wasn't with you in India. He went to India for three months to see his ma," Broodje explains to Allyson. "He was in a movie over there."

"Are you famous in India?" Allyson asks.

"I am Brad Pitt in India," Willem says.

"And maybe not since he came back. But shit, after he got back from Paris, he was a mess. And in Mexico, when he couldn't find you—"

"Okay, Broodje," Willem says. "No need to give away all the family secrets."

Broodje rolls his eyes. "Far as I'm concerned, she's family now."

Speaking of family, Allyson loves watching Willem with Broodje. Not that she needs reassuring exactly, but seeing him with Broodje is reassuring.

"I was going to take you out to eat," Willem says to her. "But Broodje beat me to it."

"We can still go if you want," Allyson says.

"I have to be at the theater in less than an hour," Willem says. "We can go out after? Just us."

"Not just you," Broodje says. "W, Henk, Lien, they're all coming. And they will all want to meet her." He nods to Allyson. "You are like the business we all invested in and now you're paying off so . . . you can be alone later."

"Wren called, too. The friend I was in Amsterdam with" Allyson says. "She wants to meet up."

And, Willem thinks, there would also be Kate and her fiancé.

Allyson and Willem look at each other, the invisible chain connecting them pulling hard. Why hadn't they taken more advantage of those quiet hours this afternoon? Why had they just sat there, her feet in his lap, when there was a perfectly good empty apartment here?

Except Allyson wouldn't have exchanged those hours with Willem for anything in the world.

And neither would Willem.

All too quickly, they part again. Willem will go ahead to his call at the theater. Wren is meeting Allyson and Broodje at the flat. Everyone will meet at the park, and after the play, they will all celebrate.

Saying good-bye is less fraught this time. They have done

it now once, like normal people: leave, come back. It builds confidence.

This time Willem kisses her good-bye. It is quick, a peck on the lips. It is not nearly enough. He wants all of her. From her lips to her feet.

"I'll see you after the play," Allyson says.

"Yes," Willem says.

But they both know they will see each other sooner than that. That they will find each other *during* the play, once more, in the words of Shakespeare.

Wren arrives not long after Willem has left. She squeals and hugs Allyson, squeals and hugs Broodje. She kisses the saints on her bracelet. Jude, patron saint of lost causes. Anthony, patron saint of lost things. She kisses all the saints. They all came through.

"I knew it," Wren says in that fluty voice of hers. "But I thought you were going to find him on the train, like you did the last time."

"I sort of found him at the train station," Allyson says. And then she explains how she'd been about to catch the train to the airport when she'd opened the packed breakfast Winston, the guy from their hotel, had made for her. And it was the *hagelslag* that did it. The bread with chocolate sprinkles, the very first thing she and Willem had talked about. It had been the sign, the accident, the nudge to go to Willem.

"How did you know where to find him?" Wren asks

"Because you told me the address, and that the name of the street was a belt."

Wren turns to Broodje. "*You* told me that."

"Foreigners can never remember Ceintuurbaan otherwise," he says.

"As opposed to the many other pronounceable street names here?" Allyson asks.

They all laugh.

They clean up the mess from the snacks and prepare to make their way to Vondelpark. Somewhere in the back of her mind, Allyson knows she has a flight home out of London tomorrow, at 4:00. She will have to figure out how to get there. She has a few hundred dollars left. If she has to blow it on the fast Eurostar train, so be it. It was a last-minute impromptu decision to go to Paris from London that had gotten this entire ball rolling. It took two hours to get from one world to another. She is fairly confident she'll be able to get back in time.

When Broodje goes to have a quick shower, Wren pats the sofa next to her. "Did you find out who the woman was, the one with the flowers from last night?" she asks.

Allyson hasn't. Last night, seeing Willem with the woman had been a deal breaker. It had seemed to confirm everything she suspected about him, the way that Ana Lucia's fury had. But now Allyson doesn't really care who that woman is. She has seen Willem. She has spent an afternoon with him. She knows that what happened to her last year, in a way, has happened to him.

"I didn't," she tells Wren.

"You could ask Broodje."

She could, but she doesn't want to. It no longer matters.

She can almost hear Melanie's scoff from across the Atlantic. Melanie had been with Allyson last summer when she'd met Willem, had been suspicious of him from the start, had not been able to understand why Allyson wouldn't let go of that one guy, that one day.

Whatever. She isn't listening to Melanie. Or her mom. Or

Dee. Or Céline. Or Ana Lucia. She is listening to herself. And she knows that everything is okay.

"You know what we should do?" Wren says, that manic mischievous smile of hers spreading across her face. "We should get him flowers."

For a second Allyson thinks this is some sort of duel, to win against the red-haired woman from last night. But then she understands what Wren means. They should get him flowers. At the flower market. Where Wolfgang works.

They ride on Wren's bicycle, Allyson sidesaddle on the rack behind. (She thinks this might be her favorite thing about Amsterdam. She wants to import the tandem sidesaddle riding back home.) It is early evening when they arrive at the flower market, but a Saturday night, and bustling. Wolfgang is there, wrapping up a big bouquet of lilies.

When he looks up and sees them, he doesn't seem the slightest bit surprised, even though Allyson is supposed to be in Croatia. He just winks. Allyson waits for the crowd to disperse and when there's a break, she hugs him. The smell of him, tobacco and flowers, feels so good and familiar that it doesn't make sense that she only met Wolfgang three days ago (except that it does).

"She found him!" Wren announces. "She found her Orlando."

"I was under the impression she found what she was looking for already last night," he says in that rumbly heavily accented voice.

Wolfgang looks at Allyson, a silent understanding passing between them. He is right. Last night, even when she'd thought Willem was a ghost she'd been chasing, she still felt like she'd found what she'd been looking for. Something harder to lose.

Because it was connected to her. Because it *was* her.

"It turns out, I found us both," Allyson tells Wolfgang.

"Double good news then," he says.

"Double happiness," Allyson says.

"That too," Wolfgang says.

"We are going to see him perform Orlando again. Can you come?" Wren asks.

Wolfgang says that one night of Shakespeare is enough for him. And he has to shut down the stall tonight. But he'll be free after ten.

"Then meet us after," Allyson says. "A bunch of us are going for dinner. You should be there."

She thinks of what Broodje said, the dinner like a banquet for the investor's circle. Wolfgang should be there. So should Dee. And Professor Glenny. And Babs. And Kali and Jenn, her roommates last year. Maybe she'll hold another investor's dinner when she goes home.

"I wouldn't miss it," Wolfgang says. "Now, would you like some flowers?"

At the amphitheater at Vondelpark, Allyson spots Broodje. He has saved several seats, up front this time. He is with a group of people, a guy even taller than Willem, a short-haired girl, another guy. He has brought a basket of food and several bottles of beer.

He kisses Allyson and Wren three times, cheek-cheek-cheek. And then he turns to the group. "Everyone. This is her. Lulu. Only she's really Allyson. And this is her friend Wren."

They all sort of stare at each other. The girl speaks first, sticking out her hand. "I'm Lien."

"Allyson."

"Wren."

Lien stares at her. "You really do look like Louise Brooks."

"Huh?" Wren says.

"The silent film actress," Allyson explains. "My hair was like hers then. That's why Willem called me Lulu."

Lien looks at her, remembering that Louise Brooks movie Willem dragged them all to. She'd known then something was up with Willem. No one had believed her when she'd said he had fallen in love.

They believe her now.

W is having a hard time understanding.

After all the methodical work they put into it, calling all the American tour companies, finding the barge captain in Deauville, the charts of all the connections, this didn't make sense. Willem going off to Mexico to look for her hadn't made sense either. It would've been one thing had the girl visited a small town during a quiet time of year, but a resort area at Christmas? The odds were ridiculous. But at least that adhered to a logic. The Principle of Connectivity, albeit stretched very thin.

But he doesn't understand this. All the looking they had done, and from what Broodje had said, the girl had done her own looking. But then she'd just happened upon him at the play last night? The play Willem was not even meant to be performing in? He'd been the understudy until last night.

It doesn't make sense. It doesn't make any sense at all.

Backstage, Willem is thinking about accidents again. And things that seemingly don't make sense, except they do. Like right out there in the fifth row. All of them, together. That makes sense.

He doesn't see Kate yet, but she has texted that she and David will be there but must leave right after the play. David is catching a late flight back to London, and she's seeing him to the airport.

Willem's cast mates slap him on the back, offer congratulations from last night, and condolences for next week. He accepts them both.

Max is by his side, as always. She is the other understudy, for Rosalind, and Willem's best friend in the cast. "You win some, you lose some. And sometimes you win and lose at the same time. Life's a bloody cockup," Max says.

"Is that Shakespeare?" Willem asks.

"Nah. Just me."

"Sounds like the Universal Law of Equilibrium," Willem says.

"The what?"

When Willem doesn't answer right away, she says, "Sounds like a bunch of shite."

"You're probably right," Willem agrees. And then he asks her if she'll come out after the show.

"I'm still hungover from last night," Max complains. "How many parties does one man need?"

"This is different," Willem says.

"How is it different?" Max asks.

Max has become one of his closest friends these past months, and yet he hasn't told her a thing. There is nothing to do now but to tell her *everything*.

"Because I'm in love."

Kate and David arrive just before curtain. She'd meant to come straight from the airport, but when she'd seen David, she had been overcome. It was a bit silly, really. It had only been a few days since she'd seen him, and they'd been together for five years. But she'd been feeling roiled since last night. A good Shakespearean performance was known to have aphrodisiacal effects. So when David arrived, she'd hustled him back to her Major Booger hotel and had her way with him. Then they'd fallen asleep and gotten themselves massively lost on the way to the park (someone should mention to city planners that Amsterdam was laid out like a rat's maze, albeit a very pretty rat's maze) and now here they are.

I hope I haven't oversold it, Kate thinks as the lights go down. She has essentially promised Willem an apprenticeship based on last night's performance, but David has to agree. She is sure David will agree. Willem had been that good. But she is nervous now. They've offered apprenticeships to foreigners before, but sparingly, because the visa paperwork and union issues are such a headache.

Willem enters the stage. "As I remember . . ." he begins as Orlando.

Kate breathes a sigh of relief. She hasn't oversold it.

It is better than last night. Because there are no walls. No illusions. This time, they know exactly who they are speaking to.

"The little strength that I have, I would it were with you."

She is his Mountain Girl.

"What would you say to me now, an I were your very very Rosalind?"

No more pretending. Because he knows. She knows.

"Fair youth, I would I could make thee believe I love."

She believes. They both do.

"I would kiss before I spoke."

The line is a kiss. Their kiss.

"For ever and a day."

For ever and a day.

"Holy shit," David says to Kate when it is over.

Kate thinks *I told you so*, but doesn't say anything.

"And this is the hitchhiker you gave a ride to in Mexico?"

"I keep telling you, he wasn't a hitchhiker." David has been giving her grief about giving a ride to a stranger for months now. Kate keeps reminding him that all people are strangers, initially. "Even *you* were a stranger to me once," she'd said.

"I don't care if he was three-legged ape," David says now. "He's unbelievable."

Kate smiles. She loves lots of things, but she especially loves to be right.

"And he wants to apprentice with us?"

"Yep," Kate says.

"We can't keep him off a stage for long."

"I know. He's green. The training will do him good. And then we can sort out union issues and get him up there."

"He's really Dutch?" David asks. "He has no accent." He stops for a second. "Listen to that. They're still applauding."

"Are you jealous?" Kate teases.

"Should I be?" David teases back.

"That boy is hopelessly in love with some American girl he found and lost in Paris. As for me, I'm hopelessly in love with some stranger I met five years ago."

David kisses her.

"Do you really have to go back tonight?" Kate asks. "You

could come out after with Willem really quickly and then we could give the squeaky bed at the Major Booger another go."

"Just one?" David asks.

They kiss again. The audience is still applauding.

Allyson notices the kissing couple. It's hard not to, because people are starting to meander out of the theater and they are still kissing. And because, much as she's looking forward to getting to know Willem's friends, what she really wants to do is what that couple is doing.

And then the couple breaks apart, and Allyson gasps. The woman! She's the woman from last night. The one she'd seen Willem with. The one she'd thought he was in love with. As of this afternoon, she no longer thought that. And now she *really* doesn't think that.

"Who is that?" Allyson asks Broodje, pointing to the woman.

"No idea," Broodje says. Then he points to the stage door. "Look, here comes Willy."

Allyson feels paralyzed all of a sudden. Last night, she'd stood at that very stage door and Willem had breezed right by her, into the arms of that other woman. The one who is now in the arms of that other man.

This is not last night. This is tonight. And Willem is walking right toward her. And he is smiling. Wren thrusts the bouquet Wolfgang prepared (an enormous bouquet; it almost capsized the bike on the ride to the park) into her arms.

The bouquet is smashed in about five seconds. Because Willem doesn't seem to give a shit about the flowers or the crowd of people waiting for him. He seems to be heeding Orlando's words tonight.

"I would kiss before I spoke."

And for the second time in a day, he does.

And, oh, what a kiss. It makes the one this morning seem chaste. It makes the flowers smashed between them bloom all at once. Allyson could live in that kiss.

Except she hears laughter behind them. And a voice, an unfamiliar one, though Allyson knows at once that it belongs to the redhead.

"I take it you found her then," the voice says.

It takes ages for them all to troop out of the park. There are so many of them: Willem, Allyson, Broodje, Henk, W, Lien, Max, Kate, David. Wolfgang and Winston, the guy from the hotel whom Wren has been spending time with, are joining them later. The logistics are complicated. This one left a bike back there. This one is meeting them over here.

But it's the introductions that take longer.

Kate is a theater director. Whom Willem met in Mexico, while he was looking for Allyson.

David is her fiancé, whom Willem has never met, who is going on about how good Willem was tonight, the vulnerability he brought to Orlando, what a brave way to play it.

Wren is the friend Allyson met in Paris and bumped into again in Amsterdam. "I wouldn't have found you if it weren't for her," Allyson tells Willem. "I was about to give up but she made me go to the hospital you were at."

Willem thanks Wren.

Wren curtsies.

W listens to all the introductions and still doesn't understand.

Neither does Max. "This is too bloody confusing. Can someone draw a chart?"

"That's not a bad idea," W says.

"I was kidding," Max says. "What I really need is a drink."

Wolfgang has arranged for a table at a café run by a friend of his in a neighborhood off the shrinking red light district. It is on the Kloveniersburgwal, not far from the bookstore where Willem found the copy of *Twelfth Night*, and where the bookseller inside told him about the auditions for *As You Like It* that were happening at the theater around the way.

It takes about an hour for them to get there, because they all walk together, instead of splitting up into taxis and trams and onto bikes. No one wants to be separated. Something about the night feels magical, as if a bit of Shakespeare's fairy dust has settled over them.

Wolfgang is waiting at the table, along with Winston, a pitcher of beer between them.

Everyone sits down. Allyson snaps a picture and texts it to Dee. *Wish you were here.*

She is about to put her phone away but then she texts the photo to her mother. *I am having the best day of my life,* she writes. She hesitates before hitting send. She is not entirely sure how welcome this message will be, from a bar, no less. But she thinks (hopes) her mother will be happy that she is so happy. And with that in mind, she presses send.

Wolfgang has ordered a bunch of food, pizza and pasta and salads. It starts to arrive, along with lots more booze.

Willem has hardly eaten all day and is famished. But Allyson is sitting next to him, and with everyone jammed at the table, she is right up close. And then she slips off her sandals under the table and sort of nuzzles her foot against his.

He loses his appetite, for food anyway.

The conversation is disjointed. Everyone wants to tell their part of the tale, and they tell it out of order and, as the booze flows, with increased drunkenness.

Allyson and Willem sit back and listen to this story.

"I didn't even know her, but I knew I was supposed to go with her to the hospitals," Wren is saying.

"I knew something was up as soon as Willem came back," Lien says.

"Hey, I did, too," Broodje says.

"No you didn't," Henk says.

"I did. I just didn't believe it was a girl."

"I knew something was up because he didn't want to shag Marina," Max says. She looks at Allyson. "Sorry, but have you seen Marina? Rosalind?" She shakes her head. "Maybe I'm biased because I'd like to shag her."

The table laughs.

"You have nothing to worry about," Kate tells Allyson. "He was a miserable mess in Mexico after he didn't find you."

"He was even worse after the food poisoning," Broodje says.

"You got food poisoning?" Kate asks. Willem nods. "The mystery meat? I knew it!"

"I got really sick right after you dropped me off," Willem says.

"You should've called me," Kate says.

"I ended up calling my ma, in India, and that's why I went over, so it was a good thing, the food poisoning." Sickness leading to healing. The truth and its opposite again.

"At least it paid off in the end, because at the time, that Mexico trip seemed like a disaster," Broodje says. "At that New Year's party, you were a mess, Willy."

"I wasn't a mess."

"You were. You had girls coming at you and you didn't want any of them. And then you lost your shoes." Broodje looks at the gathering. "There were these giant piles of shoes."

The hair on the back of Allyson's neck goes up. "Wait, what?"

"We went to this party on the beach, in Mexico. New Year's Eve."

"With the piles of shoes?"

"Yeah," Broodje says.

"And the Spanish reggae band. Tabula Rasa?" Allyson asks.

It's noisy in the bar but it goes quiet for a second as Allyson and Willem look at each other and once again understand something that they somehow, somewhere already knew.

"*You were there*," she says.

"*You were there*," he says.

"You were both at the same party," W says. He shakes his head. "I cannot even begin to calculate those odds."

She'd been thinking of him. But it had felt like ridiculous wishful thinking. Delusional wishful thinking.

He'd been thinking of her, too. In the water, he knew she was close, but not that close.

"I cannot believe you were at that party!" Henk says. "I cannot believe you went all the way there and you didn't find each other."

Kate and Wolfgang have only just met. But for some reason, they catch each other's eyes.

"Maybe they weren't ready to find each other," Wolfgang begins.

"And so they didn't," Kate finishes.

"That makes no sense whatsoever," W says.

Except that even W—mathematical, logical, analytical W—somewhere understands that it does.

The night goes on. Pitchers of beer. Bottles of wine. The novelty of the Allyson-Willem hunt takes a backseat to more prosaic matters. Soccer. The weather. There is a debate about what Wren and Winston should do tomorrow. Allyson tries not to think about leaving tomorrow.

It's not that hard, because Willem's hand has snuck under the table where for the last hour, it has been playing lightly on the birthmark on her wrist. (Allyson never knew her wrist had so many nerve endings. Allyson's wrist has turned to jelly. Allyson can't really think of much except for Willem's hand, her wrist, except perhaps for the other places she'd like his hand to go. Meanwhile, both her feet are now completely wrapped around his right ankle. She has no idea what *that* is doing to him.)

Wolfgang gets up to leave first. He has to work tomorrow, not so early, because it is Sunday, but early enough. He kisses Allyson good-bye. "I have a sense I will see you again."

"Me, too." Allyson has a feeling she's coming back to Amsterdam. She'll have to get a job on campus, pull double shifts at Café Finlay during school breaks to afford the ticket. The thought of coming back makes her happy, but she can't really think about the year of not being here. So she doesn't. She just concentrates on her wrist, the little circles Willem is drawing, which are reverberating through her body in ever-growing waves, like when a pebble is tossed into a pond.

Kate and David, who have been doing their share of under-the-table canoodling, use Wolfgang's departure to make their own excuses. There are hasty kisses good-bye.

Before she leaves, Kate says to Willem: "I'll be in touch on Monday. We'll have to start working on your visa paperwork right away, but we can get it expedited and probably have you out for October."

"Definitely," David says.

Willem has known since yesterday, since before he even asked Kate if he could join up with Ruckus, that this was the right thing, that it would happen, but now with David's enthusiastic support, it has become very real.

"What visa paperwork?" W asks after Kate and David leave. Dutch nationals don't need visas for tourist trips to the States.

At that moment, Allyson snaps out of her wrist-related haze (maybe because Willem has stopped caressing her wrist).

Willem has not had time to tell anyone about his apprenticeship with Ruckus, not his friends whom he will leave behind, and not Allyson, for whom the move has different implications. Which is maybe why he feels so nervous now. He isn't sure how she might react. He doesn't want her to feel pressured, like the move means he has expectations. (He has hopes, of course, especially now that he knows how close she is to where he will be, but hopes are different from expectations.)

Willem doesn't realize he's left them all hanging until Broodje says, "What's going on, Willy?"

"Ahh, nothing. No, not nothing. Something big, actually." The faces are expectant, even those of Wren and Winston, people he did not know of until tonight. "Kate and David run a theater company in New York City, and I'm going to be an apprentice there."

"What does that mean?" Henk asks.

"I'll train with them, build sets, do whatever is needed, and eventually, perhaps, perform. It's a Shakespearean theater company." He looks at Allyson now. "I forgot to tell you that."

He forgot to tell her everything. He was terrified to. He is terrified now. The ominous silence hanging over the table isn't helping. And Allyson having unraveled her feet from his ankle really isn't helping.

Maybe they aren't so in sync. Maybe what for him is good news, a reason to hope, is just too much too soon for her.

He vaguely hears people around the table offering congratulations.

But he can't process it. He is looking at Allyson.

And Allyson is not congratulating him. She is crying.

Allyson sees Willem's face, his panic, and she knows he is misreading her. But she is helpless to explain right now. Words have left her. She is emotion only.

And it is too much. Not Willem moving to American, not Willem moving a bus ride away from her. It's that this happened at all. How it happened.

Allyson has to say something. Willem is looking so upset. The table is so quiet. The restaurant is quiet. It seems like all of Amsterdam is holding its breath for them.

"You're moving to New York?" she says. She keeps it together for an entire sentence before her voice cracks and she dissolves into tears again.

It's Winston who gently touches Willem on the shoulder. "Maybe you two should go now."

Willem and Allyson nod, dazed. They offer halfhearted farewells. (It doesn't matter; good-byes with these two aren't to be trusted anyhow) and leave amid promises from Wren to call in the morning and Broodje to crash at W and Lien's place tonight.

Silently, they walk to the bike racks outside in the narrow alleyway. Willem is desperately trying to think of something to say. He could tell her he doesn't have to go. Except he *does* have to go.

This isn't about her. It was catalyzed by her, and she's woven up in it, but this is ultimately about him and his life and what he needs to do to make himself whole. He's stopped drifting, he's stopped being tossed around by the wind.

But he doesn't have to see her. It doesn't mean that. He'd like it to mean that. But it doesn't have to.

Allyson is thinking about accidents again. Which aren't accidents at all. Allyson's grandma has a word for it: *beshert.* Meant to be. Allyson's grandma and Willem's saba could've had entire conversations about *beshert* and *kishkes.*

Except Allyson doesn't know about Saba (yet) or about *kishkes* (officially speaking, though she knows what they are and how to listen to them and she will never ever stop doing this). And she doesn't have the words to tell Willem what she needs to tell him.

So she doesn't use words. She licks her thumb and rubs it against her wrist.

Stained.

Willem grabs her wrist, rubs his own thumb against it. Does the same to his own wrist, just to make it clear.

Stained.

They slam into the wall then, kissing so intensely that Allyson levitates off the ground. (It feels like the kiss that is making her airborne, but really it is Willem's arms, which have grabbed Allyson's hips, though Willem can't even tell that he's lifting her because she feels weightless. Or like part of him.)

They kiss, mouths open, tears flowing, tongues licking. It is a devouring, consuming kiss. The kind of kiss that never comes off.

Willem's knees press between her skirt and he can feel the warmth under there, and things are about to get pretty crazy in this alleyway. Even for Amsterdam.

A cyclist passes by, ringing his bell, reminding them that they are actually outdoors, in public. Neither wants to stop. But there is an empty flat somewhere with a bed and somehow, while still kissing her, Willem manages to unlock his bike.

Allyson had thought riding sidesaddle with Wren was fun, but with Willem it is something else altogether. She remembers the illegal bike ride in Paris, when she sat in the seat and he pumped in front of her and how much she'd wanted to touch him. She hadn't. She wouldn't. And then they'd gotten pulled over by the police. But this, here, is perfectly legal. And there is a place for her to sit, and she can wrap her arms around his waist all she wants. She can nuzzle against his back and lick his vertebrae if she wants to. (She does, so she does.)

At the stoplights, she hops off the bike and he turns to her and they start kissing again and sometimes stay that way until the light turns green and cyclists and motos beep at them to get out of the way.

It is a torturously labored ride home like this. Allyson is

desperate for it to end and would like for it to go on forever.

Willem is just desperate for it to end. He is so full of wanting that it is painful and Allyson keeps lifting his shirt and licking his back, which she shouldn't do while he's riding a bike because he might pass out. (But she shouldn't stop, either.)

And finally they are back outside his flat and he can barely keep his hands steady to lock his bike and he is about to attack her in the hall when he remembers condoms. He doesn't have any, hasn't needed any in months, so he drags her to a store that's still open and he buys a three pack.

"Get the nine pack," Allyson says, and he almost explodes right there.

And then they are outside his building. And fuck because Mrs. Van der Meer is downstairs walking her dog and he doesn't want to make small talk with her, but they do and he introduces Allyson, and Mrs. Van der Meer wants to talk to her about her trip to California back in 1991 and Willem has to position Allyson in front of him because it is like being twelve years old again, the lack of self control he has, but also at least with Allyson standing in front of him, against him, it's bearable (and it is also unbearable).

Mrs. Van der Meer's dog yanks on the leash and she goes out and they go in and he can't even wait. They are on the stairs and she is under him and he's got that wrist of hers in his mouth (finally!) but it's not enough, he wants all of her (the feet!) and they both know they need to make it up to Daniel's flat but the last stretch is the hardest, but somehow they do and Willem can't find his key and at this point he is going to take her in the hall because he doesn't care, and honestly, neither does she, but then she remembers she has the key! He gave her the key. It's in her back pocket.

They don't even take the key out of the lock. They don't even make it off of the floor.

A year is a long time to wait.

And Allyson and Willem, they feel like they've been waiting a lot longer.

Only later, after they have pulled the key out of the lock and put back on their clothes only to take them off again and try things more slowly this time and are having a 3 a.m. snack in Willem's bed, do things calm down enough for them to talk. They talk about things like birthdays and ice-cream flavors (March, August, chocolate for both) and scars (he fell on the deck of his family's houseboat, the one his father built; he has much to tell her about Bram). They speak of Willem's apprenticeship and Allyson's college. They spend a fair amount of time discussing the geography and transportation options of the American Northeast.

"Four hours from New York to Boston on the bus," Allyson says. "One hour to Philadelphia on the train."

"I like trains," Willem says as he nibbles her ear. "Buses, too."

"And I could come to Brooklyn on weekends," Allyson says shyly. Only not that shyly. Her hand is drifting down under the covers. Willem is glad she steered him away from the three pack. "And October is like nothing."

"It's practically tomorrow," Willem murmurs.

"I think today has become tomorrow." Allyson pauses. "Which means I'm supposed to fly home today. I have to get

myself to Heathrow in like ten hours. Is that even possible?"
(She hopes it isn't possible.)

"Anything is possible," Willem says. "You can take a train,
or one of the budget airlines. Though we should probably book
something now."

He thinks about reaching for his computer, but at that moment, her hand has reached what it was looking for and he is
useless. He closes his eyes. The girl he sees behind his lids is the
girl who is in his bed. He has no desire to do *anything* to send
her away.

Last year in Paris, she asked him to stay on with her, for just
one day. He had wanted to, but he'd been ambivalent, too. And
that ambivalence had cost him.

Or maybe it hadn't. He thinks of what Kate and Wolfgang
said. Maybe last year wasn't their time. But now is. He knows
it. Right in his *kishkes*.

"Do you have to go back right away?" he asks her.

She has the flight booked. And school starts in September.
Though September is not for a few weeks, and flights can be
changed.

"Can't you stay," Willem begins. "For just one—?"

Allyson doesn't wait for him to finish the question—hour,
day, week—because her answer is the same.

"Yes."

LOOK FOR GAYLE FORMAN'S
BESTSELLING ROMANTIC DUET!

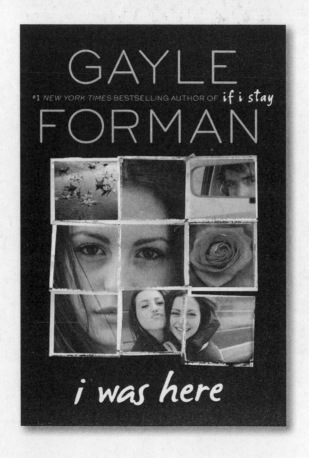